The Collier and His Mistress

ALAN DUNN

WARNER BOOKS

A *Warner* Book

First published in Great Britain in 1993 by Little, Brown
This edition published by Warner in 1994

Copyright © Alan Dunn 1993

The moral right of the author has been asserted.

All characters in this publication are fictitious
and any resemblance to real persons, living or dead,
is purely coincidental.

A CIP catalogue for this book is
available from the British Library.

ISBN 0 7515 1014 9

Printed in England by Clays Ltd, St Ives plc

Warner Books
A Division of
Little, Brown and Company (UK)
Brettenham House
Lancaster Place
London WC2E 7EN

The Collier
and His Mistress

Dedication

To Michael and Peter from Dad

Thanks

This book could not have been written without the teaching and friendship of Dave Oliver, and the companionship of the Gosforth Dancers and Caerel Cross Folk Dancers. Ian and Jean Taylor provided invaluable information on the history of coal mining, Ian St James, Merric Davidson and Graham Taylor encouraged me, Diana Tyler helped me by just being there, and David 'Shep' Kirkbride must accept responsibility for addicting me to writing in the first place. My family has supported me at all times. And Jan believed in me.

The Northumberland and Durham dances, though extremely interesting, are, it seems to me, in a sense decadent. There is a kind of perverse ingenuity about them, a striving for effect in detail at the expense of broader features, which is a very close parallel to the rather tortured cleverness of art, or of literature, which has begun to go downhill.

Cecil J. Sharp,
The Sword Dances of Northern England

The Collier and His Mistress

Chapter One

———◆———

Curl'd minion, dancer, coiner of sweet words!
'Sohrab and Rustum'
(Matthew Arnold)

He lay awake, listening to the early morning breathing of the dark room. There, that sharp repeated intake of breath, the soft sigh following, that was his youngest son, David, transformed by sleep to wide-eyed sleek-sided lurcher racing rabbits in the night-green woods above the village, leaping at the moon and flying the frost-bitten wind. At the other end of the small bed, curled tight as a fox-rolled fearful hedgehog, protecting himself from the kick and push of his younger brother, snuffled Matthew, protector of spiders and caterpillars, friend of bewildered mice and doomed earthbound fledglings.

Thomas Armstrong was his name, a good name, common, but not to be thought less of for that reason. He was a miner by trade, hewer to be precise, working at the pit-face, a hard job needing strength and agility and sometimes quick thinking. Why then was he awake at this unreasonable hour? Sleep was too valuable a commodity to be dispensed with so lightly. He knew of no worries other than those shared by his fellow workers, and those, through sharing, ceased to be worries. He was at peace with himself,

1

admittedly not content with his lot, not accepting that his
position in life would remain as it was that cold October
morning, but acknowledging that he had the potential to
change and that change took time. He loved his children,
allowed himself the luxury of a proud smile at the thought
of them, but conceded that they were not the cause of his
wakefulness. His wife then?

She lay beside him, warm against his leg and thigh,
pressing her rounded behind invitingly towards him, dreaming obediently of the husband who loved her alone with a
fire and passion she found difficult to comprehend.

'I don't know what he sees in me,' she confessed to her
mother after accepting his proposal of marriage. 'He's
handsome and he's kind and he's well-mannered, not at all
like *some* of the lads who've come courting, I might say.'
Her mother nodded, clicking her agreement through to-
bacco-stained teeth.

'He could have any of the girls round here, they all like
him. Aye, they know he's a bit strange, the way he likes to
go out by himself, the way he spends a lot of his time
reading. But that just makes him a bit, you know, special.
Different like.' She paused. 'I think he'll make a good
husband.'

A good husband he had proved to be. Other pitmen might
spend their time drinking or playing cards, paying too
regular visits to Blaydon or Rowlands Gill, out of the house
more often than in, but not Thomas Armstrong. No,
Thomas – no-one ever seemed to think of calling him Tom
or Tommy, the abbreviation would somehow have been a
false label, less than the man it was meant to represent –
Armstrong would read or write, talk to his young wife, play
games with his children, walk the fields and woods with his
family in summer, make ornately carved furniture from
scavenged timber in the winter. Other women in the row
would air their envy with their washing, hang out with neat

wooden pegs their yearning for their spouses to behave as did Thomas.

'Surely a man can't be that good all of the time?'

'Mary says he is!'

'Mary says he's good at everything!'

'Everything?'

'Aye, that as well, I heard her the other night!'

'Mm, me too. For somebody who doesn't go to chapel too often she was doing a lot of praying and calling out to Jesus!'

'I wish my Jacky was like that. He's hardly ever at home.'

'Jim's the same, he's never in.'

'And from what I've heard, when he is in, it's not long before he's out again, flat on his back snoring.'

'I'd heard that it wasn't long, full stop!'

'Go on, give over!'

Unaware of the raucous crow-laughter Mary Armstrong found herself falling more in love than she thought possible and dreamed of her husband, smiling as she slept. She was not beautiful, not in the sense that an artist might perceive beauty, although her husband would have argued the point from a matter of principle if not from true belief.

One day's early morning he had ridden the wagons down to the staithes, walked the long riverside path into Gateshead then crossed the bridge (marvelling at its size and the complexity of its construction, quaking as a train hurtled overhead) into Newcastle. Wandering, amazed, through its wide and busy streets he had found his way to the Assembly Rooms, having to ask for directions only twice. The *Chronicle* had mentioned a few days before that there was an exhibition, a collection of paintings and sculptures from the homes of some of the richest and most influential people in the area. Sir William Armstrong had sent some paintings, and Leathart, and Mitchell. Thomas had looked at books

with pictures of paintings in them, had read of the texture
and colours and light, but had been unable to understand
how any emotion could be wrought from the black and
white reproductions before him. He read the names of the
painters: Moore, Burne Jones, Dante Gabriel Rossetti,
Whistler, they meant nothing to him. But curiosity, if it was
a vice, was one to which he always fell prey. He walked
slowly, nervously, through the entrance hall, eyes cast down,
cap in hand, aware of the crunch of his hard-soled boots on
the mosaic floor, waiting for the hand on his shoulder that
would usher him back out into the street. No-one approached him, so he looked up. He found himself in front
of a painting, a picture of a woman, the most beautiful
woman he had ever seen. Bright green eyes stared at him
from beneath a sea of auburn hair. Her lips were red and
moist, slightly, suggestively parted, flushed with blood. Her
nose was slim and aquiline, her whole bearing one of
unattainable, sensual disdain. He returned her gaze, shyly at
first and then bravely, willing her to life, and eventually
turned away with tears in his eyes.

That had been, when, six years ago? No, seven, Mary had
been pregnant with Matthew that spring. Mary. Thomas
Armstrong grinned at the mention of her name. His wife, his
lover, his friend, who sought only to love him and was
therefore given his love in return, had once told him that her
face was an accident. The constituent parts, she claimed,
somehow managed to set up home before they had quite
reached their intended places of residence. Her mouth was
too large, her ears stuck out too far, her nose wasn't straight,
her eyes too close together, her eyebrows just a little too
arched. And yet put together the effect was not unpleasing.
No, he told himself frequently, the chances of choosing
worse had been far greater than those of finding better.

She breathed in deeply, exhaled, and moved against him.
He felt her warmth touch him, felt his involuntary response,

turned to slip his hand under the hem of her nightdress. Slowly, very slowly, his fingers rose up the outside of her thigh, over the curve of her hips and paused on her belly. He could remember the days when it had been taut and flat, before the boys were born, days when their love for each other was new and exciting. Life, and making love, were more predictable now. His little finger traced a delicate curve in her navel and his hand moved upwards again, pulling the cotton nightdress higher still. He eased his body back slightly to let the material expose her buttocks then moved forward again, her warm flesh against him. His hand met the roundness of her breasts, damp from the heat under the quilt and sheets and blankets. His thumb began to tease one nipple, little finger the other, a world of pleasure spanning the palm of his hand. She murmured in her sleep, dreams turning suddenly to a bright-eyed, bushy-tailed miner who insisted on her scrubbing the coal dust from his back and wouldn't let her stop there: oh no my love, there's acres more needs your attention before the night's over.

She moaned softly, even whilst asleep careful not to disturb the children, and pushed backwards. Thomas's hand circled and stroked, rolled and pulled each nipple in turn, felt their eager pressure against his finger-tips, before resuming its voyage of discovery. Down again, down over the long, fertile plain of her stomach to savour first one, then another, then a host of wiry, spring-coiled hairs. He paused for a while, gently tugging, caught in the snares of his imagination, before breaking free to seek further pleasures. His fingers felt dampness, a slick, scented moistness which brought an eager sigh from her lips and an insistent parting of her legs.

'Thomas!'

The call, an urgent whisper, came from below.

'Thomas! Come on man, it's time to get up! I've been knocking for ages!'

Thomas groaned. His passion subsided as the trapdoor at the foot of the bed was slowly lifted and a candle raised into the air.

'Thomas! Are you awake? It's getting on and . . .'

'Shut up will you, you'll wake the bairns! Just leave the candle there, I'll be right down. And leave the door too, I won't be more than a few seconds.'

The shadowy figure disappeared and in the dim, flickering light Thomas, remembering now why sleep had evaded him, reached reluctantly for the clothes left hanging on the chair beside the bed. He tiptoed carefully over to the cot, touched one of Matthew's curls back into place, slid David's arm back under the covers. Two steps and he was bending over his wife, kissing her gently on the cheek.

'Mmm,' she whispered a smile, 'I've just had a lovely dream.'

'Was I in it?'

'Yes.'

'What was I doing?'

'Oh, I don't know that I could tell you!'

'Could you show me?'

'Well, I could try. Come closer, put those clothes down, and . . .'

'Thomas! We'll never get there if you don't get a move on!' came the voice from downstairs, no longer a whisper.

'I'm sorry, love,' said Thomas. 'Tell me when I get back.' He corrected himself with a smile. 'Show me when I get back!'

'But you're on back-shift this week. It's still dark. Why are you going . . .?'

'The new pit I told you about, remember, the one opening over by Lanchester? I told you! They're wanting men of course, and they say the rates are damn good, far better than here, and the houses are newly built and really something special. They've got staircases up to the bedrooms! I *did* tell you! Anyway, Willie and me are going over to see what the chances are. We mentioned it last night!'

'I can remember you talking about it,' said Mary sleepily. 'But I didn't realise you were going today.' She snuggled down again under the covers. 'Go on then,' came her muffled voice. 'Be off with you, you don't want to be late. Hurry back. Oh, and Thomas!' She beckoned him closer and whispered in his ear.

'And me you!' he grinned in reply.

He hurried down the steep ladder into the room below. An oil lamp was set on a shelf above the blackleaded range, and in its dim glow the owner of the punctual voice could be seen, lying back in a comfortable armchair.

'I'll tell you what, Thomas me old son, if you ever decided to leave the pit you could do a lot worse than start making furniture for folk. I'd buy from you, no doubt about that.'

'You wouldn't,' came the reply, 'because you've never got any money, and I know you far too well to consider giving you credit. Anyway, you're biased. Not only are you me brother but you live here as well. You've got to say nice things about me; it's my house!'

'Aye, I suppose you're right. But you still have a talent in your hands I've never had, never will have.'

Willie Armstrong was ten years younger than Thomas. Between them came five sisters, all married to pitmen, all moved away (even if only a few miles), all somehow with less of a claim on the brothers' affections than the brothers themselves. When Willie had been born it was Thomas who spent time with him, played with him; as he grew older he showed him the secret dens for hiding, the special trees which were easy to climb, dragged him through the undergrowth in search of saplings to make bows and arrows. Thomas, the first-born, first-love of his mother, always by her side, always helping, was pleased to take on the new responsibility he was suddenly offered. His mother's smile was initially enough reward, but the bond which soon grew between the brothers became his new motivation. His mother had looked on with approval.

'It's as though he's taken on the job his father should have been doing,' she mentioned to neighbours at every opportunity.

Tom Armstrong (senior) was a handsome, talented drunkard, a philanderer whose love of the bottle and of other men's wives had resulted in sackings, bruises and broken limbs in pit villages throughout the north-east. His wife dutifully followed him as he rolled from job to job, putting up with his frequent absences because she had no alternative. Money did not seem to be a problem to him. When in work and off the drink he was a skilful carpenter; when out of work he would take his violin into Gateshead or Newcastle and tour the hostelries, playing, singing and dancing, collecting money from anyone fond of a well-played tune, a comic song or some well-turned steps. He would reappear after a few nights, sometimes a week, once three weeks, with a bag of coins and a bottle of whisky. 'Don't ask!' he would say. His wife never did.

The turning point in his life came two years before Willie was born when he was visiting his wife's brother, a genial man with whom he had always been friendly, not least because of his work as manager of a public house. That geniality had abruptly ceased when the publican found him in bed with his eldest daughter, a serving-maid in the pub. Overlooking the fact that the girl had been known to sell her favours to other customers (or perhaps angry that Tom had managed to entice her to his bed without paying) the publican had gathered together a few of his larger friends and between them they had inflicted a deal of damage to Tom's body. He never danced after that, never sang another note. And though he could remember little of the attack he recalled in every detail the publican stamping eagerly, violently, maliciously on his violin.

He returned to his wife, returned to his work, became an introverted, sullen man. His wife was happy that he no longer strayed from her side, was pleased to find that his need for drink seemed to have been assuaged. Only privately did she mourn for the loss of joy in his soul. Music and singing were no longer heard in the house. At night she would comfort him as he cried in her arms.

Thomas started work down the pit at the age of fourteen. He came home from that first day, grimy and coughing, to find Willie disconsolate on the doorstep, not even recognising him through the film of coal-dust.

'My brother's gone and left me!' he wailed.

'No I haven't,' he replied. 'And I never will. We're a team, you and me.'

And so it had proved. By the time Willie started work Thomas was a well-respected collier, a hard worker, popular. He found Willie a job, watched him grow in strength and character, encouraged him, welcomed the opportunity to work with him at the face. They became a team. Nor was the relationship one-sided. One day, just after Matthew was born, the two were drawn to one side by the pit-manager as they left the cage at the top of the shaft. He took them into his office where the Methodist minister was waiting to tell them that their mother had died. In the weeks that followed, weeks that saw their father return to his refuge in alcohol, their sisters start the drift towards independence, it was Willie who provided the strength and patience which helped Thomas cope with his loss. It was Willie who suggested that it might do them good to move away, not too far, just to the next pit, to leave memories behind. Their father had complained, of course. Who would look after him, with his wife dead, his daughters gone, and now his sons wanting to leave him to suffer in his old age? Willie, who had never known the father Thomas used to have, had no qualms about leaving; his father had barely spoken to him, indeed there were times when he wondered whether he was his father, whether perhaps his mother, tiring of the company of this depressed, uncommunicative old man, had found companionship and more from some other suitor. Thomas, however, could still remember the dancing and singing, the man who could play a set of hornpipes and perform a clog dance at the same time, beating out the intricate rhythm on the flagged kitchen floor while his mother chased him round the room with a broom, the two of them collapsing in a corner doubled up with laughter. Despite his faults there had always been laughter.

'I'll be alright,' his father had told Thomas in one of his more lucid moments. 'Don't you worry about leaving me. I've a few more years' work left in me yet, and there's still the house here, and there's the old widder woman across the road who's always eager to cook for anyone who'll add to her baccy money. Go on, you get away while you've got the chance. I don't really need you anyway.' Both men wondered at the truth of those words.

And now the Armstrong brothers were considering moving again. A new pit. It didn't happen very often. A chance to get in at the start. Everything new, everything modern. Willie's silver tongue was at work again.

'They say the owner – what's his name again, Waterhouse or something like that – they say he made his money in iron and steel in the Midlands, but he wants control of coal production to make coke for his furnaces. Seems he tried to buy some of the Cumbrian pits but they wanted too much for them, then he came up here to visit someone – Mitchell is it, that lad who joined up with Sir Billy Armstrong down at Elswick? – and he saw some surveys. Did a few test drills, found coal, dug a trial shaft then Bob's your uncle!'

'Another absentee owner, is he then?'

'No, that's the funny thing about it. He's bought Greencroft Hall and he's doing it up, moving in with his family and servants, the lot. I was talking to the minister the other day . . .' he was interrupted by Thomas's snort of derision. 'No, don't make fun, he was asking after you, he's a nice man!'

'You mean he's got a nice daughter!'

'That's beside the point. Anyway, apparently this Water-house is a very religious person, not like you at all I might say, and he believes that the lot of the working man should be improved. He's building a new village with a school and a church and a shop, he's going to employ a pit doctor you can go to for free.' Willie paused. 'There's a small problem of course. He's teetotal, so there's no pub. But it's only a mile walk into Lanchester. I could survive that.'

The sky was lightening as they walked. They turned as they crested the hill to the west of the village to look back. The silhouette of the winding gear, turning to take the cages of men beneath down the shaft into Harvey and Carrol seams, seemed almost romantic in the cool, clear morning air. The village huddled in the protection of the slag heap, the trees surrounding it beginning to shake off the steaming frost and luxuriate in the red and yellow-brown warmth of the morning sun. On the railway track leading down to the river an engine showed its pride in the new day with a plume of steam, followed a moment later by its shrill metallic whistle. In the thickets and hedges alongside the road birds were beginning to announce the morning.

'Look's nice, doesn't it?' said Willie.

'Looks even better when you're leaving it behind,' said Thomas. They walked on in silence.

There could be no doubt that they were brothers, but certain knowledge of this could only be confirmed by considering other than their physical appearance. It was true that there were similarities, certainly in height and in the strength of their bodies. But Thomas's hair was thinning (he already bore a monk's tonsure) and his moustache was turning elegantly grey, while Willie was clean-shaven with a black wiry mop of hair which could have been used as a yard-brush. Thomas's age showed in the lines around his eyes and across his forehead, and he was inclined to wear an expression of constant worry which belied his humorous approach to life.

In recent years his waist-line had shown a tendency to thicken, a result, he told those near to him, of his Mary's excellent cooking. His face retained a smooth, rounded look; Willie had once described him as an owl, wearing the bemused, slightly outraged expression of self-importance seen on that bird if disturbed from its midday repose. Thomas had replied that if he was an owl ('A most elegant and learned bird, known since Roman times to be sagacious and wise') then Willie must be a strutting peacock. In this Willie had concurred. He was invariably the first back to the house after the day's work, in and out of the bath before Thomas had walked through the front door. He spent his money on clothes, fashionable white linen shirts, colourful cravats, numerous silk scarfs, a pair of highly polished shoes. That he could do so was due in part to his living, very cheaply, with his brother; Thomas had reminded him, perhaps too frequently, that were he to get married then his expensive tastes would have to be set aside. Willie's popularity amongst the village girls (and their mothers) left both of them in no doubt that he would, one day, be caught. Many a lass went to sleep dreaming of his gypsy smile, his white teeth, his brown eyes and tanned face. But he would not be tamed for a while yet. Willie preferred the life of the socialite, insofar as that could be possible in a small village, and it would have been difficult to find a young man so well able to gossip and yet not offend any of those who were his stock in trade.

* * *

They soon left the pit behind. The road, as it would one day become, led through Rowlands Gill then back down towards the Tyne and Ryton and Prudhoe. They followed the fork to the left, heading for Consett, a well-trodden path, which led through docile fields of cows and up towards a stand of trees just below the horizon. Beyond could be seen the high heathery moors of north-west Durham, province of hardy sheep and shepherds, hardier grouse, and the occasional noble lord intent on murder of the latter. The brothers' journey would not take them that far, but they would be at least another two hours travelling.

Thomas talked of the things he had read. The schoolteacher in Blaydon, a scholarly man whose educational zeal recognised in Thomas a soul hungry for knowledge, had an aunt in London who used to send him newspapers and periodicals. These were in turn passed on to Thomas, together with the loan of books, mostly novels and poetry. He enjoyed the serialisations of Dickens and the exploded drawings of steam engines and other modern machines; he learned poetry by Tennyson and developed a particular liking for the sad verse of Christina Rossetti. He talked earnestly of the Irish problems, the finding of gold in South Africa, riots in London, the spread of socialism. Willie, who didn't read much, through lack of both volition and of skill, provided the counterpoint with tales of who in the village was doing what with whom. They sang and whistled, and soon found themselves meeting strange villages with familiar names, villages dominated by slag-heaps and wheel-topped towers of wood and metal, Burnopfield and Tantobie, Tanfield Lea off to the east, Annfield Plain, Stanley and Langleymoor.

'How's this Waterhouse getting the coal away?' asked Thomas. 'It's pretty hilly round here, I can't imagine him trying to get down to the Tyne.'

'Probably through Durham and on to Seaham, or even cross-country by train. Depends on how well in he is with the railways. He seems to have interests in everything else, and I hear he's already got a branch line built from the pit into Lanchester itself, so I don't think it'll be much of a problem. Can't be far now anyway.'

They strode the hill from Annfield down to Lanchester, found a rutted track with a hastily erected sign pointing the way to Greencroft Park.

'That's it,' said Willie, 'that's the name. We must go down there.'

'Doesn't look much to me,' said his brother warily. 'Are you sure this is the place?'

'Probably the back door,' came the reply.

The track soon widened, the grass verge to both sides becoming neater as they progressed, the tall horse chestnut trees, leaves already baccy-brown and wizened, seeming more evenly spaced. The walled and hedged fields with which they had become so familiar in the past few hours had abruptly disappeared. Beyond parallel iron railings they could see well-trimmed parkland, sheep grazing, huge ancient oaks; lines of trees showed where other paths might hide.

'Can I 'elp you gentlemen?' growled a voice, certainly not a local voice, but a voice certain of its owner's place in society. A tall, wide man stepped from behind one of the larger trees at the side of the path; any lesser trunk would not have hidden him. He was dressed in breeches and a jacket with over a dozen black buttons climbing steadily up his chest to disappear into his tangled black beard. He carried a shotgun, broken, in the crook of his arm and a yellow dog fawned at his feet.

'We're looking for a coalmine,' said Willie. 'I know it must sound daft, but we're not familiar with these parts. We've travelled all the way from Winlaton, 'cos we'd heard that a man called Waterhouse was opening a pit at Green-croft, and we saw the sign at the lonnen end, so we just followed our noses and ... well, and here we are. With you.'

'It's Mister Water'ouse t' you, young man,' sneered the man with the gun, 'though I've no doubt that before long it'll be "Sir John" or even "Lord Water'ouse" if 'e keeps on makin' money the way 'e 'as been of late. And I, young man, I am Mr Water'ouse's 'ead gamekeeper, though the devil only knows why I'm 'ere since the Master won't 'ave any shootin' on 'is land. Still, it's 'im as pays the wages in this Godforsaken place.'

'I take it that you're not from these parts?' enquired Thomas.

''Ow observant,' replied the gamekeeper with evident sarcasm, ''Ow did you guess?'

'Is this the right way to the pit-head then?' Thomas tried a different tack.

'It could be, but then again it might not be. You see, this is the new main entrance to Greencroft 'all. It wasn't, a year ago, no, it was an avenue of trees leadin' nowhere. But when they decided that the new pit village must be built right on the old main entrance, well, they 'ad to start using this.'

'So we are in the right place?' enquired Willie eagerly.

'Strictly speakin', no. And yes. Yes, this is Greencroft. Yes, there's a mine 'ere. But this is the entrance to the 'all, not the mine. So no, you're not in the right place.' The gamekeeper smiled, pleased that he had managed to explain the inexplicable to two obviously ignorant miners.

'Is it possible then,' asked Thomas, 'to get to the pit from here?'

'Why of course. You just turn round and go back the way you came. When you get to t' road, that's about a mile, you turn left and keep goin'. Then you turn left again, and again, then just follow the people, there'll be lots on t' road. It's about four mile altogither. Or you can turn right when you get to t' road, 'ead into Lanchester, then right again, that's about four 'n' a half mile but it's a prettier journey. How far did you say you'd come already?'

'From Winlaton Mill, on the banks of the Tyne,' ex-aggerated Willie. 'About eight or nine miles. We've been travelling for about two hours and we'll have to get back for our shift this afternoon.'

'Well, there is a short cut. You could get there in about twenty minutes if I showed you the way.' There was silence.

'Will you show us the way?' asked Willie.

'Please,' added Thomas. There was a further long silence. Willie wondered privately if, because of the gamekeeper's bulk, it took longer than usual for messages to travel from his ears to his brain then back to his mouth. Eventually he spoke.

'Why not. You seem reasonable enough fellers. Follow me then, not too fast mind, my legs aren't as good as they used to be.' And so they followed, Thomas listening earnestly to the gamekeeper's tales of his employer and his strange ways, the weather, the lack of work for him to do, his gout, his wife's vapours, his son's drunkenness. Willie lagged behind, mimicking the gamekeeper's rolling gait and talking to the dog.

The drive was straight for a further few hundred yards then curved round to the right. The trees closed in on one another, the spaces between them filled with rhododendrons and laburnum bushes, and beyond could be seen the chimneys and roofs of a large manor house. The gamekeeper led them towards a small gap in the foliage and onto a winding path through a dense thicket. Blackbirds churred a warning, while a nervous rabbit white-tailed it into a thick green-black tangle of brambles.

'It'll be a hard winter, mark my words,' announced the keeper in a whisper.

'Berries are fruited already. Swallows left early, and I saw geese goin' over two days ago.'

'Doesn't really matter to us,' said Willie. 'Temperatures're mostly the same down the pit, and there's usually no lack of coal. I suppose it's the same for you, you'll not need for meat at any time because of your job. We could always come to an agreement, if we got work here of course, a swap to benefit all. Meat for coal. Fuel for food.'

'If you get work,' said the keeper. 'If's a big word. There's been men seekin' work since Mr Water'ouse first made plans to open colliery 'ere, and not just pitmen, oh no. There's been 'ouses to build, and the school, and shop, and the master was most insistent that there be a library and village 'all and readin' room. 'E's even 'ad the allotment field ploughed over ready for use. Then there's the work at t'all itself, really poor state that was in when we arrived. But anyway, you'll be able t' see for yourselves. Look.'

He pushed through a hole in the hedge which had loomed before them, widening it with his passage so that the brothers could have passed through together had they so wished. They found themselves looking down a gentle slope to a neat, small village. Rows of brick-built houses, no more than four or five in each row, were grouped around a village green crowned with a duck-pond, ownership of which a mute swan appeared to have claimed as its own. A road wound its way between the houses (each of which appeared to have a garden at front and rear) before heading for a narrow gap where the trees clustered together. Beyond more houses could be seen, and a large sandstone building. The village lacked nothing but occupants; behind each window glass there were no curtains, there was no sound of children playing, no flap of washing in the breeze. And yet there was an air of expectancy, prompted perhaps by the two horse-drawn wagons grumbling slowly along the roadway, each laden with furniture and hung with a necklace of tumbling cartwheeling boys and girls.

'It's very pleasant,' admitted Thomas.

'Pleasant?' said the keeper. 'Pleasant? If you ask me it's downright luxurious. See those 'ouses? See those 'ouses? Do you realise each and ev'ry one 'as its own sink with running water? And each room 'as its own gaslight except for the parlour which 'as two? And its own – what do you call them up 'ere? – its own netty? Daft bloody language! There's no climbin' up ladders to go to bed either, no, there's a regular staircase with banisters and two bedrooms! What do you say t' that then?'

'Mary'd love it!' whispered Thomas. 'The kids'd love it. A library as well. It seems too good.'

'Where's the pit?' asked Willie. 'I can't see the pit-head or the slagheap? It can't be that far away.'

'No, just beyond the trees, that's where you'll find the pit itself. And that's where you'll 'ave to go to find out if they'll 'ave you workin' 'ere. You'll probably 'ave to join a queue, the pit-manager insists on seein' all the men who want to work 'ere, and there's no small number want that. They've all 'eard 'ow it's a good place to live, and there's the latest machinery to make work easier and safer, and the wages are better'n any others around. I 'ope for your sakes you're good or you'll 'ave 'ad a wasted journey. I won't come any further with you, the pit-manager's a bit of a strange 'un, doesn't like me – 'ow does 'e put it? – "wanderin' about on 'is patch". So I keep away from the pit and 'e keeps away from the woods. Best thing too, I wouldn't want to fall down t' shaft!' He shook his head.

'And I'm damn sure 'e doesn't want to get a blast of shot up 'is arse! I'll wish you luck lads. Look me up if you do get a job! The name's Settle, Albert Simeon Settle. Just ask for Albie, you'll find me.' He began to walk away but was turned back by Thomas's call.

'Mr Settle . . .' The keeper frowned.

'Sorry. Albie. I just wanted to say thank you. And to ask if you knew the name of the pit-manager?'

''is name? You won't need to know 'is name, you can tell by lookin' who 'e is. Just watch for the bugger with the biggest scowl on 'is face, the one everybody else is tippin' their 'ats to. But I'll tell you anyway, it's Bompas, Silas Bompas. Don't mention I sent you, it'll do you no good at all.' He wandered back through the hedge, a shiver of leaves being all that remained of his passing.

'Come on then Thomas,' urged Willie, 'let's go and find this Bompas person. I like the look of the place as much as you.'

'If it's the Silas Bompas I've heard talk of,' said Thomas with an air of finality, 'there's no chance of us working here, not so long as we're Tommy Armstrong's sons. We might as well turn round and head for home now, save us wasting his time and our time.'

Chapter Two

Not to go back, is somewhat to advance,
And men must walk at least before they danse.
(Alexander Pope, to Lord Bolingbrooke)

Greencroft Hall had once stood in isolation, surrounded by woods and parkland and a stone-built wall not quite high enough to deter night-time poachers, nor day-time visits from the children of Lanchester. John Waterhouse had bought the Hall and its grounds cheaply. The previous occupant (a relative of Lord Lambton, close enough to benefit from being associated with the nobility but sufficiently distant for that relationship to be ignored when his gambling debts began to mount) had been unaware of the rich seams of coal lying beneath his decaying manor. Even Waterhouse had not been certain of the fact. A geological survey of the area, an examination of the depth of seams in neighbouring pits, had combined to persuade him that the chances of finding coal were good. His gamble had been based on sound, scientific principles. His gamble might shortly prove to have been worthwhile.

Waterhouse and his younger brother had inherited from their father a moderately profitable Manchester cotton mill. Realising the dangers of over-reliance on one market and one product they had, led by John's ability to see where scientific theory was on the point of being developed to practical (and profitable) use, diversified into chemicals and the railways, shipbuilding and iron and steel production. The brothers complemented each other. Where John was eager to try new methods of production, new machines, new theories, Edward preferred the conservative approach, valuing tried and trusted practices, proving their worth by counting the profits they brought. They had agreed some time ago that each would serve the other best by concentrating his efforts in those areas he most enjoyed. John would be the innovator, the inventor, the inspiration behind each new money-making project they developed. Edward would then take over, consolidate matters, fine-tune the operation, bring in methods of control and accounting and administration. They worked well as a team and corresponded a great deal, but as years passed and their businesses diversified further they met less frequently. Neither welcomed the other's interference in his own province, and when they met the temptation of one to comment on the actions of the other could lead from discussion to argument to irascibility to – as happened on one occasion – the threat of violence. That threat had died stillborn in a hail of laughter from both parties, but the memory did not fade.

The elder Waterhouse was nervous. His brother had arrived late the previous evening for his first visit to the Hall. He had been tired after the long journey, had missed breakfast. It was now almost ten; surely he would come downstairs shortly. Their last meeting had been, when, nine months ago in London, just after Christmas? Events had moved apace since then.

John Waterhouse was in his office, a small room off the study, well-lit with large windows in each of the three outside walls. Hunched over a worn and battered leather-topped desk, he was surrounded by filing cabinets, a large wooden table beneath which a rack held cylinders of maps and plans, an angled drawing board, and a number of tall bookcases. The contents of some of the shelves appeared to have emigrated to every flat surface in the room. Books and magazines, papers and periodicals were everywhere, not strewn haphazardly but set in neat piles, each with a small scrap of paper pinned to the top identifying the content of the manuscripts below.

He was writing urgently, had already filled three sheets of paper with pencil drawings and small, tight-packed neat writing, and was near to completing the fourth. He paused for a moment, lifted the pencil to tap absently on the briar-pipe hanging loosely from his lips, then crossed out a few lines which had offended him. A delicate cough interrupted him before he could resume his work.

'I trust that I'm not interrupting anything important? Forgive me John, I know that everything you do is important, just as I realise that my presence here is likely to inconvenience you. But look at it from my point of view. How could I resist visiting you to see at first hand the project on which you're spending vast sums of our money!'

'Edward, you don't change,' smiled John. 'Cynicism has become part of your creed. It is indeed a pleasure to have you stay with us.'

'I can see you muttering under your breath, dear brother, your sentence should have continued "particularly when I know that you must travel on to Newcastle later this afternoon". Am I right or have you changed character and decided to be polite to me? I'll make a politician of you yet!'

Only when they smiled was their kinship evident. John, in his late fifties, was tall and angular, his long black hair turning silver as it descended to broad sideburns which strove to meet under his chin. His clothes were dark and sombre; there was no fire in the room (it had been laid but not lit) and he had not removed his overcoat after his regular early morning tour of the estate. He seemed sheathed in clouded black armour. When he stood he topped his brother by almost a foot, could gaze down on Edward's pink, polished pate, note with a private smile that he appeared even rounder than he had nine months before, and marvel at his complete lack of dress sense. He took a step back and held his hand to his eyes as though to shield them from some brightness.

'And what's the matter now?' demanded Edward.

'Nothing, nothing,' said John.

'Nothing?'

'Well, nothing much.'

'Go on, you can tell me. After all, if you can complain about my choice of clothes then I won't feel so guilty about pointing out your failings in your latest venture. Spit it out man, I can take it.'

John took a deep breath.

'You are wearing a yellow and red Paisley waistcoat. Your suit is a particularly virulent shade of what looks to be purple ...'

'Puce actually, they told me it was puce. But go on.'

'Puce it shall be. The material itself would be marginally more acceptable if the jacket sleeves were longer, the trouser legs were shorter, and if you had had it made by a tailor who wasn't blind and incapable of taking sizes from a tape.'

'Thank you, you undertaker. Is there anything else which offends you?'

'Yes. You're wearing green braces and brown shoes. You look as though you've been assembled from the diverse parts of a dozen separate people none of whom had any taste and all of whom were colour-blind. There. I've finished.'

'Are you sure? I wouldn't wish to spoil your enjoyment!'

'No, I can't see anything else wrong. Apart from the slight problems I've just mentioned everything is perfect.'

There was silence. Edward spoke first in a voice no more than a whisper.

'John, it's good to see you. Come here!'

The short fat man and the tall slim man embraced, laughed as they stepped back to admire each other, then embraced again.

'We don't meet often enough you know,' said Edward. 'Letter writing is all very well but when we come up against problems they're far easier to overcome when we can face them together.'

'Problems?' said John. 'Do you have any problems? If so, then I demand that you let me know of them this instant. I shall cure them for you immediately. That is what elder brothers are for.'

Edward smiled. 'You're beginning to sound like a character from a second-rate London play, and I suspect you're trying to distract my attention. I think you know that my side of the business is doing very well, thank you. You also know why I'm here, and that the problems I'm referring to are not too far from your doorstep. You sent me some figures a few weeks ago, some very interesting figures, showing budgets and proposed expenditure, anticipated income, the usual stuff. You must have worked very hard at them, it took me some time to digest them all.'

The brothers sat down on opposite sides of the desk. Edward took a cigar from one of his hidden pockets and placed it in his mouth without lighting it. John took his pipe from his mouth.

'Yes,' he said. 'It was a strain to get everything ready on time. As you know, I prepare most of my financial papers alone, and I worked through the night once or twice to complete the batch you're talking about. Did you find any errors? I thought I'd checked them thoroughly . . .'

'No, there were no errors. Everything made sense, it all added up beautifully. If anything it seemed too good, and that made me ill at ease. There was something not quite right, something which I needed you to explain. But you weren't there. So I read a few papers, asked some knowledgeable people some innocuous questions – in a discreet manner of course – and came to a few conclusions.' He stopped talking, tapped his cigar firmly on the desk before lighting it in his familiar slow steady manner. John realised for the first time how much that particular practice annoyed him, but what annoyed him more was the suspicion that Edward was aware of this and cultivated the mannerism deliberately.

'You see John,' he puffed, punctuating his sentences with clouds of smoke, 'I think that, in your enthusiasm, you've made one or two errors of judgement. You show us making a profit within three years when even the most optimistic alternative calculations, based on your figures and your requests for further expenditure, show us losing money for the next ten. The problem lies in your production estimates. Even allowing for the modern tunnelling machines and face cutting saws and drills you want to buy, there's no way I can agree with your calculations! You seem to be coming very close to bankrupting us this time. No, forgive me, I exaggerate. Both of us are prudent enough to know that the failure of one of our businesses would not necessarily affect our other concerns. But the amount you wish to invest in this mine could, unless everything goes exactly according to plan, cause us great harm. It would be wrong of me not to tell you of my worries.'

John had anticipated this problem, but had hoped to defer its discussion until his cash requirements (needs, he reminded himself, needs!) had been approved. He took a deep breath.

'I'm not sure that you'll be able to understand this,' he said, 'but I'll try to explain.' He took a deep breath, then shook his head.

'No, damnit, I won't explain, I'll show you! Come on!'

He rose swiftly to his feet, reached for a roll of plans from the floor beside him, then hurried towards the door.

'Come on then, follow me!' he said loudly. 'You'll have no doubts once I've finished.' Edward sighed loudly. Enthusiasm was his brother's most endearing and, at the same time, infuriating habit.

They hurried through the library and into the hall where, at John's insistence, the footman found Edward a pair of stout boots and an overcoat, both slightly too large. They walked out of the large double doors and began to march down the drive, John striding ahead, Edward struggling in his wake.

'The Hall itself has required a little work, mostly to the roof, some modern plumbing, one or two extra rooms. And redecoration, new furniture, carpets and so on. But that's more than reflected in the increase in value of the property written into my figures, don't you agree?'

'No,' panted Edward. 'And even if I did agree it's still capital tied up in property. And look at this! Suppose you did need to sell the place at some time, who's going to buy a country mansion when some idiot's built a modern village in its front garden?'

'Are you saying I'm an idiot?' demanded John in mock anger.

'Yes!' came the reply.

'Oh. Well, I suppose you're entitled to your opinion.'

They reached the main gates to the Hall, newly erected, and examined the scene ahead of them. Pillars of smoke were rising from the chimneys of two of the village houses, a horse and cart was drawn up at the front door of each where people were unloading furniture from beneath the wagons' broad, grey tarpaulins. Children screamed the chase as the swan, still sedate on the pond, ignored the noise.

'Do you like the houses?' asked John. There was no response. Edward seemed confused by the question.

'Well?'

'It's not a question I can answer. They're houses. They seem to fulfil a purpose. Where does the matter of like and dislike come into things? You might as well ask me if I like a stone, or a potato, or a sheep. I can't see the point of the question!'

'Oh, Edward, you do make things difficult sometimes. Let me see. Very well then, do you like the Hall?'

'Oh, alright, I'll humour you. Yes, it seems a pleasant enough building, quite handsome in its own way, the rooms are well-decorated and comfortable and it has an atmosphere which I found not distasteful. Now you tell me why you asked!'

John thought for a while. His fingertips danced against each other, his lips pursed, his eyes surveyed the scene before him.

'Edward, I don't think you'll understand this. I'll tell you anyway. You see, I believe that the people who are going to live in these houses, the people who are going to work for me, for us, have as much a right as you or I to live in pleasant surroundings. This isn't a new idea. It's been tried, on a smaller scale, admittedly, and in an agricultural rather than an industrial environment, but it has been tried and it works. Rowntree and Cadbury are working along the same lines, and the Levers too; they've plans for a whole new town. By giving workers the chance to live in homes they can be proud of their lives can be enriched, they can work with their employers rather than against them, and you know from your own experience how costly that can be!'

'You forget,' said Edward eagerly, 'that I am a little more familiar with costing than you. We *have* built houses before; yes, I know they were nothing to take great pride in, shared privies, no rear yards, regimented terraces, but they served our purpose.'

'Your purpose, you mean,' countered John. 'Until now my

experience has been, as you have pointed out, limited to the development of industrial processes rather than any involvement with those who might have to work in the factories I was designing. You were always the one who dealt with the other, what I considered mundane, tasks of converting my ideas to money. But you've been busy in other areas, and there have been distances separating us which have prevented us talking directly, and I have found myself growing more and more concerned with the overall principle of the way in which our society is working. That's why I've built like this. That's why there will be a church, a school and a shop and a library, a village hall for meetings and dances. This will be a place where our workers want to live. And that's not all.'

'Somehow I didn't think it would be.'

'You've seen the plans Edward, you've read the inventories. This will be the most modern coalmine in the world!'

'And the most expensive.'

'Yes, to begin with. But modern machinery will mean greater productivity. And the village will complement that. By treating the workers as people instead of a necessary but inefficient part of a manufacturing process they'll work with us, not against us. By paying them wages above the industry average we'll attract the best, most efficient workers, and we'll be giving them a life which befits their status. By making the mine a safer place to work we'll cease the stupid, casual loss of life as well as reducing the time lost through repairs and through recruiting more unskilled labour. Can't you see that it's sound financial sense to work in this way?'

'I can see that the figures you quote for the benefits of your new system can have no basis in analysis of historical information, if only because everything you're trying is so new. You're relying on guesswork in too many places, and I feel that your desire to develop your project, your experiment, may be forcing you, perhaps without realising it, to be over-optimistic in your forecasts.' Edward came to a halt. When he spoke again it was more gently.

'I'm worried about the overspending, yes, you know that. But I'm worried about you as well. You've been working hard. You're no longer a young man. If anything were to happen to you then this whole project would fail. And even if you saw things through, it still might fail. And if it did you would have no reputation and no money. We would both fall. And although your arguments are convincing and your figures are impressive, I'm afraid you've still not persuaded me, in my heart of hearts, that your proposals are sound.'

'Thank you for your concern,' said John. 'I do appreciate it. But there's no need to be worried about my health. I feel perfectly fit. And I still think that this pit – you see, the local terminology has got through even to me! – yes, this pit has a future and a profitable future at that. But don't make any hasty decisions, don't act on first impressions. Come with me, there are some people down here you ought to meet.'

He caught his brother's elbow in his and together they marched down towards the houses, pausing infrequently for the taller to point out something of interest while the smaller caught his breath. They soon arrived at the door of the village hall. The elder Waterhouse hushed his brother and gingerly turned the polished brass handle, stepped carefully inside pulling his brother behind him, and held his hand to his ear as they approached the internal doors. There came from within the sound of music, a melodic air played on some wind instrument, a flute perhaps. No, it was too high, the tune was being tongued. A recorder! The notes caressed the air, shaped and smoothed it, brought it calm and peace, soothed it with gentleness, then moved to a minor key to add sadness and a feeling of lost innocence on the final, soft note. There were a few moments' silence, then applause from a small number of hands, then a muffled sound of laughing, giggling voices which became only gradually more distinct.

'Recognise them?' whispered John.

'No, should I? There's no ... Wait a minute. It can't be! Not Margaret! She sounds so grown up! It must be, why else would you bring me here. Come on, let's go in!'

Edward pushed the doors open and bustled into the hall. Sunlight was dusting the air, and in the haze three, no, four figures paused in their labours.

'Is that you father?' said a voice, female.

'What an insult,' growled Edward, 'to mistake me for that scarecrow!'

'It's Uncle Teddy!' cried another voice, younger than the first, and a mob-capped figure in a grey dress hurled itself across the room and into Edward's arms. He caught her up and twirled her around before setting her down in front of him, an expression of delight on his face.

'No,' he said. 'I thought I heard my niece, young Margaret, but I was obviously mistaken. She looks a little like you, but she's much younger, much smaller, and not half as beautiful as you. Forgive me my lady!' He bowed deeply.

'Oh, Uncle Teddy, stop it, you'll embarrass me. I'm not a child any more. After all, I'll be eighteen next summer.' She leaned close to him. 'And besides, there are other people here,' she hissed. He nodded knowingly, but still couldn't prevent his smile from showing his pleasure.

'It's a long time since I last saw you,' he said quietly, so that no-one else would hear, 'and you really are beautiful. Take that silly cap off and let me see you properly.'

The girl removed her hat, shook her head. Her hair was long and blonde, hanging in delicate curls which framed a heart-shaped face which was, indeed, beautiful, despite being smudged with dirt and grime. Her eyes were blue, her nose *retroussé*, her lips eager to smile, for she knew from frequent visits to the mirror above the fireplace in her room that, when she smiled, even *she* could acknowledge her beauty.

'And was that you playing that beautiful tune as we approached? Those music lessons are proving their worth after all, I swear it, I was almost in tears.'

'Music? Me? But I can't play a note Uncle Teddy! It wasn't me at all, it was Elizabeth!'

'Hello Uncle Edward,' said the voice which had first queried Edward's identity.

'Elizabeth, you're here as well! How are you?' He dropped the younger girl's hands and moved forward to embrace her elder sister, kissed her formally on the cheek.

'I'm very well, thank you,' came the equally formal reply. 'I trust that you too are well. Thank you for your kind words about my playing, but it really was quite an easy piece. Did you have a pleasant journey?' – Edward would have replied but the opportunity passed before the words had begun to be formed on his lips – 'Oh, but you must forgive me, I seem to be forgetting my manners. Allow me to introduce my companions.' She turned in the half-light and motioned to the silhouettes behind her; they moved forward obediently, doing so not only from politeness but also, it appeared, from familiarity. It was as though they recognised in her words and gestures the imperative which any stranger would class as a mere firmness of voice. The air of authority was reflected in her bearing. Where Margaret was undoubtedly a girl, despite her protestations of maturity, Elizabeth was a woman. Nearer forty than thirty, though only marginally so, she was thin where her sister was rounded, with dark, straight hair cut unfashionably short and tied back into a brief knot of pony-tail. Her eyes were brown and she had the habit of staring inquisitively at a person, head tilted slightly to one side, subjecting the object of her gaze to some inner scrutiny. Her clothing was decked in shadow, almost severe in its simplicity and lack of ornamentation. Black skirt and blouse, no frills of any type, a dark brown coat which bore the marks of skirmishes with thorn bushes and battles with dried mud; she shunned any attempt to make herself appear feminine. The reason became clear as she ushered her friends forward with a smile. The smile outshone the sunlight; had she spent the whole morning preparing herself, with the attention of a dozen maids to primp and preen, to select clothing from a queen's wardrobe, the resultant mannequin would have been as nothing unless the woman within had decided to bestow a smile upon her audience.

'My uncle, Mr Edward Waterhouse. Mr Timothy Deemster, our new curate; and our neighbour Mr Henry Makemore.'

The curate was tall and bearded, his circular collar hiding like a shameful halo below a torrent of coarse red hair. His hands were broad and powerful, more suited to wielding a plough than caressing divine thoughts from a Bible, and his hearty 'Pleased to meet you Mr Waterhouse!' would have been heard even if Edward had still been standing outside the hall. Henry Makemore was, in comparison, insubstantial. His gently whispered 'Sir', accompanied by a deferential inclination of the head, suggested a young man aware of his social standing, but even more aware that although an individual's position in society might change, any movements on *his* part would be in an upward direction. The two men were of an age, twenty-one, perhaps twenty-two. The discerning eye would notice Makemore's slight limp, the beads of sweat at the curate's forehead, the way that each glanced frequently in Margaret's direction. They were competitors.

'I know that name, Makemore, Makemore?' muttered Edward.

'Sir Charles Makemore,' answered his brother, 'is our

immediate neighbour in so far as our estates share a border, although it's some distance to his home. Henry is his only son and he has been most gracious in helping us settle into the local community. He and Mr Deemster have been willing escorts to Margaret and Elizabeth.'

'Surely,' said Edward, 'Sir Charles owns one of the largest coalmines in the region! I'm sure I read of it somewhere. What does he feel about this venture of yours, John?'

'I don't think it would be any secret,' Henry Makemore replied, raising his eyebrows to the elder Waterhouse as though seeking his permission for the interjection, 'to state that my father is very interested in the coalmine here. He has made regular visits to examine the site itself and to discuss with your brother his methods of operating the extraction. Whether those methods meet with his wholehearted approval I, alas, cannot say. He intends, uh, let us say watching developments for the moment before making any comment.' John Waterhouse avoided meeting Edward's eye.

'Father,' said Margaret, 'this is boring. We've finished moving chairs and tables about, and Uncle Teddy never stays long, so I think you should allow us to show him around the estate. Come on everyone, follow us.' Without waiting for comment or permission she linked her arm with that of her uncle and pulled him with her out of the hall. John Waterhouse shrugged his shoulders and suppressed a laugh on finding Elizabeth ushering him along in the same way. They followed on, Makemore and Deemster bringing up the rear, heading back up the hill towards the house.

Edward exhausted his young niece's attention within a few minutes, and she excused herself to step alongside the curate. Makemore flashed a scowl at them which only Elizabeth noticed as she urged him forward to join her father and uncle. The conversation moved rapidly to the subject of the coalmine.

'I gather then that your father does not approve of my brother's innovations?' said Edward to Makemore. The young man considered carefully before replying.

'Oh no, sir, on the contrary, he looks upon them with great enthusiasm. He is aware that in these modern times a new outlook to coal production is to be welcomed, but at the same time he acknowledges the difficulties in applying the new methods of production to mines which have, in the majority of cases, already been in use for ten, twenty, thirty or even fifty years. The best place to try these new methods is therefore in a new mine. And here we have one with great potential.'

'Henry neglects to add,' said Elizabeth, 'that it is also in his father's interest to have someone else take the risk of trying these "new methods". His interest does not extend to a wish to invest in our project, does it Henry?' There was no reply, only a sheepish grin.

'Quite,' said Edward, 'and we haven't yet touched on the social experiments that you appear to be carrying out.'

'If I may come in there,' came the voice of the curate. 'I feel that I can offer some information on that score.' Margaret, piqued that her company should be put aside for a mere intellectual discussion, took the opportunity to detach herself from Deemster's side and take possession of Henry Makemore's willing arm. The curate did not appear to notice, continuing to speak.

'I feel that a great deal of thought has been given to the development of this mine, and I have no doubt that this planning will ultimately result in a worthwhile and profitable business venture. My concern, however, is more with those who must work here. The miners and the overmen, the managers, the clerks, their wives and their families, they just aren't used to the advantageous living conditions they're able to enjoy here. You're taking them from numerous different locations where their days are spent, if not, Lord save us, in hardship, then in awareness of their social position because of the life they lead. They're used to hard work, physical work, manual work. That's all they know. I fear that they'll be softened by their new lives of luxury, their well-appointed homes, their higher wages, and they'll cease striving to improve their lot. They just won't work. They'll take to drink and womanising and other, worse sins. It's a recipe for disaster, the vicar and I have discussed it at great length and ...' He tailed off as he noticed the grimness of John Waterhouse's face, the hurried shake of Elizabeth's head.

'I'm sorry if I've said too much,' he mumbled, 'but it would be wrong of me in the sight of the Lord not to tell you of my worries.'

Henry Makemore had not noticed the turn of the conversation. His entire being was concentrated upon the angel at his side, the angel who allowed him to gently push one of her curls back into place, the angel who laughed at his jokes and called him wonderful, the angel who, only two nights before, had not pushed him away when he kissed her, quietly, softly, briefly, on those rowan-red lips, but had sighed and murmured his name with a breathlessness that might just have bordered on passion. His well-bred ears could not fail, however, to notice the lull after the curate's outburst.

'My father did venture one opinion,' he said, 'and that was regarding the community spirit of the new village. Or rather the lack of it. You see, whenever he has had to open new seams or new mines he's always done so by moving families en bloc to the new location. A man moves, his wife and children move with him, their neighbours move. It's not uncommon to find three or four streets moved in their entirety to a new village. But that's not happening here. Your determination to employ only the best men, together with the high quality of your housing, will lead to you having a village full of strangers. My father was concerned at the social problems this might bring.'

Elizabeth could barely hide the venom in her voice.

'I suppose that you and your father have no "social problems" at all in your cosy communities?'

'You're welcome to come and see, anytime you want.'

Elizabeth resisted the temptation to enquire exactly when feeding time was scheduled.

'In fact,' continued Makemore, 'we're having a "do" up at the house in a fortnight's time. Our pitmen are demonstrating one of their dances as a sort of *divertissement*. Quite interesting if I say so myself, they use some type of flexible sword, five or six of them I believe. They tie their swords into complicated shapes and do some fast steps and somersaults. They're actually damn good; there's a sort of championship for this type of dance every summer and they've won it for the past three years. Anyway, why not come along? You could consider it an example of the community spirit I was just talking about. You're all very welcome.' His invitation was aimed at Margaret; her simpering smile confirmed that he had hit his target.

The party walked on together in silence and found themselves in front of the main gates again. John Waterhouse was the first to speak.

'Well, gentlemen, if you'll excuse us Edward and I must visit the pit-head.'

'Quite,' added Edward. 'It's been very interesting talking to you. But before I go, and I hope that you'll forgive me if I appear over-inquisitive Mr Makemore, but there's something I must ask you.' He paused, appearing slightly embarrassed.

'I am sure that I shall take no offence,' said Makemore.

'Very well. Are you fond of gambling?'

'Oh yes,' squealed Margaret. 'He's forever wagering this and that, and he nearly always wins!' The curate looked on in disdain. Makemore nodded his head in acknowledgement.

'In that case I propose a small wager. I believe that my brother's workers will be able to demonstrate their, uh, "community spirit" I believe was the phrase you employed, in a manner which you and perhaps your father will accept as proof that his theories are viable. I believe that his workers will, from amongst themselves, be able to produce a team of dancers who will compete against yours in this contest of which you spoke earlier. And furthermore I believe that they will not only defeat your team, but will win first place! Such is my confidence that I will wager one hundred guineas on the outcome. Are you willing to match that?'

Elizabeth was standing beside Makemore. Only she noticed the way he licked his lips, pulled each slightly into his mouth in turn and took a deep breath before replying. Only she noticed him force a shaking hand deep into a pocket, and the fire in his eyes. Only she felt sympathy that one so young should be so addicted.

'I'll lay odds of two to one and make my stake a thousand, Mr Waterhouse,' he replied evenly. Edward calmly nodded his agreement. Makemore continued.

'I shall let Mr Waterhouse senior have details of this competition as soon as possible. I look forward to seeing you there and,' he turned to bow to Margaret, 'I trust that we will have the pleasure of your company in a two-week at our ball.'

'I shall make a point,' said Edward courteously, 'of attending the former, but fear that I must depart this very afternoon and will be in Manchester in two weeks' time. I feel sure that the family will, however, be well represented in my absence. Goodbye Mr Makemore. Curate Deemster. Oh, by the by, does this mysterious dance have a name?'

Makemore grimaced and rubbed the bridge of his nose.

'It's on the tip of my tongue. Something of Anglo-Saxon origin I believe. Yes, yes, I have it! It's called the rapper sword dance. That's it. Rapper.'

Chapter Three

And David danced before the Lord with all his might.

2 Samuel

'Edward, would you mind telling me what that was all about?' There was no reply.

'Edward, I feel that you owe me an explanation.' Still silence.

'Please, Edward?'

'Oh, I'm sorry John,' chortled Edward. 'I couldn't help it. There you were, trying to persuade me of the viability of your project, and you find the clergy against you, the aristocracy against you, all you lacked was a reporter from one of the local newspapers to comment on the sheer silliness of your ideas and you'd have had a full house of opposition! But I digress. I was listening carefully and seriously to all that Makemore and Deemster were saying, paying them a great deal of attention and becoming less and less sure of your project, when it suddenly dawned on me that these young pipsqueaks were condemning you, the driving force behind my own good fortunes, and your ideas. And it annoyed me. After all, I'm used to being the only person able to stop you exceeding the bounds of common sense. I'm afraid I just lost my temper. But there's no going back now. I think I've just committed myself to supporting your schemes. For a while, at least. And in the most indirect manner I can recall during the entire span of our partnership!'

'Edward,' said John, 'you are my favourite brother!' He clasped the smaller man's shoulder and the two continued on their way, laughing up the road to the pit-head.

Elizabeth waited as Margaret said her fussy goodbyes to her two admirers. The curate was in a dog-cart pulled by an overweight dun pony, Makemore on his favourite black hunter. Neither seemed aware that they had offended their host, nor that his eldest daughter was angry with them. Had Elizabeth still been Margaret's age she would have rounded on them, chastised them for the boors they had shown themselves to be. Maturity, however, had brought her the burdens of courtesy, civility and restraint. Her anger was tempered by the sympathy she felt for her father, that he should have to suffer such treatment. She was aware, perhaps more than any other, of the efforts he had put into developing the coalmine. She had, since her return from London, acted as his secretary and confidante.

Once, on a cold winter's night when she had been checking some of his easier figure work, she had fallen asleep. The study had been warm, shadows leaping and curling from the fire to disappear behind the heavy curtains, and she could remember waking with a start to see the familiar figure crouched over his desk, surrounded by oil lamps, scratching at the papers before him. She had, so far as she was aware, made no noise, but still he glanced up to smile, to reassure her. During her time away she had barely thought of him, and on her return her guilt when she realised this, particularly when she considered the warmth and friendliness of his welcome, almost forced her to leave again. She had, with his help, overcome that guilt, but it was only on this occasion, on seeing his smile echoing the warmth of the fire, that she realised how much she had come to depend on him, to love him.

When she awoke again the fire was out. His jacket was draped over her, and the oil lamp was sputtering in the draught from a window he had opened, probably in an attempt to stay awake. The attempt had proved futile, and his head lay on neatly folded arms. The old clock in the corner showed it to be after four in the morning. Elizabeth stirred herself, rose stiffly from the chair, and gently shook the old man's shoulders, surprised to find herself acknowledging that he was indeed getting old. He raised his head almost immediately, opened sleepy eyes. 'Emily,' he had whispered. 'Emily, you look so beautiful tonight. How I love you.' His eyes had closed once more; when he opened them again he was properly awake. It was the first and only time since her mother's death some fifteen years before that she had heard him mention her name.

Although she called him father she was not his daughter. She had been two years old when her mother and John Waterhouse had married, two years old and skin darkened by the Indian sun, two years old and crying with the cold and damp of a Manchester autumn. She knew nothing of her real father. She had no memories of him lifting her nor playing with her, had seen no likeness of him amongst her mother's possessions, either before or after her death. Her mother had not hidden the fact that Elizabeth was not John Waterhouse's natural daughter, but neither had she encouraged any questions about her real father. When those questions inevitably arose she had refused to reply.

Two weeks after the funeral – she had been unable to venture into her mother's room until then – she had begun to examine her mother's private belongings. She had kept no diary. There had been sketches and photographs but all were of people she knew. The man she called father had proved equally reticent though no less loving than his wife. I promised your mother, he said, that the little I know I would keep until released from that promise, and having said that he would say no more, not even on the subject of the promise he swore. Elizabeth's curiosity turned gradually to sulkiness, then to resignation; with the passing of a few years she had forgotten the questions whose answers had once seemed so important.

She had not thought of her mother nor her father in this way for some time, and even then only in the misty pre-sleep moments in the warmth of her bed. How strange, she wondered, to find such memories rising unbidden to her consciousness at this moment. But her reverie was interrupted by her sister.

'Elizabeth, they're going now. Come on then, wave goodbye. Elizabeth!'

Elizabeth lifted her arm absently, saw the gesture repeated as the two young men headed down the drive.

'You were very rude to Henry and Timothy,' said Margaret in her baby's voice. 'They both noticed, though they were too polite to say. I could see it in their eyes.'

'*I* was rude? *I*? Either you weren't listening, or you didn't understand what was being said, or your silly flirting and simpering made you deaf to what was going on around you. I've never heard such insolence from two people whose ignorance is matched only by their discourtesy! If they weren't such, such ... little boys! Yes, if they weren't such little boys I'd have pointed them home with the toe of my boot!'

'You're just jealous because they don't play up to you. Timothy has already asked me to marry him. Twice! And Henry has kissed me! And I kissed him back! You're jealous, aren't you. Admit it.'

'Me? Jealous of those two? You're obviously as innocent as you appear to be. And be careful with that Henry Makemore. A kiss, however innocently given or taken or returned, can lead to a young girl finding herself out of her depth.'

'Elizabeth! I wouldn't do that. I mean, I know all about it. After all, you've explained about it when I've asked you. But I wouldn't actually do it. Not until I was married, and even then with restraint.'

Elizabeth could not restrain a giggle, and Margaret joined in without really knowing why she did so.

'When it comes to things like that,' Elizabeth said, 'restraint is something that not many people have, certainly not in large enough quantities. And before you ask what I mean, you aren't ready to be told if you have to ask. Now come on, let's find father and Uncle Edward. I want to find out how things are going with them. They should be having an important discussion.'

The pair marched up the drive, mimicking in their gait the older men who had gone before. They seemed easy in each other's company, their smiles and laughter and singing were natural, unforced. Their way led past the gates at the head of the drive and then sharp right, away from the hall and the village, on a narrow gravel path which wound through a small coppice. The road from the village to the pit-head lay further on; this short cut would save them minutes unless they were distracted on the way (as seemed to happen frequently) by a squirrel, a grubbing, nervous mouse or some new and unrecognised bird. On this day, however, nature sent nothing to delay them. Margaret, after some thought, decided that she should provide the stimulus lacking in their surroundings.

'Elizabeth?' asked the younger girl. The question warranted no reply, was hung on her arm like a walking stick, an aid to talking rather than walking.

'Elizabeth, is it . . .? Is it really as nice as I've heard said?'

'What's that, Mar?'

'You know! It!'

'You're not being very clear, are you? I'm sure I don't know what you're talking about.'

'You do, you do, you're just being awkward! Oh, I really hate you when you're like this!'

Elizabeth sighed with the resignation of one who anticipates trouble, but is not aware of its precise nature or of the direction of its approach.

'Alright then, let's assume – just assume, mind you – that I can guess what you're talking about. If it's the same thing – and remember, I'm only guessing – why should I be such an expert? What makes you think I know all about it?'

'Well,' said Margaret, 'you've been married, haven't you?'

'Am married,' came the too swift correction. 'I haven't heard from Eamon for two years now. No-one else has either, so far as I know. But I am still married to him.'

'Alright then, am married. I mean are married.' They both laughed. 'Anyway, you should know, shouldn't you! You've done it!'

Elizabeth stopped walking, stared skywards as though searching for words to assist her in dismantling this coldly logical argument. A horse chestnut leaf, thick-fingered and mottled brown like an old man's skin, whirled downward to join its companions at her feet. It would soon be winter. She disliked winter, winter brought back hard, sad memories of pinched, black days, and the wind and rain seemed to clutch at her insides during those harsh dismal months. She would be ill again, as she always was, starting in November with a cold which would become a cough, and which would then travel to her lungs. She would find it hard to breathe, be unable to eat or drink, lose weight. She feared that winter would, one day, kill her.

'Elizabeth? Elizabeth! Are you alright?' Margaret's concern was evident. Her half-sister was prone to these trances, would sometimes refuse to wake up and would be carried to her bed. She didn't relish the thought of leaving her here, nor of dragging her to the house.

'Mm? Did you say something? Have I been wandering again? Oh, Mar, I'm sorry, I can see you're worried. There's no need, I was just thinking, trying to answer your question. Now where was I?' She pulled her bottom lip into her mouth, made a small hissing sound, the ·type usually employed to attract the attention of cats. It evidently aided her concentration.

'Let me see, have you heard of a Mr Ruskin? John Ruskin?'

Margaret shook her head, wrinkling her nose as she did so. It was the only one of her many gestures which had not been modelled in front of a mirror, and was all the more charming for that fact.

'There are times when I despair of you. Listen carefully then, you might just learn something. Mr Ruskin was – is, I should say, he lives now in the Lake District – an artist and an art critic, a writer, a philosopher, a lecturer, essayist, public speaker. In short, a very learned and intelligent man, highly respected and respectable. But he had a very sheltered childhood, spent without much contact with other boys or girls. When he grew up he fell in love and married, and not long after some articles of his were published praising a young painter named Millais whose work . . .'

'I know about him,' interrupted Margaret, 'I read about him. He painted that picture of the little boy for the soap advertisement. And that other one, where the woman's floating down a river and he actually painted her while she was lying in a bath.'

'Quite,' continued Elizabeth with exaggerated patience. 'Mr Millais' early work was not received by others with quite the same enthusiasm as that employed by Mr Ruskin, so it seemed natural that Mr Millais and Mr Ruskin should become acquainted. Mr Millais was invited to dine, then to stay for an occasional weekend, and then to travel with Mr and Mrs Ruskin. But Mrs Ruskin was beautiful, and Mr Millais fell in love with her, and she with him. So great was their love that they wished to marry . . .'

'But they couldn't, Mrs Ruskin was already married to Mr Ruskin! That would have been bigamy!'

'Yes, I know, and they knew too. But there was another reason for Mrs Ruskin not wishing to remain married to Mr Ruskin. She petitioned to have her marriage dissolved because Mr Ruskin had been unwilling, or unable, to consummate their marriage. Do you know what I mean?'

Margaret began to nod her head, but turned the nod into a frowning shake.

'What does consummate mean?'

'Oh Lord, who taught you English, girl? It means that they didn't do it. They'd been married for years, but he couldn't bring himself to . . . to develop a physical relationship with her. Oh damnit Margaret, they didn't do it, they didn't make love fully. He never penetrated her. She was still a virgin. Understand?' A nod.

'Well, from what I was told, there was a reason for this. Mr Ruskin was brought up surrounded by classical paintings and sculptures, and his knowledge of female anatomy had been gained purely from those sources. So on his wedding night, when Mrs Ruskin disrobed, he was shocked, revolted even, to find that she had hair on her body and, what is more, that the hair was concentrated around her . . . her sexual organs. He couldn't go near her. He expected her to be perfectly formed, just like one of his marble statues. And she was merely human.'

It took a while for Margaret to reply.

'Well!' she exhaled. 'So what happened? You can't just leave it like that! Tell me, oh Elizabeth, do tell me!'

'The marriage was annulled. Mrs Ruskin and Mr Millais

married. Mr Ruskin continued to praise the work of Mr Millais and people thought all the more of him because of his gentlemanliness during the proceedings. There, will that do?'

'Well, yes, I suppose so. But ... what was my original question? That's it, I remember, I said that you should know what it's like because you're married, and you told me that story ...'

'Which demonstrates?'

'Which demonstrates that ... Oh, I don't know. Can you give me a clue?'

'Ignorant child! I wanted to show you that when you marry you don't suddenly become an expert on the subject of sexual intercourse! There, will that do for you?'

'No!'

'Oh, Mar, I can see that you're sadly lacking in education. How can I explain? Look, you mentioned that Henry Makemore kissed you. Did you feel anything?' Margaret tilted her head to one side and reached for the memory. She smiled.

'Yes, as a matter of fact I did. I felt his hand moving slowly down from the small of my back to the top of my bottom. I moved it away, of course.'

'I should think so too. But I wasn't thinking of physical senses, I meant any emotions that you experienced. Do you know what I mean?'

'Well, it was nice, I suppose, though he did taste a little of cigars. It was, it was sort of tingly, deep down inside. And I felt rather warm afterwards; father said I looked a little flushed. Is that the type of thing?'

'You are young, aren't you. We're nearly home now, and this is the type of conversation which should be entirely private.' Elizabeth paused, her voice softened. 'But yes, that's the answer to your question, yes. It is nice when it's with someone you love, someone who loves you. It's nicer than anything else in the world. Most of the time it's so nice that words can't describe it. But sometimes Mar, sometimes . . .'

'There they are, over there by the manager's office!' yelled Margaret. She hitched her skirts up and began to run, crying (after she had started) 'Race you!'

'But sometimes,' whispered Elizabeth, 'sometimes it's the worst thing you can imagine.'

The pit-manager's office was one of a dozen or so grouped together forming three sides of a square. Formerly toolsheds and stores, they were low and squat, almost homely; only the lack of curtains at the windows prevented them being mistaken for a terrace of pit-cottages. Thirty or so men were gathered in an informal queue in front of one of the doors. Some were squatting down, backs against the wall, while others played pitch and toss on the well-worn cobbles. One or two were reading newspapers, the *Hexham Courant* and the *Chronicle*, and the low murmur of unforced conversation was reminiscent more of a gentleman's club than a hiring. The men's clothing was, in general, worn and patched though generally clean; to dress too smartly was to run the risk of being thought a dandy, or a spendthrift. A miner's best clothes were saved for a Saturday trip to the pub and the Sunday visit to church. Caps were common, in dull greys and browns to match the jackets and trousers, but many added a daub of colour by flaunting bright silk scarves. Those who had taken off their jackets, for the day was turning warm, sported collarless shirts rendered off-white by repeated boiling. Half of the men wore boots; the others favoured clogs.

There was an air of confidence amongst the men, almost tangible. Word had spread quickly about this new modern pit and its unusual owner; the news that he wanted capable, experienced and hard-working men had travelled fast.

Those who had come along on this fine autumn day were good workers, amongst the best, and they knew it. None were much older than Thomas, most a little younger, and they had gathered round eagerly to listen to one of the deputies describe the mine and its machinery. They had nodded their approval on hearing of the height and width of the seams, commented knowledgeably on seeing photographs of the engines. Only Thomas Armstrong had seemed less than enthusiastic.

'There's no point Willie,' he argued, 'we might as well head back now. Bompas won't take us on, not unless he's suddenly developed a very bad memory.'

'So you keep saying,' replied his brother, 'but you still haven't told me why. Did me Dad steal his wife away for a night of passion on the slag-heap?'

'I'm not joking Willie, they hate each other. And that's not all. Listen man, can you remember that lass I was courting, oh, years and years ago, she came from Throckley? Nancy she was called, trim little thing?'

Willie frowned.

'Oh yes, the one who belted me when I put a frog down her blouse? She was rather nice, far too good for you of course. Why, what's that got to do with it?'

'Well, I was rather keen on her. Her old man looked after the ponies down Throckley, and he let on that they needed more men. I wasn't very happy at home at the time; it was a bit crowded, none of the girls had left and Dad was drinking too much, and I told him I was going to see about a job. He just looked at me with that superior sort of scowl on his face,' Willie nodded, recognising his brother's description, 'and says, "Throckley? Throckley? You'll get nowt there! That's Bompas's pit. As soon as you tell him your name's Armstrong you'll have your arse kicked out of the door, out of the pit, out of the village. I'll tell you that now, save you the trouble of walking all that way." And that was all he'd say.

'I went anyway – I was at that age where if somebody says "do this, don't do that" you automatically go and do that but not this – and, sure enough, the pit-manager was called Bompas. I asked Nancy's dad about him. I think he was quite keen to get rid of her, so he encouraged me. Said he was a hard man but fair, cared about his workers and their families, stood up to the owners when there were safety problems. I went to see him. He looked me up and down, asked what type of work I'd done and where, who I'd worked with, various things I'd learned. He asked me to read from a book, the company's regulations I think it was, and to write down what he said to me then read it back. He seemed very pleased, I was sure he was going to offer me work. Then he asked my name.

'"Thomas Armstrong," I says. "Any relation to Tommy Armstrong?" he asks, "Tommy Armstrong the fiddler? Tommy Armstrong the dancer?" I nodded. "That's me Dad." He didn't say anything else to me. He just opened a hatch in the wall and shouted for somebody called Albert or Herbert or something, and this fat bald little man comes in.

'"Take this bastard away from me," he yells, "before I forget meself and kick him all the way up the bloody hill to Hebburn. And tell him that if I ever see his face again I'll make such a bloody mess of it his father won't recognise him! Now get him out of here!"'

'What did you do then?' asked Willie.

'I went. He was a big man, and I think he meant it. Nancy wasn't a bad lass, but she wasn't worth getting half-murdered over. And Throckley wasn't up to much either. But when I got back I told Dad what had happened, asked him why he and Bompas hated each other so much. He wouldn't say a word. I couldn't tell if he was secretly proud or if he was ashamed. He told me never to ask again, never to mention the name Bompas again. Then he went out, came back roaring drunk much later. I never did ask him again.'

'And that's it?'

Thomas stared vacantly, dead ahead. 'No, not quite. I asked Mam. I asked her why Dad and a man called Bompas would hate each other so much.' He picked up a small pebble and began to pass it from one hand to the other.

'She started to cry. I'd seen her cry before, once when Dad hit her – they didn't know I was watching – and again when Gran died. But this was different. She just looked at me and the tears started falling down her cheeks. She didn't say anything, she didn't make any noise at all, but her face went white. The tears were dripping off her chin but she didn't move to wipe them away, so I had to do it for her. I sat her down by the fire but it was like she couldn't see me. I was worried, and I kissed her on the cheek, just gentle, to show I cared. That seemed to bring her round. She wiped her face on her pinny, blew her nose. I asked if she was alright. She nodded. And neither of us mentioned it again.'

'Never?'

'No. And I said nothing to Dad either, about the way it affected Mam.'

'That's not a lot of help, Thomas,' sighed Willie, adjusting his scarf. 'I suppose we'll just have to take things as they come. After all it was a long time ago. By the way, have you noticed that everybody's going in through that door but no-one's coming out? Perhaps Bompas is in there,' he snarled, contorting his face into what was meant to be an evil grin, 'cutting their throats and turning them into sausages, ha ha!' He reached for Thomas's neck with taloned fingers, eyes wide in a parody of madness. Thomas smiled, and his depression moved away. Willie was right. They would have to take things as they came. But he still felt a strange nervousness, not only at the prospect of meeting Bompas – for it was surely the same man, there could be no two pit-managers with that name – but because he really, desperately wanted to work at this new mine. He wanted

Mary to live in this new, spacious house, he wanted Matthew and David to go to this new school, he wanted his family to benefit from this new life they could lead. He wanted the job, he wanted the change, and then perhaps the storm of restlessness which had been threatening him recently, the urgent desire to be somewhere else or someone else, would disappear.

'Soon be us,' said Willie.

It was the same Bompas Thomas remembered from all those years ago, and time had not been kind to him. His face was lined, shadows lurked beneath his eyes. Office work had turned his muscle to fat, age had taken away most of his hair and turned white what was left. He was tall, though his shoulders were rounded and his back showed the beginnings of a stoop, as if he had borne some great weight since his youth. He was standing in front of a fire, heels resting on a brass fender, hands clasped behind his back. His black suit seemed natural for him, matched his demeanour. As the brothers entered the room he glanced at his watch, returned it to his pocket, then glared at them. A pair of spectacles, rejected by his pride, lay on the dusty mantelpiece. He showed no sign of recognising Thomas.

'My name's Bompas,' he growled, 'Pit-manager. Before I hear anything about you, lads, I want to tell you something. You see, we all have numbers in this pit, numbers on our property, on our tools, on our work-cards. I was the first to be taken on, taken on by Mr Waterhouse himself. I'm number one. I mention this so that you know *your* position, and so that you know *mine*. Now I shall ask you some questions, speak up when you answer, I like to hear a man's voice, tells a lot about his personality. My clerk, Mr Penman, will note your personal details. First your names.'

Thomas shook his head. He was stupid to have waited, stupid to have entertained any thoughts of working here.

'Thomas and Willie Armstrong,' he muttered, resigned to his fate.

'Come on lads, I said speak up! I didn't hear a word of that!'

Willie looked at Thomas, winked, then stepped forward.

'I'm sorry about that Mr Bompas, my brother's a little shy, my name's William and he's Thomas – Thomas, help Mr Penman spell our names, especially the surname, it's rather awkward, you know the trouble we've had with it – and he does tend to speak softly, but we're both impressed with what we've seen so far and . . .'

Thomas whispered their names to the puzzled Penman then returned to Willie's side. They might make it after all.

'Quiet, boy, I want to hire a miner, not a quack salesman or politician! You,' he pointed at Thomas, 'you look almost sensible. Tell me about the work you've done. Keep your brother quiet, and for God's sake speak up!'

Thomas explained about their experiences, the fact that they were brothers and that they wished to work together, that they were fit and able, strong and willing. Bompas asked questions in return, all of which they answered carefully to the best of their ability. After each response Bompas nodded his head, then squinted at them while issuing his next examination. Eventually there was silence broken only by the rasping sibilance of the fire and the careful scratching of Penman's copperplate. The pit-manager rocked backwards on his heels, leaned forwards.

'Do you have any family?' he asked.

'I'm single.' 'A wife, two children,' they replied.

'Very well then. Mark them down for a house, they might as well live together if they're going to work together. Start a week on Monday, Mr Penman will give you your numbers. When you go out through this door,' he gestured to his right, 'give your numbers to the housing clerk and he'll arrange house keys and tell you your shift times. Thank you for coming.'

That was it! They had made it! They headed for the door indicated, clutching the tags Penman had given them.

'Oh, and by the way ...' said Bompas. They turned round. He had moved across the room to stand at the clerk's desk, was peering at the ledger before him, glasses wedged on his fat, red nose.

'Oh,' he said softly, 'I see. Mr Armstrong. Mr Thomas Armstrong. And Mr William Armstrong.' He looked up at them, narrowed his eyes. 'I recognise you now, Mr Thomas Armstrong, son of Tommy Armstrong, my old friend Tommy Armstrong. And I remember. I may be getting old, and I may be a little deaf, and my eyes may not be what they once were, but I have a good memory. And I remember the last time I saw you, when I told you what would happen if I ever met you again.' He reached under the desk and brought out a pick-axe handle.

'Mr Bompas!' yelped the clerk. If he had wanted to say more then one glance from Bompas was enough to strike him dumb. He scuttled from the room, slamming the door behind him. Thomas and Willie looked at each other, began their own retreat towards the nearest exit, the one through which they had entered only ten minutes before. Willie reached for the handle as Bompas lurched towards them, but was pushed back towards him as the door was abruptly thrust open.

'Mr Bompas, I'd like you to meet my brother Edward, Edward, this is ...' John Waterhouse glanced around as Bompas gingerly lowered the stave to his side. 'Is there a problem Silas?'

'No sir, there's no problem. I was just a little, ah, a little worried sir. I was worried that these two lads here, these two lads were getting a touch upset because I'd just told them that they wouldn't be working here sir. They looked as if they might take it the wrong way sir. You know how these men can be sometimes. Sometimes they think with their fists instead of their heads.'

'That's a lie,' yelled Willie. 'We haven't done anything. He'd as good as offered ...' He was silenced by John Waterhouse's stare.

'I think that I shall find out for myself,' he said calmly as he walked across the room, 'what has been happening here.' He stopped in front of the desk and began examining the ledger.

'According to this record, Mr Bompas, Mr Thomas Armstrong,' he looked up and Thomas acknowledged his name, 'and Mr William Armstrong have been questioned by you at length. At great length. And have, it would appear, met with your approval? And been offered work? And a house? Is that so, and before you answer, Mr Bompas, consider that this conflicts directly with your previous statement? Well, Mr Bompas? I feel that a considered reply is called for!'

'The book's true, Mr Penman always writes true,' acknowledged Bompas. 'But what it doesn't say is that, by deception and cunning, and Mr Penman will back me in this, these two jack-the-lads avoided giving me their surnames, and they did so because they knew that if I found out their true identities they'd get no work here, not so long as I'm manager!'

Waterhouse turned to Thomas. Edward, bemused but enjoying the debate, shuffled round to join his brother and eagerly scanned the pages on the desk.

'Well? Is that so?' asked the elder Waterhouse.

'No!' yelled Willie. 'I mean, yes, but ...' Once again he was silenced.

'I think you will find,' began Thomas, 'that our answers to Mr Bompas's questions were true and that on the result of those questions we are worthy of employment here.'

Bompas thought of interrupting but the Waterhouse eyes again brought a respectful hush.

'We hid our name from Mr Bompas because we were aware that, at sometime in the past, he had a ... a disagreement – and I don't know what the reason for this disagreement was, nor its result – with our father. I've tried before to get work from Mr Bompas and been rejected because of that disagreement, but my brother and I are good workers; we could be of great use to you Mr Waterhouse, and it seemed worth the small deception. For that, and that alone, I apologise.'

Edward and John conferred. There was much shaking of heads and examining of the ledger, a weary sigh, the drumming of fingers. Bompas was motioned to join them, was asked one or two brief questions, then ushered away to sulk once more by the fire. Eventually John Waterhouse spoke.

'Thomas and William Armstrong, I have no doubt that you are both good workers, and that you had good reason to keep from Mr Bompas your surname. I am sorry that Mr Bompas has any reason to dislike your father. You would seem to be the type of worker it is my wish to see employed in this mine. However,' he glanced angrily at the pit-manager, 'I am able to employ good miners much more easily than good managers, and Mr Bompas is, despite this outburst, known as one of the best. I have no wish to see argument and disruption brought into the mine before work has properly commenced, and therefore I must stand by Mr Bompas's decision, his final decision, not to offer you employment. We are, as I'm sure you realise, very busy, and we have more men to see. If you don't mind . . .' He ushered them, politely, to the door.

'And tell that fiddle-playing, step-dancing drunk of a father when you see him,' shouted Bompas after them, 'that Silas Bompas sends . . .'

'Mr Bompas! That will be quite enough! I have no need . . .'

'Just a moment John,' said Edward. 'Mr Bompas, did you say dancing? Did you say that this Armstrong man was a dancer?'

'He was that sir. He would never work if he could find somebody to pay him to play his bloody violin, or dance. And the money all went on drink.'

'What type of dancing Mr Bompas?'

'What type? All types, of course, step and clog and some fancy waltz, anything. Anything except work!'

'Thomas Armstrong, is this true?' Edward continued. 'Your father was a dancer?'

'Yes,' answered Thomas, puzzled, 'he could dance. Why?'

'And did he ever do any dancing with swords?'

'Swords? Oh, you mean rapper. Yes, of course, he even tried to teach me and some of my friends, when we were at the Sunday School. Didn't come to much though, I don't think I can remember . . .'

'Mr Waterhouse,' said Willie from the doorway, 'am I right in thinking that this dancing, this sword dancing is important to you?'

'Yes,' said Edward, grudgingly.

'Well then, this man is just the person you need. He's an expert is my brother, step dancing, sword dancing, the lot, aren't you Thomas!'

'Willie, what . . .?'

'Show me,' said Edward.

'Edward,' said John Waterhouse, 'I don't quite see why . . .'

'John,' replied his brother, a little impatiently, 'if this man can dance he may be able to help solve our problem. All I've done is ask him to show us what he can do. He's nothing to lose, have you Mr . . .?'

'Armstrong,' interjected Willie, 'Thomas Armstrong's his

name, the best step dancer south of the Tyne, mark my words. And if you want to see him dance then you shall see him dance. Come on Thomas, shake a leg, don't keep everyone waiting!' He strode outside. The shouting had drawn a crowd, eager to see and hear what had been going on.

Thomas followed his brother, shaking his head, unable to believe what was happening. He reached out, grabbed him, hauled him to one side, whispered urgently and angrily in his ear.

'I can't do it,' he said. 'You know I can't do it. How can I? You know what rapper's like, it's a sword dance and not only are there no swords hidden about my body, but I would need four, no six more dancers to do it properly. Add to that the fact that it's years since I danced it anyway and you end up wondering if you're mad for suggesting it or I'm mad for standing here talking to you instead of walking away right now!'

'You can step dance, can't you? I've seen you do that, just last Christmas. Do it now. Do anything. Christ Thomas, there are jobs to be won here, and a chance to put one in the eye of that bugger Bompas!'

'Well, Thomas Armstrong,' asked John Waterhouse, 'are we to wait all day for this spectacle?' Thomas looked up.

'I've no clogs Mr Waterhouse, I'd need clogs to do a step dance. I've only boots.'

'Clogs!' shouted Willie. 'There's a man here in need of a pair of clogs! Anyone lend a pair, size . . .?'

'Ten,' said Thomas, now resigned to making a fool of himself.

A voice spoke up and two battered clogs were handed through. Thomas eyed them carefully. The black leather was worn and undecorated, the wooden soles thick and heavy, and the irons nailed beneath worn and loose. He would have preferred his own clogs, the ones which sat by the hearth at home, tooled patterns weaving their intricate way over the polished black hide. Still, these sad, ill-used shoes would, he felt, more accurately reflect the quality of the dancing. When he was young his father had taken him along to watch him dance in competitions. He never entered in advance; other dancers wouldn't bother signing on if they knew that they were competing against Tommy Armstrong. Man and boy would walk into the hall, or pub, or bandstand, hand in hand, the dancer's best clogs round his neck, and wait to be recognised, wait for the silence which followed someone saying 'Oh no, it's Tommy.' And then he'd watch the dancing. His father always smiled as he danced, hands held loosely at his sides. Some of the steps Thomas learned himself, some of the easier ones. But for him it was hard work, while for his father it came easily. His body became an extension of the music and the rhythm, his steps adding a syncopated beat to the dotted hornpipes of 'Harvest Home' and 'The Boys of Bluehill'. He'd had a style all of his own, and even those judges who didn't like innovation would be forced to concede the quality of his dancing.

'Thomas?' It was Willie who broke the spell.

'Thomas, are you ready?'

'No, I'm bloody-well not ready, and I never will be! But that seems to be the last thing that concerns you, so we might as well get on with this stupidity.'

He undid the laces of his boots, was pleased to find that his socks had been darned, and pushed his feet into the clogs. They were old, moulded to the feet of their owner, and they felt strange. Thomas stood up, looked around. The courtyard was cobbled with the exception of a pavement of cracked sandstone which hugged the perimeter, and he headed for the broadest, flattest flag he could see. It was immediately outside the pit-manager's office. He took off his jacket as he walked, flung it at Willie who followed him closely. Immediately behind him came the crowd of miners, none of whom knew why this display was about to take place, but who exhibited a curiosity especially evident when some conflict was imminent. Bompas glowered from the doorway of the office, his clerk peering nervously from behind him. John and Edward Waterhouse stood to one side, watching carefully, awaiting developments.

'This is a clog dance,' announced Thomas loudly, 'taught to me by my father, Tommy Armstrong.' He turned slowly to stare at Bompas, turned back again to face his audience.

'Tommy Armstrong was the best clog dancer in the five northern counties bar none!'

'Aye,' muttered Bompas, 'and it was in the bar you'd most likely find him!'

'And if I've got even a quarter of his skill,' Thomas continued, silencing the laughter which had rippled at Bompas's interjection, 'I'll still be better than any other man here. I wasn't expecting this. I'm still not sure exactly why I'm doing it. And a clog dance without music is a funny type of animal. But I'll try . . .'

'What type of music would you like, Mr Armstrong?' It was a woman's voice.

'Elizabeth! And Margaret! What are you doing here?' exclaimed John Waterhouse. 'I hardly think that this is the place for you to spend your mornings, now run along to the house please!'

His daughters appeared in the office doorway, Bompas shuffling to one side to let them past.

'We heard,' said Margaret, 'what was going on.'

'And we feel,' continued her sister, 'that, to be fair, this man should at least have some music to help him dance. After all,' she added in an aside to Edward, 'we also know the reason for you asking him to do the dance in the first place. So what type of music is it to be Mr Armstrong? Come on, speak up!' She took her recorder from her pocket. 'I'm quite capable of playing, just name the tune.'

Thomas looked at Willie and shrugged. Had he glanced in the opposite direction he might have seen a similar look of bewilderment pass across the faces of John and Edward Waterhouse. All seemed resigned to accepting the leadership of the small, dark-haired woman.

'Hornpipes,' said Thomas, 'please.'

Elizabeth thought for a moment, then began to play.

'No, no, that's a reel!' said Thomas. 'Don't you know "Harvest Home"? Everybody knows it, they play it for all the competitions.'

'I'm sorry,' answered Elizabeth. 'I'm not familiar with many local tunes. I do know that one, what is it called now, "Blaydon Races"?'

'No, that's a jig, six beats. Still, it might do. Can you play it like this, sort of . . . well, sort of lumpy?' He hummed the tune nervously. Elizabeth nodded, repeated his melody, and Thomas smiled.

'That's it, keep going like that, over and over, I'll set the speed.' He listened carefully, marked time with his right foot, increased the pace a touch. Now he began to think. The steps, nothing flash, nothing complicated, the basics would do. Elizabeth reached the end of a phrase, the end of a chorus of the tune, and he started the dance. 'Singles,' he thought to himself, and his feet moved with the music. Dee-DUM dee-DUM-dee da-da-da-da-DUM went the rhythm, shuffle on the left, shuffle and toe on the right, right heel and shuffle toe-heel on the left. Repeat, other foot leading. His hands were by his sides, held open, palms pressed firmly against the rough cotton of his trousers. He normally carried himself in an easy, casual manner, almost a slouch, but now his back was straight, head held high, eyes wide and staring straight ahead, seeing nothing. Step six times, once off each foot, then break. DUM-da-da-da DUM-da-da-da dum-dum-dum; step on the left, shuffle toe right, repeat, then left foot forward, back, right foot cross over. Then all of that, all over again, with the other foot leading. He felt sweat beginning to bead on his forehead and dampen the small of his back. How long had he been dancing? Five minutes? Ten? No, half a step took no more than fifteen seconds. He allowed the clogs to take control, began to think of the next step.

Something else easy? American! No need to vary the breaks, keep them simple, let them separate one step from another. Here we go! Step shuffle left, step shuffle right, step shuffle, step shuffle, step shuffle left! His mind was accepting the commands of the music. Do it again, do it again, do it again and again and again! He allowed his eyes to come briefly into focus, saw the smiles on those ahead of him, felt Willie's encouragement at his side. He glanced at Elizabeth. Her fingers, long fingers with short nails, were moving easily over the slim black recorder, caressing each trill and ornament from it. Her lips were moist, her eyes tight closed, and she swayed slightly from side to side in time with the music. He stumbled slightly, missed a beat – did anyone notice? Did it really matter? Come on man, concentrate! Change leading feet. Think of the next step. Second turn? No, too difficult, he had had problems with that. A turn though, that would be a good contrast. Leg-over turn. He could manage that. Break on the left then turn slowly, diddle-dee-dum, da-diddle-dee-dum, keep it going, keep turning, one complete turn in the phrase, concentrate, concentrate on the beats, back to the front, break! Good, then back the other way. You're going to do it lad, you're going to do it!

All thought of the reason for him dancing passed from his brain. All that mattered was the dance. He turned slowly back, clockwise, and allowed his gaze to pass over his audience; John Waterhouse looked him straight in the eye, then looked away, looked past him and frowned; Edward stared at Thomas's feet; Penman the clerk was tapping his fingers together in time with the music; Willie was marking time too, winked as Thomas turned; of Bompas there was no sign; the blonde girl looked at Thomas, head on one side, then smiled, not at him, but at someone behind him; and the dark-haired woman, the musician, opened her eyes once for two seconds to stare at his soul.

Break, then into heels. Even six beats, the end of one clog crossing behind to click the back of the other, the toe and heel of the sole filling in the missing beats. This was good! This was easy! Break, change feet, think of the next step. Irish rolls, a bit of a challenge perhaps, but well within his capability. He began the step and regretted his decision. He had started too fast, his feet wouldn't keep up! No-one noticed the first time he missed a beat in the cross-over, but that still made him a little late on the second phrase. He hurried to pull the step back together, might even have done so had he been wearing his own clogs, but the loose iron threw him off balance. He knew that he wouldn't finish the step properly, but the music stopped abruptly before he had the chance to acknowledge defeat. He slowed to a halt, gasped for air as though he hadn't inhaled since the dance started. He turned to thank his musician. She appeared as breathless as he was.

'Oh, I'm so sorry,' she said. 'I'm afraid I just couldn't keep up with you. I hope I didn't spoil things by stopping so . . .' Any other words were lost as Willie led a belated round of applause. Edward bustled forward and put his hand on Thomas's shoulder, removed it quickly as he felt the damp beneath.

'Well done, well done Mr Armstrong, that was excellent!' His brother joined them. 'Wasn't that good John, I think we may have something here, eh? What do you think then? Does Mr Armstrong get the job? John? John! John, I'm talking to you!' John Waterhouse had been staring across the courtyard at a figure striding purposefully away, hands thrust firmly into pockets. He shook his head.

'Yes Edward, I heard you,' he said wistfully. 'I suppose that there will be a place for Mr Armstrong and his brother. It is unfortunate that I shall also have to spend some time in seeking a replacement for Mr Bompas. He appears to have left our employ.'

They followed his gaze to see the figure reach the trees. In later years Willie would tell his grandchildren the story of their great-uncle Thomas's championship clog dance, and how Bompas had, before he disappeared from view, turned to shake his fist angrily at them, and cursed them all to hell. And, he would add, what a terrible thing was a curse spoken with true spite. How often could a curse like that become a prophecy. And if one of the children should comment on his wet eyes, why, he could always blame old age, old age and sad memories.

Chapter Four

The one red leaf, the last of its clan,
That dances as often as dance it can,
Hanging so light and hanging so high,
On the topmost twig that looks up at the sky.

'Christabel'
(Samuel Taylor Coleridge)

The cart was large, a four-wheeler, pulled by a patient Clydesdale gelding. Dark brown with a white stripe down its nose, four white socks, it sifted noisily through the contents of its feed bag while Matthew and David took turns to edge along the cart-shafts and sit, legs widely bowed, on its broad back.

'Donkin and Donkin,' exclaimed the white writing on the side of the green, glossy cart side. 'Drapers, Hatters, Grocers.' In smaller writing was painted 'Carriers'. It was a Donkin who would take the Armstrongs' possessions to their new home; not one of the two named on the cart (for they were the proud owners of four shops in Dunston and Ryton south of the Tyne, Elswick and Wallsend to the north, and a grand emporium in Newcastle itself) but a third-generation Donkin, a friend of Willie. While Mary packed crockery and layers of straw into boxes, Thomas, Willie and young Donkin carried furniture out and heaved it over the high tailboard. Bedheads and feet (both wooden and brass), deformed horsehair mattresses, rocking chairs, crackets, a longsettle. Willie's dess-bed, a host of proggy mats, pictures of a young Queen Victoria and Prince Albert, black and white prints of biblical scenes – 'I thought I'd thrown those away,' said Thomas as he handed them to Willie on the cart – a hand-tinted 'Light of the World', all were slipped carefully into place. The tin bath came out filled with pieces of wood, Thomas's carvings, destined to be incorporated into items of furniture during the coming winter. Chests of drawers stuffed with linen and blankets, two screens covered with pictures and prints and scraps of coloured paper which had taken Mary's fancy during the years of her marriage, all were added to the compression of goods which were the total possessions of the Armstrongs. Last came the suitcases, brown and worn, one for Thomas and Mary, another for the children, a third, much larger, which Willie claimed, and a wooden box with the initials T.A. carved on the lid.

'Is that it?' asked Donkin.

'I'll check,' said Thomas. He went back into the house, his feet rasping the stone slabs and echoing the room. Mary stood in front of the fireplace. She turned as she heard Thomas enter, forced a sad smile to her lips.

'What's up love?' he asked. The question was unnecessary. They had discussed the move, Mary had expressed her worries, and nothing had happened since then to soften her anxiety. The words Thomas had spoken were only an outward sign of his concern for her. He walked forward, took her in his arms, stroked her hair as she tried to hold back her tears.

'Hey, come on lass! We'll be alright, you know we will. I'll look after you.' He turned her head up, brushed her hair out of her eyes, dabbed at the damp patches on her cheeks with his fingers.

'Your nose is red!'

She smiled properly.

'That's better! That's the Mary I remember. Just wait till we get there, it'll be worth it. The houses are lovely, and there's indoors water, and a kitchen for you to have all to yourself. And the kids, they'll love it, it's such a beautiful place. Oh, it'll be strange to start with, but you'll soon make friends. And we can come back every month to visit your mother. I promise.'

Mary raised her eyes and looked at her husband. She had not seen him so excited since . . . since David was born. He allowed life to drift him where it would, taking a deep breath as each wave passed, not struggling against the tide. He was slow to anger, swift to forgive, and his opinion was respected because of this. She loved him (and only in the past few days had she realised this for certain, because it was not a subject which she found the need or the time to consider) for his dependability, his immutability. Perhaps her problem lay within her, perhaps she had allowed her fear of change to transform itself into a fear of him changing, and this had caused her to see in him emotions which she had not really noticed before. He seemed to relish the new challenge which the move would provide; it had brought her tears and a feeling of dismal helplessness.

She had never pretended to understand him. He enjoyed reading while she had difficulty in spelling and could manage to write, with confidence, no more than her own name. He talked of the Arts (he spoke the word with a true respect which emphasised the capital letter) and politics a great deal when they were first married, not at all now. She told him once, just before Matthew was born, that she felt uneducated beside him, unable to contribute to any conversation he started. He had laughed at her, told her not to be so silly, insisted that he loved her for what she was, not for what she might think he wanted her to be. He had put his ear to her belly and laughed at the sound and motion within; they had made love gently, and her fears had left her. Now they had reappeared.

There were other things to worry her, things which Thomas had expected to concern her, and so she attached her fear of the change in him to more mundane matters. In this way he was unaware of the turmoil she was trying to hide. She wanted him to love her, and their children, to provide for them, and to build his life around them in the same way that she had built her life around him. But she could not find the words to say so. And so his words did nothing to help.

It would be difficult. A new house, new neighbours, strangers; and not only Willie living with them, but Thomas's father too. She didn't know him well. A restrained, taciturn man he seemed, polite, that was true, but withdrawn, always smelling of smoke and drink. Thomas had been wary of mentioning the subject to her, had approached it in a roundabout way which she had not seen him use before. He had always tried to involve her in any decisions in the past, even when she had insisted that she would rather be told what to do, but this time he had implied that there was no choice in the matter. It had all to do with this dancing that was, and this was most strange to her, part of the job. How could a miner getting a job be conditional upon how well he could dance? And the only person who could help them with this, who could teach Thomas and Willie and some others (who had not yet been selected) how to do this dance was Thomas Armstrong senior. It was too far for him to travel to teach them, so he would have to move in with them! Thomas had presented her with the facts and she had accepted them. She found it more difficult to cope with her own emotions on hearing him tapping out a rhythm one morning, clog dancing, mats rolled back to make room on the flagged living room floor. She had stood by the door and peered through the crack at the hinges, watched him perform some complicated step, and had barely recognised the exultation on his face, the triumph in the hissed exhalation, 'Yessss!', his happiness at his accomplishment. No, she had told herself, no, you won't be that stupid! You won't be jealous of a dance! You love him, he loves you, nothing else matters. And she really believed that she had convinced herself of that fact.

'It's alright Thomas, it's nothing really. It's just that, well, this house holds a lot of memories for me. It's the only home we've known, our children were born here, we've been ... I've been happy here Thomas. Oh, it's not much, so far as houses go, but it's got a lot of me in it, and a lot of you in it and, I know it sounds silly, but I just wanted to say goodbye.'

'And have you?'

'Yes, I've said goodbye. The house and me, we're parting on good terms. We'll remember each other, even if we don't ever see each other again. Come on. We've got a new life waiting for us!'

She grabbed his ears and pulled his head down, kissed him on the forehead. They looked at each other, eye to eye, then turned and left the house. He helped her up to the seat of the cart.

'Have we forgotten anything?' he asked

'No love, the only thing we seem to be missing is your Dad.'

'We did it, Thomas me lad, we did it! You should have seen the look on Bompas's face as you were dancing, he turned forty shades of purple! Oh, but you were good, my God you were good. Fancy you remembering those steps after all those years. I wouldn't have credited it! I honestly didn't think you'd be able to do it!'

'You what? You mean you put me up to that, that ...

torture, that's the word, torture! You had me up there in front of everybody and you didn't even know for certain I could do the bloody dance! Thank you very much indeed. And then you have the gall to say "We did it!". You little bugger, I'll get you for that, no, not yet! When you're least expecting it!'

Willie pretended fear, knew that his brother would forget to seek revenge long before he forgot to watch out for him. The pair walked jauntily along the road, whistling and singing, discussing their new jobs, their new home, their new employer.

'That John Waterhouse, I was a bit unsure about him at first, what with him weighing things up and deciding he needed Bompas more than us. That was before you did your stuff, of course. His brother, mind, I liked his brother straight off. There's something about younger brothers, they've got that special air about them, if you know what I mean.'

'Natural gamblers, aye, I know the type. They trifle with their elder brothers' affections, live off their hard work. It's the elder brothers who bear the burden of responsibility, sure enough. And a word of warning Willie. The name Armstrong'll be even less popular with Bompas now than it was before. He's a good pit-manager, he'll find work elsewhere. Just keep your eyes open. He might decide to come looking for you, or for me. So watch out!'

Willie picked up a handful of pebbles, threw them one at a time at an approaching tree trunk.

'I'll watch out – ooh, that was close, that one! – Thomas, I'll watch out. Oh, and I'll tell you what else I'll watch out for at the same time, eh? That lass, the blonde-haired one, Waterhouse's daughter. Margaret, yes I heard him call her Margaret. What a beauty! I'm sure she was giving me the eye while you were dancing, she kept on glancing up and, if she caught me looking back, she'd sort of smile then look away. She looks just ripe for picking, that one.'

Thomas had heard that before. Willie's affections were like thistledown, exposed to an unsuspecting world by the slightest breeze and, if allowed to take root and grow, likely to develop into an unlovely weed. His professions of love were truly meant, readily offered and easily forgotten, by him at least. He seemed unaware of the fondness he generated in young women. And in their mothers.

'No Thomas, joking apart, I do think you did well. If it hadn't been for Margaret's sister stopping all of a sudden you would really have shown them what an Armstrong can do.'

Thomas, hands thrust deep in trouser pockets, watched a flock of birds hurtle past and descend on a rowan tree, still in fruit. Redwings, winter migrants, and their larger cousins, fieldfares. Fat and bumptious members of the thrush family, their presence heralded winter. So soon in the year it might mean hard times, cold weather. Good for coal demand, although frozen seas in the Baltic sometimes meant that coal ships couldn't get through to their intended markets. If that happened miners might be laid off. Although he felt himself used to hardship, he was also aware that he and his family enjoyed a better standard of living than his father, and his father's father, had done. Life was bearable if you could stay in work. The move to Waterhouse's pit would be added insurance in that direction.

'Willie,' he said thoughtfully, picking up again the threads of the conversation. 'I didn't stop because the music stopped. It was the other way round. She stopped when she saw me make a mess of one of the steps. If she hadn't stopped then it would have made me look dafter than I felt. She must have very good eyes, or a very good sense of rhythm, or both. I must ask her, if I get the chance, how she did it.'

'Well, it was a good job she did. She must have been

watching you closely. Perhaps she liked the look of you, eh? She was probably a bonny lass in her time. Wait till I tell Mary you've scored!'

Thomas seemed alarmed. 'You'll do nothing of the sort, Willie Armstrong!' he warned. 'You know Mary doesn't find that type of thing funny. And anyway, she wasn't my type at all, far too thin, no meat on her. I much prefer a woman I can get hold of. No, Mary's just right for me, so we'll have none of your trouble-making in that direction. And speaking of trouble, we've got a problem ourselves. Or you've got a problem.'

'Problem? Me? No, surely not. What problem could I possibly have? Life's too good to have problems.'

Thomas grinned. He made sure Willie could see the grin, but said nothing.

'Come on then, out with it. What's the problem?'

Thomas inhaled deeply, tutted, pursed his lips, shook his head.

'Thomas, I'm warning you!'

'Oh yes?'

'Yes!'

'Really?'

'Really!' Thomas paused for a long, theatrical moment before delivering his next line.

'You and whose army?'

It was the beginning of the children's banter which Thomas had used frequently when they were younger. It had resulted then in a brief fight which Thomas had always won on account of his age and size, or verbal sparring which Thomas had always won because of his age and vocabulary. Willie could remember both outcomes.

'Thomas, you bugger, stop it! You just do that to annoy me!'

'Mm, infuriating, isn't it! It's about time I got my own back today.'

'Thomas, you're smaller than me now, remember that!'

'Willie, surely you're not threatening your big brother with violence? The same big brother who's just got you a nice job. Who's going to let you live with him in a nice house.' He paused, then put his arm round the other's shoulders.

'The same big brother, Willie me darling, who's going to let *you* tell our lovable Dad that we need him to come and live with us for a while to teach us rapper.'

'Damn! Thomas, there are times when I hate you!'

'Where the hell is he?' said Willie. 'He promised he'd be here on time. I even borrowed a handcart last night, went down to his house, helped him pack, then brought all his stuff up here. Nine o'clock, we agreed, nine o'clock, and he's not here yet. We should go without him.'

'It's only just turned nine,' said Thomas. 'He'll be here soon.'

'Who's going to be here soon?' asked Matthew from the back of the horse.

'Your grandad,' answered Mary. 'He's going to come with us to our new house and he's going to live with us for a little while. Won't that be nice!'

'Where's he going to sleep?' came David's voice. He was about to jump the six feet or so from the top rail of the wagon's side-frame to the ground. Thomas opened his arms to catch him as he flew down.

'Can he sleep with me?' continued the smaller boy. 'He tells good stories.'

'No,' said Thomas, 'he's going to sleep with your Uncle Willie. They can keep each other awake with their snoring.' David clung tightly to his father, the more outwardly affectionate of the two children. He was both bullied and protected by his brother, the closeness of their ages preventing the paternalism which had been forced upon Thomas in his relationship with Willie. Matthew and David played together often, almost as equals; Thomas and Willie had never experienced that luxury.

Matthew slid from the horse to land at Thomas's feet on the hard earth; no cobbles yet in this street. He pulled at his father's hand, began to climb his leg in an attempt to join his brother being held aloft. David, meanwhile, was pulling and pushing at his father's hair, his aim to cover the bald spot on top of his head.

'Now then you two, what's going on? This is a conspiracy!'

'Now then you two, what's going on? This is a conspiracy! I haven't seen the two of you together since Christmas two years since, you,' he pointed at Willie, 'since this past February, and that was only because you were visiting some young skirt down the road and her father wouldn't let you in! And the two of you suddenly appear on me doorstep, all smiles and "How are you Dad" and "Hope you're well Dad" and "We've brought you a few bottles of beer Dad." I suppose for that, at least, I should be grateful. But you want something from me, that at least I can see, so I might as well drink while you tell me what it is. Come on, pass a bottle over.'

Thomas did most of the explaining, urged on by Willie. Their father said little, drank frequently from the first, then the second, third and fourth bottles. A frown crossed his face at the mention of Bompas's name; he started to rise from the chair, but was halted as Thomas rushed on to describe Willie's role.

'He said we were the sons of Tommy Armstrong the dancer, Tommy Armstrong the fiddler, Tommy Armstrong the best musician and clogger in the north-east of England. And so I had to dance, to support the family name!'

He stood up to demonstrate the steps he had done, much to his father's amusement.

'And they gave you a job? Just because you could do four of the easiest steps known to mankind? Good God lad, Matty Harrison could do those steps and he's only got one leg!' He moved on to the fifth bottle.

'In fact,' he slurred, 'Matty Harrison's dog could do better, and he's been dead three years since!' Thomas joined in the laughter without enthusiasm. He knew that his dancing had been poor in comparison to what his father had once been capable of, but it had been many years since he had danced, and he had been forced into performing. He had, all things considered, been proud of his achievement. His father must have sensed his reticence, even through the alcohol.

'No, I'm sorry, I shouldn't make fun of you like that, really I shouldn't. You've both done very well, sticking up for each other, and for me, like that. I'm proud of you. And it's good of you to come to see me to tell me that you've got new jobs, good jobs by the sound of it. And I realise you'll be moving away. No, don't worry, I'll be alright, I've still got me little widow-woman looking after me needs. I'll be alright.' He nodded gently to himself, convinced of his magnanimity in allowing his sons to move even further away, of considering their needs before his own.

'We want you,' said Willie, 'to come with us.'

The head of the family looked at his sons. He tilted his head to one side, tried to pull his vision into focus, and succeeded only in taking on the look of a bewildered spaniel. He opened his mouth to speak but held back the words which first sprang into his mind. It was unusual, almost unheard of, for his sons to request some favour of him. He had, in his own opinion, not been a particularly good father, and this was reflected in the uneasiness he often felt in their company. He drank too much, he knew that, but his brain was not yet fuddled by that evening's intake; he was aware that his sons would not ask for anything from him unless the need was great.

'Why?' he whispered.

'We need you,' Thomas replied. 'We need you to teach us how to dance. We need you to show us how to do rapper. Because the man who's given us jobs, good jobs mind you, and a good house in a place where my kids'll grow up with a school and a library, he had faith in us when we said we could get a team together. It doesn't have to be permanent, we're not saying come and live with us full time, not unless you really want to, in which case we'd be happy to have you stay' – he saw Willie raise his eyes at that, wondered what Mary's reactions might be – 'but we have to win the championship next summer, Dad. Waterhouse chose us instead of Bompas' – his father shook his head at the name – 'and we have to show him he was right in making that decision.'

There was silence for a while. The oil lamp guttered, belched a ring of smoke to join those already emblazoned on the ceiling. The old man stood up, marched to the fire, and threw on some more coals. The orange flames dimmed, and in the shadows he looked suddenly weary. He was being asked for help, and he was aware that if he gave that help he would have to face old memories, old fears that had been hidden for many years. And Bompas, the name still filled him with anger and a deep, stomach-wrenching sickness, Bompas would still be there to play a part. He knew that. And he feared Bompas. Thomas watched his father. He could see the arguments moving over his face, unable to comprehend their meaning.

'But most of all, Dad, it'll be for us. For me. And for Willie. And for you.'

The old man smiled. He was aware that the decision had been taken out of his hands.

'When do we go?'

It was a few minutes after nine when the old man (for the

first time in his life Thomas found himself considering his father that, an old man) was deposited at the door in a dog cart. He apologised for being late, blamed it on over-zealous goodbyes the night before. He was dressed in his best suit, his best boots polished and shining, his best smile on his face. And clutched in his hand was his violin case. Mary climbed down from the wagon and kissed him dutifully, murmured an aside to Thomas that 'He's had a shave this morning! And he doesn't smell of drink!' Matthew and David clamoured for his attention, demanded a tune or a story. The old man chose the latter and climbed with the children into the back of the cart, found a seat, and began the tale of Jimmy Wilikson, who lived with Charlie the dog and Wonkie Dormouse in a hollow tree in the park down by the river. Mary and Thomas took their place again at the headboard, gazing down over the broad flanks of the horse ahead of them. Willie and young Donkin led the beast off, talking of the girls they knew, laughing at their conquests, real and imaginary.

The weather stayed fine, warm October sun raising steam from damp hedgerows as they passed. It was indeed a time of change. Leaves were being cast, hawthorn berries displayed themselves invitingly red, crab apples on branch and ground attracted blackbirds and thrushes. The air was ripe, hung with dewy cobwebs and the far-off echoes of children calling. A heron flew overhead, hotly pursued by two crows, its bowed wings hurrying it towards a small pool or pond where fishing might be easy. Late butterflies hawked at a sad clover. Thomas reached for Mary's hand. He felt content, and this helped soothe her worries. Everything would be alright.

'Thomas, this isn't really our house? It's lovely! Oh Thomas!' Mary jumped down from the wagon and stood at the gate. The house was at the end of a row of four, a garden (at this stage nothing more than rough grass and weeds) on three sides. A low wooden fence ran round the perimeter. There was smoke rising from the chimneys of two of the other cottages in the row but no sign of life, no curious curtains drawn aside.

'Here you are then,' said Thomas. He handed his wife a key tied to a wooden carving, the initial letters of their names intertwined with a heart. She lifted his hand and kissed it gently, whispered thank you at the same time.

'Come on then, lovely man, let's see what it's like inside!' she said, lifted the latch to open the gate and walked up the path to the front door. The key turned easily in the lock.

The door opened into a large room ('Isn't it big Thomas, almost as big as our whole house was!') with a blackleaded range set centrally in the wall to their left, a door beside it. On the wall opposite there were two gaslights. Beside the door through which they had just come was a single, though large, window, and ahead of them was another door. The walls had been papered with a green floral design, and the ceiling was white with no rings of soot. Mary walked over to stand by the range, ran her finger over the mantelpiece. There was no dust. She raised her eyebrows in surprise. She walked to the middle of the room and whirled on the spot.

'I don't know where to go next,' she laughed. Outside Willie and Donkin were untying ropes, David and Matthew were pulling their grandfather down to look at the swan on the pond. Thomas opened the door beside the range and ushered his wife through. This room was long and thin, a window at each end, and at the bottom a door led out into the garden. Beside it was a white enamelled sink, and beside that a curtain hung from floor to ceiling.

'Go and have a look behind that,' urged Thomas. Mary did so and gasped in surprise.

'It's a bath Thomas, a proper bath!'

'Aye luv, a proper bath. And that's not all. Look!' he

pointed at a metal pipe which ran around the wall of the room to end at a small tap beside the sink.

'That comes from the range. There's a tank in there, up near the top where it gets a lot of heat, and you can let cold water straight into it, no need to carry it in in kettles and pans and things. The fire warms it up, and then you can let the hot water out straight into the sink, or,' he moved the pipe with the tap on its end, 'into the bath. Mr Waterhouse himself invented it, there's a special valve which stops the water from boiling and the tank from exploding. If you look carefully,' he pointed upwards to where the pipe disappeared into the ceiling, 'you can just see . . .'

His monologue was interrupted by a scream of delight from outside. Mary had opened the back door and gone out onto a concreted yard. There were two brick-built outhouses, the first of which was well stocked with coal. The second contained a toilet.

'Thomas, come quick! Look, it's a proper netty!' She stood beside the open door and motioned Thomas to join her. They gazed at the contents. The bowl itself was hidden beneath a wooden seat, a tongued and grooved panel in front, a similar panel providing a shelf for a small oil lamp. A lead pipe was fixed to the wall, above it a brightly painted cistern from which hung a polished brassy chain.

'Mr Waterhouse again,' said Thomas.

'Apparently he insisted that every house should have its own netty. And it's connected up to the sewers, no need for the night-soil man to come round. You just pull the chain' – he did so with a flourish and they watched the water whirlpool around the bowl, listened as the cistern re-filled itself – 'and that's it. Now come on back in the house – wait till you see upstairs.'

They hurried in again, gave the pantry, shelved but empty, a cursory glance, then moved back into the front room where Thomas opened the other door. It showed three steps, then a landing, and twelve further steps took them to the floor above. Two doors faced them. They took the one on the left. This first, larger room was bright and sunny, its windows low in the front wall, the ceiling angled where it met the roof. There was a small fireplace, again brightly polished, and in its surround were placed blue and white glazed tiles. The second bedroom was similar to the room below it, long and narrow, a window in each of the smaller walls, a fireplace matching that in the larger bedroom.

'It's beautiful Thomas,' exclaimed Mary. 'A room for the boys all to themselves, a staircase instead of that horrible, dangerous ladder, all that garden. We could keep hens, and perhaps a pig. I can see now why you were so keen to come here. And Willie and your Dad, they'll be able to sleep in the back room downstairs. And it'll be so easy to keep everything clean, there's no damp, there's hot water. Oh thank you Thomas, thank you.'

She reached up, put her hands round his neck, and pulled his lips to hers, her tongue pushing between his teeth. His hands moved down over her behind, grasped a buttock each, pushed himself forward so that she could feel the strength of his response.

'Oh, Thomas,' she murmured.

'What are you two doing up there?' came Willie's voice. 'There's a whole wagon full of stuff to unload.' His head appeared round the door at the bottom of the stairwell, and the two separated guiltily.

'Caught you!' chided Willie. 'And I thought you were getting too old for that type of thing. We need you to tell us where you want things putting. If you've got time, that is.'

The couple sighed as one, and giggled, then moved downstairs to supervise the unpacking.

Two hours later the wagon was empty and on its way back home, young Donkin thinking of how he'd spend the profits of his day's work. The boys were playing in the garden, a kettle had been boiled, and tea was being drunk by the adults. Most of the furniture had been allocated an initial resting place; the double mattress lay in the middle of the floor, its journey to the room above halted by Willie's temporary requisition of its surface as a comfortable resting place.

'It just goes to show,' said the reclining Willie, 'you can't use the same muscles for hewing as you do for moving heavy furniture. Or why would I be lying here now with a bad back?'

'Laziness?' prompted Thomas.

'No, you're just unfit,' added his father. 'In my day you had to be really fit to work in the mines. Eighteen-inch seams, air foul as a midden, the rocks creaking and groaning around you and spitting dirty water at you. It's not like that these days. You've got it easy man.'

'Unfit?' said Willie. 'Me, unfit? I'll be the fittest man in this pit, believe you me.'

'Well why are you so sore?' asked Mary, bustling into the room, her arms full of children's clothes.

'It's him,' said Willie, pointing at Thomas. 'He was carrying that settle all wrong, he put all the weight onto me, and it's done me back in. I don't think I'll ever walk again.' He whimpered as Thomas detached a sock from the pile beside him and threw it accurately at his brother's head.

Willie reached for it and was preparing to throw it back when there came a knock at the door. At the same time Matthew and David hurled themselves back into the house.

'Dad, Dad!' yelled the youngest. 'There's two ladies coming up the path.'

'They're carrying a big basket, Dad,' added Matthew, 'and one of them's very pretty. She smiled at me,' he added boastfully.

'Probably neighbours come to welcome us,' said Thomas senior. 'Bring a cake or something – you know how it is.'

'And one of them's pretty?' smiled Willie. 'I can't wait!' The knock sounded again.

'Well I suppose I'd better let them in,' said Thomas. 'Nobody else seems capable of opening a door round here. Mary!' he yelled as he reached for the handle, 'we've got visitors come to welcome . . .'

His speech was cut short, although those in the room were unable to see round the door. He began to speak again, slightly flustered.

'Oh, hello. I'm sorry, I, er, I didn't expect it to be you. We thought it would be neighbours come to say hello. But please, come in, I'm forgetting my manners.' He backed into the room to allow the visitors to enter, making urgent though imprecise flapping movements with his hands.

'This is my wife, Mary; my father, Thomas; my sons, Matthew and David; and I think you've already seen my brother Willie.' He motioned to Willie to stand up as the two women edged past the furniture into the room, then completed the introductions.

'These are Mr Waterhouse's daughters.'

Willie's back and its attendant ills were ignored as he shot to his feet. Mary curtsied gently, Thomas senior nodded with a grunt of surly respect. David stared shyly at his feet. No-one spoke; the awkwardness stifled the room.

'Hello Missus,' said Matthew cheerily, suddenly. He inclined his head towards Margaret. 'See, I told you she was pretty!' The laughter gave them all back their voices.

'Please, sit down,' said Mary, moving piles of clothes. 'Would you like a cup of tea? We haven't any milk, I'm afraid.'

'Oh yes you have,' said Margaret, 'that's why we're here.'

'Yes,' added Elizabeth, 'we'd like to welcome you on behalf of our father, but we know that you've had to travel far to get here so we brought these for you.' She reached into the basket she was carrying.

'There's milk and cheese from the farm, some loaves of bread, a cured ham, some pickle, and some plum jam, the year's first. Oh, and there are some potatoes outside the back door, we had them brought round earlier.'

'I helped make the jam,' interjected Margaret.

'I'm sure it'll taste wonderful,' simpered Willie.

'And yes please, if you don't mind, we'd love a cup of tea,' said Elizabeth.

The children were dispatched to wash their hands and faces, returning moments later to stare at their guests.

'You're David, are you?' asked Elizabeth.

'Yes, he is, and I'm Matthew,' answered his brother.

'Do you go to school?'

'I do, and he does too but he can't do as well as me. I can write my name and I can read. Well, sometimes I can read.'

'And can you dance? Can you dance as well as your father?'

'Dad?' laughed Matthew. Even David allowed himself a smile, his hands stroking the front-door key and its smooth wooden love-knot.

'Dad dances funny. He dances with Mam sometimes. He puts a dishcloth on his head instead of his hat, and he tries hard, but he's still silly.'

'Grandad dances,' said David.

'No he doesn't!' countered Matthew. 'I've never even seen him dance!'

'He told me. He said he was the best dancer in the whole wide world.'

Everyone looked at the elder Thomas, who blushed slightly.

'I think,' he said after clearing his throat, 'I think I'll take the lads out for a walk. Do a bit of exploring. If no-one minds, that is?'

Thomas and Mary looked at each other, shook their heads. The trio disappeared with yells of laughter. While

Mary went into the kitchen to make the tea (and to hunt for her two china cups and the matching saucers, only one of which was slightly chipped), Willie asked Margaret about the size of the estate, the type of farm. The fact of communication was more important than the content; he wished only to watch this vision, and talking to her gave him that excuse. Thomas, meanwhile, crouched down beside Elizabeth.

'Miss Waterhouse, I'd like . . .'

'Mr Armstrong, my name is not Waterhouse.' She held out her left hand to show the ring on her wedding finger.

'My surname is Kearton.'

'Oh, I'm sorry, I didn't realise, I thought that, because you were here with your father, you weren't married.'

'That's alright Mr Armstrong, perfectly understandable. My husband is a businessman, he travels a great deal. He's . . .' She paused, examining her ring carefully. 'He's out of the country at the moment.'

She looked up, looked directly at him with what would have been, from anyone else, a stare. With her it was more an invitation to speak again. Thomas accepted the invitation.

'I've been wanting to say thank you for playing for me when I danced the other day.' She nodded her head in acknowledgement. 'And I also wanted to thank you for stopping when you did. You made it seem as if it was your mistake, and I know that it wasn't, and you know that it wasn't. So thank you. I wouldn't have minded looking silly . . .'

'Yes, Matthew's description of your dancing with the dishcloth tends to reinforce that statement.'

They both smiled, and he found himself looking directly into her eyes yet again.

'No, but the fact that I didn't may have helped persuade your father that it was worth hiring me. And it does mean a lot to me, and to my family.'

'Mr Armstrong, I can see how much your family means to you, and I'm pleased to see you, and them, safely here. I hope that we'll all benefit from your presence at Greencroft. So your thanks are accepted, but we'll hear no more about it. Except for me to thank you. Despite your protestations to the contrary, you are a good dancer.'

Mary re-appeared, carrying the tea which she offered gracefully to her guests.

'I think that your children will enjoy themselves here, Mrs Armstrong,' said Elizabeth. 'The schoolmaster is a very good man, Mr Campbell, firm but kind, and very knowledgeable, particularly in the technical and mathematical fields. I myself go into the school once a week to teach the girls needlework and cookery. I do enjoy the children's company, although at times they can be very exuberant.'

'And there's the library too, I must show you that,' said Thomas. 'It's open in the evenings to go and read the papers, and you can borrow up to three books at once, and there's no charge.'

'Oh good,' said Mary unenthusiastically.

'I like the village hall best,' said Margaret. 'Father says that as soon as everyone moves in we'll be able to have dances and parties for the whole village. I love parties.'

'I like parties too,' said Willie. 'Will you come to village dances at well?'

'Oh yes, I'm sure I'll be allowed to come along.' She glanced at Elizabeth. 'Providing I'm chaperoned, of course.'

'In that case,' asked Willie, 'I should consider it an honour if you would be gracious enough to consider dancing with me at some time during the evening. Whenever this dance takes place, of course.'

'Why, Mr Armstrong, you have a most gracious way with words. I'd be delighted to dance with you. I shall look forward to that.'

'I think, sister,' said Elizabeth, 'that we should allow Mr

and Mrs Armstrong to continue their work while they have the opportunity. Thank you for the tea Mrs Armstrong, it was very pleasant.'

Willie cleared his throat and appeared to stand to attention.

'May I have the pleasure of escorting you two ladies to the Hall?' he asked in a voice which, to Thomas, was a parody of his normal bantering tone.

'Mr Armstrong,' answered Elizabeth in what was clearly not *her* normal manner, her words touched with friendly elaboration, 'my sister and I would be delighted to have you accompany us. Come Margaret, let us away. Such gallantry!' Willie winked at Thomas as he pulled on his jacket. He appeared intent on enjoying his new life to the full. Polite goodbyes were exchanged and the unlikely threesome departed, only to return before the door was closed after them.

'I must apologise Mr Armstrong,' said Elizabeth. 'I was on the point of forgetting the most important part of my task in visiting you this afternoon. My sister and my father and I are to attend a dance at the home of a neighbour, Sir Charles Makemore. It is his son, Mr Henry Makemore, who has made a wager with my uncle regarding this rapper dance that you are to peform. But I digress. Appearing at this dance as an entertainment will be Mr Makemore's employees doing that very dance. My father has been invited to bring some of his own men along. I fear that this is an attempt to discourage you, however, by showing you how difficult is the task ahead of you. None the less, I trust that you will wish to attend. The dance is being held on Wednesday evening, and we depart at seven from the Hall. I would advise you to dress warmly, as it will be necessary for you to sit above the coach.'

Thomas was taken aback. Elizabeth nodded a brief goodbye again and was halfway down the path once more before he could reply.

'Miss, I mean Mrs Kearton. Yes, I'll come, but I'll need to bring my father, he's the one who knows all about this dance.' She nodded.

'And me,' said Willie, 'I'll need to be there too. After all, I'll be part of the team as well.'

'Very well. It is quite a large coach. I shall see you on Wednesday, seven prompt. Goodbye again.' Finally they left.

'What on earth was all that about?' asked Mary. 'And what is the matter with Willie? He's like a dog sniffing round a bitch on heat.'

'Mary, that's no way to talk about the daughter of our employer!'

'It's not her, it's him I'm getting at. He's no chance there, you saw them, they were laughing at him, not to his face, but in their voices. I could see that, and I'm sure you could. Why couldn't he?'

'Mary, he's old enough to look after himself. And anyway, Matthew was right. She is very pretty! But not as pretty as you luv! Now where were we before that brother of mine interrupted us?' He reached out, grabbed her round the waist and pulled her to him. Their kiss was long. His hands moved over her body, caressing and catching, pinching and pulling beneath the folds of her clothing. His fingers tugged at the bow on her apron, took away the shawl, moved up to undo the buttons of her blouse.

'Thomas, not here, not now. Please, someone might see us!'

'Who's to see us. No-one'll be back for a while yet, there's a mattress right there on the floor. Mary, I need you.'

Three buttons were undone as he spoke. His left hand was inside her blouse before he finished the sentence, seeking out a nipple to tease into life, while his right was behind her, inside the waistband of her skirt, sliding down the smooth fold of her buttocks.

'Thomas, I love you,' she whispered as she began an exploration of her own, undoing the buttons on his trousers to dart her hand inside, feel his warmth against the rough flannel. Her tongue was deep in his mouth, her other hand at his neck, stroking softly. He moaned her name as she found the opening in the material, grasped the flesh beneath, moved her hand firmly up and down.

Her blouse was now open, her breasts exposed. He pulled first at one nipple, then the other, while his other hand moved further down between her legs, fumbling at the material of her underwear. He found the soft skin of her stomach, then the wiry hair beyond, and his fingers pushed urgently into the moist opening below.

'Thomas, no!' She pushed him away. They were both breathing heavily.

'Do it properly luv,' she whispered. 'If you want to do it, do it properly!'

She bent down to unlace her shoes and her breasts fell forward. She wore no stockings, no socks. She wriggled out of her skirt – the buttons had already been undone – pulled down her bloomers and took off her blouse to stand naked before her husband. She was, she knew, not as trim as she had been when they married. Five pregnancies had seen to that, and three children suckled. She had stretch marks on her behind, and she held her stomach in as she stood, and she pushed her chest out. Her body had changed, but she still felt that same longing she knew from all those years ago when Thomas had first taken her to his bed. She knelt down on the mattress and watched as he undressed.

His boots and socks (she noticed a hole in one; best remember to darn it before it grew larger) were kicked off to join his shirt in the corner, his breeches were quick to follow. The tenting of his long-johns showed his readiness, and they were quickly pulled down. He stood for a moment. She could smell the sweat on him, could anticipate his hands on her, his manhood inside her. He looked down on her, and she could see the young man he used to be, unsure of himself, slimmer, certainly more hair on his head than there was now. But he had grown accustomed to her body, aware of her needs. They would be in each other's arms, their desires quenched, their skin slicked with moisture, he slowly retreating, and he would stroke her neck or her back or her behind and say 'We're made for each other, you and me. We're made for each other luv,' and her eyes would grow moist with the love of him.

'Come on then luv,' she said, and lay back. He knelt at her feet, ran his hands up from her ankles to her knees, then to her thighs, parted her legs, and leaned forward.

'Oh, Mary,' he husked in her ear, his tongue tracing the syllables, 'I love you.'

There was a fire burning in Elizabeth's room, scattering its light randomly over the furniture within. It was reflected from the tall and highly polished mahogany wardrobe which seemed to add its own aura of warmth to the red-brown glow, and searched out the shadows beneath the huge bed, caught the carved owls stationed sentry-like at its foot in open-eyed surprise. Dark blue curtains were drawn across the stone-mullioned bay windows; the lighter blue lilies on the wallpaper were barely visible. True, there was a light hung in the centre of the room, almost a chandelier, and fitted with light-bulbs as well; John Waterhouse had insisted during modernisation of the Hall that electricity should be installed, and the generator could be powered both by water and by coal. Elizabeth did not like its glare, however, and preferred to write by the light of an oil lamp. She had been restless that evening, had retired early and played her piano for a while. The lid was still open, a pile of music bearing testimony to her inability to find a melody which would calm her mind. She had tried reading, turned to *Hard Times* (she had absorbed most of Dickens's other works) but found its weary air of gloominess depressing; searching her bookshelves for something more cheerful she had been faced with Rossetti and Tennyson, and in despair, she had taken a leisurely bath. The steamy waters had calmed her a little, but sleep was still distant. She knew what it was, knew the reason for her discomfort, and was afraid to confront her thoughts.

She reached absently for the bellpush which would have summoned Abigail, the maid she shared with Margaret. A conversation? A game of cards? Draughts, chess, it mattered not, the ocupation was less important than the companionship. Her hand faltered as she remembered that she had given Abigail the evening off, in sympathy with the poor girl having spent the day rushing around after her younger sister. She had proposed that they do without the services of a personal maid completely, but Margaret had wept and stamped her feet, pleaded with her father, and Abigail had been retained to run where Margaret's every whim directed. Elizabeth's thoughts returned to herself and she groaned out loud, raised her knuckles to her eyes as if to block out the visions confronting her. She began to pace the room, her nightdress flowing behind her as her feet trod the path from desk to fireplace, from fireplace to window, from window to bed, then back to desk. She paused only once, to glance at her reflection in the tall mirror beside the wardrobe. The reflection twisted its face, for some reason not liking what it saw. She resumed her march.

The day had been going so well. She had risen early and walked the boundaries of the estate, met Mr Settle who had accompanied her for a large part of the way and pointed out the badgers' sett, showed her where the herons would return to nest in the spring, and made her feel almost normal with his gentle, bluff joking and unforced familiarity. By the time she returned to the Hall Margaret had risen, and together they had packed the basket of food for the Armstrongs. It had been Elizabeth's idea originally, but Margaret had added form and substance. Their father had given his guarded approval, warning them that his new employees' pride might prevent them accepting gifts which could too easily seem to be charity, but Margaret's obvious enthusiasm, her naive friendliness, always won the day. Each family, as they arrived, had been greeted by the owner's daughters bearing tokens of friendship. None had turned them away, and most had commented on their good fortune in coming to work for an employer whose philanthropy (they would not, perhaps, have used that particular word) had obviously been inherited by his offspring. Three more families would arrive tomorrow, and that was the pit's complement complete.

The Armstrongs, however, had been special. It was not just Thomas's dancing, nor his heart-felt thanks for her playing and stopping when she did; nor was it the boyish attentions of the younger brother to Margaret; the children had been charming – she had enjoyed having David climb on her knee and play with her hair – and Mr Armstrong senior, in his own way, had been almost gentlemanly. Perhaps it was Mary's sense of family? She took such obvious pride in her husband and sons, and they reciprocated naturally, spontaneously. They belonged to each other, and Elizabeth had realised instinctively how much that sense of belonging was missing from her own life. That loss, however, was not the source of her torment.

Willie Armstrong had proved a pleasant companion as he escorted them back to the Hall. He had talked of his childhood and his brother in an easy, pleasant manner which had captivated both of them. Only on reaching the gate at the entrance to the drive had she glanced into the basket she was carrying and noticed a key, a key with a carved wooden heart attached to it. Straightaway she pulled

it out, realised that one of the boys, probably David, had
dropped it while scuffling about on her knee. Willie had
been as noble in gesture as in word and immediately offered
to take the key back, then return to accompany them the last
few hundred yards to the house. Before Elizabeth could
thank him Margaret had interrupted, said that of course
there was no need to do that, Elizabeth was fond of walking
and needed the exercise, and that Willie could then continue
to guide Margaret home. She linked her arm with that of the
young miner and drew him away before Elizabeth could
protest, turning back only once to smile and wink. Elizabeth
was rarely speechless, particularly when it came to dealing
with her sister, but on this occasion graciously accepted
defeat and gave up her role as chaperone to head back for
the Armstrongs' house. True, she did hesitate. Willie Armstrong was far older than Margaret, and a man from a
different social class. Despite her own egalitarian principles
she was not sure what might be said, or gossiped about, if
the couple were seen together. But Margaret was not so
young, and probably not so innocent, as she sometimes
pretended. And Willie Armstrong did seem a gentleman, far
more so than that fop Makemore who had been calling for
Margaret more often than was acceptable for what could be
considered a mere friendship. No, Margaret and Willie
might flirt, but they would behave themselves.

It took no more than five minutes to reach the house
again, less than a third of the time it had taken on the
outward journey; Willie's conversation and Margaret's gait
were not conducive to speedy travel. It was quiet, no sounds
of heavy furniture being moved, no sounds at all. She was on
the point of knocking when she heard a gasp; the window
was slightly ajar. Her first thought was to leave the key on
the doorstep. She even went so far as to take the key from
her basket, bent down to deposit it. The key-ring was
beautifully carved, the letters 'T' and 'M' and a heart

intertwining intricately. It must have taken many hours of painstaking work to produce the smooth detail. For some reason she decided that the key would be safer on the window-sill, and she took the two steps to one side which would allow her to place the key there. She had not meant to look through the window, but when she did, she drew back immediately; her heart was beating so loudly she feared that it might be heard by those inside. Had she stood in the doorway and performed an Irish jig it would have been unlikely that any attention would have been paid to her. She ought not to have looked again – the image was burned on her retina – but she did so. She saw Thomas Armstrong standing naked before her, tall and proud and eager. Mary Armstrong was below him, beckoning to him, whispering to him, and he knelt before her, covered her, entered her.

Elizabeth had stayed for no more than half-a-minute, watched the two bodies move in unison, seen hands slide over surfaces rough and smooth and secret, heard whispers and groans and oaths. And she had left. And there were tears in her eyes.

There were tears in her eyes once more as she strode animatedly backwards and forwards across the room. Her hands flew from her face to her hair, were clenched first by her sides then crossed over her chest. She shook her head, asked 'Why me God!' and 'Please, no, not again!' cried 'It's been so long, oh so long!' She flung herself on the bed, face down, her hands continuing to flutter about her as though possessed by another, her body racked by muffled sobs and cries. And then all movement stopped. And all sound stopped.

A watcher would have thought her asleep, unless that watcher had studied her with care. It was her hands which again brought life to the scene. In the light from the dying fire and the dimming oil lamp they moved from their position on the pillow, crept purposefully down the counterpane. She was lying on her stomach; a small pressure on the knees, her backside lifted slightly into the air, and her fingers found their urgent, needy target. Her breathing grew more rapid, her buttocks clenched beneath the cotton of her nightgown. And then suddenly there was no pretence at control, no hiding the act which she had known would be her doom that night. She flung herself upright, continued the motion, pulled her shift over her head and threw it to one side, then forced herself back onto the bed, this time on her back, legs apart, knees crooked at right angles. Her right arm was draped over her stomach, the heel of her hand resting on her pubis, two fingers pulling her sex open, another pushing against her in hard circles. Her left hand was below her leg and reaching back up again, finger and thumb taking turns to move in and out, slowly, languorously.

Her breathing was now more uneven, a low moan coming from the depths of her throat. A hand would break loose from its slick administrations to claw its way up to her breasts, to tease roughly and squeeze each nipple in its vice as though seeking to punish the body for its carnal desires. A patina of sweat now covered her body, the movement from her thighs became more desperate, the fingers moved faster, searching for the particular sensation which would satisfy her. She gasped, forcing air into her lungs, drowning in the deep waters of her need. The waves which had rocked her and spun her, the currents which controlled her every motion, took her deeper into the whirlpool which would drain her of lust. She began to grunt like an animal. One hand grasped the covers, its talons threatening to break through to the sheets beneath. The other was between her legs, drowning. The grunts became regular, changed their form, grew into words.

'Uh . . . uh . . . oh . . . my . . . God . . .!' she cried, lips peeled back, teeth clenched.

'Oh ... dear ... God ... please ... let ... me! Please ... God! Too ... much!'

With one cry, almost a scream, she ceased. Her breasts moved as her lungs sought air. Her hair was lank with sweat, and the musk of her own body filled her nostrils with distaste. Later she would rise, she would go to the toilet-room adjoining hers, she would wash herself with cold water and revel in the austerity of its touch. But now, alone with her guilt, she cried and whispered to herself.

'Too much, too much. Too much, Thomas, too much.'

Chapter Five

He that lives in hope danceth without musick.
                              'Outlandish Proverbs'
                              (George Herbert)

Henry Makemore was studying the chessboard in front of him. His left hand stroked his chin while the fingers of his right beat an uncoordinated rhythm on the table. It was late afternoon, or so the sun's rays trapped by the delicate air-hung dust indicated. Henry's opponent strolled around the library, turning his head occasionally to peer at the title of a book, once or twice removing a volume to give the contents a cursory glance. He was well-dressed. His clothes had an expensive cut about them, were fashionable, respectable, yet touched with colour at waistcoat and tie; self-confidence and status were the messages they proclaimed. But the man within seemed unnatural. He was tall, at least six inches over six feet, but had none of the bulk which ought to have come with that height. He was thin, with an awkward fragility which suggested that any untoward movement might snap his arms or legs and send him toppling like a felled tree. He moved as though aware of the possibility of imminent damage, a flick of the eyes seeking a distant clearing where he might safely place a large flat foot, arms never extended their full reach for fear of their own weight breaking them. He glanced at Makemore as the young man made his move, then stilted his way across the room to fold himself neatly into a sofa set at right angles to the table. He gave the game a moment's attention, slid a bishop gently forward, then leaned back. His arms, supported by the back of the sofa, stretched their full length. Adequately supported he took a deep breath, extended his legs, and gently closed his eyes.

'It really was uncommonly decent of you to invite me up to your home, Henry,' he murmured. His voice was like his movements, precise, guarded, deliberate. It was draped with the lack of accent common in those who have taken elocution lessons.

'It's my pleasure,' responded Makemore, intent once more upon the game. 'But I would remind you that you asked me to invite you. And that you threatened to inform my father of certain problems I've had in the past unless that invitation was forthcoming. Problems in which, I add, you were involved in no small manner.'

'Henry, Henry, surely you do me an injustice!' His eyes opened in innocent surprise, peering at his companion down a slim knife-edge of a nose.

'It was to me you turned, as a friend, when your problems first arose. And as a true friend I considered it my obligation to solve those problems for you. And did I not do so?'

'The boy was too young, damnit! He was too young, he didn't know why he was there, he didn't know what to do!'

'Is that why you hit him Henry? Is that why you beat him until he was unconscious? No Henry, don't look so worried, there's no-one else here but me, no-one to overhear.'

Henry Makemore stared at the thin man, an expression of loathing distorting his face.

'Come come Henry, I know you dislike me, hate me even, but I also know that you fear me because of what I know,

and that you will come once again to love me because of
what I can do for you.' At the word 'love' Henry swallowed
nervously.

'A love,' the thin man added quickly, 'which is purely filial
on your part and, in return, paternal on mine. And financial,
of course, but being a gentleman, I shall not mention that.
But tell me, what is this rumour I hear, of you betting rather
heavily on, of all things, a dance? That is, even for me, a new
vice.' He gently stroked his moustache, allowed his fingers
to trace the outlines of his lips and tug lovingly at his goatee.
Henry smiled, relaxed a little.

'You'll see, later on this evening. Yes, it's a dance, but it's
a dance where teams compete against each other. And it
happens that the team from my father's colliery is the best
there is. So when Mr Edward Waterhouse – he's the brother
of John Waterhouse, remember I told you about him –
wagered that men from his brother's pit – a pit which has
been operating for only one week, mind you, a pit where
none of the miners know each other – could do better than
our own dancers, well I knew that I was onto a good thing,
even at odds of two-to-one.'

'You never were one to turn away from gambling, were
you Henry? That's why we're such good friends. Ah, is it
still your move?'

Henry reached out a hand; his opponent raised an
eyebrow; Henry's hand retreated. He tapped out a message
again on the table, then quickly led his knight forward to do
battle.

'Good move, Henry, good move. But it allows me to do
this,' he slid a pawn forward to expose a bishop in a position
to take Henry's queen. 'And to inform you that I will have
check-mate in three moves. But you are improving.'

Henry stood up, strode to stand in front of the fire.

'Malin . . .'

'I've told you Henry, I prefer Maichamps.'

'Very well then, if you insist.' Henry did not like the name, and when he used it his nostrils quivered as though remembering some bad smell.

'Maichamps. I need to know why you wished to come here.'

'And why, pray, do you have this sudden burning desire for knowledge? I assure you that you do not, in all reality, need to know this. You have invited me. I am here. Nothing more need be said.'

'But Maichamps, you are my guest. My father will wish to know about you, about your background, who you are, what you do, how I met you. What can I say?'

'You could tell him the truth, Henry. You could tell him that I am a procurer of personal services to the gentry. After all, for all you know he too could be a client of mine! No,' he continued without pause, 'I jest, your father is unknown to me. Really Henry, it is quite simple. You introduce me by my name, Malin Cassius Maichamps. You tell him that I am the son of a rich Parisian wine merchant, but that I live with my English mother in London where you made my acquaintance. As for a living, I import my father's wines to this country. That should suffice.'

'That will suffice for my father Maichamps, but I know it all, apart from your name, to be a lie. And it still doesn't explain why you're here in this God-forsaken backwater at the beginning of winter and . . .'

'Henry, you can be quite tiresome. You will recall the mutual acquaintance, the young man of whom we spoke earlier?'

Henry nodded. Anger returned to his eyes.

'Good. You will also recall that, after you had beaten him, after – forgive my coarse language but I wish you to remember this – after you had buggered him, after you had called me because you feared that he was dead, I took him away. I returned you to your rooms. You have had no worries concerning this matter.'

Henry nodded again.

'Well done. Now consider my options. I have a boy on my hands who has been physically and sexually assaulted. He could be near death. What do I do? Obviously I summon a physician who happens also to be a client of mine. He takes care of the boy and heals him, and then presents me with a sizeable bill for doing so. And then, when he recovers fully, I pay the boy a substantial amount to prevent him informing the police of your actions. You see now the debt which you owe me?'

'Yes, but . . .'

'No Henry, no buts. You see, I could also have had the boy taken away and his throat cut. A far cheaper option, I'm sure you will agree. But you don't approve? Surely I am correct, by the paleness in your cheeks you have no stomach for this? Thus, for your own sake, I cannot tell you what has happened to your young friend. Just as I will not tell you why I am here. And we must leave it at that, because I say that we must do so, and you have no choice in the matter. So come, sit opposite me,' Maichamps patted the cushion of the armchair. 'And tell me of this evening's entertainment. Tell me who is invited. I do so love the social life of the provinces, so much less restricted than that of the capital.'

Henry grudgingly walked around the sofa and took his seat as directed.

'It's a ball really, but not as grand as you might expect. We invite all our neighbours and some of father's friends from Newcastle with their families – they should be arriving shortly. The ones from farther away tend to stay a day or two. There'll be a spot of entertainment – that dance I spoke of before. I'm thinking of increasing the odds, perhaps as high as five-to-one, see if I can attract some other bets. I've a few friends who might be interested. But that's it. We'll eat, do some dancing, drink, perhaps play cards. Nothing special.'

'Tell me,' said Maichamps leaning forward conspiratorily, 'tell me again about this girl. The one who has caught your eye. The one you mentioned last night when you were just a little in your cups.' His elbows now rested upon his knees, his gangling limbs making him appear like a malevolent spider.

'Margaret? Did I mention Margaret Waterhouse last night?'

'Oh, most certainly. In detailed and descriptive and most ungentlemanly terms. And even I blushed when you told me what you might do to her.'

'No, surely not Maichamps. I respect her.' At this the tall man smiled and bowed his head, nodded his acquiescence.

'Yes Henry, I'm sure you do. Let us make do with the fact that she is young and blonde and charming then. Waterhouse is her name, the daughter of one of the two brothers you mentioned earlier? I'm not familiar with the family at all; are they local?'

'Midlands, or Manchester perhaps. Interests in quite a few areas, heavy industries mostly. John Waterhouse – he's the one who took a gamble on there being coal under the land – he doesn't tend to socialise. His brother Edward, I've only met once; now there's more chance of you knowing *him*. He spends time in London, not married so far as I know. Short, fat, appalling dress sense. No?'

Maichamps shook his head, examined his finger-nails.

'Anyway, you'll have the opportunity of meeting them this evening, except for Edward, he's moved on again. Oh, and there's the other daughter too, Elizabeth, she's strange.'

'Strange? Strange in what way? Does she have two heads? Or three legs? Either could prove useful to a man in my occupation. Or is it perhaps that she too easily resists your fatal charms dear Henry, and is thus beyond redemption in your eyes?'

'No,' answered Henry indignantly, 'she is definitely peculiar. There's something in her eyes, it's almost frightening.
Not always. Just ... I find her difficult to talk to, her mind
seems to drift away. You'll find out, I'll introduce you. But
don't say I haven't warned you.'

'I shall look forward to that. But forgive me please, I feel
a little tired. Your father's cellar is excellent, and I fear I
over-indulged myself last night. I shall take a nap to speed
my recovery. I shall be down at ...?'

'We dine at eight.'

'Seven-thirty then. Do have a pleasant afternoon Henry.
And don't worry. You might make yourself ill if you worry
overmuch. Let me worry for you. After all, I have the build
for it. And the temperament. And the name.'

Maichamps stalked from the room, taking a low, long
stride as he passed through the doorway. His hair, thick and
brushed back from his forehead, expertly grazed the top of
the door frame. Henry returned to the chessboard. He was
no expert, but he could see no impending mate, no matter
how the pieces were played.

It was raining heavily, grey autumn rain and a vicious wind
which, together, would soon rid the trees of their remaining
leaves. The coach driver was well-wrapped against the
elements and there was no need for great haste. His horses
moved at a leisurely trot. At both ends of his seat, again at
the rear, and within the cabin itself, the lights were lit.
Darkness squalled and scrabbled against the windows.

Inside it was warm, not surprising given that six bodies
were cramped into the small space. The two leather seats,
each designed for two people, faced each other. On one sat
John Waterhouse and his daughters; the other contained
Tommy Armstrong and his sons. It was Waterhouse who
had insisted that the Armstrongs ride inside, pointed out
that the pleasant weather of the afternoon had misled them

all. He had brushed aside their protestations explaining that the coachman was used to, and prepared for, inclement weather, while they had only their overcoats. And so they had taken their seats to be cloistered in uncomfortable silence.

'I understand that you are a carpenter by trade?' said John Waterhouse.

'Aye,' answered the eldest Armstrong, politely, but unable to summon any further words. He was not used to company such as this. Neither were his sons, but Thomas felt the need to keep some sort of polite conversation flowing.

'He's a good carpenter as well Mr Waterhouse, he can do anything with wood. In fact he's been helping your game-keeper, Mr Settle, making gates and fences and the like. Isn't that right Dad?'

'Aye.'

'He doesn't talk a lot though, especially with strangers,' Thomas said, taking up the role of apologist. His father hunched further into his seat. Elizabeth tried to dispel the awkwardness.

'Who was it taught you to dance Mr Armstrong?' she coaxed.

Faced with a direct question, forced to join a few words together, Tommy Armstrong chose those words carefully. At first he mumbled, stared at the floor as he spoke, avoided the eyes of those opposite.

'It was me Dad taught me to dance, miss. Aye, and it was him who gave me me first fiddle, and that belonged to his father. Me Dad couldn't play, and to be honest his dancing wasn't too good either, but he realised that I could do both and he encouraged me. He sent me to learn more steps from Geordie Ellwood; now he was a dancer, a real dancer, the best around. A clog dancer he was like, though some call them step dancers. They say it's a bit like they do in Ireland. As for the music, I just picked up tunes here and there on the fiddle. I found it easy, remembering tunes that is, and once I could whistle a tune, well, I could play it.' He looked up to find that the others were listening closely to every word, and his voice became more confident.

'I found I could go out nights, go to a pub or into Newcastle or Gateshead, and play or dance or sing or do all three, and people would throw money into me cap. I would have been content to do that and nothing else, but me Dad said no, you've to learn a trade as well. I could have gone down the mine but the pit-joiner needed an apprentice so I served me time with him. Made me own fiddle as well, sweetest thing you've ever heard. It got broken though, a while back, before Willie here was born. And I just sort of lost interest. Then when the lads came and told me about this rapper, well, it was like the spark came back, I just wanted to start all over again!'

'What about this sword dance Mr Armstrong, how did you come to learn that?' Elizabeth again.

'Well, word got round that I could play the fiddle. Every pit village had its rapper team in those days, but it was easier for pitmen to learn the dance than to learn to play the fiddle for the dance. So there was always a problem with getting musicians, good musicians that is, to play for rapper. Well, the Winlaton team, their fiddler'd died, and they asked me to play for them. They'd go round the big houses at Christmas time and collect money and divide it up between them. Anyway, I said yes, but also I wanted a fifth of the money they collected, which they argued about but agreed to in the end. After all, if I didn't go they'd make no money at all. There were five dancers as usual, a Tommy and a Bessy and a Bagman who carried the coats and swords and collected the money, and me, so a fifth wasn't too bad. I did a few steps as well, played the fiddle at the same time. I enjoyed it.

'Next thing I knew they were wanting me to come and

play at Swalwell and Ryton, at galas and fetes and shows and the like. I soon got to know the dance teams and their musicians. There was one lad I recall, Green I think his name was, came from over Westmorland way, he used to push a piano round with him and play it for the dances. He could even play it upside down, standing on his head! But that's beside the point. Where was I? Oh yes, how I got started dancing rapper! Well, after we'd been playing we'd go to the pub and they'd have a practice and sometimes I'd stand in. That way I got to dance in all the positions, 'cos you move in different directions depending on where you dance. And I got to learn the different figures. A team from Walbottle, they'll not do the same figures as one from Ryton or Throckley, or Holystone or Wallsend. Some of them call them the same but do them different, others call them different but do them the same. It can be a bit confusing if you're new to the team, but I managed. After a while I started writing them down, not words, I'm not much good with words, but drawings of where each man should go in each figure. I've still got them all. And those I've not written down are safe up here,' he tapped his head and nodded sagely.

'So you should have no problems in teaching your sons to do this dance?' asked John Waterhouse.

'No, no problems. Course we'll need some swords. I'll make those meself, but I'll need some tempered steel. An old bandsaw blade'll do. And then we'll need some dancers, another five. I'll put word about the pit, volunteers are better than pressed men. Then it's just a question of time, time and practice.'

Willie leaned across his father and spoke to Thomas in a stage whisper.

'I thought you said he didn't talk much?' The laughter which ensued was followed by a damburst of words, three conversations taking place at once. Thomas Armstrong and

John Waterhouse began to talk of the problems which were being encountered in the mine, especially with the new machines at the coal-face. Elizabeth asked more questions of Armstrong senior, particularly regarding the music he played and the speed of that music, the tunes which were popular. Every few minutes she would nod as he whistled a few bars of some jig or reel. Margaret and Willie whispered quietly to each other and, if you were to ask them later that evening what had been the content of their lengthy conversation, they would both express disbelief that they were unable to remember a single thing. Whatever they had said, however, had been wonderful.

It was no more than three miles to the Makemore estate, a twenty-minute journey in good weather. The half-hour it took this time was, however, enjoyed by all passengers. It was Margaret who first saw the lights of the house.

'Oh, we're here already,' she said, disappointment shading her voice.

'I'm afraid you won't be able to join us for the rest of the evening,' said John Waterhouse. 'But Sir Charles has promised that you will be well looked after and that you will be given a good view of the dance when the time arrives.'

'Father,' said Elizabeth, 'I really would find it far more interesting to remain with the Armstrongs. There's so much I would like to find out about this dancing and its music, and you know how much I dislike these balls. There are always too many people.'

'Yes my dear,' came the reply, 'but it would be bad manners to do as you wish. I can quite understand your feelings, however, I too find these occasions a trial. Perhaps you can arrange to discuss these matters with Mr Armstrong another day. Thank you all, Messieurs Armstrong, Armstrong and Armstrong, for your company. I look forward to the return journey, I do not imagine we shall be too late, as we have work tomorrow. Perhaps we will be able to talk on the way back about your ideas for alterations to the drill Thomas. I wonder if the efficiency could really be improved by as much as thirty per cent? Interesting. But we must go now, I see umbrellas approaching.'

The Waterhouse family ducked out of the coach and over the wet gravel to the entrance hall, their passage eased by footmen protecting them from the rain. The Armstrongs remained in the coach as it was led off to the stables. Once there they helped the coachman unhitch his charges. Willie, garrulous as ever, began to talk horses and ended up drying and brushing one of the mares; the Thomases, junior and senior, sat on piles of straw and watched the steaming beasts. They had not had much chance to talk since the move. Thomas and Willie had been at work during the day, and at night they seemed absorbed with discussing the work they had done. Mary and her father-in-law had spent the first day moving furniture and tidying up, and had walked down to the school with a reluctant Matthew and David. While she had prepared the evening meal he had wandered off to explore the neighbourhood. It was then that he had found Albie Settle the gamekeeper, cursing and swearing as he tried fitting a wire-mesh door, wooden framed, to the opening of a cage used to protect young pheasants from the local foxes. He had watched for a while, waited until the large man had flung the door to the ground in disgust, then stepped forward. The door had not been braced. Finding a length of timber on the ground he cut it to size, angled the ends, and nailed it expertly to the door. Although the door was now a rectangle the opening, presumably made by the gamekeeper as well, was not. A quick inspection showed that the top of the frame was narrower than the bottom. It took only a minute to knock the mismeasured piece of timber out and replace it with one of the correct size. The door could then be swiftly screwed to the frame. It worked perfectly.

108 *Alan Dunn*

The gamekeeper reached into his pocket and handed the carpenter a metal flask. It contained whisky. They both took a sip, sat on a tree-trunk and examined their work. No words were spoken.

On both of the following days Tommy Armstrong visited the gamekeeper. They found pleasure in each other's company. In the evenings he sat at home and listened to his sons. On that first day they had surprised him and Mary by coming home clean. Pit-head baths, they explained. On the second day, the Tuesday of the week, they had all visited the library together, although only Thomas had done so with any great enthusiasm; the others considered it a duty. And now, on Wednesday, they were at the stately home of Sir Charles Makemore waiting to watch a team of sword dancers.

'It usually happens,' said the old man, 'that just when I think I know about all of life's little peculiarities something new comes along.'

'Like now?' asked his son.

'Aye Thomas, like now.'

They silently nodded their agreement.

'What do you think of them Dad?' asked Thomas.

'Who? The Waterhouses? They seem fair enough. I know that Willie's got his eye on that Margaret, not that I blame him, she's a very nice little piece, but really he's just wasting his time. Mr Waterhouse seems a good man at heart. And that Elizabeth, she seems really interested in the music. They're alright I suppose.'

'He's prepared to listen to a man, that Waterhouse, he'll listen and then he'll talk fairly. And Elizabeth, she's got a brain in her head. I'm not so sure about the other one though.'

'I'd agree there son. But remember one thing. However pleasant they are, no matter how kind they seem, they own the pit, and they own the land, and they own your house,

and they own your kids' school, and they own your job and
your food. They tell us there's no such thing as slavery any
more, but believe you me, they own you. All you can give
them is your labour. And if they don't want it, well, all the
rest goes. They're a different class, they're almost a different
race from us. And though we can talk to each other we'll
never mix. Just remember that son. Remember that.'

They sat in silence again, their reverie finally interrupted
when Willie sauntered over.

'Come on then you two, the driver says we're to go over
to the kitchen. They'll be expecting us, give us something to
eat and drink. Then we should be able to watch the
proceedings.' He headed for the stable door, then turned
back when they didn't move to his command.

'Howway then, I've been working while you were gab-
bing, I'm hungry!' They rose to their feet.

They followed the coachman across the wet courtyard,
but even without a guide their noses would have led them to
the kitchen. The door opened onto a scene of steam and heat
and frenzy. Maids were running here and there, cooks were
labouring over pans and tureens at the huge range which ran
the full length of one of the walls. They could smell beef,
while one of the skivvies was removing trays of small roast
birds ('partridges' said Tommy Armstrong) from the oven.
Vegetables, raw and cooked, were on every available work-
surface, and elegant china bowls and containers were
standing in a large tray of hot water, keeping warm until
they could be filled with food.

'Out!' yelled a fat woman. 'Out out out!' Thomas opened
his mouth to speak.

'I said OUT! Don't say anything, I know who you are, I
know why you're here, just go and wait in the servants'
dining room and keep out of the way! Now!'

They headed in the direction indicated by the woman's
knife-wielding hand and found themselves in a smaller

room. It contained a table, half a dozen dining chairs and, round the outside of the room, some comfortable though well-worn armchairs. They sat and waited.

There were perhaps sixty guests that evening, few of whom were familiar to the Waterhouses. After genteel social gossip, during which Elizabeth escaped to the library and examined some of the paintings, they took their seats. Elizabeth found herself between Sir Charles and Henry Makemore. Margaret and Timothy Deemster sat opposite, and there were three or four other faces (whose names she had forgotten) who contributed little of interest to the conversation and were therefore of little interest to her. There was one empty seat.

'A friend of mine,' explained Henry, 'from London. He's staying here for a little while but is, I regret, feeling a little unwell and will be unable to join us. And I had talked so much about the beautiful and talented guests from Green-croft Hall, he was so looking forward to meeting you.'

'If it had been me who was ill,' ventured the curate, 'and I had known that Miss Waterhouse was here, I would have crawled from my death-bed to be at her side.'

'Oh, Timothy,' simpered Margaret. Elizabeth raised her eyes to heaven.

Despite having pretensions of classical antiquity the Makemores' country seat was no more than ten years old. The dining room was high-ceilinged, its plasterwork painted a pale, pastel green; delicate blue cornflowers picked out with a white border formed a relief. Heavy curtains hung at the double doors which had been placed at regular intervals around the walls, and between them hung paintings of the Makemores and their descendants. Elizabeth had found the paintings in the library too conservative for her liking, and her hopes of finding something more to her taste in the ballroom met with a similar lack of success. She stared at the portrait opposite her. Despite being some distance away the subject, a woman of considerable age and ugliness, appeared cross-eyed. She found herself snatching a glance at Henry and Sir Charles. Was this a hereditary trait? Perhaps it only affected female Makemores. At least it gave the woman a touch of humanity; the other paintings showed male members of the family on horseback, at work and at play, either fighting or hunting. The horses were more personable than the men.

At one end of the room a string quartet was playing pleasant melodies of indeterminate quality, while at the other was a huge marble fireplace with an entrance door at each side and a curtained minstrels' gallery above. It was carved, in exquisite bad taste in Elizabeth's opinion, with early Renaissance figures. Nudes draped with flimsy cloaks supported shelves on which putti smiled. She had heard that close inspection revealed some of the figures engaged in social intercourse beyond that normally associated with stately homes in the north of England, but she had not yet had the opportunity to give these carvings a close inspection. Perhaps they were hidden from general view, perhaps behind those curtains where the first floor gallery met the fireplace. That, Henry Makemore had informed her, would be where the Armstrongs would be placed to watch the entertainment.

The Armstrongs. She allowed herself a brief smile at the thought of them, forced to endure a journey with their employer and his daughters. They had, she felt, acquitted themselves well. Willie was an engaging young rogue who would, she was sure, meet his match in Margaret. His father was a little shy, but when coaxed into talking about his music and dancing, well, the smile on his face showed the obvious delight he took in performing. She had arranged to meet him one day at the Hall so that he could play some tunes for her. She did not have his talent for playing from memory and would have to have the music written down if she was ever to play the jigs and reels he had talked about so fondly. And for some reason, she couldn't understand why, she felt a need to learn more about this music. And then there was Thomas. She was worried about Thomas. He seemed too good. Already her father was talking, in private of course, and so far to her alone, of promotion, of making him a deputy, or even teaching him something of the engineering involved in designing pit machinery. She remembered the cottage, Thomas and Mary together, then her own weakness later that night. She knew that the colour would rise, she could feel her neck begin to grow red, feel the warmth deep down. She sipped quickly from her glass of wine and fixed her eyes once more on the cross-eyed portrait. If that couldn't take the demon from her mind there was no hope for her.

The meal passed blessedly quickly, the servants were efficient, the food acceptable. She did not normally drink much wine. Her father had never encouraged it (although he seemed tonight to be indulging himself more than was normal) and she disliked the drowsiness and lack of clarity it brought her. But the glass before her, regularly filled by a waiter and then by Henry himself, contained one of the most fragrant whites she had ever tasted.

"'s my friend brought them,' slurred Henry Makemore, "'s 'is job, well, 's father's job really. Wine, that is. 's French you know? The wine and my friend.' He laughed too loudly, and Elizabeth was startled to hear herself join in. She blinked, pushed her glass away from her. Anyone who laughed with Henry Makemore was very polite, very stupid, or drunk. She decided she would prefer to remain polite.

'And 'e's not well. Shame! 'e's got such a lovely name, in French *and* in English. Sh'd I tell you? Sh'd I? 's very clever! 'is name is, in English mind you, in English, "Mayfield"! So now you 'ave to guess it in French. Go on then. In French!'

'May,' said Curate Deemster, 'that's easy. May is the same. Spelled differently, M-A-I, but pronounced the same.'

'And field is "champs",' added Elizabeth.

'Quite,' continued the clergyman. 'So Mayfield becomes Maichamps. Not that I can get the pronunciation right, good Lord, French has such an accent to get your lips round, too lascivious by far! Give me the Anglo-Saxon any day, eh Henry?' Henry laughed drunkenly and kissed Margaret's hand which had been resting on the table while she talked to Sir Charles. She gasped and pulled away, saw who had attacked her, and re-offered her hand to him in mock resignation while Sir Charles, almost as befuddled as his son, looked on in red-nosed pride.

'Be not drunk with wine, wherein is excess.'

'What was that Dad?'

'I said, "Be not drunk with wine, wherein is excess."'

'That's scriptures, isn't it? Thomas, Dad's ill. He's quoting from the Bible!'

'No,' said Thomas, echoing his brother's shocked tone. 'You must have misheard. Not our Dad. Not the Bible. Your ears need cleaning out. And he isn't ill, he's just had too much beer to drink with his meal.'

'It is the Bible,' said the old man. 'It's the only bit I can remember, apart from two or three of the ten commandments. "Be not drunk with wine, wherein is excess." I've heard it often enough, preached at me from pulpit and pavement alike when I've had far more to drink than I've had so far tonight. I was rather hoping they'd send a few more jugs of ale up to us, but no, they always do the same, give just enough to tempt but not enough to fulfil. Or should that be "fill full"?'

'Do you know how the rest of that saying goes?' asked Thomas. Willie groaned.

'No, don't make stupid noises,' Thomas continued, 'just because one of us is educated enough to finish off a quotation. The whole thing goes, "Be not drunk with wine, wherein is excess; but be filled with the Spirit." It's Ephesians. I'm not sure where.'

'Bloody hell, does it really say that?' said Tommy Armstrong enviously. 'I wish I'd known that. I would have told them, I would have said "I'll stay off the wine if you give me some of the spirit!"' He launched into a deep-throated laugh which became a cough and threatened to choke him. Willie thumped his back while Thomas smiled. It was good to see his brother and father at ease in each other's company. For too long they had been strangers, avoiding contact wherever possible, sniping and harrying at each other when necessity forced them to meet. The change seemed to have come primarily from his father. He had been taciturn, withdrawn, hiding from that part of himself which Thomas had known long ago. He had accepted that the happy, carefree father of his youth had been banished, would never return; hence his pessimism when faced with persuading his father to move with them, to teach them rapper. It was strange that the task had proved so easy, that the dancer in the old man had suddenly returned. He had mentioned that to Willie as they walked to the pit-head for their first morning's work.

'I know why he's come,' said Willie.

'How's that?'

'I asked him. And he told me.'

Thomas had felt a twinge of jealousy. He was the eldest son. He had been close to his father, closer at least than Willie. Why then had his father said nothing to him?

'It's because it's the first time he's felt wanted. No, that's not right, his exact words were "Because you needed me". He felt we hadn't needed him in the past. And now we do.'

And so, because they needed him, Tommy Armstrong found himself sitting with his sons on a balcony behind heavy velvet curtains, peeping out at the ballroom beneath. The diners had left while the room was cleared, chairs and tables had been placed round the perimeter, and the first few guests were beginning to return. The quartet was playing a set of waltzes.

'If you want an example of being drunk with wine in excess,' said Tommy Armstrong, 'just look at that Henry Makemore. He's as drunk as a fart. Look at him, Miss Margaret's having to carry him in!'

Henry was not, in fact, as drunk as he appeared. He had used the privilege of his position as son of the host to escort Margaret back into the ballroom, and by staggering occasionally he was more easily able to brush his arm against the swell of her breast, to press his leg against her thigh, to feel the warmth of her back against the palm of his hand. Margaret seemed unaware of Henry's motives, or perhaps, because she was unused to alcohol, she didn't mind. Timothy Deemster, following them in, his arm linked with Elizabeth's, wore his anger like a crown of thorns. Willie Armstrong was not the type to restrain himself with such dignity.

'I swear it, I'll go down there and thump him! I'll hit him before he knows what's happening! He doesn't even deserve a warning, that one, look at him, he might as well rip her bodice off as get any closer!'

'Willie, don't worry,' said Tommy. 'Look, her Dad's coming to the rescue, he's asking her to dance, see? There you are, and the curate's dancing with Elizabeth. She moves well, that lass. And poor Henry's got to go and find someone else. Aye well, such is life.' He looked around him. Willie was still staring down at the scene below, while Thomas had pulled aside the curtains masking the side of the fireplace and was admiring the carvings.

'Are you both alright lads?' Tommy continued. 'Will you be able to see well enough? I don't want you to miss anything when it starts; after all, they're meant to be good. We might pick up some ideas, a figure or two, some stepping. Keep your eyes open.'

'Willie,' hissed Thomas, 'come here.' Willie reluctantly tore himself away from admiring Margaret through the gap in the curtains.

'Willie, look at this! Look at these carvings!' Thomas whispered. 'Look what they're doing!'

'My God!' Willie turned his head to one side, trying to see some detail from a more beneficial angle. 'She must have no bones in her legs to get into that position. And look at him! Have you ever seen anything so large? He puts Donkin's prize stallion to shame for certain, that one!'

'They're normally covered up,' said Thomas. 'They're just on the side, not on the front at all.'

'That dirty bastard Henry Makemore! He lives with this and he's drooling and pawing at Margaret. I've a good mind . . .'

'You've got no mind at all Willie, not if you're thinking of going down there and doing anything. Anyway, it's his father who had this thing built. Henry might know nothing whatsoever about it.'

'Like father like son I say.'

'We'll have to watch out then. We could both turn out like Dad!'

They turned to look at their father. His hands were holding the curtains slightly apart and he was watching those below, his foot tapping in time with the music, his head nodding sagely with appreciation.

'They're doing one I know lads. "Haymakers" I call it, but the fiddler just announced it as "Sir Roger de Coverley". They're doing it quite well Willie, your Margaret's got a very neat step to her.'

Thomas and Willie hurried across to join their father, although Thomas did so reluctantly, glancing back at the figures on the wall. Watching the dancers they failed to notice the door to their balcony open, didn't realise that they had been joined by a tall shadow of a man. Only when he coughed, a delicate and deliberate clearing of the throat, did they turn to face him.

'Gentlemen, please,' he said, bowing floridly before them, 'continue your examination of the middle classes making an exhibition of themselves. I merely wish to view from a distance. But forgive me, you are not aware of my identity. My name is Maichamps. I am a guest of the family Makemore. To be more precise I am acquainted, it pains me to admit, with the young boy Henry, and he insisted that I come with him from London to this party. I suffer, alas, from the vapours when forced to travel farther north than Hampstead, and was unable to join my hosts for the evening.' Willie raised his eyebrow to Thomas; Thomas shrugged. Maichamps continued to speak.

'I must confess that a rest has made me feel considerably better, although not quite so well that I wish to join the mêlée on the dance floor. The housekeeper told me that the view from the balcony would be excellent, although she did mention that you gentlemen were already in possession of the most favourable seats. I trust, therefore, that you will be able to bear my company for a little while, suitably ameliorated by a small bribe,' he reached behind him to produce a tray with three glasses and three dark bottles, corks removed, 'which may allow time to pass more pleasantly.'

'What the hell did that mean?' hissed Tommy Armstrong.

'It means he wants to watch from here, and he's brought us a bottle each if we let him,' replied Willie.

'Well why didn't he say so?' More loudly, 'Please, pull up a seat.'

Maichamps pulled a seat from the wall and sat down beside Tommy Armstrong. He balanced the tray on his knees (which stuck up in the air, almost as high as his chest) and poured red liquid into each of the glasses.

'Port,' he said, 'twenty-year port and damn good at that.' He passed the glasses round.

'You have the advantage over me sirs, I am aware that you are here to watch my hosts' men performing some heathen dance, but beyond that . . .?'

'Oh, I'm sorry,' said the elder brother. 'I'm Thomas Armstrong. This is my brother, Willie, and my father, he's called Thomas as well, but everyone calls him Tommy.'

'You were right,' said the latter on hearing his name mentioned, 'it is good stuff, this, and believe me, I'm an expert. Err, do you mind?' He held out his glass, already empty; it was quickly refilled.

'I think,' said Maichamps, 'that if we douse the lights' – he did so – 'and pull this curtain open a little, just so, then we should all be able to see what is happening without ourselves being observed.'

And so they watched, the self-proclaimed wine merchant and the pit-workers, as the couples circled gracefully on the floor below. Waltzes were interspersed with polkas and schottisches, a barn dance, the occasional dance-game such as 'Pop goes the Weasel', the 'Lancers', one or two recognised by Thomas and Willie as having much in common with those they knew from their own entertainments. Maichamps and the eldest Armstrong kept up a running commentary on the quality of the music, the elegance of the dancers, the ease with which dance and tune conspired to lure dancers onto the floor.

Willie spent most of his time watching Margaret, clenching his fists when she was asked to dance by Makemore, Deemster or any of the other young men present, relaxing when she was husbanded into the arms of her father or taken to one side for earnest conversation and giggling laughter with young women her own age. Thomas saw his brother's reaction and reminded himself that he should have words with him. Innocent flirtation on the parts of both Margaret and Willie was surely harmless, but his brother's emotions seemed to be taking him beyond mere coquetry and into the realms of infatuation. There was, after all, no realistic hope of any exchange of affection between the two of them, given their different stations. Thomas watched Margaret carefully. She was a beautiful young woman, that much was true, and he could see why she had so easily attracted his brother's eye. But she was, in his opinion, lacking in personality. She was too aware of her own beauty, and she knew too well the effect this had on the young men around her. Her sister, however, was different. Elizabeth was not physically beautiful, neither in the classical nor in any other sense. She was thin, almost boyish in looks, the dark shadows beneath her eyes gave her a look of permanent tiredness (belied, Thomas had to admit, by the energy she displayed in her dancing), yet she possessed an inner beauty which was a shining light for the dull moths fluttering at her side. And, ever polite, she danced with each in turn, retaining a glow of calm self-assuredness as her partners sweated lamely in her wake. Each was returned safely to gossiping wife or cooing mother while the next was greeted with the same happy and seemingly genuine smile. In the middle of one dance her escort, an elderly man, lacking both stature and tolerance to alcohol, pulled her towards him and began to nuzzle into her neck. She pulled gently away from him, whispered in his ear, and both completed the dance in good humour. As she led him from the floor – he was clearly incapable of finding his own way back to his seat and without support would have folded bonelessly to the ground – she glanced up at the balcony. Thomas leaned forward, the better to see her, and found his way blocked by Maichamps who was retreating on the same course, leaning sideways and backwards. The tall stranger's gaze was fixed, Thomas was sure, on Elizabeth. On his face was a grin, almost a sneer, of triumph. And recognition. And anticipation?

Maichamps' head and Thomas's chest collided, and the former started. Maichamps turned his head and their eyes met briefly, allowing Thomas to see that beneath the veneer of courtesy and friendliness he had presented to them was a core of diffidence, indifference, even dislike. But worse was the fact that Maichamps made no attempt to hide this from Thomas, even took pleasure in emphasising with a coy smile and raise of the eyebrows that for him to be so pleasant was a pretence difficult for him to conceal. As Maichamps rose from his seat Thomas considered asking him why he had joined them when he had been unable to hide his distaste for the company. Two things prevented him. The first was the possibility that he had been mistaken, that he had read more into a glance than he ought, that both of their senses were a little dulled by port and poor light. The second was his father's urgent hiss.

'Thomas! Thomas, they're going to be starting now, they've just announced it.'

'I'll stand,' said Maichamps, gesturing towards the seat. Thomas lowered himself into it, felt its distasteful warmth beneath him. He felt suddenly uncomfortable having Maichamps standing behind him where he could not be seen.

The room was full but the dance floor was empty. Its former occupants had crowded into or behind the seats round the outside of the hall. The murmur of conversation had not yet died when the first dancer strode into the room. He was about Thomas's age, clean-shaven, and he stood silent in the middle of the dance floor. Gradually a hush came over the crowd as the audience turned to admire him. His shirt was white, and around his neck was a royal blue velvet tie. The same colour, albeit a cheaper corduroy, was used for his waistcoat and knee-length breeches. The outside seams of the trousers and the border of the waistcoat were embroidered in red; he wore red stockings and, round his waist, a broad red sash. In his hands he carried a sword made of flexible steel, a handle at each end.

'Bit flash for me,' said Tommy, then directed his words to Maichamps. 'This'll be new to you. See that sword? One of the handles's fixed, wood blocks riveted to both sides of the steel. But the other one, the one in his right hand, it's been turned on a lathe and a hole drilled up its length, then it's been slid onto a spindle formed at the other end of the sword. One fixed handle, one rotating. Let's the dancers move that bit more easily. Most teams still use swords with two fixed. We'll have to think about it.'

The dancer waited for complete silence then took a deep breath and began to sing in a pleasant baritone voice.

> Good people, give ear to me story;
> We've called for to see you by chance.
> Five heroes I've brought, blithe and bonny,
> Intending to give yous a dance.
> Now Langley is wor habitation,
> It's the place we was all born and bred.
> There's nae finer lads in the nation,
> And none are more gallantly led.'

'Bloody hell,' said Tommy. 'They're not doing the whole song, are they? Quick, fill me glass again, I need it. Anyway, they're doing it wrong – Tommy or Bessy should be singing this bit.'

> For I am the son of bold Elliot,
> The bravest you ever have seen.
> And, I'm proud and rejoicing to tell it,
> I fought for my country and Queen.
> When the Spaniards besieged Gibraltar
> Bold Elliot defended the place.

I caused them their plans for to alter;
Some died, others fell in disgrace.

'They say,' said Tommy, 'that there used to be a whole play, and the dance was just the end of it. I've seen Earsdon do a bit of acting beforehand, somebody playing the part of a doctor, sword fights and the like, but I've always thought it a bit of a distraction from the dance itself.' The first dancer was joined by a second, similarly attired, who mimicked the first's stance, stood in respectful silence as the next verse was begun.

My next handsome youth that does enter
Is a boy, there are very such few such.
His father beat the great Duke de Winter
And defeated the fleet of the Dutch.
His father was the great Lord Duncan
Who played the Dutch ne'er such a prank,
That they fled from their harbours, ran funkin'
And they fled to the great Dogger Bank.

'He's not exactly putting his heart and soul into it, is he? You'd think he was a statue. I like a bit of movement, perhaps some stepping between the verses. Thank God there's only five dancers, think what it would be like if there were ten more to be introduced!'

My third is the son of Lord Nelson,
That hero who fought at the Nile.
Few men with such courage and talent,
The Frenchmen he did them beguile.
The Frenchmen they nearly decoyed him,
But the battle he managed so well.
In their fortress he wholly destroyed them,
Scarce one reached his home for to tell.

Tommy Armstrong was still holding forth. 'You see Mr

Mayshamps, there's normally a Tommy and a Bessy, they're dressed up as the dancers' father and mother, and it's the Tommy who gets to sing the song. 'Course, they get to join in the dance as well, if they're still good enough. Usually they're proper dancers who are a bit older, a bit like me, probably can't keep up for the whole time. They act the fool, make easy figures look more complicated, pass their sword over if one of the dancers breaks his own. A good Tommy and Bessy can add a hell of a lot to a dance.'

> My fourth handsome youth that does enter
> Is a boy of ability bright.
> Five thousand gold guineas I'd venture
> That he like his father would fight.
> At Waterloo and Tarryvary
> Lord Wellington made the French fly.
> You scarcely can find such another,
> He'd conquer or else he would die.

'Only one more to go. All these good old English heroes and who do they save till last? Just wait and see, this should please you at least Mr Mayshamps!' The fifth dancer strode on to join his companions. Their costumes were immaculate, and although two of them wore moustaches and one a small beard, they were all of similar height and build.

> Now the last of my lads that does enter
> Is a boy that is both straight and tall.
> He's the son of the great Buonaparte,
> The hero that cracked the whole all.
> He went o'er the Lowlands like thunder,
> Made nations to quiver and quake.
> Many thousands stood gazing in wonder
> At the havoc he always did make.

'Bonaparte! What's a Frenchman doing in an English dance? You'd think we could find enough heroes of our own but no, we have to drag in a bloody Frenchie. Where's that damn bottle gone, me glass's empty.'

> Now you see all we five noble heroes,
> Five noble heroes by birth,
> And they each bear as good a character
> As any five heroes on earth.
> If they be as good as their fathers
> Then their deeds is deserving record
> For all of the country desires
> To see how they handle their swords.

After the last line the dancers moved smartly into a circle, swords held straight up in their right hands, tips touching in the centre of the ring. From below the balcony came music, a violin playing a jig.

'Good tune, the "Blackthorn Stick", but too fast, much too fast. Listen for the stepping, it'll be a blur before they get properly started.'

But the stepping was crisp and measured, perfectly on the beat with its rhythmic da-da-da-DUM, da-da-da-DUM, da-da-da, da-da-da, da-da-da-DUM, reinforcing the emphatic drive of the music. There was a clash of swords and the dancers were off, moving as one, round in a circle. They were now all linked, each holding his own sword in his right hand, passing the blade over his right shoulder so that the other handle was in the left hand of the man behind. Tommy kept up his commentary, but all eyes were on the dance.

'Should be Single Guard first, whatever else they do. Yes, there he goes, number one turns off to the left while the others keep going round, lifts both his swords above his head, round the opposite way to everyone else then back into his place. Then number two, yes, he's a good mover that one, very sweet, then three, four and five. What'll they do next?'

As if in response to the unheard question the dancers moved from their close circle. A change of direction, a raising and lowering of swords, and with seemingly no effort they were facing each other, but with their leader holding their five swords, intermeshed to form a locked pentangle, high above his head. There was a ripple of applause.

'They're good, I'll give them that. They went into Nut as though they'd been doing it all their lives.'

And so the dance progresssed, Tommy praising or damning as he saw fit, finding errors where no other would have been able, naming the figures when he knew them, pausing only to drink from or refill his glass. As Thomas watched he felt a wave of hopelessness engulf him. He could not envisage himself, nor his brother, nor any other men from the pit, ever approaching this team in the quality of their dancing. It was nearly November now; they had only until June with time for one practice a week and not even a start made yet. Part of him suggested, rather too readily, that it was only a dance and that if Edward Waterhouse lost his money, well, it was his own fault for betting. And he could probably afford it anyway. But his pride would not allow that thought to triumph. He wanted to dance well, to win the competition, for his own sake. To prove that he could do it. To show that the Armstrongs could pull together and work with each other. And to gain praise from his father. That, more than anything else, motivated him. He wanted to win for himself, and for his father, and for the Waterhouses, and (he was surprised to find, for he rarely took an active dislike to an individual) so that Henry Makemore would lose. He looked up from the dance to see Makemore lounging against the wall, standing beside Margaret, but his attention was not upon the young girl. Thomas watched as the leader of the dance team raised his eyes to find his master's son, who nodded back. And from that moment the dance began to disintegrate.

It was not a gradual deterioration caused by tiredness.

That would have been understandable given a dance of such speed requiring co-ordination and skill in all five of its dancers. It was as though the will to perform well had disappeared. The dancers moved round into a circle and tied the Nut, the pentangle of interlocked swords. The precision of the previous figures was no longer present, and the pentangle was loose, misshapen. When held aloft the swords began to slip and would have fallen to the ground had not the leader swiftly brought the Nut down and the others grabbed for the handles.

The next figure involved a complicated figure of eight, the swords lifted above head height clashing and sparking as the dancers wove in and out. Thomas could see that, for all the seeming intricacies, the movements were basically simple, and that the knot of swords momentarily unravelled itself at the end of each complete cycle of the figure. Until, that is, one of the dancers – he could not tell which – turned left when he should have turned right. The resultant tangle could not be untied; the leader could only solve the puzzle by ordering his men to let go the swords with their left hands and reform the circle.

The stepping too, previously almost military in its accuracy, became unsynchronised and led to a slackness in the dance as a whole. Figure followed figure, each more disappointing than the previous in its execution, until Thomas could sense the dancers' relief that the performance would soon be over. He heard the call 'Coach and Horses' and the dancers moved into a formation he recognised, two men facing front, two behind them, and the fifth standing centrally at the back. This lone figure moved forward to step over the sword lowered by the front two, put his hands on their shoulders, then somersaulted backwards over the sword. He landed well, to applause from the audience, but his success was diminished when the ensuing Nut was held aloft by the leader. The dancers had formed a straight line, but two of them were facing the balcony while three had their backs to it. There was a hastily whispered 'Turn right' from the leader and his dancers followed his command. All four turned right through half a circle (he remained with his back to the balcony) to provide merely a variation on the previous theme. 'Face front' he then muttered, and the whole team were finally unified in their sense of direction. Relieved at this the leader held the Nut high and was rewarded by seeing the swords unlock and slide un-ceremoniously to the ground. He shouted 'Out', the music stopped, and to a rustle of muted applause the dancers left the floor. The swords remained where they had fallen.

'That was rubbish,' said Tommy Armstrong. 'They just lost their way. If they do that every time we'll have no trouble beating them!'

'Aye,' responded Willie. 'But they've got as much time as we have to get ready for the competition, and we haven't even got a team yet.'

Maichamps moved forward. He had been leaning against the wall with a bored expression on his face, cleaning his finger-nails with a toothpick.

'Am I to take it,' he said 'that the performance I have just witnessed was not of a particularly high standard?'

'Like I said before, it was rubbish!' repeated Tommy.

'Even I could see that,' added Willie, 'and I'm no expert.' Three pairs of eyes turned to Thomas.

'Yes,' he said, 'it was bad. Even somebody who'd never seen the dance before would be of that opinion. But I can't understand why it turned. They started so well.'

'It's almost as though they wanted to let people see how well the dance could be performed,' said Maichamps thoughtfully, 'then showed that they themselves couldn't maintain those high standards.'

'I think,' said Thomas, 'that they did it for us. They don't want us to see how good they really are. They know we're here, you see, and they probably want us to think we can beat them with a team that's nothing more than mediocre, and then in the competition they show how good they really are! You see, I saw the look Makemore gave them, just before things started going wrong. They're acting on his instructions.' He saw the pensive look on Maichamps' face.

'Oh. I'm sorry to talk about your host like that. I didn't mean to . . .'

'No offence taken Mr Armstrong, I can quite understand your feelings about this. In fact, having seen the dance, I am beginning to understand the strange influence and fascination it seems to be exerting over Henry and, may I say, over the three of you. Now if you'll excuse me, watching all of that exertion has quite tired me out. I really must retire.' He stifled a mock-yawn. 'I do look forward to meeting you again and trust that I may one day see you perform the dance yourselves. Goodnight gentlemen.'

'Thank you for the port . . .' began Willie, but the tall man had already left.

'Strange bloke,' he said. 'Harmless perhaps, but strange.

'Good booze though,' added his father, draining the last of the three bottles.

'I didn't like him,' said Thomas, 'but I'm not sure why. That worries me, not liking someone without due cause.'

'Aye, well despite his good wishes I doubt we'll see him again,' said his father, 'so there's no need for your worry son. Come on, we'd best be getting back to the kitchens again, the Waterhouses'll be making their excuses to leave soon and we shouldn't keep them waiting.' He rose unsteadily to his feet and, supported by Willie, headed for the door. Thomas followed, by way of the fireplace wall, running his fingers reverently over the reliefs there. He wondered idly if Mary might enjoy that particular position . . .? At the thought of his wife he grinned and left the room.

* * *

The journey back to Greencroft was uneventful. The weather had, if anything, worsened, and the driver chose to move his charges at no more than walking pace. The wind buffeted the well-sprung coach from side to side and Margaret soon began to complain of travel sickness.

'I generally feel much better with my back to the direction of travel,' she said to Thomas. 'Would you mind if I changed places with you?' So saying she took up her new position beside Willie, closed her eyes, and within minutes seemed to have fallen asleep. A few minutes after that her head fell gently to rest on Willie's shoulder bringing a beatific smile to his face.

Thomas found himself beside Elizabeth; their fathers were opposite each other in lively yet quiet conversation on the quality of the dancing that evening. Waterhouse, untutored in the finer points of the subject, was being given a swift lesson by the expert facing him, made loquacious by the port.

'Did you enjoy yourself this evening Mr Armstrong?' asked Elizabeth. Her question could have been mere politeness, but Thomas sensed a real interest in her voice.

'Yes Mrs Kearton, I did. It was pleasant to see rapper danced again, and it was interesting to be in such a fine house, watching people. It's the first time I've been in a mansion. It was . . . yes, it was interesting.'

'You're very polite Mr Armstrong. If I had been in your position I might have chosen words other than "interesting" to describe my feelings.'

'No,' said Thomas carefully, not wishing to offend, 'it was interesting. Something new for me, something different. Why, is there something else I should have felt?'

'I had merely wondered whether you considered it, let me choose my words carefully now, immoral? Yes, that's it, immoral, to be in the presence of so much ostentatious wealth when you, as an individual, have not had the advantages enjoyed by the Makemores.'

'Or by the Waterhouses?' added Thomas.

'Yes, I will include myself as being privileged. Does that not seem unfair to you? That opportunities are denied to you and your brother, and to your sons, not because of any lack of ability but because you come from a different social class?'

Thomas seemed perplexed by the question.

'It's not something I've thought about much,' he eventually replied. 'My life has been ... not unhappy. If I work hard, try to improve myself, then my children will probably benefit and their lives will be happier still. And I find it difficult to understand how you can criticise the Makemores for leading a privileged life when you live, so far as I can see, in exactly the same way.'

'I agree. And because I agree, because I appreciate the unfairness of the present social system, that's why I approve of my father's efforts to give more to his workers. Not just better pay and safer working conditions, but a better way of life. A better education for their children. The chance to do more with their lives than just work down a mine. And that's just the beginning, there'll be further change, I promise that, and not only at Greencroft. Workers will soon come to realise their own strength, you'll see.'

'I've spent all my working life at the pit. It's done me no harm, and it's valuable work. It's not just "working down a ..."'

'It's done you no good either,' interrupted Elizabeth. 'Look at yourself, there's more in you than working a life down a mine and then, when you find yourself too weak to work, sitting at home spitting up coal dust from your lungs till you die. You read and you write well, you're intelligent, a sight more than Henry Makemore is, that's for certain, and yet your life's laid out for you, and the sum total of that life is what? Absolutely nothing! Which is exactly what you're doing to change it!'

The conversation was conducted at no more than whisper level, but the passion aroused was suddenly tangible to all those still awake. Both John Waterhouse and Tommy Armstrong turned to look at Thomas and Elizabeth, puzzled expressions on both faces. Willie, in a state of pleasure verging on catatonia, took no notice of anything beyond the regular rhythm of Margaret's breathing. Thomas could feel the tension in Elizabeth; sitting beside her, their legs touching from the knees upwards, he was aware of a pressure which made him feel that she might explode. She sat perfectly still, staring straight ahead at the wall behind Willie, hands clenched in a knot. Their fathers resumed their discussions and Thomas had a brief vision of Elizabeth disappearing with a bang; he considered the mess this might make and was forced to cover his mouth with his hand to prevent his amusement being seen. The movement dampened the fire, however; the smile in his eyes was enough to prevent the fuse being lit.

'I'm sorry Mr Armstrong,' Elizabeth said. 'I've a habit of preaching which I try to control, but sometimes it just proves too much for me. I was rude to you and rude about your work and I apologise.'

'No, no Mrs Kearton, think nothing of it; my feelings haven't been damaged in any way. I can see that a large part of what you said was quite right, and it may be that the balance also proves to be that way, once I have time to think about it. So no apology is necessary.' Elizabeth was about to speak again but Thomas would not allow her to start.

'Mrs Kearton, there is a favour I would ask of you.' Her thoughts of demanding to be allowed to apologise were put aside by her curiosity.

'And what is that Mr Armstrong?'

'You'll think me daft, but the only Mr Armstrong here is my Dad. Would it be possible for you to call me Thomas? And I'm sure Willie would be preferred to be known by his first name, by both you and your sister.'

'Why Mr Armstrong, I couldn't think of granting myself such a liberty. Such familiarity, what would people say? No, I'm afraid that is not possible.' She laughed. 'Unless you also call me by my Christian name.'

Thomas scratched his chin and pretended deep thought.

'Very well then. Elizabeth.'

'Thank you,' came the reply, 'Thomas.'

From outside came the crunch of gravel and a light shone through the coach window.

'Greencroft Hall,' came the driver's shout.

Margaret opened her eyes and blinked.

'Home already?'

'Henry,' said Maichamps. 'I've brought you a present.'

Henry sat up too quickly, groaned and closed his eyes.

'Too much to drink? I think you ought to retire immediately and stay in bed until noon at the very earliest. By which time I, alas, will be gone, on my way back to London.' Henry opened his eyes again, slowly this time.

'Already? But you've only been here for two days, and most of that time you've spent in your room. It makes me wonder just why you forced me to invite you. There's more to this than I know, more than you'll tell me I'll wager. Some secret, eh?'

'Yes Henry, you're right, it's a secret. But if I told you, then it would no longer be a secret. In fact fewer people would know my secret if I printed it up as a broadsheet and gave it away at all of the mainline stations in London. And so, I'm afraid, a secret it must remain.' Maichamps lowered himself into the chair opposite his host and stared at him in the manner of an attentive though not over-intelligent lap-dog.

'Tell me Henry, did you enjoy your evening?'

'Yes. Yes, I suppose I did.'

'You were right about the young lady – Margery is it?'

'Margaret.'

'Quite. She is undoubtedly beautiful. And I believe she welcomed your attentions.'

'Do you think so? Do you really think so? Maichamps, you have no idea how much I want her.' Henry shook his head as he spoke.

'You mean you want to marry her?'

Henry considered his reply carefully.

'No, not by choice. But I may have to make that promise to get what I want. We'll see. We'll wait, and then we'll see.' The diversion over, he returned his attention to his ills, rubbing the bridge of his nose, then his temples, then the back of his neck.

'Poor Henry,' commiserated Maichamps, 'you are suffering, aren't you. I expect your pride is hurting as well, eh?'

'Pride?' said Henry sharply. 'Why should my pride suffer?'

'Oh, come now, surely you haven't forgotten already. You told me yourself how good your dancers were. And yet they put up a pretty poor show, didn't they? It wouldn't surprise me to find that a great many of your friends who were there to watch, those who knew of the financial interest you have in this dancing competition, would be pleading with you to accept a wager. Are the odds still at five-to-one for this Waterhouse's team beating yours?'

'Why? Do you want to bet?'

'It's possible. But before I decide to do so, please quench my thirst for knowledge. Have you taken any further bets?'

'Yes.' Henry spoke guardedly, suspiciously.

'Would you mind telling me the value of these bets?'

'Why?'

'Merely because I ask. Politely. Without resorting to any form of persuasion.' Henry understood the un-stated threat. He could keep nothing from Maichamps.

'Well,' he conceded gracefully, 'I suppose it wouldn't do any harm. And I must admit, after the performance tonight I wanted to lower the odds. I think that two-to-one, or evens, would have been fairer. But I'm a man of my word, and I'd told them before that I would give five-to-one, so five-to-one it stayed.'

'How much Henry?'

'Five thousand.'

'Pounds?'

'Please, guineas!'

'Including Waterhouse's bet?'

'No.'

'Mm. So you stand to win, let me see, six thousand. If your team wins, of course.'

'Yes. So far. I must admit my worries though, my dear Maichamps. In my drunken stupor I agreed to offer those odds for another week, just in case any of my friends' friends wished to take up the offer. And I fear that they will do exactly that.'

'How much Henry?'

'Another five, perhaps six thousand?'

'All at five-to-one?'

'Apart from the original bet with Waterhouse; that was two-to-one.'

'That's, forgive me for being so slow, mental arithmetic was never my forte, fifty-seven thousand you'll owe if your team loses?' Maichamps shook his head sympathetically. 'You don't have that type of money, Henry. You have nothing near that.'

'No. That's why I'm worried.'

'On the other hand, if you won it would be sufficient to pay off all of your present debts, both gambling and of a more social nature – no, don't look so surprised, I know a great deal about you Henry, more than is good for me – and leave a pleasant sum over? You agree?'

Henry nodded sullenly.

'Very well then. Let us suppose that someone approaches you, having seen your dancers perform badly, who feels that they could still improve enough to justify your faith in them. What odds would you offer him?'

'I don't know Maichamps, good God man, who would want to do that after seeing them tonight? On that performance I ought to be reversing the odds completely, giving five-to-one against for our team winning. No, don't press me, let me think! Very well then, let us say evens, to prevent any disagreement. Yes, I'd say evens.'

Henry's irritation was plainly evident. He could not see how Maichamps was developing his argument but suspected that he, Henry Makemore, would not benefit from it whatever direction it took.

'I am not a rich man, Henry. No, don't raise your eyebrows at me like that, I am not rich in comparison with, say, your father. But I do have a certain amount of floating capital at present. How would you react if I were to offer that sum to you in a wager? In favour of your team winning this silly dancing championship. Say twenty thousand at evens? How would you feel?'

Henry's puzzled expression became one of panic.

'No! No, I wouldn't take the bet! I couldn't, it would ruin me!'

'Surely not, Henry. It would be, in the sum of things, hugely less embarrassing than paying out almost sixty thousand, less my twenty, of course, to your friends. And yet that, despite your protestations to the contrary, seems to cause you no concern at all.'

'You know, don't you?' Henry's voice was low, threatening.

'Yes, Henry, I know, of course I know! I watched the dancing. I saw the way your men threw the dance away. They did it cleverly, so cleverly I hardly noticed it was deliberate, and anyone who did notice will probably think that it was done to persuade the Waterhouses to underestimate their opponents. But I noticed it. And my noticing limits your options, doesn't it.'

'How?'

'Oh Henry, have you learned nothing from me? I blackmail you! I blackmail you for half your profits!' Maichamps screwed up his face.

'Unless I can think of something else that will make me more money. Tell me Henry, how certain are you that your men will do their duty by you?'

'I'm certain. There are ways of winning that don't necessarily mean you have to get better. It just means that your opponents get worse.' A smile broke out over Maichamps' face, a smile which bore the lop-sided leer of a heavy, blood-red moon, warning of impending foul weather.

'Perhaps I've underestimated you after all, Henry. Are your men going to dance again soon?'

'No, not till the New Year. It's traditional, they go out on New Year's Day, round the local houses, dancing for money.'

'And will Waterhouse's men do this?'

'If they're ready, yes.'

'Well then, I'd suggest you make sure they do. It may just be that I can invite, on your behalf of course, some very wealthy friends of mine to help you welcome the New Year. These wealthy friends are very fond of gambling, but they tire of horses and dogs, they become bored with fisticuffs and coursing, and this new idea of a wager on the outcome of a dance may bring a spark of interest to their jaded lives. But I would depend on you, my good friend, to ensure that your dancers perform as they did earlier tonight. Because then we might be able to attract bets of a more substantial size. And they must be able to make a comparison, and judge Waterhouse's team the one with greatest potential.

And we may have to reduce the odds a little. Five-to-one is perhaps too suspicious for those familiar with judging chance. Do you understand me?'

'Yes,' answered Henry, unsure of himself.

'Changed circumstances,' Maichamps announced, 'force me to delay my departure until we have had time to discuss this matter further. I shall talk to you tomorrow. I must think carefully, and would suggest you retire immediately to do the same.'

'Very well Maichamps. But, er, when you came in you mentioned a present. For me.'

'Oh yes, so I did. Now where is it.' He patted his pockets, found nothing, then saw a small package on the floor beside his seat.

'There we are. In plain brown backing paper. It's a book, Henry, one which I feel will greatly appeal to you. I found it last year in France, the central character reminds me a little of you. Go on, open it up!'

Henry opened the book warily, as if in fear that the characters inside would take life and spring out at him.

'It's in French!'

'Yes Henry, most good books are these days. English literature offers so little in the way of excitement. You will have to spend a little time acquiring the knowledge it offers. Its title, "*A Rebours*", means something like "the wrong way round", or "against the grain". A good friend told me that it was best translated as "Against Nature". It could well be your philosophy of life. I've read it, and it's a little too flamboyant for me even. Try it.'

'Thank you Maichamps, I shall. But later.'

'Yes, later Henry.'

They moved to the doorway together, paused briefly.

'Maichamps, if you wished, I could accompany you to your room. The staircase is dark and I would not wish you to fall. And if . . .'

'No Henry, not tonight. I must think and you must rest. Goodnight.'

The tall man bent down. He kissed his companion gently on the lips, then pulled the door shut behind him. Only the embers of the fire remained to welcome the grey dawn.

Chapter Six

My men, like satyrs grazing on the lawns,
Shall with their goat feet dance an antic hay.

Edward II
(Christopher Marlowe)

Tommy chose his dancers. There was no lack of interest amongst the men; word had spread rapidly of Thomas's clog dance and Bompas's abrupt departure; the pit-manager had never been popular. The challenge between the Makemores' and the Waterhouses' dance teams made sword-dancing the main topic of conversation at pit-head, coal-face and public bar. Many an expert who had never set foot on a dance floor held forth on the advantages of clogs over shoes when performing rapper; while others debated the most traditional forms of costume, or the tunes most likely to help dancers attain an even stepping rhythm, or the figures which the dancers should perform. The truth was that very few had seen the dance at all. Their grandfathers had danced it, their fathers had told tales of it, but rapper was, to most of them, a thing of the past. Tommy passed the message around that he wanted dancers, not necessarily those with experience, a good sense of rhythm would be enough. Some asked questions. What's in it for us, they said, do we get time off work to practise, do we get extra pay? How do we benefit? And the answers came back. You practise in your own time, once a week to start with, more often if necessary. There's no extra pay. There's no benefit at all, except in keeping alive a tradition. Tradition doesn't pay us money they replied, tradition doesn't feed us. And so Tommy Armstrong was eventually faced with ten volunteers, ten willing men from a workforce of over six hundred. The job of reducing this ten to three did not prove difficult.

One man had a limp, his left leg a good three inches shorter than his right. Another walked as though the arm and leg from each side of his body were tied together, slouching across the room like a Tyne-keel crossing the river on a turning tide. A third was too fat, a fourth too tall and spindly, while the fifth was drunk and lay on the ground singing salacious songs about women's underwear and North Shields fish quay. They were quickly dismissed.

One of the remaining five had danced before, but would only consider performing if he were allowed to dance as number one, calling the figures. Tommy had wanted Thomas to carry out this task, even though the latter expressed his willingness to give way. Willie cast his vote in favour of his father; it was his brother who had, unknowingly at the time, involved them in this strange situation, and it was his brother who ought to lead them out of it.

They decided to do without a Tommy and Bessy. Even the established teams, Tommy told them, often found themselves short. That left four men chasing three places. It was one of them, Rob by name, who suggested that all four be used, one of them acting as reserve, standing in for the others when they were unable to attend practice. They agreed. The team was formed.

Tommy lined them up and played a jig, not too fast, six regular beats to the bar. He showed them the basic step he required, left shuffle, right shuffle, then watched all of them as they tried to copy him. None had, nor ever would have, the elegance which his old legs still possessed, but all would be able to learn the dance to a standard which Tommy knew would better any team he had seen perform. He stalked the line in front of them, fiddle-bow tucked beneath his arm, face contorted into a mock sergeant-major growl. He stared at each man in turn, re-positioned an arm or a hand here, pushed a stomach in there, reached up to tighten a set of braces. Each man strove to keep a straight face then collapsed in laughter at the old man's antics. He made them hop around the room while he played hornpipes, had them waltzing with each other (none wished to play the part of the lady), then forced them to practise their stepping once again. All he had to decide now was where each should dance.

Thomas was number one, that much was obvious. His experience, limited though it was, demanded that position of authority. Willie would go beside him, number five. They were used to working together and familiar with the way the other moved. That gave the team a good front pair. The putter, what was his name, Tom Delaney? He was small but strong and wore a serious look which dissolved easily into a grin when he showed his obvious enjoyment in everything going on around him. 'Don't call me Tom,' he said, 'there's too many of them about. Everybody calls me Stew anyway; it's the Irish in me.' Stew was number three.

Rob could go four, behind Willie. A young man, newly married to a wife as brash as she was plump, he was thin and wirey with strong legs which he wore bowed. He said little, brushed frequently at the unruly mop of hair which fell before his eyes. The last joint of the index finger of his left hand was missing, though he would never talk of how it had happened.

Number two now. Two to choose from for number two. One of these was Len, a handsome man in his early thirties, much sought after by the ladies. His moustache was clipped short, as neat as his clothes were untidy. He was followed everywhere by a black Labrador bitch with love in her sad brown eyes, and his teeth were clenched over a pipe which he never smoked. His competitor was Davy, tall, bearded, a southerner who worked as chief clerk. Perhaps it was the latter's height, or his accent, or the fact that he worked above ground that decided Tommy against him. Or perhaps he felt that the taller man would have a greater talent for stepping into any of the others' shoes with a minimum of fuss. Either way, Len was number two. The team was decided.

They agreed to practise once a week in the village hall, from eight until ten. Their enthusiasm often found them there until eleven, once or twice after midnight. They had their followers as well. Stew usually brought one or two of his countless children, and his wife, a stately woman with short, cropped hair and wide shoulders, would collect them about nine. Rob's wife Aileen would invariably arrive shortly afterwards, their children left safely in the care of her mother, and would proceed to make lewd comments on the physical attributes of the dancers. Most of these were directed towards Len, who replied in a similar vein. Rob paid no heed to either of them, his concentration rooted in the steps he was practising. Such ribaldry quickly ran out of steam and Aileen would disappear to drink a jar or two with one of her neighbours. As she left one of Len's admirers would arrive. The others were amazed at the variety of women he seemed able to coax into his bed, or his kitchen, or both. The first week it was a buxom woman from the village, past her prime but good-looking in a comfortable way. The week after a girl young enough to be her daughter took every opportunity to drape herself over Len whenever there was a break in Tommy's drilling. The week after that it was an old woman, wrinkled, teeth blackened, who gave him a neatly folded muslin cloth which hid within it the most delicious cakes and biscuits they had ever tasted. When questioned Len merely smiled. His secret remained his own.

Willie would normally have been jealous of such an array of attendants when he had none, but he now lived only for the daily glimpses he sought of Margaret. He would journey past the Hall each morning and evening in the hope of seeing her. He visited the library every Friday in the knowledge that she too would be there, and he would insist on escorting her home again despite the presence of either her maid or her sister or both. His father and brother had teased him at first, then worried about him, then spoken to him to express their concern. They felt that he was making himself an object of ridicule and, worse still, exposing their employer's daughter to potential embarrassment. The last remark struck home, but if the Armstrongs had been seeking to end Willie's lovesickness then they had approached him, and his devotion to Margaret, from the wrong direction. Willie visited Margaret openly at the Hall, sought her pardon, and then asked outright if his presence in any way offended or embarassed her or her family. Her reply was honest; neither she nor her father had any problems with the attention Willie was giving her. If the truth were told, Margaret enjoyed the company of the handsome young miner, was aware of the glances directed toward them, revelled in the thrill of innocent notoriety. Her father was too busy with his business to worry about Margaret's adventures, preferred to leave such matters to Elizabeth's good sense. And Elizabeth? She was pleased to see her sister in the company of anyone other than Henry Makemore and Timothy Deemster. No, if pressed she would express an affection, polite, limited even, but an affection nonetheless, for Willie Armstrong and his smile and his bad jokes and for the lumbering, bear-like way he danced.

Elizabeth and Margaret had also taken to visiting the dance practice, but only after seeking the express permission of their father (who tutted them out of the room with an absent minded 'of course') and of Tommy Armstrong, who was far more difficult to win over. He knew his place in society; when the pit-owner's daughters were present they were his mistresses. But this was in direct conflict with his position of authority as dancing master. When Elizabeth asked if they could watch he was obliged to say yes but wished to say no. Elizabeth could see and understand his problem and moved quickly to resolve it. She suggested that Tommy teach her the fiddle tunes he intended playing so that he could teach and demonstrate without having to worry about music. By allowing him to become her teacher she removed herself (and her sister) from the role of being mistresses to that of pupils.

Tommy began to enjoy teaching Elizabeth music as much as he loved teaching the others how to dance. Twice a week, each Monday and Thursday, he would call at the Hall at two in the afternoon, his violin and bow wrapped in grey sackcloth under his arm. He would be shown to the music room where Elizabeth was waiting for him, sometimes playing the piano, more often scribbling tunes onto manuscript paper. They laughed at the way the other played. Tommy, self-taught, used (except on slow airs and more graceful tunes) only a few inches of the bow near to the nut, reversing direction with each staccato note. Elizabeth, more used to classical music, slurred the notes with long easy sweeps of the bow. But she learned quickly. During their first lesson she wrote down three tunes and, before they next met, found the counter-melodies hidden within them. When they played together, albeit at a more leisurely pace than would be played for the dance, the silence Tommy accorded his partner, the nod of appreciation he gave her, were such praise as she had never before received. She soon adopted his manner of playing, despite his warnings that she would be unable to revert to her trained style. She became accomplished at writing down tunes swiftly and accurately; reels, jigs, hornpipes and slip-jigs were noted and filed neatly away. At her mentor's suggestion she stopped treating the tunes as commandments to be rigorously obeyed with each playing. He showed her how to take a tune and mould it, caress its notes into different shapes and textures, make some passages more complex and others painfully and beautifully spare and simple. She developed the confidence to play without music, began to compose melodies of her own. And John Waterhouse, from the tomb of his study, would wonder at the laughter which penetrated his doric columns of paperwork, tap his foot in time with some faintly remembered air, and be unaware of his own pleasure that Elizabeth was becoming happy again.

Waterhouse was pre-occupied with work. Production was only slightly under target, but costs were too high. He could see ways of reducing them, of improving machinery and working methods, but these required time to develop and to install. He frequently looked out of the window at the pit-head and winding gear, more often than not hidden in a whirl of steam, smoke and rain. The autumn, as Albert Settle had forecast, had been short. The first snow had fallen in mid-November and frost had haunted the nights since then. Bad weather brought an increase in demand for coal both at home and abroad, though it was likely that the Baltic ports would freeze early this year. He would have to increase production somehow. Perhaps Edward might have some ideas, he was due to stay with them all the way through from Christmas to New Year. Or that man Armstrong, he seemed to have a good head on him, had taken to the new machinery with enthusiasm and had already suggested improvements. Yes, he had proved a valuable addition to the workforce. Promotion might encourage him further. He would certainly discuss that with Edward.

Mary Armstrong would have liked to see her men

practising but it was difficult to find someone to look after the children. Her immediate neighbours all had children of their own and, if she was honest with herself, she felt wary of leaving Matthew and David in the hands of comparative strangers. Then, one bitter cold night in early December, Tommy Armstrong declared himself too unwell to attend the regular meeting. Nothing serious, he insisted, just a cold. Mary thought different, suspected influenza, but the old man huddled himself close to the fire wrapped in a blanket, a glass of whisky in his hand. After the children were asleep Mary was chased from the house with threats of retribution if she didn't have a good time watching the practice.

For three days and nights the temperature had remained below freezing. The hoar frost had hung in the air and bleached the claws of elm and oak, traced acid fingers over window panes, made a playground of the pond. A full moon threw Mary's shadow ahead of her as she followed the path warily to the hall, music and laughter guiding her. There was smoke rising from one of the chimneys, and as she closed the double doors gently behind her she could see the fire roaring in one of the four fireplaces in the main hall. The five dancers were there, and Elizabeth Waterhouse silhouetted by the flames; the weather had kept all others away. Although it was hot close to the fire (Elizabeth had removed her coat, her jacket and a woolly cardigan, draped them over the back of a chair) the rest of the room was still cold. Only two lamps had been lit, and in their dim glow the breath of each dancer could be seen rising to heaven like a lost soul. They had been working hard. There was a smell of sweat in the air, not unpleasant, touched with carbolic.

No-one had seen Mary enter. She was surprised to see Elizabeth there, having assumed that without Tommy to play there would be no music at all since neither Thomas nor Willie nor their father had mentioned her presence before. It was not what she would have expected from the daughter of a pit-owner, a well-bred lady, an educated lady. But then Elizabeth was not, in any way that Mary recognised, a normal woman. She helped in the school two afternoons each week, guiding the children in their reading and writing with a kindness and patience Mary could not remember encountering in her schoolteacher. Matthew and David certainly showed an interest in what they were learning from her, were even allowed to bring books home with them. And Elizabeth always had time for the mothers, knew them all by name, greeted them cheerfully when they came to collect the younger children. And yet there was a collective nervousness whenever she was present. Mary had spoken to the other colliers' wives, without specifically mentioning her own feelings, to find that the subject of Elizabeth arose naturally. She seemed too interested in them. She asked questions about the way they lived and whether they had any problems. She asked their opinions on matters which seemed important to her, usually to do with what was happening abroad or in Parliament or in Newcastle, but which they had not been aware of. She talked about birth-control or the universal franchise or socialism and the power of the working classes in a voice which bordered on lecturing. But she was still the daughter of their husbands' employer, so they were polite in return and smiled at her and replied as graciously as they were able to her questions. After a few weeks she became aware that she was neither influencing nor interesting the women, and the questions and lectures largely stopped. But for Mary she seemed to have a special liking. She would accompany her, the boys scampering round their feet, up the hill to their house. The conversation was usually the same. It would begin with Elizabeth mentioning some aspect of her family life, commenting on how different it must have been for Mary, then asking how it was now for Matthew and David. They discussed school, church, the size of families, clothes; every subject seemed of interest. Mary spoke willingly but felt drained by the time Elizabeth left.

She mentioned this to Thomas, who seemed pleased that Elizabeth was taking such an interest in his wife and amused that it worried Mary so much. He offered his opinion that Elizabeth was lonely; it was, after all, a new home for her as well, and she had few friends. He was sure that any peculiarities Mary could see in Elizabeth were the result of her unfamiliarity with the way women of Elizabeth's class and social standing were accustomed to behaving, and that Elizabeth was probably trying very hard to understand the life that Mary led. Mary agreed, but at the same time gave the boys permission to make their way home alone after school. She had not seen nor talked to Elizabeth for two weeks now. She felt nervous seeing her again.

She stood silent by the door, her hesitation balanced by her curiosity to see the dance which had occupied so much of her husband's time in the past few months. There was no doubt that Thomas was, in his father's absence, in charge. His voice had no competition.

'That wasn't too bad lads, but the timing was wrong. We had to pause in the middle for Willie to catch up and then Stew turned the wrong way.' The two named dancers acknowledged their mistakes with nods.

'This bit all has to be joined together without anyone seeing the joins! We'll practise it as six figures, but really it should look like one complicated figure. Let's walk it first, then we'll try it with the music. Start from Coach and Horses then into Nut, tie it tight, that's it.' The dancers moved easily into the first figure, Thomas and Willie facing front, Len and Rob behind them, Stew at the back. The swords connecting them were held easily and confidently. They moved swiftly to tie the swords together in a five-spoked star; Thomas and Len cast outwards, Willie and Rob slipped inwards, and Stew moved forwards and turned.

'Here we go then. Straight Line forward! Break and move in four, step four on the spot.' The figure was executed in slow motion, Mary could see that, but the timing was good. Each dancer had to move from and to a different position, but the progress had to be complementary because they were linked together. And the stepping, the stepping that Thomas and Willie had been practising in her kitchen, the stepping which had woken the boys with its loudness; all five men were together, their feet beating out that regular rhythm that Mary had come to recognise.

Another command from Thomas and the dancers all turned right, brought their swords over their heads to form a line in the opposite direction. Another yell and a circle was formed, the men facing outwards, then a swift turn in again and another Nut was tied, then an equally fast move and the Nut was broken as they faced centre and spun outwards again to follow each other round in a small tight circle.

'Let's tie the Nut again,' said Thomas, 'then we'll try it with music. Don't forget, it's Straight Line forward, then back, Outward Circle, Nut, Sheepskin, then Double Guard. Off we go then.'

He tapped his foot to give the musician the speed; she began to play.

'Step this time, four-four-eight.' They began to dance, a complicated cadence of movement and rhythm that thrilled Mary's heart. Step then move, step then move, but no two movements the same, the music urging the dancers along, the dancers in time with the music and with each other. And then it was over. The whole sequence took no more than thirty seconds. She clapped loudly, moved towards the fire.

'Who's that?' said Thomas. Six faces, stern faces, turned to face her as she approached.

'It's only me,' she answered. 'Your Dad sent me down to make sure you were working hard.'

'Oh, it's you luv. We're just finishing. Have you been there long?'

'Long enough. It was good. What am I talking about, I'll admit it, it was very good! Far better than I'd thought it would be.'

'You didn't notice me mistake then?' asked Stew.

'Why should she?' interrupted Willie, ruffling the smaller man's hair. 'She was concentrating on watching me, I'm such a lovely mover!'

He minced across the room, whistled on by the other dancers.

'Was it really that good?' asked Thomas earnestly. 'It's diffficult to see how it's going when you're so involved in the dancing.'

'Yes luv, it was good. I'd tell you if it wasn't.' She moved closer to him. His forehead was beaded with sweat, and she reached into the pocket of her coat for a handkerchief, applied it gently to his temples, the back of his neck.

'Thanks, Mary,' he whispered, pulled her to his side. 'And what about the music? Fitted in perfectly, didn't it.' The question was a statement.

'Elizabeth's really come on in the past few weeks, she can play at a good steady speed, and the tunes just seem to match the figures perfectly.'

The recipient of Thomas's praise had carefully put away her violin, was now encasing herself in layers of clothing in preparation for the night's chill. She smiled and nodded her head at Mary who blushed as she lowered her eyes, guilt sitting awkwardly on her shoulders.

'I assure you Thomas,' said Elizabeth, 'the credit is due largely to your father. He would have been an admirable teacher. How is he tonight?'

'Oh,' answered Mary, 'he's grumbling as usual, I suppose that's a good sign. You know what they say about a creaking gate. His cough's not improving as fast as it should though, and he refuses to go to bed. Sits in front of the fire all day. But he's as stubborn as his sons and twice as smooth-tongued, so no matter what I say to him he always gets his way.'

'Are you coming for a drink Thomas?' yelled Rob, wrapping a scarf around his neck.

'Aye,' added Stew, 'Len's got a few bottles in at his house, says we can all go round.' The bottle owner himself approached them.

'You're welcome to come round lad. You too Mary.' He raised his eyes slightly toward Elizabeth.

'You as well Missus, if you want. I've tea and cakes. And the house is tidy.'

Elizabeth had given up her attempts to persuade all but Thomas and Willie to use her first name. 'Missus' was the nearest to familiarity she was likely to be offered, and she accepted that with good grace.

'Thank you very much, Len,' she said, 'but I've had a very busy day and I really must retire early. Perhaps some other time. I was thinking that it might be nice, if you wanted to of course, to have a practice up at the house sometime, while the weather stays cold. There's a big ballroom and it's a lot warmer than here. And I'm sure I could persuade father to open a bottle or two of his own beer, purely for refreshment of course.'

The grin on Len's face (he had been counting the number of bottles his invitation might cost him) was echoed by Stew and Rob and Willie, all now coated and mufflered, gloves and hats reducing the amount of man showing to a narrow sliver of eyes.

'How about you and Thomas?' mumbled Willie in Mary's direction.

'Well I don't get out very often, it would be . . .'

'Aye, we'll drop in for a quick one,' interrupted Thomas, 'just as soon as we've walked Elizabeth home. It's a nasty night to be out alone.'

Mary waited for Elizabeth's protestations to the effect that it was only a ten-minute walk, that she would be quite safe, that there was no need for the Armstrongs to put themselves out. No such word was spoken. Instead Thomas busied himself with damping down the fire and hooking the guard onto the fire surround while the others headed merrily for the door.

'It's coming on mind, it's coming on.'

''Course it is! We're good I tell you, damn good!'

'But are we good enough? There's lots to do yet.'

'Why aye, we'll beat them no trouble, no trouble at all. If we can't . . .' The voices disappeared. Elizabeth was waiting beside the door. Thomas linked his arm with Mary's and they followed her out into the night. Orion was high in the sky. Thomas stared at the constellation, the three stars of the belt, the blue-white of Rigel contrasting with the flashing red of Betelgeuse. He had read a book about stars but could not manage to superimpose the shapes from the printed page onto the pinpricks of light above him, with the exception of the Hunter and the Great Bear. There was little else visible on this night; the moon was too full, and high now, two rings around it showing that the cold weather would continue. The path from the village hall was flagged but the stones shone with ice. They walked on the white-rimed grass to the side, feeling the cold from the earth through the soles of their shoes. They steam-engined up the slope to the path through the woods, Elizabeth monopolising the conversation.

'There were a few houses here before we arrived, of course. It was a little village for the estate workers. The pond was there, and the stocks, and the track up to the Hall.'

'Stocks?' said Thomas. 'Really?'

'Is that what that wooden pole is, down by the pond?' asked Mary.

'That's right, just down there.' They looked back. A

sentinel post, about five feet tall, cast its tempered moondial shadow on the silver of the frozen water.

'There were two poles originally, and the cross-bar with three holes in it for hands and head. They couldn't get the last pole out, they were in such a hurry to do other work, so father told them to leave it. We still have the rest of it somewhere. They found an old ploughshare as well, and a man-trap. They're all in the stables I think, we can have a look when we pass. I'd like you to see the stables anyway, it could be a very good place for a practice when spring comes.' She laughed. 'Spring! We're not even past Christmas and I'm talking about spring! I don't know what's come over me, I seem to be talking a great deal at the moment. Perhaps it's excitement. The dance is going so well, I feel elated at being able to contribute something towards it.'

'Yes,' said Thomas, 'it's going quite well. And you are helping us a great deal.' As he spoke he squeezed Mary's arm and winked at her. Mary's sigh of happiness was frozen as cold as the air around her as she glanced across to see Thomas's other arm linked with that of Elizabeth. Her lips tightened as she fought to control the green jealousy which surged through her veins and coursed hot in her imagination. She didn't notice when they stepped onto the gravel path leading to the stables. She was unaware of the creak of the door and the heavy night scent of the horses, didn't see the flicker of light from the match bloom into the warm glow of an oil lamp. She passed no comment as Elizabeth pointed out the head of the stocks jammed firmly into an empty stall, almost covered with straw, stared past the man-trap hanging bubbled with rust on the cobbled wall. She ignored Thomas's nod of approval as he tapped the stone floor firmly with his foot. She waited patiently as Elizabeth and Thomas murmured polite goodnights at the front door of the Hall, then turned to walk away as soon as she heard the door close. Thomas hurried after her.

'You're a bit sharp off the mark tonight luv. Got the taste of Len's beer on your lips already, eh?' There was no reply.

'Go on then, tell me what you think about the dance. Really. Do you think we'll manage it in time? We could do with some constructive criticism.'

'Do you do that all the time?'

'What? Those figures? Well, they're part of the dance, but we don't do them every time we get together, we have to vary . . .'

'No, not that. Do you walk Elizabeth home every time?' Thomas could feel the tension in his wife's body.

'No. At least, only the past few weeks, when it's been dark and there's been no-one else with her.' His voice became conciliatory. 'I just walked her home luv, there's no need to get upset about anything.'

'And when you walked her home, in the dark, just the two of you, did you touch her?'

'No! How could you say that? Come on luv, what do you think I am? And even if I'd wanted to touch her, or do anything else come to that, what makes you think she'd have anything to do with me? Of course I didn't touch her!'

'Not even to help her on her way? Like you did tonight?' Mary stopped walking and stared at Thomas. He looked back at her then averted his eyes. He had never been able to do that, look someone in the eyes for any length of time, and he knew that looking away made him seem guilty or ashamed. He reached out, held her firmly with both hands gripping her arms. She made no attempt to move away.

'What's the matter with you Mary Armstrong? I've done nothing to deserve this! I've been trying to behave as a gentleman would, as I hope our sons would learn to do, and all I get is accusations of chasing a woman I don't fancy, a woman I've never even looked at with any thoughts of, of . . . of anything immoral at all! And you're making me feel guilty, damnit. For Christ's sake woman, stop it! What the hell is the matter with you?' As he watched a tear formed in the corner of one of her eyes, closely followed by another, then another. She collapsed into his arms as her body was racked with sobs and he pulled her close in the darkness to comfort her, murmuring in her ear, 'There there, it's alright, I'm here, there's nothing to worry about.' She pulled away.

'Thomas, I'm sorry, I'm so sorry!' she cried, but further words were drowned as she coughed and sniffed, breathed in deeply in an attempt to regain her composure.

'It's alright luv, there's nothing to be sorry about.'

'There is Thomas, there is!' She swallowed then began to speak.

'You were right Thomas, you didn't deserve to be treated like that. I was wrong and I'm sorry. It's just that . . . It's just that I was so jealous to see you touching her!'

'But you were there as well. I was touching you at the same time!'

'I know. But all I could think of was the two of you together when I wasn't there, and what might have happened!'

'Mary, I swear . . .'

'I believe you Thomas, I believe you. I love you, and I know you wouldn't do anything to hurt me in any way, but . . . Thomas, you're too nice for your own good. You can't see yourself. You can't see how much I love you, how much I want you, how attractive you are, and not just to me! No, wipe that silly smile off your face, I know what you're going to say about being fat and going bald, but it's the man inside that people like, and you don't see that! I was so proud when you asked me to marry you because there were so many other girls you could have had just by snapping your finger. Then, after we got married, I realised that you didn't know! You didn't know that we all talked about you, how we all fancied you. And you've still got that same something that makes people, women, like you!'

Thomas hadn't heard his wife say so much since they were married. He could find no words to reply.

'You're too innocent, Thomas Armstrong. And I worry that someone will take you away from me. And I worry because you're so much like your father in so many ways, and you know what he was like. And I worry because there's something about that Elizabeth Waterhouse . . .'

'Kearton.'

'Alright then, Kearton. Thomas, I tell you there's something about her that's not right. I don't know what it is, but she doesn't treat you the way she does every other working man at the pit.' Mary's voice deepened as she strove to explain her fears with all the gravity she could summon. 'And it's you as well Thomas, you're changing, you're not the same person you were a few months ago. I don't know if it's the job, or the house, or this stupid dance, or something else entirely different, but you're changing and I don't think I like it. It's as though you've no time for me and your sons. We've become less important all of a sudden. I don't like it Thomas, I don't like it.' She began to cry again.

'Come on lass, we'll head for Len's. A drink might do you good, take your mind off things.'

'No. I want to go home.' She looked up at him. Her nose was red and, when she pulled his head down to kiss him, she tasted damply of salt.

'I want to go home Thomas. I want to go home and go to bed with you. I want you inside me. I want you to want me. And then I want you to talk to me. Come on.' They slipped out of the shadows of the wood and back across the village green. All was silent; still, calm and cold-grave silent.

There was no light in the bedroom. The curtains, heavy red fabric which had started life as a table cloth, were drawn so that the frustrated moonlight could only draw harsh patterns on the window glass. Thomas had lit the fire as they entered the room. By the time they were lying in each other's arms, Mary's physical needs sated, the flames had grown and taken hold of the coal and twigs. Thomas watched as demons danced across the ceiling, keen to possess the souls of the mortals below them, prevented from doing so only by the heavy shadow of the bed-end cast up onto the wall. No sun-shadow this, no sharp line showing the end of light and beginning of darkness. This was disputed territory, and the warring factions attacked and defended each other's positions with no mercy. The defensive wall was torn down and rebuilt then torn down again in the flickering instant of a fiery spark. The outcome was, however, predetermined; the fire would dim to a soft glow, the battlements would be rebuilt more firmly until, dismayed and disheartened, the flames died.

But other imaginations could rule. Mary, her eyes hooded in dreams, rested her head on her husband's shoulder. She could smell the heat of his love-making, could still feel the dampness between her legs. For her the flames were cool butterflies, swallowtails and red admirals lilting their fragile way through summer skies to fan her with paper-soft wings. She could feel their passage on her skin, and each small hair on her body danced in time with their movement, teasing her mind into believing that a thousand soft hands were touching her gently, purposefully, lovingly.

'You said you wanted me to talk to you,' murmured Thomas. Mary didn't reply. He tried again.

'Was there anything in particular you wanted me talk about?' Mary moved her head to look at him.

'You heard what I said before, when we were out,' Mary answered. 'You shouldn't need to ask what to talk about.' She moved her head back again and closed her eyes, snuggled against him. Thomas thought back, reflected on his wife's outburst. She seemed calmer now, relaxed. He had hoped that she would say that it didn't matter, that she realised how silly she'd been, that they could go to sleep in each other's arms and forget what had happened. He was tired, it was late, he was on early shift in the morning. Surely a postponement at least would have been possible. But Mary's tone of voice, despite her outward contentedness, showed that she would not be put off.

'Alright then. You've told me what your worries are, and I've tried to tell you that you've no need to worry. You think I've changed. You might be right. After all, no-one stays the same for ever. Look at you, for example! You've never been like this before, have you? But if I've changed, and if you've changed, it's because we've been pushed into change by something. I've started a new job, a job where my boss listens to what I say and respects my opinion. We've moved to a new house in a new village where everyone's a stranger. But it's a good job, a good house, a nice village, and the only reason we're here is because I promised I'd do this stupid dance for the stupidest of reasons. And to do it I've had to get Dad in, there was no choice. I've given me word luv, I've given me word that I'd do the best I can. And that's what I'm doing, even if it means that I'm changing. Do you under-stand?'

Mary nodded slowly but said nothing. She knew Thomas well. He hadn't finished yet.

'The best thing of all though, the thing I see every day and every night, is that it's working! Everywhere I go, down the pit, to the library, to the school to see the lads, people are asking how the dance is going, wondering if we'll win. It doesn't really matter if we win or not!' He stopped, reconsidered. 'No, that's not right, it does matter, it matters a lot to me and to everyone else who has anything to do with the pit or the village. It's important, but what's more important is that we've already done what we wanted. There's a spirit in the village and down the pit which wasn't there before, and that's because of the dance, and me, and

Dad, and, through us, you! Can you see that?'

Mary nodded again, raised her finger to rest it on his lips. In his excitement his voice had grown steadily louder. When he spoke again it was once more in a whisper.

'I suppose I have changed. I've become less of an island than I was. I care more about the people around me, not just you and the boys. But that doesn't mean that I love you or them any less. In fact it makes me love you more.' A coal punctuated his sentence with a crack and spark.

'I was going to say that I was doing this for us all, for you and me and the kids and John Waterhouse and me marras and so on. But I'm not daft, lass. I know that, when it comes down to it, I'm doing this for me. It's selfish of me, I know that too, but it's pride and ambition and curiosity all mixed in together that make me do it. But there's something about the dance as well, something special I can't explain. And if there's anything else you want me to talk about, anything else you want me to say, well I can't think what it is!'

'There's nothing else you want to say?'

'No. Not that I haven't said already. Why, have I missed something?'

Mary nodded, even at the risk of her husband losing his patience.

'I've told you, if you think there's something between me and Elizabeth you must be crazy. Yes, she talks to me and she's pleasant to be with. For some reason she thinks there's more in me than I've been able to show the world so far in my unimportant little life. I don't think she's used to finding a working man who can read and write and who enjoys doing both. I fact, she gave me a book the other day!' Mary raised her eyebrows.

'Not a reading book,' continued Thomas, 'a writing book. Just page after page of blank sheets. She said I should start keeping a diary, that we were living in interesting times and that in years to come I would want to look back and see what I'd been doing.'

'And have you done as she asked?'

'Well ... yes. I've written down a few words, just how I felt about certain things. You can look at it if you want, it's not secret. There's nothing wrong with that, is there? I've not done anything wrong in accepting some blank paper!'

'Thomas, how would you feel if you found that someone you knew, a good-looking man, had been spending time with me? How would you feel if you found that he'd been buying me presents? How would you feel if I changed because of things he'd suggested doing? And how would you feel if this was all kept secret from you?'

'But I've never kept secrets from you! If there's anything I haven't told you it's because I didn't think it was important! You're making it sound as if Elizabeth and I are ... Well we're not! Good God, I've never even looked at her ...' Mary was shaking her head.

'Thomas luv, I've never said you were carrying on with her. I was just trying to tell you what it could look like, how I felt finding out a little bit at a time. I trust you, but I can't help feeling the way I do. You're doing things and saying things you never used to.' She breathed in deeply. 'And there's other things you hardly say at all these days.'

A puzzled look appeared on Thomas's face. He sucked in his bottom lip, raised his hand to massage his temples, then pulled his thumb and forefinger down below his eyes and down the ridge of his nose to smooth his moustache. He smelt Mary's musk on his hand.

'I love you,' he whispered gently, then chased the message round the whorls of her ear with his tongue.

'That's all I need,' she answered, and trailed her hand across his stomach to find that he was ready for her.

'I love you too Thomas, I love you too.'

Much later she lay at his side, breathing deeply. Sleep had

come easily to her. But the burden which had been lifted from her mind had come to squat, fat and sullen, on Thomas's shoulders. Sleep teased him but would allow no satisfaction, only the memory of brown eyes and dark hair and a smile which held within it promises and secrets which could never be revealed to him. The knocker-upper found him grey-faced and awake.

It was beginning to snow.

Chapter Seven

All night has the casement jessamine stirred
To the dancers dancing in tune;
Till a silence fell with the waking bird,
And a hush with the setting moon.

'Maud'
(Alfred, Lord Tennyson)

Willie and Len had come to an arrangement with the landlord of the pub in Lanchester. Once a week they would drive into the village with a dog-cart to collect crates of bottled beer, returning the previous week's empties and making payment for their purchases. What had started as a means of avoiding the long walk back from the pub at night (even in bad weather it had never been a hardship to walk *to* the pub) was soon recognised as a valuable source of extra income. The supplies were stored and drunk at Len's cottage, which rapidly became an extra focal point of the community, appreciated by many far more than the library, the church, the school or the village hall. On some nights of the week it had even become necessary to turn custom away.

The snow helped. After all, what sane person would want to walk three thirsty miles to the nearest hostelry, then three drunken miles back, all through deep drifts of snow in the black of winter's night when the same warm hospitality was available a few yards away? And if anyone asked questions, well, it was a party, a private party, nothing more, nothing less. It was just that Len had a large number of friends! Although nominally the landlord, Len spent most of his time in front of the fire, his dog at his side casting loving glances in his master's direction. At his other side one of his women would usually take up station, refilling his tankard at his nod, fetching food or pipe as requested. Another of his harem could normally be found behind the table which served as a bar, dispensing bottles and taking in cash in a most efficient manner, while a third cooked and sold small pies and cakes. The idea for the venture had, however, been Willie's, and the proceeds were split evenly between the two of them. While Len kept his share under his mattress in his bedroom, Willie spent his half straightaway on clothes for himself and, more often, presents for Margaret. A small brooch, a photograph of himself (he had hoped to receive one of her in return but had been disappointed) in a silvered frame, a pair of silk gloves, all had been received with gracious thanks and happy smiles. What he sought, however, was encouragement, and this Margaret dispensed in amounts sufficient only to keep his interests alive but starving. Just when it seemed that his affection for her would expire, just as he was on the point of renouncing her as a tease and a temptress to seek solace in the arms of others, she would touch his arm or reach out absently to tuck a stray hair behind his ear, perhaps allow him to peck her on the cheek as they said goodbye after meeting at a practice or in the library. He would be raised from despair to elation, forgetting the cycle which had repeated itself before and would do so again. His friends were aware of his infatuation yet appreciated that he too could see the hopelessness of his situation and was an entirely willing victim. They sympathised without joking, at least to his face, but it still came as a great surprise to them all to find him thrusting himself into Len's parlour with a young lady at his side.

'This,' he announced grandly to the room in general, 'is my friend Abigail, who has agreed to be my partner at the dance this weekend.' He guided the girl into the room; she looked around boldly.

'Isn't she one of the maids up at the Hall?' whispered a voice, a woman's voice.

'Aye, I think she is,' came the reply, equally quiet. 'She's a bit above herself they say.'

'Well, if you can't get the organ-grinder you might as well go for the monkey!' The whispers dissolved into hisses of snake-laughter.

Willie looked around, saw Len and guided Abigail to his seat by the fire. There was a stool there and this was procured for the young lady. Willie helped her off with her coat, removed his own, and hung them on a hook on the back of the door. He then stood behind Abigail, his hands on her shoulders. She reached up to stroke his hands, and that innocent gesture told of a degree of intimacy between them which would normally only be found when partners had known each other for a considerable length of time. Len raised an eyebrow; he was not known for his shy and retiring nature.

'If you'll forgive me for saying so, this is a bit of a turn-up. I thought you'd dedicated your life to the services of this young lady's mistress!' He waved his girl away as he spoke, indicating that she should fetch drinks for the newcomers.

'Aye, you could say that. But I finally realised what a fool I was making of meself,' answered Willie. 'There I was hanging around waiting for Margaret Waterhouse to pass by so's I could kiss the hem of her garment when all the time Abigail was there, just as beautiful. I just hadn't seen it!' Abigail smiled and lowered her eyes, but the gesture was not like Margaret's would have been, practised, studied. When she looked up again the beauty which Willie claimed was indeed present, but natural, without pretence or artifice.

'He was waiting to take a walk with Miss Margaret,' said Abigail, her rural Cheshire accent smoothed by years of domestic service. 'She'd agreed to meet him by the stables but then Mr Makemore arrived. I said should I go to tell him that she would be late and she said no, she probably wouldn't be able to go at all, but it didn't matter. Then she dismissed me, but I came down to see him anyway. I didn't think it was fair to treat him like that, and I told him what had happened.'

'I was angry,' butted in Willie, 'I was so angry I was all for kicking that Henry Makemore round the house like the mongrel he is. But Abigail calmed me down. She said her mistress didn't mean to be like that, she couldn't help it. It was just the way she was.' He clasped Abigail's hands again and smiled down at her. 'Abi always sees the good in people, won't hear a bad word said about anyone. Anyway, I calmed down a bit, and Abi told me that Margaret was looking forward to coming to the dance. I asked Abi if I could have a dance with her and she said she wasn't going. No-one had asked her, and she didn't really know anyone living in the village. So I asked her, and I've brought her along tonight so she'll know at least some of the people there.'

'When exactly did this happen,' asked Len 'this realisation that you were made for each other?'

'When was it? Day before yesterday?' asked Willie. Abigail nodded.

'Hmm. You are quick workers, aren't you. Here, have a drink. It's on the house.'

'Thank you very much Mr ...?'

'Damn, I didn't introduce you! I'm sorry Abi, this is Len, my friend and fellow dancer, and ...?' Willie too was suddenly unsure of an identity. Len looked round at the girl who had brought the mugs of beer. She lowered herself easily onto his lap, flicked her dark hair back to reveal purple marks on her neck. He reached down the back of her skirt.

'This is . . .' he floundered. 'This is . . .' The girl whispered in his ear. 'Oh yes, this is Louise, Loo for short. She's my bedwarmer.' They started laughing and the laughter spread rapidly round the small room and out into the night.

'This,' Willie announced grandly to the room in general, 'is my friend Abigail, who has agreed to be my partner at the dance this weekend.'

Thomas Armstrong looked up from his writing. His father dragged himself back from sleep and opened his eyes. Mary Armstrong bustled into the room, wiping her hands on her apron. Willie had blown in with Abigail in tow and now stood beaming before them. The mugs of beer Lennie had forced upon them had become three, then four, and it was now past ten o'clock.

'Would you like a cup of tea – Abigail is it?' asked Mary.

'Why, yes please, I would,' replied the girl, 'but first, if you don't mind . . .' She hurried over to Mary and spoke quietly to her. Mary laughed in return.

'Of course love, it's just out the back, there's a night-light already on in there, helps stop the pipes freezing up. I'll put the kettle on.'

'Well?' said Willie as Abigail left the room, 'what do you think?'

'Seems a nice bit of stuff,' grumbled his father. 'She can rub liniment on my chest any time.' He punctuated his sentence with an angry, rasping cough, closed his eyes and drew his blanket around him as it subsided.

'She's Margaret's maid, isn't she?' said Thomas.

'Yes,' answered Willie, defensively, 'she's maid to Margaret and her sister. Why?'

'Oh, just asking. I've seen her about with Margaret and Elizabeth quite a lot. You have as well, I suppose. How did you get round to asking her out?'

Willie explained as he had done an hour previously to Len. Thomas allowed him to speak, nodded occasionally.

'Good,' he said eventually, 'good. She's always seemed a nice lass, the little chance I've had to speak to her. I just hope you behave yourself with her. But here she comes back again, here love, sit down over here.' He pulled an armchair towards the fire, beckoned Abigail into it.

'I was just telling my brother what a pity it was that such a nice girl should be going out with such a reprobate. We have met before, but I'm not sure if you've been introduced to Mary, my wife.' Mary, on cue, brought in a teapot and poured boiling water into it from the kettle kept permanently by the fire. 'Where do you come from, originally?' she asked.

Abigail sat back in her chair, tilted her head towards the ceiling. She had brown hair which had been allowed to grow long; she wore it plaited, and the light from the fire glinted on the pins holding it in a bun. Her eyes were darker than her hair and shone as she spoke.

'I was born in a little village called Goostrey, south of Manchester. My parents worked on the land there, I had lots of brothers and sisters, some older than me, some younger. My Ma died when I was seven and I went to live with my Da's brother and his wife a few miles away. They were house-servants at the Hall, and I helped with the scullery duties and so on.' Mary poured out a mug of tea, held out the sugar bowl.

'Oh, two please,' Abigail replied, and took the mug carefully. She sipped at the contents and sighed.

'Mm, that's good. Now where was I? Oh yes, when I was, oh, about ten, my uncle and aunt moved to Manchester to start work in one of Mr Waterhouse's mills and they took me with them. I started work too, I was a big girl, looked older than I really was. One day Mr Waterhouse, Miss Margaret's father that is, saw me and asked me how old I really was and I told him the truth. He said I was too young and he would have to let me go, but I said I had to work to give money to my aunt and uncle, so he took me home as a companion for Miss Margaret. I'm two years older than her, by the way. I've been with her and the Waterhouses ever since.'

'And are they good people?' asked Mary. 'Do they treat you well?'

'Oh yes, they taught me to read and write. Mr Waterhouse, he sometimes forgets I'm a servant and he treats me like a daughter!' She giggled. 'He really is nice, I like him. Miss Elizabeth, she's been away for a while and when she came back she was changed, really ill. I think her husband's abroad, India or Australia according to Mrs Atkinson – she's the cook – though Miss Elizabeth never talks about him. She's much better now, but I feel as though I don't know her properly. She doesn't seem to need me that much, which is just as well, because Miss Margaret seems to call for me more and more as each day passes. She's turning into a right one is Miss Margaret, a real magnet for the men!'

'But what do you do?' asked Mary. 'Do you just help them dress and look after them, or do you have other duties as well?'

'Oh, it depends,' answered Abigail, 'it depends on what needs doing, what I'm doing at the time, what the house-keeper says . . .'

'Willie.' Thomas moved to one side and his brother followed.

'She's nice Willie. I hope you won't be hurting her?'

'What on earth do you mean by that?' His brother bristled.

'I just hope that . . . Well, I hope you've asked her to the dance for the right reasons. No, let me finish. I can see by the way she looks at you that she's smitten by you, God knows why, and I know that in the past you've been with a few lasses and, give you credit, you've behaved well towards them. As far as I know, that is.'

'Well I've never had any complaints!' said Willie. They both smiled.

'It's just that a week ago you were thinking of throwing yourself down the mine-shaft because Margaret Waterhouse had passed you by without saying a word. Then the next day I had to pull you down from the ceiling after she agreed to go for a walk with you. Now you don't seem to care one way or the other. Don't get me wrong, I think there's more future for you in courting a lass like Abigail than in tilting your hat at Margaret Waterhouse. But you seem to be over her very quickly.'

'Thomas, why don't you tell me what you're on about? I'm a grown man, I can take it. And if I can't, well, I'll just thump you!'

'Yes, I think you would. That's probably why I'm not being as straight with you as I should be. Here it is then. I hope you're not taking Abigail to the dance because you know that Margaret will be there. I hope it's not an attempt to make Margaret jealous. Really I want you to tell me that I'm completely wrong, that I'm a suspicious, interfering brother and that I should mind my own business.'

'Thomas, you're a suspicious, interfering brother and you should mind your own business.'

'You didn't say that with much feeling.'

Willie made no further reply, returned to Abigail's side. She reached up to hold his hand and he smiled down at her. The smile was forced. Thomas had touched a raw nerve, and both brothers knew it.

'We should be going,' said Willie abruptly to Abigail, 'you have to be in your room by ten-thirty. Thanks for the tea

Mary, back in half-an-hour.' He hurried the startled Abigail into her coat and ushered her out of the door, allowing her only the swiftest of goodbyes. As the door slammed behind them Tommy surfaced once again from the undertow of his sleep.

'Funny lad, our Willie,' said Thomas. 'There are times when I feel so close to him, and other times when he could be a complete stranger. What do you think Dad?'

'I don't,' answered his father. 'Thinking's dangerous, it makes the brain explode. I'm away to my bed.' He stumbled into the next room still wrapped in his blanket.

'What was all that about?' asked Mary. 'I was getting on so well with Abi, we were having such a pleasant chat. Why did Willie rush her away so quickly?'

'I think,' said Thomas as he settled the fire, 'he might be finding that he has problems shortly. Despite the way she behaves I think that Margaret's taken a shine to Willie, and I can tell by looking at her that Abigail's the same. I don't know how he'll cope and I don't know how they'll cope! There's always problems when a man chases two women.'

'Oh come on, you man of the world, let's go to bed before he gets back or we'll be up all night listening to his problems. Anyway, what do you know about a man and two women?' She headed for the stairs.

'Nothing luv, nothing at all! I've got my hands full dealing with one!' He made a grab for her then moved as if to run after her. She silenced a scream.

'The kids Thomas, you'll wake the kids!'

'Me? You're the one making the noise! I'm going to be quiet, perfectly quiet, quiet as the soft, soft snow.'

He moved slowly after her, slowly up the stairs. Only the fire was left in the room, the fire and an open book. There were many blank pages in the book. Thomas had filled only three in his neat hand, but on the first page, written with a pen unlike Thomas's, was a quotation between the monograms 'T' and 'E'. 'Look in thy heart and write' was written in an angled, almost tortuous scrawl. It had taken Thomas some minutes to decipher the lines, but the words now remained in his mind. Look in thy heart and write.

John Waterhouse was in a good mood. The seam of coal that his men had been working had unexpectedly widened. This meant that production was back on target, probably even ahead of forecast. Costs were marginally higher, but that was inevitable given the weather they were having. Demand was high without the need to consider exporting coal, the railway lines had been quickly cleared of snow and distribution was proving no problem. He was looking forward to Edward visiting them again, looking forward to demonstrating that his faith in the pit had not been unwarranted. His brother had originally planned on spending Christmas with them but had been distracted, according to his message, by business in London. That could have been true, John admitted, but it was more likely that he had found some new woman on whom to lavish money and presents, a woman who would be lauded as the most magnificent creature under the sun for at least – how long had the last one been in fashion? – three months? Three months in return for a small annual settlement, a suite of rooms in a residential hotel for a while until something else turned up. Edward looked after his women. But at least he had promised to tear himself away in time for the New Year party.

John Waterhouse did not normally enjoy celebrations, whether they were for birthdays or anniversaries, home-comings, departures, memorials, weddings or christenings. The enforced jollity, the meeting with long lost relatives most of whom had not been misplaced but discarded, usually combined to depress him. He avoided celebrations whenever possible; when they were unavoidable he arrived late and left early, sometimes conspiring to merge the two events into one. But this one, this he was looking forward to. Elizabeth had made the initial arrangements. The dance was to be held in the village hall with Tommy Armstrong organising the music and the estate providing the food. He must have been in a good mood when she sprang that one on him! There was even to be free ale since it was a once-a-year occasion and there was no work the following day. In the interests of good morale, of course! Thomas Armstrong's rapper team would give a first performance of their dance, and there would be games for the children and small presents for the women-folk. Then Margaret began to take an interest.

'Wouldn't it be nice,' she said one morning at breakfast, 'if we could invite some of our neighbours to the dance.'

'Which ones were you thinking of in particular?' asked Elizabeth with excessive politeness.

'No-one in particular,' came the icy reply, 'but since we moved here there have been one or two who have been polite enough to call on us, have even invited us to their own homes. It would surely be our duty to return the compliment.'

'Margaret,' said Elizabeth, 'your words have the signature of someone else behind them, and I have no doubt that the someone is Henry Makemore who has been calling on you recently with a frequency which might cause concern if father was less deeply involved in his work.'

'Now then ladies,' said John Waterhouse. 'Is there any need for such an argument so early in the day? Let us talk away our problems. Margaret, has young Mr Makemore been calling to see you?'

'He has visited the house recently, yes father.'

'How often my dear?'

Margaret furrowed her brow. 'Three times in the past week father.'

'Four!' interrupted Elizabeth. 'He called twice last Tuesday!'

'I say three!' countered Margaret. 'He was visiting a friend and called for refreshment on the way there and on the way back but that, in my mind, counts as one visit!' Elizabeth tossed her head, considering her point proved.

'No matter,' continued John Waterhouse, 'it would appear that Mr Makemore has certainly been making his presence felt. It requires a deal of effort to travel in these present conditions. Did he mention why he found it necessary to call so frequently my dear?'

Margaret blushed, turned her head down, fluttered her eyelashes. Elizabeth inhaled, would have passed comment on the silliness displayed by her sister had her father not caught her eye, silenced her with a conspiratorial, almost imperceptible shake of the head.

'I would have thought it was obvious father,' said Margaret. 'He called to see me.'

'Oh, so *you* are the object of his attention! And I thought, suspected, that he was calling to see how the mine was progressing!'

'He does mention that, when he calls to see me,' admitted Margaret, oblivious to the irony in her father's voice.

'And does he ask,' said Elizabeth, 'about the dance team? Does he mention it at all?'

'Well, yes. The subject does normally come up, in polite conversation.'

Elizabeth continued to press her point.

'I don't suppose the suggestion came from young Mr Makemore that he be invited to the party?'

'No!' said Margaret. 'Certainly not. It was I who invited him, and his father of course, though I doubt he'll be able to come, he's got gout at the moment. And his friends, he did mention that he would have some guests staying with him over the holiday and I felt I ought to . . .'

John Waterhouse raised his hand.

'Did I hear you correctly Margaret? You've already invited Henry?'

'No! I mean, yes. That is, I didn't think there'd be any problem, after all it's only a miners' party.'

'That is precisely the point, young lady. It's a party for the miners, for *our* miners, not for our wealthy neighbours and their guests. It's meant to be a celebration of the season but also of the community spirit which is developing amongst them. You have, by your precipitate actions, placed me in a potentially embarrassing situation. I shall have to think further about this, as should you my dear. I would suggest you do that now for the rest of the morning in the seclusion of your own room. I shall discuss the matter with you at lunch time.'

Margaret stamped away from the table, slamming the door behind her.

'Are you really embarrassed father?' asked Elizabeth.

'No, not really,' sighed John Waterhouse. 'We do have an obligation to invite the Makemores and, since it's a dance, we should also invite their dance team I suppose. They were good enough to have the Armstrongs along when we had dinner with Sir Charles. But I find it difficult to hide the fact that I dislike young Henry, and it annoys me that I have, as yet, no real reason for displaying that emotion. No, I shall write to Sir Charles today with a formal invitation, and I must tell Thomas Armstrong that there may be some interested observers to see his team's first public performance. And as for you Elizabeth, I'd be obliged if you would keep a weather eye on your sister. She is inclined to be flighty and silly at the best of times and I do not approve of the attention being given her by Henry Makemore. Please take care of her.'

'Yes father,' said Elizabeth. 'I'll see she does nothing stupid. I shall be the guardian of her morals.'

* * *

New Year's Eve. The village hall had been decorated with coloured paper and evergreens, the tables laid with white linen and crowned with candles and holly. At one end of the room a makeshift platform had been built, and it was there that the musicians were to play. Tommy Armstrong had removed himself from his sick-bed (and in doing so his health seemed immediately to improve) and spent the days since Christmas with Albie Settle. The gamekeeper had acted as chauffeur, the pair driving round the neighbourhood visiting pubs and private houses, hunting out Tommy's old acquaintances to invite them to play at the dance. Most had accepted readily, lured by the promise of free beer and a floor for the night; the side-room at the hall had been appropriated for this purpose. The Dunn brothers would be there, one on flute, the other on violin, and Micky Oliver had said he would bring his accordion. One of Stew's friends played the Irish drum and the bones, while Stew himself, it appeared, was capable of battering a tune from an old banjo. In the pub at Lanchester (their journeys regularly brought them back by way of the place) they had come across a slow-moving white beard beneath which hid an old man called Eric. He was capable of playing anything on the mouth-organ as long as it was in the key of 'D', and he had duly been invited to play. One of the putters confessed to owning a melodeon and was instantly drafted, even though his ability was questionable; he was at least able to move the bellows in time with the rhythm, while his wife could play the tin whistle with skill and conduct the band with her swaying hips at the same time. There was Tommy himself, and Elizabeth, and anyone else who cared to join in. The only question was whether the stage would be large enough to hold the band.

The food was prepared during the day and brought to the hall just before nightfall: meat pies and pasties, sausages and cheeses of numerous types and varieties, apples and plums and pears, cold potatoes and rice in spicy sauces, biscuits and cakes and cream. Willie had volunteered to arrange the bar and four casks of ale, both mild and bitter, had been carefully and lovingly installed the previous night, sampled at regular intervals during the day and pronounced perfect only at three in the afternoon. The judges made their way unsteadily home to prepare themselves for the evening's excesses.

The party was scheduled to begin at seven but the hall was filling by six-thirty. The younger children yelled and screamed their way across the floor, sliding and diving over each other into piles of bodies, while their elder brothers and sisters preferred, for the moment, to stay outside and play Montekitty up against the wall. The thump of their success could be felt within. Groups of people formed, clustered together round the walls of the room, congregating at fireplaces. Although individuals moved from one group to another the sexes remained apart; a husband and wife might arrive together, but social requirements demanded that they then separate. The only exception to this rule was Elizabeth Waterhouse. She moved easily from a clump of women to a circle of men, knowing at least one by name and most others by face. She ruffled the hair of children as she passed, enquired after the health of sick relatives, passed favourable comment on a dress or shawl, and was met in return with politeness and possibly even affection.

It grew warmer as more people arrived. Jackets and shawls were draped possessively over the backs of chairs, mugs refilled more frequently. The Armstrong family arrived. Matthew and David were dragging their grandfather after them, eager to head for the stage and the bran-tub containing presents, keen to join in the games being organised by the ladies of the Sunday School committee. Thomas and Mary had on their Sunday best, but appeared a little uncomfortable in stiff collars and unbroken shoes. They smiled as they came in, and although Elizabeth made for the door to greet them they had been absorbed by the crowd by the time she fought her way through. She was left facing Willie and Abigail.

Willie was dressed in his finery, a silk-faced Paisley waistcoat with matching bow-tie, crisp white cotton shirt, expensive suit, shoes spit-polished. At his side Abigail was beautiful. She was wearing a dress which Elizabeth had given her a few months ago, a dress of dark red satin material which had been embellished with brocade and ribbons. She wore a simple silver chain at her neck, and her long hair had been allowed to hang loose and fall down her back almost to her waist.

'Abigail,' said Elizabeth, hugging her maid, 'you look wonderful!'

'Thank you Miss Elizabeth, thank you for the compliment, and the dress.'

'Both are deserved, Abigail, the dress never looked so well on me as it does on you. But I didn't even know that you were coming this evening! Are you and Mr Armstrong . . .?'

'He asked me a week ago.'

'And what of Miss Margaret?'

'She's all ready and waiting up at the Hall, Miss. I believe that Mr Makemore is calling for her.'

'And does she know that you were planning on coming?'

'I don't know Miss Elizabeth. She never asked me what I was doing.'

'And you too, Willie,' said Elizabeth, 'look magnificent, most handsome. You and Abigail make a fine pair!'

'Thank you Miss Elizabeth. Can I get you a drink? Your father sent down some bottles of wine and some glasses – they haven't been opened yet.'

'Thank you Willie but no. I think the music is about to commence and I shall need all of my wits about me if I'm to keep up with your father and the rest of them. I'll talk to you both later.'

As she made for the stage Elizabeth realised that she herself had made no special effort to dress for the occasion. She was in black again, for she felt that the colour suited her, but it was so long since she had felt the need to make herself beautiful (as Margaret insisted on calling the act of sitting in front of the mirror for three hours applying powders and perfumes and colours which she all too obviously did not require) that it was becoming second nature to dress down. No matter, she had no intention of attracting men to her that night, nor any other night. She was there to play the violin, to enjoy herself, and she was going to do exactly that.

She climbed up to stand beside Tommy Armstrong. He had managed, in the short time he had been there, to drink at least three pints of beer and this had loosened his tongue just a little.

'Come on lass, we're just tuning up. Take the note from Mick on the accordion – give us that "A" again will you Mick – lovely.' He turned to address all of the musicians. 'Now, we haven't played together before, so I'll count everything in by four and we start with a chord. I'll yell "Out" to finish, and if the time's wrong watch me foot, I'll stamp to let you know the right beat. Everybody got that? Let's go then, one two . . .'

'Tommy,' hissed Elizabeth, 'what are we playing?'

Tommy Armstrong lowered his bow.

'Did I not tell you?' He looked around. The other musicians shook their heads.

'Damn! Right then, we'll do the Cumberland Square Eight for them – that's "My Love She's But A Lassie Yet" in "D", twice through, then "Atholl Highlanders" in "A" – that's a sixty-four bar tune mind – and back to "My Love" in "D". Just play the tune once to start with, it'll let them know we're ready for them. Right, ONE TWO THREE FOUR!'

They were off, dashing through the first tune before Elizabeth realised how much she was concentrating, her attention fixed on Tommy's bow and his foot tapping out the beat and her own efforts to keep up with the rest.

'Come on then lads and lasses,' he yelled, 'get yourselves onto the floor, I'm doing this for love, not for money! Square sets, that's what we need, square sets, each couple with their backs to a different wall of the room. Come on lads, don't be shy, if you don't ask her to dance somebody else will!' He turned to one side and spoke to Elizabeth.

'It's going to be hard work tonight, to start with at least. All they want to do is natter on to their friends. I'll get them going though. COME ON!' he yelled suddenly. 'If you don't get out on that floor I'll close the bar down. Don't worry, I'll tell you what to do. Have we got enough yet, let's have a look?' His eyes roved the room, making sure that each set was complete. Eventually he was satisfied.

'Start off, men, by putting your partner on your right. Will somebody show Billy Thompson which hand's his right? That's better. Now make a square. That's a pretty peculiar square you've got down there in the middle, but I suppose it'll do. Now where was I? Oh yes, the Cumberland Square Eight.

'This is what you do. The tops, that's everybody with their backs to me and facing me, you all gallop across the room, eight gallops out and eight gallops back. Good! If you haven't got room to gallop just bounce up and down a bit. Er, Fred, Fred Welton. Could you stop your wife bouncing, just for a minute. She's distracting the band. And she looks as if she might bruise her knees as well.' The instructions were called out with good humour and impeccable timing. Tommy seemed to know instinctively who would react favourably to his joking.

'SIDES, you're the ones who aren't tops, you just copy everything the tops do, so you gallop across as well. Try not to bump into anyone. That's it, well done!

'Now the tops again, you do a right-hand star, that's sticking your right hand into the middle – no Billy, your right hand, RIGHT hand Billy. Oh, just go backwards then, I don't care – and walk round in a circle, then do a LEFT hand star to get back again. Sides copy that. Good!

'Now the next bit's difficult. Just listen to start with before you do anything. Tops meet in the middle and the two men grab each other's wrists behind the ladies' backs, ladies put your hands on the mens' shoulders, and you spin round with your right foot somewhere near the middle. That's right, if you don't know what you're doing watch Dickie Dundas and his set, they've got the hang of it. Sides do the same.' While the side couples practised Tommy reached down for his mug. His forehead was slicked with sweat and he removed his waistcoat quickly.

'Nearly finished now. All four couples circle left, yes skip it if you want, that's how they do it across in Carlisle. Then promenade back, arms crossed in front of you, holding hands with your partner till you get back where you started from. And that's it once through, second time through the sides lead all the figures. If you get lost try to listen to me, I might just be watching you. Not that you'll hear me anyway, but I can always jump down and clip you round the lug. Off we go then, honour your partner on the chord for the CUMBERLAND SQUARE EIGHT!'

His count of four led into the dance and with a loud whoop the dancers began. It was obvious that a large proportion of those participating were familiar with the dance, and their influence kept the others less sure of themselves, mostly young, in line. Some of the styles were more suited to the football pitch than the dance floor, but enjoyment rather than accuracy was the benchmark for the night. Those who hadn't joined in clapped along with the music and yelled encouragement to those doing particularly well or, conversely, making fools of themselves. Elizabeth was pleased she had memorised the tunes. None of the other musicians had any music, and it meant that she could glance up to watch the dancers. All too soon the dance was finished; the floor cleared quickly.

'We'll give them a decent break between dances,' said Tommy to his musicians. 'Put a few waltzes in to slow them down or they'll never last the night out. HEY, THOMAS!' He raised his hand as his son looked up, indicated that his mug required filling again. Thomas nodded, wiping his forehead with a red and white handkerchief, and strolled to the stage.

'Hello Elizabeth,' he said. 'How are you finding life amongst the ranks of the exalted? Can I get you a drink?'

'To deal with the last first,' she answered, 'a glass of water would be very welcome, and as for the first, I'm really enjoying it up here. Your Dad's so good, I don't know how he controls the music and the dancing at the same time. He should do this for a living!'

'There's not enough demand,' explained Thomas, 'it's a dying art, this dancing. It'll soon be nothing more than a curiosity, mark my words, so you'd better experience it while you've got the chance. Speaking of which, could I trouble you, Mrs Kearton, for the pleasure of a dance at some time later in the evening?'

'Why Mr Armstrong, I'd be delighted, providing my employer will allow me time off.'

'Dad,' said Thomas, 'will it be alright for Elizabeth to have a dance later on?'

'That depends,' answered his father, 'on how quickly you get yourself back here with my mug of bitter and Miss Elizabeth's glass of water.' Thomas was gone.

'LADIES AND GENTLEMEN, and anybody else out

there, we have some entertainment for you later on tonight, the Greencroft Hall Rapper!' There were cheers from all sides. 'But until then it's your turn! We'll play some waltzes first and then follow that with STRIP THE WILLOW!'

And so the evening moved on, bar by bar. John Waterhouse arrived at about eight-thirty with a tired-looking Edward fresh (although he would have questioned the use of that particular word) from the train. The former was rushed straight onto the floor by Abigail to join in the dancing, while the latter collapsed gratefully into a seat, appropriated a glass, and reached into his deep coat pocket to bring out a large bottle of whisky. He seemed quite satisfied to sit and watch barn dances and waltzes, the Haymakers Jig, Corn Rigs, the Allendale Swing, the Long Eight, the Dashing White Sergeant. At nine-thirty, during a break when the band had gone to absorb some refreshment, Margaret arrived. The doors were held open by some men whose faces were familiar to Elizabeth but only barely so. As Henry Makemore entered, Margaret on his arm, Elizabeth realised that they were the sword-dancers she had seen at the Makemores' party. There were some other men too, five or six of them, well dressed, who seemed to wish to remain in the entrance hall. She was probably the only one to notice them; all other eyes were on Margaret.

Her dress was elaborate, fashionable, and quite unsuitable for a dance of this type. Elizabeth had not seen it before, could only assume that her sister had had it made specially for the occassion. It was of royal blue silk, gathered firmly at the waist, its *décolletage* guarded by a pearl necklace. It fell majestically to the floor in a series of sweeps and curves, a single white ribbon emphasising the thinness of Margaret's waist.

'She's forgotten the crown,' whispered a voice at Elizabeth's side.

'That's alright,' came the reply, 'she can send her butler

back to get it.' The remark was aimed at Henry Makemore who had come equipped with full dress suit, including gloves and top hat. The silence was too long to be respectful. Both Henry and Margaret began to look around, but all eyes were upon them and no words were spoken. They fidgeted, but there was no retreat. There were no empty tables, no free seats. It was Tommy Armstrong who rescued them.

'Whey lads and lasses,' he yelled from the stage, 'divvent they look bonny. I think they're here to audition for the jobs of Tommy and Bessy!' There was a roar of laughter and the unfortunate couple took the opportunity to move to one side. John Waterhouse stood up to offer his daughter a seat, a second was vacated for Henry Makemore.

'We've got time for one more dance before you see rapper done as it should be done,' said Tommy pointedly. 'So take your partners please for a waltz!'

He emptied his mug once more and bent to put it on the floor. As he stood up again he swayed to one side, put his hand out and was fortunate to find Stew beside him.

'Are you alright man?' he asked anxiously. Elizabeth looked across. The old man's skin was suddenly grey, and he seemed small, as if he had shrunk in the past few minutes. He took a deep breath and was once more in control.

'I've been talking non-stop for nearly two hours,' he said. 'When I've not been talking I've been playing. I've had, what, six or seven pints just to stop me voice from breaking down? I've been breathing that in,' he gestured outwards at the smoke-filled room, the product of tobacco and the fires in the hall, 'as well. It's hot as hell in here, look at the walls and the ceilings, they're dripping. Until two or three days ago I was an invalid.' He paused and threw a punch at Stew.

'Of course I'm alright man! Now come on, let's get playing. Scottish waltzes I think, "Leaving Uist", "Crovan's Galley" and so on. Six in and off we go, ONE two three, TWO two three . . .'

The band played well together. The musicians became aware of each other's capabilities, and from what had at first been an open assault on the tunes with everyone playing everything, there emerged an approach in which instruments complemented each other. By the time the third tune was reached only Tommy and Elizabeth were playing the melody and a soft, haunting harmony, Mick Oliver providing muted chords on his accordion. The tune was in a minor key; Tommy had played it for Elizabeth but had not known its name, and even now she remembered it as 'Unknown'. Its ethereal qualities, the way it could be played almost as a slow air, lured her into more complex, more beautiful harmonies. As the tune approached its end Tommy whispered 'Again. Play it again luv, that's grand,' and Elizabeth closed her eyes and was lost in its magic. And on the floor the dancers whirled.

As the tune took hold the random conversation dusting the hall slowly ceased. Couples stopped dancing, the better to hear the delicate melody and counterpoint, until there were only three left. Thomas and Mary Armstrong looked around them, seemed surprised to find the floor virtually empty, then stopped. Willie and Abigail were lost in each other's presence, while Henry Makemore and Margaret Waterhouse were formally determined to finish the dance. Henry's limp was hardly noticeable; he had been to dancing classes, as had Margaret, and they danced well. Willie and Abigail had never danced together before, but they possessed a natural grace and elegance (certainly not present in Willie's accurate but ursine bearing in rapper) which no amount of tutoring could have cultivated. They circled each other, circled the room, and those watching became dizzy as they marked their passage. Such was the hush that everyone heard Tommy's quiet 'Out this time', and the music slowed and finished on a major chord. Henry bowed and Margaret curtsied. Willie and Abigail opened their eyes on that chord and, for one brief moment, occupied each other's soul. They smiled, and he pulled her towards him, embraced her, and kissed her. The applause which followed could have been for the music, or for the dance, but was most likely for the kiss. The participants had the good grace to blush as they took their seats. Margaret stared at her maid in unforgiving disbelief.

'The lads are going to do rapper now, just as soon as they've got changed,' announced Tommy, 'so please charge your glasses, this is something worth watching closely, I've never seen a better team in . . .'

The hall doors burst open and in walked five dancers. It was Makemore's team.

'What the hell's going on here?' shouted Tommy. 'Get those bloody men out, we're dancing, not you! You're here to watch, not dance!'

'What's the matter old man?' sneered the leader. 'Frightened of competition?'

John and Edward Waterhouse rose to their feet to be motioned back by Elizabeth.

'I think you'd better let them sort it out themselves,' she said. 'They aren't children. I don't think there'll be a fight, there are only five of them after all.'

Thomas hurried up to the stage, ready to join the argument. He was closely followed by the rest of his team.

'Now look,' said the Makemore leader again, 'we don't want any trouble. It's New Year, isn't it? And it's traditional to do rapper at New Year, anywhere you want. That's right, isn't it?' There was no reply.

'You're all new to this, aren't you? You don't even know that! Tell them old man, tell them.'

'He's right,' said Tommy. 'Free access, it's always been the way. Then if one team finds a good spot and another comes along they can share the take. If they're good enough!'

'Oh, we're good enough old man. And we've given up our

time with our families just to come along tonight and show you how to dance properly. So if you'd like to clear the floor we'll do the dance just for you. Feel free to watch, you might pick up one or two good figures. Come on lads.'

Tommy returned to the stage.

'Ladies and Gentlemen. LADIES AND GENTLEMEN! Give us some hush, please! These lads here are from the Makemores' pit.' The rumble of discontent which Tommy had hushed grew noisier.

'SHUT UP WILL YOU! Now they've come along specially to dance for you tonight. They say it's so you can see how a good rapper team dances. It might just be that they're a little curious themselves to see what a Greencroft team can do!' There was a roar of applause. Tommy held up his hands again.

'This is your chance to see for yourselves. Give them a chance.' He climbed down from the stage. 'Oh, and don't hold their bad manners against them, they can't help the way they were brought up!'

He motioned to Thomas who hurried to his side.

'Get the lads changed. We go straight on after this, straight into the dance, no calling on song. Keep it crisp, keep it tight. Go on, off you go.' Thomas called to Willie, beckoned to Stew, Rob and Len. They disappeared into the cloakroom.

'Come on then,' chided Tommy, 'get on with it!'

'We're just waiting for our music,' came the reply, and, the cue having been delivered, the strains of the "Blackthorn Stick" sounded from the entrance hall. Tommy recognised the man who walked in playing the violin, though he hadn't seen him for twenty years or more. What hair he had was white; he was stooped and fat hung about him where previously there had been muscle. He wore glasses on his mottled red nose, and as he stared at Tommy there was hate in his eyes. But he could play the violin. Tommy sank to his seat and Elizabeth heard him mutter beneath his breath. She too knew the man – it was only a matter of months since her last encounter with him.

'Silas Bompas,' she whispered.

'Aye,' echoed Tommy Armstrong. 'That bastard Silas Bompas!'

The dance was better performed than at the Makemores' ball. Efficient, effective, still full of strange mistakes that were out of character with the dancers' overall ability, but better than last time. Tommy felt his confidence growing to the extent that he allowed his attention to stray from the dance. He could see Thomas pulling on his breeches over by the door to the cloakroom, desperate to catch a glimpse of the competition, almost falling over in his attempts to reconcile the two objectives. A change of tune, a slight increase in tempo, brought Tommy's ear back to the dance. Bompas was playing well. But then he always could play well. If only he could have put more joy and less precision into his music, he would have been up there with the best of them. Might even, thought Tommy, have been as good as me.

Elizabeth was not watching the dance. She was looking around the room, curious to find ... There he was! Henry Makemore had left Margaret with her father. While they were absorbed in the drama taking place in the hall he had moved away from them. Even as Elizabeth watched he reached the entrance door. There was a crush of bodies there, but five or six stood out from the rest. It could have been that they were strangers; it may have been the way in which they carried themselves; it might even have been the clothes they wore which, at Elizabeth's distance, seemed too fashionable for Henry's local set of friends. A combination of these was the most likely reason for her noticing them, but having done so she found it impossible to bring her concentration back to the dance. Makemore greeted them with a nod of the head, shook hands with one or two. They were with him, that much was certain, but not well known to him. Why were they there? There was something wrong, something which preyed on her mind and made her feel uneasy without her being able to determine the cause. She watched them carefully. There were six of them, six plus Makemore, and ... only six? No, surely not! There was someone else there as well, someone hidden from her view behind the door. She could tell by the way in which each of them turned his head that they were listening to someone else. Three of them nodded at the same time. The hidden man had said something important. Elizabeth rose to her feet and made for the doorway.

The passage was difficult. People were standing with their backs to the wall, others were on seats, still more sat on the floor, knees drawn up to their chests. She could have cut across the floor but that would have meant Makemore and his friends seeing her. She considered going through one of the side doors and stealing around the outside of the building, but that would have taken a few minutes more and she could see that the dance was almost at its end. Instead she moved around the perimeter of the room whispering excuse mes, standing on an occasional toe and scattering apologies as she passed. As she neared Makemore she could see the faces of his friends in more detail. They seemed older than their host (she assumed that they were staying with him over the New Year) by at least ten years, and they wore their affluence without ostentation. She had thought it inevitable that Makemore would witness her approach, but so intent was he on the performance that she reached the rear wall of the room without his noticing her. He was standing some five to six feet inside the room and she was now behind him. The double doors had been forced back as far as they would go by those eager to see the spectacle, and she hoped to worm her way through the press of bodies into the entrance hall.

'A good move, that!' said a voice which she felt ought to have been familiar. Makemore turned to give his assent and saw her.

'Why, Elizabeth! Seeking a better viewpoint? You may join me if you wish.' Although the words were directed at her, Henry Makemore's glance was aimed behind her. She heard the outer doors slam, felt a draught of cold air and knew that her quarry had escaped. She moved forward instead to stand in front of Henry Makemore. His team's dance was almost finished, the dancers were in line abreast, the swords tied in a Nut and held aloft.

'Some of my friends from London,' said Henry.

'I thought so,' answered Elizabeth.

'I was telling them how interesting life was up here. They practically forced me to invite them! Strange, eh?'

'Very strange,' acknowledged Elizabeth.

Makemore's dancers left the floor to subdued applause which was less than they deserved from the partisan audience. They stood by Henry, breathing heavily. Silas Bompas left the stage to join them; his slow walk across the room was met with perfect silence. Henry nodded briefly at him, ignored the dancers. Elizabeth muttered an excuse me and hurried away across the space in the middle of the room to join her father and sister.

'That was a surprise!' said John Waterhouse. 'I knew that Henry was planning on bringing his dance team, but certainly not with the intention of them upstaging our men! I think I'll have words with young Henry!'

'I don't think there'll be any need, father,' soothed Elizabeth. 'I've a feeling it's just what Thomas and the rest needed to fire them up. Just you watch!'

Tommy Armstrong was tuning his fiddle while those around the outside of the room whispered to each other.

Satisfied with the fine adjustments he took up his place, not on the stage where Bompas had stood, but on the floor. Light from one of the mirrors on the wall was reflected straight at him and he stood silent in its beam, his face half in shadow, violin tucked under his chin, bow at the ready. The whispering ceased, but he made no move, spoke no word. Just as it seemed that the tension would squeeze a cough or a nervous laugh from somewhere in the room Thomas led his team onto the floor to stand in front of the musician.

Their breeches and waistcoats were black, although the insides of the waistcoats were red. They wore knee-length white stockings and white shirts. Around their waists were wound black sashes reversed with red, and around their necks black handkerchiefs were tied. On the right breast of each waistcoat and again on each sash where it was tied and hung down over the leg was embroidered a Nut of five blood-red swords held triumphantly aloft by a strong hand. On their feet were polished black shoes. Each held a gleaming rapper sword at waist level, slightly bowed.

The dance was initiated not by the musician, as was normal, but by the dancers. At a nod from Thomas they moved round into a circle and raised their swords in their right hands. A swift, guttural 'one two three four' and they began stepping, crisp, sharp, together as one dancer. As they clashed swords and lowered them to their shoulders, following each other round in a circle, the music began. 'Saddle the Pony' thought Elizabeth as the dancers moved into Single Guard, the first of their figures. She recognised other figures too, and those she didn't she could sometimes hear Thomas calling; Rank, Curly, Figure Eight, Coach and Horses, Rotate, Bedlington, Choker. The fast middle section came all too quickly; Straight Line Forward and Back, Outward Circle, Nut, Sheepskin, Double Guard and Prince of Wales Spin. The dance was reaching its climax. She had seen one or two mistakes, although there might have been others which had passed her by; a moment of panic when Len had lost his sense of direction, a figure where Willie had turned instead of slipping and had had to pirouette rapidly on the spot to allow the Nut to be tied. But the dance itself was unaffected by these mishaps, was being carried along by the enthusiasm of those dancing and watching. There was an effortless ambience between the performers and their audience. They were living the dance together.

'Coach and Horses,' said Thomas, and the dancers formed into the familiar shape.

'Single Tumbler,' he said and looked back over his shoulder at Stew. The music began a new phrase and the dancers stepped for four beats. The sword between Thomas and Willie was pushed down almost to the ground and Stew moved forward to step over it. Still holding onto his own swords he placed his hands on the shoulders of the brothers; the sword between them was held in the small of his back. They stepped another four beats then Stew pushed his left foot back, his right came forward and he turned a complete somersault to land exactly on the beat to the rapturous applause of those watching.

'Did you see that?' cried John Waterhouse to Elizabeth. 'Did you see that?'

'Just wait for the next figure,' she answered. 'Watch!'

'Double Tumbler,' yelled Thomas above the noise. The five opened the circle out, facing inwards. Thomas and Willie stepped over the swords held down in Stew's hands; they were now facing one direction, the others the opposite. Their hands were placed carefully on the shoulders of their supports, Willie's on Len's and Stew's right, Thomas's on Rob's and Stew's left. Elizabeth silently counted them in. Step two three four, back forward over land. The two somersaulted together. Thomas, a little less agile than his brother, landed first; Stew, slightly off balance, lurched to

one side and was prevented from falling only by Rob's
barging him upright again. There was confusion as Thomas
called the next figure and it was lost in the uproar from the
floor. Thomas yelled again, louder.

'Nut!' he cried and the Nut was tied and held up, brought
down inverted. The dancers took hold again and began to
spin, and the drive of the music was reinforced by the
clapping of the onlookers, a regular rhythmic explosion
which lifted the dancers to new efforts. The spin slowed and
the Nut was held aloft again; the dancers couldn't hear their
stepping though the tumult of clapping and screaming of
support. And then suddenly, abruptly, the dance was over.
They stood in a line, Thomas, Rob, Stew, Lennie and Willie.
Sweat stained their shirts and dripped from the ends of their
noses. Their hair was matted, they were clutching for breath,
yet at Thomas's word they turned to his father and bowed,
applauded the musician who had been the architect of their
triumph. He bowed back but needed no acknowledgement
of his contribution. The cheers, the smiles on the faces of
those watching, were enough for him. Mary, Matthew and
David rushed forward to hug Thomas, a host of Stew's
children dived upon their father. John and Edward Waterhouse struggled through the crowd shouting their congratulations, reached Willie and shook him enthusiastically
by the hand. Elizabeth and Margaret danced a jig around
each other.

Only Tommy Armstrong was immune to the infectious
good humour. He stepped up onto the stage and looked
across to the doorway. Henry Makemore's guests were
wrapping themselves up against the cold, on the point of
leaving. The rapper team had been ushered out by Henry
himself. Only Bompas remained, carefully wiping his violin
before putting it away in its case. He did so, fastened the
leather strap around the case, then looked deliberately
across at Tommy. Their eyes met. Bompas put down the

case. He lifted up the index finger of his left hand, held up his right to form a loose fist, then pushed his extended finger slowly into the cylinder of his fist, then out again, then in again. His face held no emotion. He turned round, picked up his violin, and left. Tommy Armstrong stared after him. He felt suddenly old, old and lost and alone.

'Are you alright Tommy?' Elizabeth's voice woke him from his reverie.

'Me? Alright? After that performance? How could I be anything but?'

'It was good, wasn't it!'

'Aye Miss Elizabeth, it was good, considering. But it could be better, much better. There's one or two figures need a bit sharpening up, the judges'll not be as sympathetic as this lot here tonight. And I think Makemore's team were still holding something back, though I'm not sure why. No, the competition itself'll need a lot more careful preparation. We've still got work to do. But even I would admit that it was good.'

'And what do we do now?'

'Now? I think we'd better start playing again. We've got an audience out there you know!'

The rapper dancers found it difficult to escape their admirers. Drinks were thrust into their hands, congratulatory arms were draped over their shoulders. They appeared resigned to spending the rest of the evening in costume. Only Willie fought back.

'Right, I'm getting changed. That outfit cost even more than the dancing costume and I'm damn sure I'm going to get me money's worth out of it. Anyone else coming?'

Thomas shook his head; Edward Waterhouse was plying him with a glass of whisky, and his chances of escape seemed small. Stew was being dragged onto the dance floor by his eldest daughter, Rob was already there with Aileen, and Len had disappeared with one of his women.

'I'll see you later then. By the way, has anyone seen Abi?' There was no reply. Willie began to unbutton his shirt as he headed, muttering under his breath, for the cloakroom.

'Do you think,' asked Edward Waterhouse, 'that you'll be able to dance as well in the competition?'

'It's not a question of doing as well,' said Thomas. 'We'll have to do better, because it's certain that Makemore's lads will do better as well. They were just coasting tonight, holding back, and we were right at our limit. But it's six months yet till the competition, that's six months of practice and hard work. We'll get there.'

'Oh, I've no doubt of that Mr Armstrong. Here, have another drink, quick, before my brother comes round. He doesn't approve but I say a drop in moderation does no harm at all.' The whisky was poured before Thomas could refuse. He was taking a sip as Mary and the children came towards him, wrapped in the bulk of their outdoor clothes.

'I'm just taking the lads home,' she said. 'I'll put them to bed and stay till they're asleep, shouldn't take long. Mrs Tweddle says she'll listen out for them and I'll leave the door on the snib for her. Won't be long.' Thomas bent down, hugged the two boys.

'See you in the morning,' he said. 'We'll be able to build that snow-house if we get up early. Sleep tight!' They each kissed him and were hurried on their way.

'Good-looking boys,' said Edward Waterhouse.

'Aye,' answered Thomas, 'they take after their mother in their looks.'

'And if they have their father's brains they won't go too far wrong in this world.'

'Why, thank you Mr Waterhouse. It's nice of you to say that.'

'Well, my brother's been talking to me about the pit. He's spoken very highly of you, very highly indeed. You could go far if you show half the potential he credits you with. Stick in there Mr Armstrong, stick in there.' He slapped Thomas heartily on the back. Thomas had a sudden feeling that he was in the presence of a caricature, an escapee from a novel and a poor novel at that. He had to fight down the urge to laugh. Just then the band started playing.

'I'm sorry Mr Waterhouse,' Thomas blurted, 'I promised your niece that I would dance with her. Would you excuse me?' Thomas handed Waterhouse the glass, still full, and threaded his way to the stage. His father was in the process of announcing the dance.

'Square sets ladies and gentlemen, square sets for a local dance called "La Russe" which, as you all know, is French for the Russian Woman. That's how you can tell it's local. Take your partners please.'

'Dad,' Thomas smiled, 'can I borrow your lead violinist?'

Tommy looked across at Elizabeth.

'Aye, I suppose so, but make sure you bring her back in one piece, she hasn't finished her night's work yet.' Thomas held out his hand and Elizabeth put down her violin and bow to be assisted from the stage. They took up their places at the head of one of the sets.

'This is what you do do then,' yelled Tommy. 'Walk past your partner, on to your corner – that's the next lad or lass along – set to him or her and have a little swing. That's right, not too long, you might start enjoying it. Then go back to your starting place and do the same with your partner. Top couple, that's the one nearest the band, keep on swinging.'

It was crowded on the dance floor. Perhaps everyone thought that they could emulate the rapper teams with their own skill at stepping. The result was that Thomas and Elizabeth found themselves pressed close together by those around them. They were swinging elegantly; Elizabeth had been receiving lessons in the finer points of dancing from Thomas's father, and they were able, to Thomas's surprise, to move at a good speed. Those around them were not so fortunate. A couple behind them lurched sideways, bumped Elizabeth as they did so. Thomas's balance was upset and, in an effort to prevent himself overbalancing he changed his grip, moved his left arm from Elizabeth's hand to her waist. They spun to a halt clinging desperately to one another.

'We were nearly over that time!' said Thomas. Elizabeth tried to force her lips into motion but could say nothing. She was, for a brief moment, in his arms, holding him tight. She could smell him, feel his hands on her waist, taste his breath. She looked up at him and saw the concern in his eyes. She wanted nothing more than to hold him even more tightly, to rest her head on his chest, to let him encircle her.

'Oh there you are!' came Margaret's voice. 'I've been looking all over for you. Have you seen Willie? He promised me a dance and I can't find him anywhere.'

'No,' said Elizabeth. With one word the magic Thomas had unknowingly woven was destroyed.

'No,' she repeated. 'I haven't seen him. Not since rapper.'

'I have,' said Thomas. 'He said he was going to get changed. If he's not getting himself a drink he's probably still in the cloakroom.' He didn't hear Margaret's hurried thank-you, didn't notice her move away.

'Are you alright?' he asked Elizabeth. 'You looked as though you were going to faint,'

'Yes, I'm alright,' she replied, recovering her composure. 'I just felt a little dizzy for a moment. It must have been that swinging, I'm not used to travelling that fast.'

'Do you want to sit down?'

'Good Lord no! I've been playing all night. This is my only chance for some exercise! Come on, listen to your father!'

The dance started as Margaret reached the cloakroom. She looked around to see her sister and Thomas Armstrong and felt a stab of jealousy. It was unusual for her to be watching as Elizabeth danced. She had not planned on dancing with Willie that evening but neither had she counted on his inviting Abigail. She had wanted him to be jealous of her spending the whole of her time with Henry, but instead was feeling that very emotion after watching Willie and Abigail together. She would not, she told herself, normally seek out a young man in this way, particularly one who had snubbed her by refusing to behave like a lovelorn buffoon.

Henry Makemore, however, had refused to partner her in this or any of the other country dances, saying that he could manage waltzes with ease, but that he would not lower himself to perform these working-men's shuffles. To be truthful – which Margaret very rarely was – least of all to herself, she was tiring of Henry's company. His sense of fun and adventure was, for such a young man, so, so ... so elderly! He laughed infrequently, talked incessantly of horse and card games and smelled of tobacco. And yet there were times when he whispered softly in her ear and touched her gently on her neck, times when he helped her into and out of coaches and held her for just that brief moment too long, times when ... Just that evening, for example, he had been waiting for her, together with his friends, in the drawing room. She had appeared, been introduced and promptly forgotten all of their names, and as they left she glanced at her reflection in the mirror. A piece of fabric at the neckline (could it be called that? Even she had balked at wearing the low-cut gown that night, but time had been pressing and there was no alternative) had been a little misaligned. She had fluffed it back into place and looked up again to find Henry standing behind her.

'Allow me,' he had said, and his gloved hand had gently repeated the movement she herself had just carried out. Staring at her reflection he had then firmly, courteously even, placed the same hand over her breast. She should have turned immediately, slapped him, screamed even. She did none of these. She stood still, and quiet, and felt a warm flush of blood course through her body.

'Come Margaret,' Henry had said, 'we must go.' He had reached for her fur coat, helped her gently into it, and she had said nothing. Even now, as she stood outside the cloakroom door, she remembered not Henry's touch, but the warm feeling it had brought her. She knocked quietly, almost mischieviously. Perhaps Willie would still be changing. She had a sudden desire to see him, not naked, that would be too much, but certainly to admire his chest and upper torso. She was sure that he would have an admirable upper torso.

It was cold in the cloakroom; there was no fire. The room had been formed into a letter 'E' with the insertion of rails bearing coathooks. Below these a continuous wooden shelf cum seat had been fitted some eighteen inches above the ground. Margaret closed the door softly behind her. In the dim light she could see that most of the pegs were filled with coats and cloaks, while the floor beneath the wooden seat was awash with outdoor boots. She heard a sound from the far corner of the room and made her way on tiptoe to see its cause. Her breath misted as she crept closer. She heard a groan. Was Willie in pain? Had one of the swords cut him, perhaps he had turned his ankle during the dance. She parted the coats ahead of her to peep through the gap she created.

The groan was of pleasure, not of pain. Willie was there alright, and he wore no shirt. She could see his back clearly. He was kneeling on the floor, kneeling between the legs of Abigail Anderson. Her maid was sitting on the wooden bench-seat, her arms high above her head clutching two of the hooks. The skirt of her dress was up around her knees and Margaret could see Willie's hands, stroking those knees and moving slowly, inexorably higher. Her breasts were bare. Willie's lips moved from one nipple to the other, biting and teasing, his tongue tracing circles on the pale skin. For a few seconds Margaret felt that same warmth she had felt earlier that evening. She watched as Abigail groaned again, watched as Willie's hands rose higher still, watched and imagined that it was she, not Abigail, who was enjoying Willie's attentions. And then, at that thought, something broke.

'You slut!' she yelled, bursting from her hiding place. 'You whore, you ungrateful little trollop!' She strode over to where Abigail was rising, desperately trying to cover herself, and slapped her, forehand and backhand, across the face. Abigail slid back down again to her seat, sobbing. Margaret felt Willie behind her, his arms pinning her elbows. He underestimated her strength, her determination. She stamped down on his foot and, as he let go, kicked him firmly on the shin and again in the groin. He fell to the ground.

'You needn't bother coming back to Greencroft Hall, you harlot, I never want to see you again!' she yelled at Abigail. Two deep cuts on each of the maid's cheeks showed that Margaret's hand had been bearing rings. Ribbons of blood began to flow.

'Margaret,' groaned Willie, 'Margaret . . .'

'And as for you, you fornicator, whore-monger, you nasty, sordid little pimp! I thought that there was some . . . some affection between us! I know you now for the true lustful lecher you really are. I hate you Willie Armstrong, I hate you!' She stormed out of the room, slamming the door behind her. She looked desperately around. Henry Makemore was leaning against the wall in one of the corners, watching the dancers. She marched across to him.

'Henry, I feel ill. Would you mind taking me home?'

Henry looked surprised. He had just plucked up the courage to ask one of the miner's daughters to dance, a pretty little thing she was too.

'Henry, please!' He looked down at her. Tears were in her eyes. He reached out, put his arm around her shoulder, and was rewarded by her burying her face against his chest, her arms around his waist.

'It's alright,' he said, 'I'll look after you. I'll just tell your father we're going.'

'No!' she said sternly. She looked up, saw that her father and uncle were engrossed in each other's company. She didn't want them to see her like this, didn't want them to know that she could be so upset by the amorous dalliances of a mere miner.

'No Henry. Just take me away from here. Now.'

They slipped away quietly. The snow which had been falling all night took only minutes to hide their footprints.

Chapter Eight

Did you not hear it? – No; t'was but the wind
Or the car rattling o'er the stony street;
On with the dance! let joy be unconfined;
No sleep till morn, when Youth and Pleasure meet
To chase the glowing Hours with flying feet.
'Childe Harold's Pilgrimage'
(Lord Byron)

The Armstrongs' house was quiet. Sleep had come to all, though some had found it an elusive bedfellow. Thomas had set fires in all of the bedrooms, so cold had the weather turned, driving snow and sleet slowly giving way to clear skies and a starry, angular frost which crept under doors and slid through the cracks in windows. The cold made children whimper and old men groan. Night-loving cats hugged the hearth. Sheep and cattle huddled together in barns, ignoring the whiskering attentions of rats and mice made brave by hunger. Winter had planned carefully. Snow to drive all living things away or cover them where they stood. Wind to mould the snow into strange shapes, to hide walls, to burden trees with ornaments of sculpted white. And frost to make permanent the season's hold on the world, to make the familiar foreign, to post a warning that a new master ruled the land.

They had huddled round the fire in the parlour clutching mugs of steaming tea. Tommy stared at the flames while Mary and Thomas whispered to each other. Willie sat in the large armchair with Abigail curled in his lap. Their arms were round each other, her head resting on his shoulder.

'What do we do now then?' said Tommy abruptly.

'What do you mean by that?' countered Willie.

'I mean what I say. What do we do? We're in a difficult situation here, all of us. We need to think carefully about what's happened. We need to plan what we're going to do.' He coughed and spat through the guttural sound at the hissing fire.

'The only "we" in this place is Abi and me,' said Willie. 'The rest of you don't have to worry on our behalf!' Abigail shook her head, agreeing with him.

'I should never have come here. I should have gone after her, begged her forgiveness. She would have had me back, I know it.' She was near to tears.

'You just hush now,' said Mary, 'you'll be alright with us. Let's talk things over slowly and carefully. I'm sure,' she glared at Willie, 'that we'll be able to make some sense of things. Now what exactly did Miss Margaret say when she . . . when she came across the two of you?'

'Aye,' said Tommy. 'Tell us what she said when she caught you both bare-tit naked.'

'Dad!' said Thomas. 'That kind of talk won't help matters!'

'It's true though! Bloody hell son, she could have come in a few minutes later and then what would she have seen? She's the pit-owner's daughter, for Christ's sake, she just needs to say something to her father and we could all be out of a home!'

'I don't think Mr Waterhouse would do something like that,' said Thomas. 'What do you think Abigail?'

'No,' came the soft reply.

'Right then. I don't really think we have to worry about losing the house. Let's see how we can go about repairing the other damage.'

'She's not going back,' said Willie. 'I'll tell you now, I won't let her! Not to work for that madwoman!'

'Willie lad,' said Mary, 'you can't say that! Abi's got a mind of her own. I think she can decide for herself what she wants to do.' She knelt before the young couple, looked Abigail in the eyes, reached out and stroked her hair. 'Isn't that right Abi?'

'Yes. Yes, I suppose that's right. But Willie and I . . .' she faltered and Willie burst in.

'Abi and I were talking. We've decided. We're going to get married!'

There was silence. Thomas and Mary looked at each other.

'Congratulations,' said Tommy without raising his eyes from the fire, 'I don't suppose it'll be a long engagement. Can you wait till tomorrow for the wedding?'

'If you weren't my father and more than twice my age . . .!'

'Willie! Dad! For Christ's sake stop it! Will you both just listen!'

Thomas sat down on the arm of his father's chair. When he spoke the words came slowly, deliberately, but did not permit interruption.

'The first thing we're going to do is get some sleep. Abi, you can share the bed with Mary. I'll stretch out down here – there's a spare mattress, don't worry – and we can think about things. Like where the two of you are going to live, when you get married that is, 'cos there isn't enough room here, not really. We can think about Abigail and what people might say about her. Nobody knows what happened tonight. Margaret left without speaking to anyone, and the two of you,' he nodded at Willie and Abigail, 'rushed up here just as fast. If anyone asks we can say you fell and cut yourself, God knows it's slippy enough!

'What might set people talking is news of a sudden engagement. There's usually only one reason for that.' He looked straight at Willie who shook his head.

'Right then, we'll discount that. So the main problem is Margaret Waterhouse. What might she say, to her family or to anyone else for that matter? When you think about it we're in quite a strong position. After all,' he said direct to Abigail, 'you aren't just maid to Miss Margaret, are you? You do other duties, help Elizabeth out. And you were hired direct by John Waterhouse?' Abigail nodded.

'So think, what can she possibly say to her father. "I'm sorry, I dismissed my maid because I caught her with Willie Armstrong and I'm jealous?" She's not so unintelligent that she won't realise how silly that'll sound! And how stupid it'll make her look! I honestly think that if we send word to the Hall tomorrow morning, say you slipped and cut yourself but you're alright and you'll be back by midday, no-one, not even Margaret Waterhouse herself, will say anything against you. And that gives you, both of you, time to think clearly about other matters that concern you. What do you think?'

Thomas looked at each of the others in turn. Mary beamed proudly and nodded her assent. Willie and Abigail glanced at each other; he kissed her lightly on the forehead.

'Aye,' he sighed, 'we'll try it.'

'And you Dad?'

'Agreed. But I think you should also mention to Miss Elizabeth exactly what happened. I think she'd understand, I think she's on our side. She likes us. If Miss Margaret does tell her father then Miss Elizabeth, knowing about it in advance, might be able to help the cause. Eh?'

'It sounds good Dad,' said Thomas, 'but who's going to do the telling? I'm damn sure I won't mention it to her!'

'Me neither!' echoed Mary and Willie.

'I'll tell her,' said Abigail quickly, 'I think she'll understand alright. I'll tell her tomorrow.'

'Good,' said Mary. 'In that case let's away to bed. Come on Abi, the bottle's been in for ages. Goodnight lads, Thomas, can you settle things down here?' She kissed her husband, brother- and father-in-law in that order. Abigail stood up and hugged Willie fiercely for a long minute, moved to Thomas and took both of his hands, squeezed them firmly. She then bent before Tommy.

'Goodnight Mr Armstrong,' she said, 'and thank you for your help.'

'It's Tommy, lass,' came the gruff reply. 'At least it is till you change your own name to Armstrong, then I'll allow "Da".' He beckoned her closer, whispered in her ear.

'I'm sorry lass. I'm sorry if I said things which might have hurt you. It wasn't intentional. It's just that, for the first time for more years than I can remember, I've found myself being happy, here, with my family, and all I could think of was that it might all disappear. And I do love them all.'

'There's no need to apologise Mr ... I mean Tommy,' Abigail whispered back. 'There's no offence taken. And I can understand why you're so happy, why you love them. I've found out tonight that they're a bit special. Goodnight.'

She kissed him on the cheek and followed Mary up the stairs.

'What was all that about Dad?' enquired Willie.

'That? Oh, that was nothing. That was just Abi telling me she could see where me sons got their good looks.'

'Howway you two,' said Thomas, 'it's past three and I'm for bed. The fire's on next door Dad. Willie, I'll need one of your mattresses and a quilt. In fact I think I'll just curl up in front of the fire here.'

'Thomas, thank you,' said Willie. 'You talk good sense, I don't ...'

'Willie, tell me in the morning. Shut up and go to sleep!'

* * *

The embers were barely glowing when Thomas was dragged from sleep. It sounded as though someone was trying to break the door down. 'Come on, open up!' shouted a familiar though muffled voice. Thomas threw the eiderdown to one side. He was still fully dressed. A twist of paper shoved into the coals brought a flame which served to light the gas mantle above the fireplace.

'Alright, I'm coming!'

He reached the door and braced himself for the blast of cold air which the wind would surely blow at him. A twist of the key, a turn of the handle and a large, stout figure was revealed, a figure which almost blocked the doorway. Without invitation it lumbered into the room. Before closing the door Thomas could see that it was still dark outside and that, although the wind had died down, it had not spent the night in idle contemplation of its domain. Snow had been drifted across pathways and driven into hollows, pushed against walls and sucked into strange supernatural shapes which hung fragile as hope from gutter and branch.

'About bloody time too,' announced the figure, stamping the snow from its boots and unwinding a long frayed scarf from its neck. 'I thought I'd 'ave to break t' bloody door down!'

'Albie! What's the matter? What brings you out at this time? What time is it anyway?'

'In reverse order, it's nigh on 'alf-past-six on this New Year's Day morning. I'm 'ere because you've been invited by none other than Mr Water'ouse 'imself to join a party. The only thing bein', it's a search party. And the matter is that a certain young lady is missin' from'er room at the 'All. 'Er bed's not been slept in this night. I 'ear your brother 'as a little interest in this young lady so 'e'll no doubt want to come along as well. We've to meet in the stable courtyard at seven to decide on a search plan. I'll 'ave to go now,

I've others to get from bed yet.'

'Albie,' said Thomas as the gamekeeper turned to leave, 'wait on man! I might be able to save you a journey and save a few other folks some sleep.' The gamekeeper turned again, a puzzled look lurking beneath the folds of his hat and scarf.

'There's a simple answer to all of this. Abigail's here. That's why I'm sleeping on the floor, she's upstairs sharing a bed with Mary. There was a bit of a do at the dance last night so we told her . . .'

'Abigail? Abigail Anderson?' interrupted the gamekeeper. 'She's nobbut a maid, there'd not be this trouble for a maid Thomas. I doubt anyone's noticed she's not theer. No, it's not some slip of a maid we're lookin' for. It's the boss's daughter. Margaret Water'ouse 'erself. She's the one's disappeared!'

Thomas hurried the gamekeeper on his way then went in to raise his brother. Willie blinked his way into consciousness, listening carefully to what Thomas said. He swore briefly.

'Christ Thomas, it's all my fault, this. I didn't mean for it to happen. I only wanted to make her jealous to start with. I didn't realise I'd fall for Abi. What a bloody mess!'

'Aye, it is that,' countered Thomas. 'But there's more important things to think about at the moment. Come on, get yourself up.'

They dressed quickly and Thomas slipped upstairs to whisper to Mary, to tell her of Albie Settle's visit and their task. On reaching the ground floor again he found Willie in a heated, though quiet, argument with their father.

'Tell him Thomas. Tell him he can't come with us. It's bloody daft it is, have you seen how cold it is out there? He's only been out of bed a day or two and now he wants to go out playing heroes! For Christ's sake tell him to stay behind!'

'He's right Dad,' said Thomas, 'you're not well enough yet. I don't think you should go.'

'He called me a silly bugger,' said the old man, thrusting his hands angrily into his coat sleeves, 'a silly bugger! Let me tell you me lad,' he wagged his finger at Willie, 'while you've been cavorting these past few months I've been out and about with Albie. I know me way round here almost as well as he does. I know the places to look for a young lass who's run away. There's a better chance of me finding her, for all me being a daft old man, a silly bugger, than there is of you two finding a … finding a … finding a whore in a brothel!'

He seemed rather pleased at the phrase and mouthed it again silently. Willie turned away in frustration.

'Look Dad,' said Thomas, 'we know you want to help. But you haven't been well and last night took a lot out of you. There'll be upwards of a hundred men out looking for Margaret, and they'll be covering ground quite fast. What happens if you fall ill? We'll have to get everybody out to look for you! I really think it would be better if you stayed here. I know I'd worry less.'

Tommy Armstrong thought for a while. He could have argued more, but Thomas's words had struck home. And he didn't feel as well as he ought to.

'Alright then. I'll stay here. But if you've no luck come back and tell me, I might be able to give you some clues about where to look.' The two nodded as they put on their hats and scarves and gloves.

'And lads,' he added, and stressed his advice with a pause. 'Be careful.'

They were among the last to arrive in the stable courtyard. It was still dark, though a pale blue in the eastern sky heralded the arrival of a new day. Torches had been lit and attracted clusters of moth-like men, arms flapping and feet stamping in an effort to drive away the daggers of cold. Few of them were talking. They wore mufflers round their mouths to protect their lips from the ice in their breath. A crust of ice had formed on top of the snow, a crust which seemed firm until all of a man's weight was placed on it; then it gave way. Walking was difficult, there was sheet ice where the wind had scoured the snow from the soil and each step was like that of a tightrope walker. Where the snow was shallow it was possible, though tiring, to kick a track through the cloying crystals; where it was deeper each laborious step was followed by another, the foot being lifted high to clear the surface then breaking through to sink down two or three feet. In some places where drifts were higher than a man's waist no passage could be forced. A body hidden beneath one of these drifts would remain there until the thaw.

Such a thought had obviously occurred to John Waterhouse. He and his brother and Albie Settle could be seen inside the tack room, a map of the estate spread out on the table. The gamekeeper was pointing at then marking the map, nodding then shaking his head. Once he shrugged, and Edward Waterhouse moved to put his arm round his brother's shoulder. When the three of them came out John Waterhouse looked old and grey, a desiccated husk of the man he'd been the previous day. He seemed heartened, however, by the number of those who had come to help in the search. Albie Settle had dragged a chair with him, and this was placed foursquare in front of the trio. John Waterhouse used his brother's shoulder to help him climb onto the seat. All eyes were on him. There was no sound save the whisper of the torch flames.

'Gentlemen,' he said, and his voice reached no further than those immediately in front of him. He swallowed, took a deep breath, began to speak again, louder.

'Gentlemen! I must first thank you from the bottom of my heart for leaving your beds on such an inhospitable morning. I would not have asked for your help unless there was some emergency, and all of you will be aware that Margaret, my daughter, is missing.' His grip on his brother's shoulder tightened. Edward's hand reached up, sought the cold fingers which clutched at his coat, covered them gently with his own.

'She left the dance last night with Mr Makemore and has not been seen since.' A murmur of sound crept around the yard; it was stilled by John Waterhouse's raised hand.

'I have sent word to Sir Charles Makemore. He, like me, has had a thorough search of his home carried out. Every room, every cupboard, every outhouse and attic and cellar has been examined. No trace was found of his son, nor of my daughter. The carriage in which Henry Makemore travelled to the dance is missing.'

'Per'aps they've eloped!' cried a voice from the back of the crowd. There was a low snigger from the same area which died stillborn.

'The roads and railways are all blocked,' continued Waterhouse, 'they cannot have travelled far. I fear that the carriage may have strayed from the road and overturned, possibly injuring my daughter and Mr Makemore. If that is so then the intense cold of last night may have rendered them unconscious, incapable of movement. Or they may have attempted to struggle on foot to the lights of a distant farmhouse. They may even have been able to take shelter in a barn or a thicket somewhere. I ask you therefore to search carefully in even the most unlikely places. I ask you, please, find my daughter!'

He stepped stiffly down from the chair and was helped back into the comparative warmth of the tack room. Albert Settle took charge of proceedings.

There was no need for the gamekeeper to stand on the chair, quite apart from the danger of him causing it to collapse. He was tall enough to see over the heads of most of the men present. He quickly divided them up into groups of five or six (motioning to Thomas and Willie that they should stay with him) and told them which area they should search. Shovels were handed out, and long canes with which to test the depths of drifts. They were instructed to return immediately they had thoroughly examined their ground to be allocated another patch. Within minutes the yard was cleared. Albie stepped into the tack room and spoke to the Waterhouses then returned to Thomas and Willie.

'I've left rest of arrangin' wi' them,' he gestured over his shoulder. 'It'll give 'em summat to do. Us four'll 'ead down to t' quarry. Come on.'

'Why the quarry?' asked Willie.

'Because,' answered Albie, 'I thought I saw what might 'ave been tracks 'eadin' in that direction. And because it's easy to take t' track down theer in mistake for t' road to Makemore 'all.'

'You said four,' mentioned Thomas. 'There's only three of us.'

'Four,' said the gamekeeper as they rounded the corner. Even the copious layers of clothing could not disguise the slight figure standing before them.

'Thomas. Willie. I won't say good morning.'

'Elizabeth!' said Thomas. 'What are you doing here?'

'I would have thought,' she answered, 'that that would be self-evident. I've come to help look for my sister. It's obvious that my father would not have approved had I joined you earlier on, so I persuaded Mr Settle to allow me to accompany me and him. My father will be annoyed when he finds out, of that I'm certain, but I'm sure he'll agree that I couldn't be in better nor in safer company. But I think we should be on our way. The sun is up.'

Even as she spoke a dull redness appeared in the mist ahead of them, a haziness which, as they walked, resolved itself into the morning sun. Its presence served only to remind them of the harshness of the alien world in which they found themselves. There was no wind. The trees in the wood to their right were encrusted with snow. There were no birds abroad, no sound to break the monotony of their slow, crunching steps save the rasp of their breathing. They struggled over fallen trees and lurched through swamps of snow. The sun rose in the sky but brought no warmth. Instead it conspired with the snow to dazzle them, forced them to stare painfully through pinched eyelids. But none of them would stop.

'I can't see any tracks,' said Willie, and the sound of his voice startled him as much as it did the others. Albie motioned the young man to his side and they bent together, their eyes low to the ground. There was, from that angle, a slight depression, two parallel tracks which snaked along the road ahead of them.

'It could be t' way snow's drifted,' acknowledged the gamekeeper, 'or it could be a reflection of t' ground underneath, where there's already wheel tracks. But it could be 'Enry Makemore's carriage as made them last night. We'll see lad, we'll see.' He laboured on his way, breaking a trail for Willie to follow. Behind him came Elizabeth, light enough to walk on the surface of the snow where it had frozen hard. Thomas brought up the rear.

'Did you see Margaret last night?' asked Elizabeth abruptly. She continued without waiting for an answer from either brother.

'I hear she left in a hurry, though I must admit I didn't see her myself. I was just wondering if either of you knew of something which might have upset her?'

'Well, you'll probably find . . .' began Willie.

'Actually,' interrupted Thomas, 'Margaret and Willie had a little argument, something about Willie paying too much attention to Abigail – watch your step, there's a branch hidden under that drift – and she stormed out in a temper. Jealous if you ask me.'

'Margaret? Jealous?'

'Aye, jealous! Surely you've seen it. Your sister's had my brother on a string for weeks now, and I don't think she liked it when he decided to break free. She lost her temper, hit Abigail as well, I might add. Then she stormed off with Mr Makemore. I think she'll realise how silly she was, when she thinks hard about it.'

'I hope she has the opportunity to do so,' said Elizabeth, 'and we'll only know that if we find her.'

'When we find 'er,' came Albie's deep voice. 'Look up ahead. Those's carriage tracks for certain, you can see where they pass t' rocky outcrop, where there's been shelter. Come on.'

He quickened his pace, moving with a speed which seemed at odds with his ungainly bulk. The others found it difficult to keep up. The trees to their right grew smaller, more stunted, and began to climb up a bank which soon became too steep to support any but a twisted dwarf rowan. To their left the flat open fields gave way to hillocks which crowded together to form a wall blanketed with snow. This protection had allowed the path to remain, for a short while, free of the drifts which had hindered the searchers' progress so far. And, as the gamekeeper had promised, two parallel lines (sometimes becoming four as the path curved sinuously between hill and rock) pointed the way. He turned a corner ahead then reappeared, waited for the others to catch up, placed his large and well-rounded posterior on a boulder, and lit his pipe.

The warm smell of tobacco made the valley seem more desolate than it already was. The sun, even as it rose higher towards mid-morning, would not touch this soil. The cold took on a malevolent air.

'Come on then,' puffed Elizabeth. 'We'll just cool down if we sit around, let's keep going. This is the entrance to the quarry isn't it?'

'Aye, it's t' quarry lass, but it'll not do us much good. Just look round t' corner.' He gestured with his head. Thomas and Elizabeth took up his invitation while Willie sank to the ground at Albie's feet. He looked up with pleading eyes; no sound was made, but the message was understood. A bottle was passed to the younger man, a bottle containing a golden liquid. Willie opened it feverishly, poured some down his eager throat. He breathed in, savoured the warmth in his stomach.

'Mmm, whisky,' he sighed.

'Best not take too much lad, we might need it later.'

The bottle was spirited away into the depths of the gamekeeper's clothing. Thomas and Elizabeth trudged wearily back into view.

'There's a drift ahead,' said Thomas. 'It's at least twenty feet high and no way of telling how far back it goes.'

'No drift,' said Albie. 'T' snow's come down off t' tops. We'll 'ave to climb up sides to get round, but watch out. It's come down once, might just 'appen twice. Move slowly, stay in my steps. And be quiet!'

'What does he mean?' asked Willie. 'Why do we have to be quiet?'

'Avalanche,' hissed Elizabeth. 'Look up there.' She pointed skywards. To their right the rocks formed a cliff, perhaps a hundred feet high, but vertical. Its surface was largely bare of snow; the avalanche had probably fallen from that face. But at the top there was an overhang, a snow cap some seven or eight feet wide and at least that thick. Its leading edge was clear, solid ice, coloured and highlighted by a sun they could not see. Even as they stood they were able to watch drops of water cascading down into the void below.

'Could go anytime,' whispered Albie.

To their left the slope was less steep, probably grassy beneath its smooth white surface, but there was no indica-

tion of the snow's depth. Albie's first steps took him only
ankle deep, and he turned to smile his appreciation at those
following.

'Won't take long if it's like this all . . .' His words were cut
off as he floundered into a drift, snow up to his thighs
preventing his legs from moving while his body continued its
forward motion. He tried to stand up but in doing so slid
back down to where he had begun his climb. Twice more he
attacked the slope, twice more he was defeated. Not caring
what the others saw he reached into his pocket, brought out
his bottle, and shamelessly drew a large mouthful. Elizabeth
frowned and stepped around him. Within a few seconds she
was ten feet up the slope.

'You're just too heavy!' she murmured. 'Why not go back
and work your way around the side. One of you' she looked
at Thomas and Willie, 'had better go with him.'

'I'll keep the whisky bottle company!' said Willie, giving
Thomas no chance to argue. Thomas struggled up the hill
after the dark figure of Elizabeth while the other two back-
tracked, intending to skirt the hills by a longer but less
hazardous route.

Progress was slow; Thomas echoed Elizabeth's small steps
up the hill, but still found himself sliding back. Although the
surface was iced the snow beneath was slick and smooth,
allowing little purchase for hands or for feet. But still they
moved on and found themselves above the top of the
blockage. It stretched around another corner, and their
traverse, if continued, would take them away from the
smooth snow and beneath a rocky outcrop. Beyond that
they could not see.

'Couldn't we just go across the top of the fallen snow?'
asked Thomas. The question itself acknowledged that
Elizabeth was in charge of this half of the expedition.

'No,' came the hissed reply. 'It'll be too deep, too soft. We
wouldn't be able to move, either over it or through it. We'll

have to keep on at this height.'

She moved on again, and Thomas could see in the urgency of her motion the anxiety she must be feeling. It was difficult work, physically demanding. Even Thomas could feel the aches and pains hidden inside each muscle waiting for the opportunity to escape. He sweated when moving, but the sweat turned to ice each time he stood still. He had lost all sensation in his hands and feet. How then must Elizabeth, whose slight body had not been trained by the harsh conditions down a pit, feel? He ignored his pains and followed her. She kicked footholds in the near vertical snow approaching the outcrop, glancing over her shoulder at the ice overhanging the opposite side of the valley. It was now bathed in sunlight, groaning threateningly. Thomas watched carefully. The monotonous drip drip they had witnessed only minutes before (Thomas took his watch from his pocket; minutes? They had started the climb shortly after nine thirty and it was now almost eleven!) had become a regular flow of water. There was suddenly a loud crack, the sound of a whip or a dead branch breaking, and the entire overhang fell in one slow, orgasmic slide to the floor of the valley.

'Thomas! Move!'

It was Elizabeth calling. Thomas turned to see her safe beneath the rock outcrop. A powder of snow drifted down from above his head. His fingers were too cold to feel the slight tremor which followed, but his body was pressed tightly to the slope and he felt the movement deep inside. He lurched across the gap separating him from Elizabeth, kicking his feet into the ice. He missed one of the holds and slipped but recovered quickly and moved on. Twenty feet, fifteen feet, and the whole of the hillside was trembling beneath him. Ten feet, halfway there, and he could see the agonised look on Elizabeth's face. Was this how he would meet his end, not in the depths of some black mine, crushed by tons of rock, but by being rolled down a hillside by a snowball? He laughed as he scuttled sideways, laughed as the snow beneath his feet finally gave way, laughed as his hands grabbed for and found solid rock. He laughed as Elizabeth hauled him into the shelter of the outcrop, the sound of thunder in his ears, his eyes tight closed against the visions of death which still tried to suffocate him with soft, cloying whiteness. And the noise ceased.

Thomas felt his arms round Elizabeth, felt her arms holding him equally tightly, squeezing the breath from him. He opened his eyes a lifetime later, pushed her away slightly. She was staring at him. Her face was dirty, apart from two lines which stretched from her eyes down across her cheeks.

'It's alright,' he said. 'I'm still here. You don't get rid of an Armstrong that easily.' He hugged her close again, felt her sobbing against his chest. He waited for her to calm down.

'Thank you,' he said. 'How did you know that the snow would come down on this side as well?'

'Just a guess,' she sobbed, wiping her red nose on the back of her glove. 'I felt it. And I didn't think you'd make it.' She began to cry again and Thomas tilted her head up, looked down on her. She sniffed once or twice, then stopped. Still they looked at each other, still they remained locked in each others arms.

'I think we'd better be starting down,' he said. 'At least the path's clear now.' He pointed along the ledge. The tumble of rocks and crags ahead of them had, only a few moments before, been covered with snow. Now a track could be picked out, a path which might be followed with care, a path which lead to the lip of a deep quarry. And there, at the very edge, was a dark patch in the otherwise virginal white of the snow. The sun which had been hidden from them in the valley was revelling in its freedom where the rocks and hills had been hacked away by generations of quarrymen. So bright was the reflection that even with their faces pinched, even with their hands held up to try to shade their eyes from the glare, Thomas and Elizabeth were unable to resolve the amorphous shape into any recognisable form. They pressed on, glancing up every few steps only to return their attention to negotiating the razor rocks leading down to the bottom of the gully.

'Thomas! Dear God Thomas, I think it's a body!' Thomas looked up. It was possible. The shape was still not defined, but it seemed to have two, perhaps four legs, thin shapes sticking out at peculiar angles from the main body of the darkness. Two arms and two legs? Two bodies even? There was no sign of movement. Elizabeth's walk became a run and Thomas followed as well as he was able through the thick snow. They grew nearer and nearer, then Elizabeth stopped.

'Oh Thomas!' she cried. 'Thank God!'

Thomas could see nothing. Elizabeth's abrupt halt had blocked his view. He too slowed to a halt, walked around her. He turned to look at her.

'It's Makemore's horse, isn't it?' he said. Elizabeth nodded. Thomas approached the body. Its eyes were wide open, its neck and legs twisted beneath it at strange and cruel angles. He bent down to touch its hide, felt no warmth. He looked around.

'There're tracks heading off that way,' he pointed round the rim of the quarry. 'It might be that they dragged the carriage away, it certainly looks like it. At least there's no sign,' he inched towards the edge and peered into the depths below. 'Aye, there's no sign of them going over the edge. Mind you, if the horse collapsed here they were damn close!' Elizabeth was already away, following the tracks in the snow. Thomas swore and hurried after her, wondering aloud where the hell she found her energy.

Elizabeth's attention was fixed firmly on the two lines scrawled in the snow, two lines which now contained between them the smudges of footprints. They led round the rim of the quarry, at times skirting the edge dangerously, then veered away. Beyond a slope of shattered rock Thomas could see a finger of grey smoke rising, untroubled by any breeze, slowly dissolving into the hazy air. He nudged Elizabeth; she altered course. They rounded what was obviously a waste heap to find before them, no more than fifty or sixty yards away, a small brick building. Its slate roof was black with melt-water, showing that the fire within had been burning for some time. The windows and door appeared in need of a coat of paint but were intact; none of the glass was broken. It was a strange sight, a small piece of human creation surrounded by a huge monument to destruction. The redness of the bricks fought against the white broken rocks all around. The crude building was the quarrymaster's cabin, unused on this New Year's Day, usually servant to those who blasted rocks to provide ore for the smelters at Consett. Its functional ugliness was suddenly beautiful to Elizabeth and Thomas.

There was what appeared to be an upturned boat outside the door.

'That's Makemore's carriage, they've taken it to pieces,' panted Elizabeth as they hurried on.

'Must have wanted to burn the wood in it,' suggested Thomas.

Sure enough, the skeleton of what had once been a four-wheeled coach languished beside the door. Two of the wheels were broken, the leather roof had been torn away from its mounting. The glass had been smashed and the doors removed, and much of the panelling was missing.

'I hope to God they're alright,' said Elizabeth. She reached the building and tried to peer through one of the windows. It was crusted with dust and running with condensation. She could see nothing. The door had been forced and stood slightly ajar; a considerable amount of snow had been blown through the gap during the night. Thomas leaned against the flaking green paintwork and the opening grew larger. Inside was a small lobby with two further doors, each as dilapidated as the first. Thomas opened the one on his right and entered the room. Elizabeth followed close behind him.

There was a smell of unwashed bodies. A metal bucket containing some foul liquid shared one corner of the room with three empty spirit bottles. A pile of splintered wood, many pieces lacquered with polished black paint, lay in front of the fireplace; so close to the fire was some of the kindling that the varnish itself was blistering. In the middle of the floor lay a pile of muddied, wet clothing, travelling blankets, some dirty material which might once have been curtains, a stained tablecloth. And from beneath this heap of detritus came the faint sound of snoring.

Elizabeth pointed at a foot. It was bare and dirty but the body to which it was attached had to have been female. She bent down and touched it. It was warm.

'Margaret,' she whispered. 'Margaret. Wake up Margaret, it's Elizabeth. I've come to take you home.' There was a groan, a muttered unintelligible word or two. Then a shock of tousled blonde hair appeared from out of a heavy woollen coat. The blue eyes beneath surfaced slowly and blinked, once at Thomas, once at Elizabeth. Through the grime on her face rivulets of tears had marked their passage. Margaret Waterhouse was beautiful even in times of suffering. Her mouth opened, she swallowed.

'Elizabeth,' she croaked and held her arms out. As she did so the coat slipped down from her chin to reveal her breasts. Her nipples were ringed with red-blue bruises; her neck bore the same marks of another's passion.

'Oh Margaret love, Margaret, what's he done to you!' cried Elizabeth. She bent down, wrapped her sister again in the coat and hugged her. Margaret began to cry.

Thomas could only watch. Elizabeth was by turns gentle

then, in the same sentence, violently aggressive. 'It's alright Mags, I'm here now, you'll be alright now. I swear he'll hang for this, by God he will! Calm down love, we'll soon have you safe at home. How could he do this? He'll roast on all the fires in hell, I swear by my mother's grave he will, I'll kill him myself! Shush now, stop crying, you know how it makes your eyes red. Where is he? He's worse than the devil, the perverted, lecherous cur? Where is that snivelling Makemore runt?'

Thomas heard all that and more. He learned new words and new meanings of old words. He found himself wondering at the education a lady must receive to be so familiar with so much bad language. He was about to leave, to cover his own embarassment as much as that of Margaret Waterhouse's, when there came a light, almost genteel cough from behind him.

'Did I hear someone taking my name in vain?' slurred Henry Makemore.

He was leaning against the doorpost, his eyes blurred. His clothes were crumpled and stained with mud. He was drunk. Elizabeth rose quickly and strode towards him. Thomas moved too; he expected her to slap Makemore, was concerned that Makemore might respond with violence. He need not have worried. Elizabeth's first blow was a punch to the stomach. Makemore doubled up and she rabbit-punched him on the back of the head. He collapsed to the floor retching and as she drew back her foot to kick him Thomas grabbed her round the waist, pulled her away. She whirled on him, hate in her eyes, her fist already drawn back for another punch as he thrust out his hand to encircle her wrist. He felt the tension in her arm slowly subside.

'I'm sorry Thomas. I'm sorry, but what he's done to Margaret, it just made me remember . . .'

'Elizabeth!' cried Margaret, 'Elizabeth! You're wrong! It wasn't Henry! It wasn't him at all! Look!' She scrabbled at the clothes and material with one hand, the other holding the coat up to her neck. She pulled away a curtain to reveal someone's back, a broad back, its pale flesh covered with downy red hair.

'Stobbit!' said a deep voice, ''s cold!' A large broad hand fumbled in vain for some cover. Henry Makemore whimpered beside the door.

'Wash goin' on?' said the voice again, and its owner turned wearily to face them.

'Timothy Deemster!' hissed Elizabeth.

'The curate!' gulped Thomas.

'Jesus Christ!' groaned Deemster, his eyes blinking in the sunlight.

'Get them out of here!' said Elizabeth urgently. Thomas did as he was told. He pulled the still moaning Makemore through the entrance hall and into the adjacent room. One of the carriage seats was on the floor and the young man was dumped unceremoniously across this. The curate was half dressed by the time he returned, stumbling round the room looking for a shirt and some shoes.

'Come on me old son,' said Thomas gently, 'out we go. I'll come back for the rest of your stuff.' He manhandled Deemster out of the room, found that Henry Makemore was now able to sit up, and positioned the curate beside him. He left them there, each mimicking the other's posture, two heads in two pairs of hands, two voices making vocal the physical pain each was feeling. He returned to the two women. Margaret too, assisted by Elizabeth, was almost dressed. Both women appeared calmer.

'Thomas,' said Elizabeth, 'have a look outside will you. I think your brother and Mr Settle are coming, I heard a shout a moment ago.'

Thomas wiped away the dirt and damp from one of the window panes. Willie and Albert Settle were indeed running towards the building, the fat gamekeeper showing a surprising turn of speed for one so large.

'Aye, it's them,' he said.

'Thomas,' said Elizabeth anxiously, 'could I ask a favour of you?'

Thomas nodded. Elizabeth left her sister's side, took Thomas's arm in hers and walked him to the door.

'I think it would be best,' she said in a voice which begged accordance, 'if we kept details of what happened ...' She stopped abruptly. 'Of what we believe *may* have happened, based on what you and I have seen and heard, I think it would be best if we said nothing to anyone else. Until I've had a chance to talk further with my sister.'

'Why, aye,' said Thomas. 'I'll say nothing beyond the fact that we found them here and that Mr Makemore and Mr Deemster are a little ill through drinking too much.' He looked at Elizabeth's face. It was lined, worried, she seemed suddenly old. He reached out and brushed away the hair from her eyes, first one side, then the other. Her hand moved too, grasped his in a gesture of thanks, gratefulness, friendship even. The grip was warm and, for a woman, strong.

'I'd best get outside,' he said, 'sort things out for getting back. You see to your sister.' He opened the door, then turned back. Elizabeth was at her sister's side again.

'And don't worry,' he smiled, addressing both of them. 'Everything'll be alright.'

The story Thomas told his brother and the gamekeeper was not untrue; their own eyes told them that much. Makemore and Deemster had both been drunk, were indeed suffering from hangovers which would be unlikely to abate within the day. Margaret had not borne her misfortunes well (the real extent of these was of course a secret) and was tearful and confused. Only Thomas's insistence that Margaret be left undisturbed for a while prevented Willie from seeking the evidence of his own eyes that she was unhurt. He was instead drawn into discussions on how best to deal with the problem of returning the three young people to the Hall. It was now well after noon, perhaps three hours of daylight remaining. They agreed that an hour would see them able to make a sledge from the remains of the carriage, and that Margaret Waterhouse could be borne on this vehicle. Willie and Albie had found an alternative, slightly longer route into the quarry, avoiding the snow in the valley, although using it on the return journey would make it impossible to reach Greencroft Hall before darkness fell. With reluctance they decided that one of them should set off immediately to take word to the other rescuers in order that a party could meet them with lights and transportation and warm clothing. Willie refused to volunteer for this; the others appreciated his reasons for this even if they did not condone them. That he blamed himself for Margaret's misadventure was clearly evident. Albie Settle stated the obvious; he was stronger than Thomas and more able to drag a sledge through the deep snow. There was therefore no choice.

Thomas went back into the building. Margaret appeared almost normal again, her face clean, her emotions under control. No explanation was required; the sisters had overheard the conversation outside, could hear now the sound of wood being torn from the carriage to make a sledge. Thomas's goodbye was therefore brief, the memory of Elizabeth's and Margaret's urgent gratitude hurrying him on his way.

The track was easy to follow, two pairs of footprints leading round the edge of the quarry and through a narrow though sheltered defile to rejoin the main path at the entrance to the valley where the avalanche had occurred. Thomas moved at a regular pace, the cold kept at bay by self-generated warmth. Only when he stopped to open his coat a little did he realise that a wind was blowing down from the north, that clouds were once again gathering, that another storm would soon be upon them. His steady walk became a slow, shuffling, jogging run.

It took no more than sixty or seventy minutes to complete the four miles. It was still light when he stumbled into the courtyard and burst into the room where John and Edward Waterhouse were still poring over their plans. His story brought immediate action. Men and sledges, two huge Clydesdales, torches, shovels, blankets and coats were procured without delay. Thomas, forced to sit in front of a fire with a cup of steaming tea in his hands, was on his feet again as the party was led away by John Waterhouse himself. His way was barred by the round body of Edward Waterhouse.

'You've done enough today Mr Armstrong,' he said, 'and besides, you're needed elsewhere. Come on, I'll tell you as we walk.' He motioned to Thomas to join him and the pair headed for the village.

'John sent for the doctor from Lanchester this morning, just in case his services might be required. It's just as well he did. About an hour ago a man was found. He'd fallen into a ditch, right through the ice. The water wasn't deep enough for him to drown but he broke his leg and couldn't get out again. If he'd been left there another hour or two he would have died; as it is the doctor's very concerned about him. It's your father Thomas.'

Thomas broke into a run, Edward stumbling desperately at his side.

'He wasn't well . . . to start with . . . His lungs . . . and his heart . . . very weak . . . Doctor's doing . . . everything he can . . . doesn't know if . . .'

At the edge of the wood sloping down to the village Edward had to stop. He didn't know if Thomas had heard what he said. He stood with hands at his waist, breathing deeply in an attempt to control the pain beneath his ribs. He watched Thomas disappear into the misty, smokey gloom which was hung between the houses, small rectangular glows of yellow and orange proving the existence of life in the cold wintry evening. He thrust his hands into his pockets and began the journey back to the Hall.

Chapter Nine

'O come ye in peace here, or come ye in war,
Or to dance at our bridal, young Lord Lochinvar?'
'Marmion'
(Sir Walter Scott)

'Thomas! Oh, Thomas love,' cried Mary, 'I'm so glad you're back!'

'Where is he?' panted Thomas, 'where's me Dad?'

'He's in our room, but the Doctor says ...'

'It might be best, Mr Armstrong,' lisped a strange, hesitant voice, 'if your father were allowed to rest for a little while. He is very poorly and ...' The doctor's entreaties were wasted. Thomas was already halfway upstairs taking three steps at a time, ignoring his wife, ignoring his children, ignoring the doctor, not even noticing that Abigail too was in the room. He checked his pace outside the bedroom door, took a deep breath then gently turned the door handle. The door opened and closed with the same slight click.

The curtains were drawn shut and the fire was lit. There was no other light. Thomas moved quietly to stand beside the bed. He looked down on his father. The top of the sheet was folded neatly over the blankets and eiderdown, tucked under his father's arms which were lying straight by his

227

sides. His eyes were shut, his hair had been combed, he wore a clean flannel nightshirt. His hands lay palms downwards, motionless. He looks like a corpse already thought Thomas, laid out for friends and relatives to pay their last respects too late, to say how peaceful he looked and wasn't it a good thing he didn't linger, but life goes on anyway, another cup of tea would be most welcome. Only the rasp of shallow breathing, the slight rise and fall of his chest showed the lie. Thomas realised that he had been holding his own breath and exhaled.

'Is that you, son?' whispered his father.

'Aye, it's me Dad,' came the reply in similar tone. 'It's Thomas.'

The old man's face twisted into what was meant to be a smile, and Thomas began to understand the pain he must be feeling.

'Did you find her?'

'Aye, we found her. I came on ahead, they'll all be back shortly. She's alright Dad. She's alright. But what about you?'

'I'm just a stupid old man, son, a stupid old man.' The effort of speaking seemed to exhaust him, his breathing grew more unsteady. Thomas reached out to take his hand but there was only a feeble twitch of the fingers.

'Why did you do it Dad. Why did you do it?' he asked, not wanting a reply but desperate to keep talking, as if words would reinforce the slender threads by which his father was clinging to life. The door opened behind him.

'Thomas,' said Mary, 'Doctor Burton says it would be best if you let him rest for a while. Besides, he's got to go now, he wants a word with you. Come on love, there's nothing else you can do at the moment.'

Thomas looked at his wife and acknowledged her message. He followed her reluctantly downstairs.

The doctor was about the same age and size as Thomas,

a well-built man whose eyes held a sadness indicating the suffering he had witnessed in his years. He stood as Thomas reached the bottom of the stairs, held out his hand. His shake was firm. Thomas motioned him back into his seat, nodded at Abigail. He sat down and his sons appeared at either side of the armchair. He nodded and they slipped onto his knees. His arms went around them, granting and seeking reassurance. Their eyes were red. They had been crying.

'Mr Armstrong, your father is very ill, you don't need me to tell you that.' Thomas nodded.

'I've made him as comfortable as possible. There is little else I can do, the strength needed to begin to make a recovery must come from him. I'm not sure if he has that strength.'

'But what is it, what is the illness?' appealed Thomas. The doctor sighed, chewed his bottom lip.

'He has broken his leg. That is perhaps the most easily diagnosed problem and the one which is easiest to treat. It is not a good break, not a clean break, and I fear that the wound is infected. He was lying in a ditch of dirty water for some time. His leg has been splinted. Were it that alone I would be more optimistic about his recovery, despite the seriousness of his situation. But he is also suffering from exposure to the cold and that has lowered his resistance and sapped his strength. He realised, I think, that if he allowed himself to lose consciousness he would undoubtedly have died. He would not close his eyes, used his pain to keep him awake. Hence his overall weakness. He has snow-blindness, he reacts to light, it causes him pain. If he survives I fear he may lose his sight.' The doctor took a sip from the cup at his side.

'He was unable to respond to some of my questions. I took the liberty therefore of asking your wife about his habits, his previous health. I understand that he did not do a great deal of work underground?'

'No, he was a carpenter and joiner above all else.'

'Mm. That in itself is not a good thing. Sawdust, particularly of hardwoods, can be as destructive as coal dust if it reaches the lungs. And he drank to excess I believe.' Thomas looked at Mary.

'I had no need to ask your wife that question Mr Armstrong, I was aware of the answer before I asked you. He has been a drinker in his time – there are symptoms which I recognise.' Thomas nodded.

'He is very weak. His body seems unable to fight back. If he survives the night I feel that he will make a full recovery. Beyond making that statement there remains very little more that I can do to help.'

'And what about us,' asked Thomas, 'what can we do to help?'

The doctor stood up and Mary helped him into his coat.

'Keep him warm, get him to drink as much water as he can manage. Don't over-tax him, try to keep him quiet. If he becomes feverish send for me – I intend staying at the Hall tonight. Do what you can. Talk to him even if you feel he isn't listening. And pray.'

'Does that last medicine often work?' asked Thomas. The doctor smiled and shook his head.

'No Mr Armstrong, but it moves some of my burden of helplessness and guilt to a higher plane, and for that I, at least, am grateful. Please send for me if you need me.'

'I'll do that,' said Thomas, 'but I fear that you'll be a busy man this evening. We've found Miss Waterhouse, and Mr Makemore, and Mr Deemster. They are well, all things considered, but I feel they may need you to examine them. And listen to them. More than anything else Miss Waterhouse may need someone to listen to her.'

The doctor picked up his bag.

'But I must hurry! I shall call later, regardless, but send for me if your father appears to be suffering. Goodbye.'

He scurried into the night like a velvet mole, and Mary closed the door behind him. She sat down at Thomas's feet, pulled off his boots and his socks.

'These're soaking!' she exclaimed. 'I'll have two of you ill in bed at this rate. What about the rest of you? Come on, let's have a look.' She ran her hands up his trouser legs and onto his jacket and the woollen waistcoat beneath.

'They'll do, I suppose. There's some broth on the stove, you should have some of that. You won't have eaten yet, eh?' Thomas made no reply, merely stared at the flames in the grate. Matthew and David, sensing their father's need, sat quiet, their heads on his shoulders. Still he said nothing. He was remembering a night when he had been unable to sleep and had crept down the ladder to find his mother knitting, his father whittling at a piece of wood. They had glanced up and he had expected to be sent back to bed, possibly even with a bottom paddled for his disobeying the rule; once in bed, stay there! Instead his father frowned but invited him down, sat him on his knee and began to sing soft gentle songs of miners and keelmen, beautiful women and proud noble lords. And there he had fallen asleep, proud to have a father who was undoubtedly the best any four-year-old could be given. The memory brought a smile to his face and moisture to his eyes.

'Come on you two,' he said abruptly, 'time for supper and then . . .?'

'B..E..D..,' they chanted obediently.

'Good lads. Your Mam'll put you to bed, I'm going to sit with your Grandad. I'll take a bowl up,' he said to his wife as he stood up, scattering children to the corners of the room, 'and have it up there. Oh, by the way, we found Margaret Waterhouse.'

'So you said,' replied Mary, ladling a thick stew into a large bowl. 'Dumplings?' Thomas nodded. 'Don't worry, you can tell us all later. After all, it's not really important now, is it? Here, don't spill it. It's hot mind. I'll pop in when the kids are in bed.'

Thomas took the bowl from his wife, kissed her thank you on the cheek.

'Thomas,' interrupted Abigail's voice, 'is Willie alright?'

'Oh Abi, I'm sorry, I've not said a word to you since I came in. Yes, Willie's alright, at least he was when I left him. He's helping Mr Settle bring them back, Margaret and Henry Makemore and the curate. He should be here within the hour.' For some reason he neglected to mention that Elizabeth Waterhouse had been part of the search party. He could not, in all honesty, claim that it had been a slip of his memory.

'He should be back soon, no more than an hour away I'm sure. I'd consider it a great favour if you could go up to the stables and wait for him, tell him what's happened. Tell him to hurry back here. Could you do that?'

Abigail nodded eagerly, was already reaching for coat, hat and gloves, keen to demonstrate her willingness to help. As Thomas made his way back upstairs he heard the front door slam at her leaving.

His father had not moved. Thomas sat in the chair beside the bed and ate voraciously, realising as he did that it was his first proper meal that day. He was sure that at any other time, under any other circumstances, the stew would have tasted delicious, but now it was dry as dust, and to swallow it was an effort. Still he forced himself to empty the bowl and with stomach full leaned back to watch his father, reached out his hand to cradle that of the old man. He must have dozed, though for how long he could not say. The fire was still burning brightly, it may have been for no more than a few minutes. His hand was being held tightly.

'It's alright Dad, I'm here. Don't hold so tight, you need all your strength.' The grip relaxed slightly.

'Here, you'd better have a sip of water.' He reached for

the mug on the floor at his feet, tilted a small volume of the liquid into his father's mouth. Some dribbled down the side of his face and was quickly dabbed away, the rest was swallowed.

'Willie,' whispered the old man.

'No, it's not Willie. It's me, Thomas.'

'Thomas son, get Willie. Please. I've got to talk to him.'

'I don't think he's back yet Dad, I'll just go and see. I won't be long.' He put down the old man's hand and hurried downstairs. Mary was getting the children ready for bed.

'Hasn't Willie come back yet?' he asked urgently. Mary shook her said.

'Damn! He's asking for him, says he has to talk to him. He's getting quite agitated about it. I'll just have to tell him. Look, when he comes back send him straight upstairs will you?' Mary nodded. Thomas returned quietly to his vigil, hoping that he would not be heard entering the room.

'Is that you Willie?' came his father's voice, weakly, desperately.

'No Dad, he's not back yet. He'll come straight up . . .'

'Thomas!' hissed the voice. 'There's no time! Thomas, I need him! Go and get him, please son! Please!' The last syllable died away into a snakelike sibilance. Thomas rushed downstairs and opened the front door, peered through the mist. He saw no-one. He ran back in again, trying to make as little noise as possible in mounting the stairs, fearing that the worst would have happened during the minute he was away. And then he stopped. He stopped outside the door to the bedroom. He swallowed and opened the door.

'Dad?' he said.

'Is that you Willie?'

'No Dad, it's me, it's Thomas. But Willie's here. He's just coming. Do you want me to stay with the both of you?'

The old man's body relaxed. 'No,' he sighed.

'Here he is now then. Give us a yell if you want anything.' He entered the room, closed the door behind him. He didn't care that he was deceiving his father. He would tell him when he was well enough, just as he would tell Willie when he came in, tell him what he had done and tell him whatever it was the old man had deemed was so important. He would tell them both, and they would all laugh at the thought of it, him playing Jacob to Willie's Esau and their father the regal Isaac, son of Abraham.

'Willie?'

'Aye, it's me Dad.' Thomas's voice sounded, he felt, nothing like that of his brother. But the old man seemed satisfied.

'Give me your hand, Willie.' Thomas held his hand out, quickly removed his wedding ring and slipped it into his pocket, and took hold of his father's hand. His father sighed again.

'Let me speak. Let me say what I want to say. Don't interrupt. I haven't got long, no, please don't interrupt. Just listen.' Thomas, about to speak, sat in silence.

'I love you Willie, I really do. There's been times when it hasn't seemed that way, God knows that, but I've tried hard. And it hasn't been easy.' The old man opened his eyes and Thomas feared discovery. The eyes remained open, but they saw nothing.

'Your mother as well Willie, I loved her too. She deserved better than me, far far better.' He coughed, and an extra notch on the rack would have brought less pain.

'I left her Willie. I left her one dark night, before you were born, to go after another woman. I left her to look after all the kids, her kids, my kids. She loved me, at least I think she did. And I left her for some spit of a lass who smiled nicely at me and spent me money. She spent me money then she kicked me out. Two months, and she kicked me out. So what did I do? I crawled back to your mother. I crawled back in the middle of the night, sick with drink. The door wasn't locked, and I crawled up those stairs and I heard noises. I heard noises Willie. I heard the noise of your mother and some man. They were there together in that room, in that bed, and she was moaning and groaning and gasping and he was doing the same. I don't blame her, not now at least. I was a drunken bastard, I'd left her to look after all those children. And I think he loved her too. He wanted her to come away with him, he wasn't married, he had a good job, he would look after her. I stood outside the door and when they'd finished making love they talked and I heard it all. I don't blame her now, but I blamed her then. And him. I was drunk Willie, it was the drink made me do it.'

Tears appeared in sightless eyes. The old man's breathing became more ragged.

'Dad, have a rest, for Christ's sake, you're not strong enough ...'

'You sound more like your brother every day,' he hissed. 'Now shut up! Let me finish.' His voice diminished further, Thomas had to bend his head to hear the words.

'I crept downstairs again, I'll never know how they didn't hear me, and I got a length of timber from the fireplace, like a bloody fourteen pound hammer it was. I went back and I kicked the door open, started laying about me with the damn thing. I was lucky I suppose, made contact with one of the first blows and knocked him unconscious. I hit him again, and kicked him. I might have killed him if your mother hadn't stopped me. So I started on her instead. I'd lost the timber but that didn't matter, I had me fists. I punched her all over the room. I was clever though, even then, even in the middle of a drunken fit. I didn't hit her face where the neighbours might see, oh no, I went for her body instead. I punched the living daylights out of her. Nothing would stop me. Not even ...' he coughed again. Thomas ladled more water into his mouth.

'She said she was pregnant. She said I wasn't the father. She said he was. And I kept on punching her till she wouldn't even defend herself. I was still in a fury and I kicked him down the stairs, threw his clothes into the street and him after them. Then I saw who it was. I knew him. I'd grown up with him. He'd been me best friend and now he was me worst enemy. It's him who's your real father, not me. It was Silas Bompas.'

Thomas waited for him to go on. He could say nothing.

'He came back the next day, bold as brass knocking on the front door. He wanted to see your mother but I wouldn't let him. I told him she was pregnant and if he came round again, if I so much as heard that he'd been talking to her, I'd kill her and the baby. I would have done as well. He knew it. I don't think he ever saw her again. As for your mother, she was frightened of me. I still loved her, I told her that. I told her I still wanted her, that she could have the baby and I'd say it was mine. I told her I'd not leave her again. I would have said anything to get her to stay. And I threatened her as well. She knew I'd be able to find her. So she stayed. But it wasn't the same, it couldn't ever be the same. We never touched each other again. And even when she died she waited, waited till I was away at work, just to prove that she didn't need me. It wasn't that she hated me. It was just that she didn't love me anymore.'

'Dad, it's alright. It's not important. I still love you. You're still the only one I know as me Dad. The only one I'd ever want as me Dad. I still love you.'

'Willie, you're like your mother. Oh Willie, you remind me of your mother.'

'How is he? Is he alright? Thomas man, how is he?' Willie's headlong rush into the house echoed that of his brother only hours before. Thomas stood up. He embraced his brother.

No words were necessary. They both began to cry, great shuddering lung-searing tears which stopped their breathing, a sobbing which each tried to contain by burying his head in the other's shoulder.

'He was asking for you,' said Thomas. 'He was asking for you as he went. He wasn't in pain, he just slipped away.'

'What did he say?' sniffed Willie.

'He said he loved you. He said tell Willie I love him. Those were his exact words.' Thomas held his brother close again, whispered in his ear.

'Tell me other son I love him.'

Elizabeth spent the early part of the morning in her room. The news of Tommy Armstrong's death had affected her more deeply than she would have thought possible. Her disbelief gave way quickly to tears. The letter she tried to write to Thomas and Mary could not hope to express her sorrow and was eventually consigned to the fire. She eventually found comfort at the piano playing from memory a melody which he had plucked from the air one night, the first tune she had been able to learn without resorting to pen and paper. She had asked him its name. 'Lizzie's way,' he had said with a smile on his face. She found the smile still there as she played, followed it with a smile of her own. She would call on the Armstrongs to express her condolences in person. But other matters called for her attention first. At the stroke of eleven she made her way to her father's study. Edward was there, his journey south delayed not only by the weather but also by the events of the previous day. He had been asked to stay by his brother. John Waterhouse appeared grey. His skin, his hair, even his clothes seemed to bear the pallor of concern and worry. He had slept little the previous night.

'Elizabeth, do come in. I'm sorry to drag you away. I too have heard of Mr Armstrong's death. You were very fond of him.' Elizabeth nodded, her silence a sign that she didn't feel able, at that time, to talk of that matter any further. The older men understood.

'Elizabeth, Margaret will say nothing to me,' said John Waterhouse abruptly.

'We spoke last night. No, that is not technically true. I spoke. She will say nothing, nothing at all! She has confirmed the bruises which you reported, I saw those around her neck myself, but she will not talk of anything which happened. She will only say that she is ashamed of what she has done. I could do nothing but secure from her permission to ask you what happened. She claims that she has told you everything, and that you may tell me what you see fit. I urge you, put my mind at rest or confirm my worst fears.' Elizabeth moved to stand in front of her father, took his hands in hers.

'Father,' she said firmly, 'Uncle Edward. Margaret is in her room this morning. She is alive and physically well. She is surrounded by those who love her and care for her. In that we are all fortunate and in that we should all be thankful. As for yesterday, I shall tell you as she told me and you must yourselves make judgement.' Edward and John nodded.

'Well, let us start by sitting round the fire. Our bodies may benefit from the warmth even though our hearts may be chilled. How should I begin?'

The three did as Elizabeth suggested, the two men sharing a small settee opposite Elizabeth's high backed armchair.

'It started at the dance. Margaret interrupted Willie Armstrong and Abigail . . .'

'Abigail Anderson?' asked John.

'The very same. She walked into the cloakroom as they were indulging themselves in a little loveplay. She was jealous . . .'

'Jealous? Jealous of Abigail? Because she was with the Armstrong boy? Good Lord, I like the family, but that's taking things a little too far. After all, he's only a miner!'

'He's a young man father. He's a young, handsome man who has impressed Margaret with his lack of airs and graces, with his natural kindness, with his irresponsibility if you like. While it was acceptable for her to flirt, to pretend affection for him, perhaps not even to pretend, it was in her mind inexcusable of him to dally with another. At least before she had had her fun with him. Before she had dismissed him. And she was jealous. She has admitted it.'

'Very well. I find it difficult to believe but I will acknowledge it as a fact if you tell me that that is the case. Go on.'

'She struck them both, rather more than a glancing blow I fancy.'

'Well well,' said Edward. 'The girl has spirit.'

'And then she swept out of the hall. She desperately wanted to get away, and the first person she saw who was capable of taking her away was Henry Makemore. He was a little drunk at the time and was unaware of the cause of her distress, but he had a carriage waiting and he agreed to take her home. He suggested, for a reason known best to him, that she could spend the night at his home if she wished. She accepted because she wished you, and perhaps me, to worry at her absence. She felt unloved.'

'Unloved! How could she feel unloved? Women really are the most illogical creatures under the sun, I shall never understand them!'

'No father, I don't expect you will.' Elizabeth reached out, touched her father's hand gently.

'On their way out they met the curate. He had, apparently, been there for some time. He dislikes dancing for what he has stated are religious and moral grounds which I suspect are actually based upon his complete lack of rhythm and the fact that he is tone deaf; but that is beside the point. He asked for a lift and they could not refuse. The curate, at that time, was not drunk but had been drinking a little. The three of them climbed into Henry's carriage and off they went.

'It was snowing by then, Henry was, as I have already stated, drunk, and he was trying to steer from within the carriage. He claimed that the horse knew the road anyway, but it too must have been put off by the snow. One way or another the wrong path was taken. They were, albeit unknowingly, heading for the quarry. It was cold in the carriage, despite the blankets stored under the seats, and Henry passed around bottles of whisky and port and other spirits to fight off the chill. They all drank too much.'

'Even Margaret?'

'Yes father, even Margaret. None of them noticed that they were on the wrong road, they couldn't see much at all because of the storm. And then they stopped. Henry got out to see what the problem was. The horse wouldn't move. No matter how much he whipped it and lashed it the beast refused to go forward. He began to whip it harder and harder, the poor animal reared in the air and lost its footing. It slipped and fell and broke its neck. Even Margaret could see that it was dead, but apparently Henry kept on whipping it until he could barely stand himself. Then there was a lull in the storm. It stopped snowing, the moon came out, and they could all see just how perilous their situation was. They were perched at the edge of the steepest part of the quarry. The horse refusing to go on had saved their lives.

'Luckily Henry recognised the place, even in his drunkenness. He'd been through a week or two before chasing a fox. He knew of the quarryman's cottage and suggested they pull the carriage there, no more than a few hundred yards. Margaret thought that he and Deemster would do the pulling. It took all three of them, however, to do the job.'

Even John Waterhouse could not resist a smile at the thought of Makemore, the curate and Margaret hauling a carriage across the snowy quarry wastes.

'They forced the lock. The building was sound but there was no wood to light the fire, so they started breaking up the carriage. They took out the seats to sit on, and all the blankets and coats, found some curtains and sheets in a cupboard which they also used. By the time the storm started again they were quite cosy. And of course, they still had quite a few bottles of spirits left. Margaret can't quite remember anything clearly after that. They sang songs to keep their spirits up, she recalls dancing with Makemore while the curate sang "The Holly and the Ivy". They realised it was past midnight, well past midnight, and the New Year was upon them and they kissed each other.'

'Was kissing all they did?' asked Edward suspiciously.

'I'm coming to that now. Please remember that Margaret is not used to alcohol. She had been emotionally upset and then subject to extreme physical exertion with which she is again unfamiliar. She cannot really be held responsible for her own actions. As I said, she danced with Henry Makemore but he had had a little too much to drink. He had to sit down, so she sat between the two young men. They kissed each other again, but Makemore again had to stop. He went to sit by himself. That left Margaret and Timothy Deemster beside each other, in front of the fire. They were both drunk, both amorous. She remembers them lying down together, she even remembers helping him to remove his trousers.'

'Oh my God no!'

'I'm afraid so father. There are no entirely innocent parties in this little story. Intercourse took place. From what Margaret tells me Mr Deemster was as unpractised as she at this, but she was in no way an unwilling partner.'

'But he's a curate!'

'He's a man father, a man. And a man far more than a curate now. He has already left, early this morning. He's hoping to get to Durham to resign from the ministry. He left me a brief note urging that I keep the matter secret. I'll show it to you later. But the story is not yet over. Sometime in the night she woke again. Perhaps I should say she was woken. She says that Deemster was on top of her but this time he was rough and he was hurting her. He was pinching her and biting her, hence the bruises you saw, father; she was frightened, but when she fought back he put one hand round her neck and threatened to strangle her. She believed him so she didn't struggle any more. He had his way with her.'

No-one spoke. Elizabeth glanced at the faces of the men opposite her. She was glad that Deemster had left. Had he still been at the Hall his life would have been in danger. And she had not yet finished.

'There is more I'm afraid.' She lowered her eyes and breathed in deeply, gathering strength for the final denunciation.

'He then rolled her over. She couldn't move, his weight was on her and he held one arm behind her back. She couldn't fight him at all. He committed . . . he . . .'

'It's alright Elizabeth, there's no need to say it. Both John and I can guess what it is you mean.' Edward put his arm round his brother's shoulders. John Waterhouse was crying.

'When he finished he just lay there. She couldn't move him because of his weight. Eventually she managed to crawl out from underneath him. Deemster was snoring, sound asleep, and she looked around for something to hit him with. She found nothing. Makemore wasn't in the room at all, she went to look for him and found him in the room next door, sound asleep and drunk. She couldn't wake him. By this time she was getting cold again. What could she do? She had no choice. She couldn't even find her clothes it was so dark. She found a sharp piece of wood and took it back to bed with her, determined that if Deemster should molest her again she would use it to pierce his heart. But he didn't wake up again. The next thing she remembers is seeing me and Thomas Armstrong. The rest you know already.'

'I swear I'll murder him!' said John Waterhouse. His fists were clenched, his face a mask of rage.

'He won't be able to hide from me! I'll not rest till every bone in his body has been slowly broken! I'll have him skewered and roasted over a fire! I'll have him!'

'John, John, calm yourself.' Edward tried reason.

'If everything happened as Elizabeth says, and we have no reason to doubt that, there is no doubt that Margaret was, to begin with, a willing party to Deemster's advances. And after that? There were no witnesses. One word against another. There is no case to answer in a court of law.'

'Who mentioned courts?' stormed John Waterhouse. 'There are other means of administering justice! That's my daughter you're talking about, a "willing party" indeed!'

'Father, she told me so herself!'

'She's my daughter,' he continued. 'My only natural daughter!' Waterhouse realised as he spoke that his words had hurt Elizabeth, though she tried to hide the fact. He stooped to comfort her.

'Oh Lizzie my love, forgive me, I didn't mean to hurt you by saying that. I forget, I forget that you too have suffered in reliving these horrible deeds. Please forgive me!'

She put her arms around him, hugged him to her.

'There's nothing to forgive father, nothing at all.'

'But what do we do now?' asked Edward. 'Margaret's honour has been compromised, that much is certain. Revenge will not bring back her virginity. We must act to make sure that as few people as possible know of this. Who, apart from the three of us, are aware of the exact circumstances of the incident? Elizabeth?'

'Well, there's Margaret. And Thomas Armstrong will no doubt have his suspicions, though without being aware of the details. I have, however, asked him to keep this secret and have no reason to doubt that he will do so. I can think of no-one else.'

'Makemore?'

'According to Margaret he was not present when the acts took place. Certainly he was not in the room when I arrived. I feel that I may owe him an apology. I caused him a little personal damage without, it now appears, due cause.'

'Your apology is accepted,' came the voice of Henry Makemore. 'Though I trust that you will be more gentle with me when I become your brother-in-law.'

No-one spoke; all faces were turned to the doorway.

'What was that you said?' asked Elizabeth incredulously.

'Henry has proposed to me,' announced Margaret, stepping calmly into the room. She walked up to Makemore and linked her arm with his. Her face was pale, but she forced her lips into a brave smile.

'He has proposed to me, and I have accepted his proposal.'

'It only remains,' Makemore continued, bowing to John Waterhouse, 'for you to give your blessing.'

John Waterhouse considered himself a calm and reasonable man. When others were losing their tempers, becoming over-excited and garrulous, he would listen carefully until the arguments were spent, then deal with the matter under question in a logical, even-handed, fair manner. So he saw himself, and this view would not normally be considered false by those around him. But there were exceptions. And this was an exception.

'You must be mad,' he exploded, 'both of you! You are mad, the events of the past few days have affected you far more than you both realise! What makes you think, what makes you both think, that my blessing, my permission indeed, will be forthcoming? Because without that permission you will not marry! And I have no intention of allowing any marriage when one of the parties, my own daughter, has suffered such, such deprivation only one day since. I will not give my permission!'

Margaret began to speak. Her voice was quiet but firm. The bruises to her body may still have been causing her pain, but this pain seemed only to strengthen her resolve.

'I have told Henry all that happened, just as Elizabeth has told both of you. He is mortified that he should have contributed to such vile practices, even if only through his negligence. The experience has served to make both of us realise how much we love one another. And we believe that marriage will help solve the problems confronting our families because of this sad event. Henry is not motivated by misplaced sympathy. He first asked me to marry him months ago. He doesn't feel sorry for me; he loves me. And I, in return, love him.'

John Waterhouse had taken the opportunity given by his daughter speaking to re-load and prime his cannons, but the powder was dampened by the forthright manner in which she spoke. He held the touch, pondered his dilemma. He had never been able to gainsay his daughter anything, even when he felt that she didn't really want that which she so readily stated was her heart's desire. He had never wanted to refuse her. But now, when she expressed her need for something, seemed willing to defy him for it, he felt in his heart that she would be better persuaded not to go ahead with her wild and impulsive plan. But still he could not say no.

'I am willing,' he said slowly, 'to acknowledge the depth of the emotions you both feel. I will go that far. But those feelings may be the result of your recent misadventure. You are both under stress. All I ask is that you wait a little while, a few months perhaps, before setting yourselves on a course which is irrevocable. Is that too much to ask? And if you feel the same way in, say six months' time, then I will grant my permission with pleasure.'

'No father,' said Margaret, and took a deep breath. Henry

Makemore patted her hand, and she looked up at him. She swallowed, and Elizabeth could see she was trembling.

'We wish to marry immediately. Within the month. And if you withhold permission then we will marry when permission is no longer needed. And in the meantime the good name of the family may be besmirched by persons unknown informing the press and the general public of the salacious goings on which we all so deeply deprecate. Do you wish your daughter to be known as a fallen woman? A strumpet? A whore?'

'You wouldn't dare, young lady! You wouldn't go to those lengths simply because I refused to let you have your way!'

Elizabeth watched John Waterhouse rise to his feet. She had never seen him so angry, never seen him so out of control. She prepared herself for action, fearful that he would attack Henry or Margaret or both.

'Father,' said Margaret, her words barely audible, 'I'm not a "young lady" any more. I know what I want, I want to marry Henry. I love him, and I love you too, and that's why I'm asking you to give us permission to wed. Because I know that you love me too. And because I know that you would never deny me anything I wanted which was within your power to grant me.'

'I could disown you! I could order you to leave my house! I could alter my will, leave you with nothing!' He was shouting now, but Margaret remained calm. John Waterhouse looked at Elizabeth. She lifted her eyebrows and shrugged, helpless, unable to give advice because she did not know what advice to give. She could not remember one instance when Margaret had not got her way in the past. Edward too shook his head to show that the matter was out of his hands. Only John Waterhouse himself could make this decision. He had no doubt that Margaret would, if her demands were denied, carry out her threats. The end result would be the same no matter what he said. All he could do was attempt to circumvent the self-inflicted damage she seemed only too willing to carry out.

'Very well,' conceded John Waterhouse. He hung his head, gracious in defeat. The battle was over, he had been overwhelmed by an enemy he had never wanted to fight.

'What can I do? Margaret, I love you too much.' The words were soft, quiet, but heard by all.

'You have my permission.' Margaret smiled and her body relaxed. Elizabeth thought that she might faint, but Henry was supporting her; he led her to a chair and sat her down.

'Thank you, father,' she said. 'Thank you.'

'I understand that congratulations are in order Henry.'

'Why, Maichamps! Thank you. I must confess that I am surprised to find you still here. I had thought that your friends from London would have drawn you back to the sins of city life.'

Maichamps shook his head, tutt-tutted to himself.

'When you grow a little older you will find that even sinning can become boring. Novelty quickly becomes tiring and over-familiar, as you may find out to your cost one day. But enough of my ramblings, I have stayed behind for a reason. I wish to hear a tale. The tale of your recent adventure.'

'Oh, I'm sure that you've already heard what happened. There is very little I can add to the stories circulating the house at present. My nobility and gentlemanliness are admitted by all. What can I add?'

'Well,' said Maichamps, pretending to inspect his finger-nails, 'why not start with the truth Henry, a commodity with which neither you nor I are, it pains me to admit, greatly familiar. The truth will suffice.'

Henry Makemore sniggered. He and Maichamps were alone once more in the library. Each held a glass; both glasses had been refilled often in the course of the evening. Maichamps was curled snake-like in a chair while Henry Makemore was stretched out on the floor in what looked like a vain attempt to match his colleague's height.

'Very well then, the truth. But first tell me what you already know.'

'I know of nothing certain,' came the guarded response. 'I saw you at the dance – my friends were most impressed with the show, by the way, our potential winnings mount daily – and then we left, rather abruptly I seem to remember. You warned us away, is that right?' Makemore nodded.

'Just as well,' continued Maichamps, 'given the bad weather in which you became lost. The next thing I hear is that you are found, betrothed to the young Miss Margaret, to marry within four weeks.'

'That is so.'

'I know that you found her attractive. I know that you wished to have her. But marriage Henry? Is that not taking things a little too far?'

Henry sat up. He rubbed his hands together. Then he began to speak, slowly at first.

'I have already had her, Maichamps. I have had her, and I begin to own her, though she is not yet aware of that fact. And through her I have her father. And through him I have his money. The word "marriage" is not enough to describe what I will achieve, Maichamps. Marriage is the means alone.'

'You intrigue me Henry, as I am sure you mean to do. A more detailed explanation is called for if I am to believe these somewhat extravagant claims.'

'You are correct dear friend. And you, the most deceitful knave I have ever had the pleasure to meet, will be the only one to know the truth.'

Maichamps nodded his approval at the compliment. Henry Makemore stood up, warming to his role as lecturer.

'Margaret came to me upset. She had come across her maid and one of the miners at each other like dog and bitch. Not that I could blame the lad, the maid is a well-built creature – I've had designs in that direction myself. Perhaps I can persuade Margaret to bring her along when she moves in here? But that's by the by. As I say, Margaret was upset, she wished to be taken home. My carriage was waiting, I made the gentlemanly offer although my thoughts were far from gentlemanly at the time. I suggested that she return here with me, that it would do her family good to worry about her for a while. The poor girl really does have feathers for a brain. I anticipated taking advantage of her once we were alone then whom should we meet but that buffoon Deemster in the hallway. Margaret asked him to accompany us. He said yes. My heart sank.

'It was beginning to snow but my horse knew the way. Then we reached a fork in the road. Instead of taking the path here I diverted him onto the other track. It leads to the quarry. I planned losing us, knowing that the quarryman's house would be an ideal refuge. I anticipated having to throw Deemster over the cliff-edge or abandon him in the snow so that Margaret and I could be alone, but he found the spare bottles of whisky and sherry I'd brought along and began to open them. I have drunk with him before, I knew that he would, given the opportunity, drink himself insensible. I was surprised too at the amount of alcohol Margaret was capable of absorbing. I, of course, drank sparingly. I knew that I would need my senses kept clear.

'The weather deteriorated considerably. I miscalculated the distance, lost my bearings completely, and when the horse stopped I thought we were still a mile from the quarry. I whipped him, God, my arm was sore, he bled and he bled but he wouldn't go on. He fell, slipped, broke his neck. It quite hurt me. I was fond of the beast. There was a lull in the storm then, I was quite shocked to find us so close to the quarry edge and disaster. I told them where the quarryman's house was, suggested we pull the carriage to the door. I knew how cold it would be, knew we'd need the carriage for fuel and light. I swear I dragged the thing myself, Deemster kept falling over, Margaret was crying. I was asking whether the effort was worth it by the time we got there, what with having to rip the timber from the carriage myself while the others sat inside. No, no, I tell a lie. I threatened I'd lock Deemster out unless he took his turn. He did as he was told.'

Makemore was now acting out his part in the drama, hauling a make-believe cart across the snow, rubbing his hands in front of the newly built fire.

'It was quite cosy. We sat and we warmed ourselves and we drank. They drank more than me. Margaret became very ... very familiar with both Deemster and with me. Yes, familiar is perhaps a polite way of putting it. She tasted wonderful, a mixture of saliva and alcohol, a smell of woman. It excited me, I'll admit that, God knows the effect it was having on Deemster! You see, I had an advantage over him. He really was in love with her.'

Maichamps had now sat up. His attention was firmly fixed on Henry. Every minute or so he licked his lips and swallowed.

'He'd confessed to me some time ago his feelings for Margaret. I played on them. We sat together in front of the fire. First she would kiss me. I swear I could have had her there and then but I wasn't sure how Deemster would react. She was ripe for picking. She would kiss me and then she would kiss him. I felt sorry for him. He was ungainly, he didn't know where to put his hands. She was asking him to take her, she would have done so if he'd been her damn brother! I had to leave them to it. I had to trust that their carnal desires would overcome his reticence. I feigned sickness, crept outside then sneaked back in. They were on the floor together. He must have let instinct take over, he was quite gentle. It was quite touching really, I almost joined in.' He giggled at the thought.

'I saw her flinch when he penetrated her. She was a virgin after all! I think they both enjoyed themselves, I certainly did and I was only watching. They fell asleep quickly. He had his arm round her. It seemed a pity to disturb them, but I needed her. My God, by that time I needed her! I undressed, it was still damn cold, pulled him off her. He was in a different world, I could have shoved a red hot poker up him and he wouldn't have moved. I did consider it actually, but there were more pressing things on my mind. I pulled back the clothes from Margaret. She's beautiful Maichamps, she's really beautiful. I began to kiss her softly, on her lips, her breasts, her stomach. She smelt glorious, it thrilled me to taste the sweat on her, it excited me knowing that she had just been with another man. You know me Maichamps. You know I can't control myself. I didn't mean to do it.' He stopped speaking, abruptly.

'Go on, Henry,' urged Maichamps. 'Go on. You promised, Henry. You can't break your promise. Not to me, Henry, not to me. Go on.' Henry swallowed, licked his lips nervously, looked about him. He found no-one hidden in the shadows.

'I wanted her to think it was Deemster. I knew she'd wake up, you see. I was lying on her, I was using my lips and my teeth, my fingers and my nails. I knew that I was hurting her but I couldn't help it. She woke up. I knew she would see me so I put one hand up, round her throat, and squeezed. And all the time I was biting and pinching. She fought back so I squeezed harder and she stopped, she let me do it, she let me do whatever I wanted, and she was sobbing and crying "No Timothy" but she couldn't say it out loud because she could hardly breathe. Then I turned her over, just flipped her over onto her front. I held her arm behind her back, her head was in a pillow from the carriage, I knew she could hardly breathe. She was still struggling though, she was trying to get up, so I had to lie on her, full on top of her, to get her to lie still. She wouldn't stop, she kept on wriggling and I felt myself growing hard again. I couldn't help myself. Part of me was saying stop, the rest of me was saying go on. So I did it.' He raised his hands to his head, covered his mouth and his eyes, sank to the floor to kneel in front of Maichamps. His body was shaking.

'What did you do Henry?' whispered Maichamps. There was no response.

'What did you do?' Henry shook his head but remained silent.

'She didn't want you, did she?' Henry shook his head again.

'But you wanted her?' A nod.

'You raped her.' It was a statement.

'Did you rape her as a woman?' His head still in his hands Henry began to sob. When he moved his head he did so slowly, deliberately, from side to side.

'You took her as you would a man?' A single nod.

Maichamps shook his head. He moved forward from his chair to kneel facing Henry, put his arms around him, held him close.

'Come come Henry, less of these tears. Why do you weep so? Over a mere woman? You have done your duty, and done it right proudly I may say! Come, Henry, look at me!' He pulled the young man's hands away from his face, tilted his chin upwards.

'You have achieved your first desire. Power! You have taken what you wanted in a manner which does you true credit because the blame has been attached to another. And what an act! Why Henry, you have, in one action, raped and buggered a woman and in doing so you have defrocked a priest! What an achievement dear boy!' He shook his head in disbelief.

'He wasn't a priest,' muttered Henry, 'he was only a curate, a big, well-meaning, stupid, lovesick curate.'

Maichamps spoke quickly.

'What matters is the winning or losing, not the score Henry. Well, not yet. Winning by a margin is best left to those with greater experience than you, but I have no doubt that you will learn. After all, your teacher is one of the best. And as for Margaret, why, she's yours! You possess her, you possess her soul! How did you manage to persuade her that a speedy marriage would be to her benefit? No, don't tell me! Let me say what I would have done!' He held Henry at arm's length, his eyes wandering the room.

'I know! You called on her to offer your sympathy. No, not sympathy, apologies. You had overheard a tale of her misadventures. Surely it wasn't true? If so you should have been there to help her, to protect her, but you were not. It was all your fault. You burst into tears, throw yourself at her feet, beg forgiveness. She pulls you up, sits you beside her. She too is crying. You ask if it was as bad as you have been led to believe and she confesses the whole tale. You are shocked! You are horrified! You will kill Deemster (knowing that he has already left hours before); you will protect Margaret since, in her despoiled state, no other would lower himself to do her that honour. You will even marry her. "Oh yes Henry, yes!" she cries. Curtain falls, end of drama, drum roll, audience exeunt. But was it a comedy or a tragedy?'

He allowed a grin to flicker briefly across his long face.

'Well? Was I right in my estimation?'

Henry nodded. 'Near enough,' he muttered.

'Good. But back to your little story. There still remains a little more to tell, I believe, unless you spent the rest of your time lying inelegantly across the back of your paramour?'

Maichamps retreated to his seat, hugging his legs in delight. Henry Makemore stood up. Just as Margaret had sucumbed to his will, just as she would do again in future, so he must run to Maichamps' command. Even in realising this he was unable to escape. He lay at night in bed, those nights when he chose or was forced to sleep alone, wondering at his inability to rid himself of his demon. But he knew now that the demon possessed him, that he had no wish to rid himself of its evil. He welcomed its presence.

'I achieved satisfaction, but I didn't move. I withdrew slowly but held her beneath me. I feel now that I could have held her with one finger, but I wasn't sure then. I managed to pull Deemster back, moved away from her and laid his arm across her. She was frightened, still very frightened, but also exhausted. I stroked her hair but said nothing. She fell asleep and I left, lit a fire in the room next door. I slept well.'

'And you had no regrets?'

'Not then.'

'And now, now also you must have no regrets. Listen to me Henry, listen carefully. You have power in your grasp, and power is the headiest vintage in the whole of creation's cellar. But regrets sour the palate. Regrets dull the senses, regrets poison the pure soul, regrets are evil. You must have no regrets. Cleanse yourself of them!'

'I only wish . . .'

'Remember my words Henry!'

Henry turned to face his master. His grin was a scowl.

'I wish that when Margaret's sister had hit me, I wish that I'd laid her out, I wish that I'd buggered her as well!'

Far upstairs a servant girl heard the loud, braying laughter and crossed herself. On a night like this the devil was afoot.

Chapter Ten

A time to weep, and a time to laugh;
a time to mourn, and a time to dance.

Ecclesiastes

The undertaker was a suitably nondescript man, neither old nor young, short nor tall, imperious nor servile. He wore his studied sadness with a professionalism born of tradition; his father, grandfather and great-grandfather before him had dedicated their lives to others' deaths, and he was training his own son in the finer arts of their vocation. They had already moved the coffin into the house. It stood on trestle legs in the centre of the room, the furniture moved back to the walls or taken away. The wood was cheap pine with little ornamentation, handles of black iron, a lining of red cotton. Thomas had felt the need to explain. His father had been a carpenter, had never seen the point of burying good wood, allowing it to rot underground when it could be carved and seen and touched and appreciated by those fortunate enough to remain, until mortality touched them also, above the earth. The undertaker assured his complete comprehension of the situation while admitting to his son his surprise that the old bugger hadn't made his own coffin for just such an eventuality.

Willie had taken the boys out for a walk. At the undertakers' request Thomas and Mary closeted themselves in the kitchen while the body was brought downstairs. They listened to the bumps and thumps, the gasps and laboured breathing, the scrape of wood on wood as the lid was laid gently over the body. The body. A lifeless husk, nothing more.

Once, when Thomas was a boy, a blackbird had made its nest in a hedge opposite the house. He had woken every morning to its song, had watched as the brood had grown and eventually left the nest. The hen, dull and mousey brown, had always kept herself well-hidden. But the cock, loud and brassy as a harlot, had perched on fence-posts and tree-tops to proclaim his vanity to the world. He was a proud bird, a narrow streak of white flaming from his orange bill across his eye and down his neck. He seemed to take pleasure in chasing other birds away and crowing his triumph, boasting of his strength and the beauty of his voice. One morning, the first frost of winter chilling the air, Tommy Armstrong found his eldest son crouched in the backyard drenching the dead bird's body with his tears. He held his son close, comforted him with wise words. The blackbird had died, what was left was unimportant. It was nothing more than an empty shell. The important bit was still there, the essence of blackbird, it still lived on. It lived on as long as there were other blackbirds to welcome the dawn. The fledgelings, they were part of it. The hen too. And Thomas himself. Thomas stopped crying, sniffed and wiped his nose on his pullover.

'How?' he had asked.

'Lots of people have heard that bird sing,' said Tommy, 'one or two might even have wished he'd be a little quieter. You've seen him, haven't you, sitting on that tree outside your window? You can see him now, if you close your eyes. You can hear him, can't you? And as long as you can hear him, as long as you can see him inside yourself, it doesn't matter whether he's there in front of you or in your memory. Sometimes there's not a lot of difference between the two. And sometimes the memory's better than the actual object or person anyway.'

Standing in his kitchen, his arms around his wife, Thomas remembered the blackbird and its song, his father and his words. But still the tears fell.

All that day and during the evening visitors struggled through the melting snow, came to pay their last respects. Pitmen filed through the room, doffed their caps and left without saying a word. Children, hushed into solemnity, touched the coffin with reverence and raised their hands to be lifted, the better to see inside. Strange faces uttered comforting words, strange voices talked of Newcastle and Durham and all the villages between, of dancing at Alnwick and singing at Seaton Burn, of playing together at Wideopen and drinking at Hexham. The Waterhouse family (John and Edward, Elizabeth behind, all in black; Margaret was still recovering) brought flowers, though how they had come by them no-one could guess. The next day, the day of the funeral, was a Monday; John Waterhouse announced that, as a mark of respect, the pit would stay closed.

Thomas and Willie sat up all night. They talked of their childhood, their father, times good and bad. One or the other would doze in a chair, then wake to find the other smiling across the firelit room. Their conversations started with, 'Do you remember...?' or, 'Was it really ten years ago that...?' They smoked and drank tea and polished their best boots and, as dawn crept grey under the curtains, Willie stood and stretched. He reached into his jacket pocket and brought out a bottle of whisky, poured some into Thomas's mug, some into his own, another measure into the horn tumbler their father was fond of using.

'To Dad,' said Willie, raising his mug. Thomas realised

that he could never tell his brother the secret his father had
passed to him just before his death.

'Safe journey,' he whispered. They drank their fill. Willie
threw the tumbler and its contents onto the fire in a hiss of
flame and crack of smoke.

The funeral procession left the house at eleven o'clock. The
black hearse had once been a phaeton, one of its seats
removed to make room for the coffin. The horses, decked in
black, their harnesses wet with polish and drizzle, were led
by the undertaker and his son. Thomas and Mary and the
children followed close behind, Willie, his arm linked with
Abigail's, a step further to the rear. Silent watchers materi-
alised at windows and doorways. Some, dressed like the
Armstrongs in Sunday best black, joined the procession.
They were led slowly out of the village to the chapel where
others were waiting in the rain, a parliament of bedraggled
rooks.

The bearers took their places at the rear of the hearse.
Rob and Len, Stew and Davey, each shook Thomas and
Willie firmly by the hand before joining them to bear the
coffin through the doors and into the chapel. It was a simple
building, brick and slate, plastered and painted white inside.
The pews were newly varnished, the floor neatly laid with
diagonals of parquet. There were three aisles. That in the
middle led up to a pine pulpit; those at the sides were
escorted by windows of plain glass, simple gothic arches.
The coffin was placed softly on the white linen covered table
and the bearers retreated to their seats.

The preacher had visited the day before. He had tousled
the boys' hair and asked them gentle questions about their
grandfather, then talked similarly to Thomas, Mary and
Willie. Thomas explained that his father had not been
religious and that neither he nor his family were religious
and the preacher had nodded. Mary appeared to be about

to say something but remained silent. Thomas continued, mentioned that they had considered holding the memorial service in the village hall. Again the preacher nodded but said nothing. Willie added that they had finally decided against that, had also decided against using the church in Lanchester, but that they all felt that the service should reflect, as far as was possible, their father's beliefs or, as Willie wryly put it, lack of them. Again the preacher nodded, asked them what hymns they would like, then left. And there he was now, mounting the three steps to the pulpit, grasping the lectern firmly, looking round the chapel. Thomas turned to follow his gaze. Every seat was filled, there were people standing at the back and along the sides. The preacher began to speak.

He was in his late thirties, tall and thin with an angular face and a soft voice, its origins a little to the north of the Tyne. He cleared his throat.

'Tommy Armstrong was not a religious man,' he began. Thomas feared the worst. If this turned into a fire and brimstone 'repent ye sinners' diatribe then he'd leave in the middle of it, dragging his father's coffin after him if he had to!

'Tommy Armstrong didn't come to church regularly.' His voice was quiet, matter-of-fact.

'Tommy Armstrong didn't approve of the church at all.' He looked around him, taking in each face as though memorising it.

'And yet there are more people here today than I have seen in this chapel since I began to preach here. And I must ask why. Is it that you have all suddenly seen the light and been delivered to God's heart? Perhaps you've heard of the superb oratory, the wise sermons, the overwhelming love we practise in this house of God? Or could it be, I ask myself, something to do with Tommy Armstrong?' He took a sharp breath and continued quickly.

'But then I say no, how can this be? Tommy Armstrong was no church-goer. Tommy Armstrong was not a religious man. Tommy Armstrong was, as most of you know, fond of the bottle. He was a man of weakness, a man easily distracted by the material things of life. Sometimes that material was to be found clothing a shapely ankle, and in saying this I say nothing that I have not been told by his friends and his family in the past few days. For I didn't know Tommy Armstrong.' He paused for effect. He had the ears of the whole room.

'I did not know him, but I knew of him! I knew of him because others spoke to me of him. In passing the time of day they would mention that Tommy Armstrong had been waiting outside the school playing his whistle and all of the children were listening and dancing and clapping. They would tell of the sword-dancing competition and how Tommy Armstrong's team was coming along, and how proud they were when they saw them all dance together. And they'd say how happy he always seemed, how he was always willing to spend a few minutes with them, how he knew everybody's name, and their children, even their dogs! And when they mentioned his name they smiled! And I would think, how can they be so proud of such a man? Because Tommy Armstrong was not a religious man!

'And so I had to do some thinking myself. If such a man could be held in such respect by so many goodly people, did the problem perhaps lie with me? Was I the one who was mistaken? Is it necessary to go to church to be religious, I asked myself? Is it possible that true religion, true belief, lies not in the midst of a shell of bricks and mortar, of timber and plaster and glass, but in the heart and soul of every man? And in asking these questions I came to the following conclusions.'

Thomas felt himself growing angry. He glanced to his side to see Mary in rapt attention. Beyond her even Willie was staring at the preacher with a beatific smile rendered to his face. Was he the only one who could see what the preacher was doing? It wasn't that he'd said anything about his father that was demeaning or derogatory. On the contrary, what he'd said was basically the truth. And no doubt he would continue in the same vein, bestow praise where none was due, make his father if not a saint then certainly one of the holiest sinners the church had ever known. Thomas could put up with that, he had been to funerals before, he knew what happened. But the preacher was going beyond this. He had a captive audience. He knew that he was speaking well, he was giving them what they wanted to hear, they were in his hand and he had no intention of letting them go. He wasn't doing this for Tommy Armstrong or his family, he was doing it for himself! Thomas looked straight at the preacher and recognised the expression on his face. He had seen his father like that when he was dancing, when the audience were watching his feet and listening to the beats, when he knew that as soon as he stopped there would be a moment's silence, then the crowd would start their applause, each vying with the next to make the greatest amount of noise. The dead man and the one delivering the requiem were both addicted to the adulation which only the latter could now receive.

'There is a community spirit in a pit village which exists as of right. It exists because the men of that village share their lives underground. It exists because of the understanding these men have with each other, usually unspoken, that they have a common destiny. It exists because their wives and families are aware of the faith which binds them together. This spirit has no name. It cannot be seen or touched or written down, it cannot be conjured into being if it does not already exist but, by the same token, it cannot wilfully be destroyed. Yet some men can taste it in the air around them. They can scent it in the very coal-dust which is a by-product of their labours. And, though they may not know what they do, they can use that spirit to fortify their own lives and in doing so give back to the spirit a hundred-fold what they themselves were given!

'Tommy Armstrong was such a man. A scoundrel? Yes, sometimes. A philanderer? Perhaps, in times of weakness. A drinker to excess? Undoubtedly! These are human failings and, deplorable though we may find them, we should not condemn them lest we too find ourselves wanting when temptation becomes our companion. Tommy Armstrong was fortunate. He possessed that rare ability to sense the spirit around him, to weave it and bind it, to make it stronger with his own faith in himself, in his family, in his music and his dancing!' The preacher's voice was louder now, filling the room with its deep, trust-me resonance.

'Tommy Armstrong helped bring pride to this small community, pride and a sense of belonging, a warm feeling of contentment which emanated from his joyful spirit, a delight in life itself which was far greater than could have come from his mere physical self. But Tommy was not alone. The spirit was working with him, in him, through him. And if, as Cowper says in his immortal hymn, God moves in a mysterious way, then why should he not choose Tommy Armstrong to be the instrument of his love in this village? And can you not feel that love around you now? Your very presence here today demonstrates that you can feel it, and in coming here to mourn the loss of a loved one, to celebrate his passing to a new and better life, you are showing that you too have been touched by the spirit which lived in the heart of Tommy Armstrong.'

The preacher sipped from a glass of water at his side, though Thomas felt sure that he was not thirsty.

'I spoke to Tommy Armstrong's sons about a suitable hymn. We discussed one or two but they admitted that they had never heard him singing hymns, so they left the choice to me. I spent some considerable time on this matter, knowing how important music had been to Tommy Armstrong. I will admit that I prayed for guidance. None came. Then, in making arrangements for the burial which, as I am sure you will realise, must take place in the consecrated ground of the Anglican church, I found myself waiting at Greencroft Hall where the vicar was engaged in discussing weighty matters with Mr Waterhouse. Whilst there I was entertained by one of Mr Waterhouse's daughters, Elizabeth,' he nodded towards the rear of the church, 'who informed me that Tommy Armstrong had, of late, been teaching her some tunes for the violin. Tommy had told her the following story.

'There was once an Irish harpist who was travelling through Scotland. It was the custom in those days for musicians to play at the houses of the nobility and to be rewarded for their efforts with food and lodgings and gifts. The harpist was invited to the home of Lady Eglington and commenced to play for her guests, but could not be heard above their idle chatter. Since they would not be quiet he picked up his harp and left, even though the night was fierce with storm and rain. Lady Eglington noticed his absence and ran after him, apologising for the bad manners of her guests. She pleaded for him to return and he did so. Lady Eglington entered the hall first, stood at the door and waited for the silence of her guests. When that was forthcoming she held out her hand to bring the harpist back into the room. He replied by composing for her a tune, a haunting melodic tune called in Gaelic "Tabhair dom do Lamh".

'This was one of Tommy Armstrong's favourite tunes. Secular it may be, but I feel that the honesty of emotion it conveys is more appropriate for this occasion than any hymn might be. Mr Waterhouse's daughter, Mrs Kearton, has agreed to play that tune for us today, to play it for Tommy Armstrong. The tune has a name in English which we might, in troubled times, all care to remember. It's called "Give me your Hand".'

Elizabeth had already stood up and she began to play almost before the preacher's words had died. Thomas recognised the tune. It *was* one of his father's favourites, and Elizabeth's playing reflected his father's teaching. But it was nothing more than a reflection, and Thomas suddenly found himself longing for the reality of his father's presence rather than this pale echo. He felt the tears well up, tears and anger at the way the preacher appeared to him to have manipulated the service for his own ends, tears and sorrow that Elizabeth should have become involved in this, tears and shame that he had not loved his father more, guilt that he had been unable to express that love. And now it was too late. He felt Mary's arm round his shoulders, her hand reaching out to squeeze his, and he held back the tears. Not here, not now. There would be time enough for tears later. Time for him to be alone.

The silence which followed Elizabeth's playing was pure and natural and even the preacher seemed loath to break it. His words, when they arrived, seemed stretched, thin and taut.

'Let us pray,' he creaked, and reached again for the water. This time the need was real.

'Lord, we offer our prayers for the soul of our friend Tommy Armstrong, a giver and receiver of love. We pray that you will welcome his soul and that the music of heaven will be further glorified by his presence at your side. Amen.'

'Amen,' came the chorus. Thomas was ushered to his feet and took his place as the coffin was carried back down the aisle to the hearse. Late that night he would lie in bed, unable to sleep, dealing the day's events onto the table of his memory like a pack of cards. Someone, however, had taken the cards away, shuffled them, lost some of them, substituted cards from a different pack. His memory of the short walk to the Anglican church and its cemetery was distorted, as though he was watching from a hill or some other distant vantage point. And when the coffin was lowered into the grave (had it been dug that day by men thankful for the thaw? Or had they prepared a number of convenient graves in cryptic anticipation of the winter's mortality?) he saw faces, his own included, staring down at him as the first handful of muddy soil was thrown into his eyes. He remembered the rain and the ugly grey remnants of snow hiding behind damp-slick walls. He remembered pencil-lines of leaden smoke rising from chimneys. He could recall hearing the faint bleat of a new-born lamb, and stopping at a gate to watch it lurch away from him, drunk with the warm potency of its mother's milk. He knew that words had been spoken to him, and that he had replied, but the words themselves and the identity of the speakers had been lost. He remembered sitting in front of the fire, in the seat which his father had claimed, and listening to the note that Willie read out, the note from his and Willie's sisters, the note explaining briefly why they would not come to the funeral to honour a man they didn't love. He remembered seeing the note burning on the fire but was not sure whether it had been he or Willie who had thrown it there. He remembered voices, and hands reaching out towards him, and the smell of baking and warm, sweet tea, and the door opening and closing, and children on his lap. He remembered Mary's warm body pressed against his and the gentle sound of her breathing, and the certain despair of knowing that he would not sleep easily that night.

The next day he was on backshift, down the shaft at one-thirty, working at the face by two. Neither Mary nor Willie questioned him when he left the house at ten without saying goodbye. They both realised that he had not yet grieved, hoped that he would, given a chance to be alone, be able to allow his emotions to escape. They watched from the window as he trudged down the path and into the village, shoulders bent, head staring at the ground before him.

The weather was mild with the promise of false spring. The fields were sodden with rain and melt-water and Thomas found himself avoiding those tracks and paths which might make passage difficult. He did not feel it essential that he spend time alone. He knew that what he wanted, what he needed, was to talk, and that it did not matter if he talked and no-one listened. But if someone did listen, they would have to do so with an understanding which, at the moment, neither Mary nor Willie could give him. He decided, therefore, that he would have to be his own audience.

He walked towards the Hall, towards the mine, but turned right before he reached the stable block. The path was gravelled and he lightened his tread for some reason, as if fearful that he would be heard and admonished for entering what was, strictly speaking, private land belonging to the Hall. Suddenly aware of this and faced with a choice of routes he disdained to take that which would lead him onto the Lanchester road, instead opted perversely for that which wound its way through the gardens and shrubberies at the front of the house. His father was uppermost in his mind. His voice, his mannerisms, his touch and smell, the sound of his singing and dancing and music masked all other thoughts, made the gardens and lawns around him disappear. Give me your hand. The melody sought him out. He ought to have offered his father his hand more often.

The gardens at the front of the Hall were slightly terraced, the first two being a close-clipped lawn and a series of formal flower beds surrounding a fountain. The third terrace, again lawned, led down a natural slope to a narrow ribbon of small trees and bushes. Two or three paths led through this elongated thicket to converge on a small summerhouse, its verandah overlooking the pastures and parkland of the rest of the estate. Thomas had not been aware of the existence of the summerhouse, even now with the trees and bushes bare of leaves it was barely visible. He found himself meandering slowly in that direction when the realisation came to him that the music he was hearing was not only in his head. That it was coming from the summerhouse was certain; the identity of the violinist, however, was another matter. It sounded like his father. The melody contained the same subtleties, the same nuances of expression which had been missing in Elizabeth's playing the day before. Thomas wondered whether he might have dreamed his father's death; when that seemed, after consideration, to be unlikely he faced the possibility that he might be mad. Could a madman question his own sanity? He altered his approach, crept through the long wet grass to the rear of the ship-lapped white-washed wooden building to peer through the side window. The large double doors were wide open; that was why he had so easily heard the music, and even though the musician was not facing him he recognised Elizabeth. And he realised, because the music told him so, that at the funeral she had played because she had been asked to do so; today she was playing because she wanted to. Thomas turned his back to the wall and decided to leave. The emotion in the music was such that he felt he had no right to interrupt. Elizabeth might want to be alone. The music stopped as he began to ease silently away, was replaced with a heartfelt sobbing. He closed his eyes, clenched his fists, then turned back.

Elizabeth was leaning against the doorpost, her forehead resting on her crooked left arm. Her right hand held her violin and bow loosely at her side. She was crying, her body racked with sorrow, shudders running down her back. Thomas watched her for a full minute. He realised the importance of being able to weep, knew that when the moment came he too would be able to find release in tears. Slowly the lamentation ceased; he heard her take a deep breath, then another.

'Are you alright now lass?' he asked artlessly, mounting the steps to stand before her. She spun round, an expression of horror on her face, ashamed that she should have been witnessed in a moment of such weakness. Her eyes were red, her nose shone, there were small rivers of tears running down her cheeks. Then she recognised Thomas, without warning hurled herself across the room and into his arms. She began to cry again, muttering incomprehensibly as she did so. Thomas could pick out only one or two words, 'father' and 'Tommy' and 'love', interspersed with long periods of sobbing. He could feel the violin pressing in the small of his back, Elizabeth's suffocating, damp warmth against his chest. His hands fluttered uselessly in mid-air then, as if of their own volition, one settled gently at the top of her back, the other simultaneously began to stroke her hair. As he touched her she started, a sudden intake of breath followed by silence. Both could hear the beating of the other's heart. She buried her face deeper into the rough, homely, bread-and-butter smelling warmth of his coat; he bent his cheek to touch the top of her head.

'Are you alright?' Thomas asked again. Elizabeth nodded but did not speak.

'Are you sure?' Again a silent nod.

'If you want to talk I'm willing to listen. I'm a good listener, a very good listener.' He paused for a while, thought of all he'd been wishing he could have said to his father.

'Aye, I'm a good listener. It's only talking, saying things I really ought to say, that I find difficult.'

Elizabeth pushed her face away and looked up at the mist in Thomas's eyes. At first he avoided her gaze, appeared to be staring at the faded grey picture of Queen Victoria hung on the rear wall of the summerhouse. His glance flicked down, but his viewpoint was suddenly that of an onlooker who saw him embracing a woman not his wife, a woman who felt warm and comfortable against him, a woman who was staring at him with a look of desperate longing. He felt vulnerable, frightened, let his hands move to her shoulders and urge her gently away from him. She swayed, he thought she might faint and started towards her, but she recovered, shook her head.

'I'm sorry,' she said.

'There's no need to apologise,' he answered. 'There's nothing to be sorry for. You were upset, that's all.'

She wanted to shout at him. She wanted to say that she wasn't apologising for crying, not even for embarrassing him by falling into his arms. No, she was sorry only that she hadn't had the courage to tell him the way she felt about him, she was sorry he'd pushed her away from him, she was sorry that he appeared unable to tell her *his* feelings. Or perhaps she was telling him what a sorry, vile, wretched creature she felt herself to be. Thomas was about to speak and, overcome with self-pity, she felt tears once more come to her eyes, was sure that there was nothing he could say or do which would prevent her drowning in her own despair.

'I wish I could find tears,' he said softly, then turned, sat on one of the steps and placed his hands on his lap. His head fell forward. Elizabeth was suddenly aware of the pain Thomas was feeling and this drove away all thoughts of herself. She placed her violin carefully on the floor and sat down beside him. Her hand was raised, her arm seemed about to drape itself around his shoulders and pull him towards her. She wanted to comfort him, but was frightened of destroying the empathy which even now tied them to one another. She placed her hands in her lap.

'What is it?' she asked. 'Why can't you cry?'

'I don't know.'

'Is that the truth?'

Thomas turned to face her.

'Look at me,' he said wide-eyed. 'Look at my hands!' He held out his arm; his fingers were trembling.

'Look at my face! Look at my eyes!' His skin was grey. His eyes red-rimmed and bloodshot.

'My Dad died, and I loved him, despite the fact that he could be a bastard at times, and I know why he was like that, and that makes me love him more.' He sniffed; his voice was raw, it scattered his words like crows to a storm.

'Elizabeth, I loved him, I really did. But I never told him. Not once. I never told him what I felt about him, I couldn't find the right words, or the time was wrong. Perhaps I was frightened of him laughing at me. Perhaps I was frightened that he didn't feel the same way about me. But I never told him, and now it's too late!'

Elizabeth lifted her hand to her eyes, rubbed them wearily, then began to speak with careful deliberation.

'You know Thomas, you can tell someone you love them even if they aren't with you.' Thomas stared at her, not understanding.

'You can tell them by the things you do and by the way you live and by the memories you keep. You didn't need to say anything to your Dad! I could tell, anyone could tell, how you felt about him, how he felt about you, just by the way you talked to each other, by the way he'd wink at you when he was telling you how to do a step, by the smile you gave him when you got something right. He *knew* Thomas, he knew exactly what you felt. He didn't need to have you say anything, he might even have been embarrassed if you'd said anything outright. I think you said everything you ever wanted to say to him; it's just that you didn't use words to do it.'

Elizabeth moved round to kneel in front of Thomas. His head was still in his hands, and she reached out, took hold of his wrists, forced his arms down.

'Look at me Thomas.' He raised his head slowly.

'It's still not too late!' She stared into his eyes.

'You can show how much you loved your father. You can do rapper and you can win the competition. You can keep his memory strong in your mind, you can talk about him and sing his songs and play his tunes. You can be his son, because in being his son you're a part of him still living. You can laugh when you think of something which would have made him laugh, you can be angry when he would have been angry. And when it's needed, when you have to, you can cry Thomas. Never, never be afraid to cry.'

Thomas's eyes filled, but still no tears fell. Elizabeth pushed herself to her feet, picked up her violin.

'Stand up Thomas Armstrong!' she ordered. 'Stand up and look at me!'

Thomas did so. His shoulders were rounded, his back hunched, he seemed to have shrunk. Elizabeth began to play, a jig, a fast jig in a minor key.

'Dance, Thomas,' she said quietly. Thomas stared at her as if she were mad.

'I said dance. Dance, Thomas Armstrong.' He didn't move.

'Your father played this tune a lot. He liked it, said it expressed the way he felt. That's why I'm playing it now Thomas. For him. For his memory. Now will you dance?'

Thomas shook his head from side to side, slowly, oh so slowly.

'Dance will you!' spat Elizabeth. 'Dance! Do it for me! Do it for yourself! Do it for your father! But dance, damnit!'

The music increased its pace and Thomas's feet began to move, out of time and with an uneven rhythm, but they moved. Elizabeth laughed out loud.

'With the music man, with the music! And stand up straight! Your father would have been ashamed of you!'

Thomas seemed to make the effort. He breathed in deeply and the action lifted his shoulders; he tried to step with the music's regular six beats only to find that Elizabeth had increased the pace again. He swore under his breath.

'It's no use swearing, Thomas Armstrong, I can play faster than this and I'm proud of it. I had the best teacher there was. His name was Tommy Armstrong. You might have heard of him.'

Thomas speeded up again, caught her pace and stayed with it. His feet were moving fast now, the floor of the summerhouse was alive with their tattoo, the walls shouted the beat back at him. He danced for two, perhaps three minutes, the steps becoming more elaborate and complex as the seconds passed.

'Who are you dancing for?' whispered Elizabeth through clenched teeth. Her bow arm was moving almost as fast as the stepping.

'Dad,' came the reply, almost inaudible.

'Why are you dancing for him?'

There was no response.

'I said why!' shouted Elizabeth.

'BECAUSE I LOVE HIM!' screamed Thomas back at her. The music stopped, he stopped dancing, tears coursing down his nose and cheeks, his chest rising and falling. His arms hung limp at his sides. His eyes were closed.

'Because I love him,' he gasped. 'And I miss him. And I wish he was still here.'

'Oh Thomas,' said Elizabeth. 'Thomas Armstrong, you are such a good man.' She put down her violin again, moved towards him. 'Such a good man' she whispered as she put her hands around him, lowered his head onto her shoulder. 'Such a good man,' she cried softly to herself, and in the welcome release of his grief the mingling of their tears went unnoticed.

* * *

They walked together through the park, in silence, caught in the spider's web of their own thoughts. Thomas had accepted his grief, had accepted Elizabeth's help in allowing him to express it. As they walked, skirting puddles, keeping to the paths and away from the wet, muddy grass, he watched his companion carefully. She seemed tired. There were dark shadows under her eyes, her hair had been hastily tied back into a short pony-tail and wisps of it kept straying into her eyes. She wore her habitual black.

'Why were you there?' he asked abruptly.

'Pardon?' she replied, genuinely surprised.

'At the summerhouse, with your fiddle? Why were you there?'

'Oh, I just felt the need to be alone for a while. Alone with my thoughts and music.'

'I'm sorry I disturbed you, if I'd known I would have ...'

'Thomas, please! I didn't mean alone like that. And besides, being with you is, is ... well, it's enjoyable.' He smiled and lowered his head.

'The truth is, Thomas, I wanted to be by myself but I also wanted to be away from certain people visiting the Hall at the moment.'

Thomas remained silent. It was not his place, he felt, to ask the identity of the individuals whose presence drove Elizabeth from her home. His suspicions were, however, confirmed.

'I can put up with Sir Charles Makemore, in small doses. But Henry is insufferable at the best of times, and my sister's even worse now that she and Henry are to marry. They're pushing ahead with things, the ceremony's to take place at the end of the month. That's why Sir Charles and Henry are here. To discuss arrangements.'

They walked on. Thomas felt unable to comment and was about to say so when Elizabeth pre-guessed him.

'I don't need you to say anything Thomas, I know that

this doesn't really affect you, but I feel I need to talk to someone. That's why I was alone. I have no-one to talk to.' Thomas felt her sadness. Having helped him unburden himself of some of his grief the least he could do was act the silent listener. And if he felt the need to comment, well, she was under no obligation to listen to him.

'I'm worried about Margaret. Henry's no good for her, I know that, I suspect she knows that as well. And there's something about her story of that night at the quarry – you haven't told anyone, have you? About what she said?' Thomas shook his head.

'There's something doesn't quite fit, but I don't know what it is. I don't trust Henry Makemore, though he seems to have some affection for my sister and she idolises him. He reminds me of ...' Her voice drifted into nothingness and she stopped walking. Thomas looked back at her, her head tilted to one side in the helpless, eager to please manner of a lap-dog awaiting a titbit.

'I hope she doesn't make the same mistakes ...' Elizabeth continued, her voice quiet and introspective. Thomas took a step towards her.

'Are you alright?' he asked. He seemed, he reminded himself, to be asking that question very frequently.

'Mmm?' she said, surprised, blinking. 'Oh, yes, I'm sorry. Of course, I'm alright, forgive me. I was caught for a moment, trapped by a memory I thought I'd escaped a long time ago.' Her voice was almost perplexed.

'If you want to tell me ...' offered Thomas. Elizabeth's mouth opened in horror.

'Oh no, it's nothing I could tell you about, it's ... it's long past, long past now. I can't worry about it, it can't harm me any more. Not now. And anyway, it's Margaret who really concerns me. She's making a mistake and there's nothing I can do to change her mind.'

'Perhaps you're wrong,' said Thomas. 'Perhaps young Mr

Makemore's intentions are entirely honourable. After all, you've no evidence that he intends Margaret any harm.'

'That's part of it,' Elizabeth replied, 'he's being too nice, to me, to my father, to everyone. Too nice by far. And he's so attentive to Margaret, opening doors, fetching things for her, touching her, giving her little kisses. It's not like him, not like him at all.'

Thomas thought of a question, discarded it, then summoned up the courage to ask anyway.

'Are you jealous?'

Elizabeth seemed unconcerned at the allegation, continued to talk in the same level, measured tones.

'No, I'm not jealous. How could I be jealous of Margaret when she's likely to end up with Henry Makemore? I've already told you how much I dislike . . .'

'No,' interrupted Thomas, 'I didn't mean jealous in particular. I meant in general, jealous of the fact that Margaret's about to get married, she has someone who appears, as you yourself have admitted, to love her. Whereas you . . .'

'Whereas I,' continued Elizabeth with a wry smile, 'am well on my way to becoming a middle-aged spinster. I have no-one to love me, no-one to care for me, no close friends. Put like that, when I consider the question carefully, jealousy would be a natural emotion, would it not?'

'You're not a spinster, at least that's what you've led me to believe. You haven't told me about your husband, nor anyone else, but I assume he's still around somewhere. And . . .'

'And?'

'And you do have friends. There's your father. And, even if you feel estranged from her at the moment, there's your sister.' Thomas stared at her, lowered his eyes, then looked at her again.

'And there's me.'

Elizabeth's smile was natural, unforced, friendly, thankful. Its exuberance was infectious, and Thomas felt his own lips curve into a crescent of relaxed pleasure.

'Thomas, you are too kind, really. I consider it a great honour that you should feel me worthy of your friendship. There are few people I feel able to trust, few people in whose company I feel at ease, yet you are ... Thomas? Are you laughing? Thomas, what's the matter?'

'It's nothing.'

'No, tell me.'

'I can't!'

'Please?'

Thomas took a deep breath.

'It's just that I've never heard anyone try to say "thank you" in so many words before!'

Elizabeth looked puzzled. Her eyebrows crept together as she considered Thomas's statement, then she too began to laugh. She had never considered herself verbose in the past; could it be her age? And her worries over Margaret's future, were they a reflection of her own troubled past or perhaps, as Thomas suggested, the sub-conscious emergence of her own need to be loved? Either way Thomas had shown her that worrying would do nothing to help her, and her depression had lifted sufficiently for her to see the humour in her concerns. She didn't, she concluded, laugh enough.

'It's nice to see you smile,' said Thomas. 'Would you like me to walk you back to the house?'

'The pleasure, Mr Armstrong, would be all mine.'

They talked of the world around them. Thomas, first and most, regaled her with stories of his father dredged from his youth, tales of how he spent his childhood, the games he would play with his friends, the way he looked after Willie. He told Elizabeth about his own children and how he saw them developing, his hopes for their future.

Elizabeth was more reticent. Although she was willing to entertain Thomas with details of her childhood, would even go on to tell him of her teens, her interest in music and literature, it was as though she were holding something back, hiding some part of her past. He was curious. She had ignored his earlier remark that she was not a spinster, and now appeared to be skirting round the subject of her marriage. He decided, simply because he wished to know more about her, to bring the conversation back to that subject. He told her about Mary, how they had met and how he had proposed, their first house together, the rats and mice which clattered through the roof space at night. Elizabeth listened attentively, showing genuine interest in the way Thomas had lived.

'And you?' Thomas then asked. 'How did you meet your husband? Is he abroad at the moment, I'm sure you mentioned something about him being out of the country. What does he do for a living?'

It was the first time Elizabeth had been asked a direct question about her husband. She had known that it would come, she had planned the answer carefully, rehearsed its telling frequently. And yet it hurt her to lie to Thomas.

'My husband is in South America, he left almost two years ago. He's part of an exploration team; he's a zoologist. I haven't heard from him for over twenty months now.'

'Had he planned to be away for this long?'

'No. He should have been away for no longer than nine months, a year at the outside.'

'I'm sorry. I shouldn't have asked. It must upset you to talk about him like that.'

'No, I'm used to it now. Besides, he's a very resourceful man. He has a habit of turning up when you least expect him. It wouldn't surprise me to hear from him one day soon, to find that he's discovered some exciting new species of animal or come across a lost tribe of natives in some distant valley. I still have hope.'

'You must love him?' It seemed a strange question to ask, and Elizabeth had not anticipated it. She thought carefully about fact and fiction, compared what she did feel with what she ought to have felt.

'I must have loved him,' she almost confirmed. The conversation seemed over as they rounded the corner of the Hall to find the Makemores' carriage still waiting.

'I should really be going,' announced Thomas. 'The shift starts soon.'

'Are you back at work already?' Elizabeth seemed surprised. 'I would have thought a few days off would not have gone amiss. I shall speak to my father on this, a man needs time to mourn properly, for his own sake, let alone . . .'

'Elizabeth, it's my own doing. Your father suggested Willie and me have the rest of the week off, with pay. It was generous of him, and we thanked him for it, but we both felt we'd be better off back at work. It's what we know, keeps us busy. Anyway, we'd have felt guilty taking money and not working for it.'

'Well, I suppose it's up to you. Though I don't know what your union would say if you told them what you've just told me. I was under the impression that better conditions were one of the things you fought for, yet here you are turning them down. They're not like that in Northumberland; I hear that they're going on strike. The owners want a fifteen per cent reduction in the sliding scale, but the men'll not have it.'

'Yes,' said Thomas, 'but exactly the same'll happen this time as did in '77 and '83. They'll stay out for a while, then they'll have to go back on the owners' original terms or worse. Anyway, it won't happen here, your father pays well above minimum rates. And besides, I'm not in the union.'

'You're not in the union?'

'No. Nor Willie. Nor most of the others, leastways the underground lads. Even at the last pit I was at there were only about, let's see, half the lads in the union, and the conditions there were far worse than anything here. Lower pay as well, and I already told you about the houses. We just accepted it.'

'But surely,' said Elizabeth, exasperation suddenly to the fore in her voice, 'surely if something's wrong it makes sense that you try to change it. I thought that was the whole point in combining together in a union, to improve matters?'

'Yes,' acknowledged Thomas, surprised at the sudden turn in the conversation, 'but within limits. There's no point in trying to make things better if the improvements you get mean the pit has to close down. Or men have to be laid off. Or your work targets get so high that you have to do the job dangerously. You end up worse than when you started, no roof over your head, no food for your bairns.'

'So you're actually on the side of the employers? You're saying that they know best what they can and can't afford to do with their pits and their workers and their workers' families, so there's no point in joining a union because, even with the strength they'd have in combining, the workers would have to agree with the employers about everything.'

'No,' said Thomas, 'that's not what I'm saying at all. And why this talk about unions all of a sudden, and being on the side of the employers? After all, it's your Dad owns the pit!' Thomas could not hide his anger at his motives being questioned, while Elizabeth seemed unaware that Thomas was in any way upset. Her voice became more authoritative, her manner more like that of a schoolmistress.

'My father owning the pit is irrelevant Thomas. It doesn't alter the fact that you, and the men you work with, and hundreds of thousands of other men and women throughout the country, have a huge amount of power in your hands ...'

'Power?' spat Thomas, exasperated. 'Power? We've got no power at all, our lives aren't our own to control, even if we combine in unions. Power lies in the hands of those with money, and position, and authority, not with the likes of us!'

'You're wrong Thomas! That's the whole problem, you and the rest of the working class can't think beyond your own little circle. Don't restrict yourself to this pit. Don't limit your thoughts to pits in Durham, or even the northern coalfield. Think nationally, and then move beyond mining to ship-building, chemicals, the railways, iron and steel manufacturing, the whole lot! *That's* where the power lies! In the hands of the workers in all these industries who could, if they would only rid themselves of their in-bred parochialism and subservience, take real control of their lives!'

'Does your father know?' asked Thomas quietly, firmly.

'Does he know what?' answered Elizabeth.

'Does he know his daughter's a – what do you call it – a socialist?' He might have been swearing as he spoke the last word.

'Yes, he knows. I've discussed the way I feel with him. We've talked about Robert Owen and Carlyle and Mills and the rest of them. He might not agree with everything I say but at least he had the decency to listen to me and to think about what I was saying, which,' she hurried on, the words rushing from her mouth, 'is far more than you seem capable of doing!'

'Oh Mrs Kearton, I can listen! I can listen alright, and what I hear is a theoretician. What I hear is someone who's never had to do a day's work in her life. What I hear is someone who's had time to sit down and read good books, and if she didn't have them, well, she could afford to go out and buy them. I hear someone who's talked long and hard to others exactly like herself and formulated elegant proposals in bloodless, condescending debates about working men and the "power" they have, someone who talks about the pride and honour of workers while sipping glasses of sherry and stuffing their faces with food earned from the sweat and toil of those very same workers. Let me tell you something, if one of me marras came to me talking the way you've been doing I'd laugh at him, I swear to God I would. But I know none of them would do that. You see, we know what we can and can't do. We know the limitations we have. And we know that upper class socialists like you are living in a different world to the one we occupy!'

'That's not true, Thomas, I know how hard ...'

'You don't know anything lass, nothing at all. When have you ever been down a pit?'

'I haven't.' The words came slowly, grudgingly.

'Exactly! And you'll never know what I'm talking about until you do go down. Look, you won't hear me and Willie and the rest of the lads talking about work. You won't hear us going on about how much we've hewed, or what conditions are like down the pit. Even here, even in a good pit – and believe me this one is good, one of the best – we don't talk about it. It's a job. It lets us live. But it's so bloody awful at times we'd all go mad if we thought overmuch about it, or you'd never get us underground again. That preacher the other day, he was fond of the sound of his own voice, that's for certain, but what he said was right. Pitmen are a breed apart, and they're bound to each other because they depend on each other not only for their livings but for their lives as well. It doesn't need a bloody dance to do that, that's nothing to do with it at all. Put a hundred strangers down a pit to get coal and by the end of the day you'll have a community working together. And that's why it galls me so much to hear you talking about unions and "combining" and the "power of the workers". You know nothing lass, despite all your book-born knowledge and your endless talking, you know nothing!'

Elizabeth was silent. She had never heard such passion in Thomas's voice, had never seen such anger, albeit well-contained. His eyebrows had grown together, his finger had punctuated his sentences, his words had been emphasised with quiet deliberation. And she could not counter his arguments. She had formed her opinions from hearsay, well-informed admittedly, but hearsay none the less.

'You're right Thomas,' she said. 'I have no practical knowledge of this matter, though I still fervently believe in it. Will you teach me?'

Thomas's face contorted into a question mark.

'Will I teach you what?'

'Teach me about working in a pit. So I can speak with experience.'

'I told you, there's nothing I can teach. You need to ...' He stopped.

'Oh no, I can see the way you're thinking! You don't want me to take you underground?'

'Why not?'

'Because it's dangerous. And because I get paid for working, not for looking to the whims of some, some ...'

'Yes? You're not normally at a loss for words.'

'Alright then, the whims of a spoiled child who thinks that because her father owns the pit she can do whatever she likes with it and with those who work in it!'

Elizabeth was almost amused by Thomas's outburst, and even more convinced that she should find out first hand how he and his fellow pitmen worked.

'Surely,' she mocked 'you're not going back on your argument now. How can you accuse me of being naive, of having no practical experience to back up my social theories, then deny me the opportunity of gaining that practical experience?'

It was Thomas's turn to think. He could not, in all honesty, find a way to oppose Elizabeth without abandoning his own reasoning. This did not mean, however, that he would allow her to defeat him with good grace. Why he felt

threatened at the prospect of her accompanying him underground, even if only for one day, he could not say. But his
emotions were clear in his disgruntled tone.

'Alright then. I'm on early shift tomorrow. Be there, at the
pit-head, on time. You'd better clear it with your father, but
knowing your silver tongue I can see there'll be no problem
with that. And you'd better get him to tell the overman.
Wear old clothes; you'd be best in trousers. If you're not
there I'll go without you and there won't be another
chance.'

He turned and walked away without saying goodbye, but
even the surliness of his departure could not take the smile
from Elizabeth's lips.

She had hoped to escape to her room without being noticed.
The voices coming from the library were those of her father
and Sir Charles Makemore, and as she paused outside the
double doors she considered whether a swift rush or a
delicate glide would be the best means of secretively passing
by. Neither option was, however, put into action. She failed
to noticed the maid approaching with teapot, cups and tray,
and the crisp, 'Afternoon Miss Elizabeth' was heard by
those within.

'Ah, Elizabeth, do come in,' came John Waterhouse's deep
voice. 'We are in desperate need of your assistance.' She
shrugged to herself and strode into the room.

Sir Charles appeared to be sober, although the empty
glass in his hand and his urgent glances at the decanters on
the sideboard boded ill for the future. Her father was
studying a sheaf of papers; although they were not in his
hand she could see his writing in the margins. She curtsied
to Sir Charles who grunted in reply; she kissed her father
gently on the cheek.

'Sir Charles and I have been discussing the arrangements
for the wedding,' he announced wearily. 'I had hoped, given

the circumstances of the occasion, that it might be a small affair in the village church, with guests returning here afterwards and perhaps a celebratory ball in the evening. We haven't really had the opportunity to entertain here yet, have we my dear?' Elizabeth shook her head.

'I have, however, been out-voted in this. Both Margaret and Henry were insistent that they required a more grand affair, and to that extent Henry has, a little presumptuously on his part, made enquiries of the cathedral in Newcastle. With a reception in one of those large hotels in Grey Street. Margaret has expressed her approval of this course of action, and I must confess I feel unable to gainsay her wishes. Sir Charles has brought along a most,' he coughed slightly, 'concise guest list which numbers some two hundred and fifty souls in total. A small number of these are mutual acquaintances and will, therefore, reduce our own list. The organisation of the wedding at such short notice is, however, quite a demanding task and I was wondering if you might . . .?'

'Of course father, how could I refuse. And I'm sure,' she turned to smile sweetly at Sir Charles whose eyes were about to close, 'that Sir Charles will be equally willing to devote some time to the arrangements.'

'Oh, yes, quite,' blustered the old man. 'I'd love to help, of course! There is only one,' he held up his hand, forefinger and thumb almost touching, his eye pinched to peer through the gap, 'small problem. Business. I've to be in London in a week's time, won't be back until the day before the wedding. Damned shame really. I would have loved to help more, what with Henry being my only son, but alas, time is so precious. I have tried to do what I can, of course, hence the paperwork your father is perusing at this instant. It's not just a list of guests, oh no! It has suggestions – proposals only I should add, no obligation – for the content of the meal. Hymns to be sung. Types of carriages, where to get them, hiring of a train for the journey to and from Newcastle, rooms to be provided at the hotel, that sort of thing. Just to help out, of course.'

'Yes,' said John Waterhouse with a sigh. 'I'm still wading through these suggestions. I must say Sir Charles, given the short notice it's a remarkable achievement of yours to have this information committed to paper. It's almost as if it had been prepared in advance.'

'Really? I can assure you John – I may call you John? After all, we're almost related now – that none of this was discussed until Henry brought me the good news a few days ago. Yes, I'll admit that I've been thinking about Henry marrying for some time, not someone specific of course. But I'm an old man, in my spare moments I may have jotted down an idea or two. And as I say, there's no obligation.' He twisted uncomfortably in his chair and Elizabeth suspected it may have been with embarrassment.

'Would you excuse me John, I just need to ...' He stood up, headed for the door.

'It's this cold weather, plays hell with the bladder.' He left the room at a sprightly pace surprising in one who claimed to suffer so badly from old age and gout.

John Waterhouse shook his head, smiled at Elizabeth with disbelief. She moved to his side to read the papers over his shoulder.

'Has Henry been engaged before?' he asked Elizabeth.

'I've no idea. But now that you mention it, Abigail said something to me a few months ago about a girl in Consett Henry was supposed to have been seeing. I can't quite remember the details but she was the daughter of a merchant in the town, reasonably prosperous but well below Henry's social standing. It seems she suddenly disappeared, then her parents moved away as well. Said they'd come into some money. No talk of engagements. I can ask Abigail for more details if you want. She's still down at the

Armstrongs'. Mary Armstrong's looking after her. She and Willie are to be wed, or so I hear. I'd like to find some way of keeping her in employment if you don't mind, she's a little wary of returning after Margaret's upset.'

John Waterhouse's attention had returned to the papers before him.

'Mm? Oh yes, of course, find something for her. And there's no need to ask her anything else of Henry's alleged paramour, the past is sometimes best left untouched. I'm damned sure, mind you, that Sir Charles's list here is the result of much thought, not all his, over a considerable period of time; and I'm equally sure that I shall disregard a large part of its contents. I think we must discuss this some other time, I can hear him coming back. Margaret was wanting to speak to you as well, something about wanting you to be matron of honour, though don't tell her I told you so. She and Henry are around somewhere behaving like a pair of doves, you might want to see if you can find her.' Sir Charles lumbered back into the room and made straight for the sherry decanter.

'By all means, help yourself to a glass before you leave Sir Charles. I've been looking at your, ah, proposals and I'm afraid to say that I feel them to be a little over-indulgent. Oh, Elizabeth, when you find Margaret could you tell Henry that his father will be going shortly. Now where was I? Oh yes, fifty carriages? Is that not going a touch too far?' The voices faded as Elizabeth climbed the stairs to the first floor and headed for Margaret's room. She knocked loudly, waited, then entered. The room was empty, the fire unlit. Margaret was fond of her comfort, and it was safe to assume in the lack of a fire that she had not been there since rising that morning. Elizabeth stalked the corridor again, saw the short, squat bustling figure of the housekeeper, Mrs Dougherty. She, it transpired, had seen nothing of the young couple all morning. Elizabeth thought carefully. She had walked most of the grounds within the past two hours, both with and without Thomas, and she had not seen her sister. She and Henry had left the library an hour before Elizabeth's arrival but had been seen by no-one. There remained only one place inside the building where they might remain in comparative privacy; the nursery wing.

When the house was built, before John Waterhouse's most recent extensions, it had been decided that the arrival of children would not result in any inconvenience to their parents. The nursery and its attached bedrooms were contained in a wing to the main house, attached by the slenderest of bones, the thinnest of muscles. The main corridor of the house had rooms to either side. Library, study, a small ballroom, music room. One door, however, led only into a further narrow corridor, its draughty windows glazed with obscure glass. Some thirty feet long, at its far end another door opened onto the nursery itself. It had never been used as such. No children had ever graced the Hall, and the brightly painted walls had dulled with the passage of time. A three-legged wooden horse lay drunk in one corner; all other toys had long since disappeared. A basin in the room upstairs had leaked, and water had marked the ceiling with black stains. It was as if the nursery had been crying. Elizabeth ignored the sadness and climbed the stairs at the far end.

The space above was divided into four. A long corridor ran the full length of the wing, windows on one side, three doors on the other. The first of these led to a bedroom for girls; the second to the nanny's room; the third to the boys' bedroom. Elizabeth listened carefully as she stood at the top of the stairs. She could hear a faint noise but could not tell its source. She considered calling her sister's name but decided against it. If Margaret and Henry were doing what she imagined them to be doing (and she could think of no reason why they should be here unless they wanted privacy to make love) then she had no wish to disturb them in a moment of passion. She bent her ear to each of the doors in turn. Only at the third could she hear any sound from within. She retraced her steps. The door to the middle room was locked, but the girls' bedroom was open. She entered quickly and quietly, skirted the bed (the only other item of furniture in the room was a large wardrobe) and tried the connecting door to the nanny's room; that too was open.

The curtains in the nanny's room had been closed and it was dark. Fearful that she might trip, Elizabeth waited for her eyes to become accustomed to the darkness. The walls must have been made deliberately thin because the noise coming from the room beyond was now much louder; although the words were lost, the voices were undoubtedly those of Margaret and Henry. She crept to the door and softly turned the handle, hoping that the occupants of the room would be too involved in each other to notice the slight sound it made. A gentle push showed that this too was locked. Elizabeth looked around the room for the key. In the dim light she could make out an empty table and ramshackle chair, a single bed without sheets, a bookcase, wardrobe and chest of drawers. Light patches on the wallpaper outlined those places where pictures had hung. On two of the walls, the ones adjoining the children's bedrooms, two circular plaques had been left at head height. No more than four inches in diameter, they appeared to be plain, painted pieces of wood. Only when Elizabeth reached out to touch one and found that it moved did she realise what they were. Peepholes, allowing the nanny to check the children without going into their rooms! She gingerly lifted the one to the boys' room and raised her eye to it. She could see nothing but a dim darkness, although she could now hear Margaret's voice.

'Henry, I'm cold!' Elizabeth recognised the poor lost-little-girl tone Margaret used to such good effect.

'Henry, please will you get me my coat. Please?'

Footsteps approached her and Elizabeth started back as light suddenly stabbed at her eye. She blinked quickly then returned to the spy-hole to see Henry Makemore's retreating figure. He was dressed in long-johns, nothing else, and was carrying Margaret's coat; it had obviously been hung over the other end of the spy-hole. He threw it casually at Margaret who was sitting shivering on the bed. She quickly wrapped herself inside it; Henry sat at the foot of the bed, head in hands. Margaret looked at his back for a while then shuffled across to press herself against his back, her arms around his chest. He seemed oblivious to her actions.

'It's alright,' she said. 'It doesn't matter, there'll be other times, lots of other times. Please Henry, don't worry about it.' There was no reply.

'I'm sure it must happen quite often. I mean, neither of us are very experienced at this type of thing, are we?' Silence again.

'I'll do everything I can to help. I can ask Elizabeth if you want, she's been married, she might know if there's anything we can . . .'

'Will you hell!' exclaimed Henry whirling around, pushing Margaret away from him. 'And what will you say? "Excuse me sister dear, Henry and I were playing stallion and mare recently. At least, we should have been, but he couldn't manage it. He couldn't perform. What would you advise?" And what do you think she would say? Do you think she'd offer to come along and watch? Perhaps give me a hand? Don't you dare mention me to your insufferable sister!'

'I'm sorry.' Margaret's voice was small, contrite. She reached out to touch Henry's shoulder; he flinched.

'I'm sorry Henry, please forgive me.' Again there was no response. Elizabeth could see Henry clearly. He was staring straight ahead of him, his hands clenched in his lap. Behind him Margaret appeared almost distraught, her eyes wide, her hair falling over her face. She pushed it to one side and, as it fell forward again, she began to cry. If she had hoped to soften Henry by this, even to gain sympathy, she was mistaken.

'And you needn't start that whining and snivelling like some soft little lap-dog hoping for some attention!' Henry's voice was as harsh as his words.

'Just leave me alone Margaret. Get dressed. Go away.' Her clothes were scattered around the room and Margaret trudged slowly from one item to the next, lumping them together, sniffing as she did. She muttered to herself as she walked.

'What was that?' asked Henry.

'Nothing,' came the sullen reply.

'It wasn't nothing. What did you say?'

Margaret found courage again. She dropped the clothes and stood to face Henry. Her coat fell open, she put her hands on her hips and began to berate her fiancé.

'I said I don't know why I agreed to marry you! You're nice to me in public when everyone can see you but when we're alone you're rude and bad-tempered. When I try to be pleasant to you you call me names, you tell me to go away. Is it worth us getting married?'

Henry forced a smile to his face.

'My, you're lovely when you're roused. And such a fetching outfit!'

He looked around, searching for his clothes. Margaret, incensed at being ignored, took him by the shoulders and made him face her.

'Henry, I'm being serious. Do you really want to marry me?'

'Good God woman, have you no brains at all inside that head? Why do you think I'm here in this freezing cold room, half-dressed, talking inanities at you. It's because I want to marry you. Can't you even understand that?'

Margaret had always had a temper, as Elizabeth had found to her cost in the past. Even from a distance of over twenty feet Elizabeth could see the red mark her hand left on Henry's cheek. He was not slow to respond, grabbed her by the arms, threw her onto the bed and straddled her. She was at him in an instant, raining blows to his head and body, and for a moment he was too taken by surprise to protect himself. The pain of a punch in the eye brought his arms up, and his hands grasped at her wrists and held them tight, pushed her back down onto the bed. She spat at him.

'You strumpet!' he gasped, wiping the spit from his face with his arm. 'I've a good mind to send you back to ...' He stopped. Margaret's glance had travelled from his eyes and down his body; Henry too was staring at the erection which had pushed aside the cotton of his pants, was now resting on Margaret's stomach.

'Oh Henry,' she whispered, 'I knew you could manage.'

Henry seemed surprised. He looked up, then down again, then back up.

'Let me go now,' said Margaret. 'Let me help you.'

'No!' he shouted. 'No! Fight me! Fight me!'

He held her wrists more tightly, moved his knees to prise her legs apart, bent his head to bite fiercely at her breasts and nipples. She began to struggle, and Elizabeth had difficulty in telling if this was real or not. She broke free and reached down, guided him into her with a groan, then ran her finger nails down his back in a line of long red welts

'Harlot!' he screamed and pounded against her and into her; she pushed up against him, gyrating her hips, freeing her other hand to pull his head down to hers, darting her tongue into his mouth. He pulled away, took his weight on his hands and began to move faster. Margaret began to pant, moaned in time with his thrusting. They were both making a great deal of noise, and Elizabeth suddenly found herself wondering why she was there. Was she becoming a voyeur? Watching other people making love seemed to be happening too frequently, yet the situation was not one she sought. She left as she entered, quietly, but with the vision in her mind of Henry Makemore as he made love to her sister. There had been no ecstasy there, no joy, no love. Instead, as he had stared straight at her spy-hole, Elizabeth had seen only distaste and disgust embroidered boldly on his noble face.

Chapter Eleven

Bid me discourse, I will enchant thine ear,
Or, like a fairy trip upon the green,
Or, like a nymph, with long, dishevell'd hair
Dance on the sands, and yet no footing seen:
    Love is a spirit all compact of fire,
    Not gross to sink, but light, and will aspire.

                  'Venus and Adonis'
              (William Shakespeare)

Thomas enjoyed working foreshift. In summer it felt good, providing he had been able to take to his bed early the night before, to be up fresh with the dawn walking the path to the pit-head for five o'clock. And in winter there was something reassuring in stepping out into the darkness and seeing other shadowy figures moving silently on their way up the hill, whispered greetings helping guide him on his way. There was, whatever the season, optimism brought by the knowledge that at the end of the shift, even after bathing and cleaning up, the whole of the afternoon would be his to spend in the open, away from the claustrophobic confines of his job. But this morning brought only a deepening doubt of his wisdom in inviting Elizabeth to join him at work. It was Willie who had sown the first seeds of Thomas's confusion.

'We might have somebody watching us work today,'

Thomas told his brother as they left the house.

'Oh aye? And who might that be? Not some inspector I hope, checking we're working properly and safely. Or some manager trying to make us go faster, I'm having none of that.'

'No, it's neither of those.' Thomas said no more.

'Well come on then, out with it man! Who is it?'

'It's somebody who wants to know more about mining. They've led a sheltered life, and they think it would be best to further their education by watching us work.'

'They? I thought you said it was one person?'

'Aye. Aye, I did. Anyway, she wants to watch . . .'

'She? Oh no Thomas, don't tell me. It's that woman again, Elizabeth. She can't seem to keep away from you, she's even following you down the pit now! I don't suppose Mary was very happy to hear about this?'

'Aye, you're right,' sighed Thomas, 'it's Elizabeth. And Mary hasn't said anything because I've not said anything to her and I'd be obliged if you'd keep the same silence. And don't blame me, it wasn't my idea.'

'Then whose idea was it? And why didn't you say no? It's not that I dislike the lass, goodness knows she's been good to us with Dad and the kids, and I know Abi likes her. But for some reason Mary's worried about her and you when you get together – admit it Thomas, you do seem to get on well with her, you've said it yourself that you like her – and I don't want to see Mary upset. Why's she coming anyway?'

Thomas explained about meeting her the day before without mentioning that they had spent time alone together in the summerhouse. He told Willie about their argument.

'It was you then Thomas,' said Willie angrily. 'It was you. You as good as told her to find out what it was like down a pit. How do you expect her to react to that? I don't know, for a grown man you seem to know very little about the way women's minds work.' Willie shook his head. 'Never mind, if her Dad's got any sense he's probably told her that a pit's no place for women, not any more. With a bit of luck she won't even turn up.'

Willie's prediction seemed to have every chance of being correct. Amongst the crowds at the pit-head there was no sign of Elizabeth, though the brothers craned their necks for her slight frame amongst the taller, thickset bodies of their companions. Men came up to them and patted them on the shoulders, expressed their sorrow and sympathy at Tommy's death. Others could be heard talking of football matches or pigeons, pigs and gardens and whippets. Some had copies of newspapers, were holding them open in the dim light of the gas mantles, reading aloud stories of the Northumbrian miners about to strike. The winding gear above their heads was spinning, driven by the hiss and roar of the steam pump in the engine house away to their right. The cages arrived at ground level with a rattle and clang of machinery, metal barriers being slid to one side as the occupants hurried black into the chill morning air. Names were thrown backward and forward.

'How-do then Matty!'

'Johnny lad, rather you than me!'

'I've been keeping your bed warm Si, and your wife!'

'You're welcome Jack, I prefer yours to mine anyway.'

'What's the news Billy?'

'Nowt new lads, nowt new.'

'Has wor lass pupped yet? Has anybody heard owt?'

'No, not yet Davie, not yet. Midwife's round though, you'd best hurry!'

'Did you hear about …' 'Is anybody goin' down town tomorrow or …' 'Where's that bloody son of mine, he's never …'

'It doesn't look like she's coming Thomas,' said Willie as he and his brother joined the queue for the cages.

'Probably just as well,' came the reply. 'I can't imagine

what she'd do with herself anyway. I mean, it's not as if she's going to do any hewing, is it?'

The cages were tiered, some twenty feet tall altogether and divided into four separate compartments. Each held some twenty men, ten on each row of dirty wooden seats which were folded back when the cages were to be used for bringing wagons, both full and empty, to and from the shaft bottom. All four cages could be filled or emptied at the same time by means of steps, ramps and platforms which allowed access to the bottom and third tier cages from one side, the top and second tier from the other. Thomas and Willie chose the top tier, as was their habit, and watched the other men file into their places.

'Come on now lads,' urged the overman, 'get a move on. Let's have your tags.' Each man had a numbered tag which was hung on the appropriate hook on a board above the overman's desk. On the wall beside this was a number of buttons connected to lights and bells, a display mirrored in the winding man's room over in the engine house. By this means messages could be passed ordering the great steel cables to be wound or unwound round the huge drum of the engine.

'Everybody ready lads?' asked the overman. There was a chorus of ayes and the red button was pressed twice; the cages lurched as the clutch was let slip.

'Hang on man,' said a rough voice from the top tier, 'There's two boys on their way in, look at them run!'

'They'll have to be quick then,' said the overman, 'I've already passed the message.'

'Twopence on the biggun!' shouted another to general laughter as the cages swung slightly. There was indeed a disparity in the sizes of the two figures hurtling along the slick cobbbles and through the gate, but the smaller of the two, holding grimly onto his cap, seemed to be making up for his lack of height with a surfeit of determination. Elbows pumping he skidded into the winding hall and headed for the cages; his companion, breath clouding the air, appeared to have given up. The bottom cage had already disappeared, the second was on its way down the shaft, and the overman decided that the boy would be too late to enter any of the others. He shut the gate, barring further entry, but the boy avoided his outstretched arms (to the cheers of those watching), slid under the barrier and ran on. Cage three had gone, but without breaking his stride the boy leaped for the gap in cage four, ended up lying on the floor between the two rows of pitmen.

'Did he manage it?' came a shout from below.

'Aye, he managed it, the idiot,' said Thomas, reaching down to pull the boy into a space beside him.

'You could have killed yourself then,' he admonished. 'You need a damn good hiding lad!'

'I know,' came the soft reply. 'But then I had something to aim for, didn't I. A day down the pit watching you work.'

The face which looked up at him was familiar. Elizabeth had appeared after all.

'Were you hoping I wouldn't come?'

'Yes.'

'Oh!'

'Well, what did you expect me to say? I mean, for years and years they've been trying to get women out of pits and you want to come down! It doesn't make sense.'

'Yes it does, you said it yourself. How can I talk about working down a mine when I haven't seen for myself what it's like. So here I am, whether you like it or not, and here I stay, for a day's work at least.'

The hasty whispers which formed the conversation ceased and the cage continued to fall in dark silence. Two lamps were hung at each level of the cage; when her eyes became accustomed to their dim light Elizabeth could see the other passengers around her. They sat in quiet contemplation, their own unlit lamps on the floor between their feet. They all seemed to have adopted the same uniform. A flat cap and grubby handkerchief knotted around the neck; collarless shirt, for one or two a serge waistcoat or knitted pullover, topped by a torn and dirty jacket. Although some wore their trousers long, particularly the older men, the majority seemed to have cut the legs off just above the knee. Their socks covered their lower legs up to the knee, and their boots covered their ankles. Elizabeth felt out of place. Her clothes belonged to one of the stable lads (she hoped to have them washed and replaced before he noticed that they were missing) and although they smelled a little of the animals their owner cared for, they were in far better repair than those of her companions. She felt that all eyes were on her, that she would be recognised and thus prevented from carrying out her self-imposed task. She lowered her head.

'What did your father say?' Thomas whispered.

'I didn't ask him,' she replied. 'He was too busy to be concerned with this. Anyway, he would have said yes.'

Thomas raised his eyes and muttered. Elizabeth thought that the words were 'Bloody Hell!'

The cage slowed then juddered to a halt. Elizabeth made as if to stand up but felt Thomas's hand on her leg pushing her back down.

'Bottom level first,' he admonished. 'There's not enough room for all four to unload together.' After a few seconds the cage moved once more, then again a few seconds later. Thomas jerked his head to one side and Elizabeth followed him out.

'Willie,' said Thomas, 'we've got a new boy with us today. Thinks he might be wanting to take up a career in coal-mining. Come and say hello.'

Willie sauntered across, a welcoming smile on his face.

The smile disappeared and he shook his head as he recognised Elizabeth.

'You must be mad, both of you!' he said. 'It's your own business though, nowt to do with me. Come on, let's get some work done.' He set off down a brick-framed tunnel, chasing the other shadows who had already set off for the face. Thomas made as if to follow, but was restrained by Elizabeth's arm on his sleeve.

'I don't think Willie's very happy,' she said.

'You're a good judge of people's emotions,' said Thomas. His sarcasm went unnoticed.

'There's a breeze! Thomas, I can feel a breeze!'

'Aye? And what's so strange about that?'

'Well, we're hundreds of feet under the ground. No natural breeze should come down that far.'

'You really were telling the truth when you said you knew nothing about mining, weren't you! I tell you, I'll get no work done today for teaching at this rate. Come on, I'll tell you while we're walking.'

He headed for the tunnel down which Willie had disappeared, pausing only to light his lamp.

'There's two shafts in this pit, in every other pit as well these days, though it wasn't always so. Only one's used for taking men and coal up and down, and even that's got plenty of room round the outside to let air past. The second shaft's to help with the ventilation, the stale air goes up one shaft, fresh air comes down the other. You can do the same with just one shaft, dividing it in two or three up the middle, but that's too dangerous. If anything happens to the shaft or anywhere around it in a single shaft pit then everyone's trapped underground.'

Elizabeth shuddered. She noticed that Thomas automatically hunched his shoulders as they entered the tunnel, that his head was within hairs of the ceiling. She, however, had no need to copy him.

'How do they get the fresh air down here?' she asked.

'Steam pump. It's a bit like the engine working the winding gear, but it's used only for getting good air down to the coal face. And then they use doors built across the mouths of tunnels, to make sure the good all goes where it's needed. It wasn't so long ago, mind you, that they circulated air by building a fire at the bottom of a shaft. Or at the top. Or even halfway up!'

They walked a little further in silence, Elizabeth looking around her at the limited scenery.

'Thomas, this isn't coal at the side of the tunnel. It seems to be a wall, built of brick.'

'Aye, it is.'

'But I thought that you dug through coal and left most of it behind to prop up the roof, like pillars? At least that's what I'd been told.'

'You can do that. Most other pits round here do it that way, that's the way Willie and me used to work. It's called "Bord and Pillar". Like you say, most of the coal's left behind, to start with at least, and the men work at lots of different places around the mine. Sometimes they're in pairs, or threes or fours even, but there's not usually a lot of room at each stall. We don't do that here. We work longwall.'

'Longwall.' Elizabeth appeared to savour the word, tasted it gently.

'And what does longwall mean?'

'Like it says, the coal's taken out from one long wall. Well, three actually, though they aren't all being worked at the same time.'

'But you just said that when they worked, what was it, pillar and stall?'

'Pillar and bord.'

'Quite, pillar and bord. When they work that way they have to leave lots of coal behind to stop the ceiling from falling down. How can they work a whole wall of coal without that happening?'

'You'll see. Listen, can you hear the noise? We're almost there.'

The end of the tunnel was lost in a haze of dust and a cacophony of grinding and screeching. Thomas yelled at Elizabeth.

'Stay beside me! The noise'll stop eventually, and the dust'll die down, but be careful! Your Dad'd throw me down the shaft if I went back to say that his daughter'd fallen into a cutter!' He marched foward again, Elizabeth clutching at the tails of his jacket.

The machine which was making the noise was a low, grey-black beast mounted on two tracks running parallel to the coal face. Thomas led Elizabeth towards its shuddering form and pointed over the top of it. She leaned forward but could see nothing but black dust, leaned further forward to find Thomas's hand grab the waistband at the rear of her trousers. This added support meant that she could see the rotating wheel cutting into the coal seam at floor level, could make out the teeth as they bit through the soft rock, and the slow movement of the chassis along the track. Thomas pulled her upright and they walked on, past some men shovelling coal into trucks, past others wielding pneumatic drills. Opposite the coal face Elizabeth noticed tunnels heading back towards the shaft, some with railway tracks fixed to their floors, others without. At the mouth of one tunnel a pit pony stood, resting for a moment as its driver hitched it up to a full wagon. Thomas motioned Elizabeth to follow him down one of the tunnels.

'That's all new,' he said proudly, 'all that machinery's your Dad's idea. Production's way up above what we'd normally get, and we've done comparisons by having some of the lads work normally, on this face and the others. The machines beat them hands down.'

'But surely they cost far more?'

'True, a lot more. But they can work harder, longer hours than the men, and it means you don't need to have so many men working at the pit-face. So it's far safer as well.'

'So there are fewer jobs?' Thomas thought for a while.

'At the moment,' he conceded. 'Yes, less than there would have been. But once we start expanding the mine faster we'll be able to take on more men than we could ever have hoped for if we'd been hewing by hand.'

'Thomas, you're beginning to sound like a capitalist.' The miner felt that his employer's daughter was not being complimentary but could not find the words for a suitably stinging reply. Instead he continued with his lecture.

'Anyway, with longwall, especially in a new pit, they can organise things in whatever way they want. Here they started from the base of the shaft and worked their way outwards, building tool stores and stables first, and a machinery shop. They dig out along the face and as they go forwards they fill in the gap behind them with goaf. That's the rubble, the waste. They pack it in behind brick walls leaving tunnels for men and wagons to go along to get to the face. And it's always moving forward, the face. What's more, you can work three or four long faces all at once, if the coal's good enough.' As he spoke he gazed around him. 'Look, I'm sorry but I'll have to find Willie now, get some work done. You can watch. Don't wander off, there's lots of tunnels and tracks around and you could easily get lost. Come on.'

Willie was already at work. The cutter had chiselled a groove some two feet deep at the bottom of the coal face, and in doing so some coal had already fallen to the ground to make the groove v-shaped. Small lengths of timber had been forced into the neck of the 'v'.

'They don't look strong enough to hold that lot up,' said Elizabeth. Willie turned round, glowered at her. Abigail had returned to her duties at the Hall but came back to see Willie every evening and had reported that Margaret was refusing to speak to her. Although Elizabeth had done nothing to harm Abigail, had indeed been both sympathetic and polite, Willie was reluctant to allow the friendliness he had previously shown his master's daughter to come into conflict with the need he felt to protect his fianceé.

Willie was also concerned about Mary, was worried that she and his brother seemed unable to talk to each other of late. He was aware that Mary attached a large part of the blame for this to Elizabeth, though he had told her time after time that her anxieties were misplaced. After all, he had said, what man in his right mind, given the choice between you and that flat-chested, hard-faced old biddy, would do anything other than run after you? And he had put his arms around her, cuddled her, and had warned her that if his brother ever did wander then he, Willie Armstrong, would be first in line to offer her his worthless body and soul. To find the object of his suspicions and derision watching him work caused him more than a little annoyance, and he could not hide the aggravation in his voice when he spoke.

'They'll hold,' he growled, 'I put them there meself. They'll hold alright.'

'But what are they for?'

Willie raised his eyes, shook his head, exaggerating both movements to make sure that Elizabeth was aware of the disdain with which he treated her question.

'The cutters kirved the coal, and . . .'

'The cutters what?'

'Good grief woman, don't you know anything? Kirved! It's what we call under-cutting the seam there, so when we get at the coal it drops down automatically. And those bits of wood, they're sprags; they're to stop the coal from falling all at once. Not that it does that too often, but if it does go, if you see or hear one of the sprags breaking, you know it's

time to get back up one of the tunnels. Do you understand?'
Elizabeth nodded.

'Are you sure?' She nodded again, biting back the
accusations of rudeness and discourtesy which rose to her
lips. Instead she leaned back against the wall to watch the
brothers at work.

First they raked out the loose coal which had fallen into
the – what was it called, the kirve? – together with small
lumps which had flaked away from the face. This was
hurled into a waiting wagon, using wide-bladed shovels,
until the floor had been cleared along a twenty-foot length
of the face. Thomas explained as he worked.

'This,' he grunted 'is small coals. Not worth a lot, but we
can't get it mixed with the large stuff. Have to get it out of
the way.'

Next he and Willie examined the face, pointing out cracks
and small natural holes, marking some with a chalk cross, in
other places drawing lines. Willie hurried away to return in
only half a minute with a tall metal pole through which
there appeared to be poking a long drill-bit. Willie wedged
the pole, by means of a ratchet, between the floor and the
ceiling then commenced to turn the handle of the drill. The
bit ate its way into the soft coal.

'You won't see these for much longer,' said Thomas.
'Hand operated drills are on the way out. The cutter, that's
worked by compressed air, with the engine pump up at the
surface. We've already ordered some drills working the same
way.'

'Why is he drilling it? Wouldn't it be easier to hammer in
a wedge to make the coal fall?'

'Aye, it would, but he's not trying to make the coal fall.
He's boring a hole for blasting, and that's far quicker, in this
sort of seam, than hand-cutting. He'll do a few more holes
– see how quick he is? – and then we put in some of these
. . .' he reached into his pocket, brought out a wooden box

and carefully opened it '. . . to finish the job.' Elizabeth could see eight or ten rolls of red-brown, oily paper, like cigars smoothed with wax.

'Dynamite,' announced Thomas. Elizabeth pushed herself back against the wall.

'There's no need to worry, it won't go off. Not yet.' He lifted his head.

'What can you hear?'

'Nothing,' Elizabeth answered.

'Exactly. The cutter's been switched off. They've come to the end of the wall. What they do now is to wheel it into a tunnel up at the far end, so's it'll be safe. Now there's pitmen drilling holes up and down the whole length of the wall, just like Willie's doing, then they're packing the holes with these. Just hang on a minute, you'll see.'

Thomas watched Willie pull the drill away then inserted a cartridge of dynamite in each hole.

'Dynamite first, then a fuse and detonating cap, gently does it. Then we pack the rest of the hole with . . .' he looked around him, gestured at Willie, 'with anything handy, as long as it's not coal. Come on lad, there's some bits of brick over there, that'll do!' Willie handed him the shards of brick and stone which Thomas placed in the entrance to each hole then pushed firmly down towards the charge with a long copper rod. The job was soon finished.

'There was a time when you'd light the fuse then run like hell,' Thomas giggled. 'And many's the time I've been bowled head over heels by a charge going off too early.'

'Or it'd hang fire,' added Willie, attaching light metal wires to the head of each fuse, 'and you'd just think it was safe to go back, you'd start to move down the tunnel, you'd get to the corner, then BOOM!, the whole bloody thing'd go up in your face!'

Elizabeth looked at the two men. She thought at first that they might have been trying to frighten her, but closer

inspection of their faces, the way they moved, the tone of
their voices, suggested that they were looking forward to the
forthcoming explosion. From the other end of the wall came
three long blasts on a whistle; Thomas blew three blasts
back in return. From out of the dust appeared four pitmen
carrying long-handled picks. They ignored the brothers, dug
the picks under one of the rails which served as a track for
the mechanical cutter and heaved it from its moorings. They
then manhandled it until it was pressed against the wall
furthest from the face, did the same with the second rail, and
moved on.

'Friendly,' muttered Elizabeth. No-one heard her. Thomas
and Willie were now unwinding their coils of wire and
backing up the nearest tunnel.

'Come on then,' yelled Thomas, 'lend a hand. Grab those
shovels and picks, hoy them into the tub and push it back
along the track!' Elizabeth did as she was told, was proud to
find that she could move the empty wagon, albeit slowly and
with great effort. Suddenly that effort became less. She felt
that she must have reached the top of an incline until
Thomas's familiar voice came from the front of the wagon
where he had been pulling.

'That'll do then, it'll be alright here. Come on, follow me.'
She squeezed past the dirty wooden tub-sides, realised that
she must be just as dirty, and hurried after Thomas. He
turned left at one of the crossroads they had passed on the
way to the face, and when she turned the corner she found
him and the other face workers crouched in the tunnel.
Thomas motioned her to his side then returned to his work
connecting two wires to a small wooden box at his feet. This
done he nodded to Willie who blew two blasts on his whistle
while removing from an inner pocket a large watch. After a
minute he blew his whistle again, just once.

'Righto, lads,' said Thomas, 'here we go!' All of the men
bent down, some placed their hands over their ears; Eliz-

abeth copied them but kept watching Thomas. He turned the handle attached to the box, quickly, sharply, then pressed a button on top of the box. The effect was instantaneous. Elizabeth had expected an explosion and there was, truth to tell, a loud crack; but she felt rather than heard the fall of coal from the face, felt the earth beneath her tremble, felt the pressure of expelled air push at her ears until they ached, felt the attack of tiny particles of coal and rock on her face, felt the welcome rush of cool air back down the tunnel as the dust slowly settled around her. She lifted her head and found to her embarrassment that at some time during the previous few seconds she had grabbed at Thomas's sleeve and even now was holding it tightly.

'Five minutes!' shouted Thomas, gently unwrapping her fingers. He reached again into one of his capacious pockets to bring out a metal flask which he offered to her. She took it gratefully, unscrewed the cap and lifted it to her lips then lowered it to sniff gingerly at the contents.

'Water,' said Thomas, 'just water. No booze down a pit. Go on, have a sip. Not too much though, it's got to last us the whole shift. I doubt you've brought anything to eat or drink, have you?' Elizabeth shook her head.

'Here, have one of these then.'

He handed her a package wrapped in brown paper. Inside were four slices of dark brown bread; she took one and bit eagerly into it. She had had no breakfast that morning.

'What is it?' she mumbled, her mouth full of crumbs which tasted of strong flour and roast meat.

'Bread and dripping,' he answered, biting into his own portion. 'That'll put hairs on your chest!' After a few minutes he checked his watch. 'Righto then, back to work lads!' At his command each man clambered to his feet and the march back to the face began. The dust grew thicker, and the feeble light from each man's lantern served only to increase the opacity around them. When held above head

height the lamps gave each man a halo so out of place with
the surroundings that Elizabeth had to force back her
laughter. Later that day, soaking in her third bath, she
would reflect on that moment and concede that she had
been wrong. If there were angels (and she would usually be
willing to argue against that point) why should they not
inhabit those regions where the purity of nature had never
existed, where the world had been wrought by human
hands, where the environment was such that strength and
courage was demanded of all who ventured there? Surely
there was no more fitting place for an angel to dwell than in
the deepest and darkest of mines.

'Come on lad,' said a husky voice, 'shift your arse. There's
work to do around here, get a bloody tub down to the face!'
Elizabeth heard Thomas's laugh, felt a heavy boot make
firm contact with her behind.

'Why you …!' she began but was interrupted by Thomas's voice.

'It's alright Jack, he's helping me out today, just as a
favour for the boss. Mind you, so far the little waster's
proved himself to be a bit of an idle bugger. Still we'll soon
find out, eh? Go on then lad,' he nudged Elizabeth. 'Go and
fetch a tub, or you'll feel the point of my boot as well, and
it's bigger and harder than Jack's!' Elizabeth sulked off in
search of the correct tunnel, carrying a lantern with her,
sounds of laughter chasing her on her way. She tripped over
a rail and deduced that this was a good indication of the
tub's presence; even with the lamp she bumped into it before
she saw it. She pushed her way past it, felt over the top to
make sure that it wasn't full, then began the slow heave back
to the coal-face. Just when she knew that her arms would
fall from their sockets, just as the muscles in her legs were
beginning to tie themselves into knots, the wagon bumped
gently into the wooden buffers at the face.

'About bloody time too,' complained Willie. 'Come on then

lad, you might as well give a hand in loading it as well, Sammy'll be here to make the change in a couple of minutes.' He reached into the wagon and brought out two shovels, handed one to Elizabeth, and started to throw coals into the wooden walled vehicle. From the other side Elizabeth could hear Thomas doing the same, and she too felt obliged to join in. Her contribution was, she was sure, small; for every half shovel she lifted over the side boards the two men would pitch four or even five full of large, heavy lumps of black, viscous coal. Just as the first tub was filled, just as Elizabeth was feeling relief that she would be able to sit down for a while, a pony appeared. It was harnessed up to the full wagon and led away leaving another empty one in its place at the entry to the next tunnel down. Thomas and Willie moved smartly down to it, taking off their jackets and shirts as they went. They said nothing but looked back at her, as if willing her to give up, to plead the advantage of her weakness, her femininity. She stamped angrily after them, determined not to give way, and joined in the work again. Sweat smeared the dust on her face, ran down her back, and still she would not give in.

'Your lad's not such a bad 'un after all,' she heard the gruff voice say. She offered up a silent prayer to the Lord for the Jacks of this world.

'Perhaps,' was all Willie would offer.

'Mind you,' continued Jack's bass monotone. 'He'd get on a lot better if he'd take off his jacket and shirt.'

'You know,' said Willie as an impish grin (which even a layer of black dust could not hide) slid slyly over his face, 'I think you might be right there Jack. Aren't you hot lad? Go on, take your shirt off! Let's see those muscles you've been developing this morning!'

Elizabeth shook her head violently from side to side, went back to her shovel. She looked around but there was no sign of Thomas; her forward thrust was halted by a huge hand on her wrist.

'Look lad,' came Jack's stentorian tone, 'you'll be able to work far easier without all that on your back. Here. I'll give you a hand.'

He pulled at the jacket, grabbing at the collar from behind, and Elizabeth's arms were pulled backwards with the sleeves. At such an angle her arms were soon released and she spun round immediately. The man facing her was more than large. Where Thomas and Willie had had to lower their heads to avoid the roof this man would have had to bend double. He stood, knees bent, his thick arms hiding the lost jacket behind his back, his large stomach quivering with laughter.

Elizabeth put down her shovel and stared at the man. She knew now how David had felt facing Goliath, could appreciate Ulysses' fear on being confronted by Polyphemus.

'Please may I have my jacket back?' she asked politely.

'Oh my oh my!' laughed the giant. 'We do have a nice boy here, don't we! Willie me lad, I'm right jealous of you. Such a smart lad, such a well-spoken, polite lad, such a nice lad!'

'Come on Jack,' said Willie wearily, suddenly aware of the danger of his joke, 'you've had your fun. You've shown us all what a sense of humour you've got. Now give the lad his coat and we'll get some work done, eh?'

'That was a quick change of heart Willie Armstrong,' said the giant. 'You were all for a bit of fun a few minutes ago. I think the lad ought to pay a forfeit, to get his coat back like. I think he should come with me for a little while. I think the lad should do me a little favour. It wouldn't take long, and he'd get his coat back, and I'd be really grateful, like.'

'No Jack,' said Willie, looking over his shoulder, 'I don't think that would be a good idea.'

'I would like my coat back!' said Elizabeth firmly.

'Your coat? Why lad, you haven't even shown me your muscles yet! Come here!' He reached forward, his hand

moving with a speed which surprised both Elizabeth and
Willie, and grabbed the front of Elizabeth's shirt. He pulled
her towards him while his other arm snaked round to stop
Willie's advance. So intent was the big man on his first
quarry that he failed to notice how close Willie was to him.
What was intended (or so he would claim later, pleading his
innocence in the pub in Lanchester) was to push Willie
gently away; what was achieved was a very effective
jackhammer punch to the jaw which sent Willie quickly
down to the coaly floor. Elizabeth, calm until then, started
to flail about with her arms and legs, to kick and punch, but
she made no contact. Jack, still laughing, hooked his finger
down the front of her shirt and flicked it downwards. It
ripped all of the buttons away, pulled the tails up from the
trousers, exposed Elizabeth's chest to the eyes of the brawny
miner. She stood still, breathing heavily; he looked at her,
head on one side.

'There you are then!' he mumbled. 'Don't know what all
the fuss was about. Nice little chest you've got there lad,
nothing to be ashamed of. Bit puny I suppose, but working
down here'll soon build some muscles. And don't worry,
you'll soon grow some hairs on it, you'll see. Now about this
little favour I was going to . . .'

'Jack! Jackie Benson! Now what are you up to?' The big
man drew to one side as Thomas pushed past.

'What the hell's been going on here?' asked Thomas, his
eyes taking in Willie's groaning body, staring hard at
Elizabeth.

'Tuck yourself in lad,' he muttered.

'It were just a bit of fun boss!' said Jackie, 'I didn't mean
no harm! Willie just, he sort of walked into me fist!'

Thomas bent to help his brother to his feet, slapped his
cheeks gently, looked into his eyes.

'Can you speak Willie?' he asked. Willie nodded, blinking.

'Well? What happened? Was it an accident?'

'No, it damn-well wasn't a bloody accident!' Willie shook his head and stared at Jack Benson. 'That stupid bastard was trying to get Miss . . .'

'It was an accident!' Elizabeth butted in. 'Mr Benson was making a joke, having some fun, and Willie misunderstood. He thought Mr Benson was harming me and he stepped forward to help. Mr Benson hit him, but it was an accident, I'm sure of it. There's no harm done, just a little pride been damaged.' Elizabeth's glance pleaded with Willie to agree with her; he nodded slowly, unwillingly, and sat down to rub his jaw.

'Go on then Jackie, on your way,' Thomas jerked his head at the big man, 'and we'll be having no more trouble with you this week, or else!' He turned back to Elizabeth and his brother as the burly miner ambled away.

'I've seen pit props with more brains than that,' he said.

'Aye,' mumbled Willie, pushing his chin out and poking it. 'But he's a damn site more solid than a pit prop!'

'What really happened then?' asked Thomas. Elizabeth, acknowledging Willie's aching jaw, explained.

'I thought it might come out,' she finished, 'who I really was that is, if there were any formal complaint. And I didn't want to get you into trouble for having me down here. I'm sorry.'

'Don't apologise to me,' said Thomas. 'It's him you should be saying sorry to!' He pointed at Willie. 'It's him you should be thanking as well. You haven't heard of Jackie Benson, have you?' Elizabeth shook her head.

'Jackie's the biggest, strongest man in the pit, probably in any pit round here. He can do the work of two men or more, but he's, well, he's just a little strange.'

'How strange?'

'A little.'

'How little? Tell me Thomas.' Beneath the black dust

Elizabeth was sure she could see a reddening of Thomas's neck.

'Well, it's like this. His wife died a few years ago. Cholera I think he told me it was, they were living down by the river. He was devoted to her, swore he would never look at another woman. And he's kept his word. The only thing is, he needs his release. He needs to be ... cared for. He needs someone to help him achieve satisfaction, to – I can't quite think how to explain to you – to do something for him, to...'

'For Christ's sake Thomas,' interrupted Willie, his speech still not back to normal, 'say what you mean. He likes somebody, preferably a young lad, to stick his hand down his trousers and play with him!'

'Oh.' There was silence for a while.

'I hope you're not shocked,' said Thomas. Elizabeth said nothing.

'We warn the lads to keep out of his way, but some of them look out for him. He pays them, if they don't mind, and he keeps on working hard, well, there's nothing we can do. Besides, we all know him. He's not that bad really.' Still silence.

'Are you alright? Do you want me to take you out?' Elizabeth came round, as though from a trance.

'No,' she said. 'There's no need for that. I'm alright, and I'll feel a bit more secure when I get this damn jacket on again.' She reached down to pick up the garment, shrugged her way into it.

'Come on then, let's get back to work,' she urged. 'I don't want to be accused of slacking.' She drove her shovel into the coal, then stopped.

'He didn't even notice,' she said.

'What?' asked Thomas.

'Oh, nothing. I don't suppose that Mr Benson has poor eyesight?'

'Not so far as I know. Why?'

'He didn't notice. He ripped open my shirt, and he stared at me. And he didn't even notice that I wasn't a boy.' She shrugged, Thomas smiled, and they returned to their work.

Each time Elizabeth saw the coal climb to the brim of the wagon, each time she felt able to slow the rate at which she threw the black lumps over the side boards, Willie would heave it away and Thomas would beckon her on to the next empty truck. The ground was still strewn with coal, and Thomas told her that the fall had been a good one. There would be no need to blast again on that shift, and that meant greater production and a greater bonus.

'You work in twos or threes, perhaps four at most in other pits, and the talleyman keeps notes of how much each team produces. The more coal a team gets, the more money they get. The trouble is, there are some places in a pit where it's easy to get coal, and others where it's slow work, difficult work. If it's a narrow seam you could spend the whole shift lying on your back in a couple of inches of water. Normally you draw lots, to see who works where, but that's open to cheating. And how you divide your pay up inside your team, that's up to you and your marras to decide. But here it's different, bonus is worked out for the whole shift together. It means everybody's working for everybody else, so there's no slacking. After all, it's one thing for a manager to tell you to get a move on, but when it's your marra, well you know you're doing him and everyone else out of their money. Come on, it's not bait time yet.' They commenced shovelling again, the muscles in Elizabeth's back and shoulders and arms almost frozen into painful immobility.

'You'll hurt tomorrow, mind,' said Thomas, catching the circular motion of Elizabeth's shoulders as she preceded him to the next work-station, her hands reaching back in a vain attempt to restore some sensation to the place where her arms used to meet her body.

'Come here,' he said, moving close behind her. He began to massage her shoulders, his thumbs digging deep into her back. She gasped with pain.

'Too hard? Sorry, the last time I did this was when Willie started with us, years ago. I'll try to be a bit more gentle.'

Even through the thickness of her shirt and jacket Elizabeth could feel the jagged nail edges of Thomas's thumbs as he pushed and pulled at knotted muscles. She allowed her mind to escape, to look around her into the dark dust of the coal face. All of the men (and she too, she realised) were black. She could taste the dust, feel it on her tongue and the back of her throat, smell it caked in her nostrils. Everywhere her skin was touched by cloth the small particles of grit could be felt, rubbing, irritating. Although the pit was new, and the face quite close to the shafts, the air around the miners was warm and stifling, filled with the cloying scent of sweat. She watched a shape loom out of the darkness and draw a nebulous cloak around it to become a man who deftly unbuttoned his trousers, urinated against the reverse wall, then floated away to become once again a shade. The muffled slide of metal on rock floor, the clang of hammer on spike, the almost silent exhalation of breath from numerous lungs as coal was hurled up and into wagons, they all joined to form an inhuman chorus to the damp darkness. There was no singing, no whistling, only whispered and distant conversation.

'Is it always as quiet as this?' asked Elizabeth.

'Quiet?' answered Thomas, his fingers and thumbs dancing a hornpipe on her back. 'Quiet? This isn't quiet! Just wait, wait till the end of the shift, then you'll know what quiet is. Anyway, I'll have to stop now, we've a tub to fill. Don't forget what I said before. Everybody depends on everybody else.'

Willie joined them again, and the tub was filled quickly. Elizabeth was surprised to find that Thomas's massage had provided her with some relief. As the last load was shovelled Thomas reached into his trouser pockets and brought out his watch. He glanced at it, nodded, then from his other pocket extracted his whistle which he blew loudly.

'Bait time,' he said, throwing down his shovel and picking up his shirt. 'Come on, we might as well find somewhere comfortable to sit.'

Elizabeth hurried along behind as the brothers retreated up the tunnel towards the shaft, then took a number of turns to the right and left. There was a new smell in the air.

'Stables,' announced Willie. 'This's where they keep the ponies. And the straw makes a damn sight more comfortable seat than coal!'

'Here,' said Thomas, 'have one of these.' He handed Elizabeth a pasty and a slice of bread, unbuttered. Willie was already tearing at his own, mouth full, crumbs round his mouth and littering the floor.

'Are you sure?' asked Elizabeth, suddenly hungry. 'Will you have enough for . . .'

'Mary's trying to fatten me up,' said Thomas, 'there's enough. Eat.'

And so they did. A bottle of warm water was passed around, shared, some retained in case of need later in the day. Thomas looked at his watch again.

'Ten minutes,' he said. 'Time for a sit. What do you think then, of being down a mine?'

'It's hard work,' answered Elizabeth, 'I'll grant you that. I won't pretend I like it, I don't think I ever could.'

'You wouldn't need to,' said Willie. 'Anyway, not now. Thanks to the Mines Act.' Thomas saw the puzzled look on Elizabeth's face.

'You're down here today against the law,' he said, 'according to the "Act to Prohibit the Working of Women and Girls in Mines and Collieries etc, 1842". You see, we don't just have to dig coal. We have to know all about pits themselves, and why they work the way they do, because our lives depend on that knowledge, even when it's to do with Acts of Parliament.'

'Aye,' said Willie. '1842 saw Inspectors in as well. Then no boys under 12, unless they could read and write.'

'That was 1860,' said Thomas, 'and it covered ventilation and safety lamps and so on. And then in 1865 they brought out a law saying that all pits should have two shafts . . .'

'And in 1872 there was a consolidating Act tying all the bits and pieces together . . .'

'And there's another one on the way this year, though I doubt it'll be in force till next. It'll mean managers and under-managers'll have to have certificates. They'll have to sit exams.'

'You fancy that, don't you?' said Willie. Thomas smiled and nodded his head.

'Aye, why not? I could do it, I know about mining, I can manage men. And Mr Waterhouse, he says I should consider it. Why not?'

'I think you'd make a good manager,' said Elizabeth.

'We'll see,' said Thomas. 'We'll see. But we'd best get back to work now. There's still the rest of the shift to work through.'

'He's halfway there,' muttered Willie, climbing to his feet, 'already acts like a bloody manager.'

Elizabeth tried to stand up, was in fact pulled up by Thomas and Willie, but felt incapable of movement. Every muscle seemed to have relaxed then refused to work properly again. It was obvious that the brothers were aware of her pain, though they did nothing further to assist her beyond offering words of encouragement. She managed to follow them back to the coal face and then leaned against the wall, shovel in hand, to watch them resume their work.

'A nice hot bath'll do you the world of good,' said Willie.

'And a massage,' added Thomas. 'Get Abigail to rub your back with liniment, and your arms and legs. She's good at that, so I hear.'

'You watch yourself, brother!'

'Me? What did I say? Did I say anything at all? It's not my fault if you've got a guilty conscience!'

'Oh, shut up and keep working. You talk too much, that's your trouble. You'll never be a manager if you talk too much.'

'You're jealous, you are, that's your trouble. Just because I've got brains, *and* I can work harder and faster than you even if I do talk!'

'Oh aye? And who says that?'

'It's common knowledge, everybody knows it. And I'm better looking than you as well!'

'You? Better looking than me? It'd be hard to disfigure you with a pick-axe handle, man, that's how good-looking you are! I always said Mary needed glasses! I mean, look at that nose . . .'

Elizabeth was unsure at first whether the entertainment was for her benefit or was perhaps some ritual play which the brothers acted each time they worked together. Certainly neither appeared to slow their efforts as they spoke, and it would be a skilful man who could judge either as working harder than the other. She came to the conclusion that although the words were spoken in jest the emotions they expressed were not diluted by the words' humour. Willie was jealous of his brother's ability to get on with the other men, while appreciating the fact that Thomas had sheltered him throughout his working life, taught him his job. Thomas, on the other hand, still felt that he ought to protect his younger brother. He found it difficult to appreciate that Willie was a grown man now, did not depend on him so much. And yet they still loved each other.

Elizabeth felt suddenly alone, threatened by the warmth Thomas and Willie felt for each other because the emotion was completely alien to her. The problem was, she felt, within her. She and her mother had been rejected by her natural father, she was sure of that, and although John Waterhouse held her in the highest affection she was not and never would be his daughter. And Margaret, whom Elizabeth had loved as a sister, was suddenly distant, spurning the friendship she continued to offer. Margaret had found love elsewhere. And her husband? The love he had taken which she had offered so freely he had turned against her. She could see no other answer. There was something within her, something which made it difficult, impossible, for others to know her, to love her. She sank to the ground, drew her legs up, hugged them close, and began to cry, quietly. No-one noticed her self pity. Thomas and Willie assumed that she was resting after her exertions; they said nothing of it to her, but each felt pride in the way that she had coped with the physical drudgery of the day. Elizabeth may have dozed. If so then Thomas's whistle to indicate the end of the shift brought her quickly back to her senses. She struggled painfully to her feet, wanting only to wash herself and retire to her bed, to luxuriate in her misery. Willie set off down the nearest tunnel and Elizabeth turned to follow him. She was halted by Thomas's hand on her shoulder.

'Hang back lass. Are you alright?'

She swallowed, nodded, unable to trust her voice.

'I told you I'd let you listen to quiet, didn't I? Well you just wait here awhile.'

One by one the faint lights disappeared as the miners made their way back to the shaft. Thomas had left one light beside her, had taken another as he roamed the coal-face.

'Just checking,' he said when he returned, 'making sure there's no-one left behind, that everything's safe for the next shift.'

'Just like a manager,' Elizabeth prompted.

'Aye, I suppose so. Anyway, it seems alright. Now come here.'

She stood in front of him and he held out his hand for the lamp. She gave it to him and he put it on the ground beside his. He looked at both lamps carefully.

'No gas,' he said, and blew out the flames.

Elizabeth realised that she had never experienced total darkness before. Even on still winter mornings, long after the fire in her bedroom had ceased to glow, just before the sun rose into a moonless cloudy grey sky, she would find some shard of pale light reflecting from the glass on the chandelier, or creeping beneath the door from the hallway beyond. But now there was nothing. No light. No sound, save the barest whisper of a breeze more felt than heard.

'Thomas?' she said.

'Aye, I'm still here lass. Don't be frightened.'

'I'm not frightened. I just wanted to make sure you were still there.'

'I'm here.'

They were silent, both of them, for at least a minute.

'Beautiful, isn't it!' whispered Thomas conspiratorily, though there was no chance of his being overheard by any other.

'Yes,' replied Elizabeth. By turning her head and listening carefully she could hear Thomas's breathing, could imagine that she knew his exact position. She felt safe, helpless but safe.

'Time to go,' he said, 'they'll be waiting for us. Come on.'

She heard the scrape of flint on stone, saw the flickering sparks followed by the dull glow of a lighted taper, waited as the lamps were lit once again. What had, a few minutes before, seemed a feeble light was suddenly too bright to be looked upon directly. Thomas looked at her, his teeth splitting his face with a white smile.

'Well done,' he said. 'There's some pitmen've worked years underground who can't bear to be without light. I can't explain what it is, but I never feel afraid if me light goes out, just sort of . . .'

'Wondrous?' suggested Elizabeth.

'Aye, something like that. Privileged. After all, there's not many people have seen darkness like that, are there?'

'Yes, I suppose you're right.' Elizabeth followed Thomas down one of the tunnels, picking her way over railway sleepers, walking between rails.

'Can you actually do that?' she asked. 'See darkness, I mean!' Thomas chuckled to himself.

'I'm a pitman, not a philosopher. You'll have to talk that over with some of your friends more learned than me. But at least you'll be able to do it with direct experience rather than using your imagination, eh?'

Before Elizabeth could make any reply Thomas stopped suddenly, so suddenly that she walked into him.

'Listen,' he said, 'can you hear that rumbling noise?'

'No.'

'Bend down, touch the rails. Can you feel anything?'

Elizabeth did as she was told. There was, perhaps, a slight vibration.

'They're sending some empty tubs back. It's downhill from the shaft halfway to the face, the tubs can pick up speed over the downhill then slow down as they get to the face. We're just about at the halfway point so they'll be coming fairly fast. We're not really meant to walk in this tunnel but it's quickest.'

'What do we do then? Go back?' Elizabeth's voice was touched with panic.

'What? No, don't worry. There's not really enough room for them to pass us, but there's little cubby-holes set into the wall every few yards, just in case this should happen. Come on, there's one just round the corner. It'll be a bit of a squeeze with both of us but we'll manage.'

Thomas was right. Let into the brickwork forming the tunnel wall was a small niche, no more than a foot deep and two feet wide. He peered ahead then pushed her into the opening.

'It's alright,' he said reassuringly, 'they won't be long. Squeeze in tight!'

There was a rush of cool air and a rattle of wheels on uneven tracks. Elizabeth felt the rough brickwork pressing against her back as Thomas joined her in the recess. She felt him against her, touching her along the whole length of her body. Her face was against his chest, she could taste the dust and warmth and sweat of the day's labours. She could feel the buckle of his belt pressing against her ribs, the muscles of his thighs on her stomach. She pushed back at him, put her arms around him as though seeking protection, clung to him, pressed her groin against him as the tub passed with a noisy grind of metal on metal and streak of dirty grey.

'Stay there,' he hissed. 'There should be two more.'

She tightened her grip on him when the second tub passed; as the third approached she felt his hand move to press her head harder against his chest. She could feel the wiry hairs of his chest through the coarse cotton of his shirt.

Then there was silence. They stood, arms around each other, Elizabeth's lamp on the ground where, at some time in the last minute, it had fallen, Thomas's still in his hand. In its meagre light they stared at each other. Thomas swallowed.

'We should be going,' he said, 'the others . . .'

'To hell with the others,' gasped Elizabeth. She reached up to his neck, felt the curls of hair there, pulled his head down, kissed him. It was no more than the brushing of lips; she intended no more, was unsure of the reaction this small act of intimacy might bring. She pulled herself away only to find his mouth searching once more for hers, his hand pulling her head forward again. His tongue parted her lips and touched hers, traced patterns on her teeth and tasted the soft flesh on the inside of her mouth. He tasted salt and warmth and dampness and his hand moved down her back to cup her buttock gently and force her against him. She felt his roughness and responded, closed her teeth on his tongue. Neither of them noticed the light approaching, swinging down the tunnel towards them.

'Is that you Thomas Armstrong?' It was a deep voice, as large as its owner.

'Jackie Benson!' swore Thomas. The huge miner was standing before them. He looked at Thomas, then at Elizabeth behind him.

'It's alright Thomas,' he said. 'I won't tell anyone. I know exactly how you feel, he's quite a pretty little mite in a skinny, boney sort of way. I won't say a word. I'll want a share though, next time he's down.'

His shovel of a hand reached past Thomas to stroke Elizabeth's cheek.

'There's not really time now Thomas, you should know that. Bait time, that's the best time, that's the best time in the world. Can I have him tomorrow Thomas? Tomorrow bait time?'

'Go on Jackie,' said Thomas, 'away with you. We're right behind you.' He turned to Elizabeth.

'That never happened!' he hissed. 'Do you hear me? That never happened!'

'Yes Thomas,' said Elizabeth.

Elizabeth lay in her bath. This was the second refill she had had and the water was now clean. She offered up a silent prayer to heaven, thanking her private angel for allowing her father to have installed a system of freely available hot water. The heat had done something to soothe her aches, but she still felt that each muscle in her arms and back, her legs and stomach, had been subject to attack from some particularly violent and aggressive demon with a poison-tipped pitchfork. She could remember little of the journey up the pit-shaft, save that she and Thomas had been in different parts of the cage. He had avoided her when they reached the surface. She could have found him, she was sure of that. All of the men had headed for the pit-head baths, and in her disguise she would have readily gained admission. There would, however, have been nothing to gain from this, other than being able to gaze upon the naked bodies of the pitmen in their communal baths. She could not have confronted Thomas, not in front of his workmates. In any case, she was not sure what she would have said. Instead she sneaked back to the Hall and into her room, taking pleasure in cleaning herself thoroughly and completely. The first bath removed the worst of the grime from her body and her hair, though she was forced to clean out the bath before turning the tap to admit more hot water. This time she soaped herself thoroughly, was surprised that there should still be so much dirt on her body. The third time she lay quiet.

Her hair was dark, clean, lustrous. She was relaxed, as long as she didn't move, and she had time to think. The melancholy of a few hours ago had disappeared. She was once more in control of her emotions. She felt her face growing pink with the heat, stood up with some difficulty and stepped from the bath, wrapping herself in a huge white towel. Her dirty clothes were in a pile in the corner; she must get those cleaned and returned. She hurried into her room to stand in front of the fire, took the small towel she had left there and proceeded to dry her hair vigorously. She took a step to one side to look at herself in the mirror, dropped the bath-towel to the floor to stand naked before her reflection. She cupped her hands to her breasts. Not much there, she thought to herself, though her nipples were dark and erect. She could hardly blame Jackie Benson for thinking that she was a boy. She turned sideways. Her stomach, however, was flat and firm. She picked the towel up again, dried under her arms, her chest, down across her stomach, the triangle of hair below. She could still feel Thomas's heat, still taste him, see the look in his eye; she could sense his need.

'It's no good Thomas Armstrong,' she said to herself. 'No matter what you think, no matter what you say, there's no escaping. You're mine, Thomas. All mine.'

Chapter Twelve

If you find him sad
Say I am dancing; if in mirth, report
That I am sudden sick.

Antony and Cleopatra
(William Shakespeare)

f Thomas thought that Elizabeth would pursue him, hunt him out, then he was mistaken. He returned home burdened with guilt, certain that his sin would be evident to his wife and family, but found no change in the way they treated him. His relief did not help him sleep that night, and his moral frailty was further confused when Mary's hand reached for him in the dark and he found himself responding, unable to withold his tumescence from her. He made love unenthusiastically and lay afterwards with Mary sleeping peacefully in his arms. He listened to her breathing, felt the rise and fall of her breasts against him. She would turn away from him soon, as she always did, push herself against him in an invitation to fit himself around the curved spoon of her behind, and he knew that he would be unable to do this. When she moved he remained still, waited for her to settle, then slid to one side so that there was no longer any physical contact with her. He put his hands behind his head and stared at the dark ceiling.

It was a kiss, he told himself, nothing more. There was no promise of anything more. How could there be? He was married, with children, her husband was abroad but might return in due time. She was the daughter of the pit-owner, a wealthy man; he was one of his employees. No, he should get the matter into perspective, it was a kiss and nothing would come of it. He would not allow anything to come of it. Why then, asked a voice within him, why was he even now lying beside his wife, still damp with her musk, and thinking of another woman? Thomas found it difficult to deny the logic of that point. He could have considered that both he and Elizabeth had recently suffered a loss, he his father, she, in a way, her sister. They were both suddenly isolated, lonely and in need of succour, and had stumbled upon each other. Instead of this he sought to rationalise his feelings, to explain to himself why he felt the way he did, why the image of Elizabeth was still in his mind, why he still longed for the taste of coal-dust on her lips.

He and Mary had been virgins when they married. Their courtship had been short, the opportunity to indulge in any sort of sexual experimentation limited. Their houses were full at all times, privacy there was impossible. They could walk and talk together, find some lonely spot, a barn perhaps, or some secluded spinney, where it would be possible to kiss and fumble beneath what seemed to be numerous layers of frustrating, voluminous clothing, but only marriage would allow them the freedom to lie together whenever they wished. It was strange, but neither he nor Mary had fought against these restrictions. When he thought about it, thought hard, sent his memory back to those days of tortured innocence, the opportunities to indulge themselves had been there.

He had taken her to see the badgers' sett he had found, and they had sat in delight as first the boar, then the sow, and then two or three cubs had poked their snouts into the

warm summer air and slowly emerged into the dusty
evening sunlight. The badgers played and cuffed each other
until some other creature, probably a fox, disturbed them,
and they hurried back into the sett chased by the alarmed
churr of a blackbird. Thomas and Mary had smiled at each
other and embraced, kissed and drank in the taste of each
other, their senses heightened by the heady, intoxicating
smell of woodland flowers and damp green. They ought to
have made love. It was not long until the wedding, it would
have made no difference. They both wanted each other, that
much was certain. Thomas could recall with grim certainty
his own need, was sure that Mary had felt the same, and on
that day they had all but forgotten their resolve. Thomas
recollected his feelings, his excitement as his hands made
their way furtively into Mary's blouse and fumbled at the
buttons, cupped her breasts and teased at her nipples. He
remembered the warm glow of anticipation as her own
fingers snaked their way into his trousers and stroked and
squeezed him through the thin cotton of his pants. This they
had done before with almost equal shares of pleasure and
frustration, but any further attempts at intimacy on his part
had met with a friendly though firm rebuttal. He expected
nothing less this time, bent his head to allow his lips to take
over where his fingers were circling Mary's nipples, freed his
hands to allow them to begin their journey down into
unexplored territory.

The region below Mary's waist and above her thighs was
forbidden; Thomas's surprise at his hand being allowed
there at all, albeit resting on three or four layers of cloth, was
made greater as Mary raised her head to nibble at his ear
and groan with pleasure as he pushed harder with his hand.
He took the opportunity, forgot his surprise, moved his
hand down onto her knee then up again, pushing cotton and
serge before him in an attempt to reach his target. He
remembered Mary's words, had to suppress a laugh at the

thought of them. He knew that she enjoyed his physical attentions, but had not realised that her needs might be as great as, perhaps even exceed, his own. 'They're too tight,' she'd whispered, 'pull them down.' And he had done so, tugged as she had lifted her bottom, wriggled her bloomers down to her ankles then folded them neatly and laid them beside her. He recalled his mounting excitement as she pulled her skirts and petticoats up to her waist, took his hand and sat it, trembling, on the nest of her pubic hair. His fingers had time only to tangle themselves in the moistness, to reach and stroke and tug gently. He reacted to her own hands and fingers and tongue and the groaning which could have been his or hers. His body stiffened and all motion ceased. It was Mary again who found the words. 'I think we'd better stop now. You seem to have had a bit of an accident.'

They lay in each other's arms, quiet, secure, as the sun set and the badgers once more felt happy enough to scent the air. She tore a square from the bottom of her already patched and worn petticoat, handed it to him, then turned her back as they made themselves presentable once again. They strolled home, reached Mary's house and kissed goodnight, their tongues teasing memories, tasting pollen and sunshine.

That, thought Thomas, was a kiss. That was a kiss prompted by love and respect, not brought about by loss and loneliness and, yes, admit even that, by lust. His feelings for Elizabeth had been nothing more than an aberration, the result of a moment of madness, and he had now talked himself back to sanity. He would speak to her, explain how he felt, and she would understand. She must understand. No doubt, he persuaded himself, the same thoughts had passed through her mind. She would understand. He turned on his side, fitted himself to his wife, felt her warmth touch him. He leaned forward.

'I love you,' he whispered in her ear, unsure whether or not she heard him, and unaware that the words had been spoken because of his need, not hers.

Thomas did not go to see Elizabeth. He made no visit to explain matters to her. He was not, he told himself, avoiding her. She would be very busy with the arrangements for her sister's wedding, just as he was in helping organise that of Willie and Abigail. He had been pleased when Willie asked him to be his best man, and even more honoured when Abigail had taken him to one side and explained that, since she had no family to speak of, she wanted him to escort her down the aisle, to give her away. They had decided on a spring wedding, and Abigail was found frequently closeted with Mary discussing her dress, the guests, the arrangements for feeding and entertaining them, and, to a chorus of laughing and whispered giggling, the honeymoon.

Willie too was busy. He made an appointment to see John Waterhouse, informed him officially of his intentions, and asked that he be given the chance of renting a house. There were two in the village still empty, one of them with only two bedrooms, and permission was given for the young couple to make this their home as soon as they were wed. Thomas had suggested that the ceremony should be kept as simple as possible, but Mary had disagreed. She championed the preacher with what was, for her, unusual passion, and managed to win Abigail to her side. The two women went to see him, for an initial discussion, and returned laden with enthusiasm and eager to offer their excess to those lacking the commodity.

'He's got such a beautiful voice, he really knows how to use words to move you,' said Mary.

'He says he'd be delighted to marry us,' added Abigail. 'He really did seem pleased that we'd asked him. I'm sure it'll be a wonderful wedding!'

'And he was so pleasant! He asked how we all were, including the children, hoped that he'd been able to help in some little way with the service at your Dad's funeral. I told him he'd been a great comfort to us all, and he said he hoped we might come down next Sunday.'

'And what did you say to that?' asked Thomas.

'I said that I'd come, even if no-one else wanted to.'

'Me too,' said Abigail, 'and I think it would be best if you,' she nodded in Willie's direction, 'came as well, just to show face.'

'What's his name?' asked Thomas ungraciously.

'Pardon?' replied Mary, suspicion in her voice.

'I said what's his name? This preacher, what's he called?'

'Why, I think it's Proudfoot. No, I'm wrong, it was on the board in front of the chapel, with the times of services. Proudlock, that's it! Jonathon Proudlock. Why?'

'I just wanted to remember, for when he's not a preacher any more. 'Cos if he can persuade the three of you to start going to church he won't be long in the clergy, he'll be a politician before you can say "Our Father"!'

'And what do you mean by that?'

Thomas stood up, reached for his jacket.

'Well,' he said with mock politeness, 'we all know what knaves and scoundrels politicians are, how they give with one hand and take away twice as much with the other, how they love the working man just as long as he's doing exactly that, working. And it just seemed to me that our Mr Proudlock might have a bit of the politician in him, nothing more. Now I'm off to find the boys, they're out playing somewhere.'

Thomas didn't slam the door, but those left in the house tensed their shoulders in expectation of the action.

'What's the matter with him?' asked Mary.

'He was alright before,' answered Willie, 'then you came in talking about that preacher and that was it!'

'It'll take him a while till he gets over his Dad dying,' suggested Abigail. 'I think it affected him more than he shows.'

'That's the trouble with Thomas,' added Mary pensively, as if reluctant to tell a secret. She weighed the matter for a moment then went on.

'You see, he listens when you tell him there's something wrong with you and he helps sort you out. But when there's something the matter with *him* he turns all strong and silent, as if he's the only one who can do anything about it. He goes off for walks, sometimes he just sits and talks to himself, then he comes back and says "Right, I feel better now", and the strange thing is, he is better. But you never find out what the problem was, whether it was something important, something to do with his work, something to do with his family. And if I ask him to tell me, to talk to me, he just says that it'll make me feel bad and he doesn't want to do that. He always says he can sort it out himself. So far he has done. But one day, I said this to his face not long ago, one day he'll find some problem he can't cope with, and he'll be so used to keeping it to himself that he won't be able to share it with anyone at all. And that problem might be the one that's too big. He'll still try to fight it by himself, but he might just lose.' She breathed in deeply, looked at Willie and Abigail in turn, shrugged her shoulders.

'He's a complicated man is our Thomas. I think that's why I love him so much.'

Thomas followed the sound of laughter and raucous screams which echoed around the village, slowed his pace as the voices became louder. He enjoyed watching children play, particularly his own children, especially when they were unaware that they were being watched. What game would they have chosen today? It depended, he theorised, on who was there. The older ones preferred games where they could demonstrate their agility, ball games such as Kingo or even football, chasing games like Whiplash. The rough-and-tumble of Bulldogs was often too much for the younger children; they preferred Hide-and-Seek where their size was an advantage in securing unusual places to secrete themselves. It seemed only a few years since Thomas was watching Willie play games with the other children. Willie had been a quiet child, not keen to leave his mother's side. When forced to do so he inevitably followed one of the older girls round, clutching at her legs, demanding to be carried. Neither Matthew nor David were like that, though David was as likely to be found playing houses with girls as joining with the other boys in climbing trees or throwing stones. The path wound between the gardens of two rows of houses, and from a wooden hut thrown up in one of them Thomas could hear his younger son.

'I've just come in from the pit and I've had me bath and I'm buggered,' came the familiar voice.

'David Armstrong!' said another voice, that of a girl. 'I'll not have you use words like that in my house!'

'It's my house as well, I can say what I want!'

'It's not your house, it's in my Dad's back garden, so I can decide what you can say!'

There was the sound of a chair scraping on a wooden floor. Thomas bent his head closer to the side of the hut.

'Well I'm not playing this stupid game then! It's stupid not being allowed to say what you want, just because it's your Dad's stupid hut and his stupid garden! *My* Dad always says "I'm buggered" when he comes in from work, and he flops himself down in his big chair, so *I* can say it as well!'

'It's rude!'

'Don't care!'

'David! Be quiet, somebody'll hear you, then we'll both be in trouble! I'll tell you what, you can say . . . you can say that word, if you want, but you've got to say it quietly. And you've got to promise that you'll only hit me softly.'

'Alright.' There was a moment's silence. David spoke again.

'But I don't want to hit you.'

'You have to.'

'Why?'

'It's part of the game. That's what Mams and Dads do. The Dad comes in from work, sits down, has his tea . . .'

'Says "I'm buggered".'

'Alright, says that. Then he smokes his pipe and has some beer and the Mam washes up and bakes and cooks.'

'And the Dad plays with his kids.' Thomas grinned.

'Well, I suppose he can if he wants. But then the kids go to bed, and then the Mam and Dad argue, and then the Dad hits the Mam. Then they go to bed and make babies.'

'My Mam and Dad don't do that,' said David.

'What, make babies?' The girl seemed surprised, Thomas wondered how old she was. Older than David surely, but no more than eight, perhaps nine.

'No, stupid! They don't argue! And my Dad never hits my Mam!'

'Doesn't he? Isn't he strong enough?'

'My Dad's very strong! I bet he's stronger than your Dad!'

'I bet he's not!'

'I bet he is, and I'm nearly as strong as he is, and I'll thump you if you don't say my Dad's strongest!'

Faced with the prospect of physical violence the girl appeared to reconsider.

'Have you got a brother or a sister?'

'I've got a brother. His name's Matthew and he's nearly two years older than me and he's even stronger than me and he'll thump you as well!'

'Well, even if your Dad is stronger than mine,' the girl conceded, 'I've got three brothers and two sisters so mine's better at making babies than yours! So there!' Thomas could almost imagine her tongue out, eyebrows raised, head on one side, hands on hips.

'My Dad can make chairs and tables and beds,' countered David.

'Now who's stupid?' taunted the girl, ignoring the riposte. 'I bet you don't even know how to make babies.' There was no reply.

'La-la la-la-la, I know something you don't know!' jeered the girl's voice again. David said nothing.

'Do you want me to tell you?' David must have nodded. The girl's voice dropped to a whisper.

'The Mam lies down on the bed with her legs open and the Dad takes his trousers off – go on, I'll show you – and his peanut gets bigger and . . .'

Thomas swallowed sharply then banged on the side of the hut.

'David? David Armstrong, are you in there? It's tea-time, come on out, we'll have to go and look for Matthew.' The door flew open and David skidded round the corner, flung himself at his father. Thomas caught his son, threw him skywards and retrieved him easily. He was thin-legged and light, and no matter what he ate his ribs seemed always to be prominent, his arms long and skinny. Despite that he was robust, always the last to find that he had grazed his knees or bruised his forehead. Thomas moved him deftly to his shoulders and they headed off in search of his eldest son.

A patch of green on the other side of the path from the pond appeared to have been claimed as a football pitch, four piles of coats and pullovers marking the goalposts. Thomas could see seven or eight boys playing there, Matthew in the thick of the play. He was the smallest player, stocky and solid, but the others seemed in awe of his attempts to win the ball from them, stepping to one side before his sliding tackles began. This did not stop him from carrying them through, and had not done so for most of the game, Thomas felt; Matthew's clothes were a uniform muddy brown colour, as were his legs, his hands and most of his face. As Thomas and David watched he gained the ball, danced round an opponent, then fired the ball under the keeper to claim a goal. Thomas trapped the ball neatly as it came towards him.

'Seventeen-six,' said the scorer running to retrieve the ball. 'First to twenty ... Oh, hello Dad. Can I have the ball back please?'

'It's time for tea,' said Thomas. 'I think you'd better be away now. Say goodbye to your friends.'

'Ah, Dad, it's first to twenty wins! Can I stay for just a little bit longer, it won't take a minute to score another three goals. Promise.'

'Go on then, but be quick.' He tapped the ball back.

'Oh, and Matthew?'

'Yes?'

'Try not to get yourself too dirty.'

Matthew nodded, stopped in his tracks, looked down at himself. He turned, flashed a smile at his father, then ran back to the pitch.

'Your brother,' said Thomas to David, 'is growing up very quickly.'

'He's bigger than me,' came the reply, 'but I've got a bigger peanut than him. Do you want me to show you Dad?'

Thomas and Elizabeth managed to avoid each other during January. This was not a deliberate action; had either seen the other coming along the road they would not have hidden or hurried away. Thomas had considered the possibility of a chance meeting, had decided that, if they were alone, he would broach the subject of their kiss and apologise. As each day passed he felt happier in his belief that Elizabeth felt the same way about the unfortunate occurrence and that nothing more would come of it. He found welcome comfort in the warmth and safety of his home with his family around him.

It had taken Mary a while to get used to Thomas's absences when he was learning rapper, practising at least once a week, spending time with his brother and father. She had not been used to this but had reconciled herself to Thomas's wishes, and now found that the cycle had returned her husband to her. The death of Tommy Armstrong seemed to have taken away Thomas's enthusiasm for the dance and the competition. Although Elizabeth had offered to provide the music for practices she was, for the present, too involved in helping organise her sister's wedding. Willie and Abigail had, much to their surprise, been given the keys to their house and spent much of their spare time there, at least during the day. Thomas, therefore, stayed at home. He carried on writing a diary, as Elizabeth had suggested, haltingly at first, then with more confidence. He did not restrict himself to details of his own life but commented upon the news of the day, what his wife and family had been doing. He copied out fragments of poems he had found in library books, sometimes a verse or two, often a single line, even solitary words which he would repeat to himself, enjoying their resonance and taste on his tongue. At first Mary asked him what he was doing and he would read back to her the contents of a page, but she could take little interest in his words, even less in the dense language of the poems he seemed to enjoy most. She was happy that he was at home, with her, and nothing else mattered.

The pit was closed on the day of Margaret's wedding to Henry Makemore. All men had been given the day off work and a free train had been laid on for those who wished to see, if not the service, then at least the arrivals and

departures of the honoured guests. The Armstrong family
agreed to make use of the free journey. It would be the first
time that Matthew and David had travelled into Newcastle;
Mary was eager to experience the grandness of the occasion;
and Thomas felt it his duty to his employer to be present.

Abigail would be there, by necessity. Although Margaret
had now begun to speak to her again the maid was not
permitted to serve her former mistress. Those duties had
been given to a girl lent by the Makemores, plain of face and
surly of manner, used to being treated with diffidence and
threatened with violence. Elizabeth, however, had asked
Abigail to act as her personal maid, at least until she married
and moved in with Willie. Abigail had been pleased to do
so.

Willie declared that he too would like to see the wedding.
Thomas took him to one side, gently questioned his motives.
Willie seemed honestly affronted at Thomas's implication
that he still had some feelings for Margaret. He wanted to
be there simply to see Abigail, he protested, and it was unfair
of his brother to suggest otherwise. Thomas retreated
gracefully.

Friday, 28 January 1887. It was a cold, crisp morning, with
a slight frost hung in the hedgerows. Mary was up early
preparing a basket of food, sausages and cheese, bread and
butter, apples, pickled eggs and onions. She laid out the
children's clothes, newly pressed, then woke Thomas with a
cup of tea. He had spent the previous night polishing his best
boots, but in the dull morning light he evidently felt that he
had not been thorough enough in his devotions and once
more took up the polishing rag. He cajoled the toe-caps into
mirror brightness while his brother rushed around searching
for collar buttons and cuff-links, his meditation secure even
against Matthew's and David's waking and breakfasting.
Eventually satisfied he dressed quickly and helped the

children while Mary disappeared upstairs to prepare herself. They were ready when, at nine o'clock precisely, Albie Settle's carriage drew up to the door. The gamekeeper himself was driving, his son beside him to bring the vehicle back from the railway station.

'Is your wife not coming along?' asked Mary. No-one, not even Tommy Armstrong on his visits to drink at the Settles' house, had managed to meet the mysterious Mrs Settle.

'Alas, no. There she was, all ready t' come out, and she 'as one of 'er fits. 'S such a pity, there's us wi' seats in t' cathedral an' all. I don't suppose you'd care t' take 'er place beside me Mrs Armstrong, only it seems such a waste if there's no-one there?'

Mary lifted her hands to her mouth.

'Oh Thomas, do you think I might? I'd so love to be inside, to see the ceremony, Miss Margaret walking up the aisle. Would you mind? I'm sure it wouldn't take long, and Willie'll help you with the boys.'

Thomas smiled.

'I don't mind lass. No, you go in with Albie. You can tell us all about it afterwards, so make sure you watch every detail. Now come on, or we'll miss that train.' He helped his wife up onto the high step and into the coach, lifted the two boys in beside her. He followed quickly, and Willie brought up the rear.

The journey to Lanchester station was short, and on the way they waved at and were greeted by others walking the same road. Willie alone remained impassive, staring out of the window into the bright sunlight.

'Are you alright lad?' asked Thomas.

'Aye,' came the reply, a brief nod of the head confirming that a word had been spoken.

'Sure?'

This time the nod alone. It didn't seem worthwhile pursuing the matter further.

John Waterhouse had wanted to invite all of his employees to his daughter's wedding. When Elizabeth had demonstrated that this kindness would have been both wildly expensive and, in practical terms, impossible, her father had decided that his workers and their families would at least have the opportunity to share part of the day. The Waterhouses and the Makemores had decamped to Newcastle days before, but John Waterhouse's instructions had been clear. The engine waiting to pull the train into Newcastle had been cleaned and polished, its North Eastern Railways green and gold and brass reflecting the cleaned and polished faces of its passengers. There were four red carriages, and the Armstrongs found that there was enough space for them and Albie Settle to claim one of the compartments for themselves. The seats were of leather, the wooden trims of mahogany, and above both seats was a posy of dried flowers. There were, Thomas estimated, about 150 people on the train; the air was scented with their good humour.

The railway track lay in the bottom of the valley, staying mostly to the south of the River Browney. The train whistled through Langley Park, paused to allow the London express to precede it into Durham, then headed north. Thomas pointed out the castle and the cathedral, the Wear winding around them both as if trying to form an island. They saw the Wear again as they rattled through Chester-le-Street, and it was only minutes then before they slowed through Gateshead and crept onto the High Level Bridge over the Tyne.

'There's a road underneath us,' Thomas explained to his sons, 'to let carriages and people cross the river. And if you look down there,' he pointed to the east, 'you'll see another bridge, a little 'un. And do you know the name of the man who built that?' The boys shook their heads.

'Why, Armstrong of course! William George Armstrong, Lord Armstrong as he is now. Not that he's any relative of course, but I did have an aunt lived at Shieldfield who said that

Lord Armstrong's father was her father's cousin, so you never know. And he was a very clever man, this Armstrong, just like your uncle Willie. You see, he had a factory at Elswick, up that way,' he pointed west, 'which made ships. But he couldn't make them very big because they couldn't get under the low bridge which used to be down near the river. So what he did, he designed the bridge that's down there now, the Swing Bridge. See that little dome in the middle? Well there's big levers in there, and when the bridge keeper pulls on one of them, the whole bridge turns round so that instead of pointing across the river, it points up and down the river. That way really big ships can get down to the sea.'

'I wish I could share his money instead of just his name,' muttered Willie enviously.

The track bent round, past the old keep ('That's why Newcastle's called Newcastle,' said Thomas, keeping up his history lesson. 'From the days when that was new, 800 years ago') and into the Central Station. Albie Settle was impressed.

'I didn't think civilisation'd got as far north as this,' he said, gazing at the elaborate decoration of the arched portico.

'Aye,' said Thomas with the pride of a native, 'and opened by Victoria and Albert themselves.'

'Mind you,' added Willie, 'that was twenty-seven years ago, and they've never been back since. You see, they had a banquet, to celebrate the opening, and the manager of the hotel gets introduced to the Queen. He bows deeply, then gives her a piece of paper. She thinks it's a scroll or something, to commemorate the occasion, so she opens it straight away. And what was it? It was the bill for the banquet! And whenever she's passed through since then she always pulls the blinds down in the carriage!'

'That's just a story,' said Thomas defensively.

'It's a true story!' protested Willie.

'What time is the wedding Mr Settle?' said Mary in an attempt to stifle the impending argument.

'Noon,' said the gamekeeper, 'and it's just after eleven now. I don't suppose you know where this cathedral is, do you? Will we 'ave to take a cab? I mean, Mr Waterhouse and the rest are all stayin' 'ere,' he pointed at the entrance to the Station Hotel, 'but they'll 'ave carriages and the like.'

'We won't need a cab,' said Thomas, 'it's only a few minutes' walk. Come on, we'll show you the way, then we can walk up Grey Street. If you think the Central Station's special just wait till you see Grey Street!' Albie Settle, looking back, noticed a church.

'There it is!' he shouted. 'You're taking us the wrong way!'

'Wrong church,' said Thomas, 'that's Saint Andrew's. Or is it John's? Yes, I think it's John's. Anyway, it's not the cathedral. Follow me.'

They walked past the glass windows of the shops, staring at the goods inside. Mary stood open-mouthed in front of a draper's shop, her eyes made wide by the exotic and expensive materials. Willie peered at the clothes on display at a Gentleman's Outfitters of Renown, compared them to his own smart, though in comparison not very well cut, suit. The boys inhaled the scents of a coffee shop until its proprietor bustled outside to move them along. Albie Settle wasn't sure where to look. He first stared at a horse-drawn tram hurrying by, then his eyes lighted on a similar vehicle, travelling more slowly, but with wisps of steam rising from a funnel at its front. So intent was he on his surroundings that he kept bumping into passers-by, apologising profusely, then repeating the accident. And Thomas? Thomas was absorbing it all, the sights and sounds and smells of the city. He felt strangely at home here, despite the fact that, when away, he felt no longing to be there. It was as though the city was an old friend, always there when needed, undemanding, asking nothing but an infrequent visit and a knowing smile.

'And that,' said Thomas rounding a corner, 'is St Nicholas's Cathedral.'

The gamekeeper was unimpressed.

'It's not exactly big, is it? Or grand in its setting? Or imposing? I mean, I saw t' cathedral at Durham from t' train, and believe me, that's a big bugger, pardon my language. I mean, this 'un's not bad, I like the spire wi' its crowns, but it's not . . . it's not inspirin', is it?'

'Well it's not been a cathedral for long, only five years. It was an ordinary church before then.' Thomas found himself defending the building.

'Its setting's not bad either; there's the castle beyond, and Grey Street just round the corner. And just behind us, across the road there, that's Balmbra's Music Hall. That's where Geordie Ridley first sang the "Blaydon Races".'

'The what?'

'Oh, come on Albie, your memory's not that bad! We've sung it for you before, I can remember Dad playing it for you, and me and Willie singing. You know, it goes "I went to Blaydon Races, 'Twas on the ninth of June, Eighteen hundred and sixty-two on a summer's afternoon . . ."'

'We took the bus from Balmbra's,' continued Willie, 'And she was heavy laden, Away we went along Collingwood Street, that's on the road to Blaydon . . .'

Albie nodded his head vigorously, a smile of recognition creeping onto his face. He added his bass to the chorus.

> Oh, lads, you should a' seen us gannin,
> Passin' the folks alang the road just as they were stannin,
> There was lots of lads and lasses there, all wi smilin faces
> Gannin alang the Scotswood Road to see the Blaydon Races.

A man passed by and looked at them with suspicion; they all began to laugh.

'We'll get arrested mind,' said Willie. 'Why don't we go and have a drink in Balmbra's. I'm sure they wouldn't mind if we sang a bit in there.'

Albie Settle nodded enthusiastically.

'What about Grey Street?' asked Thomas. 'Don't you want to see it, and the monument?'

'Will there be time,' asked the gamekeeper, 'to see it after the wedding?'

'Aye,' said Thomas. 'I suppose so.'

'Well in that case I must admit to bein' a trifle thirsty, and Willie 'as just tipped me the wink that there's decent ale in that Balmbra's place, so if you don't mind . . .?'

'Philistine!' Thomas was not really annoyed. 'Why don't you join them,' he said to Mary. 'I'll take the boys for a walk. Take something from the basket, something to eat, you don't know how long the service might last. I'll see you outside afterwards, by the main doors.'

Mary seemed a little unsure.

'Come on lass!' said Albie taking one of her arms.

'We'll look after you!' added Willie taking the other. Together they headed for the Music Hall, Albie's tuneless hum escorting them through the doors.

'Just us now,' said Thomas to his sons. 'You take the basket Matthew, it's not too heavy, and then you can each take a hand. Everyone alright? Let's go then!'

It was still cold in the darkness of Moseley Street. The sun was almost at its highest but the buildings were too tall to allow any light or warmth to the pavement. The Armstrongs hurried along, their breath rising like plumes of steam from three racing engines. They reached a corner and turned left, then stopped.

'There are some scenes,' wrote Thomas in his diary that night, 'which remain in a man's mind from the day they first assault his eyes until the day of his death. Some may rise unbidden from the depths of his nightmares, pictures of death, of sorrow and suffering, of fatherless children and widows shrouded in black. I have lived these pictures, I have suffered these nightmares, and I have no wish to meet them again though I know they will continue to haunt me. But there are other visions which a man might seek to remember, and today I was witness to one of these. I was in pleasant company, the very best, none other than my sons Matthew and David. I feel privileged to have shared with them the majesty of the panorama which appeared before us. Grey Street. The name means so little to those who have not seen the magnificent buildings there, the stately elegance of the curve up to Grey's Monument, the striking similarity of style of each and every building, closer inspection revealing their subtle and well-planned individual characters.

'On this winter morning the sharpness of the air had no doubt kept many at home. There were carriages and cabs passing us, a coster-monger with his barrow, a brewer's dray whipping its way into the centre of the town, but few people walking. We could only pause every other step to marvel at the new vista, to wonder at the men who created such buildings. Some may talk of Paris or Rome or Venice, I would commend Grey Street to any man as the finest such in Europe, and therefore the finest in the world.'

The three wandered uphill, taking in the scene as if no other day would be quite like this. Each clutched a sausage and munched absent-mindedly as they walked. No doubt Thomas's sense of awe had been passed to his sons; had he been aware of this he would probably have approved. Matthew haltingly read out the attractions currently showing at the Theatre Royal from a sandwich board borne too quickly by him; he managed no more than the name of the theatre and the introductory sentence. David, meanwhile, was standing by the roadside waving frantically at a passing carriage.

'Don't do that son,' admonished Thomas, 'it's a cab. He might think we want to hire him.' The cab had slowed, turned carefully, then made its way back up the hill.

'See what I mean? Now I'll have to explain that we don't really want to hire a cab. I hope he won't be too annoyed.'

'It's the person inside,' insisted David, 'I was waving at the person inside! It's Miss Elizabeth!'

Thomas swallowed nervously as the cab drew alongside and the familiar face of Elizabeth Kearton smiled down at him.

'David! Matthew! How lovely to see you here! Have you come to see Margaret's wedding?' The two boys nodded shyly. Although she was warmly dressed and wrapped in a number of blankets Elizabeth's face was aglow with the cold.

'It's Margaret,' she explained to Thomas. 'She suddenly decided that she needed some ribbon and brocade for her dress, and I was the only person able to get it for her, simply because I was fully dressed and ready for the wedding. So off I must go to the nearest haberdasher's, then the next nearest because the first didn't have exactly what Margaret required. Take my advice boys, *never* get married! But enough of me. Are you enjoying your day out?'

Matthew and David nodded again.

'We're just looking at the buildings,' Matthew offered. 'Dad says it's one of the best streets in the world!'

'It probably is,' said Elizabeth. 'I would tend to agree with your father. It was designed and built by men whose names will one day be known throughout the country, you mark my words. Remember where you heard first about Mr Grainger and Mr Dobson, the Green brothers, Wardle and Walker. And think of the man whose name was chosen for the street itself, a very important man as well. I'm sure your

father will show you his statue, it's at the very top of the
column at the top of the street. But really, I must be going.
I'm sorry you won't be able to see the ceremony from inside
the church, but to tell the truth, it's all rather boring anyway.
Make sure you wave if you see me later; I'll try to wave
back. Goodbye!'

'Elizabeth!' shouted Thomas.

'Yes?'

'I've been meaning to speak to you.'

'Is this the right time Thomas? Is this the right place, and
the right company?' Elizabeth's voice was reproaching;
Thomas felt like a schoolboy caught misbehaving.

'Probably not. No, you're right, I'll come up to the Hall
to see you, if I may. We need ... that is, I need to make
something clear, I don't want you to misunderstand what
happened. But I'll come tomorrow, or the day after, if I
may.'

'Thomas, you may visit me whenever you wish. But if
you're referring to something that happened earlier this
month, well, I can only say that I was asked by the other
party to forget what happened. And I do believe that I have
done exactly that. I hope that your mind is eased a little by
that statement, and if you need to say or to hear more please
call on me. But now I really must fly! Goodbye again!'

This time the cab managed to escape.

'What a funny lady,' said David.

'She's nice,' added Matthew. 'At least, *I* think she's nice.'

'Yes,' said Thomas, 'you're both right. She is nice. And I
suppose she's just a little bit funny as well.' He took hold of
his sons' hands, hoping that they would not notice the
racing of his heart, the cold sweat on his palms. Together
they headed for the tall column at the end of the street, the
statue of Earl Grey at its summit beaming benevolently at
the city below.

'Who is he?' asked David. The three stood, heads back,

gazing up at the figure above them bathed in sunlight.

'Earl Grey,' answered Thomas.

'Yes,' said Matthew, 'but *who* is he? What did he do? Why is he up there?'

'There's a bird sitting on his head,' added David, feeling that this information might add some lightness to what might become one of his father's long lectures. He glowered at his elder brother who realised too late that the door had been opened to such a discourse.

'I'm sorry lads, I don't actually know a lot about him,' said Thomas. His sons smiled.

'But I do know he was once Prime Minister, and he helped abolish the slave trade, and when Wellington resigned – remember I told you about him, and the battle of Waterloo, and how he became Prime Minister – the King asked Earl Grey to form a Government.'

'What's a gubbyment Dad?'

'No,' laughed Thomas, 'that's Government David. I'll show you how to spell it when we get home. It's the people who run the country. Or at least they're meant to. Anyway, the King, it was William the Fourth I think, asked Earl Grey to be Prime Minister, and he said yes, and he passed a law called the Reform Act which allowed more people to vote for who they wanted to be in the Government.'

'Was he a nice man?' asked David.

'I don't know. He died in, let me see, 1845. That's more than forty years ago, before I was born.'

'Was he a good man?' enquired Matthew. 'I mean, everybody must have thought he was a good man if they built a column as big as this and then put his statue on top. There's a door at the bottom there, can we climb up?'

'Well son, it would be easy to say that he must have been a good man simply because some people admired him enough to have a statue erected, but I'm not sure that it would be right to say that. It depends on your viewpoint I suppose.' He looked up at the tall column. 'He was an Earl after all, an aristocrat, so he wouldn't have known what it was like for ordinary people to live in those days. I'll have to find out more, then I'll be able . . .' He looked down at his sons. Each was standing with his head on one side, eyes crossed, shoulder hunched, tongue sticking out. Their legs were bent at the knees, elbows sticking out. They resembled two small scarecrows. Thomas's face cracked into a smile.

'Alright, I'm sorry, it wasn't meant to be turning into a lecture.' He reached out, tousled their hair.

'Come on then, we'd better go and meet your Mam and Uncle Willie and Albie. We'll have to see if we can climb the column another day. Back down this way, step lively. Now see that building over there, on the other side of the road, that's the Theatre Royal. I'll go there one day, when I've earned enough money, and I'll take you with me. And over this side . . .'

There seemed to be more traffic about now, more cabs, more people shopping. At the bottom of the street a lady of indeterminate age (but of high station given the number of footmen bustling around her) was organising her entry to a large and well-polished carriage. She wore a large grey cloak which covered her completely with the exception of her hands. The fur muff into which these appeared to be thrust occasionally lifted its head and barked lazily at no-one in particular, as if to reassure itself that it had not fallen asleep. The footmen and a small army of shop assistants were, under her firm and not very gentle instruction, placing parcels on top of and inside the carriage. Her voice travelled well.

'No, no, you silly girl! That is too, too fragile to be considered mere luggage, it must travel inside with me. And you, you there, the young man with the oily hair and the disagreeable complexion! Yes you! That is a present for my nephew and should be in a case, not wrapped, please take it back inside and do it immediately!'

Thomas was still talking.

'And if you keep going down the hill, right down to the quayside, you'll come to the Guildhall, and Bessie Surtees' House, she eloped with John Scott who became Lord Chancellor. Now watch out lads, there's a dray unloading here. Best wait a minute.'

There were two draymen, one manoeuvering huge wooden casks on the flat back of his wagon and pushing them, one at a time, over the lip of the dray to drop onto a large padded cushion. His colleague would then roll the barrel down a ramp into the cellar of the hotel. Matthew and David, halted by their father, stared up at the blinkered horses, heads hidden in sweet steam-breathed nosebags.

'Hello horse,' said David to the nearest of the beasts. It snorted.

'I said "hello horse",' repeated the small boy. 'There's no need to be so rude!' He turned to complain to his father only to find that he, and his brother, were peering into the cellar. He could have joined them. Instead, seeking a reaction from the animal in front of him, he stepped into its line of vision and jumped up and down, waved his arms about and shouted 'Hello Horse!'

The drayhorses were well-trained, and the boy was rather too small for them to consider more than a minor nuisance. The nearest horse did, however, step back slightly. That was enough to move the cart by a few inches, and the barrel which the first drayman was holding at the edge left his hands too early. It caught the cushion at the wrong angle and, instead of remaining where it fell, lurched to one side and began to roll down the street. The drayman on his cart leaped down and would, if he had not tripped over the kerb, have halted the barrel before it did further damage. Two men walking up the street and seeing the barrel's progress moved easily to one side to avoid it; had they been aware of the rate at which it would increase its speed they might have combined their strength to hold or divert it. Only Thomas remained, therefore, to see the imminent danger; that the barrel was gaining speed and bearing down on a group of innocent people, their attention elsewhere.

He yelled as he started running; they did not hear. His first thought, that he might catch up with the barrel and push it to one side, was discarded immediately. It was travelling too fast, its momentum such that it would have broken his legs.

'Move!' he shouted, and someone looked up. Only twenty yards to go and the barrel still ahead of him. Another five yards and he had caught it; those in its path were beginning to shuffle to one side. Five yards more and he was ahead, bodies scattering in his path. Only a figure in a grey cloak, facing down the street, was in his way. Three more strides and he launched himself in a tackle. When he told the tale to Mary and Willie and Albie, sitting comfortably in the lounge at Balmbra's, he was quite clear about his thoughts at the time.

'It was like Montekitty!' He drew on his pint, licked his lips.

'All I could think of was playing Montekitty when I was little, seeing all these backs linked together and Jimmy Murphy's huge backside right at the end and then up I'd go and up and up. Man, it was like flying, I thought I'd never come down! And it was the same before! But I did come down, and it wasn't a nice soft landing on a platform of other kids' backs, I can tell you. Yes, I managed to move the silly woman out of the way, the barrel missed both of us, but we sort of twisted as we fell and I ended up on the bottom. I bruised me back, hit me head on the carriage wheels. And after all that did I get any thanks? Did I buggery! I tell you, she was up and away before I could even open me eyes and stand up straight! And that's not all! Go on, you tell them lads.'

'She had a dog,' said Matthew, 'and it ran away . . .'

'It was a white dog,' added David.

'And it ran up the street straight at us, and I dived for it . . .'

'It was white and it was little and it was barking.'

'I dived for it and I missed it but . . .'

'He missed it!'

'But I caught its lead!'

'He did. He caught its lead!'

'Well done lads,' said Thomas. 'Then what happened?'

'We took the dog up to the man who was . . .'

'I want to say,' wailed David, 'I want to say what we did!'

'It was me who caught it,' insisted Matthew, 'I should tell the story. Anyway, I know words better than you!'

'I know "Government",' said David. 'And I know "Prime Minister", and I know you fancy Helen Hardwick and you kissed her in the woods yesterday!'

'I did not! And I'm going to get you! I'm going to . . .' Matthew aimed a kick at David's behind and made fleeting contact. David collapsed in fake tears and agony.

'I shall finish the story then,' announced Thomas gravely, reaching round to pick up both children, one with each hand, and sit them each on a stool, one at his left hand, one at his right.

'Behave!' he glowered. Matthew stuck out his bottom lip; David feigned innocence but said nothing.

'I was still on the floor, mind, by meself. The woman had got up, or been lifted up I suspect, and they'd left me lying. But I saw these two in front of the shop. They were handing in the stupid dog, it was whining and yapping, and the man, he looked like the manager, took it off them and told them to wait. Anyway, this woman re-appears and says something to them, and Matthew does a deep bow, and David does a little one . . .'

'It was a curtsey Dad, it was a curtsey!'

'Alright then, it was a curtsey! And I heard her. With me own ears I heard her. She says,' he adopted a strange, clipped, mincing tone, ' "Thank you for catching Salome for me. I don't know what I would have done if she had been hurt. Please accept this." And she gave them half-a-crown each! Half-a-crown! I ask you, is that right when I've just saved her life and I'm lying in the gutter bleeding?'

Mary reached across, touched the small scratch on his forehead and tutted in sympathy.

'And that's not all! She looks at me, at least I think she does, 'cos I can see nothing of her face under that daft cloak, she looks in my direction, and says "You should be proud of your boys my man", then she turns on her heels and disappears back into the shop. I didn't know where to put meself! Anyway, the drayman, he was pleased at least, it would have been his fault if anybody'd been hurt, he helped me to me feet. He knew who it was as well, the woman that is. "Lady Montague," he says, one of the nastiest most stuck-up women it'd ever been his displeasure to know. He even said I should have let the barrel break her neck, but that's going a bit too far. So I made sure I was alright, dusted meself down, and came round here. And to be perfectly honest, I'm beginning to feel a bit funny now!'

'That's not surprisin',' said Albie, 'you've probably given your 'ead a bit of a knock. 'Ere, let's 'ave a look.'

His long, rough fingers searched Thomas's scalp. Thomas winced as they found a bruise.

'Are you alright Dad?' asked Matthew.

'We're proud of you' said David. He stood up and kissed his father on the forehead.

'Yes, I'm alright. And I'm proud of you two, too!' He held out his arms and his sons curled themselves into his embrace. Above his head a clock chimed the three-quarters.

'You'll survive,' said Albie. 'But we won't if we don't get

to our seats in time! Come on Mary, we'd best be off. We've a weddin' to attend!'

Willie, Thomas and the boys stood at the main entrance to the cathedral. There were others there they recognised, from the pit, one or two from Lanchester. They chatted quietly as carriages drew up and discharged their contents rapidly through the majestic carved doors. Most of the wedding guests were unknown to the spectators. 'Friends of the Makemores,' they guessed. Henry Makemore himself hurried past with his best man, a small, foppish individual whose lazy, laconic manner made the groom appear nervous and over-active. Neither acknowledged any of those watching. Edward Waterhouse, up from Manchester for the occasion, took the opposite viewpoint. He was sharing a coach with Elizabeth, and he seemed delighted that so many of his brother's employees had made the journey. He smiled and shook hands, bent down slowly and carefully to admire children (formal dress did not allow flamboyant movement) and exchanged pleasantries with one or two of those he recognised. Noticing the Armstrongs he rolled over to stand beside them.

'Mr Armstrong!' he announced grandly, 'not to mention Mr Armstrong, Mr Armstrong, and Mr Armstrong!' He bent down.

'I hope you two are taking care of your father and your uncle,' he said, winking extravagantly at Thomas and Willie. The boys nodded shyly. David shuffled backwards to take refuge between his father's legs.

'I think he's drunk,' he whispered; Thomas placed his finger gently over the boy's lips.

'Beautiful day for a wedding, eh? And wait till you see Margaret, she looks beautiful, a princess! What more do you need, apart from,' he touched the side of his nose and spoke more softly, 'a groom worth tipping your hat to, which is decidedly lacking around here. Still, Margaret appears to have taken a shine to him, so he can't be all bad. And I hear congratulations are due to you Mr William! Abigail's to be the lucky lass, eh?'

'That's right Mr Waterhouse,' mumbled Willie, 'we're getting married at the beginning of March.'

'Well damn good luck to you both, that's all I can say! Let me give you a bit of advice. When it comes to your wedding night, not that I've been married, but I am a man of the world, so to speak, make sure . . .'

'Uncle Edward, Margaret will be here shortly. I think we'd better go in.' Elizabeth had glided to his side. She had foresaken her traditional black for a rich, dark blue dress (trimmed in white brocade) with a slight bustle, gathered severely at the waist, a white silk blouse preventing the low neckline from seeming too unsuitable for the occasion. A cloak of the same colour protected her from the cold. Unlike most of the other women who had entered the cathedral she wore no hat. She was smiling at those around her, but her purpose was evident; her uncle must be persuaded to take his seat within.

'Yes Elizabeth,' he grumbled. 'I'll be with you in a moment, I'm talking to young William here.'

'Uncle Edward, Margaret's carriage is here. We must get in before her.' She linked her arm with that of her uncle and pulled him away.

'He started celebrating a little too early I think,' she whispered to Thomas and Willie. 'We must go now, I hope you enjoy yourselves.'

There was a hush as the next coach arrived. It was the finest yet, drawn by two white stallions which danced nervously when brought to a halt. It had been polished and lacquered, its paint black as a mirror, and hung with twists of white ribbon. A footman leapt from the rear and opened the door for John Waterhouse to step slowly down.

'He looks tired,' said Thomas to Willie. There was no reply. Willie was standing on his toes trying to see over the heads of those beside him, trying to see Margaret Waterhouse emerge from the coach. She timed her exit well, waiting for a moment to ensure that all eyes were upon her. A gloved hand reached out. John Waterhouse placed it delicately upon his own as though it were engraved on Beilby glass. The whispers which had sprung up when the father appeared died down once more as the daughter stepped out into the day, softly patting her dress of pure white silk embroidered with sunlight. Her veil was pulled back over her head, her hair was in ringlets. She walked majestically toward the doors, looking neither to right nor left. The hush became a tremor of whispers, and then voices which yelled their approval, and then wild, stamping applause.

'She *is* a princess,' breathed Matthew; David stood, incapable of movement, his right hand raised, fingers lifting and falling in an unseen wave. Just before the door Margaret halted and turned elegantly. The footman bearing her train scuttled sideways bent almost double, determined that he would not block anyone's view. Margaret waved in a disinterested manner, moved her head slowly from right to left to survey her admirers. She basked in their adoration, drank in their approving cheers and applause and happy smiles. She had looked at herself in the mirror before leaving the hotel, aware that there would be a sizeable number of her father's workers outside the cathedral, unsure of which face, which demeanour to wear. Friendly? Approachable? Aristocratic? Should she allow them to see her face without the veil? Should she acknowledge their presence at all? Just as she had tried numerous gowns before selecting the final one, so she wore each face in the mirror before moving to the next, discarding some out of hand, returning to others for greater consideration. It did not take her long to decide on the imperious, condescending, aloof manner. It was, she felt, what they would want. It would give them something to remember while reminding them of their station. They would love her.

But there was one face showing no emotion. One pair of eyes staring at her without any warmth. One pair of lips refusing to curl into a smile. And that face drew Margaret. Her eyes met those of Willie Armstrong and the applause, for Margaret at least, dissolved into a hollow, aching clangour on the fringe of her awareness. She stared at him, willing him to look away, but his strength was greater than hers and she found herself unable to break loose from his glare. Even when he turned, slowly, deliberately, she had to watch him as he pushed his way through the crowd. He looked back only once and spat at the ground, continued walking down a long grey tunnel to oblivion.

'Margaret? Margaret, are you alright?' John Waterhouse's voice pulled his daughter back into a world of light. She blinked, held her hand out. He moved to support her.

'Do you feel faint? Is there something the matter Margaret?' She inhaled deeply, patted her father's hand.

'I'm alright father. It was just that ... I thought I saw someone I once knew. A friend. But when I looked closer, it wasn't that person at all. I'm alright now. I think we'd best go in, I don't want Henry kept waiting too long!'

Mary was awake early, though she was not at first sure why. It was Sunday, she knew that much, and she normally slept late on a Sunday. Of late, however, she had taken to going to church, not every week it was true, but certainly two or three times a month, and ... That was it! The wedding! The first Sunday in March, Willie and Abigail were getting married! And that was today!

She resisted the impulse to leap from her bed. It was barely light, and through her mounting excitement she remembered that it had been almost two in the morning when she had gratefully fallen asleep. There had been so much to do! Abigail, of course, had no family to help her, and Thomas and Willie had sent word of the wedding to their sisters only grudgingly; they still felt that the girls should have come to their father's funeral. A note came back saying that they would make every effort to attend but that distance and difficulty in travelling might prevent it. There would be no assistance from that direction. The neighbours, however, had been more than generous. This was, after all, the community's first wedding, and it was turning into a celebration for all. Gifts had been delivered to the new house, Willie's and Abigail's house, almost daily. Crockery and pots and pans, some new; bed linen; the Waterhouses had sent down a sideboard! Willie himself had, with Thomas's help, built a double bed and chest of drawers, and they had bought a table and chairs and a very comfortable settee from the salerooms in Durham.

Any items the couple had not bought or been given were graciously lent. Cutlery and plates, extra seats, tablecloths, even the tables themselves. Mary had suggested that they move the wedding breakfast to the village hall where there was more space, but Willie had insisted that he would entertain his guests in his own home. He had found little difficulty in gathering an impressive amount of beer and ale, wines and spirits and cigars; the choice of food had been left to Abigail. Mary smiled at the thought of her future sister-in-law. When Tommy died Abigail had given Willie the strength to cope, and Mary felt a growing warmth for this woman with whom she shared a love for Tommy Armstrong's sons.

Mary wished that she had been able to help Thomas in the same way. It was not for want of trying. She felt in her heart that her husband had needed to find his own comfort, but had been willing to help if he needed her. He had not had to turn in that direction. The last few months had, however, seen him return to something like his normal self. Mary believed it was the rapper. She did not say as much, she kept her feelings to herself, but she had felt that she was losing Thomas as soon as he started doing that dance. Even the preacher had mentioned to her that he'd seen the dance for the first time that Christmas and he was shocked that the swords had been held up reverentially in the form of a pentangle. Was it the devil's dance? Certainly the music was fast and quickened the heartbeat, made the feet tap as if by magic. And it certainly seemed to have had some sort of hold over Thomas, just as it had had over his father. But since Tommy died rapper hadn't been mentioned, at least in her presence. Mary was happier. And she felt that Thomas, despite his new-found interest in writing and his new habit of sitting staring at the fire, as if expecting his future to be written in the flames, was happier as well. She stretched out her hand, felt her husband's broad back and the soft hairs at the base of his spine.

Mary shrugged mentally. Enough of me and Thomas, there's two other people far more important than us today. After all, you only get married once. And their marriage would certainly be different to her own wedding.

That had been on a Wednesday morning; Thomas had been on backshift. His original choice of groomsman had been moved to foreshift, so he had had to find someone else to stand in his place. Try as she might she couldn't recall his face nor his name. She had had a friend as bridesmaid, Betty Sarginson it was. She'd moved away not long after, never been heard from since. They'd walked to the church – the ceremony had taken no longer than ten minutes – and walked back feeling somehow different. The wedding breakfast had been a simple affair, tatie-pot and ale, and then everyone had taken themselves off for a walk in the park leaving her and Thomas alone. They'd spent two hours in bed before he had to get up and go to work. And that was it. Two months later she was pregnant, and two months after that they had their own house, if you could call it that. More like a home for starving rodents. But Abigail and Willie, they were more lucky, they were starting off miles further up the road. She reached out to Thomas again, moved her hand round onto his thigh, felt him stirring. Yes, Abigail and Willie were lucky. But she didn't envy them at all. Not at all.

The preacher had offered Willie and Abigail a free choice in the time of their wedding. Before, after, even during morning service, mid-afternoon; it didn't matter at all. We must place our priorities in strict order, he said, and a wedding outranked all other considerations on that day. He had suggested, however, that it would be propitious to have the ceremony immediately following the morning service.

'Course he'd say that,' scoffed Thomas, 'increases attendance at a stroke!'

'Thomas Armstrong!' scolded Mary, 'sometimes I think the devil's taken your tongue!'

'Rest of his body's not worth having, that's for certain,' said Willie softly, ducking in time to avoid a cushion thrown in his direction. 'Anyway, it means I get a bit of a lie in. Don't have to be there till five-and-twenty past eleven.'

Willie was, however, up long before Thomas and Mary. Abigail had stayed the night with them, so Willie had moved out early on the Saturday evening, resolved to spending the night alone in the new house. He had moved furniture here and there, usually no more than an inch or two, tidied up (although Mary and Abigail had earlier that day washed, polished or scrubbed everything that didn't move), set out his clothes for the next day. He had sighed and yawned in an attempt to persuade himself that he was tired, had even opened (but immediately laid down again) a book. Sure that he would not sleep he had retired at nine o'clock, not even removing his boots; but his clock showed five-thirty when he awoke, certain that he would not sleep again. He splashed cold water at his face and thrust his arms into his coat. A walk would do him good. It was a clear night, the sun would be up shortly, and, he realised, it was the first time since Christmas that he'd had the opportunity to be out alone. It felt good.

He strode out of the village, headed south and onto the road which led from Lanchester up to Consett. This he ignored. He leapt over a wall and followed a path across the dewy fields, scaring rabbits into their white-bobbed burrows. Lazy cows followed his progress with steamy-breathed indifference. Sheep scattered before him as his pace quickened and his walk developed into a run. An old fox almost lame with rickets snarled at him as he disturbed its rooting for insects in a rotten tree-stump. He hurdled the wire fence at the end of the field and clipped it with his foot, found himself tumbling and laughing down the railway embankment. He rose quickly, didn't even pause to dust himself down, crawled hand over fist up the steep, slick grass on the other side. Backgill Burn was taken in a single stride, the heron caught fishing there beating its retreat with strong, bowed wings. Dogs barked as he ran through Newbiggin; a goose considered chasing him but he was past before the thought could be translated into action.

He could have taken the lane leading to Upper Houses but instead chose to wade through the remnants of last year's bracken in the field beside, up the hill and through the wood, yelling breathlessly at the revolving head of a barn-owl. The way became steeper and he slowed down. He caught his foot in a rabbit-hole, measured his length on the wet turf and slid a yard or two back downhill before his hands clutched at some long grasses and his toes dug into the earth. More slowly, more carefully, he continued his climb to arrive panting at the top.

The sun was already up, Venus still in fawning attendance. There were no clouds to be seen in the sky which
moved over him from white to pale blue to black, thrown
with stars and promises. Cole Pike (if that was its name. The
maps gave the hill no title, it could as easily have been
Hollingside, for that was the other farm on its western
slopes) looked down from its lowly heights over misty fields
past Quebec to Langley and Esh Winning, Ushaw Moor and
Bear Park, on to Durham itself. Willie sank to his haunches
as a hare loped past on its easy way, ears aloft. High above
his head a lark was flung into being. He closed his eyes and
drank in the morning elation coursing through his veins.

The countryside below him was being transformed. Its
sepia tones became brushed first with pale pastels and
washes, then slowly took on the vibrancy and colour of a
pre-Raphaelite landscape, touched with deep-hued blues
and greens and varnished with the gloss of a new day. The
day he would be married.

There was no heat in the sun, not yet, and although
Willie's exertions had warmed him, he ought to have cooled
by now. True, his breathing had returned to its normal
steady deepness, but he felt nothing of the dawn's chill. He
did not question this. His thoughts had moved on, away
from the countryside and the beauty of the day, away from
the birdsong and soft V of geese in the distant sky. Today he
would be married. And the day itself, beautiful though it
might be, was less so than his bride to be. He rocked
forwards, hugged his knees, rubbed the stubble of his chin
against the rough cloth of his breeches. Abigail. They had
seen so much of each other in the past two months that he
had forgotten how life had been before he met her. There
had been no gradual transition from a single life to one of
commitment, no slow erosion of what others might consider
to be his freedom. It was as though he had been changed, his

outlook altered, not subtly but completely, by a full half-circle. He had no wish to return to the days of gossip and girls; it simply felt natural for him to be with her.

So he had told himself as they had carried blankets and sheets into their new home. Small items of furniture, curtains, rugs and mats, wall-hangings, prints, a coal-scuttle, a bookcase (he could see little use for that!); the bed, which he himself was making, was upstairs in the room which it would ultimately grace; domesticity beckoned.

From the parlour he had heard Abigail moving about upstairs, had noted the lowing staccato rattle of drawers which had to be forced from side to side in order that they would open. She had called for him and, on reaching the landing, he had found one of the bedroom doors closed. From the other room there came the glow of a candle. He entered slowly. Heavy curtains had been hung and there was no natural light in the room save a rectangle of glow showing where the window ought to have been. As his eyes became accustomed to the darkness he noticed a pile of cushions and pillows on the floor formed into a low bed. A movement caught his eye as Abigail stepped forward.

She was wearing a shift, too light and delicate to be cotton, and when she moved to stand in front of the candle flame the silhouette of her body was etched on the garment. She reached down to the hem, lifted it, brought the shift over her head and dropped it on the floor to stand naked before him.

'Willie,' she said. 'I love you.' She held out her arms and he came to her, and they made love.

'Abigail!' shouted Willie from the height of the hill. He stood up, raised his arms to the skies.

'Abigail!' he yelled. 'I love you!' He turned to begin the walk back home. In the valley below the sun was reflected from the windows of a large, square, white stone building. Makemore Hall was stirring.

* * *

There were only two at breakfast. Henry was still in bed and would, Margaret knew, wake with a hangover. Sir Charles was, once again, away on business, though she suspected that the business had more to do with the disposal rather than the acquisition of wealth. Sitting opposite her was Henry's friend from London, Mr Maichamps. She did not think it strange that he should be known only by that single name, nor that he appeared to arrive and depart at whim. Henry had many strange friends, and Maichamps was at least kind and considerate in his dealings with her. This was his third visit since her wedding, and each time he had brought her gifts. A small item of jewellery, scented oils and perfumes, elegant writing paper. He was charming, she had decided, in a vaguely sinister sort of way; perhaps it was his height. His company was certainly more welcome than that of her husband. Foul-breathed and smelling of stale sweat he had come to her in the early hours of the morning and, when her attentions had not been given quickly enough or her response had been judged lacking in enthusiasm, he had turned her over, thrown her onto her front, and struck her backside. Even now she could feel the pain, was forced to shift her position slightly. He had threatened to take a whip to her, and though she doubted that he would do this it was enough to persuade her to succumb to what she considered to be Henry's darker requirements. When he left she immediately reached for one of the bottles he forced her to keep by the side of the bed (usually the gin) and washed her mouth out. Sometimes she would swallow.

Maichamps had been in the dining room when she arrived, reading a local newspaper. He put this down straightaway, took her hands, kissed her on both cheeks. His cologne was delicate, attractive, his manner natural.

'Margaret my dear, you look tired this morning. The rigours of marriage I suspect? You need to be cosseted, to be cared for. Allow me.'

He shepherded her to her seat, fetched her coffee and toast, butter and marmalade. Only after she assured him that she had everything she required did he take a plate himself, place on it a small portion of scrambled egg. His coffee was black and unsweetened. They ate in silence but, when finished, Maichamps seemed eager both to talk and to listen. He asked about their honeymoon in Italy, though Margaret was sure that they had already covered that subject in a previous conversation. He expressed his admiration of Classical Roman statuary and, when she admitted no great knowledge of the subject, he gave her a brief, humorous though educational lecture. He reminded her of a peacock as he strutted around the room, sketching furiously on scraps of paper, pulling books down from shelves to illustrate a point, pausing to preen himself each time he passed in front of the mirror.

'I'm sorry,' he said after twenty minutes of this, 'I forget myself. I must be boring you.'

'Not at all,' she replied, 'you are both interesting and entertaining and, if I am honest, I must confess that there is very little other conversation in this house which justifies the use of either of those adjectives.'

Maichamps laughed, shook his head. He had sat down beside her and was now leaning forward conspiratorially.

'I fear that neither Henry nor his father show much interest in the fine arts.'

'Nor the performing arts,' added Margaret, 'unless the performer happens to be a dancer, female but definitely not a lady, and preferably on the stage of a music hall!'

'Philistines perhaps,' said Maichamps, 'but good men at heart.' Margaret shifted her position again. Maichamps looked at her, pursed his lips as if about to say something, shook his head to show that he had changed his mind, then went on regardless.

'Forgive me for saying this my dear,' he said, 'but it is very

Alan Dunn

rare that a marriage is entirely fulfilling in all directions. I have visited this place often, I am a good friend of Henry's, I know a little of what your life here will be like. I feel – and I must assure you that this is only my opinion – that there will be times when you feel alone, unable to confide in anyone. Henry is, alas, not a good listener. May I be so bold as to suggest that you consider me a distant, though ever willing, confidant? You may write to me anything you wish and I shall reply with equal candour. When I visit you may talk to me, question me, and I shall do my utmost to assist you in any way possible.' He reached out to her, held her hands.

'My dear Margaret, do not answer me now. Think on the matter for a few days, you will lose nothing by agreeing to this, gain nothing by declining the offer. I have not known you for long, but I feel that we have a great deal in common. I see in you much that I admire, and I would wish to be your friend. Think on.' He rose to his feet, picked up the newspaper he had been reading.

'Please consider my proposition. For the moment, however, I must be away. I look forward to meeting you at luncheon.' He headed for the door, then stopped.

'I see that there is an item of news from your father's domain, I ought to have mentioned it earlier. Now where are we ...?' he rustled the pages, flicked them over casually. 'Ah yes. Announcements. "The wedding will take place on Sunday 6 March of Miss Abigail Anderson, maidservant of Mrs Elizabeth Kearton, Greencroft Hall, Lanchester, and Mr William Armstrong, miner, of Greencroft." Abigail Anderson? Wasn't she your maid at one time? There was a little trouble I believe? And William Armstrong, he's one of those dancer-people? Should be an interesting little affair. But duty calls, until later dearest ... Margaret, are you well? Is there something the matter?'

Maichamps hurried back to Margaret's side, bent down

before her. Her eyes were closed, one hand holding the other up to her mouth, her teeth gnawing at her knuckles.

'Margaret! What is it?'

'It's nothing,' she said firmly, 'nothing at all. Just a thought, an unpleasant thought, but it's left me already.' She looked up at him and smiled.

'Thank you for your kind words Mr Maichamps. I need no time to consider your offer any further, I would be delighted to talk with you and to write to you and shall look forward to your replies. But please, I hold you back. Until this afternoon . . .?'

'I shall spend the morning in anticipation. Goodbye my dear.' He kissed her hand and left, made straight for his room, then walked past. Three doors down he entered another room without knocking. The air was stale, the closed windows hidden behind velvet drapes. He stumbled to the bed and stood over it, watching the body sleeping and snoring beneath silk sheets and a bulky, quilted eiderdown.

'Henry,' he said. The body moved, and Maichamps helped it escape from sleep by shaking it thoroughly. The result was a groan.

'Henry, you sound like a pig and you smell like one. Do you intend getting up today?'

'No!'

'I have come to report, Henry my dear. I have come to report that your wife has agreed to confide all her secrets in me. She may not yet be aware of this, but she will do it, in time. But you too must continue to play your part. Do you hear me Henry?'

'No! Go away!'

'Attentive as always, eh Henry? You must continue to behave badly towards Margaret. You should beat her, lightly but regularly. You should insist on her fellating you. Make her think that you're a little depraved Henry. I'm sure that you can do that. In fact, I believe that this little play will require no acting from you at all. Just be yourself Henry, be yourself. And you will get your reward, there is no doubt about that, you will be rewarded.' Henry Makemore groaned again.

'Verbose little creature, aren't you? Let's see if I can make you say something else, eh?'

Maichamps' hand sneaked under the quilt, under the sheet, to find its target.

'Oh, dear God!' cried Henry.

'Oh no my dear,' was the whispered reply, 'not him. Most certainly not him.'

It was late in the evening, and Mr William and Mrs Abigail Armstrong were entertaining friends and family in their new home. The whole village was there, and the nobs from the Hall, and everyone else for that matter. There was music and singing, children were hiding from each other inside, chasing each other outside, panting through the chill air. If spring had woken that day to claim the world then winter was showing that she had done so without his permission, and that he was still capable of wrapping the night in his dark cloak. But the fire was lit, good ale warmed the body, and friendly conversation warmed the heart.

'What a spread! I don't know how they did it, they must have worked like Trojans. Did you taste that trifle? Did you taste it? Mary did that, I tell you she's wasted, she could make a living out of trifles she could, I told her so to her face.'

'I'm not a great one for sweet things, they go for me teeth. But that boiled ham and pickle went down a treat, and as for the roast beef, well, I tell you, Royalty wouldn't have been ashamed to eat as we've done this evening . . .'

'. . . and didn't she look wonderful? Decorated the dress herself they say! And that Willie, what a handsome man. I only wish I'd been a bit younger, I would have been after him alright . . .'

'. . . go on, sing "Waters of Tyne" for us. I'd do it, but I can't stand up straight . . .'

'. . . well I thought Mr Proudlock did very well. You could hear everything he said from anywhere in the church, which is more than I can say for that vicar up in Consett, and he was so nice to everyone afterwards. Did you see him earlier on? Aye, he was here, just for a little while. And that's another thing about him, he knew that nobody would start drinking while he was here so he made sure he left sharpish, not wanting to spoil things. That's the sign of a man who knows his congregation. And he's not married either, now he'd be a catch!'

'Mam! Mam, I want a wee!'

'. . . so we'll need a better means of getting the coal from the face to the shaft bottom, a faster engine to get it up the shaft, and a way of sorting it that's more accurate. Now I've one or two ideas I'd like to show you, since you have the practical experience, then I can have them costed accurately . . .'

'. . . it's true! He was in love with a pigeon!'

'. . . is there any more of them steak pies left, I could murder a steak pie.'

'Where's our Albert? Where's he gone? That Ellie Pattinson's not here either, the floosie, he'll be with her, I'll guarantee it! I'll find them, then I'll give them both what for, you mark my words . . .'

'That Miss Elizabeth, she's damn good on that fiddle. Did you watch her playing "The Maggie", you could hardly see her fingers and she was sawing away with the bow so fast I though she'd set the damn thing alight. And she looked happy for once! A dour woman that one . . .'

'. . . so much good, after all, they've had a bad year so far. But they look well now, Thomas and Mary, and Willie and Abigail. Such nice people, such nice people . . .'

'Get into this house now, before you catch your death of cold!'

'Willie, I want to go to bed now. Do you think anyone'll notice if we slip upstairs?'

'Aye love, they probably will. But I don't think they'll mind. I think they'll understand. Howway.'

'. . . and thank you very much, it was very nice, I enjoyed playing the fiddle again, I've hardly picked it up since . . . since . . . Oh, and I've a favour to ask you Thomas. There's a meeting on Easter Monday, at Ryton Willows. Tom Mann will be there, and there's talk that he'll be bringing William Morris with him. Somehow I think they must have been talking to father – they heard about your dancers. Anyway, they want some entertainment, and I thought you could do rapper. I'd play for you. And they'll pay as well, ten pounds. I think we'd have to practise a little, it's a while since you've danced. What do you think?'

'I'm so pleased Thomas is settling down. I just didn't know what to do with him when his Dad died, I never actually thought they were that close! But he seems alright now, there was a time when I never saw him 'cos of that daft dance he was doing. Yes, he's alright now. But your plate's empty Mrs Bainbridge, do have one of these cakes, I made them meself and they're rather nice, even if I'm the only one who says so . . .'

'Aye Elizabeth, why not? It'll be good to dance again, I'm sure the rest of them'll agree. Aye. Easter Monday. Ryton Willows. I'll look forward to that.'

Chapter Thirteen

He capers, he dances, he has eyes of youth, he writes
verses, he speaks holiday, he smells April and May.
The Merry Wives of Windsor.
(William Shakespeare)

The wagon was full. Elizabeth had arranged to borrow it
from a neighbouring farmer; she had had it cleaned and
a tarpaulin fitted as a roof in case of bad weather, but
this precaution seemed likely to be unnecessary. Easter
Sunday had been fine all day, and the Monday seemed to
have every intention of improving on that performance.

Len was driving, his dog on one side, a woman on the
other, his pipe, unlit as usual, clenched between his teeth. He
had brought three cases of bottled beer but Thomas had
suggested that they limit themselves to a bottle each on the
outward journey, in case the dance suffered. Stew was there,
playing cards with Davy and Rob. Rob's wife Aileen had
insisted on coming and no-one had been brave enough to
deny her; her broad plump figure was sprawled at the rear
of the wagon. She sang ballads, off-key and in no particular
rhythm. The words, however, could be heard quite clearly,
and their bawdiness would have made a keelman blush. Her
companions were aware that she would soon be quiet; she

knew only three songs and, after singing them twice each, she would behave herself until the return journey.

Willie and Abigail sat close to each other, his arm around her shoulder, their backs to the driver's seat. They were lost in each other's presence. Although they would answer a question when asked, would even initiate a conversation, at no time did they cease touching one another. Abigail would reach across to pass a bag of apples round, and Willie's hand would slide down from her shoulder to her waist as she moved, across her back, down the outside of her thigh, even if he had to lean forward to do so. When he stood up to point the way Abigail's fingers scratched lazy circles on the back of his leg.

Thomas and Elizabeth sat opposite each other, a chest containing the dancers' costumes between them. They said little, seemed to be avoiding each other's gaze. Thomas's attention was, for a large part of the time, elsewhere. Mary had disagreed with his proposal that the team dance at Ryton, despite the rest of them agreeing that it would help them to go. That disagreement had remained politely unresolved until the previous night when it had degenerated into a loud and vociferous argument. Mary had never shouted at him before.

She had told him as soon as he tried to organise a practice that she disapproved of him going. She had hoped, perhaps naively, that he would be content to let the matter drop but, when he explained that he felt an obligation to dance, both to the Waterhouses and in memory of his father, she felt obliged in her turn to express her feelings more strongly. She could understand Thomas's argument, even if she didn't like it. Practices, yes. But a day away at Ryton Willows? Why was there any need for that? Why travel all the way there to dance when they could equally well do the same in the village hall and take no more than half-an-hour from their day?

'It's not the dancing itself that matters love,' Thomas had tried to explain, 'it's the circumstances of the dancing. It's a crowd of people to win over. It's hearing them cheering and applauding. It's knowing that there's five of you and you're doing something well, something nobody watching can do. It's the teamwork and ... oh, I don't know, I can't find the words for it!'

'Well that makes a change Thomas Armstrong, you can normally find words for anything else if you want to. I don't like it, I can tell you now. You're a different man when you start that dancing, you change. I mentioned it to Preacher Proudlock and he says ...'

'You did what?'

'I mentioned it to Preacher Proudlock. He asked me what was troubling me, which is more than you've done of late, so I told him that when you started doing this dancing you changed.'

'You mean you talked about me? With that ranter? Dear God woman, the man's swallowed a dictionary and farts words!'

'There's no need for language like that, Jonathon is a ...'

'Oh, so it's Jonathon now? Getting to know him well, are you?'

'There are times when I feel I know him better than you Thomas. There are times when I just don't know you at all.'

They paused. Mary was on the verge of tears. Thomas sighed.

'Come round here, love, come and sit down.' He positioned her on the seat then knelt on the floor in front of her and took her hands in his.

'We've never argued like this before, have we?'

Mary shook her head.

'There's something wrong, I know that. Despite what you've said about me, I know that something's different. Now, it might be me. I'm prepared to acknowledge that, you could be seeing something in me that I haven't noticed meself. If that's the case, well, I'll try to find out what it is. But even if I do find out, I might not be able to change things back to the way they were. People change love, sometimes without knowing it. And you should bear in mind something else as well. It might not be me. It might be you.'

Mary shook her head, began to speak again, but Thomas raised his finger to her lips.

'No, let me finish. If I can say that there's a possibility I've changed, even when I don't feel any different, then can't you see that the same thing could have happened to you? You could have changed in some way without even noticing. Or it could be both, we could both have moved, perhaps moved away from each other. And the way we feel, the way we *both* feel at the moment, is because we know that we've drifted and we need to pull ourselves back together. But it's something that involves us both, don't you think?'

Mary nodded.

'I'll stop dancing,' said Thomas. Mary's heart leaped only to sink again as Thomas continued.

'I'll stop dancing as soon as the competition's over, I swear it.'

'And Ryton?'

'I've got to go now, can't you see that? We've practised, I call the dance, they're expecting us. I can't back out now. Look, why not come with us? We can take the boys, or somebody'll take care of them for us. Don't cry love, please don't cry!'

Thomas raised his hand to wipe away Mary's tears but she brushed his hand away, ran to the stairs. There she turned.

'You're so full of your own importance Thomas, you can't see anyone doing anything without you! I've begged you not to go, I've pleaded with you, but you won't listen to me. I love you Thomas, can't you see that, and I wouldn't ask you to do something, I wouldn't ask you not to do something unless I thought it was for your own good! If it's for your good then it's for my good and it's for the good of Matthew and David, because we're a family! I can't explain how I feel because I feel emotions and you, you seem to deal in nothing but facts these days! Go on, go to Ryton, take your precious dance team and your precious violinist with you, see if I care! One day you'll find what it is you're looking for Thomas, one day you'll find it and you'll look back and you'll see that what you really wanted you left behind! And by then it might just be too late!' She stamped upstairs and slammed the bedroom door. Thomas looked at the clock. It was two in the morning. He decided to sleep on the settee. He had to be up early. He had a dance team to lead.

It took them an hour and a half to get to the Willows, a piece of rough heath beside the railway line on the south side of the river. It was popular with visitors from further down the Tyne who would ride up on the boat bringing with them their families and picnics. There was a fair with shuggy shoes and a helter-skelter, gaudily painted Galloping Horses chasing each other round a steam-powered organ, a boxing booth and stalls selling food and drink. Enterprising local farmers had brought their ponies along and were charging children for rides, while those who preferred less expensive entertainment could watch a football or cricket match for free. A large marquee had been erected and a wooden floor laid inside with a stage at one end, but already it was warm enough to have the side flaps lifted to allow a breeze to enter. Five surly musicians were setting up drums and moving a piano from a cart which bore a large placard announcing that there was to be dancing throughout the day to Tom Garvey and his syncopated sextet, admission six-pence.

'Now where?' asked Len. His eyes seemed to be searching

for somewhere to leave the wagon and horses, but he could equally well have been on the lookout for a beer seller. Elizabeth had taken it upon herself to organise the outing; the duty to reply was hers.

'There won't be any speeches until later this afternoon, but they asked us to be ready to dance at noon and again at three, then possibly after William Morris finishes speaking, if there's time. It means us staying until late evening unfortunately, but I'm sure there's plenty for us to do.'

'Right then lads,' said Thomas, 'and lasses – sorry Aileen! We're on at twelve, it's half-past ten now; let's meet in an hour's time. That'll give us time to get changed and have a quick run-through. I'll find out where we've to dance, the cart'll be under the trees there. That's it then. Don't be late!'

The evacuation was swift. Soon only Thomas and Elizabeth remained.

'If you sort out the wagon, I'll find out where you're dancing,' said Elizabeth, 'and I'll meet you back here.' She strode away; Thomas did as he was told, tethered the horses and fetched them some water in stout leather bags. There was no sign of any of his companions, so he took a blanket from the wagon and laid it on the ground, fetched one of the bottles of beer, and sat in the dappled sunlight. He closed his eyes, the better to listen to the world around him, but found himself instead reflecting on his argument with Mary. She would be up now, doing the washing or the baking, perhaps taking the boys out for a walk since it was such a fine day. Yes, they would have gone walking, probably down to the burn where David would be standing shivering while his brother was swimming. Matthew didn't seem to feel the cold, but David, there wasn't an ounce of fat on his skinny little body, and he suffered in cold weather. He smiled at the thought of his sons.

'That's better,' said Elizabeth's familiar voice; Thomas opened his eyes and blinked at her.

'I'm sorry, I didn't mean to intrude,' she continued. 'It's just that you looked so tired and miserable, then suddenly you smiled. Is there anything the matter?'

'No,' answered Thomas lifting the beer bottle to his lips, 'nothing's wrong.' He wiped the neck of the bottle with his hand and offered it to Elizabeth, expecting her to decline. Instead she took it from him and gulped eagerly at its contents.

'I didn't realise I was so thirsty,' she admitted. 'I'm sorry, I seem to have finished the bottle.'

'That's alright, there's more.' Thomas stood up, reached into the wagon.

'Do you want another?' he asked over his shoulder.

'I shouldn't really. But, go on then, just this once.'

'I'm sorry there's no glasses, I can go and find one if . . .'

'I can manage with just the bottle thank you.'

They sat in silence, each wary of the other and the secrets they knew.

'Mary and I had an argument last night,' said Thomas suddenly. He was not sure why he said it, he had never talked about his personal problems in the past with anyone, not his father, nor his mother, not even Willie. Perhaps it was revenge. Perhaps he was jealous that Mary had confided in the preacher and he needed to balance the equation. Or perhaps he simply needed to talk.

'She doesn't like me dancing. She doesn't like me dancing rapper, that is. And I think she's jealous. I think she's jealous of you.' He looked up as he said the last six words, pronounced them slowly and clearly as if making certain that she should hear them first time, that there should be no need for repetition. He thought he saw a trace of colour rise to her neck. It could have been a shadow.

'Why should she be jealous of me?' asked Elizabeth. She chose her words carefully.

'Does she know anything which might cause this jealousy?'

Thomas shook his head.

'In the past,' he said, 'I've not done anything without Mary. Even things not involving her, like reading or writing, I've stayed at home and done it in the house, with her knitting or sewing by the fire. I think she finds it hard to come to terms with me having something not involving her. She seems to want me to stay at home, to be with her all the time.'

Thomas's head had sunk again. His hands rolled the beer bottle between his palms, he took a drink then returned his attention to the ground. Elizabeth looked at him, her head on one side.

'So what will you do?' she asked.

'I've already decided that. I'll stop dancing as soon as the contest's over, I told her that straight away.'

'And did that help?'

The time between question and answer was lengthening.

'No.'

Elizabeth stood up. She walked over to the nearest of the horses, stroked its neck firmly, scratched its ears.

'Perhaps you're wrong,' she said. 'Perhaps the answer is to continue doing what you want to do but to reassure her that your feelings for her haven't changed. I don't know how you'd do it, I don't know either of you well enough. But it's an alternative. And it would mean you could keep on dancing.' Thomas grunted non-committally.

'I mean it Thomas! Damn it, you can dance, you can dance well, you know that! And you can teach others to dance, which is probably more important. You said it yourself, these dances are part of your life, your history, and they're dying out! And you're going to stop, just like that?' She shook her head angrily.

'There's something else as well Thomas,' she continued. 'I've watched you when you dance and you come alive. It doesn't matter where it is or who's watching, it could be a practice, you could be doing a step dance in your kitchen for all I know, but that's what you live for! I can see it Thomas, I can see it and I can feel it, and it affects me too. When you and Willie and the rest of them are dancing it makes me play better, it makes me proud to be playing for you, it makes the hair rise on the back of my neck. It does that for me and I'm only watching, God knows how you must feel, when it's going well, when you know that you're good! Am I right?'

Thomas shrugged his reply.

'Yes, you're right.'

'And you're willing to give that up?'

'Aye.'

'Thomas Armstrong, you're either the biggest fool in the world or you love your wife far more than I'll ever understand.'

Thomas looked up again.

'You're probably right,' he admitted, 'on both counts.'

They sat quietly, watching the others make their way across the open field towards them. Abigail and Willie were the first, Len and his woman and his dog not far behind, the rest in a large group. Elizabeth stood up and waved to them, then turned to Thomas.

'One day, Thomas, you'll reach a point in your life where you have to make a decision. It'll be a turning point. It won't be repeated. When that time comes remember what I'm saying now, what I've said before. Because I don't want you to go through the rest of your life forever looking back, saying "I could have done it, I could have broken the chains then" and regretting that you didn't. There's something about you, I don't know what it is, but it makes you different from anyone else. It gives you a spark of excitement, of individuality. But there are too many people in this world who don't like those who are different. They're the ones who can put out that spark. I'll say nothing more. Just remember.'

* * *

In the centre of the field they found a platform some four feet above the ground, and in front of it a number of table tops, their trestles discarded, had been laid to form an area some twelve feet square. William Morris would speak from the platform; they would dance on the boards. Stew wandered amiably onto the dancing surface, jumped up and down a couple of times.

'It's better than grass,' he said, 'but not much.'

'Hadaway,' said Len. 'We'll get a good bounce on this and a lot of noise. The trouble is we've been spoiled, it's such a good floor in the hall. Good God, think about it man! We could have become so used to dancing on level ground that we might not be able to dance on anything that's not perfectly flat!' He fell to his knees in mock horror, hands clenched in a fearful prayer.

'Get up you daft bugger,' said Willie, 'people'll think you're a right loonie.'

'You mean I'm not? Oh thank you kind sir, thank you for your kind words!' He crawled across to Willie's feet and began to polish his shoes with his sleeve.

'He's right you know,' said Aileen. 'You are a bit daft. I mean, just look at you, look at your outfits. They're not normal, are they? And what are you going to do? You're going to do a dance. Five men, and you're going to do a dance. And not only are you going to dance together, but you're going to do it with little bendy swords in your hands. Little bendy swords with a handle at both ends. Now *that* is what I call daftness!'

'That's what I call tradition,' laughed Thomas, 'but if we *are* going to do it we'd best have a practice now, before we get an audience.'

They went through the motions of the dance without music, a strange futuristic ballet which attracted a crowd of one, a small brown mongrel. They missed out the stepping altogether, concentrating on the movements within the figures and the order of the figures themselves. There were no mistakes, it took no more than five minutes, and the troupe returned to the wagon (guarded jealously by Len's dog) to change. Out of deference to Elizabeth – somehow the rules of modesty did not seem to apply to any of the other women – the men put on their costumes hidden behind one side of the wagon while the women lounged at the other. Only Aileen felt it necessary to crawl beneath the wagon and peer at the dancers in various stages of undress, and then to be theatrically upset when they ignored her ribaldry.

There was no crowd when they returned to the platform, but the sight of the men in their costumes soon drew a few curious onlookers. Thomas whispered something to Elizabeth, and she began to play her violin, a reel called 'The Badger Bag'. More people stopped. The tune moved easily to a familiar set of hornpipes; Thomas strode to the centre of the stage and began stepping, some of the easy steps, nothing too strenuous. The crowd grew. One or two even sat down, unsure of what was about to happen but determined that they would have a good view of whatever it might be. As Thomas began to wind down the other dancers took up their positions behind him. He finished with a 'Double and Treble', accepted the polite applause, and as he stepped back into line Willie marched forward to sing the calling-on song.

They had decided that the first and last verses would suffice, more than that tending to bore those watching, and that Willie ought to sing these. His voice could be politely described as raucous. He started, as he always did and despite Elizabeth giving him the correct note, too high. He knew, the dancers knew, and the audience knew through his pantomiming that he would not reach the top note. He scuttled across the stage, made rude gestures with the sword, put it down his shirt, down his trousers, between his legs.

Each note of the song may not necessarily have been in tune with any of the others, but if they lacked accuracy they certainly possessed power. By the time he finished the second verse those watching were four or five deep, all curious to see what was going on. The dance was begun.

Seven minutes, perhaps eight at the outside, that was all it took to reduce five dancers and one musician to a state of sweaty exhaustion and convert two hundred onlookers into enthusiastic followers of the ancient tradition of sword-dancing.

'We'll be on again at three!' shouted Thomas. 'Come back then, bring your friends, your families, husbands, wives, dogs, pigs and sheep! But most of all bring your applause!'

'That sounded like a very poor Music Hall line,' said Abigail.

'Can't have been,' panted Thomas, 'I don't go to places like that. Must have been Willie who taught it to me.'

He looked around. The dancers were draped over wooden seats or squatting on the floor. Aileen and Len's woman were handing round bottles of beer, Elizabeth had put away her violin and was standing with her hands raised to the sky. Dark shadows under her arms showed that she too had put much effort into the dance.

'Too hot?' asked Thomas.

'Overdressed,' came the reply. 'If I'd suspected it was going to be this warm I'd have dressed in something a little lighter.'

'Well, it is a fair we're at. You could always have a look round, there's always someone selling clothes. You might find something cooler.'

He reached for two passing bottles of beer, handed one to Elizabeth without thinking. She shrugged and began to drink.

'That was good lads. Let's see if we can do better next time, eh? We'll have a bigger crowd then, 'specially if we

wander round now in our costumes. Back at five-to then.'
He gathered in the swords and, after a nod from Elizabeth,
the violin, and put them under the speaker's platform. The
others were beginning to drift away.

'Just the two of us left?' he said.

'Yes,' answered Elizabeth. 'I think I'll have a look round,
see if I can find something a little looser to wear.' She picked
up her bag.

'You're very welcome to accompany me. If you wish.'

Thomas shrugged and looked around him, as if searching
for something better to do. Finding nothing, he nodded.

'Aye,' he said, 'I'd like that.'

They wandered the heath, finding no trace of the willow
trees which the name suggested ought to have been there,
nor coming across a stall selling clothing, but discovering
much else to fill their afternoon. There were other enter-
tainers there, jugglers and a Punch and Judy show, a band of
players who had set up a makeshift theatre and were
presenting 'The Red Barn' in all of its melodramatic glory.
They watched a foot-race (which Thomas declined to enter)
and applauded the skills of a one-man-band whose dancing
monkey snatched coins from outstretched fingers. They
bought baked potatoes and meat pies and drank more beer
(Elizabeth confessed that she was beginning to enjoy both
the taste and the effect) and eventually found themselves in
Ryton itself. The shops were all open and Elizabeth was
delighted to find one with a selection of dresses in the
window. Thomas waited outside for a mercifully brief few
minutes, his costume drawing the attention of those passing
from the railway station to the fair. It was hot on the
pavement, he would have preferred to be back with the
wagon under the shade of the trees. A cough drew his
attention.

Elizabeth was standing in the doorway. Gone was the stiff
black dress and tight-bodiced waistcoat, in its place a simple

white blouse and loose skirt in light blue cotton. Her feet, only a moment before in ankle-length black boots, were now cossetted in light leather sandals; her toes peeped out from beneath the hem of the skirt. Thomas nodded approvingly.

'Very nice,' he opined. The shop assistant appeared from behind Elizabeth and warbled with delight.

'Your husband approves, it would appear. Do you wish me to wrap your other clothes?'

'I'm not ...' began Thomas, then stopped. Elizabeth gave an anguished shrug as she followed the woman back into the cool of the shop.

'Oh Thomas, I'm sorry,' she said as soon as she walked out of the door. 'I didn't say anything to her, she must just have assumed ... I mean, I only said that I'd have to get another opinion before saying yes. I'm sorry.'

'It's nothing, Elizabeth, it's not important. Don't worry about it. And thank you for valuing my opinion enough to ask me about your clothes, they do look very nice. Black suits you, but not all the time. But now I'm in need of a sit down, I've never known an Easter so warm, and we've a busy afternoon ahead.'

They walked back slowly, Thomas carrying Elizabeth's parcel for her. Although they chatted with the ease of a couple who knew each other well, a disinterested observer would probably have noted that they avoided touching each other. When they met a crowd and passage was awkward, forcing Elizabeth to step in Thomas's direction, then Thomas too would move away. Like train-tracks they remained a constant distance apart. When they stopped to buy ice-creams (Elizabeth making the purchase) she took care to hand Thomas his without allowing their fingers even the most innocent of touches. It was as though each were primed with charges, short fuses fitted, and that a touch would provide the spark to ignite all. Neither seemed willing to take that risk.

They resisted the temptation to try the rides and returned to the shade of the trees by the wagon. Thomas lay again on his blanket sipping cool beer; someone (he suspected it had been Len) had requisitioned one of the horses' drinking bags and placed half a dozen bottles inside it. Elizabeth brought out a book from her bag, one she had plucked from her shelves that morning. Long ago, she remembered, she had written three words inside the front cover and signed her name. 'To my love' were the words, and she had wept when the book had been flung back at her unread. The memory meant nothing to her now; she began to flick through the pages. She glanced at Thomas infrequently, just as he did at her. Once their eyes met and they smiled.

Despite her calm appearance Elizabeth's emotions were adrift in a turbulent, stormy sea. She had spent weeks looking forward to this day, simply to spend time with Thomas. She suspected – no, she knew that she was falling in love with him. This admission had been wrested from within her months before, not when they had talked after Tommy's death, not when they had kissed, but on the day of Margaret's wedding when she had seen him with his sons in Newcastle. His love for his sons was self-evident and was, in its way, a barrier to Elizabeth's own emotions. She could not at first understand why she was so affected by seeing him then, and she had sat in the church, even as Margaret was taking her vows, questioning her own sanity. And then she realised. Coming across him like that was a reminder not only that he was married but that he and his wife were happily married, that they had had children to signify their love for each other. And in some way Thomas's devotion, his sense of duty, his love for others, only combined to make him seem more attractive to her. He was a good man, and in remaining distant from her, avoiding her, even rejecting her, he made her want him more. She had remembered a line from Milton, had written it down and even now could have spoken it aloud: '... The fruit of that forbidden tree, whose mortal taste brought death into the world, and all our woe, with loss of Eden.'

If Thomas was her forbidden fruit then picking that fruit, biting it, tasting its richness would surely be wrong. So much could be lost. It might be that the taste was too sweet, that one mouthful was sufficient, that she would then tire of its cloying scent and discard the uneaten portion to rot where it fell. But to leave it as it was now, ripe for picking and within her grasp, was more than she could bear. She looked up again. He was watching her, and she knew that part of his inner turmoil was that he was attracted to her. He would not admit it to himself, let alone to her, but the attraction was there. She wondered how long they would be able to live like this, returning to her book in an attempt to drive all other thoughts from her mind.

'What is it?' asked Thomas.

'Pardon?' she replied, suddenly afraid that her emotions had been visible to him. If that was the case then it was too early; she was unprepared.

'What is it, the book you're reading?'

'Oh, that!' She sighed with relief. 'It's called *Sesame and Lilies* by John Ruskin. Have you heard of him?' Thomas nodded.

'It's not fiction, it's social comment, political comment as well I suppose. After all, the two can hardly be separated. I read a lot of Ruskin a few years ago so I thought I'd re-read him now. He was involved with the pre-Raphaelites, William Morris included, and I was sure I could remember not liking what he wrote but couldn't think why. I was right, I didn't like it, and I can see exactly why now.'

'Do you want another beer?' Thomas had understood only part of what Elizabeth had said and felt that he was about to receive a lecture.

'Yes please. He really does go too far you know. He says

that you can't talk of one sex being superior to another because they work in separate spheres of influence. That seems fairly straightforward. But then he goes on to say that man is, now where is that passage? Here we are. Man is,

> '... the doer, the creator, the discoverer, the defender .... The man, in his rough work in the open world, must encounter all peril and trial:- to him, therefore, the failure, the offence, the inevitable error: often he must be wounded, or subdued, often misled, and *always* hardened. But he guards the woman from all this ...'

And that's not all! He suggests that women are useful as icons, their presence alone is a reason for men to go out and work or fight so that they can come home and be praised by their wives. A woman may not be active. She may have no thoughts of her own, may not contemplate a career, should not work other than at wifely duties in the home, should sublimate her own wishes and desires if they do not coincide with those of her husband. Don't you think that's ridiculous?'

'Would you like me to open the beer for you?'

'Thomas, you haven't listened to a word I've said!'

'Oh, but I have.'

'Well then? What are your feelings on the matter?'

'I don't have any,' he replied. 'And before you say anything else, because you look as if you're going to, let me say one thing. Let me read the book, then I can give my comments, if I have any, on an equal basis. I don't trust anyone who holds a book up, a book with so many hundreds of pages and thousands of words, then tells me in two minutes exactly what that book says. It makes me want to find out for myself what the writer wants to tell me.' He stopped speaking.

'That's it,' he added, 'that's all I wanted to say. You can go on now.'

'You'd better have this, then,' said Elizabeth tossing him the book. 'I'll look forward to discussing it with you.'

'Thank you,' said Thomas. 'I'll read it later.'

The second dancing session was, if anything, better received than the first. The sun seemed hotter, the crowd was undoubtedly larger and more appreciative, and the dancers were more relaxed. Rob in particular was so relaxed that he fell over just before they were due to start. His place was taken by Davy who was so nervous that he performed the whole dance with his trousers unbuttoned, to the great amusement of Willie who noticed the mishap halfway through the dance and could not resist pointing it out, first to the dancers and then very loudly to the audience. As they finished, a well-dressed man approached Elizabeth, mopping at his brow with a large white handkerchief. Thomas motioned to the rest of them not to disappear yet, and they waited until Elizabeth came over.

'That man,' she said, 'is one of the organisers. He thinks you're good. He thinks you're very good, particularly the way you pretend to be drunk then carry out all those complicated movements. I told him you really were drunk, but he wouldn't believe me. Anyway, they expect the speeches to start at six and they want us to dance for the last time just before then, to attract the crowds. They're putting up notices around the heath saying that.'

'In that case, back here at ten-to-six,' said Thomas. 'And no more booze till we get back in that wagon. Aileen, see if you can get Rob sobered up. See you all later.'

Elizabeth and Thomas headed for the river, this time with Willie and Abigail as company. The young couple had exhausted the entertainment at the fair, and Thomas's suggestion that the tea-shop by the river would be a pleasant place to rest for a while met with their approval, particularly when Thomas offered to buy the tea. He hoped that their presence might lighten the increasing seriousness of his conversation with Elizabeth.

There was a bend in the Tyne here; the view was restricted up and down river. Immediately opposite were Newburn and Throckley pits, and Lemington, and smoke and steam could be seen rising from Lord Armstrong's Elswick works out of sight to the east. From there to the sea there were factories and pits, docks and shipyards to both sides of the river. To the west the aspect was more rural, the river narrowing and becoming shallower.

'They could never decide where its source was,' said Thomas as they took their seats outside the small wooden hut which served as tea-rooms.

'There are two rivers joined you see, out beyond Hexham. The one from the north starts up on Kielder Moor, in the Cheviots, while the one coming from the south has its source on Alston Moor, not too far from where the Tees has its source. Anyway, they sorted things out by calling them the rivers North Tyne and South Tyne. It didn't sort out which was the source, but there were no more arguments!'

'I suppose that's the important thing in life,' said Elizabeth, sipping her tea. 'Make sure there are no arguments even if it means not solving the problem.'

'Have we missed something?' asked Willie. 'That seemed a bit of a funny thing to say.'

'I'm sorry, your brother and I were talking earlier this afternoon about problems in life. I tend to face them out and talk about them. I'm like a dog with a bone, I won't stop chewing at it until it's of no more use. He seems to prefer a more conciliatory approach, less confrontation. What do you think is the best approach?'

Willie and Abigail looked at each other. 'Yes!' they both said together, and began to giggle. Elizabeth conceded defeat.

'Alright, I apologise. It wasn't exactly light conversation. Let's change the subject.'

They talked instead of the river and the mine, of the dancing and the quality of the performance, their hopes for the future. Abigail decided that she would like children, lots of them, at least eight. Willie turned pale at the prospect. All he wanted, he admitted, was a quiet life, going to work, finding everything as it ought to be at home, going out for a pint sometimes. And children, he acknowledged, but he could make do with four or five. Elizabeth wanted an end to inequality. She wanted women to have the same opportunities as men in all spheres of life, she wanted a fairer distribution of wealth. It did take her quite a few minutes to express those wishes, but the others listened politely and watched the steamer from Newcastle come in. And then it was Thomas's turn. He would not say at first, merely shook his head. Only when Willie threatened to throw him into the river did he give way, and even then the result was less than satisfying.

'I used to dream of the future,' he said. 'I used to dream, but now I can see nothing ahead. My dreams, the real ones, the ones I have when I'm asleep, are all of the past. My hopes for the future seem hidden by concerns with the present.'

He would say nothing more, and, though the sun continued to shine as brightly as it had done all day, it was as though a cloud had passed before it.

'Who is this William Morris anyway?' asked Abigail in an attempt to bring the group back together again.

'He's a socialist,' answered Thomas.

'Oh, I see.' Abigail was no wiser.

'He's a very interesting man,' said Elizabeth. 'He studied for holy orders but decided instead to become an architect. He met the painter Rossetti, who persuaded him to become a painter for a while, which he did; then he began to design wallpaper and furniture. He also writes poetry and novels and he was one of the founders of the Socialist League.'

'So now you know,' said Thomas. 'But you really don't know any more than I told you, do you?'

'Thomas,' growled Willie, 'what's the matter with you? Even I can see that that's being rude.'

'No, no,' said Elizabeth reassuringly, 'Thomas is right. I haven't really explained about the man himself. He's a philosopher really. He thinks, and he writes his thoughts down, and many people, like me, believe that his ideas are worth listening to, worth considering as a way to run our lives, to run the country even, in future.'

'Why's he here then?' asked Willie. 'Why come to Ryton? It's not exactly the centre of civilisation in the north-east. And he sounds a bit too high in the clouds for the likes of me.'

'Oh no, not at all. Look at it this way. If there was to be an election tomorrow how would you vote?'

'I don't know. I'd have to see who was standing, wouldn't I. But I suppose I'd vote Liberal.'

'And you Thomas?'

'Probably the same.'

'The question doesn't unfortunately apply to me or to Abigail. Yet! Now, will the Liberals actually do anything for you? As working men?'

'I doubt it,' said Thomas, unsure of where this was leading. Willie shook his head in agreement.

'Who does do things for you then?'

'Well, we do it ourselves,' said Willie.

'All alone? You as an individual?'

'No. No, we help each other out as a family. And the neighbours, and our friends, they help as well.'

'You mean people from Lanchester, they're your neighbours? Or some of the farmers round about?'

'Of course not, you know they'd do nothing for us, living in their posh houses and ... Present company excepted, of course! I didn't mean to ...'

'No offence taken Willie, it's alright. What I'm trying to say is that you'll only get help from others in a similar situation. It'll be those around you, and they'll be your fellow workers from down the pit. And when it comes to bigger problems, problems involving, let's say, a reduction in the selling price of coal leading to the owners pressing for less pay, then miners from lots of pits combining together will be far stronger than those from just one pit. And if you take it that far, why stop with coal mines? You've more in common with shipwrights, boilermakers, chemical workers, engine drivers and steelworkers than you think! And when you combine you've got power! Why vote for a Liberal or a Tory who doesn't care about you except as a means of increasing the nation's wealth? Workers have the power to have their own political party; that's what William Morris believes, and it'll come one day, and that day won't be too far off, believe you me!'

Thomas started clapping.

'Well done, well done! A wonderful speech, we needn't stay to hear Mr Morris now, we can leave straight after the dance!'

Elizabeth rose to her feet, her chair falling backwards to the ground. She flashed a look of anger at Thomas then turned and stalked away.

'Well, big brother, you did it that time,' said Willie.

'Did what? What did I do?'

'You never were any good at being sarcastic, were you? I think you'd better go after her and apologise, we're going to look damn silly dancing rapper in front of five hundred people without a musician!' Willie looked almost pleased at his brother's obvious discomfort, leaned back on his chair and grinned broadly.

'Alright then, I'm going, I'm going!' he huffed. 'Bloody women, they can't take a bloody joke.' His voice trailed into the distance. Elizabeth was almost at the wagon by the time he caught up with her. He danced around her, tried to block her way.

'Look, I'm sorry if I upset you,' he said with feeling.

'No you're not!' Elizabeth walked round him.

'I am, I am! It was rude of me, I meant it as a joke but it didn't come out right. I'm sorry!'

Elizabeth stopped walking to confront him.

'Are you sorry you were rude, or sorry that your joke didn't come out right?'

'I don't know! Which would you prefer me to be sorry for?'

'No Thomas, that's the wrong answer! You're doing it again, not facing up to your problems, trying to get round them by smoothing the way. Well it won't work this time!' She started walking again.

'Alright, alright! I'll try again!' He was walking backwards, trying to keep up with her more than swift pace and talk to her at the same time.

'I am sorry! I'm sorry I tried to be funny at your expense. And I'm sorry that the joke went wrong. But most of all I'm sorry because I know that what you were saying, you were saying for me, and for Willie, and for the rest of us. And I know that you're right.'

'Thank you Thomas,' said Elizabeth primly. 'I have only two things to say to you. First, I accept your apology. And second, there's a bench behind you and you're going to fall . . .'

She soon stopped laughing.

'Are you alright?' she asked.

'You mean apart from this broken leg and bruised ribs, the hole in my head and the severely dinted pride? Yes, I'm alright!' As soon as he too started laughing the cloud moved away from their collective sun.

'The quality,' panted Thomas, 'of the dance' (he took a deep

breath) 'is directly proportional,' (he reached for the pro-
fered bottle) 'to the size of the crowd watching it!'

The crowd had numbered some seven or eight hundred,
perhaps more, and their applause continued long after the
stand behind the dancers was occupied. One of those on the
platform held up his hands for silence and the first speaker,
a well-dressed, handsome man, his moustache waxed into
luxuriant sweeps of curl at each end, rose to his feet.

'Come on Tom!' shouted someone. 'Tell us what it's all
about!'

'My name is Thomas Mann,' said the speaker. 'Thank
you for coming here to listen this evening. I'd like to talk to
you about socialism.'

And talk he did. Even Thomas Armstrong, arch cynic,
had to concede that the speaker was eloquent. Eloquently
mad perhaps, with his revolutionary notions of workers
taking over and running their own industries, but no less
persuasive for all that. He seemed to say a lot; although
much of what he said was not easily digestible he knew how
to handle a crowd, and the few hecklers who cared to
interrupt were summarily dealt with. Elizabeth, Thomas
noticed, was wearing a look of religious serenity which
would not have been out of place on the face of a nun at
prayer. He had seen that look before; Mary's face took on
the same expression of wondrous awe when she listened to
her preacher. Thomas was left puzzling over the effect
simple words could have on women.

After Mann, William Morris was something of a disappointment. He was short and round, somewhat dishevelled and unkempt in appearance, as if he had shrunk since
he put on his clothes and someone had left him overnight in
a trunk. He had unruly black, curly hair and a thick beard.
He was more conservative than the previous speaker,
believing in 'evolution, not revolution', although his proposals seemed at times Medieval in their harking back to

craft-guilds. His loathing of mass-production and belief in the nobility of free craftsmen were luxuries, Thomas felt, which a man could only afford if he had never tasted the bitter and sparse fruits of manual labour. He seemed to have his supporters though, and when he warmed up a little he was entertaining, and spoke some common-sense when talking of the future of trades unions. Thomas could see where Elizabeth found her inspiration.

These were the only two speakers, and it was beginning to get dark by the time Morris finished. Someone in the crowd, probably paid for doing so, yelled 'Three cheers for the socialists' and a fair number joined in with the shouts of approval. Thomas made his way back to the wagon feeling strangely alone. Elizabeth had gone to collect the dancers' fee from the organisers with the hope, Thomas suspected, of being introduced to William Morris. He had never seen her like that before, almost girlish in her wish to be away, to meet her hero. He found it hard to understand. Someone less clouded in emotion might have said that he was a little jealous.

'Did you see him?' Thomas asked when she returned.

'No,' she said, clearly disappointed. 'They'd already taken him down to the river and onto a boat. Apparently he's due to speak in Newcastle later this evening. But you'll be glad to know,' she raised her voice so that everyone would hear, 'that I have been paid!'

'That's better news than anything Morris said,' rumbled Len from the back of the wagon.

'What's the share-out?' asked Aileen, then proceeded to answer her own question. 'I think it should be divided amongst the dancers' girls!'

'That sounds fair to me!' laughed Abigail, holding her hand out only to have Willie playfully snatch it away.

'Yes, why not?' continued Aileen. 'I'll have Rob's share, Abi can have Willie's, what's 'er name up there can make do with Len's.' She turned to face Elizabeth.

'Don't worry dear, you won't go empty-handed. You can have Thomas's money.'

Everyone was quiet. All had heard. Had the sun not already set the flush rising to Elizabeth's face would have shown her embarrassment and confusion. Thomas saw her move, thought that she might have run away.

'That's enough of that,' he roared light-heartedly. 'You lasses have had an easy time of it, sitting on your bums all day watching the best rapper team in the north! Now then,' he held out his hand to Elizabeth, she handed him the bag of change, 'there's ten pounds here, six dancers and a musician makes seven, and – how much for the beer Len?'

'Ten shillings'll do Thomas.'

'Ten shillings to Len, that leaves nine pounds ten divided between seven which is . . .' he closed his eyes, re-opened them quickly, 'One pound seven shillings and a penny each, with fivepence left over. Let's say twenty-seven shillings each, and Aileen can have the shilling that's left if she promises not to sing on the way home!'

He ducked Aileen's well-telegraphed blow to the head and retaliated with a kiss to her forehead which brought a heart-clasping, highly exaggerated swoon. He divided up the cash, giving Elizabeth her share as they climbed into the wagon. 'Thank you, Thomas,' she whispered, touched his sleeve, and he knew that the acknowledgement was for more than the mere apportionment of their reward.

The night drew close as they left the valley behind, oil lights at the head and tail of the wagon and one under the canopy swaying in time with the horse's gentle motion. The moon rose briefly only to be hidden minutes later by a billow of dark clouds hurrying in from the horizon. The day's gentle breeze grew stronger, slapped at the tarpaulin, forcing the passengers to take refuge under the blankets which Elizabeth had packed. Len, still at the reins with dog and woman, took from his pocket a bottle which he passed to the rear of the wagon.

'To keep yous all warm back there,' he chortled.

'Whisky!' coughed Aileen, the first to sample the liquid.

'Nice,' said Willie as his turn came round.

Elizabeth said nothing, merely grimaced as she took a sip. Thomas smiled approvingly and tapped Len on the back to allow him his tilt.

'No need,' came the reply. 'I've got me own up here!'

The bottle circled the host twice; when empty was replaced by a second which Len produced from another pocket. Thomas drank sparingly, passed the bottle by when he began to feel its effects. After a short while the rocking motion, the alcohol, the warmth under the blankets, all combined to coax the party into sleep. Rob and Aileen lay under one blanket, Willie and Abigail were entwined under another. Stew and Davy pulled drowsily at a third, neither giving way, until they too found themselves huddled together for warmth. Thomas and Elizabeth had a blanket each, but after one rutted jolt of the wheels Thomas felt Elizabeth's head rest delicately against his shoulder. It seemed a natural reaction for him to lift his arm and let her fall towards him, to pull her blanket close around her, to let his arm lie gently on hers, to feel her warmth. He could not pretend that the feeling was unpleasant.

He too must have dozed. The wind had increased and it was beginning to rain, the canopy was flapping raggedly and beating a tattoo against its metal supports.

'Len!' Thomas yelled, 'where are we?'

'Dunno,' came the slurred reply, ''s too dark t'see.'

'Oh no,' Thomas groaned. 'You're drunk!'

He untangled himself from Elizabeth's arms and in doing so woke her. She looked around anxiously as Thomas climbed up beside Len, bundling his dog into the back of the wagon. Of Len's woman there was no sign at first; further inspection proved that she had, at some time in the journey, made her way back to snuggle between Davy and Stew leaving Len with only a bottle as consolation.

'Whoa there!' said Thomas, hauling on the reins; the horses came to a halt.

'Give me a hand,' he yelled above the wind, 'he's going to fall off if we leave him up here.'

He helped the driver, now as fluid as the drink he had been consuming, into his own place and Elizabeth covered him up. Together they lowered the canvas sheet at the sides and front of the wagon and tied it securely so that those inside would not suffer if the weather worsened. As Thomas climbed up to take the reins Elizabeth mounted the seat from the other side.

'I don't recognise this,' she said, peering into the darkness.

'Neither do I,' he answered. 'But then I wouldn't expect to anyway. All we can do is push on, hope we come to a signpost. Go on, you go back, this rain's not going to get any better. You'll get soaked.'

'No, I've been this way before. I might recognise the road, or there might be a milestone on this side. I'll get our blankets, then I'll keep watch with you.'

She reached behind her, under the tarpaulin, and brought forward two blankets. They draped them over their heads and round their shoulders but they did little to prevent the rain from soaking them to the skin. Thomas shrugged his off but Elizabeth picked it up and placed it back around his shoulders.

'No, keep it on,' she insisted, 'even if it's wet it'll keep you warm.'

The rain grew heavier, the wind stronger. The tarpaulin behind them was lifted.

'Are you two alright?' came Willie's voice.

'Yes,' answered Thomas wearily, 'we just love sitting out here in the wind and rain while you stay warm and dry in there.'

'Oh! That's alright then. Wake me up when we get back.'

Twice they took a wrong turning where there was a fork in the road and no sign. They asked directions at two farmhouses, and at one of these Thomas had to lead the horses into the farmyard to find sufficient room to turn the wagon round. The cobbles were wet and slick, there was little light, and he slipped twice. Back on the road again he climbed up to the seat, but did not notice Elizabeth move away from him.

'Did you hurt yourself?' she asked.

'No,' he answered, blowing the rain from his moustache, 'no, the ground was quite soft really.'

'I don't think it was ground you fell on,' she suggested. 'I think it was something else.'

'Like what?'

'Well, you smell as if it was something unpleasant. A midden heap perhaps?'

He swore.

It was almost eleven when the lights of the village showed themselves through the razored blades of rain. Elizabeth was shivering violently, and Thomas could barely feel the sharp leather of the reins in his numbed fingers. He pulled the wagon to a halt at the top of the hill.

'Right you lot!' he shouted, beating on the canvas behind him like a drum. 'Out you get! You walk the last few yards, rain or no rain!' One by one, eyes bleary with sleep or alcohol, the passengers stumbled into the night.

'Are you not coming?' asked Willie, Abigail tucked under the side of his jacket, eyes still closed.

'Aye, of course I'm coming! But some idiot's got to stable the horses, and since I've been sitting up here in the rain for the past three hours it would seem I'm best qualified for the job. Now go on, go to bed. I'll see you tomorrow.'

'Right you are then, far be it from me to stop you being a martyr.' Willie and Abigail began to walk away. 'Have you noticed that funny smell around here, must be the drains I reckon . . .' Willie smiled to himself.

'I need to get warm Thomas,' said Elizabeth from his side, her teeth beating out a rhythm which Thomas's clogs would have done well to emulate. 'Come on, head up to the stables before I freeze.' Thomas did as he was told.

'There's no-one there!' he said. Sure enough, the stables were in darkness.

'The groom will have gone to bed. Look, I'll open the doors and put the light on, you can unhitch the horses and lead them in. They'll need drying, and feeding and watering, but I can do that once I've warmed up. You bring them in and I'll do the rest.'

While Thomas fumbled at the buckles connecting the horses to the wagon Elizabeth swung open the doors and disappeared inside. Thomas saw one gaslight flare into existence, then another, then a third in the tack room and a fourth in the office. Elizabeth scuttled outside again, a large overcoat wrapped around her.

'Thomas, you wouldn't believe it, the stove's still on! Oh, it's so warm in there! Leave the wagon, the groom will see to it in the morning, we'll just get these beasts in.' She took the first horse, led it straight into one of the stalls; Thomas followed with the second and Elizabeth shut the stable door behind him.

There was a smell of warmth and dampness, a sense of safety and security. The rain clawed at the roof and was dashed against the windows but could not overcome the sputter of the gaslights and the soft champing of the horses at their mangers. Thomas could feel his fingers again.

'Oh, I wish you could see yourself,' Elizabeth said

teasingly, throwing her coat to one side, 'you do look a sight!' Thomas glanced down. His clothes were a uniform brown colour, stiff with mud or worse, hung with gaudy pieces of yellow straw. His hands were a similar shade of dun, and he had no reason to suspect that his head had escaped the combined attentions of rain, wind and midden heap.

'I'd let you have the mirror straight after me,' answered Thomas. 'I've a feeling we'd make a good pair of scarecrows.'

Elizabeth had not escaped the deprivations of the night. Her hair was wild and windblown, her thin clothes, newly bought that afternoon, were plastered to her body. Where Thomas had been painted brown Elizabeth had been dashed by the spray from the wheels a broad and even piebald. She looked at herself and began to laugh.

'I'll deal with the horses,' she said firmly. 'You go and dry yourself in the office, that's where the stove is. The groom always leaves some spare clothes in there, but I don't think they'll fit you. The sink though, that's connected to the hot water supply. You should be able to wash yourself down. There's soap and a towel, oh, and some blankets to wrap yourself in.'

She joined the first of the horses in the stalls, began to brush it down with strong, easy movements. Thomas didn't move. He wasn't used to taking orders from a woman, it made him feel like a schoolboy again.

'Oh, and Thomas.' Elizabeth spoke again without looking round.

'I'd make sure it was a good wash if I were you. You do smell a little high.' She continued with her work. Once again Thomas found himself doing as he was told.

It didn't take long for Elizabeth to finish her work. What remained unfinished or poorly done would be put right in the morning by the groom. She wondered how Thomas was getting on. There was a patch of light by the office door. The door, she remembered, had never closed properly, it had no lock and had been hung so that it always opened itself a little. She moved closer, slowly, so that she wouldn't be seen or heard. She lowered the gaslights as she passed them so that, by the time she reached the empty stall, the one filled with hay and straw, she was hidden in the shadows. She glanced at the door then hurried away, as if she had forgotten something. When she re-appeared she was carrying three or four clean horse-blankets. She laid them over the straw and sat down.

Thomas was standing at the sink with his back to her. He was naked. She could make out his clothes hanging around the stove at his left hand. Just like a man, she thought to herself, what's the use of trying to dry something so foul that it'll just have to be washed anyway? She watched him carefully. The sink was full of water, hot water, she could see the steam rising. There was soap but no flannel. First he dipped his head in the water, stood up and pushed his hair back so that small streams of water ran down his neck and back. He rubbed the soap in his hands, lathered it well, then scrubbed his hair, his face and the back of his neck, down his arms, back up under his armpits. Rinsing was carried out in the same order with much spluttering and coughing. More soap and he moved onto his chest and stomach, round onto the small of his back and then over his shoulders. There was a patch of skin in the middle of his back which could not be reached from above or below; Elizabeth felt an urge, forcibly restrained, to run into the office and cover the dry skin with soapy water. When he rinsed she could hear the hiss of water splashing the stove.

He looked round and reached behind the door for something. She saw him place a chair to one side, lift one foot, his left foot, and place it on the seat. He was now half-turned toward her, facing the stove. One of the horses stamped restlessly and Thomas looked up, straight at Elizabeth, but could see nothing in the shadows. He continued to wash himself. She could see each muscle in his leg in shadowed relief, calf and thigh, and the hairs on his chest, and the slight folds of flesh at his stomach. He rinsed again, brought his foot down and, as he lifted his other foot, pushed at the door. It closed a little, just a little, but enough so that Elizabeth's view was restricted to a foot, a leg and a chair, hands washing, head looking down. The door was pushed again; Elizabeth could see nothing. She cursed silently then realised that she was suddenly warm, that she was hugging her legs, her head resting on her knees, her thighs pushed hot together, a strange ache in her body. And then, slowly, the door began to open again.

Elizabeth saw a foot, a leg, an arm upraised, muscles tensed as Thomas stretched. It was his right leg, his right arm; he would be facing her. She watched his body, hidden in the shade of the office light, emerging from the penumbra of the door's protection. His chest was covered in fine hairs which twisted and whirled between his nipples, swept down over his stomach, a dark central line disappearing into the shadow of his navel. She felt a longing to thrust her tongue deep into the cavern of his navel, moved her hand into the tight hot space between her legs. The hairs on his stomach were straight and led downwards, a trap for unwary fingers which entered that impenetrable forest, forever pressing on and down, making retreat impossible. And then they grew tight and curled, fierce tendrils which could not, would not relinquish their hold. His upper legs too were covered with a lawn of hair, the whole encircling his genitals with a crown of thorns. Genitals. She smiled. Such a clinical word, so detached and remote. Like penis and testicles, so cold and inhuman. She knew other words. She recalled words from the past, words whispered in private, words savoured and tasted and rolled around the mouth, words moistened with

saliva before being offered soft and raw to the tongue of a
lover. He looked around him, took his dirty clothes from the
fireguard by the stove and held them up to his face. He put
them back down again, his nose wrinkling, and began to
wrap himself in a blanket as Elizabeth crept away to the
main door of the stable. She opened it slightly and went
outside into the rain, headed for the wagon and climbed into
the back. The chest which held the dancers' costumes was
still there. She undid the clasp and pushed back the lid.
There was a smell of old sweat and tobacco. She rummaged
about inside, searching for Thomas's costume, then in
desperation reached in and took all of them. She held them
up to the rain, dropping a shirt and two pairs of trousers in
the process, picked them up and dawdled back across the
yard and into the barn.

'Thomas!' she shouted.

'I'm in the office,' came the reply.

'I think the groom's outfit will be too small for you ...'
'This groom's suit is far too small, I can't ...' They started
and stopped together, then began together again.

'After you,' said Thomas from behind the door.

'Thank you. I've been out to the wagon, I thought you
could wear your dancing costume so I've brought it in, but
it seems to be rather wet. Someone had left the trunk open.'

'Damn! I'll just have to wear it damp, can you pass it in
for me?'

'No, I won't hear of it. It'll take no more than a few
minutes to dry it out on the stove, and anyway, I need a
wash as well. Just wrap yourself up in a couple of blankets
and get out of there. Come on, you're not the only one who
needs to get some sleep.'

Thomas again did as he was told. The novelty of being
ordered about by a woman allowed him no room for
objection. He padded meekly out of the office to let
Elizabeth take his place. She passed his soiled clothes out to

him, a distasteful expression on her face, and began to hang the dancing costumes, virtually dry, on the fireguard.

'There are some blankets and rugs over there somewhere. Make yourself comfortable, I won't be long.'

While the office had had carpets strewn about the floor, threadbare but clean, the stable was paved with large slabs of stone. These were cold, and Thomas tip-toed across to where, in the dim light, he could see blankets spread on a bed of straw. He sat down on one of these and pulled the others around his shoulders and waist, wrapped a third around his feet and draped yet another over his front so that he was swaddled in clean, fresh though rather stiff and irritating material. He felt tired and lay down, the backs of his hands grazing the straw piled up behind him. It had been a busy day, especially the journey back. He had enjoyed himself, he decided, he had enjoyed being in Elizabeth's company despite her ridiculous idolisation of that William Morris, despite the impractical dreams Morris and Mann were proposing. And the dancing had been good, and Elizabeth's playing. She looked so much better in that skirt and blouse, he decided, rather than the prim, matronly dresses she wore as a rule. He ought to tell her that.

At the thought of Elizabeth he sat up and glanced at the office door. It was ajar, just a little. He remembered it being so when he had washed. He could see nothing of Elizabeth inside, and considered whether he should warn her that if she stepped in front of the sink she would be directly in his view. Before the thought could be translated into action Elizabeth appeared before him. Her back was to him, he could see her turn on the taps to fill the sink with hot water. First of all, though, she wiped around the sink with a rag. Thomas cursed, he always forgot to clean the sink after he'd used it. She threw away the rag and, for a while, stood with her head bowed, as if in prayer. Thomas wondered what she could be doing, then realised when she shrugged out of the blouse she was wearing, buttons all undone. The skin on her back was caressed by the shadowed light to a warm brown colour; she had worn nothing beneath the blouse's flimsy material.

Thomas swallowed. He was unable to move, unable to speak though he knew that he ought to have done one or the other, both, to warn Elizabeth that he could see her. She placed a blanket on the floor then took off her shoes, placed them neatly together. She turned off the taps and began to wash herself, hands and face first, then her arms and her upper body. She still had her back to him, still wore her skirt, and Thomas found himself silently urging her to turn round. She didn't do so, but lifted the hem of her skirt from the front and, almost invisibly, tugged down a pair of white, baggy drawers which she quickly discarded.

There was a sudden rattle of wind and rain, a tattoo of hailstones on the roof slates. Elizabeth looked up at the office window and turned slightly to her left. Thomas caught a glimpse of one breast, small and rounded. He was reminded of his sisters when they were still growing, the shyness of their puberty forced by necessity to hide beneath towels that were too small hung on a flimsy wooden clothes horse each bath night.

'Tell him to go away!' they'd cried, hands flapping at chest and groin as he'd decked his face in the most lascivious of grins, especially for them. 'Don't be stupid!' his mother had scolded, his lewdness displaced by false innocence the moment she glanced at him. 'He's your brother. And you can put your hands down and get yourself washed, good Lord, there's nothing there to hide anyway!' But there had been, he had known it, and his sisters had known it. They had danced a slow gavotte around each other, he eager-eyed to glimpse what otherwise could only be enjoyed by paying Annie Thomas a farthing, they confused by his sudden attention but sure that it was something to be avoided. Then one night his mother had noticed him watching too closely, realised perhaps that her daughters had too quickly become young women. He was sent to bed early, could only listen jealously from his exile to the laughs and giggles of a foreign race.

Elizabeth's back was turned towards him one more. She pulled her skirt down and stepped out of it, soaped her hands and began to wash her groin and her legs. She moved her hands down to her feet and, as she bent, Thomas saw a thin line of dark hair between her legs. For a brief moment he closed his eyes; when he opened them again she had gone. When she reappeared from behind the door she was carrying a chair, the same one he had used. She placed it carefully in front of the sink and put the blanket over its seat, then sat down on it. She was facing him but despite her nakedness appeared conservatively prim. Her knees were together, legs touching from ankle upwards, heels raised from the ground. Her hands nested in her lap, her eyes were closed. She remained motionless like that for a minute or longer; when she began to move it was with the smallest of circling motions of her head, so slight that Thomas could not say when he first noticed them. She turned her head clockwise and anti-clockwise in larger and larger circles; then her shoulders crept into the dance, first right, then left, then both. Her head was lifted back, she inhaled deeply, and the shadows under her breasts grew to blood-red crescents. She raised one arm high, turned it and allowed the fingers to waltz with each other and taste the air. The other arm was lifted too, fingers and thunbs touched their opposite numbers in an arch of perfect symmetry.

Thomas had not realised how dark she was. He had always assumed that the colour of her hands and face had more to do with her being frequently outdoors, but that was before he was offered the opportunity of closer inspection.

The light was poor, certainly, but even allowing for that her skin seemed to take on a sultry hue. There was a ghost of deeper shade under her arms where he was sure she must recently have removed the hair.

She brought her arms down slowly, as if in prayer, placed one hand delicately just behind each knee, thumbs pointing inward, fingers splayed. She began to massage her legs, first moving her feet forward and pointing her toes to relax the muscles, taking pleasure from each press and push and pinch of firm flesh. Her fingers forced their way in between her knees to feel for aches, travelled higher and pushed her legs further apart until she was sitting with them fully open, a black 'V' of shadow only partly obscured by her hands. Her mouth opened slightly, her tongue flicked out to smell the snake-thick air, she bit at her bottom lip. One hand, her left, continued its journey onto her stomach and higher, crept spider-like to rest on her right breast and spin a web of teasing, silken touches on and around the swollen nipple. The fingers of her right hand formed a claw which dug into its nest of hair, tightened its hold, then pressed and pushed and pulled. One finger broke loose to move down; the muscles in Elizabeth's legs tensed, she inhaled sharply, moaned softly as she breathed out again. The finger was joined by another; together they began to rub, small circular motions interspersed with a faster to-and-fro movement. Her head began to move from side to side, her left hand became rougher and more urgent in its demands. She swallowed, then pushed her tongue to the top of her mouth, trapped a pool of saliva there, transferred it reverently to the swiftly raised fingers of her right hand which returned hastily to their duty.

The rhythm became more regular. Circle, then a lateral movement which never failed to make her gasp, then fingers diving down into the darkness to reappear moments later slick and damp. Thomas watched, suddenly aware of his

own excitement and the tenting of the blanket covering him.
He reached down and felt the heat of his erection but could
not look away from the woman seated before him. The
speed of her movement increased, her legs began to tremble,
her mouth opened wide and her head fell back. Small
childish whimpers tumbled over each other to join hands in
a low, feral growl, her left hand moved from one breast to
the other bullying each nipple into tumescence, her whole
body rocked backwards and forwards in an ever-quickening
race towards oblivion. And then she was, suddenly, still.
Each muscle was tensed into immobility. She slumped slowly
forwards, head on arms, arms on knees. Thomas found his
own movement slowing, the rapid pumping of his hand
ceasing before he had achieved any release. It was impossible
for him to continue now that she had stopped.

Elizabeth sat, still and quiet, while Thomas looked on.
She took a deep breath and the inhalation spread through all
of her body. She sat up, her head lifted, her eyes opened,
blinking and searching for the light as a flower at dawn. She
glanced around as though unsure of her whereabouts,
swallowed, absent-mindedly picked up her skirt and stepped
into it. She put on her blouse but remembered to fasten only
the bottom three buttons, turned to empty the sink, moved
the chair back, tidied up as she saw necessary. And then she
was coming towards him. The light from the lamp in the
office was weak but it still served to outline her body
through the thin material of her clothes. As if aware of that,
as if knowing the effect she had had on him, Elizabeth
stopped at his feet and looked down on him.

'You could see me,' she whispered, but did not look back
to confirm that her statement was correct. Thomas mouthed
'Yes,' but no sound came from his lips. Elizabeth knelt down
beside him, put her hands on his shoulders. He flinched but
made no effort to move away.

'Thomas,' she said, 'I'm sorry, I can't help it.' She lowered her lips to his. It was no polite, demure kiss. Her tongue was between his teeth, in his mouth, soft as a knife. She felt him shrink from her and then respond, almost against his will, and she stretched out her legs so that she could feel him all the way down her body. The kiss became theirs, not hers, and they clung together.

'Oh Thomas, I've wanted you for so long, for so long.' Her right hand was at the back of his neck holding tightly the damp curls of hair; her left hand traced whorls on his chest.

'Since the first time I saw you doing that silly clog dance I knew, I knew that I had to have you.' Her nails ploughed gentle furrows through the hairs on his chest, a finger pushed itself curiously into the hollow of his navel then moved on, she took his erection firmly in her grasp. When she spoke her voice was low and filled with slow desire.

'I've waited so long Thomas. Too long.'

'No,' he said. 'No Elizabeth, I can't. It's wrong, I just can't do it!' He sat up, pushed her away, but she pushed back, pushed him back onto the blanket, her hands on his shoulders.

'Wrong?' she hissed. 'How can it be wrong? I want you Thomas, and you want me, you can't deny it! I've seen what you want, I've touched it!' As she spoke she lifted her leg over his body to rest on his stomach.

'I can't help the way my body reacts,' said Thomas, 'but my mind tells me no!'

'Don't listen to it Thomas, don't listen to it! Listen to this instead!'

She kissed him again but this time there was no response. She reached for his hand, moved it inside her blouse. It was warm and rough against the smoothness of her breast, made her breathe in sharply, her nipples demanding to be touched.

'Feel that heartbeat Thomas! That's how much I want you!'

She lifted herself and her skirt up, forced his hand between her legs; it came away wet and she pushed it up to his face, rubbed it against his cheek.

'That's how much I want you!' Thomas's eyes widened and he grabbed her wrists.

'Elizabeth! I can't! I won't!'

'Liar! You're a liar Thomas Armstrong! I'm not blind, I can see for myself. You want me as much as I want you, you just won't admit it!'

'That's not true!'

Elizabeth's voice became persuasive, gentle.

'Thomas, Thomas,' she whispered. 'I'm not an innocent young girl, I'm not going to bleed like a virgin. I know what I'm doing. I know what I want to do. I know more than you can believe, and I know what you want as well.'

Her voice was suddenly hard again.

'Now lift your arms up!'

'What?'

'You heard, lift your arms up, above your head! Now!' She hit him on the chest, hard enough for him to consider retaliating. She shrank back as though she felt that he might indeed do that; instead he raised his arms, a look of bewilderment on his face. Attacked physically and verbally by a woman, a woman who had used force and words he would not have thought her capable of using, rendered him incapable of independent action. Elizabeth bit her lower lip and exhaled, her face graced with a brief expression of relief that Thomas had obeyed her.

'Feel the wood?' she asked. He nodded; the timber was smooth with two semi-circles cut into it about twelve inches apart.

'Now do as I say. Put your wrists in the notches.' He tried to turn his head but she pulled it back.

'Do it Thomas! Come here!' She slid up his body, he could feel the heat and the damp and the roughness of her hair, and pushed his wrists into their places. She moved higher; Thomas caught a scent of her musk as she reached over his head, then felt the pressure of a second piece of wood encircling his wrists. There was a rasp of metal on metal.

'The stocks!' he mumbled. 'I'd forgotten . . .'

'Yes!' crowed Elizabeth triumphantly. 'I swore I'd have you Thomas, and I shall have you!' She moved back down over his chest and stomach, fumbling at the buttons on her blouse then ripping it off, thrusting to one side the blankets which still covered Thomas's lower body.

Her whole weight was on him, but even then he could have escaped. The stocks had been jammed between the wooden walls of the stall but were not firmly fixed, he was sure he would have been able to move them. And he was strong, he was used to physical exertion, the muscles in his thighs and legs were capable of circling her waist and holding her, squeezing her, hurting her. But the will to fight had disappeared. He knew that she had spoken the truth. He knew that he did want her as much as she desired him. She pulled her skirt off over her head and threw it to one side, reached behind her, grasped his erection, positioned herself carefully and pushed down on him.

'Oh God that's good!' she husked as she took him inside her; Thomas merely groaned. She rocked backwards and forwards, one hand pinching her nipples, the other behind her back cupping and caressing him. She leaned forward, stretched herself towards him, offered him her left breast. His tongue stabbed out, his lips drew the nipple into his mouth, his teeth bruised and abused it. His legs were bent at the knee, his pelvis pushing at her with an easy motion which suddenly grew more urgent. She sat back, began to push down at him as he pushed up at her.

'Yes,' she whispered. 'Come on, I can feel you! Come on my love, come on, come on . . .!' Thomas's lips were pulled back in a rictus of small death, his arms strained against their stays, his back arched and threatened to throw Elizabeth from him. He held that position ... and then it passed. He collapsed as though deflated.

'Oh my love, my love, I told you it would be alright, I told you it would be good.' Thomas began to cry.

'Oh no, please, don't do that. Don't cry Thomas. Here let me loose you.' They separated, Elizabeth crawled up his body and he felt a warm flood of semen trickle from inside her to pool on his chest. She opened the stocks and kissed his wrists.

'I'm sorry, I'm so sorry,' she whispered. 'I didn't mean to hurt you.'

'You didn't hurt me,' said Thomas. 'I'm alright.' He wiped at his eyes; Elizabeth rolled off him to lie at his side, staring into his eyes. Her hands fluttered about him, touched his back then his stomach, his cheeks, his head.

'We shouldn't have ...'

'We should Thomas, we should! Even if we have nothing else there's been tonight. I won't chase you, I won't threaten you or blackmail you. It's enough to know that you care. You do care, don't you?'

Thomas spoke slowly, his voice cracked as an old plate and veined with hopelessness.

'I care Elizabeth, oh, how I care. It would have been easier if I didn't, but I do.' She bent her head to his chest so that he would not see the tears that misted her eyes. In an almost involuntary reaction his arms went around her, pulled her tight against him.

They lay together, for a while, quite still until Thomas pulled the scattered blankets around them.

'What do we do?' asked Thomas suddenly.

'Nothing,' replied Elizabeth, 'there's nothing we can do. For the moment at least. You have to go away and think Thomas. You have to think about what this means, and you have to do it alone. If you want me, if you need me to listen to you or talk to you, anything, then leave a note in ... yes, leave a note in the summerhouse. Behind Victoria's portrait. I'll go there once a day, probably in the afternoon. Let me know a place and a time, better make it the day after your visit. I'll be there waiting. If you want me.'

Thomas nodded, his forehead furrowed with worry.

'And Thomas.' Elizabeth looked at him, took his chin in her hand to force him to look at her.

'I'll understand. If there's no note, that is. I'll know that there will be no more than tonight.' She leaned forward and he met her halfway, his eagerness now matching hers. She found him erect again, mounted him immediately, smiled her approval as his hands moved across her breasts and down her back, held her buttocks firmly. Her hands rested on his chest as she moved against him, thrusting her pubis at him, gasping with each urgent movement.

'Yes!' she cried. 'Yes! Oh Thomas, this is ... I've waited ... wanted ...' She moved faster; he pulled harder at her nipples, her fingernails began to raise weals in the flesh at his ribs. She moaned, loud and long.

'Oh Lord!' she wept. 'Oh no, no, no! Yes, Yes! Thomas, hold me, for Christ's sake hold me!' She stiffened, then fell forward onto him. He held her close.

'Thank you Thomas,' she said, shaking her head. 'You don't know how much I ... That is, I think you ...' He put his finger to her lips and rolled her over, not separating from her, until he lay between her open legs. He kissed her gently and began to move, lifted himself up onto his knuckles so that he could look at her.

'Tell me,' she urged. 'Tell me how you feel,' but he seemed incapable of speech, could only grunt like an animal.

'Oh yes!' Elizabeth encouraged him. 'You feel good!' She shuddered as he reached one arm down and raked his nails across the soles of her feet, continued the movement to hook her knee with the crook of his elbow, pull her leg round in front of him. The other leg followed, her feet were now around his neck. He thrust harder and faster.

'Harder!' screamed Elizabeth. 'Harder! Oh, that's so good, so deep! Thomas, I love you, I love you, oh dear God I love you!'

Thomas's silence was broken by a soft, suffocating sob and he sank down on top of her. Their sweat mingled. Her hands stroked his back and he mumbled into her shoulder.

'What was that?' Elizabeth asked gently.

'I love you,' Thomas confessed, 'Elizabeth, I love you.'

Chapter Fourteen

Vous chantiez? j'en suis fort aise.
Eh bien, dansez maintenant.
(You sang? I am delighted.
Well, dance now.)

'La Cigalle et la Fourmi'
(Jean de la Fontaine)

It had all but stopped raining, though the clouds had not yet moved away to the east. The storm had passed and the night smelled fresh; the air was cool but not unpleasantly so, and touched with the scent of newly cut grass. When Thomas reached the corner of the square he turned. He knew that Elizabeth would be there, in the doorway, and when he raised a hand she echoed the gesture. She had insisted that he leave, that she would remain behind to tidy up, but leaving was not easy. They had embraced and kissed and Thomas had felt his erection grow once again. Elizabeth had responded by holding him tighter, pushing herself hard against him, and they had made love again. Eventually she pushed him out into the courtyard and sent him on his way. He watched the shaft of light, making mountains of the mirrored cobbles, narrow into darkness as she closed the door, and he began the short journey back to the village.

He felt like a boy again, his heart was leaping in his chest as though it were trying to escape the confines of his body, to broadcast to the world his elation. He was aware that these emotions bordered on insanity, that he had no right to feel this way, but he was unable to hold back his happiness. He looked down on himself from the boughs of a horse chestnut tree sated with the season's new buds. Was that Thomas Armstrong passing below? Was that the same man who had felt such pangs of guilt on giving way to one furtive, dusty kiss? And what have you been up to Thomas me lad, heading back home so late at night, so early in the morning? What is it brings a smile so easy to your face bonny lad?

Why man, I've had the boss's daughter. Not once, not twice, but three times I've tupped her.

And was it good lad?

It was good man! It was like nothing else I've ever known!

And what about her Thomas? Was it good for her as well?

She wouldn't keep quiet man! She was groaning and yelling, I've heard nothing like it! I don't think she'll have any cause to complain, I can tell you that!

So now what?

What do you mean?

I mean, what are you going to do now?

I'm going to go home. I'm absolutely buggered, I'm going home to bed, and I don't care if I don't wake up for a week.

You misunderstand, Thomas me lad. Your life has just become very complicated. The woman you've just 'tupped' has said she loves you. Unless I'm mistaken I'm sure I heard you say that you loved her. Those were the very same words you used no more than a week ago when you 'tupped' another woman who happens to share a bed, and a house, and a life with you. Do you love them both, Thomas? Perhaps Elizabeth can move in with you. Perhaps she can share a bed with you and Mary. You're a good joiner, I'm sure it wouldn't take you long to make the bed a little wider.

Howway man, be serious!

I'll be serious lad, will you? Come on, I'll walk with you a while, we can talk together. What are you going to do?

I don't know! I can't think straight, I don't know what to do!

Well at least you've stopped smiling, that's a start. What are your choices? Think about them, carefully. Are you going to leave Mary? Are you going to take the boys? She lives for those boys Thomas, she lives for them, you know that, it'd kill her if you took them away.

Jesus Christ, I know that! You don't need to tell me that! *I* love them as well! They're *my* sons as well!

So you leave them with Mary and you go away with Elizabeth. You'd have to go away of course, you couldn't stay around here. But Elizabeth loves you, she told you so, so I'm sure she wouldn't mind. Wales? Nottingham? Scotland? You'd get a job easily enough, with your skills. And Elizabeth, well, she'd soon learn how to look after a pitman, how to cook for him, sew, wash his dirty clothes, keep the house tidy. It would be hard, yes, but you love each other. You'd manage.

I thought you were going to be serious!

I was, Thomas lad, I was! But I see what you mean. It might be hoping for a bit much, when she's not used to that type of work. Perhaps she could keep you? After all, her dad's loaded, he could make you both quite comfortable. You could be her kept man. No work to do, just lie around in bed all day and enjoy yourself. No, I can see by your face you wouldn't consider that. So make a suggestion. Tell me. What are you going to do, Thomas me lad?

I'm going to think. I'm going to think things through, like Elizabeth said. I'm going to see what I can sort out that'll help everybody in the long run. I just need some time, just a little bit of time.

Well lad, I wish you luck. You might find that time's got a habit of running away from you just when you needed it most. But you'll find me there to help you. Or hinder you, depending on how you feel. We're home now. Let's go in.

The door wasn't locked, the fire was still aglow, and on the table by Thomas's chair a nightlight burned in a small glass jar. Thomas took his shoes off and left them by the door, suddenly tired. Mary always left a light burning if he was out late. He'd told her that it wasn't necessary, that he could find his way around the furniture even on the blackest night. She had replied that the light meant more than him being able to see. To her it was like a beacon, a lighthouse, guiding him back home to safe harbour. He smiled at the thought and then noticed the envelope beneath the jar. It had his name on it, written in Mary's ornate but laborious hand. He pulled the flap open, felt that there was something small and weighty inside, but ignored it for the moment to concentrate his attention on a single piece of white paper. He unfolded it and held it close to the nightlight, but the glass of the jar distorted the weak flame and made it impossible to read the flickering letters. He moved off the seat, knelt in front of the fire, and began to read.

'Dear Thomas,' he mouthed, 'I'm sorry. I kno I hurt you and Im sorry. I love you so much Im fritend I mite loos you. I dont like it when your away and doing things withowt me, Im fritend you mite not come back. I wont stop you if you wont to keep on dooing your rapper but I wont you to kno how much I love you. My Gran gave me this, I wont you to have it from me and keep it with you so you think of me when Im not there I love you Thomas. From Mary.'

Thomas reached into the envelope and brought out a silver heart hung on a thick brass chain. The heart was hinged and Thomas prised it open with his thumbnail.

Inside was a scrap of thin red tissue which he unfolded and laid flat on the floor in front of him. It had been carefully trimmed and cut into the shape of the letters 'T' and 'M' intertwined with one another. On it, in fine black ink, was written 'Thomas I love you Mary'.

Thomas carefully refolded the tissue and put it back into the heart, closed the lid, then put the heart and the accompanying letter back in the envelope. He held it close against his chest and began to weep.

Margaret looked at herself in the mirror. It was something she found herself doing less often than in the past. She took no pleasure from the action now, it seemed to matter little to Henry how she looked, and there was no-one else who would care about her appearance. Today, however, curiosity had the better of her. She looked tired, pale, ill even. Her hair was dishevelled; she reached for a brush and began to pull it painfully through the knots of her depression. She would spend some time on her appearance today, she would bathe and choose her clothes carefully, she would powder and perfume herself. She must look good. Maichamps was due to arrive late in the afternoon.

Her maid had drawn her bath only minutes before and the room was filled with steam. Although Margaret would have welcomed kind hands to soothe away her pain the maid was dismissed before she began to undress. It would not have been seemly to allow a member of staff to see the bruises and cuts on her body. Henry had been particularly angry two nights before, for no reason that she could see. She had done all that he had asked of her, fear forcing her to overcome her revulsion, yet still he had beaten her, not just with his hand but also across her buttocks with his riding crop. The memory of the blows returned as she lowered herself into the hot water. Why did he do this? She had asked herself the question so many times, had demanded an answer from Henry as often, but received only a surly grunt and the threat of a further beating if she persisted in aggravating him. During the day he was a gentleman, or as much a gentleman as he was ever likely to be. It was only at night that he seemed to change. He needed to dominate, she could understand that. But he became rough, then violent, and if she was submissive then he would beat her. What he really wanted was for her to fight back, to attack him in return, but when she did this he would redouble his efforts and she would be forced to succumb to his fists. If she had sufficient energy she fought him; the bout was over more quickly, she was left with more time to lick her wounds. But when she was tired the slow, deliberate torture would last half the night.

Sometimes he gagged her, though there was no need. His threats were enough to secure her silence. Sometimes he tied her, though if he had told her to remain perfectly still her fear would have held her safe as a thousand cords. And afterwards, when she lay sobbing, his tears would outnumber hers and he would beg forgiveness. He would tell her how much he loved her, that he hated to hurt her but was unable to control himself. And she would comfort him in her blood and agony, hold his head to her breast, admit that she loved him in return. She could not lie to him.

Why? That was what she kept asking herself, not one question but many. Why did he hurt her, keep on hurting her? Why was there within him this need to express his needs with violence? Why, despite his protestations of love, his remorse, his promises that he would never violate her again, why was he unable to restrain his base instincts, his foul, bestial nature? And why, the last why, the most important why, the why with which she nightly scoured her soul, why did she not leave him?

She *had* loved him, she was convinced of that. Before they

were married, definitely, even when they had been together in the nursery wing, the first time she'd felt uneasy in his presence. But that had been different, how she'd wanted him then, wanted him to love her, wanted him to understand the passion she felt for him. And when he'd fought her as they made love she believed it was a manifestation of his love for her. Yes, she'd loved him then.

The change in him had been gradual. Sometimes she thought that he was ill, there was a side to him, a vicious side, which was so at odds with the mannered, courtly gentleman she thought she knew; illness could be the only explanation. And it was her duty, as a wife, as a lover, to care for him despite that sickness; because of that sickness. His roughness, which she'd come to accept, even enjoyed a little, became more and more a trial of strength which he was certain to win. The first time he hit her (not too hard, she'd barely noticed it) he was crippled with tears. She'd comforted him, said it was nothing and known it, believed it. She'd loved him then.

It was a question of degree. She could not remember when the pain had started, so insidious had been its approach. During its application she felt that there could be nothing worse in the world. But afterwards, when he and his tears filled her arms and soothed and calmed her, when she was proof that the human mind cannot, in the interests of its own sanity, remember pain, she would lie with him and force herself to believe that she still loved him.

She did not mention her troubles to her family. To do so would have been a gesture of defeat, an acknowledgement that they had been too right in their assessment of Henry's character. Then there was the matter of her own pride, her refusal to accept that she might have been wrong. Yet more than this there was her determination to see the matter through, to show Henry that their love, her love, would overcome this problem. If Henry would only learn to accept her love then he would no longer need to hurt her so, to debase her.

Anyway, her family, she was sure, were all too busy with their own lives to listen to her. The letters she received from Elizabeth talked of nothing but the mine and Elizabeth's precious dancing. Her father's brief notes read like newspaper advertisements selling the benefits of life at Greencroft Hall. They didn't know her, they just didn't know her. She longed for them to see through her deception, to realise how miserable, how desperate she really was, she longed for them to take her away from Henry. Why couldn't they see? When they asked how she was and she replied that she was in good spirits, when they asked how she enjoyed married life and she answered that it was everything she had ever hoped for, all she wanted was for them to take her back home.

She needed help, not just a confidante, but someone who would supply her with physical, material aid. She knew that both her father and Elizabeth disliked Henry; the assistance they could offer would in one way answer her needs: they would tell her to come home. But she didn't want to desert Henry; her own pride coupled with the love she thought she felt for him still outweighed her fear of him. And so she sought advice elsewhere: she wrote to Maichamps.

Margaret's letters were at first reserved, hinting at problems, telling how she had passed the time of day and how beautiful the countryside was becoming as spring hurried towards them. She was amazed that from this scant information Maichamps seemed to be able to see into her soul, could read not what she wrote but what she felt. She could not have suspected that this was due, in part, to Henry's correspondence providing Maichamps with specific, almost pornographic details of the debauchery he was inflicting upon his wife. And, just as Maichamps' replies to her calmed her with conciliatory advice, so he wrote to Henry detailing further excesses to which he should subject her. Margaret's letters too became more explicit as she strove to explain the conflicting emotions which struggled inside her, and these emotions were relayed to Henry in his turn. Both Henry and Margaret danced to the puppeteer's tune.

'Elizabeth my dear! You do look well, the sun has caught you! Come, tell me how your day went. How was the dancing? I hope that the journey back wasn't too bad, the weather seemed to take a turn for the worse yesterday evening. Let me pour you some coffee.'

'Thank you father,' said Elizabeth. She took a seat by his side at the large dining table and reached for a slice of toasted bread, spreading it lightly with damson jam, no butter. She found herself smiling for what, to a bystander, would have been no reason. Her father caught the happiness.

'It was a good day then?' Elizabeth nodded, and John Waterhouse smiled back at her. There was a time when he had thought that he would never see his step-daughter happy again, and asking her to move with him to Greencroft, to help him organise the opening of the pit, had been something of a gamble. The enthusiasm she had shown in this task had never been questioned, but her involvement with the music and dancing seemed to have gone further, to have banished her dour outlook, to have brought a little youthfulness back into her life. She had lost the care-worn expression which she had worn like widow's weeds for so many years.

'The day was wonderful, the dancing was the best I've ever seen, the music ... the music, my dear father, was out of this world!'

'I'm pleased you don't believe in false modesty,' said Waterhouse with mock gravity. 'But please, do go on.'

'The speeches were ... acceptable, let us say. Mr Morris

is not a particularly good speaker, but his ideas are interesting. Mr Mann, however, is a most eloquent orator, and I felt it a shame that his rhetoric should contain so little of practical use. It was fascinating to hear them both, to contrast their theories and their presentation. You really should have made the effort to come father, you would have enjoyed listening to them both. You would have enjoyed the whole day!'

'No doubt, my dear, but I felt that my presence there with your dancers would have forced them to behave in a more restrained manner, and I had no wish to impose myself upon them. It is enough for me to know that you enjoyed yourself.'

'Yes,' sighed Elizabeth, 'I certainly did that.'

She had slept little. Elation had too strong a hold on her, she was unable to descend from its heights to something as mundane as sleep. Instead she curled in the warmth of her bed, quilt and covers pulled over her head. She could smell Thomas's heat still on her, feel where his rough fingers had touched her, and his presence beside her was almost tangible. She had dozed eventually and dreamed of his lop-sided, wry, almost contemptuous smile, and when she awoke to the sound of early morning songthrush and blackbird she was surprised to find that he was not lying beside her.

'Elizabeth? Elizabeth, I do believe you haven't heard a word I've said!'

'I beg your pardon. Oh, I'm sorry father, I was in a different world. Please forgive me, what was it you were saying?'

'No, it's alright. I'll wait for you to come down to earth.'

'Father, you're teasing! My attention is yours and yours alone. Or rather, yours and this cup of coffee's. Now please, tell me what it was you wanted.'

John Waterhouse leaned forward, elbows on the table,

fingers tapping each other. He breathed in through his teeth, the pause designed to ensure that Elizabeth should be aware of the gravity, the importance of his speech.

'I shall be going away shortly, for no longer than a week. First to Manchester, then to Nottingham, then to London. There are machines I wish to buy for the mine, but before I do so I wish to inspect them on site. Hence the reason for the Nottingham visit. Edward has asked me to look at one or two problems in steel production, and then I must discuss some matters of finance with our bankers. I had hoped that in my absence Edward would be here as nominal director of operations. I had even considered taking you with me, Elizabeth, to learn a little of other aspects of the family business. Edward has, however, written to me to say that he is forced to remain in Manchester. In these circumstances, and I am reluctant to place this burden on you, I wish to ask you if you would be prepared to run operations in my absence.'

'To take charge of the mine?' asked Elizabeth excitedly, 'for a week?'

'You wouldn't be alone,' said her father, mistaking her eagerness for apprehension. 'My clerks are, after all, used to carrying out your instructions, and they control most of the day-to-day administration. You would be in charge, of course, but I anticipate no problems.'

'If you feel I could manage, father, I'd love to help. I'm proud that you should ask me. Yes, yes, of course I'll do it.'

'Good. I didn't doubt for a moment that you would help me. To be honest, I feel you'll manage far better than Edward would have done anyway. There is, however, one other thing.'

'Yes?'

'You have no experience in underground work. You are an able and efficient administrator, but you lack knowledge of that part of mining dealing with the actual extraction of coal.' Elizabeth resisted the temptation to tell her father of her recent trip to the coal-face. She was not sure whether he would have been impressed by her determination to further her education or annoyed by her not asking his permission to venture underground. She merely nodded her head, acknowledging his statement.

'I have it in mind to help you with this shortfall in your learning, and at the same time be of assistance to others. May I explain?'

'Please do,' said Elizabeth, silently urging him on. Curiosity was, for her, elevated almost to the status of a vice.

'The Armstrong brothers,' said her father emphatically. Elizabeth's breath ceased. She swallowed nervously. What did her father know? What had he guessed, had someone seen her with Thomas?

'Yes,' she whispered encouragingly.

'They are held in good respect, I believe? By their friends and neighbours?'

'I think so.'

'No stains or blemishes on the name? Apart from that little incident at New Year with Abigail and William, and even that turned out for the good.'

Elizabeth shook her head.

'Good. I expected nothing less, of course, but you seem to know them rather better than I, through this dancing and music.'

'Why did you want to know?' Elizabeth asked.

'Promotion Elizabeth, promotion! But forgive me, I should keep to the point. Thomas has been, to all intents and purpose, running whichever shift he works on. The other pitmen seem to take to him, and although I've been carrying out some of the duties I'd hoped to have done by a pit-manager above ground, he's been doing a great deal underground. I've never acknowledged his contribution, other than in personal terms . . .'

'You mean you haven't paid him for the extra work?' Elizabeth interrupted.

'Quite. You have a very perceptive and incisive view of matters my dear. May I go on?'

'Please do,' Elizabeth answered with exaggerated politeness.

'The new Act, we spoke of it some months ago, will introduce written examinations for pit-managers. I believe that Thomas Armstrong will be of enormous benefit to me and to this mine if he can pass these examinations. I have spoken to him on many occasions and have been impressed with both his knowledge of mining and his ideas for the future of the industry. I cannot, however, comment upon his ability to express himself in writing, or his potential for becoming an administrator. I suspect that he will be able to do both with ease, but I would value your opinion in this.'

'Why? Do you feel that I know him so much better then you do? After all, I've played violin for him to dance, but beyond that I hardly know ...'

'Elizabeth, Elizabeth! Would I ask you something when I was perfectly aware that you didn't know the answer? That is precisely why I mention it now. While I am away I want Thomas to work alongside you. I want you to show him how this mine is run. And I want him to tell you about face work. You will both be able to help each other, and by the time I return, my dear, you should have found out a little more about Thomas Armstrong the man and his value to us. What do you think?'

Elizabeth tried to contain her excitement. A week with Thomas at her side! But what would he say? Perhaps he had decided that he would have nothing further to do with her. He might decline the offer, choose to remain a face worker.

'And of course,' went on her father, not waiting for her to reply, 'that would leave me with the chance to let William Armstrong take on more responsibility. I'm sure he's capable, it's just that he always seems to be in his brother's shadow. But I've heard good reports of him as well. We could benefit from this all round, the company, you, Willie and Thomas.'

Elizabeth ignored the fact that her coffee was cold, drained the black liquid to the dregs, enjoying its dark bitterness.

'I think that it's an excellent idea father. I think that Thomas and I could teach each other a great deal.' She put down her cup. Her next words were whispered softly so that her father heard nothing. 'I just hope that he feels the same way.'

'That's it then. It's all settled. I shall see Thomas towards the end of this week and arrange matters with him.'

'Will that be soon enough?' Elizabeth enquired. For some reason she believed that her father's departure was imminent, perhaps within a day or two.

'Oh yes my dear, there'll be plenty of time. When do I go, let me see ...' he reached into his jacket pocket and pulled out a neatly folded piece of paper, 'the fifth of June! I've to be in Manchester on the sixth but I prefer travelling on a Sunday. So you'll be in charge for the whole of the following week. Is that a problem?'

'Oh no father,' she replied, hiding her disappointment. 'No problem at all. I only thought, by the way you broached the matter, that there might have been some urgency. But we've months to spare.'

'I do like to arrange things like this well in advance. Well, if you'll excuse me, I've work to do.' Elizabeth, lost in thought, looked up as her father pushed back his chair.

'Oh, yes, I'm sorry, yet again my mind was elsewhere. I'll be along in a moment.' She reached for the coffee pot although she was not thirsty. For a few minutes she had believed that fortune was smiling on her, that luck had finally been won over to her side after so many years opposing her. A week with Thomas, a week which would give them the opportunity to be, during the day at least, alone together, alone with no chance of interruption. But that prospect was now in the distant future, two months away, and she felt that she should take some positive action to satisfy the aching desire which even now was invading her body. She stood up, hurried back to her room, took out writing paper and pen.

'Dear Thomas,' she began ...

'Dear Elizabeth,' wrote Thomas. 'I had hoped that I would not need to write this letter. The fact that I have done so (and that I have had to do it so soon after we parted) will, I trust, indicate the turmoil which is threatening to engulf my mind. I am unable to drive you from my thoughts.

'I write at my table and must go to work in an hour. The children are at school but Mary is in the house. Even that knowledge cannot stop me from thinking of you. I must see you, speak to you, touch you. Am I mad to want you so much? I cannot understand the emotions I am feeling, the pressure which is building inside me, and I am frightened. Suddenly nothing seems as important as being with you. I hate myself for feeling this way, for being unable to control myself, for betraying all that I thought believed in, but that hatred does not lessen my need for you.

'I shall be at the summerhouse tomorrow morning at ten o'clock. You would do well not to be there, because if you are then I shall know that your feelings for me are as strong as those which torture me now. Stay away! We have the power to destroy ourselves and so many others if we pursue the course of action which our meeting will dictate. Thomas.'

Willie woke to a bed empty, but still warm from Abigail's body. He lay still. She would be back in a few moments, back from lighting the fire and setting the kettle on the hot plate. It would take a little while before there was enough heat to boil the water, twenty minutes perhaps. Enough time for them to snuggle close to each other, enjoy each other's presence, touch and stroke and rub and scratch. He could smell her perfume on the pillow beside him, a light, airy cologne which, even if scented on other women, brought her face immediately to his mind. Willie was content, happy with his lot. He had, he decided, not known real love until he married Abigail. Yes, he was in love with her before they married, but he had been in love so many times before. Being in love was a state of mind, a sudden rush of blood to the head and the loins, a few moments of ecstasy. But loving someone was a commitment, as was accepting the love which that someone gave in return. Willie was not a man of many words, and if asked to express his feelings would probably not have been able nor have wished to do so. But he knew how he felt, and he knew that he loved Abigail and that she loved him.

He heard her light tread on the stairs, watched from eyes almost closed as she entered the room. She was carrying the clothes they had discarded the previous night, clothes dampened by rain as they had run from the wagon along the road to their house. As he had fumbled in his pocket for the front door key she had reached out her hand to his chin and turned his face to hers, had kissed him and been kissed by him, rain darkening their hair and cascading down their faces. He eventually managed to open the door and they had stumbled into the room. Made drunk by the lack of light they had fallen onto the sofa and begun to make love, only Willie's discomfort prompting them to separate and continue their tryst in bed.

Abigail draped the clothes neatly over the chair. Willie closed his eyes fully and tried to guess her movements. She would go back to the door and take off her dressing gown;

he heard the rustle of material as she took her arms from the sleeves, the slight creak of hinges as the garment was hung on the hook on the door. Then she would come to the bed and sit down, take off her shoes; his back was to her but he felt the mattress depress as it took her weight. She would slide beneath the covers and mould herself to him, her knees behind his, her breasts against his back, her breath warm on his neck. Her hand would come to rest naturally on his behind, or creep round to pull gently at the hairs on his chest; he waited; he felt nothing.

He lay still for a moment then turned, sat up. It was not dark in the room, dawn had come two hours before, and in the half-light Willie could see his wife sitting hunched on the side of the bed, her head in her hands.

'Abi love,' he said, worry in his voice. 'What's the matter?'

'I'm not well,' she whispered back.

'You didn't have too much to drink yesterday, did you? No, you couldn't have, no more than a bottle or two of beer. What is it exactly?'

'It's not me head,' she replied. 'We were sharing bottles, remember, and you drank more than half. No, I feel really ill.'

'Do you want me to run for the doctor?' He was already half out of bed when her hand grabbed his, pulled him back. He shuffled across to sit beside her, his arm around her shoulder.

'No, I don't think I need the doctor, not yet.'

'Where does it hurt then? Come on love, if you tell me I might be able to help. It's not women's troubles, is it?'

'No Willie,' she smiled, 'it's not that. I just feel sick.'

'It must have been something you ate then. I told you that pie smelled a bit off but you wouldn't have it, you said it was just the seasoning. I'm glad I didn't have any, I can't afford to be off . . .'

'Willie love, it's not something I've eaten.' She swallowed, looked straight at him, began to speak slowly.

'I've been like this on and off for nearly two weeks Willie, I just haven't told you. You were on early shift, it didn't really seem important. But I was due to start last week and I didn't, and I'm normally so regular. And the past few days the sickness has been worse and . . .'

'Are you sure?' Willie demanded.

'It's not something I know much about love. But I think so.'

Willie's smile broadened. He stretched out his hand and let it rest on Abigail's stomach.

'If it's a boy,' he whispered, 'would you mind if we called him Tommy?'

Henry brought Maichamps from the station. Margaret had hoped that her husband might allow her some time alone with his friend; on any other day he would have been out on horseback or visiting some local inn. Perhaps he sensed her wishes and stayed in deliberately, to annoy her. It was more likely, she conceded, that he was attempting to be a good host. Maichamps, she knew, was a capable horseman but he did not seem to enjoy himself riding. Unable to go out without offending his guest, Henry decided to make the most of a bad job. He began drinking at lunch and moved from wine to spirits early in the afternoon. He and Maichamps played chess and then backgammon; Henry lost at both. They talked of unknown mutual acquaintances, sometimes glancing at her as she sat reading or embroidering, more often ignoring her as they laughed loudly at some private joke. When Henry staggered away on what he persisted in calling an 'errand of mercy', chortling at his own sense of humour, Maichamps rushed to her side.

'Oh, Margaret,' he said, kissing her hands, 'I am so sorry. I should have come earlier, your letters touched my heart.

But I am here now, and I shall do everything in my power to improve your situation. I am not without influence over Henry but I may have difficulty in broaching the subject. But he will return in a moment, listen carefully.' He looked around, almost theatrically, then spoke clearly and rapidly.

'I must wait for him to talk to me about you, so that I can bring the conversation round to the way he treats you. He will not do so while you are here. When he returns you must make an excuse and leave, do not join us for dinner. Come to my room tonight and I shall let you know the outcome of my entreaties. Will you do this?'

'Yes,' Margaret nodded, 'I shall be there. But please, for my sake, do not allow him to drink too much. He is so much stronger when he drinks, so much more cruel, I fear that he may kill me if . . .' Henry's footsteps sounded their clumsy way along the corridor. Maichamps bounded back to his seat as Margaret collected her embroidery and folded it carefully into her bag. She met Henry at the door.

'I'm feeling a little unwell,' she said. 'I shall lie down for a while. I'm sure that you and Monsieur Maichamps will forgive me, you must have so much to talk about without my distracting you. I may be forced to miss dinner.'

'I am sorry,' said Henry. He leaned forward to peck her on the cheek. As his lips made contact with her skin she closed her eyes and swallowed, determined to hold back the revulsion she could feel rising in her throat.

'Shall I have your maid bring you something?' he enquired. She shook her head and hurried away. As she turned the corner to mount the stairs she looked back and saw him leaning against the door to the drawing room. He waved, a flick of the wrist which served to dismiss her rather than show any shadow of affection. She ignored the gesture and sought the fragile sanctuary of her room.

'Has she gone?' asked Maichamps as Henry sat opposite him. The young man nodded.

'Good. She trusts me Henry, she really trusts me. I feel encouraged, my talents to deceive are not waning. She is a ripe fruit is that one, ripe and ready for plucking. And tonight my dear, if all progresses as it ought, if you carry out my instructions, we shall both taste that fruit.' He leaned forward, an action copied by Henry.

'But the real miracle is, my lovely one, that the fruit may be tasted again and again without ever losing its sweetness. No matter how corrupt its flesh may appear at the end of the night, the morning will find it perfectly formed again and ready to challenge the lips and teeth of the adventurer brave enough to reach to the highest boughs for its rarest delights. Henry, does not such a challenge excite you?'

Henry nodded eagerly. Maichamps read the incomprehension in his eyes, the idle offspring of indolence and alcohol, but did not care. Tonight he would triumph again.

'Thomas, I can't find the clothes you went out in yesterday. Where are they?' Thomas's hand sneaked into his jacket pocket, rested on the envelope containing his letter to Elizabeth. It felt suddenly large, and the coarse wool of his jacket transparent, and Mary's eyes all-seeing.

'I came back in my costume, love. I must have left my other clothes in the trunk, they'll still be there. I'll call in for them on the way in to work, don't worry.'

'How did it go? Yesterday I mean.' Mary wandered in from the kitchen, wiping her hands on her apron. The smell of baking bread followed her.

'It was good, very good. Ask Willie and Abigail when you see them. We're getting better every time we dance.' He looked down at his feet, then back up again.

'I just wish you'd been there,' he added.

Mary seemed a little embarrassed.

'Did you get my note?' she said brightly. 'I left it on the

table by the fire, I noticed it wasn't there this morning when I got . . .'

'I got it when I came in. And the present. Thank you very much, I know how much that heart means to you, there was no need . . .'

'I had to say sorry somehow, Thomas. I thought about you a lot yesterday. It was strange without you, I didn't like it. I missed you.'

'I appreciated it. I would have said thank you last night but you were so peaceful when I came up, it seemed a pity to wake you.'

Mary sat down by the fire and stretched.

'There was a time when you would have woken me, Thomas. I don't mean by shaking me or making a loud noise, nothing like that. Not so long ago you'd have found a way to wake me up so's I didn't know where dreaming ended and real life started. Do you think those days are past now, love?'

'No!' protested Thomas, 'Of course not! But it was late, and you . . .'

'. . . looked so peaceful lying there! Oh Thomas, I'm sorry, I'm teasing you again. You seem to have become so serious recently. I mean, look at you now! You're hopping from one foot to another. What's the matter man?'

'There's nothing love, really, nothing at all. It's just hard to come back to being ordinary, that's all. Yesterday we had a crowd of five or six hundred people watching us, all cheering and clapping. Today there's nothing. It takes a bit of getting used to.' He moved in front of her, sat down in the seat opposite. A shaft of sunlight raised dust in the air of its passage and he sifted it with his hand as he sat. It seemed as though he was trying to catch the individual motes of light in his palm, but each trawl only made them more agitated, more difficult to capture.

'I know Thomas, the place needs a good spring-clean. I'll

start on it later today. It looks nice though, the sunbeam. It's a pity really. Even if you could catch all the little bits of gold, they'd turn out to be nothing but dust. I'm pleased mind, that the dancing went well. Really. Do you think you might win? The championship, that is?'

'Aye, if we can keep improving we might just do it. It'll need practice mind, but the lads won't mind that.'

'Do you know yet when they're being held? And where? It was Durham last year, wasn't it?'

'It won't be Durham this year, not twice in a row. I've heard Peelwell's the most likely place, and the date's to be the twenty-first of June. It's a Tuesday.'

'That's daft! Nobody'll come and watch on a Tuesday, they'll all be at work. What about you lot, how will you get time off?'

'Oh, we'll manage. You can come as well, and the kids. You see, we won't be at work, and they won't be at school. It's a holiday for everybody. It's Victoria's jubilee. That's why they're holding it at Peelwell, that hill overlooking the Tyne, the one with all the old drift mines. We went there once, years ago.'

'That's right, I can remember. You told me it was dangerous, there were lots of vertical shafts near the top. It doesn't seem a very good place to hold a rapper competition.'

'Well, perhaps there aren't as many shafts as I said. It was before we got married, wasn't it? Any excuse to have you hold on to me!' Mary raised her eyes and feigned a simpering blush.

'The important thing is that it's a good high spot, you can see it from miles around. You see, they're going to build a whole chain of bonfires across the country to celebrate the jubilee, each one visible from the one before and after, and they'll light them at dusk. There'll be one at Peelwell, and we should be able to see the next one over at Penshaw, and the

one across at Kenton Bar, perhaps all the way up to Tosson
at Rothbury if it's a clear night. It should be quite a day. A
day to remember.'

They both sat back, lost in their thoughts. Thomas could
see himself holding up the rapper swords locked into a fiery,
burning pentangle, though whether the fire was a reflection
of the jubilee beacon or the setting sun he could not say.
Mary looked back to her younger self holding Thomas
tightly, filled with an irrational fear that he might suddenly
slip away from her down some hidden mine shaft. The fact
that she too would fall with him did occur to her, but what
mattered more was that she should be with him.

'Well, I must go,' said Thomas, standing abruptly.

'You're early,' said Mary, 'you don't start for an hour.'

'I've got to get me other clothes,' said Thomas, 'remember? And I'll have to tell Willie to meet me at the pit.'

'Alright then. Take care. Don't forget your bait.' She
stood up and they kissed each other lightly. As he left
Thomas convinced himself that he had told no lies. He
would arrange to meet Willie at the pit. He would collect his
clothes from the stable, explain their dirtiness by saying that
he'd dropped them on the way back home. And as for his
detour to the summerhouse, well, the less Mary knew about
that the better.

Spring had arrived, and the children in the playground
chased and butted each other like new lambs. David
Armstrong could be found with the others, skinny as a lath,
coat left in the cloakroom, cardigan undone, running after
girls with a roar of shout and pockets full of glassies. The
hurry and bustle of the season seemed to have afflicted the
children with the same symptoms which urged the animals
and birds around them into activity. They ran where they
could have walked, shouted when they should have merely
spoken, played games with an intensity and competitive

spirit which verged on warfare. Some, however, seemed immune to this illness.

Matthew Armstrong lay quiet on the brief strip of grass at the bottom of the hedge, gaze fixed on an early season bumble bee searching for some brave nectar-clad flower. 'Not here!' whispered Matthew to the bee. 'Not here! There's primroses and violets up at the woods, and there's daffodils on the lawns at the big house. Go on, off you go!' He blew at the bee and it flew drunkenly away. It had, so far as he was concerned, only been of passing interest. What he was really looking for was the hedgehog. He had noticed it when staring out of the window during the morning's first lesson. It was a thin, emaciated creature newly woken from hibernation, snuffling for grubs or earthworms, plants or carrion, anything to fill its winter-hungry stomach. He was sure it was still there; all he had to do was to keep still and watch.

'What you doing?' came David's strident voice.

'Go away,' said Matthew politely. He had been scolded by the teacher for being rude to David, had been smacked and sent to bed by his mother when found sitting on him. The trouble was, David was smaller than him. He was also more inclined to ask for cuddles, to sit on people's knees, to put his arms round their necks and give them wet kisses. They would say 'Aah' and 'What a lovely child' and 'Isn't he sweet.' But the David Matthew knew was all elbows and feet, jostling and kicking and annoying him when he wanted to be quiet, aggravating him beyond adult comprehension. And then, just when Matthew meted out the punishment which his younger brother so richly deserved, David would cry out and someone would turn round and catch Matthew doing once what had been inflicted upon him a dozen times. He had therefore decided not to rise to the bait which David scattered so generously upon the still waters. He would ignore him.

'What you looking at?' asked David again.

'Nothing,' answered Matthew truthfully. David lay down on the ground beside him and stared at the dead leaves at the bottom of the hedgerow. They barely breathed, David's glancing at his brother the only sign of movement.

'There's nothing there,' whispered the younger boy.

'I know. That's what I told you,' came the curt reply.

'Why you looking at nothing?' David's question proved difficult to answer easily.

'It helps me think,' said Matthew, suddenly inspired. 'It's like when Dad's asleep, only he's not really, he's just got his eyes closed. And when you ask him why he's got his eyes closed, he says it helps him think. That's what I'm doing now. Thinking.' Surely, he thought, David would be satisfied by this statement of the obvious and would leave him in peace.

'What you thinking about?' came the inevitable question.

'Nothing!' hissed Matthew. 'Now will you go away!'

'Yes,' replied David, 'I'll go away. And I won't tell you me secret!'

'What secret?' asked Matthew.

'Not telling!' answered David. This was obviously an opening gambit. David desperately wanted to tell Matthew his secret, but only if Matthew begged him to do so. And Matthew would not beg his younger brother. Some negotiation was necessary.

'If you tell me your secret,' proposed Matthew, 'I'll tell you why I'm really lying here. I'll tell you what I'm looking for.' David thought for a while.

'Alright,' he said, 'you first.'

'Oh no,' said Matthew. 'If I go first you'll listen to what I say then you won't tell me your secret.'

'I will!' protested David. 'Honest! Cross me heart and hope to die!' He crossed his cardigan with a muddy finger. Matthew looked at him suspiciously. Could he trust him?

He decided that he had no choice, if the matter was to be resolved before the bell rang to call them back into their classroom.

'I'm watching for a hedgehog,' he said, and proceeded to tell David why he was doing so in this particular spot. The younger boy did not seem impressed.

'Is that all?' he said. 'Well you won't find it here. That's why I came to see you. Amy Pearson's found your hedgehog over by the bins. That was my secret!' As Matthew struggled to his feet the bell sounded.

'Damn!' shouted Matthew. 'Why didn't you just tell me! You're stupid you are, stupid!'

'I'm not stupid!' came the vehement reply. 'You're the stupid one!'

'No I'm not. I know more than you, I know lots more than you, I bet I know everything you know and more besides!'

'No you don't!'

'Yes I do!'

'Prove it then! Tell me something you know about that I don't!' They were on their feet now, jostling each other as they joined the lines waiting to go into the school.

'I know where frogspawn comes from,' said David.

'So do I, that's easy,' countered Matthew.

David did not think it worthwhile questioning Matthew's statement. His brow furrowed with concentration.

'I know what twelve-sixes are!' he announced.

'Easy-peasy – seventy-two. You'll have to think harder than that. Come on, you've got one more.'

'No!' cried David, 'you didn't say just three things!'

'It's always three! Three wishes, three guesses, it's always three. You've got one more!'

David squeezed his head with his hands.

'I know something about Mam and Dad you don't know!' he said triumphantly, went straight on, unable to keep his news to himself. 'They shout at each other!'

'No they don't,' said Matthew, puzzled. 'I've never heard them.'

'They did, they did! You were asleep. I woke up for a wee and I heard them. They were shouting at each other and Mam ran upstairs and banged the door and I heard her crying.'

'Are you sure?' asked Matthew, a worried look on his face.

'Honest! I wouldn't tell fibs about that.' The line began to file into the school.

'I didn't know that,' said Matthew. 'I didn't know they shouted at each other. And I didn't know Dad did things that made Mam cry.'

Elizabeth was nervous. She had spent the morning trying hard to help her father with his work, writing letters, filing, passing instructions to clerks, collating information. The tasks were not demanding. She could have left them for others to do but was afraid that she would be unable to apply herself to anything which required more than a modicum of concentration. She found herself gazing idly out of the window, watching trees sway in the wind, wishing that she were out in the park amongst the daffodils and crocuses. She held her breath as a figure headed along the path at the side of the house, moved somewhat furtively in her direction. Only when he drew close did she breathe out as she recognised one of the gardeners carrying a sack of mouldy leaves to spread amongst the rose bushes. It might have been him, she told herself.

She found her pen had a will of its own, drawing the letters 'T' and 'E' without her permission on the paper before her. She hastily scribbled over them in case others should see, then laughed at her paranoia. Who would see? And what could they say?

In the afternoon, she had told Thomas, she would go to the summerhouse in the afternoon. But Thomas was on late shift, she had read his name on the roster, if he had left a message it would already be there. But perhaps he had not turned in. Perhaps he was waiting for her even now. Perhaps he would appear later in the day, in the afternoon, when she had said she would be there. She must be patient. Two o'clock, she would go at two o'clock.

She could not eat lunch. Even the soup was indigestible. She excused herself and went to the music room, began to toy with the piano but found her fingers unable to reach the keys she wanted; her violin playing was equally poor. She wandered into the library but could find nothing which would hold her attention, tried playing patience but the cards refused to be dealt. Despairing of ridding herself of her anxieties she climbed the stairs to her room and lay down on her bed. If thoughts of Thomas were impinging upon her life then she would allow herself the luxury of concentrating on those thoughts.

She fell asleep willing herself to dream of Thomas, wanting only to relive the night before, to hold him and their moments together in her memory. But the man who came to her was not Thomas. She knew him but could not say his name. He pursued her but did not catch her, though she was aware that he was stronger than her, and faster than her, and seemed to know exactly which way she would turn in the labyrinth of corridors and passages which made up her world. And then she saw Thomas, and he was running too, but chasing someone only recognisable as a distant shadow against a blood red, fiery flame of night. He couldn't see her, and whenever she moved towards him her pursuer would appear to block her path with hands that were claws and a smile that showed sharp, razored teeth in a mouth of evil.

She woke in a sweat of horror. Somehow she had managed to wrap herself in her quilt. The heat of that had, she reasoned, influenced her mind and taken her into her nightmare. As she sat up the clock struck two.

Margaret waited for Henry to fall asleep. She lay on her back, her nightclothes a ruff around her neck. Henry's arm was draped across her, his head resting in the hollow formed by her neck and her shoulder. His breath still reeked of alcohol, but the regular rise and fall of his chest against her side showed that he was in a world of dreams. Margaret drew back her lips over her teeth in what might have been a smile; God knew what depraved beasts haunted his dreams! Yet they could be no worse than the animal which her husband had become, the animal which made her own life a nightmare of pain and misery.

She turned slightly away from him, as though she too were asleep. More than once he had pretended to be dormant and she had moved away from him, only to be pulled back and accused of desertion; she had been punished with further beatings. This time, though, he *was* asleep. She moved again, pushed his arm from her, rolled onto her front and winced with pain. He had whipped her this time, raised welts on her thighs and stomach and across her breasts, on her back and buttocks. But she would suffer him no longer. Maichamps was waiting for her. He had promised to help in some way and she trusted him. She had to. There was no-one else.

She lowered her feet to the floor and slid from under the bedclothes, pulled her shift down to cover herself and crept to the door. It opened quietly, and there were no lights in the corridor. Henry and Margaret shared this wing of the hall with no servants, no guests, lest others hear, literally, of Henry's sadism. There were rumours amongst the maids and footmen of course, they heard noises which could only have been cries of pain; and the housekeeper tutted over the lines of blood which too frequently graced her sheets and pillows, wondering why the mistress ever fell in with such a bad lot as Master Henry. But they said nothing and did nothing, for they were servants.

Margaret limped slowly along the corridor. She had to stop twice when dizzinesss threatened to overcome her, leaned against the cool wall until her strength returned, but soon found herself outside Maichamps' room. There was a blur of warm light at the bottom of the door. Given the circumstances she felt that knocking was unnecessary. She turned the handle and went in.

Maichamps looked up. He was in bed, his back propped up against some pillows, a book in his hands. At first he didn't seem to recognise her, then as she approached he leaped from the bed and ran towards her.

'Margaret, oh Margaret,' he gasped. 'What has he done to you?' He took her hands and looked at her face; even now she could not cry. His dressing gown was on the bed, he laid it gently over her shoulders and shared her pain as she flinched at its pressure.

'Sit you down,' he comforted. 'It's past now. I won't let it happen again. Come on, come over here.'

He moved her to the bed, sat her down, lifted her feet and covered them with the counterpane.

'You just sit there, be still, calm down. No, don't speak yet. You can tell me in a while, once you've recovered. I'll just get . . .'

He stood up and she grabbed at him, panic in her eyes. Her taloned fingers held the sleeve of his nightshirt, would not let go. He touched her wrist lightly, unwound her fingers. Her eyes seemed fixed upon the material, captivated by the light and dark blues painted on the white background in floral whirls and petals. He leaned forward and she could smell his cologne, a faint odour of mint and apples and woodsmoke.

'You need something to calm you Margaret. I've just the

thing, it's over there, on the desk. I won't be out of your sight, I'll come straight back. Let go Margaret. Let go.' His voice was soothing, hypnotic, and Margaret felt herself relaxing. She let go Maichamps' sleeve and he hurried away to the desk, returned immediately with a decanter of red-brown liquid and a glass. He put them on his bedside table then, before she could reach out for him again, set off once more on some mysterious errand.

'I've some creams and lotions which might soothe you,' he explained. 'They're in my travelling bag but I'm not sure where the boy put them. Perhaps,' he threw himself down onto his hands and knees, 'they're under here.' He peered under the bed and gave a snort of triumph, pulled a dark wooden box out and placed it beside the decanter. If his fussy manner was designed to calm Margaret then it did so. His bony arms and legs projected from his nightshirt like the branches of some heath-blown bog oak, gnarled and angular. When he walked it was like the scuttling of a crab. He looked like an emaciated scarecrow, and when he finally sat down beside her Margaret smiled.

'That's better,' he said. 'Now then, drink this.' He filled the glass with the brown liquid and passed it to her. She sniffed suspiciously.

'It's a blend of fruit juices and herbs and just a touch of alcohol, some cinnamon, a little essence of rosemary. Take just a sip to start with, if you're worried.' He watched as she drew some of the liquid onto her lips with her tongue, then took a sip, then swallowed a mouthful.

'And then it also contains crushed dung beetle, dead rat ...' Margaret's smile almost became a laugh. She emptied the glass.

'There now, feel any better?' She nodded.

'Well then, have a little more. Here we are, I'll pour it for you. You look better already.' He lowered his voice.

'Did he beat you?' She nodded, solemn again.

'I'm sorry, I tried to stop him from drinking but it was no use. Then I thought I might get him so drunk he was incapable of moving, but he seemed to become bored with me and left without even saying that he was retiring. I ran after him and stood in his way but there was no stopping him. We almost fought.' He lowered his head. 'I should have fought him. I might have saved you this!'

'Dear friend,' said Margaret, 'it would have been of no use. He has the strength of an ox when he's drunk. He would have struck out at you and he would have knocked you down without remorse, and my lot would have been worse with him so inflamed. And then you would not have been here to help me when my need was great.'

'What did he do?' whispered Maichamps.

'He whipped me. Like a horse or a disobedient dog, he whipped me. He calls me that as he does it. He calls me a bitch. He was standing over me, on my bed, and I saw the whip in his hand, the short one, the very one he uses when he rides out. I begged him not to hit me. He ordered me to lift my nightdress. It was one he bought for me when we were in Italy. He said he didn't want to damage it. And then he whipped me.' Margaret broke down, her body racked with tears. Maichamps reached towards her and took her hand.

'More,' he ordered in a kindly voice, holding the glass up to her lips. She drank gratefully.

'And where did he ...' He seemed unable to utter the words, held back, ran his tongue over his lips as if forcing them to say words abhorrent to him.

'Where did he whip you?'

Margaret looked straight at him. The liquid she had been drinking was everything he had promised. Her pain was now bearable, she felt calm and in control of her actions.

'Here,' she said, holding her hand to her breast. 'And here,' the other hand rested lightly on her stomach, 'and here,' she touched her thighs, 'and on my back and on my behind. At least, those are the places I hurt.'

'And did he break the skin? Did you bleed? Oh Margaret, let me go fetch a doctor, you may be disfigured unless you receive the right treatment!'

'No, no doctors! No-one must know! But you spoke of a cream, some oil you said would help?'

'It's here. I've used it for burns so I suppose it would help on anything similar, it soothes the pain and the skin seems to heal more quickly. But I haven't seen the damage done, so I'm not sure if . . .'

'I'll show you,' said Margaret.

'I couldn't! This would compromise you even more than . . .' He was unable to complete the sentence. Margaret silenced him by turning around so that her back was to him. She sat on her heels, then pulled her nightdress slowly over her back. Maichamps watched as the hem of the garment revealed her hips and her waist, her back and her shoulders. They were covered with narrow red stripes. On two or three of them blood had hardened into scabs.

'Oh, dear God!' he breathed.

Margaret pushed her legs and buttocks down under the sheet, reached behind her and pulled it up to her waist. Maichamps leaned forward to examine her back more closely.

'Very well Margaret. I'll try it on your shoulders first. Tell me if it hurts.' He unscrewed the cap of one jar and laid it neatly to one side, then did the same with another, and a third. He dipped the index and middle fingers of his right hand into the first jar. It was made of blue glass, virtually opaque, and the cream inside it was almost white, almost liquid. He touched it gently to the unblemished skin at the tip of one of the red weals, jerked his fingers back as Margaret inhaled sharply.

'Painful?' he asked.

'Cold,' she replied.

He smoothed the cream onto her skin, one finger on either side of the stripe of pain, then turned his hand sideways so that both fingers together could run their tips along the raised flesh.

'That helps,' said Margaret, 'I can hardly feel it now. Please do the rest.'

Maichamps repeated the treatment on each of the marks along Margaret's shoulders and upper back. Where the skin was broken he used a different jar, this time of green glass. The ointment inside was stiffer, a yellowish paste which stuck to his fingers, and when he applied it Margaret winced.

'Yes, it feels different, but don't worry.' His voice was quiet, reassuring.

'This one's stronger. It deadens the pain more effectively and causes the skin to heal more quickly, but it isn't as soothing as the other. Lie still my dear, you should be feeling better already.'

'Mm, I am.' Margaret spoke dreamily. The pain was disappearing, and not only from those parts of her back which Maichamps had treated. The tonic, medicine, call it what she would, was also proving effective. Despite the fact that there was no fire in the room and that her back was bare she felt warm. No, more than warm, strangely content and almost happy. Maichamps' magic fingers and wonderful, sorcerer's potions were working their spells.

'Do you want me to go on?' he asked, his voice deep and sonorous, soothing her mind. She nodded, almost imperceptibly.

'That is good,' he intoned. 'It's so good that you trust me, that you want me to go on, that you want to feel my hands touching you, healing you, taking away the pain.' He recited his mantra, the regular rise and fall of the soft incantation driving away all worries.

'That feels good, so good, you feel safe, you are in my care.' He pulled away the sheet covering her buttocks, left it draped below her knees. 'You want me to help me, don't you.' It was a statement. 'It's good that you want me to help you. It's good that you want to tell me that. You do want to tell me that, don't you?'

'I want you to help me,' murmured Margaret sleepily. Maichamps' hands were now moving over the cheeks of her behind.

'And what else do you want?' he asked, then answered the question himself. 'You want me to protect you. Isn't that right?'

'I want you to protect me.'

'You want me to soothe away the pain.'

'. . . soothe . . . pain . . .'

'You want me to touch you.'

'. . . touch me . . .'

'You need me.'

'. . . need you . . .'

'You want me.'

'. . . want you . . .'

'That's good. That's very good. Because I want to help you. I want to protect you, and heal you – you can turn over if you want now – and I want to touch you, take away your pain. And I want you to need me. And I want you to want me.'

The words were not important, the message was lost in the calm authority of Maichamps' tone, and Margaret's will was as one with that of her confessor, her healer, her master. She rolled onto her back. Maichamps was right. It felt good.

'He did a good job of work, your young man, but we'll soon put things right. We'll start down here, where I can reach, then I'll work my way up, is that alright?' He began to rub the white cream onto the front of her thighs, slowly, softly, his fingers feeling for the ridge of tender skin as his eyes climbed Margaret's body. She lay quite still, a smile on her face, her skin flushed, arms at her sides. Henry's whip appeared to have been applied more sparingly to the front of her torso, leaving lines across her stomach and rib cage and across the flesh of her breasts. The valley between them was moist, as was her forehead and upper lip.

'You're getting a little hot my dear, it's so warm in here. You're still wearing that sad old nightdress; it never did suit you, did it?'

Margaret shook her head.

'Perhaps you'd better take it off. You didn't like it, did you? That's it, reach up, pull it over your head. Just put it to one side, that's a good girl, it might turn chilly later. Now relax again, feel my fingers, listen to my voice, I'm here to help you. What am I here to do my love?'

'... help me ...'

'That is right my angel, that is so perfectly right. And you are an angel as well, so beautiful. No wonder he wanted you, no wonder hurting you causes him pain. But that's over now, that's over. Relax my love. Relax.'

Maichamps' hands moved over Margaret's thighs. They hovered over but then ignored the nest of hair between her legs, so fair that nothing of her sex was hidden, so fine that she might have been a girl of twelve. Instead they stayed a while on her stomach, then continued their journey to rest briefly at her breasts, breasts which showed that she was no twelve-year-old but indeed a woman.

The blue glass jar was almost empty. Maichamps scooped out the last of the cream and smoothed it sparingly into the last two weals. Margaret lay utterly still, as if sleeping. Only her monosyllabic responses to Maichamps' solemn invocations proved that to be false.

'Margaret my angel, my love, has the pain gone?'

'Yes.'

'Have I cleansed you? Is your body now pure?'

'Yes.'

'You have felt the benefit of my devotions, I have taken away the pain, the suffering, the hurt. I have drawn the poison from your soul, the venom from your heart, I have banished the serpent from your presence. You are floating, floating in the love of your own existence. The perversions of your mind, the desecrations of your body, they are not even memories. They have been cast away. You are a vessel, an empty vessel waiting to be filled with the love you need.'

'. . . need.'

He paused and reached for the third jar. The glass was clear, as was the liquid inside, though thick like treacle when he dipped his finger in, lengthening into a long string of silver which parted abruptly to be drawn back into the jar.

'I have given you my help, my comfort, I have cured your pain. And now I shall give you more. I will satisfy your needs, I will fill the empty vessel you have become with my love, and ask for nothing in return save the knowledge that you have asked me to do this.'

'Do it,' Margaret whispered

'Do what my love?'

'Fill me with your love!'

'Why must I do that my angel?'

'Because,' she breathed, 'because I want you. Because I need you. Because I love you.'

'Oh, my sweet!' Maichamps took his finger, still glistening with the clear syrup, and touched it to Margaret's mouth; her tongue snaked languorously out and ran its damp trail over her lips. He touched her mouth again but this time allowed his finger-tip to trace the same course her tongue had run, then, as she opened her mouth, rested it lightly on her bottom lip. Her tongue danced once more, weaving its sinuous way around the whorls and curves of his finger. She drew it further into her mouth, bit at the soft flesh and hard nail alike. He pulled away and she whimpered, but his hand went only as far as the jar and returned to tease her tongue into motion. Nor was his other hand idle. It too had dipped into the liquid and delicately smeared the mead onto first one and then the other nipple, then returned to stroke and caress them into life, favouring neither, ignoring neither. Margaret breathed more deeply and, though her arms did not move from her sides, her fingers gripped the sheet beneath her and her hands shrank into knotted fists.

'It's good,' whispered Maichamps. 'Taste the goodness. What can you taste my love? Tell me what you taste.'

'So good!' came the mumbled reply. 'Warm and sweet . . . sugar . . . mint . . . wine . . . oranges. Feels . . . good! Touch me again. Touch me!'

He did as he was told but this time used fingers of both hands to excite her, to rub and stroke, pinch and pull at her breasts. She moved her hips slightly.

'You want more?' he asked. She nodded urgently.

'Then you shall have it.' He reached for the jar itself this time, brought it to her and tilted it carefully over her. She winced at the coolness of it, felt the liquid run down between her breasts to pool at her navel then overflow to both sides.

'Such a waste!' said Maichamps putting the jar down again on the bedside table. 'There must be something we can do with this surfeit. I think I may be able to help.'

He dammed the rivers which had strayed from their course with his palms, moved the flood back onto the plain of her stomach, then formed a canal to direct the flow down again around the island of her pudenda; but even that atoll would soon succumb to the relentless pressure placed upon it. Maichamps laid his hand, his left hand, high upon her chest and slid it down her body, fingers spread wide. The excess liquid collected between his fingers as they trawled their way down the canyon of her breasts and onto the sea of her belly. She moaned out loud as his hand anchored between her legs, fingers and thumb pushing open her thighs. She gave way to the pleasure of his touch, the tips of his fingers, so soft, his tongue, delicate and inquisitive, his nails, hard, disciplined, his mouth, warm and safe, his lips, insolent, self-confident, knowing.

He managed to remove his nightshirt without her realising that he had done so, and when he entered her it was as though every nerve in her body had been waiting for that moment. The surge of satisfaction was not allowed to die but was taken further by his ardent administrations. She felt the weight of his body upon her and, sundew-like, snaked arms and legs around him to bind him to her. She pushed herself hard at him, he responded by grinding his pelvis down upon her, and she was rewarded with another wave of euphoria. She heard a strange voice, low and guttural, crying words unrecognisable as such, no more than bestial grunts, and a small detached part of her mind confirmed that the beast was her. She could not move now, but still the frenzy was upon her, still she climbed the mountain of pleasure, reaching each false summit only to find herself led higher and higher until, at the very peak, she threw herself skyward with a scream of death and delight in falling.

She felt Maichamps' sudden rigor, a warmth within her; his body fell like a rake across her. His ribs pressed against her like the laths of a cheap wooden seat, spaced too far apart for comfort, and his heartbeat rattled inside his chest as though a boy were running a wooden stick along his bones. He said nothing. He moved not at all, save for the insidious retreat of sated male flesh. Margaret felt pain returning, she flinched and moved herself slightly where Maichamps' elbow lay against one of her sores. Each striped ache announced its presence with an irritation she recognised, one which she knew would become a sting then a stab of pain. She pushed at Maichamps' chest in an attempt to move him from her.

'Finished so soon?' asked a familiar voice from the shadows. Henry stepped into view at the foot of the bed. Maichamps rolled over and, in the same instant, Margaret grabbed at the bedsheet and pulled it up to her chin.

'Hiding? From me?' slurred Henry. He had pulled on his trousers but was naked from the waist upwards. He glared at Margaret then turned his eyes upon Maichamps who seemed unconcerned at his nakedness. Maichamps wiped himself on the corner of the sheet and, as he stood up, ripped it from her.

'No!' she cried, covered her sex with one hand, her other hand and forearm raised to her breasts.

'Too late for being shy,' said Henry unsteadily. His eyes were fixed on her again. 'Was she good?' he asked almost as an aside.

'I've had some better,' said Maichamps with disinterest, wrapping the sheet around him, 'and some worse. Of course the ointments helped, and the liquor. Average, I suppose would be the answer. But with potential. Definitely some potential.'

'And now?' Henry licked his lips.

Maichamps looked at Margaret. She had drawn her knees up to her chest, her arms were protecting her head from the likelihood of a further beating, and she was crying.

'Well, Henry my boy,' he said, standing beside his protégé, 'it looks to me as though you need to relieve a little tension.' He put his hand on the front of Henry's trousers, raised his eyebrows in appreciation.

'And we are, I believe, already on the way to achieving our objectives. The night is still largely ahead of us. Should we proceed?'

Henry nodded grimly. He and Maichamps advanced on the weeping girl.

Elizabeth was out of breath. She had left the Hall at a sedate pace, nodding at those servants she passed, wearing a look which she hoped would demonstrate that she was on urgent business and did not wish to be diverted from her task. That much at least was true. Her walk had quickened as she crossed the gravel path, had become a run as she passed the end of the house. She arrived at the summerhouse to find it empty, had expected this, but had harboured some secret hope that Thomas might, perhaps, be waiting. She stood at the entrance, hands on hips, waiting for her heart to resume its normal beat. She could see the picture of Victoria. It seemed to be exactly as she remembered it, there was no sign that it had been moved. He hasn't been, she told herself. He's thought about what happened and decided that he doesn't want me.

'No,' she whispered as she advanced, Victoria's unsmiling countenance showing her evident disapproval of her being used in this way. The picture was almost beyond her reach; she pulled it away from the wall, expecting a note of some sort to flutter down, but received no reward for her efforts.

'Damn!' she swore. 'Damn you Thomas Armstrong!' She sank to the floor, her head resting against the wall as if in prayer. The elation which had carried her through the morning was gone. She was lost.

'I won't cry!' she said to herself. 'You won't have that satisfaction, Thomas, of me shedding a single tear for you. Not a tear!' She raised herself to her feet and stalked to the door, flung it open. The skeletons of the autumn's leaves still clung to spider-webbed corners of the verandah, a broken branch left by winter's storms lay at her feet. But summer would soon be here; a swallow dipped into view, chasing early insects across the park, and fresh mole-hills had erupted between the oaks. A new cycle had begun.

'Bastard!' shouted Elizabeth, not caring who might hear her. She bent down, picked up the broken branch, and hurled it with unerring accuracy at Victoria's smug face. The glass in the frame broke, the cord which had held the frame to the wall snapped, and the whole fell to the ground. Even from where she stood Elizabeth could see a small rectangle of white still fixed to the back of the frame. She rushed across.

'You stupid, stupid man!' she said. 'Oh Thomas, fancy jamming the thing behind one of the nails.' The envelope had her name written on it. Despite her burning curiosity she opened the envelope slowly, trying not to tear it too much. She took out the letter and read it, then read it again.

'Oh Thomas,' she said softly, 'Thomas, you poor, poor man. I'll help you. Thomas, I love you so much.'

Chapter Fifteen

―――――◆―――――

They teach the morals of a whore, and the manners of
a dancing master.
  (Samuel Johnson, on Lord Chesterfield's Letters)

Thomas and Elizabeth were careful. They knew the risks
they were taking in continuing to see one another. They
could be seen together, but only in circumstances where
suspicion would not be aroused. For this reason dance
practices were recommenced on a regular basis, sometimes
twice a week, and in the ballroom of the Hall instead of in
the village hall; the floor, Thomas informed the others, was
better for dancing. They were only too eager to spend time
in the luxurious surroundings of the big house, to admire the
paintings and, during their short rest breaks, sit on large,
comfortable, velvet sofas. And if Thomas would never join
the other dancers in a jar of ale at Len's house afterwards,
well, that was his choice. After all, he had the music to
discuss with Elizabeth, and his clog dance to practice. The
dancers all agreed with him, the clog dance came in handy
as an introduction to the real business of rapper itself.

And so it was that after the others left Thomas and
Elizabeth would repair to the ante-room (to which she
possessed the only key) beside her office, nothing more than

a large windowless cupboard containing a desk, a chair and a single bed. The bed had been her idea.

'It's in case I'm working late at night, father,' she told John Waterhouse. 'I often take papers up to my room only to find that I need other files which are still down here. So in future if I want to work, especially during the periods when you're away, I shall just sleep here. Everything will be at hand.' John Waterhouse had voiced his approval. Elizabeth was taking a real interest in the mine and in his other businesses, and her enthusiasm was a relief to him. He had often wished that Emily had borne him a son, but he was coming to realise that ability was as important, no, more important than gender.

The room was in a part of the Hall visited infrequently by servants during the day and not at all during the evening or night. Elizabeth had put blankets and sheets on the bed herself; she made sure that the desk was always well stocked with towels; and the jug and bowl sitting on its polished surface were always filled with fresh water. If anyone noticed that Thomas left the Hall an hour after the others then they would also have been aware that he still arrived home long before the rest of the dancers staggered away from Len's unofficial hostelry. And if his name came up in conversation it was his prowess as a pitman, not as a lover, which was discussed.

The news that Thomas was to be groomed for the post of pit-manager came as no surprise to his friends. They had accepted his leadership both below and above ground, and all welcomed John Waterhouse's decision. His working day changed immediately. Although he would still have to go underground this would happen no more than once or twice a week. At other times he could be found working alongside Waterhouse, or learning from the clerks and storemen, the joiners and carpenters, engine drivers and winders. Given such a schedule it was hardly surprising that each lunchtime he felt the need to take a walk in the grounds of the Hall. Sometimes that walk took him home to see his wife; more often he visited the summerhouse to meet with another.

Mary suspected nothing. Aware of his wife's past worries Thomas was, if anything, more attentive than he had been in the recent past. He told her straightaway that he would, for some of the time at least, be working alongside Elizabeth. In effect he sought her approval, implied that if Mary was in any way dissatisfied with this then he would decline the offer of promotion. She was aghast that he should even consider this, but at the same time was both proud and thankful that he should have mentioned it to her. The fact of consultation was more important than her feelings on the matter; there was, of course, never any doubt that he must take the job. His new position brought her a measure of reflected glory, the extra wages were always helpful, and if he complained of fatigue, well, his tiredness was understandable. He often mounted the stairs before her and was asleep before she joined him, but that was a small price to pay for the opportunity to progress in the world.

'Do you still make love?' Elizabeth asked him one evening. The bed was narrow; they could lie beside each other only by turning onto their sides. She was facing the wall, he cupped into the small of her back, mimicking her position. One of his arms was underneath her, reaching round to rest on her breast, tracing lazy circles around each nipple in turn. The other was spiralling love-knots in her damp pubic hair.

'Yes,' he replied, not ceasing the motion of his hands.

'Very often?' He was still inside her, barely erect, but by pushing her behind against him she could still feel him.

'Not as often as in the past,' he said sleepily.

'How often?' she responded quickly. 'Every other day? Twice a week? Only at weekends?'

'Why? asked Thomas. 'Does it matter?'

'Yes,' said Elizabeth, 'it matters a lot.'

'Tell me why that is, then,' said Thomas. Elizabeth remained silent.

'Come on, you might as well tell me. You know you will anyway, you might as well make it sooner rather than later.'

'You wouldn't understand.'

'Try me.' Again there was no sound.

'Oh well, I suppose I'd best be away,' announced Thomas. He slid his arm from under Elizabeth, eased gently out of her and, taking a cloth from the desk, placed it between her legs. He splashed water from the bowl onto his chest and stomach and genitals and rubbed himself with soap.

'I'm not jealous,' Elizabeth said, her face still turned towards the wall. 'I know we discussed this, how I . . . we need to be with each other as often as possible. I know the guilt you felt, still feel. I know that you won't leave her . . .'

'Can't leave,' interrupted Thomas almost angrily, 'I can't leave her. I still feel for her. I don't know what it is, God knows we've talked about it often enough, you and I. It might still be love for all I know. Love isn't black or white, it's all shades of grey in between. I still care for her, and I won't leave her. And then there's the boys . . .' It was his turn to fall silent.

'You can't leave,' continued Elizabeth. 'I can understand that, and anyway, there are other difficulties. How would we live? If you did leave – no don't interrupt, I said if – then who would care for Mary? Who would feed your children? I know the limitations we set ourselves Thomas, I took them on knowing you could never be wholly mine. But I never thought . . .'

'Yes?'

Elizabeth's words came in a sudden rush, a damburst of syllables tumbling over one another in their haste to be free from the logjam of her mind.

'I never thought I would want you so much. I can't help

it, I resent the time you spend away from me. I resent the time you spend with her. I watch you leave here knowing that you'll be in bed with her, and that she's your wife, and that you lie to her about where you've been. I know that you can't ignore her because that would cause suspicion; you have to behave as you normally would. I know that you'll be lying beside her and touching her the same way you touch me, and that she'll want you the same way I want you, and that afterwards she'll be warm in your arms saying that she loves you. And I know that you'll say the same to her, DON'T DENY IT THOMAS, just don't say a word, let me finish! And whether you mean it or not, you're with her, and married to her, and I'm all alone living for the next few minutes we can spend together, either here or fumbling on the floor of the summerhouse. Do you realise what it's like for me? Sometimes you're beside me, when you're working or dancing, and I love you so much all I want to do is touch you, put my hand on yours, see you smile at me. But I know I can't, that there's nothing I can do to show you how I feel, and it's as though I've been stabbed through the heart. We're trying to squeeze our lives into these frenzied moments together and I don't know if I can do it! I'm going to go mad, I swear it Thomas, I'm going to go mad!'

'You're not!' hissed Thomas. 'You won't go mad. You're already mad, you're like me, a lunatic, just waiting to be taken away and locked up! Listen, can you hear them?' He knelt down by the bed and turned her face roughly towards him, pretended to be waiting for a distant noise to sound again.

'They know alright. They can smell madness, and they're all around us, just waiting for us to drop our guard. Then they'll be onto us, and we'll be in strait-jackets and padded cells before we know it! Of course we're mad, Jesus Christ woman, even a madman could tell that!' He giggled.

'I could do it, you know! I could persuade meself, if I had

a mind to, that I really was mad. I'll end up in the asylum yet.' He stood up and began to dress himself, regained his composure.

'Look love, I don't like the situation either. But it's all we've got. And it's better than nothing, isn't it?' Elizabeth nodded.

'Come on then. I'll have to be going. Will you be at the summerhouse tomorrow?' She nodded again. He pulled on his socks and sat down beside her to fasten his shoes.

'I don't like to leave you like this. Will you be alright?' She nodded once more. He leaned over her, kissed her lightly on the cheek.

'Till tomorrow then.' He stood over her but didn't leave; his face was filled with concern. She sprang to her feet, threw her arms around him.

'I'm sorry,' she cried. 'I didn't mean to make your life so complicated. I just wanted to love you.' He hugged her back, felt her warm saltiness against his neck.

'Come on love, I really must get going.' He pushed himself away from her, turned the key in the lock. 'You'd better tidy yourself up mind.' He nodded his head at the floor. Gravity had done its work, his sperm was dripping from her to pool on the faded and worn rug lying at her feet. She nodded slowly, gave a feeble, weary half-wave, then sat down with her head in her hands as he closed the door behind him.

Thomas was at first amazed, then concerned, that deception came so easily to him. He had always considered himself a man of morals. His lack of religion did not hinder him in this; on the contrary, he argued that it allowed him to reflect upon the salient points of any argument and then judge it by his own standards, not those imposed upon him by a God in whom he did not believe. Whatever criteria he applied to his own predicament, however, he always arrived at the same conclusion. That he was wrong to have made love to Elizabeth, was wrong to continue seeing her, and was wrong to have deceived Mary. But knowing this was different to acting upon it. He tried to tell himself that this was not love but an addiction, that it required nothing more than strong will to break the habit. More than once, lying in the heat of Elizabeth's arms, their bodies glued together in the aftermath of their sexual fervour, he decided that this would be the last time. The next day he would be strong. The next day he would tell her that these liaisons must end, the ridiculous pretence that they loved each other must cease. But the new day's dawning brought with it his need renewed, renewed and more intense than it had been the day before, and he knew that he would say nothing.

Instead he planned each day carefully. If he must deceive his wife then he would do so properly. He told Elizabeth that he feared for Mary's well-being if she should ever find out about them.

'I don't know how she would cope. I mean, it's not as though it's something that's happened before. I can't guess at what she might do. She might go mad, she might decide to attack you! I just don't know. But I think that the sense of rejection, that would cripple her, knowing that there's someone else. Someone else above her. That's why I worry about her.'

Elizabeth did not suggest that Thomas might be excusing his duplicity by dressing it in the guise of protecting Mary. She suspected that he was already aware of this possibility, but if he felt it necessary to justify the subterfuge in this particular way then she would not argue with him. She had to cope with her own reality; she had fallen in love with a married man. Far worse in the eyes of any outsider (should they ever be discovered) was the fact that he was not of her class. Each time they lay together they would discuss their next meeting. Although they would see each other during their working day they would allow no sign or signal of intimacy to pass between them, even if they were alone.

Such weaknesses bred carelessness, which would just as surely lead to discovery. They could meet and make love only after dance practices or at midday in the summerhouse (making their way there separately and by different routes) which Elizabeth had now had decorated and made weatherproof, furnished with seats and curtains and a large wooden chest filled with blankets. They would make a bed with these, undress quickly in the cool air and make love before departing.

They did not see each other at weekends. They made no contact whatsoever, but found that their spare moments were spent in thoughts of each other, thoughts expressed in words and writing, in long and abstract poems filled with despondence and gothic darkness which would be lifted only by their being once more in each other's presence. And Thomas kept up his pretence of normality.

It was the first week in May when Thomas was summoned to John Waterhouse's study. The old man was bustling about, thrusting sheafs of paper into a large black bag. Elizabeth was there, sitting relaxed in an armchair beside the grate. Although the fire was laid it was not lit; the day was warm with the promise of summer. Thomas stood before the desk, legs slightly apart, hands grasping each other behind his back, gaze fixed firmly ahead of him.

'Good Lord man, you're not a soldier!' John Waterhouse paused in his packing and marched round the desk to his seat.

'You make me nervous standing like that. Go on, get a seat, make yourself comfortable!' He looked across at Elizabeth, raised his eyes in supplication. Thomas placed a round-backed, embroidered dining chair in front of the desk and sat down.

'Good man. Thomas, you will no doubt have guessed by the state of panic in which I am rushing around that I am a little agitated. I received a telegram from my brother this morning requesting my personal assistance in an important matter. He gives no details, but for him to ask me for help tells me that his need is great. I would imagine that his problem concerns machinery, or the reorganisation of production.' He leaned forward and looked directly into Thomas's eyes, 'Or a woman. I don't think, Thomas, that I am giving away any secrets by including that last possibility. Anyway, I am forced to leave at regrettably short notice. Now then young man, I had planned on allowing you a further month before taking a scheduled trip, a month in which you would have been able to spend a little more time familiarising yourself with those parts of the mine beyond your past experience in coal extraction.' He stopped, savoured his own choice of words, then moved quickly on.

'I have discussed with Elizabeth the various options open to me. She feels – we feel – that you have the ability to assist her in managing the mine while I am away. This may be for a day or two, hopefully no longer than a week. Are you willing to assist us in this way?'

Thomas felt suddenly vulnerable. From his seat he could see only John Waterhouse, who was looking over Thomas's shoulder at Elizabeth and smiling. It would have been impolite of him to turn to see Elizabeth, although he was sure that she was pulling faces. Why else would her father be smiling at her?

'Well?' asked John Waterhouse.

'Oh, of course!' answered Thomas, flustered. 'Of course I'll help. I'll do whatever you require.'

'No Thomas, not me. Elizabeth. She'll be in charge. But she needs your experience as well. So look after each other. Neither of you can do the job properly by yourselves, but together, well, you complement each other. Understood?'

'Yes,' came Elizabeth's voice. Thomas nodded his head.

'Very well then. I shall go immediately, I've a connection

to make at Durham. If there is an insurmountable problem then do contact me, but consider that it will take me at least a day to return. I shall, however, write as soon as I am in a position to estimate the period of my absence. Now was there . . .?'

'You'll miss your train, father,' Elizabeth reminded him.

'Yes, I know, I know. Take care.' He embraced his daughter.

'No, don't come to see me off. You two have a great deal to discuss. I shall leave you now. Goodbye Thomas.' He extended his hand; Thomas shook it.

'Remember what I said! Work together!' He picked up his case of papers and hurried away leaving Thomas and Elizabeth alone together. They broke one of their rules. They touched hands and smiled at each other.

The Armstrong family was gathered around the table. Mary was serving the meal from a brown earthenware pot, ladling stew and dumplings onto each of the four plates in turn. She put down the pot and retreated to the kitchen.

'Mashed potatoes for anybody?' she cried. There was a chorus of eager yesses, and she reappeared carrying a long-handled soot-blackened pan.

'Some for you,' she said, scooping the steaming white potato onto David's plate. 'And a good helping for you because you're growing so fast,' a larger portion was deposited on Matthew's plate.

'And for the head of the family . . . the smallest share of all!' Thomas's plate was indeed less full even than that of his younger son.

'Why's that?' he asked, unsure of his wife's motives. She seemed to be in a good mood, so he assumed that this was some sort of joke.

'You can have some of mine Dad,' whispered David.

'The reason,' said Mary, 'is quite clear. If you work down

a mine, doing hard work all day, with lots of physical labour, you need to have lots of good food. Builds up your strength, doesn't it?' Thomas nodded.

'But why . . .?'

'Don't interrupt! But now you're not working down a mine. You're a manager. You're sitting behind a desk most of the time. You don't need so much food. In fact I've noticed a definite trend for just a little bit of thickness round the waist of late. What do you think lads?' She crossed behind his chair and pinched the flesh at his stomach; David and Matthew dived after her, began to do the same.

'Stop it,' laughed Thomas. 'That tickles! It's not fair, three onto one! No! Oh no, not the shirt out of the trousers! Matthew, your hands are cold! What are you doing with that spoon Mary? Don't you dare! Don't you . . .'

Mary put the spoon on the table.

'It's alright love, I was only joking. Mind you, you are putting on a bit of weight. But you help yourself to what you want. Sit down and eat lads, your Dad'll play with you after supper.' She went back to her place and served herself.

'We've got a surprise for you Thomas,' she announced, 'me and the boys.' She looked at each in turn; they nodded eagerly. Thomas looked up, his expression equal parts curiosity and suspicion. He had experienced surprises in the past. Matthew had surprised him with a live frog in his bed one summer; and David had once given him a dead rat as a birthday present. He looked at his eldest son whose smile of angelic innocence could have hidden a thousand evil thoughts. David was more open, David's face would tell him what to expect; but the small boy was staring fastidiously at his stew, scooping it eagerly into his mouth, avoiding his father's attention at all costs. And Mary? She merely raised her eyebrows.

'After we've eaten,' she said, 'you'll find out then.'

The silence was broken only by the scrape of cutlery on

plates, David's snort as he managed to control his volcanic laughter. Thomas finished eating before the others and sat back in his seat, looked surreptitiously around the room to see if there was any clue to the nature of this surprise. All seemed normal. What about the flowers though? He suddenly noticed that one of the vases (a hideous gold and white creation, a present from some distant, dusty aunt) was filled with wild flowers and leafy twigs; the room was touched with a delicate scent of summer to come. Could this have anything to do with the surprise? No, Mary liked flowers as much as he did, she would often bring them into the house. This was the first time she had done so this year, that was why he had noticed.

There was nothing else he could see which was unusual, no new pictures or tracts (he had moved 'God is Love' from its position above the fire to a less prominent station beneath the stairs), no lacy anti-macassars to nestle the chair backs. His eyes ceased their wandering, returned to the table where he found that the others had finished their meal and had, in their turn, been watching him.

'Well?' he said.

'Close your eyes Dad,' said Matthew.

'Tight shut,' added David, 'and put your hands over them so you don't peep!' Thomas did as he was told under the watchful eyes of his sons. He heard chairs being drawn back and Mary's footsteps receding then returning. Something was put down on the table in front of him. He felt the presence of his sons, one at each side of his chair.

'Go on then,' said Matthew.

'You can open your eyes now,' added David. Thomas lowered his hands and slowly opened his eyes. In front of him was ... something. What it was he couldn't tell; it was covered with a clean white linen tea-towel.

'Take it away,' said Mary. He reached for the corner and pulled the rectangle of material away to reveal a cake, light brown at the sides and smelling of oranges. The top of it was spread with white icing, and on this was written in large red icing 'Well Done Thomas (Dad)'. Below, more difficult to read because the writing was smaller and the icing had spread, he could make out 'Love from all of us'.

'It was their idea,' said Mary, gesturing at the boys. 'They wanted to congratulate you for doing so well at the pit.'

'But Mam made the cake,' shouted David in his father's ear. 'And she did the writing as well! Isn't it good!' Thomas nodded.

'And I've got another present for you,' said Matthew shyly. 'I made it meself.' He reached into his pocket and brought out a small bundle wrapped in newspaper and handed it to his father. Thomas glanced at Mary who shrugged her shoulders; this was evidently a surprise to her too.

'I'll tell you what love,' he said to Mary, 'you cut the cake while I have a look at this, eh? What have we got here?' He took his time unfolding the paper, aware that the attention of the others was on him. Each angle of print was peeled back slowly to reveal a stone, almost circular, some two inches across. It was black and had been polished to a high lustre.

'It's not really any good,' said Matthew as his father turned the stone over to reveal the carvings on its reverse. Etched into its surface was a lock of five swords, the handles (Thomas noted with pride) overlapping one another in the correct order. They had been picked out in white paint, while around the perimeter were inscribed five words, one at each point of swords. Thomas mouthed the words silently.

'Thomas Armstrong, King of Rapper.'

He put the stone down carefully, reverentially.

'Did you do that yourself?' he asked.

'Aye,' answered Matthew. 'I used an old nail, and I got the paint from school, and the varnish. It's not much good, not really.'

'Matthew,' said Thomas, reaching out to pull his son towards him, 'it's beautiful. It's one of the most wonderful presents I've ever been given. Honestly, it's, it's . . .'

'I've got a present as well!' said David, determined that he too should have some attention. 'It's a big kiss 'cos you're the best Dad in the whole world!' He leaped for Thomas's neck and deposited a large, wet, gravy-stained kiss on his father's lips. Thomas put an arm round each of the boys.

'Thank you both. And you Mary, thank you all. I've got the best family ever. I really have. I really do love you all, more than you can imagine.' He kissed both children, squeezed them tightly.

'Don't cry Dad,' said David, puzzled at the tears in his father's eyes. 'You don't cry when you get presents!'

'What did you tell Mary?' asked Elizabeth. She was in bed, her own double bed in her own room, with the sheets pulled up to her neck. Her nightdress was folded neatly over the chair beside her dressing table; she was naked.

'I told her what we agreed. That I needed to see how the night-shift worked, how they carried out repairs and so on. That I wanted to check on safety. You know, we talked about it.'

Elizabeth had given him full instructions. He was to enter by the side door (she had given him the key) and make her way direct to her room. If any of the servants were to see him then he was to ask them directions to the room, pretending that there was a matter concerning the running of the pit which required her immediate attention. He was dressed in his work clothes, so there would be no suspicion of anything untoward, but he felt wary, uncomfortable. There would be no excuses if he were discovered now, in Elizabeth's room.

'Are you coming to bed then?' she asked. He began to remove his clothes.

It had been her idea. She wanted, she had said, to spend the night with him, to make love without being pressured by time, to fall asleep in his arms; and her father's forced absence seemed to give them the ideal opportunity. Thomas found himself agreeing despite his misgivings. His guilt had been given extra weight by the surprise presents he had received. He had told Elizabeth about them, but it did not cross his mind that her desire that they should be together for a whole night might be to counteract those guilty feelings. He felt himself drawn onward by a force beyond his control, by emotions he couldn't understand. But that did not stop him. It seemed that nothing could stop him from wanting to be with Elizabeth.

He slid between the sheets, felt their cool touch give way to warmth as Elizabeth made room for him. He expected her to be as passionate as usual; willing though he was, it was always she who initiated their love-making. But this time, when he reached out his hands, she retreated.

'No Thomas,' she said. 'I've something to tell you. And when I've finished . . .'

'Oh shit!' muttered Thomas, his eyes closed, fists clenched. 'You're not pregnant, are you?'

Elizabeth forced a smile to her face.

'No, I'm not pregnant, though I suppose that could have something to do with it, the possibility that is. Or otherwise But that's not all. I've been thinking a lot about you, you know that, and . . . Well, you've always been honest with me. So I thought I should be the same with you. You see, I haven't been entirely truthful, about my past. I haven't told you a lot anyway, but when I have it hasn't always been the truth. I haven't wanted to lie, but I didn't know how involved I'd get with you. I didn't know how much I'd grow to love you. I didn't know if you'd return that love.' She was lying, one arm propped up on her pillow, her head resting in her hand. Thomas copied her position, looking at her with serious eyes. The sheet had fallen away slightly and her left breast was exposed, one dark nipple peeping out to smile encouragingly at him.

'All I want to do is tell you, about me,' she continued, 'without you interrupting. And when I've finished you can do what you want. If that means you getting out of bed, getting dressed and going home, well, I won't stop you. Do you understand?' Thomas nodded.

'Very well. I'm not sure how much of this you already know, but I think I ought to start at the beginning.' She swallowed nervously and turned onto her back, stared at the bed canopy.

'I've never met my real father. My mother, whose name was Emily, returned to this country from India when I was still a baby. She never spoke of my father, my real father that is. I'm quite dark-skinned, so it may be that he was an Indian, or perhaps a half-caste. I doubt that I'll ever know for certain. Soon after we came back my mother met and married John Waterhouse. They were happy together, at least my memories tell me so. My mother was very young when I was born but she had no further children, not until I was nineteen, when Margaret arrived. The birth weakened her, certainly she was never well again after that. She died two years later.' Thomas noticed Elizabeth's hands; their fingers were interlocked in an attitude of white-knuckled prayer.

'I was naive. I'd led a very sheltered life, I was schooled by governesses, I had no friends of my own age save the children of servants, and then only when I had been a child. It was I who brought up Margaret, almost as my own child. My father – John Waterhouse that is, I'd naturally come to look upon him as my father – was so involved in his work that Margaret and I hardly saw him; she used to cry when he came into the nursery and picked her up. I don't know why he stayed away. It may have been that seeing her, seeing me as well, reminded him of my mother. He took her death hard, it was cholera. He blamed himself, that's why this place has fresh water and other amenities.

'We moved house fairly frequently, as my father opened new businesses. He liked to be close to his work, he always was more interested in innovation and invention than organisation and administration. Uncle Edward's the opposite. I think that's why they work so well together. I found it hard to meet people, hard to make friends. No sooner did I begin to get to know someone than we'd be off somewhere else. And men didn't seem to find me attractive. I was shy, I always thought I was too small, too thin, too ugly. Anyone who visited us always said how beautiful Margaret was, even when she was a baby. No-one ever said anything like that about me. So I stayed at home, read a lot, played the piano and the violin, reconciled myself to becoming an old maid.

'When I was, let me see, just turned thirty, we went to live in London. It wasn't to be a permanent move so we took a short lease on some rooms in Knightsbridge, not too grand. Uncle Edward visited us a lot; he's far more outgoing than father, and he used to take me out to balls and dinners, the theatre, opera. I became a little more self-confident. I stopped blushing when men complimented me. I even began to realise that I was not unattractive, in a small, thin sort of way.

'I was, of course, too old to be accepted as eligible for marriage. There would have been inevitable questions asked about why I had received no proposals before coming to London, why so little was known about me. But I enjoyed my new life, even if it was without any particular direction. I met interesting people. My reading habits changed, I devoured books on politics and philosophy, and I began to form my own opinions rather than just adopt those of my father. I visited museums and galleries on my own, during the day at least, attended recitals and concerts. At one of these I was introduced to Eamon Kearton. He was with some people I had met at a party once or twice, and I thought little of him. We talked briefly of politics, he said he was a businessman, had been in the City for only a few weeks. I met him again a few weeks later; I had been to the theatre with Uncle Edward and we dined afterwards, and Kearton was in the same restaurant. He came across and reintroduced himself to me, and Edward must have thought by his manner that I knew him rather better than I did. He asked him to join us from politeness and I think that both of us were surprised when he agreed to do so. It turned out to be a very interesting meal.

'He had something about him, did Eamon Kearton. He was not handsome, certainly not handsome, but striking, yes. I thought him tall, but from my viewpoint most men have that attribute. He had a nose slightly too large for his face, but a charming smile that more than made up for this. He wore his hair a little too long for fashion but he was beautifully, elegantly dressed. He said that his family came from Dublin but he had no trace of the accent, so I assumed that he was fairly well off. His voice was quiet, hypnotic even. When he said something people stopped talking to listen to him, and he could argue the most ridiculous of opinions simply because he enjoyed debate so much. Both Uncle Edward and I were taken by him, and when he asked if he could call to see me I was sufficiently flattered to say yes.

'We walked together through the parks, and talked, and I told him everything about me. He told me of his childhood. He was from a large family, and I felt rather jealous at the homeliness he could capture in his tales. When I told him of this (he seemed able to persuade even strangers to divulge their most private thoughts and feelings) he said that I need never feel lonely again. He was my slave, my vassal, and would do anything I commanded.

'We spent a great deal of time together. He was meant to be looking for business opportunities for his father who owned a number of breweries but wanted to expand into the hotel business. For a month we never dined at the same place twice in succession; he was always moving on from one hotel to another, testing the competition, he said. It was impossible to contact him; he was always the one who would call or write or arrange to meet in some strange, out-of-the-way place. I enjoyed being with him and I knew that I was falling in love with him, but at the same time part of me was warning me to hold back.

'Father broke the news, suddenly, that we would be moving north again in a fortnight's time. When I told Eamon he did not at first seem upset, he went away that evening promising to see me again the next day. I waited for him but he didn't appear. I waited the next day, but again there was no sign of him. On the third day he appeared on the doorstep. His face was bruised and cut, his clothes were torn and dirty. I took him into the house and sat him down, gave him some whisky. He told me what had happened.

'He had been walking home when the realisation dawned on him that he might lose me. Until then he was not aware how much I had come to mean to him. He had wandered, without noticing, into a disreputable area, and was set upon by ruffians who stole every penny he possessed. They tied him up and left him in some rat-infested warehouse down by the docks, lest he describe their appearance too readily to the authorities. But he escaped and returned to his rooms to find that the same scoundrels had used his keys to pilfer everything of value that he held there, including a chest of money which was his deposit for the purchase of a hotel which had just come onto the market. He was distraught. "But the loss of all of these," he said, "is as nothing when compared to the fact that I might lose you!" He was sitting in the drawing room, crying, bleeding on the carpet. I didn't know what to do.

'I ran a bath for him, found him a dressing gown. I must confess that I too had a glass of some spirits or other, I'm not sure what it was. I found some tincture of iodine. I took him into my room. He had to lean on me, he was shaking, and I put him to bed. Then I tended his bruises and cuts. I could remember the iodine being painful but he didn't wince, didn't complain at all. He asked for another glass of whisky, to calm his nerves, and it seemed to help him. He thanked me for looking after him personally, he said that anyone else would have had servants do the work. He relaxed even more when I told him that one was out with Margaret, the other doing the shopping, and father's manservant was having a half-day; we didn't have a large staff.

'I'm not sure how it happened. He was holding my hand and then kissing me. I had never been kissed by anyone like that before, with such passion and feeling, and I could feel myself responding to him. He pulled me across the bed towards him and I could feel his hand undoing the buttons on my bodice. I tried to pull them away but he was strong and I don't suppose I tried very hard. Then his hand was inside my clothes and touching my flesh and I couldn't resist him. He was so gentle. He managed to undress me so easily, I must have been helping him. I didn't stop to think that he might have been practised at the art. He put his hand between my legs and began to rub me and I knew that nothing in the world could ever be as good as this. I think he was surprised to find, given the apparent ease with which he achieved his conquest, that I was a virgin. He apologised in case he hurt me, but there was no pain, just a sense of relief. I orgasmed, he made sure of that. And then he asked me to marry him.

'My father had met him once or twice but was unaware of our feelings for one another. Eamon asked his permission as a matter of courtesy. I was, after all, thirty years old, and he was not my natural father. He didn't approve. He had no proof, he said, of Eamon's background or his good intentions. He was unable to confirm or deny that Eamon would be able to keep me in the manner to which I had become accustomed. He was unable to find out anything definite about Eamon's background at all, and that was not for want of trying, but I was too much in love to care. I told him that we would marry anyway. He gave way, eventually. I share a certain stubborness with my sister, we must have inherited the trait from our mother, and he could see that forbidding me to do this would have no effect. And so we married a week later, just before father returned to Manchester.

'There was no time to invite Eamon's family from Dublin; a few of his friends from London were there, and I had no-one apart from Uncle Edward, father and Margaret, together with one or two acquaintances. We stayed on in the rooms father had leased, he had agreed to allow us to use them until the lease expired. He granted me a monthly income. I was, I suppose, the happiest I had ever been in my life.'

Elizabeth looked tired. The dim light, shining obliquely on her face, coloured her forehead with deep shadows and painted seas of darkness beneath her eyes. She looked at Thomas, not sure how he might react to the rest of the tale she was telling. She'd noticed, when she'd told him of Eamon Kearton making love to her, that his hands had framed themselves into white-knuckled fists; his eyes had filled with questions, but no words had passed his lips. Elizabeth gathered her thoughts before proceeding; she needed to explain, she had to tell Thomas everything despite the pain it would cause her, despite her fear of his reaction.

'We spent a great deal of time together in the first few weeks. Mostly in bed, when I think about it. He was kind and gentle, he taught me not be ashamed about my body or my feelings. He showed me how to give pleasure as well as how to take it, and I enjoyed it when he would look at me and say "That was good!". He didn't go out to work at all. We would go out to parties until the early hours then lie in bed until well into the afternoon. He invited people to stay, some for days at a time. Some brought their friends, and then their friends brought friends. The parties started coming to us, but the people were strangers and their habits were strange. They drank to excess and smoked peculiar substances and seemed, by any standards, to be weird. I mentioned this to Eamon and he laughed, but the parties stopped.

'He began to go out by himself, during the day, and occasionally stayed out late. The lease came to an end and we had to find other premises, a smaller house in a rather run-down area. Eamon said that business wasn't good, that this was all we could afford, and I couldn't argue with him because I didn't know how good or bad our finances were. He disappeared for a night, said that he'd been playing cards. After that he stayed in for a while and things were as good as they'd been to start with, but then he stayed away for two nights. I accused him of having a lover. He seemed affronted. "Why ever would I need a lover?" he said. "After all, I'm married to the best there is." At first I felt quite flattered. It was only much later that I realised that that was how he saw me. Someone to satisfy his sexual needs.

'About that time he introduced me to a friend of his. He was a sad man who had ambitions to be a poet. He was rather young and melancholy, spent his time translating Norse sagas into English. He visited frequently, always gave me flowers. I suppose I enjoyed his company because Eamon was, at that time, away so often. He was tired as well, especially at night, and he seemed to have lost all interest in the physical side of our relationship. I was growing more and more frustrated. I had even . . . I had even taken to pleasuring myself.

'One night he brought his friend, the poet, home with him. They had both been drinking and they insisted I join them. If I were to be truthful then I would say that I welcomed the company, I had spent too many evenings alone. The alcohol must have loosened our tongues a little, we talked of matters which worried us or gave us cause for personal concern. Eamon was the first to confess. He said that business was so bad that he (I think he meant we, but this was the first I had heard of it!) was near to bankruptcy and that this was affecting his libido. He looked at me, as if for confirmation of this fact, and I found myself nodding my agreement! The poet then spoke out. He said that he had never been with a woman before. He was in tears, I felt so sorry for him. He'd tried prostitutes but was unable to perform, he felt so depressed that he had thought of killing himself. At that Eamon went over to him, sat beside him, hugged him. He motioned me over and I did the same and we all cried together and then laughed together and drank some more. Eamon invited the poet to stay the night and we all went to bed. I had hoped that the alcohol would have given Eamon a certain amount of release from his troubles and I was pleased when he offered to massage me. Unfortunately all he could do was arouse me and then leave me perched below a peak of anticipation with no means of reaching the heights I craved.

'I'm sorry,' she said. 'I'm sorry to talk of matters like this. You may think me crude and vulgar to do so, but the past has made me the woman I am today, the woman who loves you, Thomas. And I cannot hide my past.'

Thomas said nothing, merely waited for Elizabeth to regain control of her emotions. She lowered her eyes, and her voice.

'Eamon couldn't manage . . . that is, he was unable . . . he couldn't achieve an erection.' She forced herself to go on. 'It was then that he made a suggestion, something which seemed so outlandish when he first mentioned it, but which, on further consideration, became the only logical course of action. I needed release but my husband was unable to assist me; our friend needed gentle encouragement and instruction in the art of sexual intercourse; and Eamon wanted to help both of us. Why did I not spend the night with our friend?

'I was horrified that he should even broach the subject and told him so. He seemed quite hurt, protested that he was only thinking of me. If I required pure physical release then the identity of the individual granting that release was surely immaterial. And if, in achieving that release, I was also making two other people happy, then the act was so much more to be approved. He was unable to see why I did not share his viewpoint and insisted that I go with him into our guest's room to discuss the matter further. He could be most persuasive. I pulled on my nightdress and followed him and we sat on the bed and talked about morals and sexual desire for at least thirty minutes. Then Eamon stood up and said that the choice was ours, and he left. I'm not sure, even now, why I didn't go with him. It may have been the look of need on the poet's face; it may have been my own state of excitement; perhaps it was a hidden wish to increase my experience of men, since my husband had obviously made love to a large number of women. Whatever the reason I found myself closing the door which Eamon had left open and slipping my nightdress over my head. I stayed the night.' She shook her head as if unsure of her own sanity in carrying out both the deed and the confession.

'My poet came back each week and we slept together. It was new for me, to take control of the situation. He was so willing, so pliant, so young, so obedient. And Eamon's passions too were suddenly rekindled, it was more like the days of old. One day, when Eamon was out, the poet appeared with a friend of his own, a handsome boy even younger than himself, and suggested rather shyly that I might help this friend in the same way that I had been of assistance to him. I refused, of course, and told Eamon as soon as he came in. He told me, in a matter of fact way, that I was wrong to have done this. I had a rare talent, he said, a talent to excite and raise passions in others as well as to care for them, and I ought to be thankful for this, to use those talents. Did I feel no pity for this young boy who had come to me, desperate, encouraged by the news that I had been so helpful to his friend? Did I feel no shame that I had turned him away in his hour of need? I was, truth to tell, too confused to be able to think properly at all. When the poet and his friend appeared the next day I took the young boy to my bed. He called again two weeks later when my husband was at home. Eamon welcomed him in, gave him wine, sent me upstairs to prepare myself for my visitor. After he left me I noticed that he had left his gloves behind in my room and, wrapped only in a shift, I hurried after him. Eamon was saying goodbye to him at the door. He shook his hand and the young boy, I swear he was no more than eighteen, gave him some money.

'I asked Eamon what the money was for, though I already knew the answer. I wanted to hear him lie, but he refused me even that satisfaction. "That," he said, "was payment for your services. And damn good payment it was too. I told you that you had a natural talent, didn't I? This proves it." He waved the money in front of me. "You've turned me into a whore," I screamed at him. He didn't shout back, his voice was as calm as it always was. "You've always been a whore," he said. "You just didn't know it." I ran upstairs and cried myself to sleep. When I woke up the door to my room was locked.' There were tears in Elizabeth's eyes, but Thomas did nothing to wipe them away. His face, his whole body, was tense like the coiled steel of a rapper sword, he was a hunting cat poised before the spring. But Elizabeth could see nothing of this; her gaze was fixed on the bed canopy – she saw nothing but her memories.

'He came in to talk to me. I tried to hit him but he slapped me and then held onto my wrists until I promised that I would be quiet, calm. He showed me a letter from my father which he said he had hidden from me (a letter I later found had been forged; he knew the scum of society, did Eamon Kearton) dated a few weeks before, telling me that he and Edward and Margaret were going to America for a while, six months at least. There was no forwarding address. I was alone.

'Eamon told me that he had no rich father in Dublin, that he had no means of income other than gambling and prostitution. That day he had come to see me, the day he had proposed to me, he had been telling the truth when he said that he had been attacked. But the thieves had been seeking repayment of gambling debts, and they had taken his stable of whores as well as his money. Since then his losses and gains at the tables had been even; he had, in fact, been living on my income. A few weeks before, he had, however, lost a significant amount at cards. His creditor had agreed to let him repay the debt over a few months, but the regular payments exceeded our income. My role, therefore, was to provide the extra by selling myself. And he told me the alternative. His creditor would appear one night, un-announced, with a number of large helpers. He would hurt Eamon. He would take what furniture could be easily removed, whatever money was in the house. And, knowing that Eamon was pimping again, he would take the only other thing of value he possessed. Me. His whore.

'I didn't have any choice. He locked me in, brought me food, brought me customers. He was, I suppose, quite rigorous in selecting these. They were always monied, well-dressed, well-educated. I think he charged a lot, after all, it

was evident that I wasn't born in the gutter. He didn't need
to encourage me to be enthusiastic, I was aware that my
future depended upon my performance. I'd heard about the
brothels in some parts of London and I knew I didn't want
to go there, so I did as I was told. At first there was one a
night, then two, then three, then four, going right the way
through to dawn. After one I was acting anyway, so the
number didn't really matter. I suppose I became used to it.
He had a door put up on my landing. It was kept locked, but
it meant that I had access to a bathroom, and another room
for reading or eating. He even had my piano brought
upstairs. One night I couldn't sleep and I heard laughter
from above, a woman's voice. I asked Eamon about it in the
afternoon when I woke up. He unlocked the door and took
me upstairs. There was another locked door on the next
landing and he opened it, took me in. The rooms were
similar to mine, somewhat smaller with lower ceilings. He
introduced me to Stella, said we should get to know each
other, then left. I told her my name. She asked me how I got
into the business and I told her that Eamon was my
husband. She laughed. Apparently he was married to her as
well.

'It was inevitable that I became pregnant. When Eamon
found out he made me have an abortion. I had four
abortions in two years. The last one went wrong, I caught
an infection of some type. I was ill. He got me a good doctor
though, a real one, and I came round. But I don't think I'll
ever be able to have children.' She swallowed, then went on,
quickly, frightened that if she slowed her pace Thomas
might say something, might even leave.

'There were, at the most, four girls in the house. It must
have been a good income for Eamon, he even took on an old
woman to cook for us all, change the beds, do the washing,
and a doorman in case anyone turned awkward and refused
to pay. I didn't see the others very often. They were all

younger than me, but Eamon would still tell me that I was the best.' Elizabeth looked at Thomas. It was the first time she had given him any attention for a while. His face was drained of colour and, when he caught her eye, he held out his hand to her.

'No, Thomas,' she said, 'not yet. Wait until I finish. If you touch me I'll cry.' She took a deep breath and once more regained her self-control.

'Yes, I still slept with Eamon. There was nothing there now, not even hate. I'd come to realise that he wasn't worth hating. Sometimes, when he'd had a lot to drink, he brought one of the other girls with him. He couldn't do anything, the alcohol affected him that way, so it was up to us to entertain him. Sometimes he brought a client with him and asked if he could watch. It didn't matter to me, not any more. I just did as I was asked.

'After a while I noticed that the customers were more common. Less well-dressed. Rougher, in all senses of the word. I think Eamon must have been gambling and losing, he was taking anyone who wanted a woman and who had the money. Some of them had strange needs. One or two needed to be tied up. Others just wanted to talk. Some could only enjoy themselves watching others. One man came in, said he wanted a boy. Eamon offered him me instead; the other girls were all big-breasted. The man still wanted it as though I were a boy but I said no. He started to hit me, he was big and strong. He knocked me about until I was almost unconscious then he threw me onto the bed. He pulled out a knife and threatened to kill me if I screamed. He turned me over, face down, and I could hear him taking off his boots and trousers. Then I felt his breath on me, his body against my back. Luckily I'd made a lot of noise as I'd been bounced off the furniture and Eamon and the doorman rushed in and pulled him off me. I was bruised and battered, I'd broken a rib. It took nearly a month for that to mend, but it was a month for me to think. I knew that I'd have to get out. I knew that if I didn't I'd be dead, by my own hand or by someone else's. I'd thought of escaping before but hadn't been able to figure out a way of doing it. But things were different now. I needed to go. And under my pillow was the knife my attacker had dropped when Eamon and the doorman had pulled him off me. And I knew that I wasn't afraid to use it.

'There were other difficulties. Even if I managed to get through the locked door I had nothing to wear. All of my day clothes had been taken from me. It was almost two years since I had set foot outside my prison. And there was the brute my husband had hired as doorman; he would surely try to stop me. I decided to deal with each of these problems as it arose.

'I waited until one of Eamon's visits. Either he was growing tired of me or his need was less than it had been in the past. He only paid his calls when the doorman was on duty, and he made sure that the imbecile locked him in. This was, I suppose, one of his insurances. I waited for him to wake after his exertions then went with him to the door. He pulled at the rope which rang the bell signalling that he had finished his business. The doorman, I knew, would open a grille in the door to make sure that it was indeed his master who had summoned him. Only then would the door itself be opened. I heard the slow shuffle of the guard's tread on the stairs and, moving behind Eamon, pressed the point of the blade to his back. "Yes," I said, "it's a knife, and I'll take great pleasure in sticking you like the pig you are unless you do as I say. Get him to bring me some clothes. Tell him we're going out, you and I. Or I'll kill you." He did exactly as he was told.

'"You won't do it," he said as we waited for the clothes. "I could call for help now and you wouldn't do a thing. You don't have it in you." I knew, though, that the very fact he mentioned it meant that he wasn't sure. I didn't know if I could kill him, but he didn't know either. He started to turn round but I pressed harder and he whimpered.

'"Put your hands straight out ahead of you," I said, "palms against the wall." He did so. I took the knife away from his back and before he knew it was gone I'd slashed it across his wrist then brought it back again. He swore, the blood was spurting, he grabbed his wrist with his other hand. "You bastard," he said, but he didn't move any more than he had to. I used the knife to cut off the bottom of my nightshirt and handed to him. He wrapped it around his wrist above the cut. "I could bleed to death!" he hissed. "I know," I said, "and that was just to show you what I can do. I'm leaving. Don't even think of trying to stop me!" I gave him instructions on what to do next. The thug brought an armful of clothes and left them on the landing, unlocked the door then went away. I waited for him to disappear and ordered Eamon into my bedroom. I told him to stay there then went to see what I could wear.

'He must have thought that, in a face to face fight, he would have the better of me even if I had a knife, even though he'd already been cut. He chose his moment carefully. I'd pulled off my nightshirt and was standing there naked, trying to sort out the ruck of clothing, when I heard the door open. He charged straight at me. I'm not sure exactly what happened, or how it happened. I know that with one hand he managed to pin one of my arms against the wall, the one holding the knife, and the other was at my throat. He was a big man and his weight was against me. I couldn't move my knife arm or my legs. My other arm was jammed between our bodies. I couldn't breathe, his face was only inches away from mine. There was no fear or fright in his eyes, no hate, no look of revenge. There was only sadness, I think that I had seen fit to disturb the serenity of his life. I could feel myself losing consciousness and I knew that he would kill me and there was nothing I could do about it. But he had been bleeding a lot, he was weaker than both he and I realised. He must have felt his grip weakening, he moved his weight slightly, and for a moment my arm, the one between our bodies, was free. I thrust it down. He could feel me doing it, I know. He had an erection! He even smiled! He was enjoying this! I just grabbed at him, dug my fingers into his testicles and squeezed as hard as I could. He doubled up straight away and I kicked him as he went down, it hurt my foot. I couldn't think what to do next. He was lying there, groaning, his wrist was still bleeding. I began to dress, frantically. I was shaking, one hand pointing the knife at him, the other trying to pull clothes on. Somehow I managed it. I realised that the doorman had brought no shoes but that I had a pair in my bedroom. I crept past Eamon and into the room, found the shoes and went out again. Eamon had stopped groaning. He was lying still. I thought that he'd passed out, through loss of blood, but I didn't care. I hugged the wall as I passed by. The door was ajar. Freedom beckoned.'

Elizabeth pulled herself upright, sat with her back against the pillows. She stared ahead of her, hands wringing. She was filmed with a coat of sweat. Her speech grew faster.

'He'd been pretending. I felt his hand on my ankle, he pulled me to the floor and dragged himself to his knees then dived at me. I brought the knife up as he did so. It was very sharp. I felt it move easily into his flesh then jar against a bone and he hissed at me, no words, just a hiss which started at the back of his throat and stopped as he rolled off me. He ended up against the wall, half sitting, half lying. The knife was in his side and he was staring at it. Then he stared at me. "Help me," he said. I was stupid. I bent down to see what I could do and he grabbed me. He grabbed my hair and pulled my head down past his. All I could see was the knife and the blood around it. I took hold of it, pulled it out of the wound and stabbed him again and again and again. I felt his grip slacken, I found that I could stand up. I ran down the stairs and opened the door to the street. As I looked back I could see him. He had managed to crawl to the top of the stairs and was looking at me. His mouth opened but I could hear nothing. I knew what he was saying though. Whore.

'I knew that I'd killed him. I wasn't sure what would happen if I was discovered; I suspect that the authorities would have allowed me my freedom. But I didn't want to wait to find out. He might have had friends. But what could I do? Where could I go?

'I decided to head north. I told lies to the ticket collector on the train, told the cab driver to take me to the Waterhouse residence, and found myself, within eight hours of escaping from my now dead husband, standing outside the door of a house I didn't recognise in a part of Manchester I'd never visited before. The servant who answered the door was a stranger to me but I could hear my father's voice inside. I was home again.

'I told my father everything. He showed me the letters I had written saying that Eamon and I were spending the year touring Europe and then going to America. They were good forgeries. I still have nightmares. I still feel Eamon's hand clutching at me, still see his eyes following me. And . . .'

'And?' said Thomas, grimly.

Elizabeth was crying.

'And I couldn't have gone on loving you without letting you know all of this. It would have been wrong of me. I would have been as bad as Eamon Kearton if I'd gone on deceiving you. And anyway, part of me, part of the way I am, is a result of the life I've led. You take me as I am, Thomas Armstrong. You take me as I am or not at all.' She wiped her eyes on the sheets, sniffed, looked across at him. He'd copied her position, sat himself up, but moved no closer to her. He seemed unable to look at her directly; his eyes could only dart to one side and back.

'Well?' she said.

'It's a lot to take in at once,' he said.

'What should I have done?' she sobbed. 'Serialised it? Told you a little at a time, finished each month with a last paragraph full of suspense? What's going to happen to our heroine? Read next month's exciting episode!'

'That's not what I meant. Don't be so damned defensive, woman, I'm not the one who turned you into a whore!' He realised at once that the remark hurt.

'I'm sorry, I didn't mean it. What I just said, that is. Forgive me. I don't know what to say.'

'I do,' said Elizabeth. 'At least I know what I want you to say. But I don't want you to tell lies. I've told you all about me, I've told you the truth. At least grant me equal treatment. Don't lie to me. You know what I've been through, the worst that you can say will hurt me, but no more than I've already been hurt. Be honest, Thomas. Be honest.'

'I'll be honest, then,' he said, 'as honest as I can be. I don't find words easy at the best of times, and this isn't the best of times. I ...' He looked at her, once, then stared again at the wall in front of him.

'I've listened to what you said. It wasn't easy. It's not a good feeling, to find that someone you think you know so well is really a stranger. You've suffered, dear God you've suffered, and I know that you can't be blamed for what's happened to you. But ... But to have done what you did! And kept on doing it! I didn't want you to tell me, I swear it, I didn't want to know, I was going to leave, I was ready to go! I was disgusted, to think that you'd done such things, all I wanted to do was get away!'

Elizabeth was sobbing now, her hands raised to her eyes. Thomas ignored her.

'But I couldn't leave. I couldn't go. And the reason was ...

Oh God, how can I tell you this, how can I say it? Elizabeth, I was horrified, I felt sickened! But at the same time, against my will, despite my fighting against it, I was excited. My mind was filled with pictures of you doing the things you described to me, and I ought to have felt sympathy, or revulsion even, and yes, I did feel those emotions, but I was also aroused, I imagined you with me, doing the same things. And now, now I'm so filled with confusion, I can't think properly. I hate myself for feeling that way I even ... I even hate you, for making me feel like this!'

Elizabeth stopped crying.

'And is that all you feel, Thomas?'

'Isn't that enough?' he yelled angrily.

'I don't know! I'm like you, Thomas, I don't know anything.'

'No, then, no, that's not all I feel! I feel angry, as if I want to fight someone. I want to hurt everyone who's ever hurt you, I want to protect you, to hold you tight, to let you know that no-one can harm you. I want to love you, I want ... Jesus Christ, I don't know what I want!'

Elizabeth's voice was quiet.

'Thomas, I know what I want. But I won't say it first. I can't say it first.'

Thomas was drained. He thought that there was no emotion left in him, that he was incapable of thought or action, his mind and body numbed by Elizabeth's revelations. And yet from somewhere he found words.

'Come here,' he said. She moved closer, into his arms. He kissed the tears from her eyes, but the salt he tasted did not only belong to her. And the words he found were the words she wanted.

'I love you,' he whispered.

Elizabeth looked at her lover asleep. He had turned in the night, turned his back towards her. His arms were crossed over his chest, his knees drawn up. She reached across him to touch the stubble on his chin and he stirred slightly.

'It's five o'clock Thomas,' she said. 'Time for you to finish your shift. Time for you to go home again.' His eyes flicked open suddenly, he looked around him in panic, then saw Elizabeth's face.

'I wondered where I was,' he said. 'I saw the room and the furniture and the canopy. I thought I must have died and gone to heaven. Then I saw you, and I was *certain* I'd gone to heaven.' Elizabeth took a pillow and hit him with it, laughing.

'No, no, not the pillow!' he cried. 'Anything but the pillow!' He grabbed at it and pushed her back onto the bed, lay across her and kissed her. Her mouth tasted sour, of salt and sweat and hot bodies, and he was sure that his own tasted the same to her. He was suddenly excited, guided one of her hands to his erection and moved his own hand down between her legs. She pressed her thighs together, surrounding his hand with flesh.

'Oh no,' she said as he struggled to escape, 'not again. I feel quite sore as it is, and you've to get home. Go on, get dressed. We can do this again in a day or two's time.'

'Why not tonight?' asked Thomas.

'We don't want to arouse suspicion. And we should do some real work as well.'

'Alright then.' He climbed reluctantly out of bed and began to dress.

'The summerhouse?'

'No,' she answered. 'There's a practice tomorrow, I'm sure you can restrain your lust until then.'

'I can't,' he said. 'I'll explode. Someone'll come running in to see you and say that Thomas Armstrong has been the victim of spontaneous combustion and has plastered himself all over your office. And you'll know why. And you'll know that only you could have prevented it by sacrificing your body to his quest for carnal knowledge!'

'Thomas, you're wasted as a miner. You should be a writer, or a preacher, or even a politician. Yes, a politician I think.'

'Couldn't do that,' grunted Thomas, pulling on his boots, 'too honest.'

'Too modest!' came the reply. 'I don't think!'

'I'm ready then,' said Thomas.

'Just a minute!' said Elizabeth. 'I've something for you.' She threw back the covers and ran to her desk, opened the top drawer.

'For Christ's sake woman put some clothes on, or I won't be answerable for my actions. Here!' He flung a shift at her and she scrambled into it as she walked towards him. She held out a small package and he took it from her carefully. It was a small box. He opened it carefully to reveal a ring, a metal ring, but instead of a jewel it was mounted with a small lock of rapper swords. At its centre were his initials.

'It's beautiful,' he said, 'absolutely beautiful. But I can't wear it, you know that. What would Mary say?'

'Nothing,' Elizabeth replied, 'nothing at all. Not when every member of the rapper team is given a similar ring as a token of my father's appreciation. Theirs are made of silver, Thomas, but yours is solid gold underneath the silver. And look inside the ring. Can you see any writing?' Thomas could see nothing at first. Only when he moved it could he see the faint script within the band. 'To Thomas from Elizabeth with her love' it read.

'I can give you nothing in return,' he said sadly.

'You can,' she replied, 'and you have, and you will. Now give it back, they'll all be presented together. Kiss me and go, Thomas. I'll be waiting for you.'

He left as he had entered, unseen, and headed for the village. The sky in the east was lightening to blue, and already hidden blackbirds and thrushes were announcing the dawn. Thomas sang cheerfully back to them. He was, he decided, a very lucky man.

Chapter Sixteen

He took her soft hand, ere her mother could bar,—
'Now tread we a measure!' said young Lochinvar.
                                          'Marmion'
                                   (Sir Walter Scott)

Thomas woke at midday to the sound of children playing outside his window. It was dark in the room; the curtains had been drawn. He could feel his heart beating fast, he was hot and his body was covered with sweat. You're at home, he told himself, there's nothing to fear. But the mention of that word alone made him realise that his fear was real, that something *had* frightened him, frightened him to the extent that he found himself forced to breathe deeply to quell the panic which had been about to suffocate him.

He told himself that it had been a nightmare, nothing more. He had had nightmares in the past. He had woken screaming as rocks crushed him in the darkness, or the flash of burning gas set him alight and he watched his fingers burn to the bone before him. He had drowned in black dust, and watched the pale, blind faces of long-dead miners appear before him to carry his broken body down, down into their hell below. No-one who worked in a pit could claim that they had never suffered from nightmares.

But it was not about the pit this time; in his dream he had not been underground. There had been light and the smell of flowers, and birdsong, not choking blackness and charred dust and the drip, drip of old water. It had been that day, long ago, when he had gone with Mary to see the badgers' sett, and they had lain down on the grass and kissed. But this time they went further. They had taken off their clothes and were making love, rolling down the grassy slope, first him on top, then her, and they had been happy and laughing. Then the laughing stopped. He had hit his head on a rock and was telling her to stop, he was holding his hands to his head, desperate to take the pain away. And Mary had pulled away from him, left him. When he looked up she was running away, deeper into the wood, so he ran after her, calling her name. It grew darker. He realised that he was lost, it was beginning to grow cold. He started to run back the way he had come but hands started appearing from the grass, hands which clutched at his ankles and pulled him to the ground. When he looked up he saw Mary. She was lying on the ground in front of him with a man on top of her, a man who looked just like him, and they were both moaning and groaning as they moved together.

He remembered grabbing the man, grabbing himself, putting his arm round his neck and hauling him away, but as he did so he changed shape. He was no longer a second Thomas Armstrong but became the preacher, Proudlock, who ran screaming away. He looked down on Mary who was still writhing and twisting on the ground; he knelt between her legs and entered her and she pushed back at him then rolled him over. He closed his eyes and when he opened them it was Elizabeth astride him, and in her hand she had a knife. He couldn't move. He could only watch the blade of the knife as it danced before him, its motion becoming more and more complex as Elizabeth moved faster. She stiffened; when she opened her eyes they were black, and she drove the knife into his chest. He screamed in agony as she stabbed him again and again, as she became Mary, then Willie, then the preacher, then John Waterhouse, then Elizabeth again, he screamed at the pain and the blood. And then he woke up.

Recollection helped drive the fear away. Once exposed as a dream there was little to fear in the dream itself. But the cause? That was another matter. Was he frightened that Elizabeth might to do him what she had claimed to have done to her husband? Or perhaps Mary, if she found that he had been unfaithful, would attack him in that way. And the others, why had they appeared? Was he worried that their disapproval might display itself in such a violent manner? The sleep which was meant to rest him had only succeeded in making worse his anxieties. The optimism and happiness which had so fortified him the previous night had all but disappeared. He was deceiving his wife, his good and faithful wife, for a woman who was a murderess, by her own admission. And if her confession were by any chance untrue, a fabrication designed to win his sympathy, then she was surely mad! He groaned and sank back into his pillow. How could he extricate himself from his own stupidity?

He heard Mary's footsteps on the stairs and watched the door open slowly.

'I'm awake,' he said. 'You can come in.' She entered bottom first, carrying a tray. She put this down on a chair beside the bed.

'Watch your eyes,' she said, 'I'm going to open the curtains.' She did so with a majestic sweep.

'It's a beautiful day Thomas,' she continued. 'I was wondering if you might find time for a walk later on. I've brought you some tea and toast and a pot of jam. I mean, you might have to be back at work later, I'm not really sure. There's some butter there as well. I know you're busy, but I've hardly seen you lately. Damn, I forgot the sugar!'

'It's alright love, I can do without.' He looked at her, silhouetted by the light from the window. 'You're a bonny lass you know.'

She put her hands on her waist and swung her hips from side to side.

'Do you have to go back then? Today?'

'I should, really,' he replied. 'But not for long. I'll probably have to do another night later in the week, mind.' He cursed himself silently. Why did he do it? He had all but acknowledged his own madness in going back to Elizabeth time and time again, virtually sworn to stop it! Yet here he was making plans to do the same thing once more, but it wouldn't be once, or twice. Perhaps she was a witch. Perhaps she had cast a spell on him! Witches? In 1887?

'Are you alright?' asked Mary. 'You looked as if you were trying to say something.'

'Aye,' sighed Thomas, 'I'm alright.'

'Are you sure? Don't you feel well?' Mary sat down beside him on the bed. 'You haven't drunk your tea yet, it'll get cold. Come on, I'll butter your toast for you and you can decide what you want to do.'

Thomas had already decided. He wanted to reach out and touch Mary. He wanted to hold her tight, to tell her how sorry he was. He wanted to pull her to him, to feel her familiar warmth. He wanted her there, beside him, naked and selfish in bed with him for the rest of the day. He wanted her love, her forgiveness. All of this could be his, all he need do was reach out. His fingers moved slowly towards her cheek.

'Here you are,' she said, placing the teacup in his outstretched hand, 'I'll nip downstairs and do some baking. We could go out later, if you want to.' She blew a kiss at him from the doorway. The moment was lost.

Rapper practice was going well. The dance and the music

had been married, were happy in each other's company. When they danced well, which was most of the time, each dancer seemed to know exactly what the others were doing, even what they were thinking of doing, and the swords became extensions of their arms. Even when performing Double Tumbler, the backward somersault over fixed swords which Thomas and Willie did together, the take-offs and landings were perfectly synchronised. They went through the whole dance twice then stood, gasping for breath, waiting for Thomas's verdict. He handed round towels (Elizabeth had brought them each week since finding Stew mopping the sweat from his face on the ballroom curtains) and looked at them. Willie and Stew were sitting on the floor, Len was flat on his back, and Rob was bent double, his hands on his thighs. Elizabeth's brow was damp from her exertions.

'Well,' said Thomas eventually, 'that was . . .'

'NOT BAD!' chorused the others; five towels found their target.

'I wasn't going to say that!' protested Thomas.

'You always say that,' said Rob, 'even when we're bloody marvellous.'

'Like then,' added Stew.

'Aye,' said Willie, 'that was good. It must have been good. It *felt* right, all the way through.'

'Aye, it must have been good,' said Len sagely. 'After all, you didn't call me a pillock halfway through.'

Thomas laughed. There was little time to point out dancers' errors in the course of a performance, but he had found that a carefully chosen profanity thrown in the right direction would ensure that the mistake would not be repeated.

'Alright then,' said Thomas, 'I'll admit it. It was good!' Cheers and hurrays echoed from the walls.

'But it could still be better! We need that little bit extra, that little edge, and we'll be there.'

'Are we good enough to win?' asked Stew. Thomas thought before replying.

'We'll be better with an audience. It always makes a difference having people there to watch you, to cheer and clap and shout. If everything goes right on the day we should beat Makemore's team.'

'Stuff Makemore's team,' said Stew. 'Beating them's not going to be good enough for me. I want to win!' There was a murmur of agreement from the rest of them.

'We'd better get on then and practise, hadn't we!' said Thomas. 'The beginning could be a bit crisper, we need to get the stepping spot on. And Single Guard through Curly into Figure Eight, it needs to be really smooth, to contrast with the . . . what's the word Elizabeth?' – 'Staccato,' – 'Aye, that's it, staccato. It needs to contrast with the staccato bit at the beginning, before the music joins in. Come on, we'll go through it now.'

'But will we win?' persisted Stew.

'Aye,' said Thomas quietly. 'We'll win.'

They did the dance twice more, and each time they felt the improvement without being aware of what they had done to make the performance better.

'That's it!' said Willie. 'No more! I'm absolutely f. . .'

'I'm tired as well,' said Thomas, gesturing at Elizabeth.

'It's alright,' she said. 'I don't mind. In fact I'm quite flattered, knowing that you don't behave differently because I'm here. It makes me feel part of the team.'

'In that case,' said Willie, 'do you fancy a pint? I'm f-f-fantastically thirsty!'

'Willie!' admonished Thomas.

'He's joking,' said Elizabeth, 'he knows you've to practise your clog dance.' She raised her voice, 'Before you go lads, I've something to say. Can you gather round?' They looked at each other warily as they approached, keen to be away, fearing some long speech, but essentially curious. Elizabeth began to speak, softly at first, her eyes fixed on her feet as though she were embarrassed.

'I'd just like to say thank you. I know that I'm not as good as your Dad,' she glanced up at Thomas and Willie, 'never will be for that matter. I play from my head; he played from his heart. But I'd like to think that over the past few months I've got better as you have, and I hope that you've enjoyed it as much as I have.' She looked up, her voice grew stronger.

'I've got something for you all. You see, I wanted to remember – I wanted you all to remember – these past few months. They've been special for me, certainly. So I've had these made for you,' she reached behind her and took a cloth from her violin case, 'and I hope that you'll be able to look at them when you're old and grey and remember when you danced together, and perhaps think of the silly woman who stood and scraped at the violin while you were doing it. And remember how proud she was of you all.'

She put the cloth on the table at her side and unfolded it to reveal seven silver rings emblazoned with a rapper nut.

'There's one for each of you,' she said. 'There you are Thomas, and Willie. They're adjustable, you can make them fit, whatever the size of your finger. One for you Stew, and Rob. There you are Len. There's one for me and an extra one for Davy. Mind, you'll have to take them off when you dance, they might catch in the swords.'

'They're lovely,' said Willie.

'There was no need to do that love,' said Len. 'But thank you. They're really nice.'

'No-one's ever given me anything like that before,' said Rob.

'Elizabeth,' said Stew standing in front of her, the only one of the team not to dwarf her, 'you're special.' He put his hands on her cheeks and kissed her on the forehead. She smiled and blushed.

'Go on then,' she said. 'I'm sure you're even thirstier than you were half-an-hour ago. I'll see you next week.' She watched them leave, then she and Thomas headed for the room beside her office.

'It started as an excuse,' she said, unbuttoning his shirt. 'The idea of having rings made, that is. You were the only person I wanted to have one. But now I'm glad I did it, for everyone. I wasn't pretending when I was speaking to them before, I meant every word. I do feel part of the team, and I feel proud of you all.' She peeled his shirt from his back. 'My God, you're sweaty! You smell wonderful!'

By the time they had finished making love they were both wet with sweat.

'You're special,' said Thomas, brushing her hair away from her forehead as she lay above him.

'I wasn't sure you would feel that way,' she replied, 'after what I told you about me. I thought you might just go off with the others. I wouldn't have said anything; I wouldn't have told anyone about us. I would have understood how you felt. You see Thomas, no matter what you do I shall always love you. I don't care if you can never love me in the same way. It's like rapper. Even if it stopped now there would always be memories of playing and dancing and practising, thinking about the things people said and did. And if you were to walk out of my life now I'd still have memories of you and me, lying together, talking together, being together. And I'd be thankful that I'd had some joy and happiness with you, because there are so many people who have never experienced those emotions. Do you understand?'

'I know what you mean,' said Thomas. 'There are times when I feel the same way. I feel . . . I feel content when I'm with you, and when I'm away from you I feel such a need I can't describe it. But sometimes there's a devil tearing me in two. I can't think, I just want to stop what I'm doing and cry. I feel guilty, you know that, I've told you often enough. I feel ashamed of myself. Sometimes I think you're a witch; it's the only way I can explain the emotions you create inside me. But I know that you're a woman. And that you're special to me. And . . .'

'You don't have to say it Thomas. You don't have to say you love me. I don't expect it.' She pushed away from him, their bodies separating reluctantly, and looked down on him.

'But I do,' he protested, 'I do love you.' And they both wanted to believe those words, and they clung together as if hoping to conjure reality from hope.

'Can I spend the night with you tomorrow?' whispered Thomas in Elizabeth's ear.

'We can't,' she said desperately, 'father sent a telegram. He's coming back tomorrow. The problem in Manchester was quite easy to solve. It wasn't Uncle Edward, it was a design problem with one of the machines. So he'll be back here by late afternoon.'

'Damn!' Thomas rolled her onto her side, followed her as she turned.

'What next then?'

'We just keep going. He's away again in June, for a whole week. There'll be time then. It'll give us something to look forward to.'

'If I survive that long,' said Thomas. 'I think I'm becoming addicted to you.'

'We'll see each other during the day. We'll manage.'

'Will we? Do you honestly think we can go on like this? And if we can, for how long? Another month or two? A year? Ten years? A lifetime?' Despondency was the question mark at the end of each sentence. 'I don't think I can do it.'

'That depends on us,' said Elizabeth. 'It depends on what we want to do. And at the moment I can't tell in the morning how I'll feel on the same day's afternoon. I only know that I want to spend as much time as possible with you, and that's why it hurts to remind you that you ought to be going.' She pulled away from him, stretched to one side for a cloth.

'I'm sorry,' said Thomas, 'I always seem to get this way when I have to leave you. Sad. Morose even.'

'I feel the same way. But I'll see you tomorrow, and we can go to the summerhouse. We'll survive Thomas, we'll survive.'

He left slowly, and Elizabeth tidied up then returned to her own room. She felt too tired to bathe, promised herself that she would do so in the morning, and so took to her bed with the smell of Thomas and their love-making still on her body. And lying there alone she wondered if it was possible that they would make something of their love (she had no doubt that it was love), or whether survival itself would be their only objective, their only achievement. She slept fitfully.

'It's going to be a good summer,' said Mary.

She and Thomas were sitting on a grassy bank overlooking the pond. Children's laughter ran around the green, disturbing the moorhens which had nested on the small island well out of the way of stone-throwing boys and keen-eyed buzzards. Even now one of the large, lazy birds of prey was mewling high above them on invisible thermals, searching for the unwary young rabbit, the careless or unguarded chick. Swifts, newly arrived, screeched their way through the dusky air, whiskered mouths agape in hungry, insect-welcoming grins.

Amongst the nearby trees, most in bud, some with leaves already displayed in proud, fresh shades of green, blubells hugged the ground and buzzed with bees' anticipation. It was not yet late enough in the day for butterflies to have sought shelter, nor was it so early that the first moths had not ventured out; they danced through the harsh light-shadows of the early evening. Far away a cuckoo warned dunnocks and meadow pipits to beware; nearer at hand a swallow hornpiped its way across the surface of the water.

Puffing and panting, the steam-engine called David threw himself onto his father's lap. If Matthew arrived a moment later then the speck of time which passed between the events was not measurable.

'I won!' gasped David.

'Only 'cos you had a head start!' countered Matthew. 'And anyway, it was a draw!'

'Does it really matter who got here first?' asked Mary.

'Yes!' 'No!' yelled David and Matthew together.

'I think,' said Thomas sagely, 'that the answer depends on whether you arrive first or second.'

'I won, I won, na na na na-na!' sang David, capering around his parents. Thomas grabbed Matthew as the boy tensed himself for the retaliation which he considered the only answer to such provocation.

'That will do!' said Thomas firmly. 'Now come over here. Come on, one either side. That's right. Now then, I've got a question for you. What's the nicest thing in the world?'

'Sweets,' said David immediately, a smirk on his face as though suspecting that a packet of these would be produced from a hidden pocket.

'Winning at football,' said Matthew. 'No, winning at anything!' The two boys giggled.

'What about your Mam. What does she think is the nicest thing in the world?' Mary pursed her lips in exaggerated contemplation of her innermost thoughts.

'Yes, what do you like best?' asked Matthew.

'Me?' suggested David.

'No, me!' said Matthew. 'After all, I was here first!'

'I think,' said Mary the peacemaker, 'that I like all three

of you equally, but in slightly different ways. And being with you all, being here with you now, is definitely one of the nicest things I've ever known! But what about your Dad? After all, he asked the question in the first place!'

Thomas took his time before replying.

'Sweets are nice,' he said, 'but they're soon gone and they just leave you wanting more. And sometimes you just can't get more of something like that. Winning at games makes you feel good, that's true, but what matters isn't winning, it's knowing that you've done the best you possibly can. Because somewhere in the world there'll always be someone who's better than you.' He held out his arms and his sons curled into position beside him.

'Being with people you love makes you feel so happy sometimes that you can't imagine anything better at all. And the important thing is, even when the moment's over, you can look back and remember it, and suddenly your heart's filled with the same happiness you felt originally. Remembering good times is one of the nicest things there is. Times like this.' He glanced around. 'But,' he whispered, then paused for effect, looked around him as though frightened that some hidden stranger might hear this secret, 'there's something even nicer than that! And I'll show you what it is. Lie back, rest your head on the ground. You too, love.' They all four lay back.

'Cloudwatching,' said Thomas with mock solemnity, 'is without a doubt the nicest thing in the whole world. Look up at the clouds. Did you know that everyone sees clouds differently? I mean, what shape is that big one up there?' He pointed skywards. Towers of grey-white cumulus marched overhead, frothing and boiling like milk, delicate as south-facing cowslips.

'What do you think Matthew?' he asked.

'A dragon. A big dragon with teeth and claws. I can see his wings as well.'

'And you, David?'

'It's like a man. It's like Granda Tommy when he was asleep with his mouth open and his leg on the stool.' Thomas smiled at the memory.

'I think it's a castle,' suggested Mary, 'a castle in the clouds. And a beautiful princess and a handsome prince live there, and brave knights on horses, and ladies-in-waiting who dance the quadrille with their gallant protectors. Oh look! There's the princess waving from the battlements!'

'The dragon's turning into a ship now!' said Matthew; 'A steam-engine!' protested David; 'A clown,' added Mary.

'Do you want to know what I see?' asked Thomas. The others nodded.

'I see a face. It's the face of the cloudman, and he's looking down on us, and he's happy. See, see the smile on his face? And he's happy because we're looking at him. And he's happy because we can see all of the shapes he's sending rolling across the world. He's not always happy though. Sometimes he's very sad, because there are lots of people who look at clouds and see only clouds. And it's funny, because all children, everywhere, can see the shapes in clouds. It's only when they grow up that lots of them forget how to watch clouds. They're usually too busy with things happening around them. Most of them don't even look up.'

'That's sad,' said Matthew. 'I hope I don't forget how to see cloud-shapes.'

'I'm not going to grow up!' said David. 'I'm going to turn into a cloud!'

'Well in that case,' said Mary, 'the breeze is in exactly the right direction to blow you into our house and into bed. Come on!' She stood up and began to chase her younger son across the field. Matthew and Thomas rose together and, hand in hand, went at a more leisurely pace.

'I think this is one of those times you were talking about,' said the boy, 'you know, that you remember when you get old.'

Thomas tried to remember his own childhood. Were there any moments such as these? Had his father ever talked to him as he had talked to his sons? There were evenings of music and singing and dancing, and of drinking, but he had always been an outsider, a watcher, never a participant. Of course, in those days it was harder. They couldn't step out of their home into fields in the middle of a beautiful wood or green fields. They were down by the Tyne in the mud and dirt and smoke. He had memories, but they weren't always good. He hoped that his sons would fare better.

Smoke was rising from one or two chimneys. Someone was playing a harmonica, and a wavering tenor began the first verse of 'All people that on earth do dwell'.

'Old Hundredth,' said Thomas softly.

'Close your eyes son,' said Thomas. 'Listen. You can smell summer coming. You can taste it on the breeze. You can feel it touching you.' He ruffled his son's hair. 'I think you're right. We'll all remember this day.'

They walked into the house to find David naked in the kitchen sink.

'That'll teach you to be first!' sneered Matthew. Even David joined in the laughter.

'Yes,' said Mary as she fetched the hot water, 'I think it's going to be a good summer.'

The french windows in the dining room were open; the afternoon sun was hot, and Elizabeth had ordered iced tea for herself and her sister. It was the first time Margaret had visited Greencroft since the wedding, and their fitful correspondence had consisted of mild and uncontroversial letters which hid all that they might have wished to say to each other. Elizabeth was reluctant to go to Makemore Hall. Her antipathy toward Henry had, since the mid-winter incident, turned to active dislike. For her part Margaret had not initially wished to show how much she missed her family, and more lately had feared her husband's reaction to any visit. His feelings for Elizabeth were a reflection of Elizabeth's for him. Today, however, Henry had accompanied Maichamps to Durham. They were to take the train to London and spend a weekend together there, then Henry was to return with his father. The relief Margaret felt at this brief respite was apparent in her demeanour, her comparative cheerfulness. When she looked at herself in the mirror before she left she was shocked to see the shadows under her eyes and the lines on her forehead, but had managed a smile at the fact that she had even bothered to examine her reflection. It was a habit she thought she had lost, both smiling and mirror-gazing.

The decision to visit her sister came without warning. She had considered going for a walk, then thought about riding. Either of these would have been painful; she had been beaten by Henry two nights before. A carriage journey, well-cushioned, seemed a pleasant alternative on such a fine day, and she asked that the dog-cart and pony be made ready for her. It was only as she turned out of the gates that she made up her mind that she would journey to Greencroft; and no-one saw her take the road to Lanchester save a white-haired, red-nosed man trudging the path to the Makemores' colliery. But Silas Bompas marked the direction she was travelling.

The day was warm, the lane was not too rutted, and Margaret considered as she rode what, if anything, she would tell her sister. She was not sure that Elizabeth would sympathise with her. She was, after all, one of those who had warned her against such a swift marriage, warned her against Henry Makemore. And what could Elizabeth say? Leave Henry? Margaret knew what that would bring, Henry and Maichamps had explained it clearly.

She was, Henry had pointed out, an adulteress. She had
visited the room of a guest and made love to him. Witnesses,
he implied, could be procured to testify to this, and she had
no reason to doubt his word. The beatings? He would deny
them, there was no law against wife-beating, and anyway, he
would claim provocation. Then Maichamps had spoken.
Her leaving Henry would, of course, put him under an
obligation to explain himself, to counter her accusations, to
make public the perceived facts of the case. The name
Waterhouse would be emblazoned across the newspapers,
she would suffer, her family would suffer, her father's
businesses would suffer, their standing in the community
would cease to exist, as would their reputation.

Their words had been soft, persuasive. She considered
them carefully, at length. And it was true that she had had
intercourse with Maichamps, on a number of occasions.
Whether she had been willing, well, that was open to
question. The first time she had been drugged, she was sure
of that, and after that ...? If she was honest with herself
(which she could afford to be, since her thoughts belonged
to no-one but her) she would admit that sexual intercourse
with Maichamps was certainly preferable to the same act
with Henry. Maichamps was gentle where Henry was
violent, he was knowledgeable where Henry was rough and
coarse, his intent was, or so it seemed, to give her pleasure.
Henry did nothing but take from her.

She was confused. Each night before she retired the three
of them would sit in the drawing room, playing cards or
reading, discussing the day's news. And as the evening
progressed, each moment announced with grave, croaking
splendour by the tall, wide clock squatting toad-like on the
mantelpiece, she would become more tense. Ten o'clock was
the time. The chimes would set her heart reverberating with
their echo, she would count the strokes. Who would make
the announcement? The words were always the same. 'Is it

not time for bed Margaret?' Only the speaker would be different, and she could never be sure in advance who would say those words. If it were Maichamps then he would come to her some thirty minutes later, giving her ample time for her toilet, slip quietly beneath the sheets to touch her softly, carefully, efficiently. At some time, she was never sure when, Henry would enter the room, would stand quietly at the foot of her bed patiently waiting his turn. And when he pressed himself upon her Maichamps would still be there, touching, pushing, remonstrating when Henry's violence seemed about to erupt. And so thankful was she for this mercy that she could brook no objection to their wishes, would allow them their way as they saw fit, with her or with each other.

Sometimes, when Henry sent her to her bed, he would follow immediately. This she feared most of all; he would rip her clothes from her as she entered the room, tear at her breasts, force her to the bed or the floor.

There were also times when Henry delayed his appearance. This would at least give her time to prepare for him. She would attempt to relax herself, find refuge in the whisky bottle she now kept beside her bed, seek solace in the liquid's anaesthesia. Alcohol allowed her to accept his perversions with less revulsion than would otherwise have been the case.

And if neither of them spoke? Ten was, regardless, the hour of curfew. She would spend the night alone while her husband and her lover pleasured each other. She looked forward to these dark hours of solitude, but in the loneliness of her bed found her thoughts turning frequently to a matter she could not comprehend. Why, she asked herself, did she desire Maichamps' company when he had been party to so many evil and unnatural acts which had been forced upon her? Surely she could not be falling in love with him? Yet how else could she explain her emotions?

How would Elizabeth react to revelations such as these? That in itself was a puzzle. Elizabeth had always been straightforward and honest whenever Margaret had questioned her about her own sexuality. She was, in so many ways, an unusual woman, emancipated in her thoughts and her deeds. Unfortunate to lose her husband while still young (and in circumstances which had never been fully explained), Margaret feared that her half-sister's forthright opinions and uncompromising insistence upon her equality frightened most men who met her. There was no doubt in Margaret's mind that Elizabeth would end her days a spinster and was already showing signs of settling too easily into that mould. How then would she understand Margaret's predicament?

As she entered the grounds of Greencroft Hall Margaret had still not decided what to tell Elizabeth. She would have to let the conversation take its own course, she thought to herself as the groom led her pony away. Besides, the situation could be no worse than it was at present, regardless of whether anything or nothing was said.

Margaret strolled into the hall, peeped into the library. Nothing had changed. Nothing would change. Her father would be sitting at his desk, Elizabeth his faithful satellite moving around him. She smiled at the thought of them, realising suddenly how much she had missed them. She hurtled through the door of the office.

'It's me, father,' she said, 'the prodigal daughter re . . .' The figure sitting at the desk was not her father.

'Miss Margaret!' said Thomas Armstrong, rising quickly to his feet, 'That is, Mrs Makemore! Please, take a seat, I didn't know you were coming to visit . . .'

'That,' said Margaret sharply, 'is clearly evident. What are you doing at my father's desk? Where is he? Do you have his permission to be here? Come on man, I want answers!'

Thomas was flustered, suddenly unsure of himself. He looked around him.

'Well?'

'I'm helping out, while your father's away that is, and learning. Paperwork, that's what I'm doing. With Elizabeth, she's showing me how to . . .' He tailed off miserably.

'Elizabeth? I wasn't aware that you were on first name terms with my sister Mrs Kearton. Where is she anyway? I'm not sure that I believe you!'

'Oh Margaret,' laughed Elizabeth as she entered the room, 'you seem to have become something of a harridan in your old age. Is that what married life does for you?'

'Elizabeth,' gushed Margaret. She hurled herself into her sister's arms and they embraced fondly. It was Margaret who spoke first.

'Would you mind explaining exactly what is going on?' she asked imperiously.

'Of course,' Elizabeth replied. 'But why not do as Thomas suggested and sit down. You too Thomas.' The two did Elizabeth's bidding.

'Now, where shall I start? At the beginning I suppose. Thomas is here with father's permission, with his blessing in fact. He is being groomed for the position of pit-manager and we are working together, Thomas and I, teaching each other all we know about the running of the mine. He is an expert on matters underground; I know more about the administration above. We complement each other, isn't that right Thomas?'

Thomas nodded eagerly.

'Yes,' continued Elizabeth. 'We've learned a great deal about each other over the past few weeks and I think that we know each other well enough to make Christian names perfectly acceptable. Father is in Manchester on business, but he'll be back later this afternoon. Was there anything else you wished to know?'

'No,' said Margaret, 'that seems to answer all of my questions. Oh, there is one other thing: I'm longing for a cup of tea!'

* * *

'You could have apologised,' said Elizabeth.

'Why?' said Margaret. 'He looked so suspicious sitting there. And it doesn't matter whether he's a miner or a manager, he's still hired help. And I don't apologise to servants.'

'Margaret! There are times when I despair of you!'

'Yes, I know. That's really the only reason I behave like this.'

The two women were at home in each other's company. Elizabeth found in her sister a new maturity, a confidence which had not been present before her marriage, but at the expense of a loss of innocence which went beyond the physical. In the past Margaret had never been able to hide her true feelings from her sister. When, as a child, she had misbehaved, Elizabeth knew this even if Margaret's angelic face had deceived servants, governess and her father. And in later years when Margaret craved attention from her father which was all too often not forthcoming, Elizabeth was the one who saw the real hurt and disappointment. It was Elizabeth who comforted her in times of need, who cheered her up in times of sadness, who chastised her when she did wrong. She had thought that she would always know her sister's thoughts, but was now faced with a poised, mature woman who was playing the role of her sister. She was doing the job well, but without emotion; there was something wrong.

In a similar way Margaret was aware of a change in Elizabeth. The shrill termagant had gone, instead was someone happy with her life (despite not stating exactly how that life had changed), someone outgoing, almost carefree. The conversation became a duel, each woman determined to find out the other's secret without giving away any information herself. But while Elizabeth played this as a game, Margaret found herself increasingly unable to dwell upon her problems, unwilling to disclose them under any circumstances.

'So. How is married life? It has changed you, I feel.'

'How could it fail to do so? I'm a different person to the one who left here a few months ago. The caterpillar has slipped its chrysalis and become a butterfly, dear Elizabeth.'

'If that is the right analogy Margaret. There are other creatures which shed their skins, are there not? Spiders? Snakes? Crabs even!'

'Elizabeth! Are you suggesting that I resemble a snake or a spider in some way? Surely not!'

'Merely pointing out a comparison Margaret, a comparison which could be made with anyone whose character has altered over a period of time.'

'Such as you?'

'Such as me, if I could be said to have changed. Do you feel that that is the case?'

'Oh yes, without a doubt! And I'm left wondering what it is that has brought this about.'

Elizabeth pursed her lips. She disliked lying, particularly to her sister, but was not sure that she was yet ready to tell the complete truth.

'My life is in a constant state of change,' she conceded. 'So much has happened since you left us. Father has seen fit to allow me a greater amount of freedom in the way I work, I find myself with authority and responsibility. I'm still involved with music, I play for dancing regularly. There are times when I feel more at home doing that, being with the dancers, than I ever have done going to parties and balls and the like. I'm happier with myself. More content.' She looked up. 'Does that answer your question?'

'Almost,' said Margaret, 'if that's all there is. Is there nothing else?'

'Such as?'

'Such as ... a man perhaps? No, don't fluster and flap

your fingers about like that, it's a perfectly normal assumption, I know from my own somewhat limited experience the effect a man can have on a woman's life. I don't disbelieve what you've already told me, that most certainly was not my intention. But I do know you well Elizabeth, and most of what you describe was happening to a certain extent before I left. That leads to me consider other possibilities. That there may be a man in your life is just one of them.'

Elizabeth was horrified. Was she that transparent? Had she and Thomas been seen together, had someone reported that to her sister? And if that was the case, who else had been told? No, they had been too careful. This was speculation on Margaret's part, nothing more. But the fact that her sister's mind could work in such a way was itself a novel idea. Margaret had never in the past been one for logical argument. Perhaps it was time to find out whether she had learned to defend as well as attack.

'I think, dear sister, that you read more into my state of mind than is actually written there. If I appear overly content you might consider that this may be due to the pleasantness of the day, or the fact that father will be home this afternoon, or even that I'm happy to see you.' Elizabeth played the rules carefully; at no time did she deny that Margaret's allegations were untrue. She continued before Margaret could interrupt again.

'But you said that you were aware of how a man can change a woman. Does this mean that you've changed since you married? And if so, how?'

'Yes, I've changed,' acknowledged Margaret. 'I think that it would be impossible not to do so. As for the degree and the direction, I'm too involved to tell. I would have to leave that to others to consider and then let me know the results of their deliberation. Do you have any feelings on that?'

'Not yet. But I may have, if I'm given time to talk to you,

and to listen to you.' She reached out, held Margaret's hands in hers, looked into her eyes.

'There are shields around you, sister. I don't know who put them up, it may have been you, for protection. It may have been someone else, for his or her own defence. Or even to keep you prisoner. No, don't laugh, you don't mean it.' Margaret stopped laughing, looked down at her hands.

'You see,' said Elizabeth quietly, 'you don't contradict me! Your silence speaks more eloquently than any words might have done. I know you too well to believe that the new veneer you wear is the whole you. You've learned how to hide your true feelings through necessity, not through choice, and that may deceive others but not me. I shan't push you Margaret, if you want to tell me you must do so voluntarily, and it might not be here, it might not be now, but I will always be here for you. Remember that, dear sister.'

Margaret found herself in the same position Elizabeth had occupied only moments before. Her guess at Elizabeth's pre-occupation had been precisely that, a guess, and she was unaware how close to the mark that conjecture had been. Elizabeth, however, had arrived at her conclusion by deduction, by a knowledge of her sister gained through years of watching her grow older and more beautiful. Even now Margaret's beauty was evident. Elizabeth felt that familiar, far off touch of jealousy as she looked at her sister. She seemed tired, careworn, dogged by some hidden shame or concern, but still she was beautiful. No longer the playful puppy, eager to please, craving attention, she was now stately, noble, almost accepting that whatever tragedy might befall her, she would bear that burden with pride.

'Do you want to tell me Margaret?' asked Elizabeth. Margaret considered her options again. A full confession? Tell of Henry's beatings, his violence, his ... yes, the word was not too strong, his rape? Mention that she had been driven to unfaithfulness, that she was, despite herself, sleeping with a man who used her no less badly than her husband? And the strange thing was, she knew that Henry needed her, and that Maichamps did not. What should she do?

'I think I'm pregnant,' she said.

John Waterhouse returned to Greencroft Hall to find his daughters in fine spirits. On being told the reason he joined them eagerly, tempering his enthusiasm with protestations that he was too young to become a grandfather. He explained to Elizabeth and to Margaret (though the latter seemed rather bored by the discourse) that his journey had been valuable. There had been problems with some of the machinery in a mill Edward had bought. John Waterhouse had not even been aware that the brothers owned a mill, but once introduced to the building and the looms he had been able to see immediately ways in which the manufacturing process might be improved. Some of these he had described to Edward and his managers and they had put them into action straightaway. Others would require thought, planning, careful design. He would start work on them that very night.

'But father, what about the pit?' asked Elizabeth. 'Don't you want to see what Thomas and I have been doing?'

'Why?' countered her father. 'Is there anything wrong? Has something happened?'

'No.'

'Well then, you and Mr Armstrong had better just get on with your jobs. If you can run things for a day or two I don't see why you can't do it for a little longer, eh? You can start earning your wages, can't you!'

'Does that mean you're going to pay me?' queried Elizabeth.

'Don't I?' said her father incredulously.

'No.'

'Well you'd better start drawing some money, hadn't you! Back-date it a few months if you feel the need. And I suppose I ought to see last week's production figures, while we're talking about the mine. I don't suppose you could run and fetch them for me, since we do appear to have a few minutes . . .'

'You don't have any time at all,' interrupted Margaret, 'I'm here, I'm your guest, and I demand to be entertained!' She stamped her foot in mock temper.

'Oh Margaret, it's been so quiet without you,' said Elizabeth, bending down to hug her sister.

'We've missed you,' added her father. 'You must visit us more often. And is there any reason why you shouldn't stay for the night? We can dine together, I promise I won't mention mines or mills or steelworks or foundries!'

'Yes,' said Elizabeth, 'we can sit and talk, catch up on the news. You haven't told us about Italy, and France as well. We can send word back to Makemore Hall. You did say that Henry was away.'

'Well, it would be pleasant. And I would be alone if I went home.' Margaret looked up, happy. 'You've convinced me. I shall stay. But I must leave tomorrow morning. I am, after all, mistress of the manor; the whole place will grind to a halt if I'm not there!'

There was a knock on the door. Thomas Armstrong entered shyly, just as John Waterhouse rang to summon one of the grooms.

'I've finished the bookwork I was doing,' said Thomas. 'I thought I'd go home now, if there was nothing else you wanted doing.' He looked boldly at Elizabeth. 'I can always come back later this evening, if there's any pressing work that is.' John Waterhouse shrugged and turned to his elder daughter. Elizabeth had caught Thomas's glance. Margaret's presence, her news, had pushed him temporarily from her mind: seeing him there now flooded her with a sudden remorse that she had been enjoying herself without his company.

'Margaret's staying with us for the night,' she said. 'I imagine I'll be occupied all evening.' She chose her words carefully. 'There are one or two matters which we should examine together, and I've some points to raise which require your close consideration. It might be best, however, if we left those until a more convenient time. Tomorrow?'

'I'll look forward to that,' said Thomas. He turned to leave as the groom entered, was called back by Margaret.

'Mr Armstrong? Or may I call you Thomas as well, as it seems that you're almost a member of the family these days?'

'I'd be honoured to be Thomas, Mrs Makemore.' Thomas was unable to tell whether Margaret was being sincere or sarcastic.

'Good. Come, I wish to talk with you. Would you accompany me into the garden for a moment?' They stepped out, through the french windows, Thomas a respectful yard behind Margaret. John Waterhouse was instructing the groom, writing down a message for him to give to the housekeeper at Makemore Hall.

'I wish to apologise for my hastiness earlier, Thomas. It was wrong of me to take such a high-handed manner with you, particularly when you are placed in a position of trust by both my sister and my father . . .'

'There's no need . . .'

'I haven't finished yet, Mr . . . Thomas, that is.' She looked straight at him. 'I don't think I've thanked you properly for the part you played in rescuing me from my, let us call it a dilemma, all those months ago. Nor have I offered you my sincere condolences for the death of your father. In all I and my family owe you and your brother a significant debt, and I trust that we are repaying you in a coin to your liking.'

'Willie and I are both ...' began Thomas, sure now that Margaret was being sincere, but under the impression that his elevation from the pit-face was because of his good work and not a reward for rescuing his employer's daughter.

'Ah yes, Willie. How is he? I do think of him sometimes. He's married now, to Abigail I believe. Are they both well?'

'They are, and they'll be three by winter they tell me.'

'Really? Please pass on my regards to them. And my thanks to your brother in particular. Perhaps I shall meet him again some day, speak to him personally. There is so much I could say, so much which I ought to have said.' Her voice became less harsh, she seemed to be speaking her thoughts.

'I wonder if he would care to visit me one day?' She shook her head and her curls shone with honey. 'No, no, out of the question! A meeting perhaps, chaperoned of course. With my sister and Thomas, that would set the tongues wagging!' Thomas looked round uneasily, sure that he was not meant to be party to these secrets. He was not used to hearing himself addressed in the third person.

'But I would like to see him again,' she continued, talking aloud to herself, 'to ask his forgiveness. To thank him. To explain. I'll mention it to Elizabeth, she can arrange it with Thomas, they'll do it for me. I'll tell her when I tell her the rest, when I tell her my secrets. She'll understand.'

'Mrs Makemore! Are you alright?' Thomas stood in front of Margaret, she appeared to be in a trance, hands fluttering in front of her mouth like demented, flame-struck moths.

'What? I'm sorry Thomas, I must have been daydreaming. Did I say anything silly?' She regained control of her hands.

'No,' said Thomas, 'you were just saying thank you.'

'Oh good. I felt a little lost then, not quite myself. It must be the wine, we opened a bottle to celebrate. I'm going to have a baby as well you see.'

'Congratulations,' said Thomas, genuinely pleased. 'I'm

sure that you and Mr Makemore are delighted.'

'Henry?' said Margaret. 'Well, yes, I suppose he will be.' She appeared to banish her husband from her thoughts. 'But come, you must want to get back to your family, and I wish to talk further with Elizabeth. I do hope that we shall meet again.' She held out her hand and Thomas resisted the temptation to bend and kiss it. Instead he shook it gently, smiled at Elizabeth and her father, and left. There was, he felt, something not quite right with Margaret Makemore. He felt sorry for her, but was not sure why. She carried an air of tragedy with her, like the gloom of a winter fog.

The groom was in a hurry. He had been about to sit down for a meal when his master had summoned him, and he had galloped his horse at a good speed to reach Makemore Hall and hand over the message. The housekeeper there, surly as was most of her breed, glanced at the note with a lack of interest and waved him away. He was eager to return but not so bad at his job as to be unaware of his mount's needs. A few minutes to cool down, some water, then he would be on his way. He led the mare to the stable and, on entering, disturbed four men playing cards. Two of them looked up guiltily; they were young, probably stable lads to judge by their dress. One ignored him; he was an old man, wizened, probably a gardener. The fourth, however, seemed familiar. The groom addressed himself to that one.

'Can I water me horse?' he asked. 'I've just been delivering a message.' The fourth man nodded. The white hair he wore long at his ears and over his collar had abandoned the top of his hair. He was fat, that could be seen even when he was sitting down.

'Where are you from then?' he asked.

'Greencroft,' came the reply, 'Mr Waterhouse's place.'

'Ah, the mistress's father. I saw her heading out that way earlier on. There's nothing the matter, is there?'

The groom led his horse to the trough, watched carefully as it slaked its thirst.

'No,' he answered, 'nothing the matter that I know of. Miss Margaret's staying the night, that's all. She'll be back tomorrow, that's what the note said.'

'Here,' said the talkative man, 'you must be thirsty too. Have a swig.' He handed the groom a metal flask, already uncorked. The groom looked at it, nodded his thanks, then threw the contents down his throat. He coughed.

'Good stuff,' said the man. 'Pinched from Mr Henry's own decanter.' He laughed aloud. 'That's the one he keeps for himself, not the one he offers to his guests!' He slapped his knees, nudged the old man beside him. The card game seemed to have been forgotten.

'So how is Miss Margaret? She's been a little down of late, a bit too quiet. Missing her family I suspect. It'll have cheered her up, going back to see her old dad and her sister, eh?'

'I didn't see that much of her,' the groom replied, 'only while I was being given the note. She wasn't actually in the room at the time. She was out in the garden, talking to Mr Armstrong.'

'Really? Mr Armstrong you say? And what would they find to talk about, I wonder?' The question did not demand an answer but the groom spoke just the same.

'I couldn't hear them, but she was smiling a lot, and laughing, and looking thoughtful as well. And I saw her take Mr Armstrong's hand, just before I left.'

'Now that is interesting. Isn't that interesting boys! I mean, it's so nice to find the mistress able to enjoy herself in the company of old friends.' He stood up. 'Must have a piss.' He wandered away in search of privacy, muttering to himself.

'Miss Margaret with an old friend, eh? Willie Armstrong again! Just can't keep away from each other, those two.

What would happen if Mr Henry found out I don't know, I just don't know . . .'

'No,' the groom called after him, 'not Willie Armstrong, it's his brother Thomas. It was Thomas who was . . .' His words were not heard.

'Oh well,' he shrugged. 'I'll head back. I can taste that stew already.' He tugged on the reins, the horse followed him out into the yard. There was no sign of the talkative man; the groom felt he ought to thank him for the swig of whisky as well as put him right on the identity of the particular Armstrong talking to Margaret Makemore. But it wasn't really that important. He cantered out of the yard and headed back to Greencroft Hall.

Chapter Seventeen

Will you, won't you, will you, won't you,
will you join the dance?

Alice in Wonderland
(Lewis Carroll)

Summer arrived. May gave way to June in a flurry of heat and colour. The hedgerows wore dog roses and eglantine with pride, meadows and fields were decked with blue and red and gold. The still air droned with insects which were preyed upon by birds, taken to feed wide-mouthed fledgelings which in turn were hunted by weasel and cat, badger and owl.

Sundays had become days of habit for the Armstrongs. Mary would take Matthew and David to the church, where she would deposit them at Sunday School while she attended the full service. Thomas would use this time to write to Elizabeth, secret letters and secret thoughts. Some of these letters he gave to her; others he kept along with her letters to him. She asked him once where he hid them, frightened that they might be found one day; she was aware that Mary kept a tidy house. He reassured her. They were locked in a small chest, hidden inside it in a secret drawer. He held the only key, and if Mary were ever curious enough to ask about the chest's contents he could show her that they were cuttings from newspapers, poems, drawings he had been given by the children. No, Mary would find nothing in their house which would lead her to suspect the affair.

After an hour's writing Thomas would collect his sons from the church and, if the weather were fine (as it seemed always to be; rain was permitted to fall only on weekdays), he would take them for walks through the fields. He showed them the foxes' lair and they lay in silence watching the cubs play-fighting over rabbit bones. They would search the sky for the pinprick of dust that was a lark, oblivious to the world from which it sought to escape. The boys found themselves able, with their father's guidance, to identify birds easily. One day they came across a lapwing in a field of long waving grass, its wing held away from its side at some crazy angle. Above a kestrel hovered with practised ease, darting forward only to return to its position.

'It's going to kill the peewit, chase it away, Dad,' exhorted David. He bent down to pick up a stone but his father held him back.

'Don't!' he said. 'Watch carefully. Look, over there!' He pointed to the edge of the field, where the grass was shorter.

'I can't see anything,' said Matthew.

'Keep watching,' whispered Thomas. What appeared to be a brown, speckled pebble moved slightly.

'Did you see that?' asked Thomas. The boys nodded. 'That's a lapwing chick. The kestrel's after it and that's why the parent's trying to lure it away. The adult bird hasn't really got a broken wing, it's just pretending. If the chick keeps still the kestrel won't see it, it's so well disguised, and the parent will fly away once the chick's safe. But the chick's scared, see, it moved then. And the kestrel can see that movement, out of the corner of its eye, so it moves away to where the chick is. Then the parent flaps its wing again, so the kestrel moves back. It doesn't know what to do.'

Thomas felt two hands reach to hold his, and they stared at the drama white-knuckled. A second adult lapwing appeared, dived at the kestrel, screamed an aerobatic curse which was ignored. The chick, unable to remain still a moment longer, dashed for the safety of the hedge but was too slow. The kestrel swooped to take its prey.

'Damn!' said Matthew.

'It's got it,' cried David, 'it's got the baby! Why didn't you stop it Dad, why didn't you stop it!'

'Hey there, calm down,' he said. He bent down to look at his younger son.

'What could I have done, eh? Thrown a stone at the kestrel? And then what? We can't stay here all day to protect a little lapwing chick. And anyway, I might have hit the kestrel. I might have killed it. And then who would have been the bad one? That kestrel's probably got chicks of its own, and if I'd killed it I would be as good as killing them as well. And birds aren't like people, they don't know what's good or bad. They live by instinct, they only kill for food. That's what it means, being a human being. You always have the choice between good and bad. The trouble is, sometimes, even when you know what's right and what's wrong, you can't help choosing the wrong way.'

'What are you on about, Dad?' asked Matthew impatiently.

'Poor peewit,' said David. 'I'm hungry,' he added as an afterthought.

'Come on then,' said Thomas cheerily, ignoring the first question and reacting only to his younger son's statement. 'Your Mam should be out of that church by now. Let's go and see if she's made us any dinner.'

Hand in hand they swung through the summer fields and sang the path which led to home.

'Thomas?'

'Mm.'

'Are you asleep yet?'

'Yes!' He turned onto his side, turned away from her.

'Thomas?'

'I'm still here.'

'Are you happy?'

'Am I what?' he said, turning back to face his wife. It was still light in the bedroom. The window looked out to the north-west and the sun had just set.

'I was just wondering if you were happy,' said Mary. She was lying on her back, her eyes wide open, staring at the ceiling. Her hands were crossed over her breasts, her fingers interlocked. It was hot in the room and neither of them wore any nightclothes; the bedsheet (the blankets were neatly folded on a chair in the corner) was turned down to their waists.

'Do you mean happy in general,' asked Thomas, 'or happy at this moment? Is it my own happiness you're thinking about, or our joint happiness? Or take it even wider, the village's happiness, the country's, the world's? And why?'

'No, I was thinking of you, just you. Are you content? I was thinking, you see, there's been a lot happening recently. We moved here, and I must admit I wasn't sure it was the right thing to do, but you've been promoted, you've got a good future ahead of you. It's a good place to live, the boys love it. You've got a good wage, we can even put something aside each week in case we need it for the future. Everything seems to be working well. And I wanted to make sure that you were, well, you know, alright. That you were happy too. Do you see what I mean?'

'Is there anything that makes you think I'm not happy?'

Mary stared at the ceiling in silence. She licked her lips before replying.

'You don't sing as much,' she said. 'You don't laugh as

much either, and you don't talk about work like you used to. When you were working at the face you used to sit down and tell us all about what had been happening, who was calling who else names, who'd been out drinking, who was ill, who was well, whose wife was expecting, all that type of thing. I know you don't see the men as often as you used to, I know that. And I was wondering if you missed them.' She turned on her side to look at him.

'I just wanted to say that if you did miss them, if you found you didn't like being a manager, it wouldn't matter to me. If you wanted to go underground again I wouldn't try to stop you. We both know it's more dangerous, but your happiness matters. Do you see what I mean?'

'Yes love, I see what you mean. And thank you for thinking about me like that.' He stretched out his hand and stroked her hair.

'I do miss the friendliness, I'll admit that. The dancing helps, it means I can still keep in touch. And it's not as if I don't go underground, I still do, at least once a day, sometimes more. The work's different too, when I come home my brain feels so tired but the rest of me wants to go out and kick walls down! And there's not really a lot to talk about either, so I suppose I have been a bit quiet sometimes. But I'm not unhappy love. Just distracted on occasions.'

His hand moved down over her ear, onto her neck, down onto her breast. He teased a nipple into life, she closed her eyes and swallowed. He took the opportunity to look at her. She was lying on her right side, her left arm crooked above her head, her hand anchored at her neck. A tuft of dark hair sat at her armpit. Her breasts rested, one on top of the other, the two nipples almost touching. He spanned them with finger and thumb and she inhaled sharply.

She never initiated their lovemaking these days, and Thomas wondered whether she would notice if he abstained altogether. It was not that she didn't enjoy it once they had started (at least he assumed that was the case; she could, he supposed, have become a very good actress), but even then she had become increasingly passive. She was beginning to put on weight, he noticed, a slight thickening of the waist which had begun years ago but which had accelerated over the past few weeks. But he couldn't complain about that; his new sedentary life was making its presence known in the increase of his own girth. His eyes moved down her body and his right hand followed, while his left took over the other's duty. He flicked the bedsheet away to expose Mary's waist, her groin and her legs.

He had lied to Elizabeth. He had told her that he and Mary only made love when she wanted him. He had told her that he was unable to sustain an erection unless he thought of her, Elizabeth. Yet even now he could feel his penis becoming engorged as his hand reached the triangle of hair at Mary's pubis, as she rolled slowly onto her back and parted her legs. Her hand reached out to encircle him, and he felt the same guilt which troubled him when he and Elizabeth made love. He nearly laughed! The irony of it, a man who feels guilty when making love with his mistress because he's deceiving his wife, and who feels the same guilt when making love to his wife because of the lies he's told his mistress. Not that Elizabeth would accept some of those terms. She was his lover, not his mistress; Elizabeth and Thomas made love together; Thomas and Mary had intercourse.

Mary was an undemanding partner, easy to arouse, easy to satisfy. Her single orgasm came quickly providing she were aroused sufficiently. Elizabeth, however, was more demanding, more active, insistent that she should obtain pleasure from their love-making. There were times when he was envious of her ability to hold her pleasure at such a high level of tremor, to move from the crest of one wave to the next with so little effort. She enjoyed mastering him, she had told him that, moving her pelvis faster and faster, pressing down on him, knowing that she had the power to suck his juices from him, to render him flaccid. And then she would collapse on him, and he would feel her sweat and her moist warmth mingle and bind their bodies together.

Two fingers were now inside Mary, his thumb encircling her mound. He began to kiss her right breast while his spare hand still tugged at the other nipple. Her hand had let go of him; she was unable to move voluntarily, was forced like the lapwing to obey her instincts. Her arms were outstretched and her head was moving slowly from side to side.

Tomorrow, thought Thomas, John Waterhouse would be leaving for his week away. Elizabeth would want to spend a night with him, perhaps two. No, that was unfair; it was not her wish alone, *they* wanted to spend a night together. He could not deny his need to be with her. But why? Why was there such a need? Was it vanity, that a woman such as Elizabeth, a woman of rank, should be in love with him? Was it that, having told him of her past, he wished to protect her with his own stability? The thought of her being held against her will, of being forced to have intercourse with strangers, revolted him but at the same time made him desire her more. But surely that could not be all!

He rolled over Mary's outstretched leg, slid his knees down the bed and entered her slowly, softly. She moved her feet, bent her knees, pushed herself at him to increase the force of his thrusts. He responded by moving faster, his mouth and hands becoming rougher at her breasts. He felt her hands reach for his backside, her fingers claw at him, and he realised how close they both were to release. He plunged at her, raised himself up on his hands, felt her stiffen below him and then, just as suddenly relax. He slowed as she opened her eyes, lay back as he pushed and pulled slowly to his own inevitable climax, his head lifted high as warmth flooded his loins.

Elizabeth would not have allowed him to do that. She would have demanded that he quicken his pace if anything. She would have lifted her legs up onto his shoulders, forced his head to her lips, screamed and cried at him. And then, after he had shuddered to a halt, they would talk. Perhaps that was the difference.

'Thank you,' said Mary. She reached for the box of rags she kept under the bed, handed one to Thomas as he rolled off her. She sat up, then knelt. It must be the same the world over, thought Thomas as he watched her wipe herself, wriggle her hips, then wipe again. She took his rag and placed it with hers beside the bed, ready to be washed in the morning, then lay down and pulled the sheet up to her chin. Thomas leaned over her and kissed her on the lips, unaware that it was the first time that night he had done so.

'Goodnight love,' he said softly. She murmured in reply, and he fitted himself to her, his arm draped over her breasts. Darkness claimed their world.

The good weather continued. Elizabeth forecast a drought unless some rain fell, but there was no sign of a change. Her father left almost as planned, a day or two late, on the seventh of June. It was two weeks until the rapper competition. Two weeks until 21 June 1887. Two weeks until Queen Victoria's Golden Jubilee. Thomas and Elizabeth planned their time together.

They would spend the Wednesday and Thursday nights with each other, in Elizabeth's own room. John Waterhouse would be away for at least seven days, possibly a little longer, but when he returned he would bring Edward with him. Edward had insisted that he come to the dance championship. He had written to his brother making arrangements for the visit, and John Waterhouse had given Elizabeth the letter to read as he set off. She had complained of feeling unwell, was blaming the fish which she had eaten the night before. Her uncle's letter, however, seemed able to dispel her nausea far more quickly than any medicine. She sat in the office giggling, reading portions of the letter out to Thomas.

'I never realised how funny Uncle Edward was,' she said. 'Apparently London's going to be sheer hell for the whole of the week before the Jubilee celebrations, and he says he wouldn't stay there for the great day even if he knew that he'd have to dance in the championship himself. He says that the Queen has granted special dispensation for "ladies who have been innocent parties in divorce cases",' she affected a regal tone of voice, 'to be admitted to her drawing-rooms. She even asked Salisbury if innocent foreign ladies might be admitted, but he said no because of the risk of admitting "American women of light character". Good Lord, Thomas, she's refusing to wear her crown or robes of state! Edward says she'll have her black dress and white bonnet on as usual so she'll look like a Christmas pudding with white sauce on top. Oh no, I'm wrong, because it's such a special occasion she's going to have her bonnet decorated with diamonds! Won't that please the populace!'

'I'd guess from your comments that you aren't very taken with the royal family,' said Thomas. 'Are you one of these republicans?'

'I'm sure they're quite pleasant people,' said Elizabeth, 'I just can't see how relevant they are to modern society. I suppose you approve?'

'I've not given the matter much thought,' he replied. 'They don't bother me, I don't bother them. That's my philosophy.'

'That's not a philosophy,' said Elizabeth indignantly. 'That's called ignoring your responsibilities. Just because something isn't affecting you doesn't mean that you can ignore it. If you see a man lying in the street and two others kicking him, punching him, do you ignore it? If the

Northumbrian miners strike again does that mean, because
we're in Durham, that you can't discuss their reasons for
doing so? Aren't you allowed to form an opinion on the
subject? Your opinion might count for more than someone
directly involved because you can look at the subject from
outside. You can be independent. Isn't that worth something?'

'I suppose so.'

'Good God Thomas, there's a brain and a mind lurking
somewhere in that skull of yours. All you need do is exercise
it every now and then. You never know, one day you might
need it.'

'Yes miss. Please may I go to the toilet?'

'Pardon?'

'I'm using my brain,' said Thomas, slowly, deliberately.
'I'm trying to tell you, without saying it in so many words,
that I don't enjoy being treated like a schoolboy. I don't like
using sarcasm but there are times when it's called for, and
that was one of them.'

Elizabeth sat back in her seat. Thomas stared at her; she
looked at him from beneath hooded eyes. She was the first
to speak.

'I'm sorry,' she said.

'I accept your apology,' he replied. 'Now would you mind
showing me how you reconcile the quantities of coal
produced at the face with the quantities shipped out by
railway?' She moved to his side of the desk, resolving not to
go too close to him until she was sure that his spines had
retracted.

It was an interesting start to their week together, one
which meant that everything following was bound to be an
improvement. The rules they had made about hiding their
feelings were quickly relaxed without them agreeing in
words that they should do that. They smiled at each other,
touched hands as they passed when sure that no-one was

watching. Twice they had disappeared together into the window-less ante-room (Thomas insisted on calling it the broom-cupboard), locked the door and made love. They did not consider that they were, perhaps, being reckless. They had been undiscovered for so long that the thought did not occur to them. After all, why should anyone come to look for them? Neither had left any evidence for anyone to find. All of their letters were safely hidden away. And so they indulged themselves in each other's company, and the week passed quickly.

John Waterhouse sent a telegram announcing the time of his arrival at the station, requesting that a carriage be sent to collect him and Edward.

'Tuesday 14 June, three twenty-six p.m.' read Elizabeth. 'Only three-and-a-half hours more.' The lovers had become used to their comparative freedom. Elizabeth had warned Thomas that, once her father and uncle returned, they would have to be more vigilant. Edward was less involved in the workings of the pit than his brother; he might spend his days wandering the grounds, appearing when and where he was not expected.

'And then,' she had continued, 'it'll be the rapper competition. And you promised your wife that you would stop dancing after that. How often will we be able to be together then?'

'We'll manage somehow,' said Thomas. 'We've managed in the past, I'm sure we can manage in the future.'

'And then what?' Elizabeth seemed remote, pre-occupied with her own unhappiness. 'Is that what our future's to be? Snatched moments together in a dark room? Fumbling in the cold of the summerhouse, always afraid that someone will discover us? And will we continue to do that, will we want to do that until we're in our dotage? Can you imagine me when I'm sixty, lying flat on my back with my legs in the air on that summerhouse floor?'

'You're asking questions I can't answer,' warned Thomas. 'I can't even think about tomorrow or the day after, let alone when you're sixty. But neither of us have made any promises, remember that. We can get out if we feel we have to.'

'I know!' hissed Elizabeth. 'I know! But I don't want to get out! I want to be with you Thomas. I love you.' The look of helplessness which crossed her face was mirrored in his.

'We've another three hours Thomas. I know what I want to do in that time. Do you want to join me?' He nodded and reached out his hand.

Mary enjoyed housework. Having her home neat, tidy and clean gave her a sense of achievement. Goodness knows, she would complain, it's difficult enough when you've two boys whose hobby is collecting mud on their boots and in their clothes and who don't recognise a doormat when they see one. And a husband who leaves clothes lying around, who whittles away at wood while he's sitting in front of the fire; he doesn't help either. But her fussing was like that of a mother hen, proud of her brood, and if she looked upon each speck of dirt brought across her threshold as a personal affront, then the bearer of each mote, man or boy, was unwittingly helping her rise to her challenge.

It was Tuesday afternoon. Yesterday's washing had dried the same day, was now ironed and aired and put away. The evening meal was prepared, the larder was as full as decency would allow (no food was allowed to go off in this house), and it was the turn of the parlour to succumb to Mary's relentless pursuit of domestic perfection. The range had been leaded, the carpets and rugs lifted and beaten, the dust on the floors beneath chased from the room. All flat surfaces had been polished, all walls tickled with a feather duster. The windows had been washed, the cushions plumped, the furniture moved slightly so that it might not become too complacent in its static homeliness. Only Thomas's desk remained untidy. Mary was loath to touch it, despite Thomas's insistence that she might do so. His box, his private box, was on the lid of the desk. Mary looked at it for a while as if frightened that it might spring at her, then lifted the desk lid and put the box away. Little more than a week ago, she had picked up the box and found it unlocked, but her sense of privacy far outweighed her curiosity and she had put it down without examining the contents. She straightened the pens and paper inside the desk, lifted out the arrows of splinter where Thomas had sharpened his pencil. There only remained his books to set in order.

Mary did not enjoy reading. The task, for she looked upon it as such, was largely beyond her. She could read and write her name and could spell out words in newspapers, but had little interest in improving the skill. She liked Thomas's books for their feel and their smell, the way they looked with their different coloured bindings, the shine of the gold-blocked letters on some of the spines. She liked them arranged in decreasing order of size on the shelf above the desk, largest to the left, smallest to the right. Thomas had not had much time to read recently; the books, numbering more than twenty, had not been disturbed much since she had last re-arranged them over two months ago. There were, however, one or two out of place, and because she had time to spare she decided to take each book down and lightly dust along its top. She did not know individual books by title, but by colour, shape and size. The complete works of Keats was, to her, royal blue, fat and dense. Tennyson's *In Memoriam* slim, tall, black. Thomas's Bible had belonged to his mother, it too was black but short and squat, with gold lettering and wafer-thin pages. Dickens's *Hard Times* and *Oliver Twist* were twins in purple. And there was a new volume there, one she had not met before. She introduced herself to it. Small, neat, yellow and green binding. It was by someone called Ruskin, she could see that, but the title on the spine had been partially worn away. She opened the book to the title page but never did find out what it was called. She could not read well, but the words written inside the cover were inked so neatly, so legibly, so clearly. Her mouth formed the words as her finger crossed the page.

'To my love. Elizabeth.'

There was a moment when the words did not register, and then a moment when they did, and these two moments separated a time when Mary was happy from a time when her heart was taken from her and crushed. Had Thomas been there with her he might have explained simply by telling the truth; the words were Elizabeth's but had not been meant for him. But Thomas was not there. Mary was alone with her empty house and her tears.

'Calm down lass,' she told herself, 'calm down', but the voice was that of a stranger. She sat in the chair by the fireside, sat in the warmth of the afternoon sun and tried to collect her thoughts, but they had escaped to wander freely and no amount of chasing would persuade them to return to her in an orderly fashion. She imagined herself to be in control only to find her fancy feeding her pictures of her husband and Elizabeth together, and the tears began to flow once more. She saw Thomas before her telling her that it was a misunderstanding, that he had not returned the love Elizabeth so blatantly offered him, yet even as he spoke his words shrivelled and died on the floor at his feet. He would explain, surely he would find some way of telling her that it was not true. She would accept a lie, a necklace of pretty, gaudy lies, if only he would tell her that her worst imaginings were not true, that he loved *her* and no other. He would be back by tea-time, but so would the boys. She could not say anything to him then. She began to weep again at the thought of her sons. *Their* sons, she reminded herself, surely

Thomas could do nothing which might harm their sons. No, she would have to go to see him! She would go to see him now!

She ignored the books scattered on the floor as she hurried out of the house, passed neighbours without seeing them, without returning their greetings. Her walk grew faster, faster still, became a run. And then, as she neared the Hall, she slowed down, managed to control her breathing. She entered by the front door – it was the only way she knew, but there was no-one about. She knew where the offices were situated; Thomas had shown her from the outside, one evening they had peered through the windows together and he had shown her where he sat and she had felt proud for him. Pride! For him? Oh, stupid, stupid woman!

The corridor was long and dark. The first door she tried was a cupboard, the second the library. At least, she reasoned, she was heading in the right direction. The next door was ajar and she opened it quietly to find the office she had only previously viewed from outside. Everything was tidy; even when her mind was in turmoil she appreciated tidiness.

The room was unoccupied and Mary was prepared to turn away. But from the corner of her eye she glimpsed another door, almost hidden around a corner. Probably another cupboard, she told herself, or somewhere to put files and paperwork, but still she approached it quietly, turned the handle slowly. Inside it was dark, but from the light rushing past her she could make out a small bed, a table and a chair, nothing more. But where was her husband?

She slammed the door behind her and left the office, determined to find Thomas. She looked again into the empty library, then across the hall where she disturbed a maid polishing the silver candelabra in the ballroom.

'I'm Mrs Armstrong,' she said. 'I'm looking for my husband. Have you seen him?' The maid shook her head lazily.

There was no-one in the music room, nor the dining room, and Mary found herself back in the main hall.

'Can I help you?' The figure of the housekeeper, her voice as starched as her blouse, appeared behind her.

'I'm looking for my husband, Thomas Armstrong,' said Mary. 'He's not in the offices. I don't suppose you've seen him?'

'I have not,' came the reply. 'May I ask why you wish to find him? If I see him I can give him a message.'

'It's personal,' said Mary, 'and it's urgent. I'll have to keep on looking.'

'I'm sorry Mrs Armstrong, that won't be possible. I can't have just anyone wandering around the house. I'm afraid I must ask you to leave.'

There was a chair behind her; Mary slumped into it, her head in her hands.

'Are you alright dear?' asked the housekeeper. 'You aren't ill, are you?'

'I won't make a mess on your floor,' sobbed Mary, 'don't worry.' The housekeeper considered retaliating but decided that her prey was not worthy of her. It might even do her some good to help this woman; Thomas Armstrong was smiled upon by both Mr Waterhouse and his daughter.

'If you wait here,' said the housekeeper graciously, 'I'll have a look for him. He may be across at the stables or in the pit-head offices, he may even have taken a stroll in the gardens. Don't you worry, I'll find him.' She patted Mary on the shoulder. 'I'll be no more than ten minutes,' she added, then scurried away. Mary waited for her to go, then mounted the stairs to the first floor.

She found herself at a large open landing; three walls were hung with dark, oiled landscapes. Above was a roof of smudged green glass, and in the fourth wall two large windows let her see across the parklands to the farms beyond. There were two arches which led, she assumed, to different wings of the building; she chose the one to her left and looked down another corridor. Once again there were rooflights pooling their pale sunshine along the carpet at regular intervals. There were four doors, two on each side of the corridor. The first of these, on the left, was locked; when she bent down to look through the keyhole she could see some furniture, a window in the far wall, but little else. The second door, on the same side, opened quietly onto a huge room. This was obviously, she decided, John Waterhouse's bedroom. It was furnished with fine wallhangings and brightly coloured carpets, and a painting of a woman who looked like Miss Margaret but older, kinder, hung over the fireplace. Mary noticed the door she had tried earlier, this time from the inside; two rooms had obviously been converted into one.

She left quickly, feeling that she was intruding upon John Waterhouse's privacy, and tried the door opposite. In her haste she made no attempt at disguising her approach. She turned the handle noisily, swung the door wide open. She saw Elizabeth reach for the sheets to hide her nakedness, and in doing so pull them away from the man at her side.

'Oh Christ!' said Thomas. Mary turned and ran.

'Mary! Mary, come back! I can explain!' he shouted as he leaped from the bed. She was at the foot of the stairs before he reached the door.

'Thomas!' called Elizabeth, climbing out of bed after him. 'You'd better get dressed. Calm down, think things through. Think about what you're going to do, what you're going to say.'

'What the hell *am* I going to do?' yelled Thomas as he stalked back into the room. 'How the hell do I know what I'm going to do! Go after her I suppose, but I don't know what I'll say! I don't know, I just don't know! How did she find out, how did she guess?'

He sat down on the bed, fists and teeth clenched.

Elizabeth picked up his clothes from the floor, brought them to him, put them by his side. She reached out and stroked his neck.

'Don't,' he said softly. She took her hand away.

'Get dressed first,' she said. 'Then go after her. Try to speak to her. She'll probably give you a choice, though it might not sound like it at the time. It'll be me or her. And you're the only one who can decide.'

'Yes,' he said, 'I'll talk to her, if I can find her. She'll be at home, there's nowhere else she can go. Or at Willie's. She could be with Abi.' He fumbled at the buttons on his waistcoat, his socks were inside out, his shirt not tucked into his trousers. He picked up his jacket and headed for the door where he stopped and turned around. Elizabeth was still sitting on the bed, still wrapped in the sheet. She looked up at him.

'I'll be downstairs in the office,' she said, 'if you need me.'

'Thank you,' said Thomas. Then he was gone.

'Good luck,' said Elizabeth, her voice cracked and worn. She felt old, old and helpless, and she turned to her pillow and began to cry.

Elizabeth looked at the clock. Half-past five. Her father's train must have been late; he and Edward were still not back. Files lay open on the desk in front of her but she was unable to read them, unable to work. She rested her head on the desk and, when she heard the door open, anticipated her father's voice.

'Hello,' said Thomas.

'Oh dear God,' she said as she hurtled around the desk and into his arms. 'I didn't think you'd be back. I thought I'd never see you again!'

She kissed him hard on the lips, tasted salt and felt him wince. She pulled away and looked at him. There was blood at the corner of his mouth and on his forehead, his lips and eyes were swollen. As she helped him into a seat she noticed that he was limping.

'What happened?' she asked. 'No, wait until I get you a drink. Don't move!' She left the room and re-appeared a moment later with a glass of whisky which she handed to him, then left again to fetch water and towels from the ante-room. She dabbed at his eye as he told her his story.

'She wasn't at home. All of my books were lying on the floor and the Ruskin was open. You'd written in it, remember? She must have read it, thought that the message was for me.' He snorted a laugh. 'I suppose that's justice. I've done so much to deceive her but I'm found out because of something which doesn't actually have anything to do with me. Oh, that stings!' Elizabeth moved to his mouth.

'I went round to Willie's but she wasn't there, nor was he, nor Abi. I didn't know what to do, where to go. Then I remembered that the kids would be at school, but by the time I'd got there Mary'd already got them. I asked the teacher, he said that Willie and Abigail had been with her and that they'd headed off towards the manse. I might have known that's where she's go, that preacher nearly owns her! Anyway, I set off there as well, fast, hoping to catch up before she got through the door. I mean, she was only ten or fifteen minutes ahead of me. I was too late though.'

'Does anywhere else hurt?' asked Elizabeth.

'Aye, me knee. I scraped it. And me ribs, it hurts when I breathe in.'

His trouser leg was ripped at the knee and Elizabeth rolled it up to show that his knee was skinned and bleeding, small pieces of grit and dirt embedded in the flesh.

'This'll hurt,' she said as she began to clean the wound. 'Go on, keep talking.'

'I banged at the door, I suppose I must have been shouting and yelling as well. The preacher answered but I could see Willie behind him. He asked me to be quiet, said I was frightening the kids. Me! Frightening me own children! Anyway, I quietened down a bit. I said I wanted to see Mary. He said she didn't want to see me. By that time Willie was standing beside him, I think they were both worried in case I tried to force me way in. I said I had to see her, I needed to talk to her. I said she probably needed to talk to me. They wouldn't let me in though. Then Willie started at me. He asked me what I thought I was doing, was I mad, did I know how much I'd hurt Mary. He called you a witch, and one or two other names. The preacher tried to calm him down but he couldn't, he was jabbing his finger at me. He's got a bit of a temper has our Willie. I just turned away, I've seen him like that before, but he came after me, down the steps and into the street. I don't know what it was, perhaps he's resented me for a long time, me being too much of a big brother, but everything seemed to come out of him, all the anger, all the rage. He was pushing at me, and Abigail was there at the door telling him not to be stupid, to come back in. I could have pushed back at him I supposed, but me heart wasn't in it. Be careful with that leg love, it's bloody sore.

'He was going to go back in. They were going to leave me there, not let me see me own wife and me own kids. I shouldn't have said it I suppose, but I wanted to hurt him without doing anything physical.'

'What did you say, Thomas?'

'I just said "Margaret sends her love". I wasn't sure if it would do anything or not. That's all I said, just as he was turning away. No-one else heard. He turned back and he started hitting me, punching me, and I couldn't defend meself. "Fight back!" he was screaming, but I couldn't, I couldn't bring meself to do it. He knocked me down and started kicking me, I rolled into a ball. I don't think there's any ribs broken. The preacher dragged him off eventually, hauled him back into the house. He helped me up, asked if I was alright. He said I'd better go. I could see, only just, out of one eye, up at one of the bedrooms. Mary'd been watching. She had David in her arms and Matthew was there too, I could see his head above the sill. They were all crying and David had his arms out towards me and I could see him crying "Dad!" but I couldn't hear him. And then the curtains were closed. I came back here. What else could I do?'

'You did everything you could Thomas, everything you could. Right now you need someone to look after you, and that someone's me. I'll get you bandaged and tidied up and then we'll go. I'm not sure that my father would understand what's been going on, not immediately. We need to let things calm down a little. We can go to Newcastle, stay there for a little while, talk things over. We'll find some way of sorting things out, don't worry. Is that alright with you?'

'Aye, I suppose so. Whatever you say.' If Elizabeth had suggested leaping from the High Level Bridge he would have agreed with her. He had no will left of his own.

'I'll find one or two things to wear, we can always get something for you later. I've sufficient money to last for a while, I'll take plenty of towels in case we need bandages. Do you think you're well enough to travel?'

Thomas nodded.

'I'll be back in a minute then.' She left him alone, sad and lost and unable to weep.

Chapter Eighteen

There are five dancers, a Tommy or Fool, a Bessy . . .
The Sword Dances of Northern England
(Cecil J. Sharp)

Thomas spent two days in bed. The journey into New-castle had taxed him more than he thought possible, he was feverish and in pain. He refused to allow Elizabeth to call a doctor; it was as though he needed to accept his suffering as a penance for his sins. On the first day Elizabeth ventured out only when he was asleep, to buy him night-shirts and other clothes. She washed him and fed him, though he could take little but thin soup, and watched over him at night from a chair by his bedside. And then, late on the Thursday afternoon, he woke and demanded food. His temperature had dropped, his bruises were more colourful than they had been but less painful, and he seemed keen to talk to Elizabeth, to discuss their problems.

'I could go back,' he said bluntly. 'I think she'd have me back, despite what's happened. But we'd have to leave Greencroft.'

'Why?' asked Elizabeth. 'You're an important part of the business there now. You wouldn't have to go.'

'I would. Mary wouldn't have me there if you were around. And if for any reason you decided to go away I doubt that your father would want me. I doubt he'd want me to stay anyway. He'll be back by now, God knows what he'll be thinking. No, I don't think that's a possibility. We'd have to go.'

'Where to?'

'I'd find somewhere. I'm not without skills, don't you worry. No references, that could be a problem. And I wouldn't get work above ground, it would be at the face again. Perhaps that's my place, really. It would be a pity to leave. The kids like it at Greencroft, they enjoy the school. It's far healthier than any other pit village I've seen. It would hurt them to go.'

'So stay.'

'I can't, I've already told you that.'

'Stay with me.'

Thomas thought for a while.

'How could I do that? What would happen to Mary? What about the boys? I couldn't leave them, you know I couldn't leave them.'

'You wouldn't have to. You're not looking at all the possibilities Thomas, you're not thinking properly. What would happen if you went to see Mary and told her that you didn't want to go back to her but you wanted Matthew and David to come and live with you? With us?' Thomas was shaking his head before the sentence was finished.

'Oh no,' he said with certainty, 'not that. It would kill her. Or she would kill me, one of the two. I couldn't do that to her, she loves them as much as I do. That isn't a choice, I thought you'd know that.'

'I do Thomas, I wanted to make certain that you knew that as well. I'm trying to see things from everyone's point of view. Would Mary accept you living with me and her retaining the use of the house? And the children living with her some of the time, with you the rest of the time?'

'I don't know Elizabeth, I don't know! I've been married to her for almost ten years and I'm only realising now that I don't know her!'

Margaret had not mentioned her pregnancy to her husband. He had been, since his return from London, almost kind to her. Perhaps that was due to his father's presence, although the old man was rarely up before noon and his first act of devotion was a visit to whichever bottle he had left half empty the night before. Henry still came to her each night. He still hurt her sometimes, but with less frequency than in the past, and his blows seemed softer. And he drank, almost as much as his father, and he talked to her. He told her who he had slept with when he was away, apart from Maichamps. He told her of the boys and girls, and others whose sex was impossible to tell and unimportant for the acts they carried out. He made unfavourable comparisons between her and them. He chastised her for going to bed with Maichamps, then announced that his friend would soon be returning to aid them both in their search for pleasure. And if she was good, if she was very good, then Maichamps and he might just, as a reward for her behaving herself, take her to London next time. And there she would meet all of their friends, their interesting friends, and go to their interesting parties and do all sorts of interesting things. Margaret swore that she would kill herself before allowing her husband or Maichamps to take her anywhere near London.

At breakfast next day Henry was too pleasant to her. He rose to his feet as she entered the dining room, held her chair for her as she sat down, poured her wine, smiled at her. Sir Charles entered the room shortly after her, pecked her cheek and took his place at the head of the table. She decided to take the opportunity to tell them her news.

'Well?' said Sir Charles. 'There's obviously some reason

why you've had me woken so early in the day. I hope that it's a good reason.'

'Of course father,' said Henry, 'It's news which should certainly interest you. I thought that . . .'

'I have some news as well,' interrupted Margaret. Henry smiled poisonously at her.

'I'm sure father and I will be pleased to hear your news in a moment. But there are important matters which we need . . .'

'This is important too, Henry. It concerns both you and your father. You see, there will soon be another generation of Makemores.' She blushed into her napkin then looked up again. 'I'm going to have a baby.' Henry coughed and splurted wine over the tablecloth. Sir Charles looked at Margaret, looked at Henry, then threw his napkin in the air.

'That is indeed wonderful news!' he chortled. 'If it's a boy you must call him Charles, I insist! Oh well done my dear, well done!' He waltzed around the table to hug her, squeezed her tightly and breathed alcohol fumes into her face, then continued his dance to stand before his son.

'Well done old man!' He shook his hand violently. 'I didn't think you had it in you.' He laughed. 'But we must celebrate. Champagne is due I think, if we have any. Do we have any Henry my boy?'

'I doubt it father. We seem to have very little to drink at all, at least since your return. Perhaps plain wine will do for the moment. I've always been led to believe that it doesn't do to celebrate too far in advance of a birth. So much can go wrong these days, isn't that right Margaret?' He glanced at her; more pleasant smiles could be seen on death masks. 'But nonetheless, well done.' He raised his glass to her.

'Tell me,' he said, 'how long have you known about this good news?'

'I've suspected for some time Henry. About a fortnight.'

'And you didn't tell me of your suspicions?'

'I wasn't certain.'

'I see. The child's physiology will be examined with a great deal of interest I would say.'

'You've been learning new words my boy,' slurred Sir Charles. 'Would you mind translating into English for your ignorant old father.'

'Oh, merely an exercise to determine whether a child most resembles its mother or its father. My friend Maichamps will, I am sure, show particular interest in the latter.'

Margaret blanched. She had not, for some illogical reason, considered that the father would be anyone other than Henry.

'But you said that you had news as well,' said Sir Charles. 'Come on, out with it. I'm well awake now, it's a pleasant day, so I shall go out riding this afternoon, and I don't want it to be spoiled by my being over-curious at some little tidbit of gossip you've forgotten to mention.'

'It was nothing father. Margaret was quite right to interrupt me, my information is insignificant in comparison to hers.'

'Henry, you are tiresome at times. Tell me. Tell me now and tell me quickly or I shall take my riding crop to you.' It was difficult to tell whether Sir Charles was serious; Henry decided to err on the side of caution.

'Very well father,' he sighed with indifference. 'I trust that it will not be too unpleasant for dear Margaret, and I must point out that I have not had this information confirmed by a worthy source. It appears, however,' he leaned forward conspiratorially, 'that Margaret's sister was discovered in a, how shall I put it, sexually compromising position,' he giggled at his own play on words, 'with one of her father's hired men, a Mr Thomas Armstrong by name. The two of them have disappeared together, their whereabouts unknown. Mrs Armstrong and her children are being consoled at the home of Mr Proudlock, the preacher. A sad tale, *n'est-*

ce pas? Still, one good thing comes out of it. Thomas Armstrong was the leader of Waterhouse's dance team, their reliance on him is considerable by all accounts. The dancing championship is this weekend; I stand to make a large sum of money now that he's out of the way.'

'Excuse me,' Margaret cried, stood up and ran from the room.

'Was it something I said?' asked Henry.

'What do we do now then?' asked Stew. 'No Thomas, no musician. We don't stand a chance.'

'Is it really worth going?' said Len. 'I mean, Thomas held everything together.'

'I'll call it,' said Willie. 'Davy can come in as number five, that way there's only two of us not used to our places. There's bound to be a spare musician there somewhere, or we might be able to borrow somebody from one of the other teams.'

'I can see that,' said Rob. 'Silas Bompas offering to play a set of jigs for us!'

'Not him,' countered Willie, 'but we'll find someone. Look, I'm prepared to work at it if you lot are. It'll be difficult, I know that, but we can at least try. What do you think?'

There was a chorus of weary ayes.

'I'm not dancing in this, mind,' said Len. He took off his ring and threw it onto the table.

'Me neither,' said Willie. 'We can send them up to the Hall addressed to Mrs Kearton.'

'Here's mine then,' said Stew. Davy added his to the collection and they all turned to look at Rob. He shrugged.

'Mine's already pawned,' he explained, to the others' amusement.

'How's Mary taking it?' Stew asked Willie as they shuffled into position.

'I don't know,' Willie answered, 'I can't really tell. She keeps on bursting into tears, but then she'll be alright next minute. She tries to be brave when the boys are around, but they've no idea what's going on. They're confused, they keep on asking where their Dad is.'

'I hear you and Thomas had a bit of a do,' Davy said.

'Not really. I hit him once or twice but he wouldn't fight back. They saw me do it, Mary and the boys.' He shrugged his shoulders. 'It was wrong of me, I know that, I shouldn't have done it. But I was so angry.'

'And nobody knows where they are?' Stew again.

'No. Mr Waterhouse and his brother have been searching everywhere. Somebody thinks they saw them at the station, heading for Durham. Once they got there they could go anywhere.' He appeared to be thinking, and when he spoke again he tried filling his voice with enthusiasm; his efforts were not wholly successful. 'But listen, we're here to dance, not talk! We'll have to practice by numbers, but we'll go slow to start with. We've got two days to get this ready. Howway then.'

'Just one more thing,' said Rob, 'there's a rumour going round that Mary's pregnant. It's not true is it?'

'There's always rumours going around about lasses being pregnant, especially when something like this happens. I've always thought meself that they're best ignored.'

'You mean it *is* true,' Rob persisted.

'Aye,' said Willie wearily, 'so Mary says, and she should know. Thomas is probably the only one who hasn't heard about it yet.'

'Why's Dad gone away?' Mary and her sons were in bed together. David was asleep.

'I've already told you that son.'

'I know. But I didn't understand, not properly.'

'It's a difficult thing to explain, because I don't really

understand myself. I can't tell what he's thinking.'

'Has he gone away with Elizabeth?'

'Yes.'

'Because he loves her?' Mary winced at the word but continued her explanation.

'I don't know if he loves her or not. I don't know if she loves him. And "love" is such a funny word, it means different things to different people.'

'Do you still love Dad?' Why, thought Mary, do children ask such awkward questions.

'That's difficult to answer, Matthew. I don't know that either. I think I do, but I can't be sure. Sometimes you don't know how much you love someone until they tell you how much they love you.'

'But Dad might not know either,' suggested the young boy, taxing his and his mother's powers of logic. 'Both of you might love each other, but not know how the other one really feels.'

'Yes, you could be right there. We'll just have to wait and see.'

'Does Uncle Willie still love Dad?'

'I imagine so. He's your Dad's brother, isn't he. Sometimes brothers fall out with each other, a bit like you and David, but they still love each other.'

Matthew's brow furrowed as he puzzled over whether he really did love his younger brother.

'He was hitting Dad very hard,' he said, concerned.

'He was angry, he didn't know what he was doing. It's so easy to hurt the people you love most of all. Your Dad hurt Willie, and me, without even knowing what he was doing. That's why I've been crying a lot. And that's why Uncle Willie was hitting your Dad. Somehow I think your Dad will forgive him.'

'Do you know where Dad is?'

'No, I don't. I'm sorry son, I don't seem to have many

answers for you. You see, when your Dad had problems in the past, anything that worried him, he found it difficult to talk about them. It usually helps when you have a problem, to talk about it to someone, but your Dad couldn't do that for some reason. Instead he used to go out, by himself, and talk about it to himself. Then he'd come back an hour or two later and be right as rain! He didn't need anybody, or at least he thought he didn't need anybody, to help him. So he might be doing that. He might be wandering around somewhere, talking to himself. He might get himself sorted out and then appear on the doorstep, pleased to see us. I think we'd be pleased to see him as well, don't you?'

'I would. I miss him.'

'I miss him too!' said David's small voice.

'So do I,' said Mary to herself as she settled her sons down to sleep for the third time that night.

'I'm going out for a walk,' said Thomas.

'That's a good idea, a breath of fresh air would be welcome. I'll just get my coat and then . . .'

'Elizabeth.' She looked up.

'Elizabeth, I think I'd like to go alone, if you don't mind. I need to think, I need some time by myself.' She had one arm in her sleeve.

'That's alright,' she said taking off the garment again. 'I don't mind. You're right of course, you do need to think seriously about what to do next. We can't stay here for ever, can we? I don't suppose you know how long you might be.' Thomas shook his head. 'It's just that I don't want to worry about you, and I'm certain you're not fully well again, and . . . And I just want to be certain that you'll come back.' She ran to him, hugged him, looked up into his face.

'When Mary found us,' she said earnestly, 'when you followed her, it was me who actually sent you after her. I thought that you wouldn't come back, but you did. Now you're leaving again and I'm frightened again. Come back Thomas, even if it's to tell me that you're going away for good. I need to know.'

'I'll come back,' he said. 'I promise.'

Elizabeth had books and newspapers to read but was unable to concentrate on any of them. The few days she had spent with Thomas had served to remind her how much she loved him. Even in the midst of his depression, when he was surrounded by conflicting emotions and worries about his family, he was kind to her, gentle, undemanding. They had slept together for comfort; neither had felt the need to make love, it would have been inappropriate. And just as she had cared for him when he was hurt and ill, so he had soothed her brow with cool water when she complained of head-aches each afternoon. Strange stabs of pain had clouded her vision, forced her to draw the curtains, and these had been followed the next morning with sickness though she had eaten little and taken no alcohol at all. And yet, despite his displays of kindness, she had come to the conclusion that he did not love her. She was sure that he did not love Mary more than her; the question was not whether he loved one woman more than the other, but rather if he was able to give himself wholly to that emotion at all.

He was thoughtful, but his thoughts were his own and divulged to others with great reluctance. He was kind, very much so, but the kindness seemed born of his need to do what he considered was right and just. He did not lack emotion; on the contrary, he could be moved to tears by an act of tenderness, to rage by injustice; he could be soothed by music and made to laugh by clever words. He could be warm, he could be loving, but she doubted that behind those emotions there was true love. She read it in his eyes. It was not that he was incapable of loving. If she had from him half the love he had for his children she would have been content. She would be content to spend her life with him even if he did not love her.

At the beginning, when they had been drunk with each other's presence, addicted to their own lust even, she had read into his words and his letters a love which she now believed he had never intended offering her. He was in love with the idea of romantic love, secret assignations, the swearing of oaths, writing ingenious, tedious sonnets to a woman who could never be his. But now that this romance was proving to be a reality he was having difficulty in coping with what he had done. These at least were Elizabeth's feelings. She lay down on the bed and closed her eyes. She wanted, more than she had ever wanted anything else in her life, Thomas to come back to prove that her feelings were wrong.

Had Thomas been aware that Elizabeth thought him incapable of giving his love to her or to Mary he might have laughed. He was more of the opinion that he loved too many people, each of whom had sunk a poisoned dart into his flesh and was tugging on the cord attached to his or her own arrow. The pain and confusion he was feeling made it impossible for him to form any coherent thoughts; waves of raw emotion, guilt, anxiety, anger, self-hate, tumbled him down the steep streets towards the quayside. His actions since that fateful night in the barn had been those of a madman, that much was clear to him. But could a madman recognise his own insanity? And could he then cure himself? The world he now inhabited was not his own, all values were reversed, all normality scorned.

He stumbled into a pub, one of many punctuating the warehouses and merchants' offices down by the grey water. Perhaps, if nature had indeed turned her back on him, alcohol would bring lucidity and the answer to his problems.

After three pints of ale the room had taken on a more homely air. He had become used to the smell of unwashed bodies; even the painted prostitute at the end of the bar had assumed more muted, pastel tones. He could hear foreign voices in the general hubbub of conversation, French and some Slavic tongue, perhaps Russian or Polish. He tried to listen more closely, but realised that the beer had affected his powers of concentration. His fifth pint was now half empty. Two seamen in matching uniform, blue trousers and white shirts, rolled up to the bar. The prostitute made as if to approach them but was waved back.

'No time love,' said the first sailor, bearded, middle-aged.

'That's certain,' said the second who was much younger, in his early twenties. 'We're on the *Lady Montague* and we're sailing on Tuesday night, and there's one hell of a lot of work to do before then!' Their accents bore a hint of the south of England.

'Excuse me,' said Thomas, 'I know that name from somewhere.'

'What name's that me lad?' asked the older man.

'"Lady Montague,"' Thomas replied.

'That's not surprising. It's the name of a ship, an ocean-going steam yacht to be precise, the most modern vessel of its type. It's been mentioned in all the papers, so they say. Nothing but the best materials used in its building.'

'And only the best men in its crew!' laughed the younger man.

'No,' said Thomas, 'I'm sure I would have remembered if I'd read about it. Here, let me buy you another one. I'm curious now.'

The seamen were not about to pass up the chance of free ale and accepted Thomas's invitation with alacrity. They moved to a table by the window.

'I suppose,' said the elder in a slow, resonant voice, 'you might just have recognised the name as being that of the owner. "Lady Montague" is also a person, or so rumour has it. She's . . .' His sentence ground to a halt.

'Come on Sam,' said the young sailor quickly and eagerly, 'You're not usually caught for words when you're talking about the W.O.B!'

'I know Harry, but I'm trying to be polite. After all, we don't know this gentleman here. He might be her brother!' They snorted into their glasses at the thought.

'Or her fancy man!' Thomas joined in the laughter, though he wasn't sure why.

'Or even her son!' Sam slapped at the table, Harry clutched his sides. Thomas waited for them to calm down.

'What's she like then, this Lady Montague?'

'The boat or the woman?' asked Harry.

'They're the same,' said Sam. 'Painted bright colours, fast, they both look good but they're damn difficult to control . . .'

'. . . And never ready on time,' added Harry.

'That's right,' added Sam. 'Do you know, we were meant to sail a week ago and was the tub ready, was she buggery! We were up all night finishing off, loading supplies, polishing decks. But we knew what the W.O.B. was like . . .'

'W.O.B?' queried Thomas.

'Woman on Board,' answered Sam.

'Whore of Babylon,' muttered Harry under his breath.

'Quite,' Sam continued. 'Now where was I? Oh yes, we just managed to get things ready when her ladyship appears, comes on board, takes one look at her cabin and complains about the colour of the wood! It's too dark! And that sets her off, she goes round from bows to stern finding one fault after another then demands that it all be put right within three days! Now it's not our job, we're paid to sail the bloody thing, but there's no chance of us going back to the yard and getting it done, there's no time. And who's paying us?'

'W.O.B!' they chorused together.

'So we get down to work again, finish in time again, and what happens? Her bloody ladyship's dog's not well! So we've buggered ourselves for nothing! It's a madhouse, I tell you!'

At the mention of the dog Thomas's memory clicked.

'That's why I recognised the name!' he said, and told the sailors about the day his sons rescued the dog and were thanked profusely, while his actions in preventing injury to the dog's mistress were ignored.

'That sounds just like her,' said Harry. 'She's more of a bitch than her dog.'

'I don't know if I'll ever forgive you,' said Sam, 'rescuing her like that!' They began laughing again, Thomas with them, slapping each other on the back.

'Whew!' said Sam. 'I haven't laughed so much since the bosun fell in the bilges.' He wiped the tears from his eyes; his face was red. He addressed Thomas.

'Look mate, we've really enjoyed ourselves but we've got to go. We were only meant to be away for a few minutes. Thanks for the drinks, if we're ever back here we might even repay the compliment.'

'You're welcome,' said Thomas. 'Give my regards to the W.O.B!'

The seamen rose to their feet and left and Thomas's gloom returned immediately. He went out into the night, smelled the river air. For a few minutes he had forgotten his troubles, but they had been waiting outside like vultures, and no prey easier than him had passed by. The sun had set not long ago, and over to the west Thomas could see, on the south side of the river, the dark shape of Peelwell Hill. In – what, two days' time? – he should have been there, dancing. He wondered as he made his way back, up Dog-leap Stairs, how they would manage without him.

The streets were darkening rapidly. Shadows of monsters

masquerading as people hung in every corner, the glow of a cigarette or a dim gaslamp picking out some small detail. A pair of red-glossed lips smiled at him, taloned fingers beckoned; a fist clenched, white eyes glared. He turned up the collar of his coat and passed quickly by, found his way to the warmth of the well-lit hotel, hurried through the welcoming doors.

'Thomas Armstrong,' said a familiar voice. 'Oh, Mr Armstrong, I'm so pleased I found you . . .'

Elizabeth woke at midnight. She was alone, Thomas had not returned. She turned onto her face and began to cry.

She was awake again at dawn but waited until the cathedral bells chimed six before gathering together her few belongings, the clothes she had bought for Thomas, and making her way downstairs. She would go home, beg her father's forgiveness. He would probably want her to leave, for her own good, and she would do whatever he wished. She would urge him, however, to allow Thomas to stay at the pit, for his family's sake.

The hall porter called as she passed by.

'Mrs Armstrong!' Elizabeth felt the pain. It had been her idea to register in that name. She should have chosen something neutral.

'Do you require any breakfast Mrs Armstrong?' She shook her head. The thought of food made her feel ill.

'I have a message for you.' He handed her an envelope from the rack behind his desk then sat down again, oblivious to her presence. Elizabeth moved to one of the chairs opposite the desk. Only Thomas knew that she was here. Only Thomas knew that they were registered as Mr and Mrs Armstrong. She looked at the envelope again. On it the words 'Elizabeth Armstrong' were written, but in a hand which was most certainly not Thomas's. She ripped open the envelope, took out the piece of paper within, and began to read.

'Something has come up, my love, something which I must deal with immediately and alone. I shall explain everything when I see you. Meet me at Peelwell farm. You should find it without any problem. Do not tell anyone where you are going and bring this note with you. I love you, now and always. Thomas.'

Once again the handwriting was not Thomas's. Nor was the style of writing, it was too brief, truncated. Elizabeth was unsure what to do.

'Is there anything I can do for you Mrs Armstrong?'

'No, no thank you.' She headed for the door then turned, walked swiftly back to the desk, a new purpose in her stride and in her voice.

'Yes! Yes, there is something you can do. Please would you summon a cab?'

A minute later a hansom drew up and Elizabeth climbed inside.

'I'm not sure where it is,' she said to the driver, 'but I need to go to Peelwell. Peelwell farm, please.'

John and Edward Waterhouse were taking tea together.

'We know nothing for certain,' said the elder brother. 'All we have heard is rumour, and malicious rumour at that. Nothing is proven.'

'John, John, we must face reality.' Edward's voice was conciliatory.

'Granted, neither of us has spoken with Armstrong's wife. Given the nature of the matter, I'm sorry, the alleged matter,' he corrected himself, anticipating his brother's objection, 'I feel it would have been wrong of us to subject her to an inquisition. But we have questioned his brother who has reported the woman's discovery most convincingly. Why would she lie? Why else would Elizabeth and Armstrong disappear together?'

'We don't know that they have disappeared together,

Edward. That's the whole point I'm trying to make, we don't know. They may be in two entirely separate locations. It's possible that Elizabeth is being held against her will. Damnit, we don't know!'

'I'm sure that the authorities are doing everything possible to find them, I've no doubt that . . .'

'Edward, it's the bloody Jubilee tomorrow! The authorities could not give a damn about searching for Armstrong and my daughter for two reasons. The first is that they're too busy making preparations for this stupid celebration! And the second is that they believe, as do you, no doubt, that they are together, incommunicado, enjoying each other's company while the rest of us kick our heels in desperate ignorance! They don't care Edward, they don't care!'

'We are, I regret to say dear brother, powerless in this.' Edward moved to his brother's side, put his arm around his shoulder.

'I'm sorry John. We have no choice. We must wait. And pray.'

'I think this must be it,' said the cab driver. He had brought his horse to a halt at the start of a deep-rutted track bordered by tall overgrown hawthorn hedges. In their shade long grass was struggling to find a way up into the sunlight. Elizabeth climbed out and looked down the lane.

'Couldn't you take the cab down there?' she asked, opening her purse to pay him.

'Too rough,' the driver replied, fishing in his pocket for change, 'springs would go. There *is* a house there, I can see buildings.' He was speaking from the roof of his vehicle; Elizabeth could see nothing from ground level.

'Could you wait?' she asked, hoping to appeal to the man's courtesy with her helplessness.

'Sorry Missus,' he replied, 'I'll have to get back. If I'd known it would take this long I wouldn't have brought you out here in the first place.' Courtesy was obviously not an essential qualification for becoming a cabbie. Elizabeth watched as he pulled on the reins, turned the cab around and headed back up the hill to the village. She looked around her nervously.

Peelwell Hill was not large, but there was no other similar natural outcrop anywhere on either side of the Tyne. The cabbie had had no difficulty in reaching the village but had been forced (to his own shame) to ask directions to the farm. He found an answer only from the third person he stopped. Everyone in the village seemed to be in a hurry, making preparations for the double celebration which the morning would bring. The most important of these was undoubtedly the rapper championship. Locks of crossed swords could be seen everywhere, hung outside pubs and shops and even the undertaker's. Buntings and banners were strung across the street (there was only one street) and on poles leading the eye onto the hill itself. Halfway up Elizabeth could see that a wooden platform had been built in the bowl of a natural amphitheatre. Marquees had been erected, wooden benches and seats were being carried up the steep paths by a swarm of schoolchildren. Higher up still, on the flat top of the hill, a wooden castle perched. That was evidently the bonfire which would be lit to celebrate the secondary event of the day, Queen Victoria's Golden Jubilee.

The track to the farm bent around the base of the hill, and as she carefully stepped over the muddy ridges and hollows of the path Elizabeth caught glimpses through the hedge of the buildings the cabbie had mentioned. There were slates missing from the roof of the house and the adjoining barn, and most of the windows appeared to be broken. The path was difficult underfoot and twice she fell. Only then did she notice the ruts broken in one or two places; a vehicle had passed that way not long before.

The hedge gave way to a tumbledown stone wall. On one

side the field had been left to grass, on the other cows were head down in the afternoon sun, tails beating the still air. The heat was oppressive, far too warm for June, threatening thunder. A wooden gate, its timbers rotten, lay open before her. It led into a farmyard whose cobbles had long ago ceased to fight the invasion of weeds. A wagon, two of its wheels missing, its paint flaking, lay drunk against one wall of the barn. There was no door to the barn, no door to the house, and a swallow dipped under the lintel below which a window ought to have been. Surely, Elizabeth thought, this was the wrong place. Why would Thomas want to meet her here?

There was no sign of him. She yelled his name and the empty barn mocked her in its echo. Perhaps she was early? She reached for the note in her pocket, read it again despite having memorised it. There was no mention of any time, just the place. She decided to explore the house first.

The open doorway led into a small hall. There was a door on the left, another on the right, and stairs straight ahead. The stairs were lop-sided, as though some supporting timber had given way to woodworm, rot or old age. From behind the right hand door she thought she heard a sound, a soft sound, nothing more than a scratch. She turned the handle carefully and pushed the door open, peered in to catch the briefest flurry of movement out of the corner of her eye. There was another door in the rear wall, partially covered by a ripped, faded curtain, and she crept across to it, found it open. She was nervous, sweating, unable to breathe. The room beyond was dark; the shutters had been nailed closed. She took a step forward, stretched out her hand to the side and felt a sharp pain, heard a hiss of anger, saw a streak of black bolt for the exit. She calmed her heart, examined the cuts on her palm. It was not the first time she had been clawed by a cat, the beast had obviously been intent on capturing the swallow chicks which even now were boasting of their safety in their mud nest high up in the corner of the room. The scratches were a welcome sign that the demons her mind had been conjuring were imaginary, the reality mundane.

The room to the other side of the stairs was empty and part of its ceiling was missing; she could see up to the bedroom above and beyond, to the sky. That left the stairs. She tested each one gingerly. If this was the wrong place, as seemed increasingly likely, if she fell and hurt herself, no-one would know. She could break a leg, break her neck, die, and no-one would find her. And, she thought wryly to herself, there was not even enough meat on her to feed the marauding cat.

There were two doors again at the top of the stairs. That to the left was closed and led anyway to the room with no floor and no ceiling. Behind the other was the familiar scratching sound she had heard before, the sound of a cat trying to find an alternative way out of a room.

'Come on puss,' she cajoled, 'I won't hurt you, even if you scratch me. Come on.' She pushed the door wide and it complained on rusty hinges. There was furniture in this room, she could see a dressing table and a wooden chair. The bottom of a brass bed crawled into her vision as she slowly moved into the room, and . . . She stopped in horror. There was a body on the bed. It was Thomas!

She rushed to his side. He was pale, at first she thought that he was dead, but his skin was warm and a strong pulse beat at his wrist.

'Oh God,' she said, 'what's happened to you? Who's done this to you Thomas?' There was a strange, oily smell in the air, a smell which clung to Thomas's cheeks and made her feel dizzy. She tried to move him though she knew that he was too heavy for her to carry, found that one hand and one foot were manacled to the bed.

'Oh Lord!' she said, pulled at the chains. They would not

give way. She slapped at Thomas's face.

'Wake up man!' she cried. 'For Christ's sake wake up!'

She felt an arm around her neck pulling her upright, throttling her in the process, and a knee in the small of her back preventing her from twisting away. She heard a voice forced from between clenched teeth, 'How good of you to come Elizabeth,' it growled, dripping irony. And she smelled that smell again, but stronger, in the dirty cloth which was held up to her mouth and nose and pressed hard against her, and she watched the grey, cracked ceiling move down to meet her in loud and strident silence.

Chapter Nineteen

For you and I are past our dancing days.

Romeo and Juliet
(William Shakespeare)

Elizabeth woke to Thomas's voice.

'Thank God you're awake! I thought he'd killed you, you were so quiet, so still! Are you alright? Elizabeth, for Christ's sake say something!'

She looked for him, eyes barely focused, saw a shadow which might have been him.

'Fancy meeting you here,' she giggled, then went back to sleep.

She woke again, her head aching. This time she stayed awake. She forced her eyes open. She was lying on the bed, Thomas at its foot.

'Nice to have you back,' he smiled. 'Your head'll probably be sore. It doesn't last long though.' His voice was a whisper. Elizabeth tried to sit up, found that she had been manacled in the same way as Thomas had been to the head and the foot of the bed.

'Where is he?' she asked.

Thomas shook his head, 'I don't know. We were alone when I woke up. I don't even know where we are.'

'Peelwell,' she answered, 'an old farm. I don't think anyone ever comes here. I take it that it wasn't your message. The one that told me to come here.'

'No, not mine. I didn't have a chance to leave a message. Does anyone know you're here?' His voice was worried, urgent.

'Only the cabbie who brought me,' she replied, testing her chains, 'and he'll have seen me as a fare, nothing more. What happened to you Thomas? Who's doing this? Why?'

'I don't know the answer to the last. As for the who, it's a man called Maichamps. I met him at the ball we went to, at the Makemore place. He joined me and Willie and Dad on the balcony, to watch the dancing. I'd never seen him before and I'd never seen him since, until last night. I got back to the hotel and he was there in the lobby, waiting. I was surprised to see him, but he said he had some news for me, about Mary and the children. He told me to go with him and I did just that, I thought they might have had an accident, or that the kids were ill. He got into a carriage outside the door and I followed him. He helped me in and put a cloth across my face, I thought it was an accident, that I'd stumbled, and the next thing I remember was waking up here. I don't even know the man. Why the hell would he want to keep us prisoner? Why here?' He reached up with his free hand, squeezed the bridge of his nose.

'Do you know him?' he asked, raising his head to look at her.

'I've never heard of him,' Elizabeth answered, her helplessness and fear evident in her voice. 'When I arrived I found you on the bed, exactly where I am now. I thought you were dead. He must have crept up behind me and used whatever it was to knock me out too. Thomas, he must be mad. I'm frightened!' Thomas twisted his body round. With his free hand he could reach through the frame of the bed-end, and she stretched down to touch him. Their fingertips curled into one another.

'It's alright love,' said Thomas, 'we'll make it. We'll make it, don't you worry.' He slumped back to his position on the floor.

'I've already tried to get loose. The chains are too strong and the bed feels as if it's made of cast iron. What about you?' Elizabeth tried her bonds.

'The same,' she said, 'they're tight round my wrist and my ankle. What about the bed itself, will it come to pieces?'

'I've already looked. It's bolted and the bolts are rusted in place. And even if I could undo them we've an arm and two legs attached to this end, your arm fixed to the head. What could we do?' He lay back, tried to think of another path to freedom.

'Was there anyone about, when you arrived? A farmer perhaps, somewhere in the fields?'

Elizabeth shook her head.

'Why do you think he's got us here?' she asked. 'Why us? Could it be your wife or your brother asked him to do it?'

'No, they wouldn't do that.' His face slumped, as though reconsidering whether Mary or Willie could possibly have had some part in this.

'No, I can't see that at all. It was at Makemore's dance I met this Maichamps, it's more likely to be something to do with him. I mean, what have we got in common, apart from us being lovers? It's either the mine or the dancing, one of the two. Does your father have any enemies?'

Elizabeth appeared shocked by the suggestion.

'I don't think so. I'm sure it's possible, it's always easy to upset someone when you're successful in business and my father has been successful in many areas. I suppose someone could be jealous of him. But why kidnap us?'

'It might not be us,' said Thomas, 'it might just be you. I could have been a very handy way of getting you to come here, nothing more. Your father might have received a note by now, "Pay us fifty thousand in return for your daughter". He's probably getting the money together this very minute.'

'Yes, perhaps,' said Elizabeth, unconvinced. 'But you mentioned the dancing as well. Surely no-one would keep us prisoner just to stop the team doing well in the competition?'

'You'd be surprised at what goes on,' said Thomas. 'After all, your uncle and Henry Makemore have got a bet, haven't they? There's a lot of betting goes on anyway, and Makemore was always fond of gambling, so you told me. What if he's over-reached himself. He might stand to lose a lot of money if we won, if his team lost. I think I'm the only one who realises how good we are you know, we could win that competition!' He corrected himself. 'Could have won. It's a possibility, that's all. Just another idea.'

They lapsed into silence once more. The length of the shadows, the angle of the light which roamed the room, showed that it was late evening. The world outside was filled with a familiar warm, summer drowsiness of birdsong and insect buzz, the distant low of cattle. The house clicked and groaned in chorus as it settled for the night. It was Elizabeth who first heard the slow tread of footsteps on the stairs.

'Oh my God,' she cried softly, 'he's coming!'

'It might not be him!' hissed Thomas. 'It could be someone else come to look for us. Just wait!' The door opened slowly and a tall figure entered. He was wearing a cloak, the hood of which hid his face in shadow. In one hand he carried a small leather bag, similar to those used by doctors. In the other was a pistol, its muzzle pointing directly at the bed. The figure stood, watching carefully, saying nothing.

'Is that you Maichamps?' said Thomas, his voice little more than a croak. There was no sign that the figure heard anything.

'What do you want from us?' asked Elizabeth nervously.

The hood moved slightly, as if its wearer had tilted his head to see Elizabeth better. And then he moved, placed the pistol and the bag on the dressing table by the door. Still with his back to them the cloak was removed and draped over the cracked mirror to reveal a tall, angular body clothed in a neat, black, conservative suit. The bag was clicked open and a number of bottles and vials taken out, arranged neatly in rows on the flaked varnish of the dressing table.

'I trust that you are both comfortable,' came a rounded, deep, almost accentless voice.

'What are you going to do with us?' blurted Thomas. 'Why did you bring us here? Elizabeth left a message for her father telling him where she was going! They'll be here soon!'

'I think not Thomas,' the voice chuckled. 'You don't mind if I call you Thomas, do you? I feel I know you so well. We have a great deal in common you know. Isn't that right Elizabeth?' He turned round quickly and sat down, straddled the chair back, stared at Elizabeth. She whimpered, swallowed quickly, backed away from him as far as her chains would allow.

'My dear, you look as though you've seen a ghost!' He laughed, but the laugh held no humour.

'I'm afraid, Thomas, that you should not count on any dashing rescue. Elizabeth was always so obedient, she will have done exactly as she was told. No-one knows that you are here. But forgive me, Elizabeth and I have a great advantage over you, is that not right my dear? Perhaps you ought to introduce me to your paramour?'

'I know who you are Maichamps,' said Thomas with false bravado, 'I don't need any introduction.'

'No Thomas, you only think you know who I am. Elizabeth also thinks she knows who I am, although even she may be mistaken. It is only good manners, however, that she be given the opportunity to explain.' He smiled gently.

'Elizabeth?' The word was an invitation, a prompt. A threat. And Elizabeth began to speak.

'Thomas, remember I told you about when I was married?' Her voice was low, she spoke quickly and did not take her eyes from the figure before her, nor did she wait for Thomas to reply.

'I told you about being kept prisoner. I told you about the things I was made to do. I told you that I killed the man I thought I loved, the man who said he loved me. I was wrong Thomas. I should have stayed and stabbed him again, I should have made sure he was dead. I should have cut his throat, because I now know that I didn't kill him. He's here now, in this room with us. It's my husband Thomas, Eamon Kearton. This is him.'

She burst into tears, a paroxysm of sobbing brought to a halt by Maichamps' slow, sardonic applause.

'Well done my dear, well done! A magnificent performance, worthy of a far larger and more appreciative audience than this! But I am, I must confess, a little disappointed. I had looked forward to seeing Thomas's reaction when he found out that you had a husband.' He licked his lips, rubbed his hands together.

'I have spent some happy hours,' he continued, 'picturing his face when he learned of the despicable acts you were forced to commit. But you told him! Such courage! Such love! Ah, it even touches the heart of a hardened cynic such as myself.' He shifted slightly in his seat, turned his attention to Thomas.

'And you Thomas, she told you all of this? She confessed her sins and still you pledged her your undying love? You are truly a man of courage. Stupid perhaps, but with courage.' He shook his head sadly.

'Why have you brought us here Maichamps? Or Kearton, whatever your name is.'

'A good question Thomas, a good question.' He lifted his

hand to his chin, stroked his neck as he considered his response.

'First of all, the name. Maichamps will do I think. It is me in my most recent incarnation. I always feel it so important to have a name which suits one's character, one's sensibilities. That's why I change my name so frequently, it reflects the chameleon in me. In fact I feel a change coming at the moment, but Maichamps will suffice at present.' He looked at Elizabeth again.

'Eamon Kearton is long since dead. And as for your question about the reason for bringing you here, well, that is very difficult to answer. I'm not quite sure myself why you're here. Nor am I sure what I will do with you.' He stood up so suddenly that the chair almost fell over.

'That's not quite true,' he said, pacing the floor in front of them. 'I don't know exactly what will happen to you, that much is, I suppose, a statement of fact. I do know, however, that you will die. So there you are. You have the destination; only the route remains to be determined.'

Elizabeth began to cry again, but more softly.

'That still doesn't tell us why,' said Thomas. He was surprised at the calmness in his own voice.

'You are a curious soul Thomas. What with Elizabeth's expertise and your natural inquisitiveness I'm sure you must have enjoyed each other's company in quite a spectacular manner. I do wish I could have seen you together.' He ceased his walking, looked at them carefully.

'I wonder, it might just be possible . . . No, too dangerous. No guarantee that you would both be able to perform. Now where was I? Oh yes, you were asking why it was necessary to kill you.' He moved closer to the bed, but not so close that he was within touching distance. He bent down, as a woman might when talking to a child, or a man stroking a dog.

'I shall answer you, Thomas, by asking you a question which will, unfortunately, propose philosophical points which you will be incapable of understanding but which are in themselves of intellectual interest. For instance, must there be a reason for me wanting to kill you? Is an external stimulus necessary to make a man capable, no, the wrong word, to make a man wish to kill another? Don't worry, I don't expect an answer. You see, neither you nor Elizabeth need a reason, for example, to breathe. An apt choice for an analogy if I may say so. You really have no choice in the matter. The same is true for me; I need no reason to kill you. The act itself is almost second nature to me. Do you understand?'

'I hate you, you bastard,' wept Elizabeth, 'I hate you! I should have finished you off when I had the chance! I should have killed you!'

'A perfectly natural emotion my dear, don't upset yourself over it. Now then, I must confess that I have done a little preparatory work. I've taken the liberty of emptying your pockets of any money you might have, any valuables, jewellery, brooches and the like. There was not, I'm afraid, a great deal to take.'

'I always knew you were mad,' spat Elizabeth, 'but I never thought you'd stoop to being a petty thief.'

'Sticks and stones my dear, sticks and stones. You are, as always, perfectly correct. It pained me to take those little baubles, but it will be necessary to make it seem as though you have been robbed. Murdered and robbed, that is, by a person or persons unknown. Now then, any questions?'

Thomas and Elizabeth were silent.

'Nothing? Really? You're just accepting everything I say? How disappointing! I could be lying you know. I could be about to leave. Look,' he fished in his pocket, 'here are the keys for your manacles. I'm going to put them down on the dressing table for you. There we are.' He looked back at them over his shoulder.

'I could go now. If I did, it would take you no more than

a minute or two to pull the bed across the room and set yourself free. Of course, I will have made my escape by then. Or, on the other hand, I could be hiding outside the door with my little gun. Just as you think you're there, just as the key turns in the lock, I peep round the corner and BANG, BANG! No more Thomas. No more Elizabeth.'

'For Christ's sake Eamon, stop torturing us! Either kill us or let us go!'

'But my dear, can't you see? Killing you will give me pleasure, that much is clear to all of us, but it will be akin to sexual release. You more than Thomas or me should realise that a far more exquisite pleasure is derived from the actions leading up to that intense but, alas, too short elation than from the release itself! And I do find that I am sexually aroused at the prospect, not of your deaths, but of you knowing that I will, eventually, kill you.'

'So you can't manage it any other way?'

'Oh Thomas!' laughed Maichamps. 'So shy, so imprecise in your words! Yes, I can achieve an erection, and ejaculate, by having intercourse in a normal manner. I would add that what I consider normal may not coincide with your definition of the word. I have a penchant for young men.'

'Henry Makemore?' said Elizabeth.

'Oh, welcome back to the conversation my dear. Yes, Henry Makemore is one of my conquests. But then, so is his wife, your sister.'

'I feel sorry for you Eamon,' Elizabeth said poisonously. 'You're ill. You need to see a doctor.'

'Yes, I imagine you're right. But I don't think I can be cured, so all that would happen is that I'd be locked away. I wouldn't like that at all. Life is such fun.'

'We might be able to help you,' said Thomas, 'if you let us go.'

'A new tack Thomas? Sorry, it won't work. You see, I enjoy being like this. I have no conscience, I admit that, but

I delight in the power it gives me over people like you. And Elizabeth, I suppose, although I suspect that she has rather less of a conscience than you, Thomas. No conscience, no guilt. Ah, the freedom of it all!'

'I can see that there's no point in arguing with you,' said Thomas. 'There never was any point in arguing with a madman.'

'Not so Thomas, not so! If I am mad, and I do not necessarily concede that point, then my insanity is of such a pure and logical kind that it should be susceptible to detailed questioning and dissection. If you can persuade me, through logical argument, that I should let you go, then I will do so!'

'He's lying Thomas,' said Elizabeth. 'He lied to me in the past and he won't ever change. He's going to kill us. We might as well accept that and let him get on with it.'

'Brave words, my darling wife, brave words. And if that is what you wish why should we not commence immediately?' He reached into his bag.

'Do you recognise this knife? Of course, I can see it in your eyes, how could you fail to do so. It is as sharp as it ever was when you last used it on me, I test it regularly. And I can testify to its fitness for its purpose, can't I Elizabeth?' He took off his jacket and undid the buttons on his waistcoat, threw that on the floor and pulled his shirt from his trousers to expose his chest.

'You see, Thomas, the damage your beloved is capable of causing?'

There was a livid scar under his ribs, another running from the waistband of his trousers to his sternum; both were red and jagged. He let his shirt fall. His movements were swift where before they had been leisurely and relaxed.

'Should we see, then, what else this blade can do?' He strode to the bed. Elizabeth rolled desperately away from him but he reached out and hauled her back.

'Stay where you are Thomas!'

The knife was at her throat.

'I won't kill her yet unless you make some silly attempt to come to her rescue!'

Thomas had been about to do so, was ready to launch himself at Maichamps knowing that such an attack would have been suicidal. He sank back to his place but did not relax.

'That's better.' Maichamps' voice was calm again.

'Now then, a sharp knife like this could do immeasurable damage in the wrong hands, is that not so? Just a flick of the wrist, like SO!' Elizabeth screamed as he jerked the blade down the front of her waistcoat, severing all six buttons in one movement.

'Or even like THIS!' Her blouse fell open in the same way, 'or THIS, or THIS!' He slashed at her clothes and, where the knife would not cut, ripped them until they lay in shredded tatters to either side of her body. Her cries for pity served only to drive him faster, and, realising this, realising that one slip of the knife might kill her, she forced herself to be quiet, forced herself to be still. Eventually he stopped. She heard his breathing, opened her eyes to him as he stood over her. His chest was rising and falling, a vein was beating rapidly in his temple, his lips were pulled back to reveal his teeth.

'Elizabeth,' he whispered, 'you are indeed still beautiful!' He reached towards her and placed one dry, warm hand on her belly. The other still held the knife, and with its point he traced whirls and loops over her breasts, around her nipples and down to her navel. He changed his grip, smiled at her, and began to increase the pressure with his knife hand.

'Please Eamon,' she whispered. His smile broadened.

'Pleading with me now, are you?'

'Yes,' she answered, 'but not for me.' She swallowed, closed her eyes, clenched her fists.

'Eamon, I'm pregnant.'

He took his hands away from her, staggered back to his seat.

'You?' he laughed, 'pregnant? Oh my oh my, that is rich indeed! And who is the lucky father? Is it the brave Thomas here?'

'Yes.'

'Are you sure now? I mean, the four times you were caught when you were with me it could have been any one of a dozen or so different men! It might even have been me!'

'Thomas is the father.'

'Why didn't you tell me?' cried Thomas painfully. 'Why didn't you tell me? I thought you said that you couldn't . . . That is, after he'd forced you to . . .'

Elizabeth looked at him, tried to smile.

'Don't let me stop you,' said Maichamps, 'go ahead with your little discussion. It all adds to the drama. What a fortunate fellow I am, three for the price of two!'

'I didn't think it was possible,' said Elizabeth to Thomas, 'but I was late and then I began to feel ill in the mornings. I knew when we were away together but I didn't want to say anything, I didn't want to make you think that I was putting any pressure on you. I wanted you to come back because you loved me Thomas, not for any other reason. I'm sorry.'

'Oh, this is so good, so good!' Maichamps chortled, his chin on the back of the chair, his feet tapping the floor with excitement. 'This is such sweet news! Oh the irony of it, the wonderful, wonderful irony of it!'

'Why should that make you so happy?' asked Thomas. His voice was surly, low.

'It's just that I love secrets Thomas, nothing more, nothing less my fecund friend. And of course I would not be playing the game unless I had my own little secrets to tell, and do you know what my lovelies?' He giggled again. 'I have!'

'I have two secrets to tell you,' he continued, standing again. 'One concerns you,' he pointed at Thomas with his knife, 'and the other concerns you,' the blade moved and he peered down its edge at Elizabeth. 'I wasn't actually sure whether I would tell you these secrets, but you've entertained me so well that I feel I must do so. But which revelation should come first? Oh, the choice is so difficult!'

He walked around the end of the bed to stand gazing down on Elizabeth. Her arms were still in her tattered sleeves, she still wore her shoes and stockings, but she was otherwise naked.

'You remind me so much of your mother,' he said, his tongue dripping poison. He stood before her, arms crossed, head tilted to one side. Elizabeth could see that he was waiting for the reaction she had so nearly given him. She bit back her words.

'Such strength of character as you wish to display may be seen as admirable by some. I consider it nothing but foolishness. I shall therefore move to your companion.' He smiled benevolently down at Thomas.

'It would appear that we are suffering from a rash of pregnancies, Thomas. Is it something in the air? Your brother and his charming young wife are expecting, is that not right? And then there's Henry and the beautiful Margaret, though I must confess that I may have contributed as much as Henry to that.' He looked at Elizabeth who closed her eyes to him.

'An interesting thought, eh my dear? And then there's you two, happy young parents to be. Would a fourth pregnancy be a coincidence, I wonder? Would there be any truth in the rumours I heard before I set off to search for you? Obviously you haven't heard them, have you? They were circulating at Durham, that's where I was when the information was passed to me. Waterhouse's daughter run off with a man called Armstrong they said, and I thought it was Margaret and your brother, Thomas! But no, a little further careful questioning and all was revealed. It was you two! And what else was I told. What other little rumour did I hear? Should I be telling you this? But of course I should, you won't hear it from anyone else, will you! It appears that this Armstrong, this Thomas Armstrong, has left his wife behind and she's up the stick.'

'Liar!' yelled Thomas, 'you damned liar! I'll kill you for this, I swear it!' He lunged at Maichamps but was brought short by his chains.

'Threats I'm afraid you won't be able to carry out, Thomas. And please temper your language. I know that Elizabeth doesn't mind indiscriminate use of the vernacular but my ears are particularly sensitive. Anyway, there we are. You're to be a father again. Twice in the space of ten minutes. Life is interesting. While it lasts.'

He moved to the window at the rear of the room and looked out.

'The sun will be down shortly,' he said. 'The witching hour will be upon us and I must, alas, commence my duties. You see behind me,' he gestured carelessly at the dressing table, 'the means by which I shall dispose of you. Chloroform will render you insensible. There are various other potions which can kill slowly or quickly, with or without pain. I have not yet decided which ones to use, nor do I know which of you will be the first to receive my administrations. The second will, of course, have the benefit of seeing the first die. Perhaps I shall toss a coin to determine which of you may have the honour.' He reached into his pocket and brought out a penny.

'Would either of you like to call?' he enquired politely. 'No? Very well, I shall do the job for you. Thomas is heads, Elizabeth tails. Here we are then ...' he threw the coin upwards and caught it neatly '... heads! It looks like you first I'm afraid Thomas. Please don't struggle, I might have to shoot you instead, and that would upset me a great deal, such a speedy, messy death. It might upset me so much that

I would be forced to allow Elizabeth's agonies to linger for some considerable length of time. Now let me see, what can I choose ...' He turned to the bottles on the dressing table.

'Eamon,' said Elizabeth, 'you mentioned my mother.'

'So I did my dear, so I did. But I judged from your silence that you had no wish to hear my little secret. Is that not so?'

'No Eamon, I want to know. What do you know about her?'

Maichamps looked at Elizabeth, then at the ceiling, then at the floor. He shook his head and walked toward the dressing table, then appeared to change his mind. He came back, stood in front of her and began to speak in schoolmasterly tones.

'Very well my dear. I shall answer your question and prolong your lives by a further ten or fifteen minutes each.' He hooked his thumbs into the waistband of his trousers.

'You see, I am something of a detective. For example, when I knew that you and Thomas had hidden yourselves somewhere I deduced that it would have to be Newcastle, Durham was too near, too small. I set off immediately, not even leaving word for Henry, whom I was about to visit, that I would be late. Once in the great city itself I asked at the station for the addresses of hotels which were not top grade, but certainly reputable. It seemed to me that you would be likely to visit such an establishment. There were no more than six of these, and I visited each in turn asking the head porter, in return for a donation to his trouser pocket, whether a couple of your description was present. I did think that you would have had the sense to register in a name other than Armstrong, but it made confirmation of your presence so much the easier. The rest you know.'

'And did you find out about my mother by means of similar detective work?' Elizabeth asked.

'No,' said Maichamps, 'quite the opposite. I knew all

about your mother. To be more precise, I should say that I actually knew her.'

'You met her?' said Elizabeth incredulously.

'Yes,' Maichamps smiled, 'I suppose you could say that. She was the child of a soldier and she married a soldier. I don't know his name. They were posted to India and there the soldier died.'

'Was that my father?' asked Elizabeth urgently. 'I never met my father. Was he the soldier?'

'No, he wasn't. And please don't interrupt, it's getting dark and I dislike working in the dark. It's too easy to make a mess when you can't see what you're doing. Now then, your mother Emily's husband died in India. She was young, the other soldiers' wives cared for her, helped her. The regiment offered to send her back to England but she declined; there was nothing for her to return to. There was a small pension, she bought a piece of poor land. She was courted by a number of the men, former colleagues of her husband, but none was to her liking. Then one day she met a young lieutenant, a dashing blade.' He turned to Thomas, 'I'm sorry if it seems like one of those cheap penny reads, but it is true.' His attention was redirected swiftly to Elizabeth.

'She fell in love with this lieutenant, fully aware of his station, knowing that for him the relationship meant nothing. She became pregnant and he abandoned her. Her former friends would, of course, have nothing to do with her. The wives despised her; the regiment cared only for the reputation of its officers. Only the men came to see her, the other ranks. They brought her food and money because her land, it turned out, was virtually worthless. And in return she gave them all that she had: her body. Like mother like daughter, my dear Elizabeth. A whore begets a whore. Perhaps it's as well that you and your child will not be able to continue the tradition.' He scratched his nose, as if bored with the tale.

'She had no prejudices, your mother. She was popular with the well-to-do Indian merchants as well as British soldiers; white flesh was considered something of a delicacy. She eventually had enough money to pay for the passage back home. That's when my task became difficult, you see I had no knowledge of what she did after returning to England. But I persevered, examined the shipping records, followed up one lead after another. Imagine my surprise when I found that she'd married John Waterhouse. And my sadness when I discovered that she had died. I did so want to meet her again.'

'Why? Why did you want to meet her again? How did you know her in India? Come on, you might as well tell me everything, you're going to kill me anyway!'

Maichamps looked thoughtful.

'Yes,' he said, 'that is true. It's also a possibility that my story could be a lie, of course. That's for you to worry about. But only for a short while.' He smiled in anticipation.

'I was, I will admit, very keen to see your mother again. I had some unfinished business with her. I think that I would have killed her, though I was not sure of that at the time. Having found that she was dead I had no choice but to take my revenge upon her daughters, and this I have been doing and will continue to do. You may rest assured, Elizabeth, that Margaret will suffer far more than you ever will.'

'Why? What have we done to harm you?'

'Nothing. Nothing whatsoever.'

'Then why do this to us?'

'I must. I swore revenge. It's a matter of honour.'

'What did she do? What could my mother possibly have done to you to make you hate her, hate me and Margaret so much?'

Maichamps stared directly at Elizabeth.

'Look at me,' he said, 'and then consider your own face.'

He placed the knife flat on her stomach, its point resting midway between her breasts, and held it there with his left hand, held down her free hand and bent his lips to hers. His kiss was gentle at first; then his tongue forced its way into her mouth. She tried to turn away but felt the point of his knife against her, so sharp that it must have drawn blood. He backed away and looked down at her. When he lifted the knife it was tipped with red; he bent down once more, this time his head was directed to her body. Where the sharp pain of the knife's blade had cut into her she felt the warmth of his mouth, and when he stood again he opened it to reveal his tongue, like the knife, coloured with her blood. He swallowed lasciviously.

'Bastard!' she swore.

'Is that any way to greet your brother?' he replied.

Elizabeth's eyes narrowed.

'Liar!' she spat, then looked at him carefully, reconsidered.

'How do I know you're telling the truth?'

'You don't. That's the beauty of it.'

'It can't be true. She would have told me. Why didn't she tell me? She said nothing, nothing at all! She would have said something, I know it!' Confusion possessed Elizabeth's face.

'Why?' said Maichamps. 'I was part of her past. Why should she care about me? Still, at least I knew who *my* father was. I found him quickly, he was the lieutenant who first made her pregnant. I was her eldest child. He died slowly.' He crossed his legs and leaned back in the chair, deciding that further explanation was required.

'You see my mother, your mother, had no-one to look after me while she was flat on her back with her legs open, working. But the wife of one of her Indian friends would take me home, care for me. She could have no children. She grew very close to me. I suppose I grew close to her too. When my mother said she was going back to England this woman was distraught. I was, to all intents and purposes, her son. She had given me more of her life than my real mother ever did. She begged my mother not to go. Then, in the end, dear Emily decided to leave me behind. Our mother was a good business-woman. She got a very good price for me. Prime white boy. I found a copy of the receipt one day, when I was sixteen. I think that was the last time I cried.'

He stared into the middle distance, his eyes unfocused, hands hanging loose at his sides. Thomas thought that he might drop the knife and he tensed himself for the leap which might gain him the weapon.

'What happened to her? The Indian woman?'

'She died. When I was eighteen. Dysentery, not my doing. Her husband turned me out, he'd only tolerated me in the house because of his wife. He had someone else in mind to take her place. That's when I came back to look for my real mother and father.'

'What's your real name?'

'I don't know. I never knew the name I was christened with, I was always called Sanjay around the house by my other mother. In England I change names regularly. They're unimportant, labels, nothing more.'

'I'm sorry.' Elizabeth's voice was quiet.

'Yes, I do believe you are. Even after what I've done to you, even when you know what I intend doing to you, you still have sympathy for me. Well I don't want sympathy, I don't need it.'

'If I'd known I would have tried to help you.'

'Would you? Would you even have believed me? Do you believe me now?'

'Yes.'

'Then there's no accounting for your stupidity, dear sister, because I feel nothing for you, not even contempt.'

He reversed the knife, began to circle her nipple with its rough, ribbed handle.

'You used to like that,' he said. 'You used to beg me to use my tongue on you, just there.' He moved to her other breast.

'But this was always the more sensitive of the two. Can you feel it beloved?'

'Yes,' she croaked, 'I can feel it.' Tears fled from her eyes.

'And does it feel good?'

'It feels ... It feels ... God, don't torment me like this Eamon!'

'You feel good, I can tell. I know you Elizabeth, I know you too well. It's the whore in you!'

Thomas raised his head to watch. Though still held by the manacles and by Maichamps' hand at her wrist Elizabeth was beginning to move. Her eyes were closed and her head was rolling slightly from side to side.

'But you used to like this more,' Maichamps continued, and the knife moved quickly down, over her stomach; he pressed it over the mound of her pubic hair. Elizabeth gasped.

He repeated the motion and she raised her hips as he pushed down; when the knife handle was pulled up again she pushed in the opposite direction. Again and again he pressed against her and she pushed back, her moans and groans, her urging and protestations growing louder as their motion grew faster. Thomas watched in horror, not believing what he saw. What he had thought were groans of pain now appeared to be moans of pleasure; Elizabeth had seemed to want to avoid contact with the hilt of the knife, now she courted its company.

'No!' cried Thomas. 'No!' His cry went unheeded. Elizabeth's hand, her free hand, clenched at Maichamps' wrist.

'Touch me!' she said. 'Oh please, touch me!' She managed somehow to move his hand to her breast where it grabbed at her as though it would pierce the flesh. Her hand went back to its place, held tight to the bed-head.

'Do it!' she cried. 'Do it! You know what I like!' He moved closer, leaned over her and bent his head to her breast, began to bite and pull at her nipple. As Thomas watched he saw her head lift swiftly; her eyes met his and pleaded with him, sought his understanding; and her fist balled and plunged into Maichamps' groin.

There was a soft grunt of pain from Maichamps. Thomas leaped over the end of the bed, ignored the metal cutting into his wrist and ankle, and reached for Maichamps' head. He could see blood on Elizabeth's thighs, he prayed that it was from Maichamps' hand, that Elizabeth's blow had caused him to grip the sharp blade. He grabbed Maichamps' hair and pulled his head towards him, was surprised at the ease with which he slid across the bed to meet him. He banged his head hard against the cast iron grille of the bed-end, then again, and again.

'Thomas!' screamed Elizabeth. 'Stop! I think you've killed him!'

Thomas stopped. There was blood on the sheet, on the grille and on his hands and on Maichamps' head. Maichamps' body was limp. Thomas let go and rolled off the bed to lie, exhausted, on the floor.

'Are you alright?' he panted. There was no reply, only the sound of crying. He raised himself to his feet and looked at the bed. Elizabeth was trying to crawl as far away from Maichamps' body as possible but, restricted by her chains, she could not rid herself of his legs and lower torso.

'The keys!' Thomas said. 'Elizabeth, the keys are on the table! If I can drag us over there ...' First he heaved Maichamps onto the floor. Elizabeth stopped crying as the weight left her, looked at Thomas.

'I had to do it,' she whispered, 'I had to pretend. He would have killed us. I was thinking of you, I had to do it for you Thomas.'

'It's alright love, you did just right. Come on, see if you can help me with the bed. You were wonderful, I knew you were pretending. You've got blood on you, are you alright? He didn't do anything, did he? With the knife?'

Elizabeth shook her head.

'His blood, not mine,' she said. There was even a touch of pride in her voice.

Between them they managed to drag the bed to the drawers, and, once there, unlocking the manacles was easy. Elizabeth fell into Thomas's arms. They held each other tight, his hands moving down the tatters of clothing at her back.

'It's alright now,' he murmured, 'it's alright. There's nothing else to be frightened about. We're safe now.'

Elizabeth pulled away from him, then looked over her shoulder at Maichamps' body. She limped over.

'We'd better look for your bag, love,' Thomas continued, 'see if we can find some clothes for you. Did you see it anywhere?'

'Thomas,' came Elizabeth's quavering voice, 'he's still alive.'

'That's good,' said Thomas. 'We can use these manacles to tie him. He can be arrested, put on trial.'

'No Thomas. He was going to kill me, and you. He was going to kill our child.' She reached for a pillow from the bed, a damp, mouldy, misshapen thing, and dropped it onto Maichamps' head.

'Don't try to stop me!' she said as Thomas made a move towards her.

She placed the pillow over Maichamps' nose and mouth, knelt on his chest and, putting her arms and hands firmly on the grey linen, pressed down hard. Maichamps may have been unconscious but his body, in its struggle to hold onto life, acted by reflex. He began to buck and wriggle in an effort to throw the weight from him, his hands reached up to drag the pillow from his mouth and nose.

'Thomas!' yelled Elizabeth. 'Help me!' Thomas's actions were instinctive too. He flung himself to the ground, added his weight to Elizabeth's, pinned the thrashing arms and legs to the ground. They lay there for a full five minutes after all motion ceased. Thomas was the first to rise.

'Your bag's over here,' he said stiffly, 'by the door. Best get some clothes on.'

They sat on the bed. Thomas had covered the corpse with a sheet while Elizabeth had dressed. They had examined the bottles on the dressing tables and found, apart from the chloroform, some concentrated acids and alkalis, a liquid smelling of bitter almonds which Elizabeth said was prussic acid, and a juice which Thomas thought was belladonna. Still in the case were various scalpels and sharp knives, nails and pins, a small hand-operated drill. Elizabeth shivered, then put everything away and slammed the case shut. It was dark. They crept gingerly down the stairs and stood in front of the house, tasting the fresh air of a summer night. Bats dipped and whispered around their heads. From the barn there came the whinney of an impatient horse.

'Now what?' asked Thomas.

'We hide the body and leave,' said Elizabeth.

'Hide it? Why can't we just tell the police and the magistrates? We haven't done anything wrong.'

'We've murdered a man.' Elizabeth's voice was almost matter-of-fact.

'Aye, in self-defence.'

'It wasn't self-defence Thomas,' said Elizabeth primly, 'he was unconscious. He may have deserved to die, I won't argue that, but it wasn't self-defence. We murdered him. And I still think we should get rid of the body.'

'Where?' asked Thomas.

'How the hell should I know? Bury him! Dig a hole! Does

it matter?' Thomas could see Elizabeth's face in the dim light, could tell that she was near to breaking.

'I'll sort it out, then,' he announced. 'Listen, can you hear that horse in the stable? That must be how he got here, Maichamps, after he got rid of the carriage which brought me. I'll load him onto the horse. Up on the hill,' he gestured towards Peelwell, 'there's lots of open shafts. Some are adits, they go in parallel to the ground. Others are vents, they go straight down. I'll drop him down one of those, he'll never be found.'

Thomas was amazed at the ease with which he could assume responsibility for the disposal of the body. He seemed to be able to adapt readily to matters even this far outside the law, and was surprised that he felt no remorse at all for Maichamps' death.

'You'll have to make your own way back to Peelwell. Are you sure you don't want to involve the authorities?'

'I'm sure.' Thomas had to bend his head to hear Elizabeth's response.

'Well in that case you'd better find somewhere to stay for the night. See if there's a pub, leave word for me at the bar, I'll join you when I can. Have you got that?'

Elizabeth nodded. She appeared drugged.

'Go on then. Leave it to me to tidy everything up here. It's probably best not to see what I've to do. I'll see you later.'

'Promise?'

'Aye, unless I'm kidnapped again. Go on, away with you.'

Elizabeth headed for the gate which showed the track leading to the road; Thomas made for the barn and the horse within. Neither turned to wave.

Chapter Twenty

—◆◆◆—

Nunc est bibendum, nunc pede libero pulsanda tellus.
'Now for drinks, now for some dancing with a good beat.'

(Horace)

Margaret waited in her room, waited for the door to open, waited for Henry to visit her. There was no doubt that he would do so, and so she had prepared herself. Two large glasses of gin had already passed her lips, she was pouring the third as Henry entered.

'For Christ's sake woman put the bottle down!' he shouted as he stormed into the room. 'You're becoming a sot!'

'Only when you're here,' she answered him, quietly. He stopped abruptly and stared at her, his hands on his hips.

'Oh, a quick reply from the wit of Makemore Hall. How long did it take you to think of that? Have you been practising the line all day?'

His temper seemed worse than usual, but he did not approach her. Instead he paced the floor at the foot of the bed, hands thrust deep into his pockets. His lips were moving but no words could be heard. When he looked at Margaret his eyes, though almost hidden in the deep shadow of his forehead, held a glint of fire which she had not noticed before. He recommenced his dogged marching to and fro.

'I wish you wouldn't do that,' she said, 'that walking up and down. It makes me nervous.'

'More nervous than usual?' he countered.

'Yes.' The gin had given her courage. There was something wrong with Henry, something that was affecting him, making him behave differently. Twice she had answered him back, but he had not yet struck her.

'Is there something troubling you?' she asked. In their private exchanges, away from servants or Sir Charles or those of Henry's friends who visited him infrequently, they used no terms of endearment in addressing each other. There was no sentiment in their voices, they touched each other only when contact was unavoidable or when they had intercourse.

'Damn right there's something troubling me!' he said, altering his path to take him to the bed-side. He grabbed at the gin bottle and drank from it eagerly. Margaret flinched as he slammed it down again.

'You've heard nothing about your sister and her fancy man, I take it?' he enquired. He looked around him, dragged an armchair from the fireside to within a few feet of the bed and sprawled into it.

'There's been no contact,' answered Margaret. 'I don't suppose you've heard anything either? No rumours?'

'Nothing at all. I wouldn't be asking if I knew, would I?' His feet were tapping against one another, his fingers accompanying them, beating out a strange staccato rhythm on the arms of the chair.

'Is there something you wanted to say?' asked Margaret.

'No.' The swiftness of the answer, its brevity, the silence which followed it, all combined to tell Margaret that Henry did wish to speak to her. She waited.

'Maichamps was meant to be here,' he blurted out. 'He

was coming up for the dance championship. We were going together, to watch our team win again.' The 'our' referred to Henry and Maichamps, to Makemore Hall; Margaret was not, probably never would be considered as belonging to the family. She was still considered part of the enemy camp, but whether as a traitor or a prisoner she was unsure.

'The championship's tomorrow. He should have been here two days ago. There's been no word from him. I know that he has other obligations, but it's unlike him to disappear like this without letting me know why. Damnit, I'm worried!'

Margaret wanted to ask a question but was frightened of the consequences of doing so. Henry seemed particularly vulnerable, but that might change, he could become violent without warning. But his silence gave her courage.

'Do you love him?' she said quietly.

His answer was straighforward, honest. It was probably the first time he had been honest with her.

'No,' he said, 'I don't love him.' He raised his eyes, tossed a humourless laugh at her.

'It's impossible to love someone like Maichamps. I think the only person who does love him is Maichamps himself, and even then not completely. He's too divorced from himself, always looking outside himself. He seems to think he's a catalyst, not actually doing anything but, by his presence, his actions, allowing others to achieve some purpose. That purpose usually benefits him, of course, but I don't think that's important to him.' He took a deep breath and looked at Margaret.

'But I still need him. I've come to depend on him. He helps me think, he helps me decide what to do. It doesn't matter if he's not here as long as I know when I'll see him again, and at the moment I don't know. I think that there's something happened to him, I don't know what, and I feel as though something's gnawing my insides out. It's stupid but I can't help it.'

'If it's not love it's something very close,' said Margaret, almost jealously.

'It's not, damnit!' Henry's fist hit the chair, he leaned forward but stayed in the seat.

'It's not love, it's ... it's an addiction! It's like you and that bottle, or me and gambling! I can't explain it, I just need to be with him. Not physically, though I've come to terms with that part of me. I just feel ... lost!' He buried his head in his hands, his fingers clutching at his hair. Margaret pulled the sheets to one side and climbed out of bed, knelt on the floor in front of him. With a great effort she reached out and touched him.

'I'm sorry,' she said. 'I really am sorry. I'm sorry that you feel this way, I'm sorry for the way things are between us. Oh Henry, I used to love you so much!' His hand touched hers.

'I loved you too,' he confessed. She barely heard his next words.

'I still do.'

He leaned forward, placed one hand on her belly. She could feel its warmth through the cotton of her nightdress.

'The child,' he said, 'will it be mine? Or his?'

'I'm not sure,' she replied, 'the two of you were together. It could belong to either.'

'Maichamps and I are so different. I shall know, when the child grows, whether I am the father or not. Even now I am ... unsure of how I will react. I fear for the child, for you, for me. Sometimes I can't control the rage that grows within me. I don't know the cause. I feel that you, my father, those closest to me, are plotting against me, hiding secrets from me. Perhaps that's why I'm driven to consort with Maichamps. There are times when I feel that you would all be better off if I were dead!' He lowered his head to her neck, and she felt his tears run down her breasts.

'Have you told your father the good news?' his voice mumbled. He looked up at her.

'Yes,' she replied cautiously. 'Yes, I've suspected for some time that I was pregnant but the moment just didn't arise for me to tell you. You've been so unpredictable, I didn't know how you would take it. I was frightened of you. But I told my father. It was when you went away to London. I drove out one day to see him. And Elizabeth. They were both pleased.'

'Good,' said Henry, 'and I'm pleased that you told me. You see, I already knew that you'd been to Greencroft at that time, though I wasn't sure why. People tell me these things. They like to keep me in touch with what's going on. I was surprised you didn't say anything to me.'

'I didn't try to hide anything Henry. I stayed the night, I sent back word to say that I was doing so. There was nothing underhand about it, merely a visit. I wasn't even sure that I was going there, when I set off that is. It was almost an accident.'

'I'm not accusing you Margaret,' Henry's voice was steady. Margaret's head had fallen slightly, he lifted it, his fingers under her chin.

'You seem so defensive, a visit to your father's home is nothing to be concerned about. I can understand the reasons you chose to tell him and your sister of your pregnancy before informing me.' Margaret thought she detected a chill in his voice, though his hand was still gently stroking her shoulder.

'Did you see anyone else while you were there?' asked Henry.

'No, not that I remember.'

'Are you sure? Think back.'

'No-one, I saw no-one else. Wait though, I did speak to Thomas Armstrong. Yes, he was in the office at the time and

I spoke to him. I thanked him and his brother for . . .'

'Was his brother there?' The words were like schoolboy-thrown stones, sharp and hard.

'No! Just him! I thanked him and asked him to pass on my thanks, and yours too, to his brother. And condolences on the death of his father. I was being polite, that's all.'

'But you didn't see his brother?'

'Henry, why are you doing this? No, I didn't see his brother!' She was sitting up straight now, her hands fast in her lap, a frown on her face.

'You were fond of Willie Armstrong, weren't you?'

'No, I wasn't!'

His hand moved from her shoulder and twisted itself into her hair.

'Margaret, don't lie! You were fond of him, I know it. You flaunted yourself in front of him. Good God woman, don't treat me like an imbecile. You found him with your serving maid, it was jealousy which drove you to seek my company that night, not any particular fondness for my sparkling wit or Deemster's sense of humour!'

'Yes then, if that's the answer you want, yes I was fond of him. He was interesting to be with. And if I was a flirt at times you deserved it, and he deserved it. I did nothing wrong. You're hurting me Henry, you're pulling my hair!'

He wound his hand tighter, pulled harder.

'I'm hurting you, am I? Well perhaps you'd better start telling the truth! I know, you see, I know what happened! It wasn't Thomas Armstrong you were talking to, it was Willie! Admit it woman, tell the truth!'

'It wasn't Henry, it wasn't! Please, my neck, you're hurting my neck!'

He let go of her hair, stood up and, in the same motion, threw her onto the bed. If she had thought that this would bring relief she was mistaken, for he followed her hard. One hand was at her throat, his body was across hers, one leg thrust across her knees. She couldn't move, could barely breathe.

'You were seen, bitch, you were seen!' he snarled. 'Don't deny it! What were you talking about? What were you telling him? Did you just happen to mention that you were pregnant, eh, the same as you seem to have told everyone else except me? And why was that? Because you know I'm not the father, isn't it! And it's not Maichamps either, you whore! It's him, it's that Willie Armstrong!'

Margaret struggled to break free, managed to loosen Henry's grip on her wrist. With that one free hand she clawed at his face, terrified. He had never been as bad as this before. She felt her nails break the surface of his skin, saw parallel lines of blood along his cheek. He hit her, half a slap, half a punch, and her head rocked to one side. He hit her again and she felt a crack of pain as a bone broke somewhere in her jaw. She could hear someone whimpering 'No, no!' in her small distant voice. She tasted blood.

'You opened your legs for him, didn't you? You couldn't wait to get him inside you! Was he good? Was he better than me? Tell me the truth Margaret!' She shook her head and he hit her again.

'Was he as good as me that night in the quarry? It was clever of me, wasn't it, to have poor old Deemster blamed for that? And all the time it was me who raped you! It was me who buggered you!'

The words registered. Margaret could fight no more, the final blow had been struck. She slipped into brief unconsciousness.

Henry's tears accompanied her return to the darkened room, but bright lights were bursting in her head. She tried to speak and found only incoherent mumblings spewing from her mouth.

'I'm sorry, I'm so sorry!' cried Henry. 'Please forgive me!'

Margaret's brain sent a message to her fist, 'Strike him!'

it said, but she could not move. There was a pain in her chest where he had continued to hit her after her lapse into insensibility. She summoned up the last vestiges of her strength, determined to hurt him as much as was possible before she succumbed once more to pain. But her attack would not be physical.

'It was him,' she croaked. Henry stopped crying, held himself still.

'It was Willie.' The words were badly formed but Henry could hear them clearly enough.

'I had him before you,' she rasped, 'and I've had him since. You're nothing compared to him. He's a real man. He doesn't need to hurt me before he can please me.' Her jaw was askew, her lips bleeding, her face puffed and bruised. She made a last attempt to raise herself to a sitting position but fell back in agony. Henry stood before her, the emotions on his face shifting from hate to revulsion to self-pity. His eyes were wide and wild, he seemed on a precipice, his self-control about to plunge to the depths below.

'Shut up!' he screamed.

'He's so good!' whispered Margaret. 'I want him now!' She licked her lips in a parody of anticipation. Henry reached for the gin bottle at the side of the bed, held it by its neck and brought the base down on the corner of the table. He held the jagged remains above Margaret's face.

'He satisfies me!' she announced with pride, 'and I love him!'

Henry trembled, immobile, for seconds. Margaret looked up at him in triumph; whatever happened next she knew that she had won. With a howl of rage Henry raised the broken bottle higher then brought it, swiftly down into the pillow beside Margaret's head.

'I'll kill him!' he shouted as he ran for the door. 'I'll kill him!'

He stopped on the threshold.

'And then I'll come back here, whore, and I'll kill you!'

There were no hotels in Peelwell, and the three public houses were overflowing with merrymakers. The village was filled with the sound of music from indoors and out, violinists and accordionists playing traditional tunes, a pianist grinding out ballads for a trio singing off-key harmonies, a barrel-organ and attendant monkey drawing a crowd of children. Elizabeth surveyed the scene with despair. There were tents clustered on the side of the hill, some nothing more than sheets stretched over branches, while others were more substantial affairs capable of holding a dozen or more people. Fires had been lit primarily for cooking, since the night was still warm, and the smell of roasting meat reminded Elizabeth that she had not eaten for over a day.

At the first pub she was told politely that there was no room, while at the second the landlord looked her up and down and told her to get out, that 'single women such as her' were not welcome in the establishment. At the third she decided to assert her authority.

'My name is Waterhouse,' she said loudly once she had attracted the manager's attention. 'My father is John Waterhouse of Greencroft, and I sent word two days ago that I required a room for the night. Please show me to it and bring me some supper.' Through her arrogance two serving girls would spend the night sharing a bed, but Elizabeth felt no pity for them; her need was greater than theirs. She ate heartily, left word that if a man came asking for her she was to be summoned immediately, then lay down exhausted.

It was morning when she woke. A pitcher of water had been placed outside her door and she washed herself before descending to the bar. The clock showed shortly before ten but already the room was half-filled with drinkers, some of whom looked, by their general state of dress and the angle at which they leaned against their tables, to have been there all night. The air was sour and unwashed, and when the barman reported that no-one had asked for her during the night she was pleased to leave the room behind.

The scene outside was similar to that she had just left. Dogs sniffed daintily where someone had been sick, a drunk lay insensible across the pavement and passers-by stepped carefully over him so as not to disturb his snoring. The banners strung haphazardly across the street proclaimed (in bright red letters the paint of which was already beginning to run) a welcome to all dance teams, while the union flags fluttering on poles and sticks outside shops and houses had, at their centre, scowling portraits of the black-clad Queen Victoria. Here and there groups of men were talking, one or two already dressed in their dancing costumes. One quintet was walking through various figures of their dance under the guidance of a fat, whiskered captain who had difficulty turning under his own sword.

During the night (or possibly early in the morning, while she had still slept) stalls had been set up on the hillside, each gaudily decked with striped material and selling pies and cooked meats, fresh fruit, spiced buns, wooden dolls ('painted in your own team colours'), cider and milk and ice-cream; a small round-about was already attracting a crowd of children. Elizabeth wandered the grassy slopes watching for Thomas, while at the same time trying to remain as inconspicuous as possible should the Greencroft dancers have already arrived. She did not feel that she would have been welcomed by them.

In the time it took her to inspect the dancing platform halfway up the hill then return to the village the crowd had grown four-fold in size. Although she welcomed this because it decreased the chance of her being seen, she realised that it gave her little opportunity to watch out for Thomas. A worry that something might have happened to him began to blossom in her mind. She had seen two of the shafts that he had talked about, fenced in, certainly, but the timbers making up the fence were rotten and in some places missing entirely. In the dark, with the weight of Maichamps' body making movement difficult, on a steep slope, it was possible that he had fallen. He might be injured with no-one but her knowing his whereabouts, no-one but her able to help him.

She had made up her mind to climb further up the hill, then round onto its steep side, the side that led down to the river, when she saw him. He was climbing slowly, moving away from her. She called his name but there was no response. Even if he had heard her she was in the middle of a crowd, he could not have seen her. He was looking around as he walked, no doubt searching for her as she had been looking for him. Her fears banished, she elbowed her way unapologetically through the mass of bodies around her, headed up the hill to find him. They needed to talk. She felt that they should escape from the vicinity of Peelwell immediately, but the thought had also crossed her mind that Thomas would wish to stay, to see whether his team appeared, to watch them dance. But more than anything else they needed to talk.

A convoy of wagons and carts and carriages had set off early that morning from Greencroft. The dancers had brought along their families and supporters, John and Edward Waterhouse were there, Albie Settle was doing his best to bring a smile to Mary Armstrong's face. She had insisted on coming, pointed out that, if left behind, she would have only her thoughts for company.

A week had passed since she had last seen Thomas. She had believed at the start of the week that, for the sake of the children at least, he would have been in touch. That he had not contacted them was a sign, she felt, that he would probably not return. After all, Elizabeth had money. She could afford to keep him, to take him far away so that they could build a new life together. It had happened before, men had disappeared leaving their wives and families behind. She had never thought that it might happen to her.

She fought back her tears as David clambered squealing over her, Matthew in pursuit. The boys had comforted her, cried with her, tried to understand when she told them what had happened. They appeared to the casual onlooker quite unconcerned with their predicament; one or two people had indeed remarked upon it, and Mary had nodded and agreed with them, said that it was good that that should be the case. But they had not seen them waking in the night and crying for their father, holding tight to her nightgown and begging her not to go away as well, eventually falling asleep only to have nightmares pursue them through the darkness until morning. And while she comforted them, hugged them, held them close, she cursed Thomas Armstrong and wished that he was dead.

She had confessed her feelings to Jonathon Proudlock. He, more than anyone else, had provided her with the help she had tried to give to her children. He had listened, sometimes agreed with her, sometimes pointed out how wrong he felt she was. 'Love and hate are emotions which are, at times, indistinguishable from one another,' he had said, and she realised then that she did still love Thomas. It would have been easier had she been allowed to forget that love; hate was easier to understand. Love served only to add to her confusion. Love and the confirmation that she was pregnant.

Although the children, more than a dozen of them playing in the back of the cart, were laughing and singing happily, pleased to have a day away from school and a holiday, their parents appeared despondent. The dancing practices had not gone well, particularly when there was no music. Willie did not have the same authority his brother possessed, was trying to lead the dance as well as learn a new position. After early failure he was forced to revert to his old place in the dance, prepared himself against all tradition to call from five rather than one. That improved matters a little, but his lack of confidence affected the others. None of them were happy with their performances, and what should have been a journey filled with optimism became a slow march into gloomy self-pity.

They arrived at Peelwell just before noon, the time at which the competition was scheduled to commence. While the Waterhouses' carriage turned to one side to deposit its occupants at the grandstand, Willie went off to seek further instructions. He returned waving a sheet of paper.

'There are twenty-five teams dancing,' he announced, 'And this year they're doing it as on a one-to-one contest. That means two teams dance, one after the other, and the best goes through to the next round. That way the judges don't have to rely on just one performance to pick the best. Otherwise they have to try to remember whether the twenty-fifth team was as good as the first, at least that's what it says here. They judge on timing, stepping, carriage, dress, coordination, complexity of individual figures, and complexity of combinations of figures. And the good news is . . . in the first round we don't have to dance! We get a bye.'

'Great,' said Stew sarcastically, 'that means we only have to dance four times to win.'

'Is it worth dancing at all?' asked Rob disconsolately. 'I mean, all due respect to you, Willie, but we're no bloody good without Thomas, not really. He was the one held us together.'

'Aye, he's right,' added Len, 'we don't stand a chance, we all know that. It's not really our dance, is it, it's Thomas's dance. He made it up, and your Dad, of course, he taught us all.'

'Even if we did win,' said Davy, 'it wouldn't feel right, not without him.'

Willie looked at each of the dancers in turn, allowed his puzzlement, his disappointment, to show.

'Now just hold on,' he said, 'it's only a week since we got together, and decided, we *all* decided, mind you, that we'd go on without Thomas. And we've worked hard, we've worked damn hard to bring the dance round. For Christ's sake, I know it could be better, a lot better, if Thomas was here. But he's not. And instead of Thomas you've got his brother who's not even sure why he's trying to get you to do the bloody dance. He's thinking how easy it would be to say no, let's not bother, it's too difficult, we don't stand a chance. But he's not saying that because he's still got a little bit of pride, he still cares about what other people think, about him, about his family, even about his boss. They're all here today to watch us, lads, *your* families, *your* friends, the Waterhouses, everyone. But if you don't want to bother that's alright with me. But you can do your own explaining, right?' His eyes caught the attention of the others; they looked away in turn.

'Right,' he continued, 'so I'll ask again, like I did before, are you dancing?'

'I'll dance,' said Stew quickly.

'Me too,' added Len, almost in the same breath.

Rob and Davy looked at each other.

'It needs all of us or none of us,' said Willie, 'and I won't mention anybody who's depending on us. I won't mention Mary and the bairns, or the lads from the pit, our wives and kids. I promise I won't mention Mr Waterhouse and his brother, I saw them before, they're both here. I won't even mention your own pride, whether you'll be able to hold your heads up in the street again, I won't . . .'

'I'll do it!' said Rob. 'Oh hell, I'll do it, just as long as you shut up!'

Willie smiled, clapped his hand on Rob's shoulder; they all looked at Davy; he nodded reluctantly.

'That's great lads, just great, I knew I could count on you!' said Willie. There was much back-slapping, push and shove and horseplay, ruffling of grease-tamed hair.

'That's all very well,' said Davy, 'but I still say it won't be the same without Thomas.'

'I know,' said Willie, 'believe me, I know.' Whatever his own private thoughts were, he put them to one side.

'Gather round then, lads,' he said, 'and listen in.'

'By my reckoning it'll take about two hours for them to get through the first round, so we'd better meet at two up by the platform. I'll take the costumes up, and, with a little help from my assistants,' Willie looked round to find Matthew and David, 'we'll get the swords there as well. I'll see if I can find a violinist. If I can't we'll have to sing as we dance. Any questions?'

'Are we allowed a drink?' asked Len.

'No more than two,' said Willie. 'We don't want you falling over in the middle of the dance.'

'He does that anyway,' said Rob. The team dispersed.

The early rounds of the competition drew an audience partisan in its support of the respective teams. If your dancers were on stage you cheered; the opponents were booed. If your team wasn't dancing then it was far more interesting to wander around, see the sights, have a drink, play at cards. Those who remained at the arena were offered a wide variety of styles of dancing. Willie, keeping watch over the costume box and swords in his new role as team leader, resisted the temptation to stray.

Willie's limited experience of rapper had been through performing with the Greencroft team and watching the side from Makemore's pit, and he was surprised at the wide variations in skill displayed by those he was watching. One of the teams seemed to have no dancers younger than fifty, all of them rather stoutly built, and the dance was taken at a pace so leisurely that he was sure he could have waltzed to the jig. But the next dancers were young, so young they could have still been at school, and although they lacked experience they more than made up for this in the enthusiasm and exuberance they showed.

'Which pit are they from?' he asked the man sitting beside him whose yells of encouragement showed clearly which team he supported.

'Pit? Why no man, they're not pit lads! They're from Whitley and Robsons, shipbuilders. Most of the teams here today aren't from collieries either, they're from steelworks and foundries, chemical firms, shipyards. There's even a team of schoolteachers, I ask you man, what's the world coming to? Still, I suppose it's just as well. After all, everybody knows rapper's dying out in the pits.'

Having delivered his sermon he hurried down to congratulate his team, who had just won through to the next round. Willie was left to watch the next match. There were young and old, fit and unfit, dancers short, fat, thin, tall, talented, practised, nervous and over-confident. One dancer, in what had, until then, been a good performance, turned the wrong way into tying a Nut. When held up, the swords slipped apart to fall loudly onto the floor; the dancers walked off in disgust. Another team found that its musician had started too fast and, even worse, was playing inexorably faster with each turn through his one tune. Some of the dancers tried to keep up with the music, the others thought that by stepping more slowly they might bring the music back down to the right speed. The confusion led to the death of the dance by disintegration.

Some men were drunk. One fell off the stage. Willie estimated that half of the teams ought not to have been there, and that the Greencroft team, if Thomas had been dancing, would have proved to be as good as, if not better than, the top four or five. As they were they would be fortunate to win through their first match, unless they were competing against one of the poorer sides.

Willie's attention was drawn away from the dancing. Mary and Abigail were approaching, each of them clutching the hand of one of Thomas's children, each child holding, equally tightly, a large ice-cream. They were all laughing. But Willie's eyes were not the only ones attracted by the laughter. Higher up the hillside, hand held to his forehead to divert the sun's rays, Thomas Armstrong was watching his family.

'Have you been down to see them yet?' asked Elizabeth.

She was standing behind Thomas, unseen by him, but he did not seem surprised that she was there.

'No.'

'Are you going to?'

'I don't know.'

Elizabeth sat down beside him, close to him but without touching.

'Did you manage to dispose of . . .?'

He nodded, knowing what she meant.

'I was worried about you when you didn't appear. What happened?'

'Nothing. I did as you told me, I got rid of the body. And then I just wandered around. Thinking.'

'And did you come to any conclusion?'

'I thought I did. I thought about what I'd done to Mary and the boys, and I thought about what I'd done to you, and your family. I thought about how much I'd betrayed you all, betrayed your love and your trust, betrayed my duties as a father and a husband, as an employee, as a lover even. And I thought about last night. I realised that I'd helped kill a man. Oh, I know what you'll say, that it was you who killed him. But I would have done it too, when I was hitting him, hitting his head against the bed-end, if you hadn't stopped me. I didn't know I could do all of these things. And I'm not sure I like the man I've become.'

'And did that help you decide what to do, accepting that you were to blame for all the problems in the world since man first crawled from the swamps?'

Thomas ignored Elizabeth's tone.

'I thought you'd all be better off without me. You'd be able to go back to your father and I'm sure Mary would find someone. Willie would look after her for the moment; he'd do more for Matthew and David as an uncle than I could ever do as a father. I'd just go away, find work somewhere else. After a while, a year or two, you'd all forget I'd ever existed.'

'You are feeling sorry for yourself, aren't you?' said Elizabeth. 'Is that the best way of dealing with your problems? Forgetting about them? Just leave them all to someone else, they'll cope. I'm sorry, I must have made a mistake. When I saw you sitting here I thought you were someone I knew, someone I admired, but I must have been wrong. He's nothing like you, nothing like you at all. His name's Thomas Armstrong, and I happen to love him. If you see him around anywhere tell him I need to speak to him! Tell him I'd rather he went back to his wife and family and forgot all about me than end up like you!'

She jumped to her feet and marched back up the hill, taking up a position fifty feet away from him. He did not even turn round, remained mired in his own misery. In the arena below Willie was preparing his team for the dance.

'Right lads, I don't know what this other lot are like, they got a bye as well. I've found a musician, he plays the squeezebox. He's . . . well, he's better than nothing. The only thing is, he doesn't feel confident enough to pick up the rhythm from our stepping, so we'll have to let him start and then follow him. We're on first. Don't forget, the most important thing is . . .'

'Start together, finish together, and smile in the middle,' intoned Len, Rob, Stew and Davy in unison.

'Righto then. Let's go!'

Even the most benevolent of critics would have found it hard to spot more good points than bad in the dance. Willie was nervous, and his nervousness was transmitted to the other dancers. The music altered its pace throughout the dance, and they missed out a large section when Willie forgot the instructions. Davy, too, was suffering. Brought in at the last moment, he had always feared the backward somersault of Double Tumbler, had fallen twice in practice. Stew did his own backward flip and the others moved around him.

'I can't do it!' muttered Davy.

'You what? Step again!' hissed Willie. What could he do? He knew of no other way out of the figure.

'You'll have to do it!' he said, 'you won't fall!'

'I can't!'

'Come on! Step again everybody! How the hell do we get out of this?'

'We'll bring the swords down to the ground,' said Stew breathlessly. 'Just step over them!'

They did so and managed to move on, to progress to the end of the dance. They turned, applauded the accordionist, then left the stage.

'I'm sorry,' said Davy, 'I just couldn't do it. I would have fallen, I know it.'

'It's alright,' said Willie, 'it doesn't matter. I don't think any of us can claim that they were doing well out there. We'll just have to see what the others do, and if by any chance they're worse than us and we get through to the next round, we'll rework the dance, miss Double Tumbler out.' He put his arms round Davy's shoulder.

'Don't worry,' he said, 'don't worry.'

Thomas shook his head as he watched, stood up, looked around him. Elizabeth was still there. He walked up to join her.

'I'm sorry,' he said, 'you were right. It wasn't me there before. Do you mind if I join you?' She gestured to a place at her side, acknowledging his apology, accepting it and inviting him to stay with one easy movement.

'How were they?' she asked.

'Bad. Only half the dance was there, and that half they weren't good at. Willie can dance or call but not both together, he just hasn't got the experience. And Davy's not had enough practice, and his stepping's behind the rest. It was bad.'

'Well, they'll have another chance next year, I suppose.'

'Oh no, they aren't out! They were bad but the other team was far worse, they could hardly stand up! They got through. God knows how they'll get any further though.' They sat in silence. There was a slight breeze, and swifts were hurling themselves screeching around the slopes of the hill. Elizabeth lay back and closed her eyes.

'Have you eaten?' she asked. He seemed surprised by the question.

'Yes, I bought something. Took some money from Maichamps' pocket at the farm. Why?'

'Oh, I'm just concerned for you, that's all.' There was silence again, then Elizabeth took a deep breath, as if steeling herself for an unpleasant decision.

'Thomas, I think it's time you decided what you are going to do.'

'Me?' he answered. 'It's not just my decision, is it? It involves so many other people as well.'

'Yes, but you're the one who's at the centre of it all.' She sat up again. 'Look, I don't have a decision to make. I'm already committed, I'm committed to you. You say "come on, let's go" and I follow. I don't mind where, I don't mind what you want me to do. I love you Thomas, and that's enough for me.'

'How would we live? I can't quite see you as a miner's

wife, and I doubt that your father would be willing to support you, because indirectly he'd be contributing to my well-being.'

'I don't know for certain how my father would react, Thomas. But if he refused to see me again then I'd be happy with you, no matter where we lived. I'd have you. And your child.'

'Yes,' he said, 'I know. I can't even think about that. And Maichamps said that Mary was pregnant too. Jesus Christ, what a bloody mess!'

'You can't believe everything he said,' offered Elizabeth.

'But how do I find out for certain? Go and ask her?'

'Why not? You're going to have to speak to her sooner or later. I just told you that I loved you Thomas, and I told you that I'd come with you now, straight away, if you wanted me to. But if you'd said yes, we'll do that, it wouldn't have been the real you talking. I would have expected you to want to talk to Mary, to see Matthew and David, to try to explain the way you felt. I think you should go down now. And I'm saying that knowing there's a chance you'll see them and you won't come back. That's a risk I have to take, because the Thomas I love wouldn't leave without doing what I've just said. So go on. Now.'

Thomas stood up and pulled Elizabeth with him. He hugged her to him and kissed her lightly on the lips.

'Whatever happens,' he said, 'I love you.'

'Actions,' she smiled wryly to herself as he strode away, 'love me with actions, not words.'

Chapter Twenty-One

The next that I'll call on
It is big walloping Tom;
He's courted two fair women
And durst not marry one.
For if he married one,
The other he would sleight;
And the best thing he can do
Is to treat them both alike.
'The Captain's Song,' Earsdon Sword Dance.
The Sword Dances of Northern England
(Cecil J. Sharp)

Mary was surrounded by dancers and their families. How, Thomas wondered from his vantage point above and behind, would he be able to speak to her quietly without involving the others? It was highly likely that she would cry and be upset, and he had no wish to experience Willie's rather rough protection again. He waited, aware that Elizabeth would be watching him from afar.

Willie was marshalling his men. After resting and agreeing that their next opponents were unlikely to be as poor as their last, they picked up their swords and moved through the dance again, altering it where necessary, missing out Davy's double tumbler. Thomas looked on. The alterations meant that the dance was not as good as it had been; on the other hand, it was now within the capabilities of the dancers and Willie's calling. They were scheduled to dance last in the quarter-finals; a glance at the sky showed that it would be late afternoon, perhaps six o'clock, before their turn. Thomas decided to be patient. Once Mary stood up, and he too jumped to his feet. A call of nature perhaps, or some errand, would take her away from the crowd. But no, she merely stretched and looked around her, confirming that her sons were not too far away, playing safely. Thomas turned his back as her glance swept past him, just as, minutes later, he hid his head in his hands as his youngest son hurtled past him in his search for a hiding place which would evade his brother's seeking.

Eventually the moment came. The dance team moved away, closer to the stage, and most of their followers joined them. Only Mary was left guarding the costume box and sundry items of clothing, bags and boxes and bottles. Thomas swallowed, stood up, walked toward her. Her back was still turned to him. He bent down behind her.

'Hello,' he said quietly. She turned quickly, recognising his voice, then turned as quickly away again. Her hands flew up to cover her mouth, then her eyes as her head bent forward. She began to cry, great shuddering, shoulder-heaving sobs.

'I'm sorry, love,' he said, moved to her side, put his arm protectively around her shoulder.

'Don't touch me!' she spat at him. 'Don't call me "love"! Did you call her that as well?' He took his arm away.

'I'm sorry,' he said again. 'Mary, what more can I say? I'm sorry.'

She managed to bring herself under control. When she looked at him her eyes were red, her gaze clear and direct. Venomous would have been a more appropriate word, Thomas felt.

'Do you think that sorry is enough?' she asked. 'And

anyway, what are you doing here? Have you come just to apologise? Or did you want to hurt me more, by coming back and then going again. Just what is it you want, Thomas? Do you really know?' Her voice was bitter and Thomas knew that he should have expected nothing less.

'I wanted to talk to you,' he said, 'to try to explain to you what happened. I wanted to tell you straightaway but Willie and the preacher wouldn't let me. But you already know that, don't you. I saw you at the window.'

'That was a week ago,' she said. 'Where have you been since then? With her? Is she here? 'Cos if she is she'd better keep well away from me or I'll have her, I swear it!'

'I don't know where she is,' Thomas lied, deciding that some aspects of the truth were best kept hidden, 'and as for where I've been, half the time I've been recovering from the battering Willie gave me, and the rest of the time ... Well, the rest of the time I can't explain, not at the moment. I don't even believe myself what's happened.' He found that he could not look directly at her; she was too strong for him.

'How are the boys?' he enquired.

'I think you've got a damn cheek asking,' she replied. 'For what it's worth, they seem to be alright. They miss you like hell, and they cry a lot, but that isn't surprising when they see how I am. How could you do it Thomas? How could you hurt them so much?'

'I didn't mean to do it. Do you honestly think I set out thinking "Oh, I must do something to hurt Mary and Matthew and David". I didn't mean to get involved with Elizabeth, I didn't seek her out. It just ... happened.'

'Well you shouldn't have let it happen, should you? There was a time, there must have been a time, when you knew that it was wrong, when you should have said "Stop!". But you didn't. You just went on and on, making a fool of me. You're a bastard, Thomas Armstrong, a right bastard!'

He could think of no reply.

'I know,' he said quietly.

'And how long was it going on?' she said. 'Three months? Four?'

'Since Easter. Not that long.'

'So tell me why you're here. Has she got tired of you and your working-class ways? Have you come to ask me to have you back?'

'No, she hasn't tired of me. And I ... I'm not really sure why I'm here. I had to talk to you, to find out how the lads are. To find out how you are. I'd heard ... That is, there was a rumour that you were ... that you were pregnant. I had to know. I need to know, Mary.'

'Does it make any difference?' she sneered. 'Will you offer to come back if I'm pregnant, for the sake of the baby? I've got more pride than that, Thomas Armstrong! If you think I'm going to live with the knowledge that you went off with someone else and came back, not because you loved me, but because I was expecting your child, well, you've got another think coming!'

'Do you want me back?' he asked. Mary stared at him.

'I don't know,' she said, her voice suddenly soft, 'I honestly don't know. There've been times in the past few days when I've anticipated this moment, so I could tell you what I thought of you, so I could tell you to get out of my life and leave me alone. But then there've been times when I've been lying there at night, all alone, and all I wanted was for you to come through that bedroom door again and tell me that you loved me, and I'd just hold out me arms and you'd be there and everything would be just as it was before.' She was beginning to cry again.

'Look what you've done to me, Thomas, look what you've done! I just hope you're proud of yourself!' There was a sudden whoop of delight from the area of the stage. The figures of Matthew and David detached themselves from the crowd and began to run up the hill towards them. Mary took a handkerchief from her pocket and wiped her eyes, blew her nose, tried to compose herself.

'They've won!' Matthew's voice yelled. 'Mam, they've won!' He slowed slightly as he recognised Thomas, then built up speed once more.

'Dad!' he shouted, half turned to his brother. 'David, it's me Dad!'

He flung himself at Thomas, knocked him to the ground. A moment later David too landed from what felt like a great height.

'Where've you been, naughty Dad?' David's deep voice queried from the region of Thomas's midriff.

'Are you back to stay?' asked Matthew's more tremulous tones; older than David, he understood a little more of what had been happening. His eyes were filled with moisture, though he was determined not to cry.

'Hello, trouble one and trouble two,' grunted Thomas from his position of disadvantage at the bottom of the pile. He pushed their questions to one side, asking cheerily, 'How are you?'

'I've had an ice-cream,' said David, 'and Uncle Willie's just won his dance. I've missed you, Dad.'

'I've missed you too,' said Matthew. 'David and me, we've both been sad sometimes. We've been sleeping with Mam.'

'And I wet the bed,' said David proudly, 'twice!'

'Are you going to come back home with us?' asked Matthew hopefully.

'That depends,' said Thomas 'on a lot of things. Your Mam and I have got a lot of things to talk about. I don't know if we'll be able to decide on anything today. It might be difficult to . . .'

'But Dad,' said David, 'we all love you. Me and Matthew love you, and Mam loves you too. I heard her telling Uncle Willie just the other night when I was meant to be asleep but

I wasn't. Matthew was, he was snoring, but I was watching the moon out of the window and I heard her. You did say, didn't you Mam?'

Mary held out her arms to her youngest son.

'Sometimes we say things and we don't really know the meaning of the words, son. Sometimes we make promises we don't keep. Like your Dad said, we need to talk for a while.' They all looked up. The dancers were approaching.

'Yippee!' shouted David, leaping from his mother's arms and cartwheeling down the hill. 'My Dad's back! Uncle Willie, you don't have to hit him this time, he's not making Mam cry!'

'Please don't go again,' whispered Matthew.

'We'll see son, we'll see. I can't promise.'

The group mounting the hill halted. They could see Thomas with Mary and the children. Their faces were raised; Thomas could see them looking at him. The dancers were tired and hot, their shirts clinging to their bodies, but their weariness was now decked with curiosity, anticipation, pleasure even, and concern. Len and Stew were certainly smiling at him, Davy seemed eager to see him, was already wiping the sweat from his hands and face, while Rob had his eyebrows raised in some mute question. Only Willie's face was closed to Thomas, and it was Willie who halted the others then came on, alone at first, but then Abigail moved to join him.

'I didn't expect to see you here,' said Willie.

'I've been watching you dance,' responded Thomas. 'I hear you've got through to the next round. Well done.' Willie seemed pleased to have the conversation on a neutral topic.

'If you've been watching,' he said, 'you'll know we're not dancing well. And we're up against Makemore's team in the next round. I just saw that bastard Bompas, you should have seen the smile on his face. He knows we've not got you, no proper music ...' He looked around; Thomas knew that he was searching for Elizabeth. Abigail nudged him, whispered in his ear.

'How are you Thomas?' she asked, slightly embarrassed.

'Alright,' came the reply. Abigail nudged Willie again. He began to speak, falteringly.

'I ... I want to say that I'm sorry, Thomas, for hitting you like I did. I shouldn't have done it, I just lost my temper. And I know that you weren't fighting back, I could tell, and that made me even more angry. So I want ... to say ... Well, I want to say sorry.'

'There's no need,' said Thomas. 'I deserved it.'

Abigail hurried forward and threw her arms around him.

'Welcome back!' she said, 'I knew you wouldn't be able to stay away for long. We've all missed you so much.'

'Wait on,' Thomas protested, 'I came to see Mary, to talk to her. There's a lot we need to discuss, I don't know if ... That is, I can't say for certain ... It's not up to me alone, we need to talk! Do you understand?'

Abigail looked into his eyes. 'I understand,' she said, and kissed him gently. Suddenly the rest of them were around him, slapping his back, shaking his hand, putting their arms around him. Thomas looked helplessly at Mary, trying to tell her that this was not his doing.

'Thank goodness you're here,' said Stew. 'We can do the full dance, we can show that Makemore lot, we'll beat them then we'll go on to win the whole thing!'

'You can dance instead of me,' said Davy, relieved. 'I thought I was going to break me neck doing that Tumbler.'

'We stand a chance now,' put in Rob, 'a damn good chance. We might need a quick run-through, mind, but we can take them on, I know it!'

'Aye, Thomas,' added Len, 'we've missed you. It's good to have you back.'

'Hold on,' said Willie, 'we haven't agreed yet that he should come in ...'

'STOP!'

Thomas's voice hushed them all.

'I didn't come here to dance,' he said angrily. 'I told you, I came to talk to Mary.' The celebrations stopped. Faces which a moment before had been jubilant were suddenly saddened. The dancers were easily parted by a young boy pushing through them.

'Greencroft Rapper?' he panted.

'Aye,' said Willie.

'You've got five minutes before you're on again. Best get yourselves ready now,' the messenger said, then ran back to take his place at the side of the stage. All around them there was a general move down the hill as the crowd began to gather for the first of the semi-finals. Only around Thomas did everyone remain still.

'Thomas,' said Mary, 'your responsibilities go a lot further than you ever thought possible. Here you are, surrounded by your family and your friends, people who used to love you, who used to respect you. It's still not too late. You haven't lost everything, not yet. It's up to you.'

'You mean you want me to dance?' he said. 'You're the one who wanted me to stop dancing. How can you . . . Hell, I just can't understand you, Mary! What do you want me to do?'

'You can't spend your life asking other people to tell you what to do, Thomas Armstrong! The decision's yours, not mine. But don't expect to please everyone with everything you do. The world's not like that, Thomas.'

'I want to please you, Mary! I want to please you and I can't tell what *you* want! Just tell me. Tell me that you love me!' He was almost in tears, longing for the answer that would make his world right again. She looked at him, looked at him long and hard.

'I don't know,' she said, and turned her back on him.

'Right!' said Thomas. 'To hell with it! My costume had

better be in that chest!' He strode towards it. Only Willie was in his way.

'Do you have any objections to me dancing?' he asked.

Wilie took his time before replying. He allowed his eyes to rove over his brother's face, to see the anger and despair and love which were fighting there.

'No,' he said. 'You'd better call.'

In the grandstand which had been set aside for the more well-off spectators, the local dignitaries and social climbers with aspirations of position, John and Edward Waterhouse were sitting. They had invited the Reverend Proudlock to join them and this he had done, after spending the early part of the day with the dance team. They talked of the day's events until, somewhat uneasily, the preacher asked permission to broach a delicate subject. The brothers looked at each other; John nodded his assent.

'I am aware,' said the preacher gravely, 'that an employee of yours, one Thomas Armstrong, has not been seen by his wife and family for well nigh a week. Mrs Armstrong states that her husband was found, by her, in a somewhat compromising position with another woman, a lady she recognised. That woman was . . .'

'My daughter Elizabeth,' said John Waterhouse. 'Yes, I too have heard that rumour. Why do you mention it now?'

'The rumour, as you so delicately put it, has, I will admit, not been substantiated by independent evidence. I have no reason to doubt, however, Mrs Armstrong's honesty, and I mention this to you only in case you have received information concerning your daughter or Mr Armstrong, perhaps been contacted by one or both of them. Mr Armstrong has two young sons, and I am gravely concerned for them. It is by all accounts not in character for Mr Armstrong to behave in this way . . .'

'We have no evidence that Mr Armstrong nor my

daughter has behaved in any particular way, either together or individually, Mr Proudlock. Your insinuations . . .'

'Concerns, Mr Waterhouse, I assure you that they are worries for all parties.'

'Your concerns then, are best restricted to those who have shared their troubles with you. As for me, I know only that Elizabeth is missing. I have informed the authorities, and I must await their findings. Now, if you will excuse me, I think that the Makemore team is about to perform, and it will then be the turn of the Greencroft men. My only intention in coming here today has been to support my employees and I now wish to do so. I will watch them from the stage-side.'

He stood up, made his way stiffly to the exit pausing only to nod at the preacher. Edward rose to join him.

'Walk with me?' he asked the preacher, then took his arm to prevent him from exercising any choice in the matter.

'He knows,' said Edward, 'exactly what has happened. He knows that this is just as you have described in, may I say, extremely polite terms. I thrashed it out with him last night, and I can tell you I used words which would make a miner blush!' Proudlock could smell drink on Edward's breath; he recoiled slightly.

'He won't have anything said against Elizabeth. I mean, when you look back over the past few months, she's had her eyes on that Armstrong fellow for ages! And what man, what true red-blooded man, is going to say no to an invitation like that? I know about things like this, preacher, I'm a man of the world! But he'll soon tire of her, you'll see, she's not an easy one to be with, I know that. Not like her sister, not like young Margaret. Now there's a one! Do you know Margaret?'

'I have met her, briefly,' replied Proudlock. They were following the tall figure of John Waterhouse, and the crowd seemed to give way as he passed through them.

'She is beautiful, absolutely beautiful! In fact, Mr Proud-foot ...'

'Proudlock, the name is Proudlock.'

'Sorry. Proudlock. Where was I? Oh yes, the only bad thing about her is her imbecilic husband! He's meant to be here, you know? I had a bet with him and he hasn't appeared. Must know he's going to lose. I mean, there's his dancers now, up on the stage. Look at them! I could dance better than that with my legs tied together and a pit-prop balanced on my nose!'

Edward Waterhouse's low opinion of the Makemore team was not shared by many others. Thomas and Willie, the former now dressed in his costume, looked on with respect. Stew, Rob and Len were equally awestruck. The dance bore little resemblance to that which they had seen at New Year. Gone was the sloppiness, the air of weary boredom which had so marked their previous performances. Instead there was a clinical precision, a feeling of control which was emphasised by the clean tone and sharp playing of the fiddler. Silas Bompas's face was contorted, his squinting eyes set firmly on his dancers as he marked time with one foot. When they finished there was, for a brief moment, no applause at all. It was as though the spectators had not yet been able to digest the whole of the dance, or that the dancers had slipped ahead of time and were waiting, perfectly still, for the world to roll on its way and rescue them from their lost seconds. And then there was applause, and cheers, even from the Greencroft team.

'They were good,' shouted Stew in Thomas's ear.

'Well we'll just have to be better!' retorted Thomas. 'Come on, let's get going.'

They mounted the steps as the Makemore team descended.

'Well done lads,' said Len.

'Good dance,' added Rob.

Their appreciation went unanswered. The only reaction was from Silas Bompas who stared at Thomas, then spat on the ground. Thomas refused to ignore him, went over to him, stood in front of him.

'You're not so big,' said Bompas, 'nor so young that I can't knock you down if I want to.'

'I believe you,' answered Thomas, 'but I've no wish to fight. He's dead now, can't you let it be?'

'No. No, I can't. I can't forget what he did. You'll never be able to understand . . .'

'I will,' said Thomas softly, 'I do. He told me as he died. He told me everything. About you. About me Mam.' He lowered his voice further. 'About Willie.'

'The bastard!'

'No, he wanted forgiveness. No-one else knows. No-one else will know, unless you tell them. But I had to tell you. And offer you this.' He held out his hand to the older man. Bompas looked at it, looked at Thomas again, then spat once more on the ground. He walked away leaving Thomas's hand still outstretched.

Thomas walked back to his dance team.

'Not a very friendly bunch,' said Willie, 'especially that Bompas. I don't know why you bothered, Thomas.'

'Don't judge too harshly, Willie. You can never tell what makes a man do a certain thing, and we don't know what lies behind Bompas's hatred. Still,' Thomas admitted, 'he is a bit of a bugger.'

'Are we going to let ourselves be beaten by the likes of that?' put in Len.

'Are we hell!' said Willie, on cue.

'Right,' said Thomas, 'places then. Willie, does this accordionist know about the start?' Thomas looked across to where the musician was standing

'He knows,' said Willie wearily, 'whether or not he can do it is another thing entirely. He's a bit slow, he can't follow . . .'

'Never mind!' said Thomas sharply. He glanced around him. 'Ready?' Each dancer was in place, close in beside each other. They could smell each other's excitement.

'We've got a proper musician now!' whispered Thomas. They looked up to where Elizabeth had shouldered the accordionist aside, a borrowed violin in her hands. She was staring at them, daring any of them to deny her the right to play.

'Anyone want to drop out?' asked Thomas. His question was addressed to all of them but he was looking at Willie. No-one spoke.

'Remember how good the practices were? Well this has got to be better, much better! Not for you, not for me. For me Dad! Righto, three steps back!'

They moved back and stood, sword arms outstretched. Thomas looked around him. The ribbon of displaced time which had draped itself over the Makemore team fluttered over his eyes, and in one glance he took in the world around him. The sun had left the hill in shadow and all around torches had been lit, their flames dancing in the air, lighting a path all the way up to the beacon at the summit. There were familiar faces, all staring at him. Elizabeth, hard, accusing. Mary, apprehensive for so many different reasons, her eyes flickering between Thomas and Elizabeth. Matthew and David, open-mouthed in excitement. John Waterhouse, confused, his brother, celebratory. Silas Bompas, filled with sour, years' old hatred. Thomas brushed the time from his eyes.

'ONE TWO THREE FOUR!' he shouted, and the stepping began, all five of them together, crisp, fast, staccato steps which echoed across the arena and hushed those watching. The rhythm carried them on. In two three clash, turn two three clash! And the music began, and the dancers knew, and the audience knew – they were all aware that here was something special. When Willie would be old and grey, when he reminisced on long winter nights in front of the fire, his story would become a song of triumph. His arms and legs, bent with arthritis, would suddenly feel young again as he lived the dance once more. His voice and his body would move with a poetry he could only create to describe this one event, and his children and his children's children would look on, captivated by the old man's sudden transformation into arrogant youth. He described the dance both as onlooker and dancer, twisting the viewpoints around each other like rapper swords.

'SINGLE GUARD, and they followed each other round in the circle, and the smiles on their faces showed them how good they were, how good they felt ... RANK, a straight line, step over, nice and neat, step back the same, swords come over together ... CURLY, turn at the front, one and five cast, others follow, three turn to left first, then right. Can anything else feel this fine ...? FIGURE EIGHT, serpentine weaving, a deceipt of locked swords and metal scraping on metal, will they get out of it? YES, a twist, a turn the swords pull together into a lock and then into ... NUT and spin it, don't give them time to draw their breath, to see where one figure starts and another finishes, keep it going, keep it moving, but in time, in time, slow and then break ... COACH AND HORSES, just as it says, thoroughbreds, prancing, dancing, but not for long, must move on ... STEW'S FIGURE, he's the only one who doesn't move, lazy sod, standing there looking proud, but we've something to be proud about ... ROTATE, look at us, we do it the other way to everyone else, we're different, and ... BEDLING-TON, swords so tight your wrists jar, turn it round, let them all see, come out fast, one double turns, five slips inside, two and four in together so close they can feel each other's heartbeat, but we've done it in time and ... CHOKER, look at the swords crossed like armour, shine in the light ... NUT again, but don't leave it, it's the fast part of the dance, keep control, keep it tight, keep it together ... STRAIGHT LINE FORWARD ... LINE BACK ... CIRCLE OUT ... NUT ... SHEEPSKIN ... DOUBLE GUARD, yes!

'Listen to them, listen to the stamping of feet, hands clapping, yells of excitement, screams of encouragement, each turn out, double pirouette, a false turn, lift the swords, slide underneath and we're there ... PRINCE OF WALES SPIN, first time slow, keep it slow, let them wait; then faster, they know what's coming now, faster, then NOW, faster still, each step a whole circle, each stamp shaking the world to its foundations, hands sliding on thin metal, the feeling of sweat and blood but no pain, slow it, slow it, into position ... SINGLE TUMBLER, Stew steps forward over the sword hands on my shoulder, on Thomas's shoulder, step back step forward and OVER he goes, can't hear the stepping for the applause, into place, they KNOW, they KNOW what comes next ... DOUBLE TUMBLER, Thomas and Willie step over the swords and together into the air and DOWN at the same instant; God, legs are tired, not far now, NUT, tie it, hold it up and the light catches it and sets it on fire with red and burnished gold, feel its heat, feel its power, THEY KNOW, invert it, bring it down, one more spin, open out into a straight line, backs to the audience and tie the Nut once more. THEY KNOW, hold it, not yet, let them wait ... and ... TURN, HOLD IT HIGH! Step, tired, weary legs, sweat stained backs and arms, foreheads dripping moisture, thank you sweet Jesus Christ for letting me live this dance through, break step and FINISH!'

There was no doubt in the minds of judges and spectators, dancers and musicians, that there would be no better display of dancing that night; but none would have guessed, in that moment of euphoria, that the winner's trophy that year would bear no name, only the figures 1887. Thomas picked up the lock of swords from the ground where Stew had thrown it in triumph. Only he and Willie were left on the stage. Amongst the yelling and shouting of the crowd, the swirling mass of bodies dancing drunk on the potent brew of rapper and rapid jigs, he could see Elizabeth engulfed by her father's arms, Edward capering around them both in delight. Mary was holding Matthew in her arms, David was perched on Abigail's shoulders, all four were waving frantically.

'Do you think everything'll be alright, Thomas?' asked Willie, his chest still clawing for air, a towel draped around his neck. Thomas could find no answer, could not express himself nor his worries. He looked at Mary and his children and felt the warmth of fatherhood and old familiar love fill his heart. A glance at Elizabeth, still in her father's arms but now looking at him, and that warmth became a passionate fire, a desire which threatened to overwhelm him. He felt lost in uncertainty. But if Willie's question required an answer then the need for a response was about to be overtaken by events. Willie nudged Thomas; climbing the steps towards them was Silas Bompas.

'We've beaten you, old man,' said Willie. 'They may not have announced it yet, but we beat you. That was for me Dad!'

'Willie!' shushed Thomas.

'Leave him be,' said Bompas, 'I was like that in me day. Headstrong. Sure of meself. It's taken me a long time to grow out of it. That's why I'm here now. To congratulate you. Because you were good.'

'Hell!' said Willie, amazed. 'Where's the flying pigs?'

'Shut up!' Thomas scolded. He turned to Bompas.

'Thank you. I know how much rapper means to you. Praise from you is praise indeed.'

'Oh, I feel ill! I think I'm going to be sick!'

'Willie! Shut it!'

'He'll understand, one day,' said Bompas. 'I'll leave you now.' He held out his hand and Thomas took it readily, found the hatred which had been present in Bompas's eyes only minutes before replaced with a deep sadness. Bompas nodded and offered his hand to Willie. There was a pushing and shoving in the crowd, a ripple of disturbance was moving towards the stage. Willie looked at the man before him.

'Tell me why I should shake hands with you?' he challenged. 'After all you've said and all you've done against me and my family. Why should you change now, so suddenly? Why should I shake hands?'

'No reason. No reason at all. Except that I think your father would have wanted you to.' And slowly, suspiciously, two hands reached out, two thumbs interlocked. The shake was brief and formal; and interrupted.

'WILLIE ARMSTRONG!' screamed a tortured voice from hell. Willie and Thomas and Silas Bompas turned, the crowd split to reveal the madman in its midst.

'WILLIE ARMSTRONG YOU BASTARD!' screamed the voice again. A thin, wracked figure climbed the stairs to the stage, in each hand a pistol, the barrels wavering, but, none could doubt it, aimed at Willie.

'Is there something troubling you Mr Makemore?' asked Thomas, moving deftly in front of his brother.

'I'll kill you both!' shouted Makemore. He whirled round to where Len and Rob, nearest to the stage, had begun to creep up the stairs. He fired, rapidly, two shots. The reports, sudden and loudly violent, forced them to retreat. The splinters raised by the bullets as they struck the floor, inches from Len's hand, made the retreat a swift one, and one which was copied by those around the stage. Makemore turned back, ignoring the screams of frightened women, the cries of pain from those who had been knocked over in the rush to get away from the gunman. He stared at Willie who, for the moment, was more concerned to see that Abigail had escaped without injury. Thomas too was searching the twilight for Mary and his sons, for Elizabeth as well. There was no sign of them, but he could see that all of those who had fallen had scrambled to their feet and hurried away to join their comrades in a rough circle some hundred yards in diameter. None of them could have known whether they were safe at that distance; to go further, however, would have meant loss of face and might have rendered them unable to see clearly the drama on the stage.

'Mr Makemore, sir,' pleaded Bompas, arm outstretched in supplication, 'What's the matter sir?'

'Be quiet Silas,' snapped Makemore. 'My business is with young Mr Armstrong here, the strutting gigolo, the proud peacock, the foul, prating cuckoo!'

'Yes,' said Thomas, 'that sounds like a fair description of my brother. Now why don't you put that gun down . . .'

'Get back!' Thomas ceased his slow edge towards Makemore.

Not all of the spectators had fled the area. Some, seeking more solid and immediate shelter, had thrown themselves under the stage. John Waterhouse, one arm round Elizabeth, the other holding his brother down, was there. So were the rest of the dance team, and Mary, and Matthew.

'Why?' urged Willie. 'Why? If you're going to kill me at least tell me why!'

'It's too late to pretend innocence,' said Makemore. His clothing was torn, his hair blown by the speed of his travelling, the pupils of his eyes surrounded by white. Insanity became him.

'Margaret told me everything,' he continued. 'She told me that you're the one who's fathered that bastard in her belly, and when I've blasted you I'll go back and rip your bastard child from her and she can meet you in hell!

'She's lying!' said Willie. 'I've never touched her! I've never even seen her since she was married!'

'No! You're the liar! But you won't tell any more lies!'

The three men were lined up in front of Makemore, Bompas in the middle. As Makemore raised his weapons, levelled them at Willie, both Thomas and Bompas had the same idea; but Bompas was first. He moved surprisingly quickly for such a large man, for an old man, and he almost succeeded in his aim of knocking Makemore over or, at the very least, making him miss his target. He made contact, not with the gunman's body, but with his outstretched arms. And the bullets which were meant for Willie, one from each gun, the bullets which hit Bompas so easily in the chest and stomach, took his life from him so quickly that he was unable even to raise his eyes to his one, his only son.

Thomas, marginally behind Bompas, his dive lower, caught Makemore below the knees and sent him sprawling across the stage. One of the guns twisted from his grasp and fell spinning onto the grass by Edward Waterhouse's hand. Such a gift could not be ignored, and Edward squirmed from his brother's side to pick up the weapon, scuttled out into the open.

'Henry Makemore!' he shouted. Makemore was back on his feet, looking around him at Bompas's bloody body, at Thomas still spreadeagled, at Willie incapable of movement.

'I'll teach you,' he shouted. 'You won't defame my niece again!' But Makemore had fired before Edward had finished speaking. The shot hit him in the groin; Edward looked at the blood in amazement before sinking to the ground.

Makemore panicked. He was six feet from Willie. He could have raised his gun and shot him once, twice if he had wanted to, just to make sure that he wouldn't rise to pursue him as he leaped from the stage and, in the confusion, make his escape. But there was no sign that the thought crossed his mind. He had killed Silas Bompas. The man was dead before him, his blood already staining the wooden boards, forcing those huddling below to crawl to one side to avoid being touched by the sticky, salty, glutinous liquid. There was no time for them to consider from whose body the blood had come. They hid their eyes and clamped their lips together lest some treacherous word attract the attention of the madman above them, call him to seek random retribution amongst those sheltering below. But they could have laughed or screamed, they could have urged him to murder them too, and still his gaze would not have been drawn from the body of Silas Bompas. Makemore's madness had at least had purpose. His paranoia had protected him from the realisation that he was mad. But the sight of Bompas, his body not yet still, served to lower the shields in his mind, allowed his obsessions, his phobias, his manias to free themselves, to breed the ecstatic delirium of one who will never know sanity again.

He began to laugh then sprang from the stage, vaulted Edward Waterhouse's groaning body, sprinted up the hill waving his gun wildly in the air.

'Take care of him!' said Thomas to the still passive Willie, though he had seen enough to know that there was no life there to care for. He too jumped from the stage, began to run after Makemore. He didn't hear Mary's plea for him to return, nor Elizabeth's warning to take care. He didn't see the crowd part to allow Makemore and him passage, nor did he sense their following him up the slope. All of his attention was focused on the figure in front of him, and the drumming of his heart, and the voice in his head which told him that it was none of his business, that he should stop running. But he forced himself onwards, imagined that he was closing on his prey. They were nearing the summit when Makemore halted, turned slowly and fired at Thomas. Thomas kept moving, refused to halt his charge, and felt the bullet pluck at his sleeve. The slope was steep, surely a second shot would find its target. The trigger was pulled and . . . there was no sound save an almost silent click! Makemore giggled and threw the gun at Thomas, who raised his arm and so prevented the weapon from hitting his head. The shock, the twist and fall as he strove to avoid being struck, allowed Makemore to gain a few more seconds. Thomas rose to his feet and continued the chase.

Near the top of the hill a rope cordon had been looped around a number of well-spaced fenceposts to keep on-lookers a safe distance from the bonfire. On the way up Makemore and Thomas had passed several flaming brands, path markers for those who would have climbed later. The last two of these were at the gap in the cordon, a gap which showed the entrance to the bonfire itself. This was no ramshackle pile of garden debris and household rubbish. Built from best quality timber, evenly cut and matched by length and girth, it had been constructed with tunnels inside to provide through draughts and aid swift ignition. Its beehive shape had been augmented by balconies and turrets to make it seem more castle-like, fit for the Golden Jubilee of a Queen. And, in case of rain, barrels of tar had been stored in its base; there would be no excuse for this bonfire not burning.

Makemore was incapable of logical thought. Another man might have paused, looked around him, considered his options. Turn and fight? Thomas Armstrong was a large man, strong and, it would seem, determined in his pursuit. Escape then? Flight was certainly possible, the slope leading down to the river was almost in darkness now. But Makemore considered none of these. Instead he grabbed at one of the torches and ran into the bonfire.

Those following the couple up the hill, at a safe distance, saw Thomas take the remaining brand and follow Make-more. They struggled onward until they reached the cordon but went no further, stood in hushed silence. Others arrived a moment later, shouldered their way through the mass of bodies.

'What's happening?' Willie asked a short stocky man who

had been lecturing a companion on the futility of bravery. He looked around, ready to demand that this rude stranger cease interrupting his discourse. The stranger, however, was accompanied by three other large, burly men.

'You heard him,' said Stew, 'what's happened?' Len and Rob leaned forward to add urgency to the question. The short man became suddenly loquacious.

'They're in there, in the beacon, both of them. You can see, sometimes there's a light appears, or a shadow. They've both got torches with them, stupid bastards, I mean, naked flames with all that dry timber about. Asking for trouble, isn't it! I was just saying to this other lad, you wouldn't catch me . . .'

'I'm going in after them!' said Willie, and made as if to duck under the rope. As he did so the crowd gasped, not with wonder, but with dismay. High up near the peak of the bonfire a wisp of smoke appeared, smoke which would not have been noticed in the darkness had it not been followed immediately by a flare of orange fire. Other tongues of flame licked the night; Stew and Len and Rob took firm hold of Willie's arms and shoulders.

'You can do nothing by going in there,' said Stew, 'except make a widow of Abigail.'

'Let me through!' cried a voice, Mary's voice. 'Oh my God, he's not in there, please tell me he's not in there!'

'He's not finished yet, Mary,' said Willie. 'He could find his way out, there's still time.' He looked around him. 'The kids?' he asked warily.

'I left them down there, with Abi. I thought it best, in case . . .'

There was another exclamation from the crowd. The whole of the lower part of the pyre was now in flames; the heat was driving back those nearest the fire, and above its roar the muffled crunch of falling timber deep within its heart sounded like a drum-beat of doom. Others joined those watching. Jonathon Proudlock took up position behind Mary, certain now that he would be needed. Mary herself felt someone brush close against her but could find no strength to argue as Elizabeth Waterhouse took her place with those who were already mourners. Abigail arrived with Matthew and David, and Albie Settle, who intended reporting that Edward Waterhouse was suffering from no more than a flesh wound and was being taken to hospital by his brother. But the bearer of this cheerful news found himself unable to pass it on. The faces of those watching, each tear cruelly highlighted by the brightness of the harsh flames and then scorched into submission by their heat, told of the true loss.

A finger pointed, and all eyes turned. A scream and then another scream, a woman fainting. On one of the false battlements a flame appeared. No ordinary flame this, no fire born of wood or tar. At its heart was a man, a man who capered and danced for his audience as the flames ate at his clothes, his hair, his skin, a man whose screams could not be heard. He fell, not out into the night, but deep into the heart of the fire. Mary buried herself in the welcoming arms of the preacher; Elizabeth looked proudly on, showing no emotion, her lips forming the litany of her lover's name. In the distance the glow that was Penshaw's celebration burned bright. But the Peelwell fire burned brighter.

At dawn the fire was still burning, though few were present to watch it. The clouds which unfurled from the west brought a slow, hissing rain. Volunteers ventured out upon the embers, dancing back as their probing uncovered volcanic sores, allowing the drizzle, soon to become a downpour, to heal the night's injuries. One of the marquees had been brought up to the heights. In it sat Mary and Elizabeth, the preacher, John Waterhouse returned from hospital, Albie Settle. The dancers were helping in the search; the children were asleep on a mattress of coats. Faces were streaked with ashes and tears, hung with sleepless exhaustion.

'Has anyone looked down the hill?' asked Elizabeth. 'He might have got out that way. He could be lying there, injured, while we're poking about looking for bodies. Someone should look for him!'

'They've looked,' said her father, 'there was no sign. Elizabeth, why not come home with me. You can do no good here. You can talk to me about him, tell me what he was like. You see, I still don't know what really happened. All I know is . . . you must . . . you must have loved him.'

Elizabeth looked into her father's eyes, saw her own tears reflected there, nodded because her throat would not allow her to speak. Her smile was one of thankfulness that someone should recognise her feelings. She clung tight to him, kept her crying low and silent.

Willie walked slowly into the tent. He might have worked a shift at the coal face, so dirty was he. There was a table with jugs of water on it, he picked one up, drank straight from it. His lips left a grey semi-circle of ash on its rim. He found himself the centre of attention.

'We've found the remains of two bodies,' he said wearily, went straight on before questions could be asked. 'There's no way of knowing which is which; their clothes are burnt almost away. There's not much there,' he added quickly, stretching out an arm to prevent Elizabeth running past him. She didn't fight.

'I don't think any of you should look,' he said. 'I've seen some bad sights down the mine before but not like this. I'm sorry, I didn't mean . . .' He broke down, tears washing his face, and Abigail ran to embrace him, hold him close. He regained control, swallowed.

'We . . . we tried turning the bodies over, to see if there were any marks, any means of identifying them. There was nothing at first but then, almost hidden, we found something.' He looked at Mary, and then at Elizabeth.

'I think you should have them back,' he said, held out both his hands. On one lay a ring, a ring bearing five rapper swords interlocked; on the other was a heart-shaped necklace. Both had been damaged by the fire, were partially melted. Each woman took her gift. Mary began to cry, was consoled by Proudlock, but Elizabeth walked outside. The wind and the rain beat at her, tore at her hair and her clothes. She surveyed the ashes before her. Two blankets had been put down over the bodies, weighted with partly burned logs, but the wind plucking at them made it seem as though there was life beneath. Elizabeth looked up at the sky.

'Thomas Armstrong!' The words were harsh but soft. 'You didn't keep your promise! You didn't come back!'

From within the marquee a child's voice was raised in tearful anguish.

'Where's my Dad? I want my Dad back!'

And the rain kept falling.

Chapter Twenty-Two

The next salient point is the presence [in the sword dance] of drama in some degree ... whenever this element rises into the form of a play however rude, the central incident of this play is the death, or death and resurrection of one of the characters.

The Sword Dances of Northern England
(Cecil J. Sharp)

Thomas was delirious. His mind was unable to focus on any single thought; through a mist of pain he watched his life ebb away from him. It was as though he had been taken from his body and was looking down at himself from some great height, he was being borne on some chariot whose smooth motion both charmed him and, with each rock and swell, reminded him of the hurt his body had suffered.

He saw himself, through the haze, charged with the task of disposing of Maichamps' body, carrying the corpse downstairs and throwing it over the back of Maichamps' horse. The body was still warm, though lifeless.

Thomas's duties had been made far worse by the turmoil in his mind. He had to remind himself that Maichamps had intended killing him and Elizabeth, that his cruelty had caused her almost unbearable physical and mental pain in the past, and that he was in the process of hurting her sister in the same way. By concentrating on these horrors he found himself able to hold in check the self-pity which lurked ever close to the surface of his mind and which brought with it a sense of disgust that he had behaved as he did. He had helped murder a man. He had managed to impregnate two women, alienate his family and friends; and yet he still found himself loving this woman who would, he was sure, ultimately destroy him.

His confusion stalked him as he set off for Peelwell Hill and its mine shafts, his mind as laden as the mare which plodded at his side. He intended approaching the Hill from its western side, the side nearest to the farmhouse. The northern flank, dropping down steeply to the river, would have been too difficult for the mare to climb. The lower slopes of the southern face were too close to the village itself, although on its heights were the greatest concentration of shafts. By climbing the western face he hoped to reach the top, and then descend to dispose of his burden in the first available shaft.

The climb was slow, though easy; the Hill was not high. But he had made no allowance for the mildness of the night which encouraged many folk, intent on enjoying the next day's celebrations to the full, to spend the hours of darkness on the hillside, in the open. From his vantage point at the summit he could see a village of fires below him, could hear the singing and carousing of hundreds of voices; an unnoticed descent would have been impossible. To make matters worse three or four smaller flames were heading directly towards him, torches borne by those required to inspect or guard the beacon bonfire. His agitated mind refused to think clearly and he panicked, slid the corpse from the back of the horse, slapped the poor beast sharply (hoping that it would not choose the steep and perilous descent to the river) and dragged the body into the heart of the bonfire.

It was dark. The entrance was small, but opened into a corridor, and by feeling the wall beyond Thomas found an opening which he assumed was the centre of the beacon. There were a number of barrels there, all, by the smell of them, containing tar. He pulled the body around behind them and left it there, out of sight of anyone who would venture into the beacon even in daytime. He was unsure how flesh and bone would burn, but his relief at leaving the body behind outweighed any worries he might have had about its subsequent discovery.

The men with torches walked quickly around the beacon then set off once again down the hill. Thomas waited for them to go then followed. The rest of the night he spent wandering from one group of people to another, never joining them in their singing, never moving too close to their fires, always remaining on the fringes of darkness. He did not go into the village, didn't even attempt to find out whether Elizabeth had been successful in finding a room in one of the pubs. He was alone; he could not remember when he had last been truly alone, even with so many people around him, and he enjoyed the sensation. But with the sunrise his responsibilities and duties, his needs, his obligations, began to pursue him once more.

The memory receded. Mental anguish was replaced once more with physical pain. He could feel the bones of his leg grating on one another; each breath was made painful by broken ribs, and his skin, his skin was still on fire, the flames were licking their way over his whole body. Unconsciousness was a welcome escape.

Thomas had grown to love darkness. In winter he would go to work in the darkness, spend the day underground in darkness, then return home after sunset. Although at first frightened by it, he came to enjoy the total lack of light which could only be experienced in a mine. And darkness brought him comfort, a time to think, a time when he could, through a pretence of sleep, be selfish in his desire to be alone. And so he faced daylight with a premonition of doom, not fear. He was not frightened of what might occur; merely certain that his fate lay as much in the hands of others as under his own control.

The mists of those dark memories wrapped themselves around him; he drifted in their cool and hazy caresses, was taken backwards and forwards in time, saw glimpses of his childhood, his father, his sisters dancing in front of the fire, Mary in the sunlight, Elizabeth's smile. And then . . .

They had danced. They had danced the dance of their lives, and Silas Bompas lay dead before him. Thomas felt a longing to pull Willie down to him, to tell him that this was his real father, to show him why he had saved his life. But instead he ran. There was no logic, no reason in his pursuit of Makemore. The murderer would not have escaped, no matter where he had fled. But perhaps Makemore's fate, and Thomas's and that of Maichamps, were so interwoven that they were drawn to one another. Thomas never did believe in pre-destiny, but he felt that he had no choice in pursuing Makemore.

He realised that Makemore was mad when he turned to fire his pistol. His eyes, his face, showed that the mind within had been damaged. Thomas realised the danger when Makemore ran into the beacon with a lighted brand, but, in reality and in his dreams, knew that it would have been foolhardy to follow him without some form of defence. And Thomas, his body twitching and contorted, staining the clean linen of a narrow bed with his blood, found himself once again within that castle of wood. . . .

There were stairs and false passages within. Thomas had not realised the extent of the tunnels, but the walls were such that he could see the light of Makemore's torch shining through the gaps in the timbers; he assumed that Makemore was therefore aware of his own position. There was no need for silence, indeed, as Thomas pursued his prey he called to him, urging him to give himself up. He told him that he was unwell, that he could not be held responsible for his actions, but the response was limited to harsh breathing and maniacal giggles.

It was not clear who was responsible for lighting the fire. Thomas was careful as he moved around, but in his eagerness to catch Makemore he might have allowed the flames of his brand to lick the timber above or to one side of him. Given the sudden appearance and expansion of the fire it was more likely that Makemore was the culprit, and that his act was a deliberate one. Thomas could have escaped. He found himself close by the entrance, seeing flames at various points around him, but was also aware that Makemore had just entered the central room at the base of the fire. And so Thomas followed him.

Makemore turned, his brand held before him like a sword, and he moved slowly round the tar barrels in the centre of the room. He was watching Thomas closely, so closely that he lost his footing, tripped and fell, and one of the opened barrels went with him. It was Maichamps' body, perhaps an outstretched leg, which had caused him to lose his balance. Thomas saw the horror on his face when he recognised the dead man lying beside him, saw him scramble to his feet covered with dark, treacly pitch.

And then another gap, a failing of the memory, perhaps obscuring visions too painful to recall.

The clean air of Thomas's new surroundings was suddenly thick with heavy, remembered fumes of tar, patches of orange fire were bursting, smoke was fawning at Thomas's feet. The low rumbling of the flames was punctuated with sharp cracks of wood breaking, or knots firing, or resin exploding. The flames may have ignited the vapour which in turn set alight Makemore's clothes. Thomas wanted to believe that, but his memory, or dream, or nightmare returned to show him a crooked smile and wide eyes, a look of hatred, defiance, a glance at Maichamps' body. And then Makemore had held the torch to himself.

Makemore threw the brand to one side, it fell into the pitch and began to burn fiercely, but no less fiercely than Makemore himself. He was screaming as he came towards Thomas, his agonised arms outstretched, a living demon determined to hold him, to embrace him, to set fire to his soul and drag Thomas with him to hell. His hair was on fire, his skin was melting, and Thomas dived to one side to avoid his touch. Even then Makemore must have been blind, he lumbered past Thomas and stumbled towards the stairs leading up to the false battlements.

The fire of his passing had set light to the portals of the only exit from that central room. The rush of air from outside caused the flames to fan inwards and Thomas felt that he might manage to dive through that small gap in the centre of the doorway and thus secure his freedom. No sooner had he made the decision to do this when the choice was taken from him. A collapse of timber somewhere must have blocked the throughflow of air, and the flames changed direction. The exit was entirely blocked by fire. There was no way out.

The timber was very dry, for that at least Thomas could be thankful, the smoke and fumes were not too great. If the wood had been wet he would have suffocated. The heat, however, was almost unbearable. The tar barrels were now thoroughly alight, their furnace filling almost the whole of that central room. Burning logs were falling all the time, jets of flame would suddenly flash before his eyes to join their fellows in their desire to escape upwards. He took a

handkerchief from his pocket to wrap around his mouth and
nose, but he could see the hairs on his hands beginning to
char and curl; that was the moment he realised that he was
going to die. He wanted to lie down, but could not. Just as
Maichamps' body had struggled for life, so Thomas's
ignored the signals his brain was sending. He crawled
around the perimeter of the room searching for some weak
spot, a prop which was not as well set into the ground as it
ought to be, and found it halfway round the room, a single
upright which gave way slightly as he pushed at it. He
heaved again, and again. He turned around, his head
perilously close to the burning tar, lay on his back and
kicked at the timber. It gave way, cracked and snapped. The
gap was no more than four inches, but he could use that
broken piece of timber as a lever. He forced its neighbours
aside to make the gap larger then crawled through, slicing
open his knee as he passed; but he felt no pain then; that
would come later.

Thomas found himself in the outer corridor. Although the
roof was afire he could feel fresh air coming through the
gaps in the outer wall, and this was keeping the flames high.
It would not be long, however, before they descended to
engulf him. He felt a sudden scorching agony on his back,
forced himself to roll onto it to douse the flames which had
taken hold there. He could hear himself screaming with a
distant voice. The outer wall against which he was trapped
was the most solid of the pyre, supporting most of the
structure's weight. Flames were behind him, to his right and
left, and beginning to move down the wall ahead of him. He
retreated to the centre of the corridor and began to scrabble
at the earth with his bare hands. He was not trying to dig his
way out; that would have been impossible and futile. But his
body was aware of the danger on all other sides and was
acting independently; he had no control over its actions.
There was nowhere else to go.

There must have been, somehow, a build-up of vapour in the heart of the fire; perhaps one of the tar barrels had not been opened. Thomas heard the explosion and felt the pain at the same time. The force of the blast threw down the inner wall in a sheet of flame, blasted the timbers at the outer wall and broke them. He was lying in the slight hollow of his digging and the worst of the blast passed over him, but he felt something strike his leg and was aware, dispassionately, that the bone had been broken. Although the explosion passed largely over him there was enough strength left in it to pick him up and hurl him bodily into the night. Two of his ribs were cracked, breathing caused him pain, he was burned all over his body. He longed for death but was not allowed that luxury.

He could remember rolling down the darkness of the steep slope of the hill, bouncing and turning, unable to halt his plunge into welcome blackness and oblivion. It was pain which dragged him back into consciousness, just as pain was the companion of these dreams and memories; but which was nightmare, and which was truth?

He was by the river, could hear the distant lapping of soft waves, dragged his body the few feet to the bank and toppled into the cool waters of the murky Tyne. The pain of contact with that coolness caused him to lose his senses again, though only for the briefest of moments. He found himself choking and turned onto his back, and in that position drifted out into the centre of the river. He could see to one side the flame-topped Peelwell Hill, to the other the streetlights of Newcastle. Above him stars swung, and he could hear the sound of a storm-cock singing through the night.

He would have been content to die in this way. The water was soothing now, caressing away the heat, supporting his body and broken leg. Where, he wondered, would he be found? Would the incoming tide deposit him at Elswick, or further upriver at Scotswood, Ryton, or even Wylam? He couldn't remember if the tides went that far. He decided that he would prefer to be carried away to the ocean, not be found at all. He imagined himself being saluted by Tynemouth Priory on his way to the North Sea, felt rather sorry that he would not be able to return its greeting. He said his sad goodbyes (made more sad by the fact that the recipients of his affections would never know how much he cared for them, how much he regretted the pain he had caused them) to Mary and Matthew and David, to Willie and Abigail, to Elizabeth, to his unborn children, unable to separate the tears of sorrow from those of pain. And he heard music, his father's music, played on the violin as only he could play it, not a requiem but a greeting, a welcome. He began to smile. Death was near.

That was the feeling of those who pulled him out of the river and onto the deck of their boat. There were four voices. Thomas could see nothing, his eyes refused to open.

'He's dead!' said one, uncaring.

'No he's not!' said the second. 'Look, his chest's moving. He's breathing.'

The third voice was more authoritative, well-spoken. The others seemed to hold it in awe, or respect.

'Poor devil might as well be dead,' it said. 'By the look of him he's been burned, he's broken his leg badly, God knows what else there is wrong with him. But since he's still breathing we have no choice in the matter. You two stay with him, don't move him but try to keep him comfortable. I'll give the command. We'll get back to the dockside.'

'You will do no such thing, Captain!' That was a woman's voice, a harsh voice, a voice not used to having her orders disobeyed.

'He's almost dead,' said the first voice.

'I do not,' the woman's voice continued, 'expect to hear

crewmen speak without having been spoken to first.' By the silence it was clear that her wishes would be obeyed in future.

'I have already waited four weeks,' said the same voice, 'for the chance to embark from this God-forsaken spot and I have no intention of returning to the quayside to find myself forced to remain there until the authorities have investigated this person's untimely appearance. We therefore have a choice. We may return him whence he came and allow him to die peacefully, or we take him below decks.'

'I shall arrange to have him taken to the infirmary ma'am.' That was the authoritative voice, the Captain's voice, suddenly meek.

'Good. I'm sure that my doctor will welcome the opportunity to play with the facilities I've had installed for him at such great expense. If this man dies then bury him at sea. If he lives, well, we shall eventually have to find some work for him to do.'

'Yes ma'am. I shall keep you informed of his . . .'

'There's no need for that, Captain. This man's welfare is of no interest to me whatsoever. His appearance is, however, rather repellent. His presence sickens me. I think that I shall retire. Goodnight Captain.'

'Goodnight ma'am.' Thomas heard footsteps, small, rapidly repeating footsteps, fade away.

'Right you two, you heard what her ladyship said, get him below. I'll find the doctor.' More footsteps, heavier.

'Bloody hell! It's a good job there's no keelhauling these days or I'd have been under the bows before the W.O.B. said off with his balls!'

They rolled him onto a stretcher of some sort, and the pain returned. He groaned, or made some involuntary sound of complaint, because their rough treatment softened suddenly.

'Never mind, mate,' said the second voice, close to his

head, 'if you survive this you'll get a nice sea cruise on the *Lady Montague*, first stop France, second stop the Canaries, then all the way across the ocean blue. Come on, we'll just put you on the bunk like this, there you go. The doctor'll be here soon. Don't you worry.'

Thomas and his pain were left alone, alone with their thoughts, their memories. He forced his mind to leave the past behind, to focus, briefly, on the present. He was bound, if he survived, for some distant port. The thought followed him down into darkness again. Where was he going? Across the ocean? Which ocean? And the sea swell whispered to him, 'America.'

America.

But his body whispered, 'Death.'

☐	The Jericho Rose	Olive Etchells	£4.99
☐	The Summer of the Fancy Man	Sara Fraser	£4.99
☐	The Broken Gate	Eileen Ramsay	£4.99

Warner now offers an exciting range of quality titles by both established and new authors which can be ordered from the following address:

Little, Brown and Company (UK),
P.O. Box 11,
Falmouth,
Cornwall TR10 9EN.

Alternatively you may fax your order to the above address.
Fax No. 0326 376423.

Payments can be made as follows: cheque, postal order (payable to Little, Brown and Company) or by credit cards, Visa/Access. Do not send cash or currency. UK customers and B.F.P.O. please allow £1.00 for postage and packing for the first book, plus 50p for the second book, plus 30p for each additional book up to a maximum charge of £3.00 (7 books plus).

Overseas customers including Ireland, please allow £2.00 for the first book plus £1.00 for the second book, plus 50p for each additional book.

NAME (Block Letters) ....

....

ADDRESS ....

....

....

☐ I enclose my remittance for _____

☐ I wish to pay by Access/Visa Card

Number ⬚⬚⬚⬚⬚⬚⬚⬚⬚⬚⬚⬚⬚⬚⬚⬚

Card Expiry Date ⬚⬚⬚⬚

quarry edge and disaster. I told them where the quarryman's house was, suggested we pull the carriage to the door. I knew how cold it would be, knew we'd need the carriage for fuel and light. I swear I dragged the thing myself, Deemster kept falling over, Margaret was crying. I was asking whether the effort was worth it by the time we got there, what with having to rip the timber from the carriage myself while the others sat inside. No, no, I tell a lie. I threatened I'd lock Deemster out unless he took his turn. He did as he was told.'

Makemore was now acting out his part in the drama, hauling a make-believe cart across the snow, rubbing his hands in front of the newly built fire.

'It was quite cosy. We sat and we warmed ourselves and we drank. They drank more than me. Margaret became very ... very familiar with both Deemster and with me. Yes, familiar is perhaps a polite way of putting it. She tasted wonderful, a mixture of saliva and alcohol, a smell of woman. It excited me, I'll admit that, God knows the effect it was having on Deemster! You see, I had an advantage over him. He really was in love with her.'

Maichamps had now sat up. His attention was firmly fixed on Henry. Every minute or so he licked his lips and swallowed.

'He'd confessed to me some time ago his feelings for Margaret. I played on them. We sat together in front of the fire. First she would kiss me. I swear I could have had her there and then but I wasn't sure how Deemster would react. She was ripe for picking. She would kiss me and then she would kiss him. I felt sorry for him. He was ungainly, he didn't know where to put his hands. She was asking him to take her, she would have done so if he'd been her damn brother! I had to leave them to it. I had to trust that their carnal desires would overcome his reticence. I feigned sickness, crept outside then sneaked back in. They were on